Treasure Island

Treasure Island

ROBERT LOUIS STEVENSON

ILLUSTRATIONS BY
LOUIS RHEAD

KONECKY & KONECKY

To Lloyd Osbourne an American Gentleman
in accordance with whose classic taste the following
has been designed, it is now, in return for numerous
delightful hours and with kindest wishes,
dedicated by his affectionate friend, the author.

Konecky & Konecky
150 Fifth Ave.
New York, NY 10011

ISBN: 1-56852-233-9

Cover design by Studio 31

Manufactured in the U.S.A.

CONTENTS

CONTENTS

TO THE HESITATING PURCHASER

If sailor tales to sailor tunes,
    Storm and adventure, heat and cold,
If schooners, islands, and maroons,
    And Buccaneers and buried Gold,
And all the old romance, retold
    Exactly in the ancient way,
Can please, as me they pleased of old,
    The wiser youngsters of to-day:

—So be it, and fall on! If not,
    If studious youth no longer crave,
His ancient appetites forgot,
    Kingston, or Ballantyne the brave,
Or Cooper of the wood and wave:
    So be it, also! And may I
And all my pirates share the grave
    Where these and their creations lie!

PART I

THE OLD BUCCANEER

TREASURE ISLAND

CHAPTER I

THE OLD SEA-DOG AT THE "ADMIRAL BENBOW"

Squire Trelawney, Dr Livesey, and the rest of these gentlemen having asked me to write down the whole particulars about Treasure Island, from the beginning to the end, keeping nothing back but the bearings of the island, and that only because there is still treasure not yet lifted, I take up my pen in the year of grace 17—, and go back to the time when my father kept the "Admiral Benbow" inn, and the brown old seaman, with the sabre-cut, first took up his lodging under our roof.

I remember him as if it were yesterday, as he came plodding to the inn door, his sea-chest following behind him in a hand-barrow; a tall, strong, heavy, nut-brown man; his tarry pigtail falling over the shoulders of his soiled blue coat; his hands ragged and scarred, with black, broken nails; and the sabre-cut across one cheek, a dirty, livid white. I remember him looking round the cove and whistling to himself as he did so, and then breaking out in that old sea-song that he sang so often afterwards:—

> "Fifteen men on the dead man's chest—
> Yo-ho-ho, and a bottle of rum!"

in the high, old tottering voice that seemed to have been tuned and broken at the capstan bars. Then he rapped on the door with a bit of stick like a handspike that he carried, and when my father appeared, called roughly for a glass of rum. This, when it was brought to him, he drank slowly, like a connoisseur, lingering on the taste, and still looking about him at the cliffs and up at our signboard.

"This is a handy cove," says he, at length; "and a pleasant sittyated grog-shop.—Much company, mate?"

My father told him no,—very little company, the more was the pity.

"Well, then," said he, "this is the berth for me. Here you, matey," he cried to the man who trundled the barrow; "bring up alongside and help up my chest. I'll stay here a bit," he continued. "I'm a plain man; rum and bacon and eggs is what I want, and that head up there for to watch ships off. What you mought call me? You mought call me captain. Oh, I see what you're at—there!" and he threw down three or four gold pieces on the threshold. "You can tell me when I've worked through that," says he, looking as fierce as a commander.

And, indeed, bad as his clothes were, and coarsely as he spoke, he had none of the appearance of a man who sailed before the mast; but seemed like a mate or skipper, accustomed to be obeyed or to strike. The man who came with the barrow told us the mail had set him down the morning before at the "Royal George"; that he had inquired what inns there were along the coast, and hearing ours well spoken of, I suppose, and described as lonely, had chosen it from the others for his place of residence. And that was all we could learn of our guest.

He was a very silent man by custom. All day he hung round the cove, or upon the cliffs, with a brass telescope; all evening he sat in a corner of the parlour next the fire, and drank rum and water very strong. Mostly he would not speak when spoken to; only look up sudden and fierce, and blow through his nose like a fog-horn; and we and the people who came about our house soon learned to let him be. Every day, when he came back from his stroll, he would ask if any seafaring men had gone by along the road? At first we thought it was the want of company of his own kind that made him ask this question; but at last we began to see he was desirous to avoid them. When a seaman put up at the "Admiral Benbow" (as now and then some did, making by the coast road for Bristol), he would look in at him through the curtained door before he entered the parlour; and he was always sure to be as silent as a mouse when any such was present. For me, at least, there was no secret about the matter; for I was, in a way, a sharer in his alarms. He had taken me aside one day, and promised me a silver fourpenny on the first of every month if I would only keep my "weather-eye open for a seafaring man with one leg," and let him know the moment he appeared. Often enough, when the first of the month came round, and I applied to him for my wage, he would only blow through his nose at me, and stare me down; but before the week was out he was sure to think better of it, bring me my fourpenny piece, and repeat his orders to look out for "the seafaring man with one leg."

How that personage haunted my dreams, I need scarcely tell you. On stormy nights, when the wind shook the four corners of the house, and the surf roared along the cove and up the cliffs, I would see him in a thousand forms, and with a thousand diabolical expressions. Now the leg would be cut off at the knee, now at the hip; now he was a monstrous kind of a creature who had never had but the one leg, and that in the middle of his body. To see him leap and run and pursue me over hedge and ditch was the worst of nightmares. And altogether I paid pretty dear for my monthly fourpenny piece, in the shape of these abominable fancies.

But though I was so terrified by the idea of the seafaring man with one leg, I was far less afraid of the captain himself than anybody else who knew him. There were nights when he took a deal more rum and water than his head would carry; and then he would sometimes sit and sing his wicked, old, wild sea-songs, minding nobody; but sometimes he would call for glasses round, and force all the trembling company to listen to his stories or bear a chorus to his singing. Often I have heard the house shaking with "Yo-ho-ho, and a bottle of rum;" all the neighbours joining in for dear life, with the fear of death upon them, and each singing louder than the other, to avoid remark. For in these fits he was the most over-riding companion ever known; he would slap his hand on the table for silence all round; he would fly up in a passion of anger at a question, or sometimes because none was put, and so he judged the company was not following his story. Nor would he allow anyone to leave the inn till he had drunk himself sleepy and reeled off to bed.

His stories were what frightened people worst of all. Dreadful stories they were; about hanging, and walking the plank, and storms at sea, and the Dry Tortugas, and wild deeds and places on the Spanish Main. By his own account he must have lived his life among some of the wickedest men that God ever allowed upon the sea; and the language in which he told these stories shocked our plain country people almost as much as the crimes that he described. My father was always saying the inn would be ruined, for people would soon cease coming there to be tyrannised over and put down, and sent shivering to their beds; but I really believe his presence did us good. People were frightened at the time, but on looking back they rather liked it; it was a fine excitement in a quiet country life; and there was even a party of the younger men who pretended to admire him, calling him a "true sea-dog," and a "real old salt," and such-like names, and saying there was the sort of man that made England terrible at sea.

In one way, indeed, he bade fair to ruin us; for he kept on staying week after week, and at last month after month, so that all the money had been long exhausted, and still my father never plucked up the heart to insist on having more. If ever he mentioned it, the captain blew through his nose so loudly, that you might say he roared, and stared my poor father out of the room. I have seen him wringing his hands after such a rebuff, and I am sure the annoyance and the terror he lived in must have greatly hastened his early and unhappy death.

All the time he lived with us the captain made no change whatever in his dress but to buy some stockings from a hawker. One of the cocks of his hat having fallen down, he let it hang from that day forth, though it was a great annoyance when it blew. I remember the appearance of his coat, which he patched himself upstairs in his room, and which, before the end, was nothing but patches. He never wrote or received a letter, and he never spoke with any but the neighbours, and with these, for the most part, only when drunk on rum. The great sea-chest none of us had ever seen open.

He was only once crossed, and that was towards the end, when my poor father was far gone in a decline that took him off. Dr Livesey came late one afternoon to see the patient, took a bit of dinner from my mother, and went into the parlour to smoke a pipe until his horse should come down from the hamlet, for we had no stabling at the old "Benbow." I followed him in, and I remember observing the contrast the neat, bright doctor, with his powder as white as snow, and his bright, black eyes and pleasant manners, made with the coltish country folk, and above all, with that filthy, heavy, bleared scarecrow of a pirate of ours, sitting far gone in rum, with his arms on the table. Suddenly he—the captain, that is—began to pipe up his eternal song:—

"Fifteen men on the dead man's chest—
Yo-ho-ho, and a bottle of rum!
Drink and the devil had done for the rest—
Yo-ho-ho and a bottle of rum!"

At first I had supposed "the dead man's chest" to be that identical big box of his upstairs in the front room, and the thought had been mingled in my nightmares with that of the one-legged seafaring man. But by this time we had all long ceased to pay any particular notice to the song; it was new, that night, to nobody but Dr Livesey, and on him I observed it did not produce an agreeable effect, for he looked up for a moment quite angrily before he went on with his talk to old Taylor, the gardener, on a new cure for the rheumatics. In the meantime, the captain gradually brightened up at his own music, and at last flapped his hand upon the table before him in a way we all knew to mean—silence. The voices stopped at once, all but Dr Livesey's; he went on as before, speaking clear and kind, and drawing briskly at his pipe between every word or two. The captain glared at him for a while, flapped his hand again, glared still harder, and at last broke out with a villainous, low oath: "Silence, there, between decks!"

"Were you addressing me, sir?" says the doctor; and when the ruffian had told him, with another oath, that this was so, "I have only one thing to say to you, sir," replies the doctor, "that if you keep on drinking rum, the world will soon be quit of a very dirty scoundrel!"

The old fellow's fury was awful. He sprang to his feet, drew and opened a sailor's clasp-knife, and balancing it open on the palm of his hand, threatened to pin the doctor to the wall.

The doctor never so much as moved. He spoke to him, as before, over his shoulder, and in the same tone of voice; rather high, so that all the room might hear, but perfectly calm and steady:—

"If you do not put that knife this instant in your pocket, I promise, upon my honour, you shall hang at the next assizes."

Then followed a battle of looks between them; but the captain soon knuckled under, put up his weapon, and resumed his seat, grumbling like a beaten dog.

"And now, sir," continued the doctor, "since I now know there's such a fellow in my district, you may count I'll have an eye upon you day and night. I'm not a doctor only; I'm a magistrate; and if I catch a breath of complaint against you, if it's only for a piece of incivility like to-night's, I'll take effectual means to have you hunted down and routed out of this. Let that suffice."

Soon after Dr Livesey's horse came to the door, and he rode away; but the captain held his peace that evening, and for many evenings to come.

Chapter II

BLACK DOG APPEARS AND DISAPPEARS

It was not very long after this that there occurred the first of the mysterious events that rid us at last of the captain, though not, as you will see, of his affairs. It was a bitter cold winter, with long, hard frosts and heavy gales; and it was plain from the first that my poor father was little likely to see the spring. He sank daily, and my mother and I had all the inn upon our hands; and were kept busy enough, without paying much regard to our unpleasant guest.

It was one January morning, very early—a pinching, frosty morning —the cove all grey with hoar-frost, the ripple lapping softly on the stones, the sun still low and only touching the hill-tops and shining far to seaward. The captain had risen earlier than usual, and set out down the beach, his cutlass swinging under the broad skirts of the old blue coat, his brass telescope under his arm, his hat tilted back upon his head. I remember his breath hanging like smoke in his wake as he strode off, and the last sound I heard of him, as he turned the big rock, was a loud snort of indignation, as though his mind was still running upon Dr Livesey.

Well, mother was upstairs with father; and I was laying the breakfast-table against the captain's return, when the parlour door opened, and a man stepped in on whom I had never set my eyes before. He was a pale, tallowy creature, wanting two fingers of the left hand; and, though he wore a cutlass, he did not look much like a fighter. I had always my eye open for seafaring men, with one leg or two, and I remember this one puzzled me. He was not sailorly, and yet he had a smack of the sea about him too.

I asked him what was for his service, and he said he would take rum; but as I was going out of the room to fetch it he sat down upon a table and motioned me to draw near. I paused where I was with my napkin in my hand.

"Come here, sonny," says he. "Come nearer here."

I took a step nearer.

"Is this here table for my mate Bill?" he asked, with a kind of leer.

I told him I did not know his mate Bill; and this was for a person who stayed in our house, whom we called the captain.

"Well," said he, "my mate Bill would be called the captain, as like as not. He has a cut on one cheek, and a mighty pleasant way with him, particularly in drink, has my mate Bill. We'll put it, for argument like, that your captain has a cut on one cheek—and we'll put it, if you like, that that cheek's the right one. Ah, well! I told you. Now, is my mate Bill in this here house?"

I told him he was out walking.

"Which way, sonny? Which way is he gone?"

And when I had pointed out the rock and told him how the captain was likely to return, and how soon, and answered a few other questions, "Ah," said he, "this'll be as good as drink to my mate Bill."

The expression of his face as he said these words was not at all pleasant, and I had my own reasons for thinking that the stranger was mistaken, even supposing he meant what he said. But it was no affair of mine, I thought; and, besides, it was difficult to know what to do. The stranger kept hanging about just inside the inn door, peering round the corner like a cat waiting for a mouse. Once I stepped out myself into the road, but he immediately called me back, and, as I did not obey quick enough for his fancy, a most horrible change came over his tallowy face, and he ordered me in, with an oath that made me jump. As soon as I was back again he returned to his former manner, half fawning, half sneering, patted me on the shoulder, told me I was a good boy, and he had taken quite a fancy to me. "I have a son of my own," said he, "as like you as two blocks, and he's all the pride of my 'art. But the great thing for boys is discipline, sonny—discipline. Now, if you had sailed along of Bill, you wouldn't have stood there to be spoke to twice—not you. That was never Bill's way, nor the way of sich as sailed with him. And here, sure enough, is my mate Bill, with a spy-glass under his arm, bless his old 'art, to be sure. You and me'll just go back into the parlour, sonny, and get behind the door, and we'll give Bill a little surprise —bless his 'art, I say again."

So saying, the stranger backed along with me into the parlour, and put me behind him in the corner, so that we were both hidden by the open door. I was very uneasy and alarmed, as you may fancy, and it rather added to my fears to observe that the stranger was certainly frightened himself. He cleared the hilt of his cutlass and loosened the blade in the sheath; and all the time we were waiting there he kept swallowing as if he felt what we used to call a lump in the throat.

At last in strode the captain, slammed the door behind him, without looking to the right or left, and marched straight across the room to where his breakfast awaited him.

"Bill," said the stranger, in a voice that I thought he had tried to make bold and big.

The captain spun round on his heel and fronted us; all the brown had gone out of his face, and even his nose was blue; he had the look of a man who sees a ghost, or the Evil One, or something worse, if anything can be; and, upon my word, I felt sorry to see him, all in a moment, turn so old and sick.

"Come, Bill, you know me; you know an old shipmate, Bill, surely," said the stranger.

The captain made a sort of gasp.

"Black Dog!" said he.

"And who else?" returned the other, getting more at his ease. "Black Dog as ever was, come for to see his old shipmate Billy, at the 'Admiral Benbow' inn. Ah, Bill, Bill, we have seen a sight of times, us two, since I lost them two talons," holding up his mutilated hand.

"Now, look here," said the captain; "you've run me down; here I am; well, then, speak up: what is it?"

"That's you, Bill," returned Black Dog, "you're in the right of it, Billy. I'll have a glass of rum from this dear child here, as I've took such a liking to; and we'll sit down, if you please, and talk square, like old shipmates."

When I returned with the rum, they were already seated on either side of the captain's breakfast-table—Black Dog next to the door, and sitting sideways, so as to have one eye on his old shipmate, and one, as I thought, on his retreat.

He bade me go, and leave the door wide open. "None of your key-holes for me, sonny," he said; and I left them together, and retired into the bar.

For a long time, though I certainly did my best to listen, I could hear nothing but a low gabbling; but at last the voices began to grow higher, and I could pick up a word or two, mostly oaths, from the captain.

"No, no, no, no; and an end of it!" he cried once. And again, "If it comes to swinging, swing all, say I."

Then all of a sudden there was a tremendous explosion of oaths and other noises—the chair and table went over in a lump, a clash of steel followed, and then a cry of pain, and the next instant I saw Black Dog in full flight, and the captain hotly pursuing, both with drawn cutlasses, and the former streaming blood from the left shoulder. Just at the door, the captain aimed at the fugitive one last tremendous cut, which would certainly have split him to the chine had it not been intercepted by our big signboard of Admiral Benbow. You may see the notch on the lower side of the frame to this day.

That blow was the last of the battle. Once out upon the road, Black Dog, in spite of his wound, showed a wonderful clean pair of heels, and disappeared over the edge of the hill in half a minute. The captain, for his part, stood staring at the signboard like a bewildered man. Then he passed his hand over his eyes several times, and at last turned back into the house.

"Jim," says he, "rum"; and as he spoke, he reeled a little, and caught himself with one hand against the wall.

"Are you hurt?" cried I.

"Rum," he repeated. "I must get away from here. Rum! rum!"

I ran to fetch it; but I was quite unsteadied by all that had fallen out, and I broke one glass and fouled the tap, and while I was still getting in my own way, I heard a loud fall in the parlour, and, running in, beheld the captain lying full length upon the floor. At the same instant my mother, alarmed by the cries and fighting, came running downstairs to help me. Between us we raised his head. He was breathing very loud and hard; but his eyes were closed, and his face a horrible colour.

"Dear, deary me," cried my mother, "what a disgrace upon the house! And your poor father sick!"

In the meantime, we had no idea what to do to help the captain, nor any other thought but that he had got his death-hurt in the scuffle

THE NEXT INSTANT I SAW BLACK DOG IN FULL FLIGHT

with the stranger. I got the rum, to be sure, and tried to put it down his throat; but his teeth were tightly shut, and his jaws as strong as iron. It was a happy relief for us when the door opened and Doctor Livesey came in, on his visit to my father.

"Oh, doctor," we cried, "what shall we do? Where is he wounded?"

"Wounded? A fiddle-stick's end!" said the doctor. "No more wounded than you or I. The man has had a stroke, as I warned him. Now, Mrs Hawkins, just you run upstairs to your husband, and tell him, if possible, nothing about it. For my part, I must do my best to save this fellow's trebly worthless life; and Jim here will get me a basin."

When I got back with the basin, the doctor had already ripped up the captain's sleeve, and exposed his great sinewy arm. It was tattooed in several places. "Here's luck," "A fair wind," and "Billy Bones his fancy," were very neatly and clearly executed on the forearm; and up near the shoulder there was a sketch of a gallows and a man hanging from it—done, as I thought, with great spirit.

"Prophetic," said the doctor, touching this picture with his finger. "And now, Master Billy Bones, if that be your name, we'll have a look at the colour of your blood. Jim," he said, "are you afraid of blood?"

"No, sir," said I.

"Well, then," said he, "you hold the basin;" and with that he took his lancet and opened a vein.

A great deal of blood was taken before the captain opened his eyes and looked mistily about him. First he recognised the doctor with an unmistakable frown; then his glance fell upon me, and he looked relieved. But suddenly his colour changed, and he tried to raise himself, crying:—

"Where's Black Dog?"

"There is no Black Dog here," said the doctor, "except what you have on your own back. You have been drinking rum; you have had a stroke, precisely as I told you; and I have just, very much against my own will, dragged you head-foremost out of the grave. Now, Mr Bones—"

"That's not my name," he interrupted.

"Much I care," returned the doctor. "It's the name of a buccaneer of my acquaintance; and I call you by it for the sake of shortness, and what I have to say to you is this: one glass of rum won't kill you, but if you take one you'll take another and another, and I stake my wig if you don't break off short, you'll die—do you understand that?—die, and go to your own place, like the man in the Bible. Come, now, make an effort. I'll help you to your bed for once."

Between us, with much trouble, we managed to hoist him upstairs, and laid him on his bed, where his head fell back on the pillow, as if he were almost fainting.

"Now, mind you," said the doctor, "I clear my conscience—the name of rum for you is death."

And with that he went off to see my father, taking me with him by the arm.

"This is nothing," he said, as soon as he had closed the door. "I have drawn blood enough to keep him quiet a while; he should lie for a week where he is—that is the best thing for him and you; but another stroke would settle him."

Chapter III

THE BLACK SPOT

About noon I stopped at the captain's door with some cooling drinks and medicines. He was lying very much as we had left him, only a little higher, and he seemed both weak and excited.

"Jim," he said, "you're the only one here that's worth anything; and you know I've been always good to you. Never a month but I've given you a silver fourpenny for yourself. And now you see, mate, I'm pretty low, and deserted by all; and Jim, you'll bring me one noggin of rum, now, won't you, matey?"

"The doctor—" I began.

But he broke in cursing the doctor, in a feeble voice, but heartily. "Doctors is all swabs," he said; "and that doctor there, why, what do he know about seafaring men? I been in places hot as pitch, and mates dropping round with Yellow Jack, and the blessed land a-heaving like the sea with earthquakes—what do the doctor know of lands like that?—and I lived on rum, I tell you. It's been meat and drink, and man and wife, to me; and if I'm not to have my rum now I'm a poor old hulk on a lee-shore, my blood'll be on you, Jim, and that Doctor swab;" and he ran on again for a while with curses. "Look, Jim, how my fingers fidges," he continued, in the pleading tone. "I can't keep 'em still, not I. I haven't had a drop this blessed day. That doctor's a fool, I tell you. If I don't have a drain o' rum, Jim, I'll have the horrors; I seen some on 'em already. I seen old Flint in the corner there, behind you; as plain as print, I seen him; and if I get the horrors, I'm a man that has lived rough, and I'll raise Cain. Your doctor

15

hisself said one glass wouldn't hurt me. I'll give you a golden guinea for a noggin, Jim."

He was growing more and more excited, and this alarmed me for my father, who was very low that day, and needed quiet; besides, I was reassured by the doctor's words, now quoted to me, and rather offended by the offer of a bribe.

"I want none of your money," said I, "but what you owe my father. I'll get you one glass, and no more."

When I brought it to him, he seized it greedily, and drank it out.

"Ay, ay," said he, "that's some better, sure enough. And now, matey, did that doctor say how long I was to lie here in this old berth?"

"A week at least," said I.

"Thunder!" he cried. "A week! I can't do that: they'd have the black spot on me by then. The lubbers is going about to get the wind of me this blessed moment; lubbers as couldn't keep what they got, and want to nail what is another's. Is that seamanly behaviour, now, I want to know? But I'm a saving soul. I never wasted good money of mine, nor lost it neither; and I'll trick 'em again. I'm not afraid on 'em. I'll shake out another reef, matey, and daddle 'em again."

As he was thus speaking, he had risen from bed with great difficulty, holding to my shoulder with a grip that almost made me cry out, and moving his legs like so much dead weight. His words, spirited as they were in meaning, contrasted sadly with the weakness of the voice in which they were uttered. He paused when he had got into a sitting position on the edge.

"That doctor's done me," he murmured. "My ears is singing. Lay me back."

Before I could do much to help him he had fallen back again to his former place, where he lay for a while silent.

"Jim," he said, at length, "you saw that seafaring man to-day?"

"Black Dog?" I asked.

"Ah! Black Dog," says he. "*He's* a bad 'un; but there's worse that put him on. Now, if I can't get away nohow, and they tip me the black spot, mind you, it's my old sea-chest they're after; you get on a horse—you can, can't you? Well, then, you get on a horse, and go to—well, yes, I will!—to that eternal Doctor swab, and tell him to pipe all hands—magistrates and sich—and he'll lay 'em aboard at the 'Admiral Benbow'—all old Flint's crew, man and boy, all on 'em that's left. I was first mate, I was, old Flint's first mate, and I'm the on'y one as knows the place. He gave it me to Savannah, when he lay a-dying, like as if I was to now, you see. But you won't peach unless they get the black spot on me, or unless you see that Black Dog again, or a seafaring man with one leg, Jim—him above all."

"But what is the black spot, captain?" I asked.

"That's a summons, mate. I'll tell you if they get that. But you keep your weather-eye open, Jim, and I'll share with you equals, upon my honour."

He wandered a little longer, his voice growing weaker; but soon after I had given him his medicine, which he took like a child, with the remark, "If ever a seaman wanted drugs, it's me," he fell at last into a heavy, swoon-like sleep, in which I left him. What I should have done had all gone well I do not know. Probably I should have told the whole story to the doctor; for I was in mortal fear lest the captain should repent of his confessions and make an end of me. But as things fell out, my poor father died quite suddenly that evening, which put all other matters on one side. Our natural distress, the visits of the neighbours, the arranging of the funeral, and all the work of the inn to be carried on in the meanwhile, kept me so busy that I had scarcely time to think of the captain, far less to be afraid of him.

He got downstairs next morning, to be sure, and had his meals as usual, though he ate little, and had more, I am afraid, than his usual supply of rum, for he helped himself out of the bar, scowling and blowing through his nose, and no one dared to cross him. On the night before the funeral he was as drunk as ever; and it was shocking, in that house of mourning, to hear him singing away at his ugly old sea-song; but, weak as he was, we were all in the fear of death for him, and the doctor was suddenly taken up with a case many miles away, and was never near the house after my father's death. I have said the captain was weak; and indeed he seemed rather to grow weaker than regain his strength. He clambered up and down stairs, and went from the parlour to the bar and back again, and sometimes put his nose out of doors to smell the sea, holding on to the walls as he went for support, and breathing hard and fast like a man on a steep mountain. He never particularly addressed me, and it is my belief he had as good as forgotten his confidences; but his temper was more flighty, and, allowing for his bodily weakness, more violent than ever. He had an alarming way now when he was drunk of drawing his cutlass and laying it bare before him on the table. But, with all that, he minded people less and seemed shut up in his own thoughts and rather wandering. Once, for instance, to our extreme wonder, he piped up to a different air, a kind of country love-song, that he must have learned in his youth before he had begun to follow the sea.

So things passed until, the day after the funeral, and about three o'clock of a bitter, foggy, frosty afternoon, I was standing at the door for a moment, full of sad thoughts about my father, when I saw someone drawing slowly near along the road. He was plainly blind, for he tapped before him with a stick, and wore a great green shade over his eyes and nose; and he was hunched, as if with age or weakness, and wore a huge old tattered sea-cloak with a hood, that made him appear positively deformed. I never saw in my life a more dreadful-looking figure. He stopped a little from the inn, and, raising his voice in an odd sing-song, addressed the air in front of him:—

"Will any kind friend inform a poor blind man, who has lost the precious sight of his eyes in the gracious defence of his native country, England, and God bless King George!—where or in what part of this country he may now be?"

"You are at the 'Admiral Benbow,' Black Hill Cove, my good man," said I.

"I hear a voice," said he—"a young voice. Will you give me your hand, my kind young friend, and lead me in?"

I held out my hand, and the horrible, soft-spoken, eyeless creature gripped it in a moment like a vice. I was so much startled that I struggled to withdraw; but the blind man pulled me close up to him with a single action of his arm.

"Now, boy," he said, "take me in to the captain."

"Sir," said I, "upon my word I dare not."

"Oh," he sneered, "that's it! Take me in straight, or I'll break your arm."

And he gave it, as he spoke, a wrench, that made me cry out.

"Sir," said I, "it is for yourself I mean. The captain is not what he used to be. He sits with a drawn cutlass. Another gentleman—"

"Come, now, march," interrupted he; and I never heard a voice so cruel, and cold, and ugly as that blind man's. It cowed me more than the pain; and I began to obey him at once, walking straight in at the door and towards the parlour, where our sick old buccaneer was sitting, dazed with rum. The blind man clung close to me, holding me

AT ONE LOOK THE RUM WENT OUT OF HIM AND LEFT HIM STARING SOBER in one iron fist, and leaning almost more of his weight on me than I could carry. "Lead me straight up to him, and when I'm in view, cry out, 'Here's a friend for you, Bill.' If you don't, I'll do this;"and with that he gave me a twitch that I thought would have made me faint. Between this and that, I was so utterly terrified of the blind beggar that I forgot my terror of the captain, and as I opened the parlour door, cried out the words he had ordered in a trembling voice.

The poor captain raised his eyes, and at one look the rum went out of him, and left him staring sober. The expression of his face was not so much of terror as of mortal sickness. He made a movement to rise, but I do not believe he had enough force left in his body.

"Now, Bill, sit where you are," said the beggar. "If I can't see, I can hear a finger stirring. Business is business. Hold out your right hand. Boy, take his right hand by the wrist, and bring it near to my right."

We both obeyed him to the letter, and I saw him pass something from the hollow of the hand that held his stick into the palm of the captain's, which closed upon it instantly.

"And now that's done," said the blind man; and at the words he suddenly left hold of me, and, with incredible accuracy and nimbleness, skipped out of the parlour and into the road, where, as I still stood motionless, I could hear his stick go tap-tap-tapping into the distance.

It was some time before either I or the captain seemed to gather our senses; but at length, and about at the same moment, I released his wrist, which I was still holding, and he drew in his hand and looked sharply into the palm.

"Ten o'clock!" he cried. "Six hours. We'll do them yet"; and he sprang to his feet.

Even as he did so, he reeled, put his hand to his throat, stood swaying for a moment, and then, with a peculiar sound, fell from his whole height face foremost to the floor.

I ran to him at once, calling to my mother. But haste was all in vain. The captain had been struck dead by thundering apoplexy. It is a curious thing to understand, for I had certainly never liked the man, though of late I had begun to pity him, but as soon as I saw that he was dead, I burst into a flood of tears. It was the second death I had known, and the sorrow of the first was still fresh in my heart.

CHAPTER IV

THE SEA CHEST

I lost no time, of course, in telling my mother all that I knew, and perhaps should have told her long before, and we saw ourselves at once in a difficult and dangerous position. Some of the man's money—if he had any—was certainly due to us; but it was not likely that our captain's shipmates, above all the two specimens seen by me, Black Dog and the blind beggar, would be inclined to give up their booty in payment of the dead man's debts. The captain's order to mount at once and ride for Doctor Livesey would have left my mother alone and unprotected, which was not to be thought of. Indeed, it seemed impossible for either of us to remain much longer in the house: the fall of coals in the kitchen grate, the very ticking of the clock, filled us with alarms. The neighbourhood, to our ears, seemed haunted by approaching footsteps; and what between the dead body of the captain on the parlour floor, and the thought of that detestable blind beggar hovering near at hand, and ready to return, there were moments when, as the saying goes, I jumped in my skin for terror. Something must speedily be resolved upon; and it occurred to us at last to go forth together and seek help in the neighbouring hamlet. No sooner said than done. Bare-headed as we were, we ran out at once in the gathering evening and the frosty fog.

The hamlet lay not many hundred yards away though out of view, on the other side of the next cove; and what greatly encouraged me, it was in an opposite direction from that whence the blind man had made his appearance, and whither he had presumably returned. We were not many minutes on the road, though we sometimes stopped to lay hold of each other and hearken. But there was no unusual sound—nothing but the low wash of the ripple and the croaking of the crows in the wood.

It was already candle-light when we reached the hamlet, and I shall never forget how much I was cheered to see the yellow shine in doors and windows; but that, as it proved, was the best of the help we were likely to get in that quarter. For—you would have thought men would have been ashamed of themselves—no soul would consent to return with us to the "Admiral Benbow." The more we told of our troubles, the more—man, woman, and child—they clung to the shelter of their houses. The name of Captain Flint, though it was strange to me, was well enough known to some there, and carried a great weight of terror. Some of the men who had been to field-work on the far side of the "Admiral Benbow" remembered, besides, to have seen several strangers on the road, and, taking them to be smugglers, to have bolted away; and one at least had seen a little lugger in what we called Kitt's Hole. For that matter, anyone who was a comrade of the captain's was enough to frighten them to death. And the short and the long of the matter was, that while we could get several who were willing enough to ride to Dr Livesey's which lay in another direction, not one would help us to defend the inn.

They say cowardice is infectious; but then argument is, on the other hand, a great emboldener; and so when each had said his say, my mother made them a speech. She would not, she declared, lose money that belonged to her fatherless boy; "if none of the rest of you dare," she said, "Jim and I dare. Back we will go, the way we came, and small thanks to you big, hulking, chicken-hearted men. We'll have that chest open, if we die for it. And I'll thank you for that bag, Mrs Crossley, to bring back our lawful money in."

Of course, I said I would go with my mother; and of course they all cried out at our foolhardiness; but even then not a man would go along with us. All they would do was to give me a loaded pistol, lest we were attacked; and to promise to have horses ready saddled, in case we were pursued on our return; while one lad was to ride forward to the doctor's in search of armed assistance.

My heart was beating finely when we two set forth in the cold night upon this dangerous venture. A full moon was beginning to rise and peered redly through the upper edges of the fog, and this increased our haste, for it was plain, before we came forth again, that all would be as bright as day, and our departure exposed to the eyes of any watchers. We slipped along the hedges, noiseless and swift, nor did we see or hear anything to increase our terrors, till, to our huge relief, the door of the "Admiral Benbow" had closed behind us.

I slipped the bolt at once, and we stood and panted for moment in the dark, alone in the house with the dead captain's body. Then my mother got a candle in the bar, and, holding each other's hands, we advanced into the parlour. He lay as we had left him, on his back, with his eyes open, and one arm stretched out.

"Draw down the blind, Jim," whispered my mother; "they might come and watch outside. And now," said she, when I had done so, "we have to get the key off *that*; and who's to touch it, I should like to know!" and she gave a kind of sob as she said the words.

I went down on my knees at once. On the floor close to his hand there was a little round of paper, blackened on the one side. I could not doubt that this was the *black spot*; and taking it up, I found written on the other side, in a very good, clear hand, this short message: "You have till ten to-night."

"He had till ten, mother," said I; and just as I said it, our old clock began striking. This sudden noise startled us shockingly; but the news was good, for it was only six.

"Now, Jim," she said, "that key."

I felt in his pockets, one after another. A few small coins, a thimble, and some thread and big needles, a piece of pigtail tobacco bitten away at the end, his gully with the crooked handle, a pocket compass, and a tinder-box, were all that they contained, and I began to despair.

"Perhaps it's round his neck," suggested my mother.

Overcoming a strong repugnance, I tore open his shirt at the neck, and there, sure enough, hanging to a bit of tarry string, which I cut with his own gully, we found the key. At this triumph we were filled with hope, and hurried upstairs, without delay, to the little room where he had slept so long, and where his box had stood since the day of his arrival.

It was like any other seaman's chest on the outside, the initial "B." burned on the top of it with a hot iron, and the corners somewhat smashed and broken as by long, rough usage.

"Give me the key," said my mother; and though the lock was very stiff, she had turned it and thrown back the lid in a twinkling.

A strong smell of tobacco and tar rose from the interior, but nothing was to be seen on the top except a suit of very good clothes, carefully brushed and folded. They had never been worn, my mother said. Under that, the miscellany began—a quadrant, a tin cannikin, several sticks of tobacco, two brace of very handsome pistols, a piece of bar silver, an old Spanish watch and some other trinkets of little value and mostly of foreign make, a pair of compasses mounted with brass, and five or six curious West Indian shells. It has often set me thinking since that he should have carried about these shells with him in his wandering, guilty, and hunted life.

In the meantime we had found nothing of any value but the silver and the trinkets, and neither of these were in our way. Underneath there was an old boat-cloak, whitened with sea-salt on-many a harbour-bar. My mother pulled it up with impatience, and there lay before us, the last things in the chest, a bundle tied up in oilcloth, and looking like papers, and a canvas bag, that gave forth, at a touch, the jingle of gold.

"I'll show these rogues that I'm an honest woman," said my mother. "I'll have my dues, and not a farthing over. Hold Mrs Crossley's bag." And she began to count over the amount of the captain's score from the sailor's bag into the one that I was holding.

It was a long, difficult business, for the coins were of all countries and sizes—doubloons, and louis-d'ors, and guineas, and pieces of eight, and I know not what besides, all shaken together at random. The guineas, too, were about the scarcest, and it was with these only that my mother knew how to make her count.

When we were about half way through, I suddenly put my hand upon her arm; for I had heard in the silent, frosty air, a sound that brought my heart into my mouth—the tap-tapping of the blind man's stick upon the frozen road. It drew nearer and nearer, while we sat holding our breath. Then it struck sharp on the inn door, and then we could hear the handle being turned, and the bolt rattling as the wretched being tried to enter; and then there was a long time of silence both within and without. At last the tapping recommenced, and, to our indescribable joy and gratitude, died slowly away again until it ceased to be heard.

"Mother," said I, "take the whole and let's be going"; for I was sure the bolted door must have seemed suspicious, and would bring the whole hornet's nest about our ears; though how thankful I was that I had bolted it, none could tell who had never met that terrible blind man.

But my mother, frightened as she was, would not consent to take a fraction more than was due to her, and was obstinately unwilling to be content with less. It was not yet seven, she said, by a long way; she knew her rights and she would have them; and she was still arguing with me, when a little low whistle sounded a good way off upon the hill. That was enough, and more than enough, for both of us.

"I'll take what I have," she said, jumping to her feet.

"And I'll take this to square the count," said I, picking up the oil-skin packet.

Next moment we were both groping downstairs, leaving the candle by the empty chest; and the next we had opened the door and were in full retreat. We had not started a moment too soon. The fog was rapidly dispersing; already the moon shone quite clear on the high ground on either side; and it was only in the exact bottom of the dell and round the tavern door that a thin veil still hung unbroken to conceal the first steps of our escape. Far less than half-way to the hamlet, very little beyond the bottom of the hill, we must come forth into the moonlight. Nor was this all; for the sound of several footsteps running came already to our ears, and as we looked back in their direction, a light tossing to and fro and still rapidly advancing, showed that one of the new-comers carried a lantern.

"My dear," said my mother suddenly, "take the money and run on. I am going to faint."

This was certainly the end for both of us, I thought. How I cursed the cowardice of the neighbours; how I blamed my poor mother for her honesty and her greed, for her past foolhardiness and present weakness! We were just at the little bridge, by good fortune; and I helped her, tottering as she was, to the edge of the bank, where, sure enough, she gave a sigh and fell on my shoulder. I do not know how I found the strength to do it at all, and I am afraid it was roughly done; but I managed to drag her down the bank and a little way under the arch. Farther I could not move her, for the bridge was too low to let me do more than crawl below it. So there we had to stay—my mother almost entirely exposed, and both of us within earshot of the inn.

CHAPTER V

THE LAST OF THE BLIND MAN

My curiosity, in a sense, was stronger than my fear; for I could not remain where I was, but crept back to the bank again, whence, sheltering my head behind a bush of broom, I might command the road before our door. I was scarcely in position ere my enemies began to arrive, seven or eight of them, running hard, their feet beating out of time along the road, and the man with the lantern some paces in front. Three men ran together, hand in hand; and I made out, even through the mist, that the middle man of this trio was the blind beggar. The next moment his voice showed me that I was right.

"Down with the door!" he cried.

"Ay, ay, sir!" answered two or three; and a rush was made upon the "Admiral Benbow," the lantern-bearer following; and then I could see them pause, and hear speeches passed in a lower key, as if they were surprised to find the door open. But the pause was brief, for the blind man again issued his commands. His voice sounded louder and higher, as if he were afire with eagerness and rage.

"In, in, in!" he shouted, and cursed them for their delay.

Four or five of them obeyed at once, two remaining on the road with the formidable beggar. There was a pause, then a cry of surprise, and then a voice shouting from the house:

"Bill's dead!"

But the blind man swore at them again for their delay.

"Search him, some of you shirking lubbers, and the rest of you aloft and get the chest," he cried.

I could hear their feet rattling up our old stairs, so that the house must have shook with it. Promptly afterwards, fresh sounds of astonishment arose; the window of the captain's room was thrown open with a slam and a jingle of broken glass; and a man leaned out into the moonlight, head and shoulders, and addressed the blind beggar on the road below him.

"Pew," he cried, "they've been before us. Someone's turned the chest out alow and aloft."

"Is it there?" roared Pew.

"The money's there."

The blind man cursed the money.

"Flint's fist, I mean," he cried.

"We don't see it here nohow," returned the man.

"Here, you below there, is it on Bill?" cried the blind man again.

At that, another fellow, probably him who had remained below to search the captain's body, came to the door of the inn. "Bill's been overhauled a'ready," said he, "nothin' left."

"It's these people of the inn—it's that boy. I wish I had put his eyes out!" cried the blind man, Pew. "They were here no time ago—they had the door bolted when I tried it. Scatter, lads, and find 'em."

"Sure enough, they left their glim here," said the fellow from the window.

"Scatter and find 'em! Rout the house out!" reiterated Pew, striking with his stick upon the road.

Then there followed a great to-do through all our old inn, heavy feet pounding to and fro, furniture thrown over, doors kicked in, until the very rocks re-echoed, and the men came out again, one after another, on the road, and declared that we were nowhere to be found. And just then the same whistle that had alarmed my mother and myself over the dead captain's money was once more clearly audible through the night, but this time twice repeated. I had thought it to be the blind man's trumpet, so to speak, summoning his crew to the assault; but I now found that it was a signal from the hillside towards the hamlet, and, from its effect upon the buccaneers, a signal to warn them of approaching danger.

"There's Dirk again," said one. "Twice! We'll have to budge, mates."

"Budge, you skulk!" cried Pew. "Dirk was a fool and a coward from the first—you wouldn't mind him. They must be close by; they can't be far; you have your hands on it. Scatter and look for them, dogs! Oh, shiver my soul," he cried, "if I had eyes!"

This appeal seemed to produce some effect, for two of the fellows began to look here and there among the lumber, but half-heartedly, I thought, and with half an eye to their own danger all the time, while the rest stood irresolute on the road.

"You have your hands on thousands, you fools, and you hang a leg! You'd be as rich as kings if you could find it, and you know it's here, and you stand there malingering. There wasn't one of you dared face Bill, and I did it—a blind man! And I'm to lose my chance for you! I'm to be a poor, crawling beggar, sponging for rum, when I might be rolling in a coach! If you had the pluck of a weevil in a biscuit you would catch them still."

"Hang it, Pew, we've got the doubloons!" grumbled one.

"They might have hid the blessed thing," said another. "Take the Georges, Pew, and don't stand here squalling."

Squalling was the word for it, Pew's anger rose so high at these objections; till at last, his passion completely taking the upper hand, he struck at them right and left in his blindness, and his stick sounded heavily on more than one.

These, in their turn, cursed back at the blind miscreant, threatened him in horrid terms, and tried in vain to catch the stick and wrest it from his grasp.

This quarrel was the saving of us; for while it was still raging, another sound came from the top of the hill on the side of the hamlet— the tramp of horses galloping. Almost at the same time a pistol-shot, flash and report, came from the hedge side. And that was plainly the last signal of danger; for the buccaneers turned at once and ran, separating in every direction, one seaward along the cove, one slant across the hill, and so on, so that in half a minute not a sign of them remained but Pew. Him they had deserted, whether in sheer panic or out of revenge for his ill words and blows, I know not; but there he remained behind, tapping up and down the road in a frenzy, and groping and calling for his comrades. Finally he took the wrong turn, and ran a few steps past me, towards the hamlet, crying:

"Johnny, Black Dog, Dirk," and other names, "you won't leave old Pew, mates—not old Pew!"

Just then the noise of horses topped the rise, and four or five riders came in sight in the moonlight, and swept at full gallop down the slope.

At this Pew saw his error, turned with a scream, and ran straight for the ditch, into which he rolled. But he was on his feet again in a second, and made another dash, now utterly bewildered, right under the nearest of the coming horses.

The rider tried to save him, but in vain. Down went Pew with a cry that rang high into the night; and the four hoofs trampled and spurned him and passed by. He fell on his side, then gently collapsed upon his face, and moved no more.

I leaped to my feet and hailed the riders. They were pulling up, at any rate, horrified at the accident; and I soon saw what they were. One, tailing out behind the rest, was a lad that had gone from the hamlet to Dr Livesey's; the rest were revenue officers, whom he had met by the way, and with whom he had had the intelligence to return at once. Some news of the lugger in Kitt's Hole had found its way to Supervisor Dance, and set him forth that night in our direction, and to that circumstance my mother and I owed our preservation from death.

Pew was dead, stone dead. As for my mother, when we had carried her up to the hamlet, a little cold water and salts and that soon brought her back again, and she was none the worse for her terror, though she still continued to deplore the balance of the money. In the meantime the supervisor rode on, as fast as he could, to Kitt's Hole; but his men had to dismount and grope down the dingle, leading, and sometimes supporting, their horses, and in continual fear of ambushes; so it was no great matter for surprise that when they got down to the Hole the lugger was already under way, though still close in. He hailed her. A voice replied, telling him to keep out of the moonlight, or he would get some lead in him, and at the same time a bullet whistled close by his arm. Soon after, the lugger doubled the point and disappeared. Mr Dance stood there, as he said, "like a fish out of water," and all he could do was to despatch a man to B—— to warn the cutter. "And that," said he, "is just about as good as nothing. They've got off clean, and there's an end. Only," he added, "I'm glad I trod on Master Pew's corns;" for by this time he had heard my story.

I went back with him to the "Admiral Benbow," and you cannot imagine a house in such a state of smash; the very clock had been thrown down by these fellows in their furious hunt after my mother and myself; and though nothing had actually been taken away except the captain's money-bag and a little silver from the till, I could see at once that we were ruined. Mr Dance could make nothing of the scene.

"They got the money, you say? Well, then, Hawkins, what in fortune were they after? More money, I suppose?"

"No, sir; not money, I think," replied I. "In fact, sir, I believe I have the thing in my breast-pocket; and, to tell you the truth, I should like to get it put in safety."

"To be sure, boy; quite right," said he. "I'll take it, if you like."

"I thought, perhaps, Dr Livesey——" I began.

"Perfectly right," he interrupted, very cheerily, "perfectly right—a gentleman and a magistrate. And, now I come to think of it, I might as well ride round there myself and report to him or squire. Master Pew's dead, when all's done; not that I regret it, but he's dead, you see, and people will make it out against an officer of his Majesty's revenue, if make it out they can. Now, I'll tell you, Hawkins: if you like, I'll take you along."

I thanked him heartily for the offer, and we walked back to the hamlet where the horses were. By the time I had told mother of my purpose they were all in the saddle.

"Dogger," said Mr Dance, "you have a good horse; take up this lad behind you."

As soon as I was mounted, holding on to Dogger's belt, the supervisor gave the word, and the party struck out at a bouncing trot on the road to Dr Livesey's house.

CHAPTER VI

THE CAPTAIN'S PAPERS

We rode hard all the way, till we drew up before Dr Livesey's door. The house was all dark to the front. Mr Dance told me to jump down and knock, and Dogger gave me a stirrup to descend by. The door was opened almost at once by the maid.

"Is Dr Livesey in?" I asked.

"No," she said; he had come home in the afternoon, but had gone up to the Hall to dine and pass the evening with the squire.

"So there we go, boys," said Mr Dance.

This time, as the distance was short, I did not mount, but ran with Dogger's stirrup-leather to the lodge gates, and up the long, leafless, moonlit avenue to where the white line of the Hall buildings looked on either hand on great old gardens. Here Mr Dance dismounted, and, taking me along with him, was admitted at a word into the house.

The servant led us down a matted passage, and showed us at the end into a great library, all lined with bookcases and busts upon the top of them, where the squire and Dr Livesey sat, pipe in hand, on either side of a bright fire.

I had never seen the squire so near at hand. He was a tall man, over six feet high, and broad in proportion, and he had a bluff, rough-and-ready face, all roughened and reddened and lined in his long travels. His eyebrows were very black, and moved readily, and this gave him a look of some temper—not bad, you would say, but quick and high.

"Come in, Mr Dance," says he, very stately and condescending.

"Good evening, Dance," says the doctor, with a nod. "And good evening to you, friend Jim. What good wind brings you here?"

The supervisor stood up straight and stiff, and told his story like a lesson; and you should have seen how the two gentlemen leaned forward and looked at each other, and forgot to smoke in their surprise and interest. When they heard how my mother went back to the inn, Dr Livesey fairly slapped his thigh, and the squire cried, "Bravo!" and broke his long pipe against the grate. Long before it was done, Mr Trelawney (that, you will remember, was the squire's name) had got up from his seat, and was striding about the room, and the doctor, as if to hear the better, had taken off his powdered wig, and sat there, looking very strange indeed with his own close-cropped, black poll.

At last Mr Dance finished the story.

"Mr Dance," said the squire, "you are a very noble fellow. And as for riding down that black, atrocious miscreant, I regard it as an act of virtue, sir, like stamping on a cockroach. This lad Hawkins is a trump, I perceive. Hawkins, will you ring that bell? Mr Dance must have some ale."

"And so, Jim," said the doctor, "you have the thing that they were after, have you?"

"Here it is, sir," said I, and gave him the oilskin packet.

The doctor looked it all over, as if his fingers were itching to open it; but, instead of doing that, he put it quietly in the pocket of his coat.

"Squire," said he, "when Dance has had his ale he must, of course, be off on His Majesty's service; but I mean to keep Jim Hawkins here to sleep at my house, and, with your permission, I propose we should have up the cold pie, and let him sup."

"As you will, Livesey," said the squire; "Hawkins has earned better than cold pie."

So a big pigeon pie was brought in and put on a sidetable, and I made a hearty supper, for I was as hungry as a hawk, while Mr Dance was further complimented, and at last dismissed.

"And now, squire," said the doctor.

"And now, Livesey," said the squire, in the same breath.

"One at a time, one at a time," laughed Dr Livesey. "You have heard of this Flint, I suppose?"

"Heard of him!" cried the squire. "Heard of him, you say! He was the bloodthirstiest buccaneer that sailed. Blackbeard was a child to Flint. The Spaniards were so prodigiously afraid of him, that, I tell you, sir, I was sometimes proud he was an Englishman. I've seen his topsails with these eyes, off Trinidad, and the cowardly son of a rum-puncheon that I sailed with put back—put back, sir, into Port of Spain."

"Well, I've heard of him myself, in England," said the doctor. "But the point is, had he money?"

"Money!" cried the squire. "Have you heard the story? What were these villains after but money? What do they care for but money? For what would they risk their rascal carcases but money?"

"That we shall soon know," replied the doctor. "But you are so confoundly hot-headed and exclamatory that I cannot get a word in. What I want to know is this: Supposing that I have here in my pocket some clue to where Flint buried his treasure, will that treasure amount to much?"

"Amount, sir!" cried the squire. "It will amount to this: if we have the clue you talk about, I fit out a ship in Bristol dock, and take you and Hawkins here along, and I'll have that treasure if I search a year."

"Very well," said the doctor. "Now, then, if Jim is agreeable, we'll open the packet;" and he laid it before him on the table.

The bundle was sewn together, and the doctor had to get out his instrument-case, and cut the stitches with his medical scissors. It contained two things—a book and a sealed paper.

"First of all we'll try the book," observed the doctor.

The squire and I were both peering over his shoulder as he opened it, for Dr Livesey had kindly motioned me to come round from the side-table, where I had been eating, to enjoy the sport of the search. On the first page there were only some scraps of writing, such as a man with a pen in his hand might make for idleness or practice. One was the same as the tattoo mark, "Billy Bones his fancy;" then there was "Mr W. Bones, mate." "No more rum." "Off Palm Key he got itt;" and some other snatches, mostly single words and unintelligible. I could not help wondering who it was that had "got itt," and what "itt" was that he got. A knife in his back as like as not.

"Not much instruction there," said Dr Livesey, as he passed on.

The next ten or twelve pages were filled with a curious series of entries. There was a date at one end of the line and at the other a sum of money, as in common account-books; but instead of explanatory writing, only a varying number of crosses between the two. On the 12th of June, 1745, for instance, a sum of seventy pounds had plainly become due to someone, and there was nothing but six crosses to explain the cause. In a few cases, to be sure, the name of a place would be added, as "Offe Caraccas;" or a mere entry of latitude and longitude, as "62° 17' 20", 19° 2' 40"."

The record lasted over nearly twenty years, the amount of the separate entries growing larger as time went on, and at the end a grand total had been made out after five or six wrong additions, and these words appended, "Bones, his pile."

"I can't make head or tail of this," said Dr Livesey.

"The thing is as clear as noonday," cried the squire. "This is the black-hearted hound's account-book. These crosses stand for the names of ships or towns that they sank or plundered. The sums are the scoundrel's share, and where he feared an ambiguity, you see he added something clearer. 'Offe Caraccas,' now; you see, here was some unhappy vessel boarded off that coast. God help the poor souls that manned her—coral long ago."

"Right!" said the doctor. "See what it is to be a traveller. Right! And the amounts increase, you see, as he rose in rank."

There was little else in the volume but a few bearings of places noted in the blank leaves towards the end, and a table for reducing French, English, and Spanish moneys to a common value.

"Thrifty man!" cried the doctor. "He wasn't the one to be cheated."

"And now," said the squire, "for the other."

The paper had been sealed in several places with a thimble by way of seal; the very thimble, perhaps, that I had found in the captain's pocket. The doctor opened the seals with great care, and there fell out the map of an island, with latitude and longitude, soundings, names of hills, and bays and inlets, and every particular that would be needed to bring a ship to a safe anchorage upon its shores. It was about nine miles long and five across, shaped, you might say, like a fat dragon standing up, and had two fine land-locked harbours, and a hill in the centre part marked "The Spy-glass." There were several additions of a later date; but, above all, three crosses of red ink—two on the north part of the island, one in the south-west, and, beside this last, in the same red ink, and in a small, neat hand, very different from the captain's tottery characters, these words:—"Bulk of treasure here."

Over on the back the same hand had written this further information:—

"Tall tree, Spy-glass shoulder, bearing a point to the N. of N.N.E.

"Skeleton Island E.S.E. and by E.

"Ten feet.

"The bar silver is in the north cache; you can find it by the trend of the east hummock, ten fathoms south of the black crag with the face on it.

"The arms are easy found, in the sand hill, N. point of north inlet cape, bearing E. and a quarter N.   "J. F."

That was all; but brief as it was, and, to me, incomprehensible, it filled the squire and Dr Livesey with delight.

"Livesey," said the squire, " you will give up this wretched practice at once. To-morrow I start for Bristol. In three weeks' time—three weeks!—two weeks—ten days—we'll have the best ship, sir, and the choicest crew in England. Hawkins shall come as cabin-boy. You'll make a famous cabin-boy, Hawkins. You, Livesey, are ship's doctor; I am admiral. We'll take Redruth, Joyce, and Hunter. We'll have favourable winds, a quick passage, and not the least difficulty in finding the spot, and money to eat—to roll in—to play duck and drake with ever after."

"Trelawney," said the doctor, "I'll go with you; and, I'll go bail for it, so will Jim, and be a credit to the under-taking. There's only one man I'm afraid of."

"And who's that?" cried the squire. " Name the dog, sir!"

"You," replied the doctor; "for you cannot hold your tongue. We are not the only men who know of this paper. These fellows who attacked the inn to-night—bold, desperate blades, for sure—and the rest who stayed aboard that lugger, and more, I dare say, not far off, are, one and all, through thick and thin, bound that they'll get that money. We must none of us go alone till we get to sea. Jim and I shall stick together in the meanwhile; you'll take Joyce and Hunter when you ride to Bristol, and, from first to last, not one of us must breathe a word of what we've found."

"Livesey," returned the squire, "you are always in the right of it. I'll be as silent as the grave."

PART II

THE SEA COOK

CHAPTER VII

I GO TO BRISTOL

It was longer than the squire imagined ere we were ready for the sea, and none of our first plans—not even Dr Livesey's, of keeping me beside him—could be carried out as we intended. The doctor had to go to London for a physician to take charge of his practice; the squire was hard at work at Bristol; and I lived on at the Hall under the charge of old Redruth, the gamekeeper, almost a prisoner, but full of sea-dreams and the most charming anticipations of strange islands and adventures. I brooded by the hour together over the map, all the details of which I well remembered. Sitting by the fire in the housekeeper's room, I approached that island in my fancy, from every possible direction; I explored every acre of its surface; I climbed a thousand times to that tall hill they call the Spy-glass, and from the top enjoyed the most wonderful and changing prospects. Sometimes the isle was thick with savages, with whom we fought; sometimes full of dangerous animals that hunted us; but in all my fancies nothing occurred to me so strange and tragic as our actual adventures.

So the weeks passed on, till one fine day there came a letter addressed to Dr Livesey, with this addition, "To be opened, in the case of his absence, by Tom Redruth, or young Hawkins." Obeying this order, we found, or rather, I found—for the gamekeeper was a poor hand at reading anything but print—the following important news:—

"*Old Anchor Inn, Bristol, March 1, 17—.*
"DEAR LIVESEY,—As I do not know whether you are at the Hall or still in London, I send this in double to both places.

"The ship is bought and fitted. She lies at anchor, ready for sea. You never imagined a sweeter schooner—a child might sail her—two hundred tons; name, *Hispaniola.*

"I got her through my old friend, Blandly, who has proved himself throughout the most surprising trump. The admirable fellow literally slaved in my interest, and so, I may say, did everyone in Bristol, as soon as they got wind of the port we sailed for—treasure, I mean."

"Redruth," said I, interrupting the letter, "Doctor Livesey will not like that. The squire has been talking, after all."

"Well, who's a better right?" growled the gamekeeper. "A pretty rum go if squire ain't to talk for Doctor Livesey, I should think."

At that I gave up all attempt at commentary, and read straight on:—

"Blandly himself found the *Hispaniola,* and by the most admirable management got her for the merest trifle. There is a class of men in Bristol monstrously prejudiced against Blandly. They go the length of declaring that this honest creature would do anything for money, that the *Hispaniola* belonged to him, and that he sold it me absurdly high—the most transparent calumnies. None of them dare, however, to deny the merits of the ship.

"So far there was not a hitch. The workpeople, to be sure—riggers and what not—were most annoyingly slow; but time cured that. It was the crew that troubled me.

"I wished a round score of men—in case of natives, buccaneers, or the odious French—and I had the worry of the deuce itself to find so much as half a dozen, till the most remarkable stroke of fortune brought me the very man that I required.

"I was standing on the dock, when, by the merest accident, I fell in talk with him. I found he was an old sailor, kept a public-house, knew all the seafaring men in Bristol, had lost his health ashore, and wanted a good berth as cook to get to sea again. He had hobbled down there that morning, he said, to get a smell of the salt.

"I was monstrously touched—so would you have been—and, out of pure pity, I engaged him on the spot to be ship's cook. Long John Silver, he is called, and has lost a leg; but that I regarded as a recommendation, since he lost it in his country's service, under the immortal Hawke. He has no pension, Livesey. Imagine the abominable age we live in!

"Well, sir, I thought I had only found a cook, but it was a crew I had discovered. Between Silver and myself we got together in a few days a company of the toughest old salts imaginable—not pretty to look at, but fellows, by their faces, of the most indomitable spirit. I declare we could fight a frigate.

"Long John even got rid of two out of the six or seven I had already engaged. He showed me in a moment that they were just the sort of fresh-water swabs we had to fear in an adventure of importance.

"I am in the most magnificent health and spirits, eating like a bull, sleeping like a tree, yet I shall not enjoy a moment till I hear my old tarpaulins tramping round the capstan. Seaward ho! Hang the treasure! It's the glory of the sea that has turned my head. So now, Livesey, come post; do not lose an hour, if you respect me.

"Let young Hawkins go at once to see his mother, with Redruth for a guard; and then both come full speed to Bristol.

"JOHN TRELAWNEY."

"*Postscript.*—I did not tell you that Blandly, who, by the way, is to send a consort after us if we don't turn up by the end of August, had found an admirable fellow for sailing master—a stiff man, which I regret, but, in all other respects, a treasure. Long John Silver unearthed a very competent man for a mate, a man named Arrow. I have a boatswain who pipes, Livesey; so things shall go man-o'-war fashion on board the good ship *Hispaniola*.

"I forgot to tell you that Silver is a man of substance; I know of my own knowledge that he has a banker's account, which has never been overdrawn. He leaves his wife to manage the inn; and as she is a woman of colour, a pair of old bachelors like you and I may be excused for guessing that it is the wife, quite as much as the health, that sends him back to roving.

"J. T."

"P.P.S.—Hawkins may stay one night with his mother.

"J. T."

You can fancy the excitement into which that letter put me. I was half beside myself with glee; and if ever I despised a man, it was old Tom Redruth, who could do nothing but grumble and lament. Any of the under-gamekeepers would gladly have changed places with him; but such was not the squire's pleasure, and the squire's pleasure was like law among them all. Nobody but old Redruth would have dared so much as even to grumble.

The next morning he and I set out on foot for the "Admiral Benbow," and there I found my mother in good health and spirits. The captain, who had so long been a cause of so much discomfort, was gone where the wicked cease from troubling. The squire had had everything re-

I SAID GOOD-BY TO MOTHER AND THE COVE AND
TO DEAR OLD "ADMIRAL BENBOW"

paired, and the public rooms and the sign repainted, and had added some furniture—above all a beautiful arm-chair for mother in the bar. He had found her a boy as an apprentice also, so that she should not want help while I was gone.

It was on seeing that boy that I understood, for the first time, my situation. I had thought up to that moment of the adventures before me, not at all of the home that I was leaving; and now, at sight of this clumsy stranger, who was to stay here in my place beside my mother, I had my first attack of tears. I am afraid I led that boy a dog's life; for as he was new to the work, I had a hundred opportunities of setting him right and putting him down, and I was not slow to profit by them.

The night passed, and the next day, after dinner, Redruth and I were afoot again, and on the road. I said good-bye to mother and the cove where I had lived since I was born, and the dear old "Admiral Benbow"—since he was repainted, no longer quite so dear. One of my last thoughts was of the captain, who had so often strode along the beach with his cocked hat, his sabre-cut cheek, and his old brass telescope. Next moment we had turned the corner, and my home was out of sight.

The mail picked us up about dusk at the "Royal George" on the heath. I was wedged in between Redruth and a stout old gentleman, and, in spite of the swift motion and the cold night air, I must have dozed a great deal from the very first, and then slept like a log, up hill and down dale through stage after stage; for when I was awakened, at last, it was by a punch in the ribs, and I opened my eyes, to find that we were standing still before a large building in a city street, and that the day had already broken a long time.

"Where are we?" I asked.

"Bristol," said Tom. "Get down."

Mr Trelawney had taken up his residence at an inn far down the docks, to superintend the work upon the schooner. Thither we had now to walk, and our way, to my great delight, lay along the quays and beside the great multitude of ships of all sizes and rigs and nations. In one, sailors were singing at their work; in another, there were men aloft, high over my head, hanging to threads that seemed no thicker than a spider's. Though I had lived by the shore all my life, I seemed never to have been near the sea till then. The smell of tar and salt was something new. I saw the most wonderful figureheads, that had all been far over the ocean. I saw, besides, many old sailors, with rings in their ears, and whiskers curled in ringlets, and tarry pigtails, and their swaggering, clumsy sea-walk; and if I had seen as many kings or archbishops I could not have been more delighted.

And I was going to sea myself; to sea in a schooner, with a piping boatswain, and pigtailed singing seamen; to sea, bound for an unknown island, and to seek for buried treasures!

While I was still in this delightful dream, we came suddenly in front of a large inn, and met Squire Trelawney, all dressed out like a sea-officer, in stout blue cloth, coming out of the door with a smile on his face, and a capital imitation of a sailor's walk.

"Here you are," he cried, "and the doctor came last night from London. Bravo! the ship's company complete!"

"Oh, sir," cried I, "when do we sail?"

"Sail!" says he. "We sail to-morrow."

CHAPTER VIII

AT THE SIGN OF THE "SPY-GLASS"

When I had done breakfasting the squire gave me a note addressed to John Silver, at the sign of the "Spy-glass," and told me I should easily find the place by following the line of the docks, and keeping a bright look-out for a little tavern with a large brass telescope for sign. I set off, overjoyed at this opportunity to see some more of the ships and seamen, and picked my way among a great crowd of people and carts and bales, for the dock was now at its busiest, until I found the tavern in question.

It was a bright enough little place of entertainment. The sign was newly painted; the windows had neat red curtains; the floor was cleanly sanded. There was a street on either side, and an open door on both, which made the large, low room pretty clear to see in, in spite of clouds of tobacco smoke.

The customers were mostly seafaring men; and they talked so loudly that I hung at the door, almost afraid to enter.

As I was waiting, a man came out of a side room, and, at a glance, I was sure he must be Long John. His left leg was cut off close by the hip, and under the left shoulder he carried a crutch, which he managed with wonderful dexterity, hopping about upon it like a bird. He was very tall and strong, with a face as big as a ham—plain and pale, but intelligent and smiling. Indeed, he seemed in the most cheerful spirits, whistling as he moved about among the tables, with a merry word or a slap on the shoulder for the more favoured of his guests.

Now, to tell you the truth, from the very first mention of Long John in Squire Trelawney's letter, I had taken a fear in my mind that he might prove to be the very one-legged sailor whom I had watched for so long at the old "Benbow." But one look at the man before me was enough. I had seen the captain, and Black Dog, and the blind man Pew, and I thought I knew what a buccaneer was like—a very different creature, according to me, from this clean and pleasant-tempered landlord.

I plucked up courage at once, crossed the threshold, and walked right up to the man where he stood, propped on his crutch, talking to a customer.

"Mr Silver, sir?" I asked, holding out the note.

"Yes, my lad," said he; "such is my name, to be sure. And who may you be?" And then as he saw the squire's letter, he seemed to me to give something almost like a start.

"Oh!" said he, quite loud, and offering his hand, "I see. You are our new cabin-boy; pleased I am to see you."

And he took my hand in his large firm grasp.

Just then one of the customers at the far side rose suddenly and made for the door. It was close by him, and he was out in the street in a moment. But his hurry had attracted my notice, and I recognized him at a glance. It was the tallow-faced man, wanting two fingers, who had come first to the "Admiral Benbow."

"Oh," I cried, "stop him! it's Black Dog!"

"I don't care two coppers who he is," cried Silver. "But he hasn't paid his score. Harry, run and catch him."

One of the others who was nearest the door leaped up, and started in pursuit.

"If he were Admiral Hawke he shall pay his score," cried Silver; and then, relinquishing my hand—"Who did you say he was?" he asked. "Black what?"

"Dog, sir," said I. "Has Mr Trelawney not told you of the buccaneers? He was one of them."

"So?" cried Silver. "In my house! Ben, run and help Harry. One of those swabs, was he? Was that you drinking with him, Morgan? Step up here."

The man whom he called Morgan—an old, grey-haired, mahogany-faced sailor—came forward pretty sheepishly, rolling his quid.

"Now, Morgan," said Long John, very sternly; "you never clapped your eyes on that Black—Black Dog before, did you, now?"

"Not I, sir," said Morgan, with a salute.

"You didn't know his name, did you?"

"No, sir."

"By the powers, Tom Morgan, it's as good for you!" exclaimed the landlord. "If you had been mixed up with the like of that, you would never have put another foot in my house, you may lay to that. And what was he saying to you?"

"I don't rightly know, sir," answered Morgan.

"Do you call that a head on your shoulders, or a blessed dead-eye?" cried Long John. "Don't rightly know, don't you! Perhaps you don't happen to rightly know who you was speaking to, perhaps? Come, now, what was he jawing—v'yages, cap'ns, ships? Pipe up! What was it?"

"We was a-talkin' of keelhauling," answered Morgan.

"Keelhauling, was you?—and a mighty suitable thing, too, and you may lay to that. Get back to your place for a lubber, Tom."

And then, as Morgan rolled back to his seat, Silver added to me in a confidential whisper, that was very flattering, as I thought:—

"He's quite an honest man, Tom Morgan, on'y stupid. And now," he ran on again, aloud, "let's see—Black Dog? No, I don't know the name, not I. Yet I kind of think I've—yes, I've seen the swab. He used to come here with a blind beggar, he used."

"That he did, you may be sure," said I. "I knew that blind man, too. His name was Pew."

"It was!" cried Silver, now quite excited. "Pew! That were his name for certain. Ah, he looked a shark, he did! If we run down this Black Dog, now, there'll be news for Cap'n Trelawney! Ben's a good runner; few seamen run better than Ben. He should run him down hand over hand, by the powers! He talked o' keelhauling, did he? *I'll* keelhaul him!"

All the time he was jerking out these phrases he was stumping up and down the tavern on his crutch, slapping tables with his hand, and giving such a show of excitement as would have convinced an Old Bailey judge or a Bow Street runner. My suspicions had been thoroughly reawakened on finding Black Dog at the "Spy-glass," and I watched the cook narrowly. But he was too deep, and too ready, and too clever for me, and by the time the two men had come back out of breath, an l confessed that they had lost the track in a crowd, and been scolded like thieves, I would have gone bail for the innocence of Long John Silver.

"OH," I CRIED, "STOP HIM! IT'S BLACK DOG!"

"See here, now, Hawkins," said he, "here's a blessed hard thing on a man like me now, ain't it? There's Cap'n Trelawney—what's he to think? Here I have this confounded son of a Dutchman sitting in my own house, drinking of my own rum! Here you comes and tells me of it plain; and here I let him give us all the slip before my blessed dead-lights! Now, Hawkins, you do me justice with the cap'n. You're a lad, you are, but you're as smart as paint. I see that when you first came in. Now, here it is: What could I do, with this old timber I hobble on? When I was an A.B. master mariner I'd have come up alongside of him, hand over hand, and broached him to in a brace of old shakes, I would; but now—"

And then, all of a sudden, he stopped, and his jaw dropped as though he had remembered something.

"The score!" he burst out. "Three goes o' rum! Why, shiver my timbers, if I hadn't forgotten my score!"

And, falling on a bench, he laughed until the tears ran down his cheeks. I could not help joining; and we laughed together, peal after peal, until the tavern rang again.

"Why, what a precious old sea-calf I am!" he said, at last, wiping his cheeks. "You and me should get on well, Hawkins, for I'll take my davy I should be rated ship's boy. But, come, now, stand by to go about. This won't do. Dooty is dooty, messmates. I'll put on my old cocked hat, and step along of you to Cap'n Trelawney, and report this here affair. For, mind you, it's serious, young Hawkins; and neither you nor me's come out of it with what I should make so bold as to call credit. Nor you neither, says you; not smart—none of the pair of us smart. But, dash my buttons! that was a good 'un about my score."

And he began to laugh again, and that so heartily, that though I did not see the joke as he did, I was again obliged to join him in his mirth.

On our little walk along the quays, he made himself the most interesting companion, telling me about the different ships that we passed by, their rig, tonnage, and nationality, explaining the work that was going forward—how one was discharging, another taking in cargo, and a third making ready for sea; and every now and then telling me some little anecdote of ships or seamen, or repeating a nautical phrase till I had learned it perfectly. I began to see that here was one of the best of possible shipmates.

When we got to the inn, the squire and Dr Livesey were seated together, finishing a quart of ale with a toast in it, before they should go aboard the schooner on a visit of inspection.

Long John told the story from first to last, with a great deal of spirit and the most perfect truth. "That was how it were, now, weren't it, Hawkins?" he would say, now and again, and I could always bear him entirely out.

The two gentlemen regretted that Black Dog had got away; but we all agreed there was nothing to be done, and after he had been complimented, Long John took up his crutch and departed.

"All hands aboard by four this afternoon," shouted the squire after him.

"Ay, ay, sir," cried the cook, in the passage.

"Well, squire," said Dr Livesey, "I don't put much faith in your discoveries, as a general thing; but I will say this, John Silver suits me."

"The man's a perfect trump," declared the squire.

"And now," added the doctor, "Jim may come on board with us, may he not?"

"To be sure he may," says squire.—"Take your hat, Hawkins, and we'll see the ship."

Chapter IX

POWDER AND ARMS

The *Hispaniola* lay some way out, and we went under the figureheads and round the sterns of many other ships, and their cables sometimes grated underneath our keel, and sometimes swung above us. At last, however, we got alongside, and were met and saluted as we stepped aboard by the mate, Mr Arrow, a brown old sailor, with earrings in his ears and a squint. He and the squire were very thick and friendly, but I soon observed that things were not the same between Mr Trelawney and the captain.

This last was a sharp-looking man, who seemed angry with everything on board, and was soon to tell us why, for we had hardly got down into the cabin when a sailor followed us.

"Captain Smollett, sir, axing to speak with you," said he.

"I am always at the captain's orders. Show him. in," said the squire.

The captain, who was close behind his messenger, entered at once, and shut the door behind him.

"Well, Captain Smollett, what have you to say? All well, I hope; all shipshape and seaworthy?"

"Well, sir," said the captain, "better speak plain, I believe, even at the risk of offence. I don't like this cruise; I don't like the men; and I don't like my officer. That's short and sweet."

"Perhaps, sir, you don't like the ship?" inquired the squire, very angry, as I could see.

"I can't speak as to that, sir, not having seen her tried," said the captain. "She seems a clever craft; more I can't say."

"Possibly, sir, you may not like your employer, either?" says the squire.

But here Dr Livesey cut in.

"Stay a bit," said he, "stay a bit. No use of such questions as that but to produce ill-feeling. The captain has said too much or he has said too little, and I'm bound to say that I require an explanation of his words. You don't, you say, like this cruise. Now, why?"

"I was engaged, sir, on what we call sealed orders, to sail this ship for that gentleman where he should bid me," said the captain. "So far so good. But now I find that every man before the mast knows more than I do. I don't call that fair, now, do you?"

"No," said Dr Livesey, "I don't."

"Next," said the captain, "I learn we are going after treasure—hear it from my own hands, mind you. Now, treasure is ticklish work; I don't like treasure voyages on any account; and I don't like them, above all, when they are secret, and when (begging your pardon, Mr Trelawney) the secret has been told to the parrot."

"Silver's parrot?" asked the squire.

"It's a way of speaking," said the captain. "Blabbed, I mean. It's my belief neither of you gentlemen know what you are about; but I'll tell you my way of it—life or death, and a close run."

"That is all clear, and, I dare say, true enough," replied Dr Livesey. "We take the risk; but we are not so ignorant as you believe us. Next, you say you don't like the crew. Are they not good seamen?"

"I don't like them, sir," returned Captain Smollett. "And I think I should have had the choosing of my own hands, if you go to that."

"Perhaps you should," replied the doctor. "My friend should, perhaps, have taken you along with him; but the slight, if there be one, was unintentional. And you don't like Mr Arrow?"

"I don't, sir. I believe he's a good seaman; but he's too free with the crew to be a good officer. A mate should keep himself to himself—shouldn't drink with the men before the mast!"

"Do you mean he drinks?" cried the squire.

"No, sir," replied the captain; "only that he's too familiar."

"Well, now, and the short and long of it, captain?" asked the doctor. "Tell us what you want."

"Well, gentlemen, are you determined to go on this cruise?"

"Like iron," answered the squire.

"Very good," said the captain. "Then, as you've heard me very patiently, saying things that I could not prove, hear me a few words more. They are putting the powder and the arms in the fore-hold. Now, you have a good place under the cabin; why not put them there?—first point. Then you are bringing four of your own people with you, and they tell me some of them are to be berthed forward. Why not give them the berths here beside the cabin?—second point."

"Any more?" asked Mr Trelawney.

"One more," said the captain. "There's been too much blabbing already."

"Far too much," agreed the doctor

"I'll tell you what I've heard myself," continued Captain Smollett: "that you have a map of an island; that there's crosses on the map to show where treasure is; and that the island lies—" And then he named the latitude and longitude exactly.

"I never told that," cried the squire, "to a soul!"

"The hands know it, sir," returned the captain.

"Livesey, that must have been you or Hawkins," cried the squire.

"It doesn't much matter who it was," replied the doctor. And I could see that neither he nor the captain paid much regard to Mr Trelawney's protestations. Neither did I, to be sure, he was so loose a talker; yet in this case I believe he was really right, and that nobody had told the situation of the island.

"Well, gentlemen," continued the captain, "I don't know who has this map; but I make it a point, it shall be kept secret even from me and Mr Arrow. Otherwise I would ask you to let me resign."

"I see," said the doctor. "You wish us to keep this matter dark, and to make a garrison of the stern part of the ship, manned with my friend's own people, and provided with all the arms and powder on board. In other words, you fear a mutiny."

"Sir," said Captain Smollett, "with no intention to take offence, I deny your right to put words into my mouth. No captain, sir, would be justified in going to sea at all if he had ground enough to say that. As for Mr Arrow, I believe him thoroughly honest; some of the men are the same; all may be for what I know. But I am responsible for the ship's safety and the life of every man Jack aboard of her. I see things going, as I think, not quite right. And I ask you to take certain precautions, or let me resign my berth. And that's all."

"Captain Smollett," began the doctor, with a smile, "did ever you hear the fable of the mountain and the mouse? You'll excuse me, I dare say, but you remind me of that fable. When you came in here I'll stake my wig you meant more than this."

"Doctor," said the captain, "you are smart. When I came in here I meant to get discharged. I had no thought that Mr Trelawney would hear a word."

"No more I would," cried the squire. "Had Livesey not been here I should have seen you to the deuce. As it is, I have heard you. I will do as you desire; but I think the worse of you."

"That's as you please, sir," said the captain. "You'll find I do my duty."

And with that he took his leave.

"Trelawney," said the doctor, "contrary to all my notions, I believe you have managed to get two honest men on board with you—that man and John Silver."

"Silver, if you like," cried the squire; "but as for that intolerable humbug, I declare I think his conduct unmanly, unsailorly, and down-right un-English."

"Well," says the doctor, "we shall see."

When we came on deck, the men had begun already to take out the arms and powder, yo-hoing at their work, while the captain and Mr Arrow stood by superintending.

The new arrangement was quite to my liking. The whole schooner had been overhauled; six berths had been made astern, out of what had been the after-part of the main hold; and this set of cabins was only joined to the galley and forecastle by a sparred passage on the port side. It had been originally meant that the captain, Mr Arrow, Hunter, Joyce, the doctor, and the squire, were to occupy these six berths. Now, Redruth and I were to get two of them, and Mr Arrow and the captain were to sleep on deck in the companion, which had been enlarged on each side till you might almost have called it a round-house. Very low it was still, of course; but there was room to swing two hammocks, and even the mate seemed pleased with the arrangement. Even he, perhaps, had been doubtful as to the crew, but that is only guess; for, as you shall hear, we had not long the benefit of his opinion.

We were all hard at work, changing the powder and the berths, when the last man or two, and Long John along with them, came off in a shore-boat.

The cook came up the side like a monkey for cleverness, and, as soon as he saw what was doing, "So ho, mates!" says he, "what's this?"

"We're a-changing of the powder, Jack," answers one.

"Why, by the powers," cried Long John, "if we do, we'll miss the morning tide!"

"My orders!" said the captain shortly. "You may go below, my man. Hands will want supper."

"Ay, ay, sir," answered the cook; and, touching his forelock, he disappeared at once in the direction of his galley.

"That's a good man, captain," said the doctor.

"Very likely, sir," replied Captain Smollett. "Easy with that, men— easy," he ran on, to the fellows who were shifting the powder; and then suddenly observing me examining the swivel we carried amidships, a long brass nine—"Here, you ship's boy," he cried, "out of that! Off with you to the cook and get some work."

And then as I was hurrying off I heard him say, quite loudly, to the doctor:—

"I'll have no favourites on my ship."

I assure you I was quite of the squire's way of thinking, and hated the captain deeply.

CHAPTER X

THE VOYAGE

All that night we were in a great bustle getting things stowed in
their place, and boatfuls of the squire's friends, Mr Blandly and
the like, coming off to wish him a good voyage and a safe return. We
never had a night at the "Admiral Benbow" when I had half the work;
and I was dog-tired when, a little before dawn, the boatswain sounded
his pipe, and the crew began to man the capstan-bars. I might have
been twice as weary, yet I would not have left the deck; all was so
new and interesting to me—the brief commands, the shrill note of the
whistle, the men bustling to their places in the glimmer of the ship's
lanterns.

"Now, Barbecue, tip us a stave," cried one voice.

"The old one," cried another.

"Ay, ay, mates," said Long John, who was standing by, with his
crutch under his arm, and at once broke out in the air and words I
knew so well—

"Fifteen men on the dead man's chest—"

And then the whole crew bore chorus:—

"Yo-ho-ho, and a bottle of rum!"

And at the third "ho!" drove the bars before them with a will.

Even at that exciting moment it carried me back to the old "Admiral Benbow" in a second; and I seemed to hear the voice of the captain piping in the chorus. But soon the anchor was short up; soon it

was hanging dripping at the bows; soon the sails began to draw, and the land and shipping to flit by on either side; and before I could lie down to snatch an hour of slumber the *Hispaniola* had begun her voyage to the Isle of Treasure.

I am not going to relate that voyage in detail. It was fairly prosperous. The ship proved to be a good ship, the crew were capable seamen, and the captain thoroughly understood his business. But before we came the length of Treasure Island, two or three things had happened which require to be known.

Mr Arrow, first of all, turned out even worse than the captain had feared. He had no command among the men, and people did what they pleased with him. But that was by no means the worst of it; for after a day or two at sea he began to appear on deck with hazy eye, red cheeks, stuttering tongue, and other marks of drunkenness. Time after time he was ordered below in disgrace. Sometimes he fell and cut himself; sometimes he lay all day long in his little bunk at one side of the companion; sometimes for a day or two he would be almost sober and attend to his work at least passably.

In the meantime, we could never make out where he got the drink. That was the ship's mystery. Watch him as we pleased, we could do nothing to solve it; and when we asked him to his face, he would only laugh, if he were drunk, and if he were sober, deny solemnly that he ever tasted anything but water.

He was not only useless as an officer, and a bad influence amongst the men, but it was plain that at this rate he must soon kill himself outright; so nobody was much surprised, nor very sorry, when one dark night, with a head sea, he disappeared entirely and was seen no more.

"Overboard!" said the captain. "Well, gentlemen, that saves the trouble of putting him in irons."

But there we were, without a mate; and it was necessary, of course, to advance one of the men. The boatswain, Job Anderson, was the likeliest man aboard, and, though he kept his old title, he served in a way as mate. Mr Trelawney had followed the sea, and his knowledge made him very useful, for he often took a watch himself in easy weather. And the coxswain, Israel Hands, was a careful, wily, old, experienced seaman, who could be trusted at a pinch with almost anything.

He was a great confidant of Long John Silver, and so the mention of his name leads me on to speak of our ship's cook, Barbecue, as the men called him.

Aboard ship he carried his crutch by a lanyard round his neck, to have both hands as free as possible. It was something to see him wedge the foot of the crutch against a bulkhead, and, propped against it, yielding to every movement of the ship, get on with his cooking like someone safe ashore. Still more strange was it to see him in the heaviest of weather cross the deck. He had a line or two rigged up to help him across the widest spaces—Long John's earings, they were called; and he would hand himself from one place to another, now using the crutch, now trailing it alongside by the lanyard, as quickly as another man could walk. Yet some of the men who had sailed with him before expressed their pity to see him so reduced.

"He's no common man, Barbecue," said the coxswain to me. "He had good schooling in his young days, and can speak like a book when so minded; and brave—a lion's nothing alongside of Long John! I seen him grapple four, and knock their heads together—him unarmed."

All the crew respected and even obeyed him. He had a way of talking to each, and doing everybody some particular service. To me he was unweariedly kind; and always glad to see me in the galley, which he kept as clean as a new pin; the dishes hanging up burnished, and his parrot in a cage in one corner.

"Come away, Hawkins," he would say; "come and have a yarn with John. Nobody more welcome than yourself, my son. Sit you down and hear the news. Here's Cap'n Flint—I calls my parrot Cap'n Flint, after the famous buccaneer—here's Cap'n Flint predicting success to our v'yage. Wasn't you, cap'n?"

And the parrot would say, with great rapidity, "Pieces of eight! pieces of eight! pieces of eight!" till you wondered that it was not out of breath, or till John threw his handkerchief over the cage.

"Now, that bird," he would say, "is, may be, two hundred years old, Hawkins—they lives for ever mostly; and if anybody's seen more wickedness, it must be the devil himself. She's sailed with England, the great Cap'n England, the pirate. She's been at Madagascar, and at Malabar, and Surinam, and Providence, and Portobello. She was at the fishing up of the wrecked Plate ships. It's there she learned 'Pieces of eight,' and little wonder; three hundred and fifty thousand of 'em, Hawkins! She was at the boarding of the *Viceroy of the Indies* out of Goa, she was; and to look at her you would think she was a babby. But you smelt powder—didn't you, cap'n?"

"Stand by to go about," the parrot would scream.

"Ah, she's a handsome craft, she is," the cook would say, and give her sugar from his pocket, and then the bird would peck at the bars and swear straight on, passing belief for wickedness. "There," John would add, "you can't touch pitch and not be mucked, lad. Here's this poor old innocent bird o' mine swearing blue fire, and none the wiser, you may lay to that. She would swear the same, in a manner of speaking, before chaplain." And John would touch his forelock with a solemn way he had, that made me think he was the best of men.

In the meantime, squire and Captain Smollett were still on pretty distant terms with one another. The squire made no bones about the matter; he despised the captain. The captain, on his part, never spoke but when he was spoken to, and then sharp and short and dry, and not a word wasted. He owned, when driven into a corner, that he seemed to have been wrong about the crew, that some of them were as brisk as he wanted to see, and all had behaved fairly well. As for the ship, he had taken a downright fancy to her. "She'll lie a point nearer the wind than a man has a right to expect of his own married wife, sir. But," he would add, "all I say is we're not home again, and I don't like the cruise."

The squire, at this, would turn away and march up and down the deck, chin in air.

"A trifle more of that man," he would say, "and I should explode."

We had some heavy weather, which only proved the qualities of the *Hispaniola*. Every man on board seemed well content, and they must have been hard to please if they had been otherwise; for it is my belief there was never a ship's company so spoiled since Noah put to sea. Double grog was going on the least excuse; there was duff on odd days, as, for instance, if the squire heard it was any man's birthday; and always a barrel of apples standing broached in the waist, for anyone to help himself that had a fancy.

"Never knew good come of it yet," the captain said to Dr Livesey. "Spoil foc's'le hands, make devils. That's my belief."

But good did come of the apple barrel, as you shall hear; for if it had not been for that, we should have had no note of warning, and might all have perished by the hand of treachery.

This was how it came about.

We had run up the trades to get the wind of the island we were after—I am not allowed to be more plain—and now we were running down for it with a bright look-out day and night. It was about the last day of our outward voyage, by the largest computation; some time that night, or, at latest, before noon of the morrow, we should sight the Treasure Island. We were heading S.S.W., and had a steady breeze abeam and a quiet sea. The *Hispaniola* rolled steadily, dipping her bowsprit now and then with a whiff of spray. All was drawing alow and aloft; everyone was in the bravest spirits, because we were now so near an end of the first part of our adventure.

Now, just after sundown, when all my work was over, and I was on my way to my berth, it occurred to me that I should like an apple. I ran on deck. The watch was all forward looking out for the island. The man at the helm was watching the luff of the sail, and whistling away gently to himself; and that was the only sound excepting the swish of the sea against the bows and around the sides of the ship.

In I got bodily into the apple barrel, and found there was scarce an apple left; but, sitting down there in the dark, what with the sound of the waters and the rocking movement of the ship, I had either fallen asleep, or was on the point of doing so, when a heavy man sat down with rather a clash close by. The barrel shook as he leaned his shoulders against it, and I was just about to jump up when the man began to speak. It was Silver's voice, and, before I had heard a dozen words, I would not have shown myself for all the world, but lay there, trembling and listening, in the extreme of fear and curiosity; for from these dozen words I understood that the lives of all the honest men aboard depended upon me alone.

Chapter XI

WHAT I HEARD IN THE APPLE BARREL

"No, not I," said Silver. "Flint was cap'n; I was quartermaster, along of my timber leg. The same broadside I lost my leg, old Pew lost his dead-lights. It was a master surgeon, him that ampytated me—out of college and all—Latin by the bucket, and what not; but he was hanged like a dog, and sun-dried like the rest, at Corso Castle. That was Roberts' men, that was, and comed of changing names to their ships—*Royal Fortune* and so on. Now, what a ship was christened, so let her stay, I says. So it was with the *Cassandra*, as brought us all safe home from Malabar, after England took the *Viceroy of the Indies; so* it was with the old *Walrus*, Flint's old ship, as I've seen a-muck with the red blood and fit to sink with gold."

"Ah!" cried another voice, that of the youngest hand on board, and evidently full of admiration, "he was the flower of the flock, was Flint!"

"Davis was a man, too, by all accounts," said Silver. "I never sailed along of him; first with England, then with Flint, that's my story; and now here on my own account, in a manner of speaking. I laid by nine hundred safe, from England, and two thousand after Flint. That ain't bad for a man before the mast—all safe in bank. 'Tain't earning now, it's saving does it, you may lay to that. Where's all England's men now? I dunno. Where's Flint's? Why, most of 'em aboard here, and glad to get the duff—been begging before that, some on 'em. Old Pew, as had lost his sight, and might have thought shame, spends twelve hundred pound in a year, like a lord in Parliament. Where is he now? Well, he's dead now and under hatches; but for two year before that, shiver my timbers! the man was starving. He begged, and he stole, and he cut throats, and starved at that, by the powers!"

"Well, it ain't much use, after all," said the young seaman.

"'Tain't much use for fools, you may lay to it—that, nor nothing," cried Silver. "But now, you look here: you're young, you are, but you're as smart as paint. I see that when I set my eyes on you, and I'll talk to you like a man."

You may imagine how I felt when I heard this abominable old rogue addressing another in the very same words of flattery as he had used to myself. I think, if I had been able, that I would have killed him through the barrel. Meantime, he ran on, little supposing he was overheard:

"Here it is about gentlemen of fortune. They lives rough, and they risk swinging, but they eat and drink like fighting-cocks, and when a cruise is done, why, it's hundreds of pounds instead of hundreds of farthings in their pockets. Now, the most goes for rum and a good fling, and to sea again in their shirts. But that's not the course I lay. I puts it all away, some here, some there, and none too much anywheres, by reason of suspicion. I'm fifty, mark you; once back from this cruise, I set up gentleman in earnest. Time enough too, says you. Ah, but I've lived easy in the meantime; never denied myself o' nothing heart desires, and slep' soft and ate dainty all my days, but when at sea. And how did I begin? Before the mast, like you!"

"Well," said the other, "but all the other money's gone now, ain't it? You daren't show face in Bristol after this."

"Why, where might you suppose it was?" asked Silver, derisively.

"At Bristol, in banks and places," answered his companion.

"It were," said the cook; "it were when we weighed anchor. But my old missis has it all by now. And the 'Spy-glass' is sold, lease and good-will and rigging; and the old girl's off to meet me. I would tell you where, for I trust you; but it 'ud make jealousy among the mates."

"And can you trust your missis?" asked the other.

"Gentlemen of fortune," returned the cook, "usually trusts little among themselves, and right they are, you may lay to it. But I have a way with me, I have. When a mate brings a slip on his cable—one as knows me, I mean—it won't be in the same world with old John. There was some that was feared of Pew, and some that was feared of Flint; but Flint his own self was feared of me. Feared he was, and proud. They was the roughest crew afloat, was Flint's; the devil himself would

64

have been feared to go to sea with them. Well, now, I tell you, I'm not a boasting man, and you seen yourself how easy I keep company; but when I was quartermaster, *lambs* wasn't the word for Flint's old buccaneers. Ah, you may be sure of yourself in old John's ship."

"Well, I tell you now," replied the lad, "I didn't half a quarter like the job till I had this talk with you, John; but there's my hand on it now."

"And a brave lad you were, and smart, too," answered Silver, shaking hands so heartily that all the barrel shook, "and a finer figurehead for a gentleman of fortune I never clapped my eyes on."

By this time I had begun to understand the meaning of their terms. By a "gentleman of fortune" they plainly meant neither more nor less than a common pirate, and the little scene that I had overheard was the last act in the corruption of one of the honest hands—perhaps of the last one left aboard. But on this point I was soon to be relieved, for Silver giving a little whistle, a third man strolled up and sat down by the party.

"Dick's square," said Silver.

"Oh, I know'd Dick was square," returned the voice of the coxswain, Israel Hands. "He's no fool, is Dick." And he turned his quid and spat. "But, look here," he went on, "here's what I want to know, Barbecue: how long are we a-going to stand off and on like a blessed bumboat? I've had a'most enough o' Cap'n Smollett; he's hazed me long enough, by thunder! I want to go into that cabin, I do. I want their pickles and wines, and that."

"Israel," said Silver, "your head ain't much account, nor ever was. But you're able to hear, I reckon; leastways, your ears is big enough. Now, here's what I say: you'll berth forward, and you'll live hard, and you'll speak soft, and you'll keep sober, till I give the word; and you may lay to that, my son."

"Well, I don't say no, do I?" growled the coxswain. "What I say is, when? That's what I say."

"When! by the powers!" cried Silver. "Well, now if you want to know, I'll tell you when. The last moment I can manage; and that's when. Here's a first-rate seaman, Cap'n Smollett, sails the blessed ship for us. Here's this squire and doctor with a map and such—I don't know where it is, do I? No more do you, says you. Well, then, I mean this squire and doctor shall find the stuff, and help us to get it aboard, by the powers. Then we'll see. If I was sure of you all, sons of double

Dutchmen, I'd have Cap'n Smollett navigate us half-way back again before I struck."

"Why, we're all seamen aboard here, I should think," said the lad Dick.

"We're all foc's'le hands, you mean," snapped Silver. "We can steer a course, but who's to set one? That's what all you gentlemen split on, first and last. If I had my way, I'd have Cap'n Smollett work us back into the trades at least; then we'd have no blessed miscalculations and a spoonful of water a day. But I know the sort you are. I'll finish with 'em at the island, as soon's the blunt's on board, and a pity it is. But you're never happy till you're drunk. Split my sides, I've a sick heart to sail with the likes of you!"

"Easy all, Long John," cried Israel. "Who's a-crossin' of you?"

"Why, how many tall ships, think ye, now, have I seen laid aboard? and how many brisk lads drying in the sun at Execution Dock?" cried Silver, "and all for this same hurry and hurry and hurry. You hear me? I seen a thing or two at sea, I have. If you would on'y lay your course, and a p'int to windward, you would ride in carriages, you would. But not you! I know you. You'll have your mouthful of rum to-morrow, and go hang."

"Everybody know'd you was a kind of a chapling, John; but there's others as could hand and steer as well as you," said Israel. "They liked a bit o' fun, they did. They wasn't so high and dry, nohow, but took their fling, like jolly companions every one."

"So?" says Silver. "Well, and where are they now? Pew was that sort, and he died a beggar-man. Flint was, and he died of rum at Savannah. Ah, they was a sweet crew, they was!—on'y, where are they?"

"But," asked Dick, "when we do lay 'em athwart, what are we to do with 'em, anyhow?"

"There's the man for me!" cried the cook, admiringly. "That's what I call business. Well, what would you think? Put 'em ashore like maroons? That would have been England's way. Or cut 'em down like that much pork? That would have been Flint's or Billy Bones's."

"Billy was the man for that," said Israel. "'Dead men don't bite,' says he. Well, he's dead now hisself; he knows the long and short on it now; and if ever a rough hand come to port, it was Billy."

"Right you are," said Silver, "rough and ready. But mark you here: I'm an easy man—I'm quite the gentleman, says you; but this time it's serious. Dooty is dooty, mates. I give my vote—death. When I'm

"HERE'S TO OURSELVES, AND PLENTY OF PRIZES AND
PLENTY OF DUFF"

in Parlyment, and riding in my coach, I don't want none of these sea-lawyers in the cabin a-coming home, unlooked for, like the devil at prayers. Wait is what I say; but when the time comes, why, let her rip!"

"John," cries the coxswain, "you're a man!"

"You'll say so, Israel, when you see," said Silver. "Only one thing I claim—I claim Trelawney. I'll wring his calf's head off his body with these hands. Dick!" he added, breaking off, "you just jump up, like a sweet lad, and get me an apple, to wet my pipe like."

You may fancy the terror I was in! I should have leaped out and run for it, if I had found the strength; but my limbs and heart alike misgave me. I heard Dick begin to rise, and then someone seemingly stopped him, and the voice of Hands exclaimed:—

"Oh, stow that! Don't you get sucking of that bilge, John. Let's have a go of the rum."

"Dick," said Silver. "I trust you. I've a gauge on the keg, mind. There's the key; you fill a pannikin and bring it up."

Terrified as I was, I could not help thinking to myself that this must have been how Mr Arrow got the strong waters that destroyed him.

Dick was gone but a little while, and during his absence Israel spoke straight on in the cook's ear. It was but a word or two that I could catch, and yet I gathered some important news; for, besides other scraps that tended to the same purpose, this whole clause was audible: "Not another man of them 'll jine." Hence there were still faithful men on board.

When Dick returned, one after another of the trio took the pannikin and drank—one "To luck"; another with a "Here's to old Flint"; and Silver himself saying, in a kind of song, "Here's to ourselves, and hold your luff, plenty of prizes and plenty of duff."

Just then a sort of brightness fell upon me in the barrel, and, looking up, I found the moon had risen, and was silvering the mizzen-top and shining white on the luff of the foresail; and almost at the same time the voice of the look-out shouted, "Land ho!"

CHAPTER XII

COUNCIL OF WAR

There was a great rush of feet across the deck. I could hear people tumbling up from the cabin and the foc's'le; and, slipping in an instant outside my barrel, I dived behind the foresail, made a double towards the stern, and came out upon the open deck in time to join Hunter and Dr Livesey in the rush for the weather bow.

There all hands were already congregated. A belt of fog had lifted almost simultaneously with the appearance of the moon. Away to the south-west of us we saw two low hills, about a couple of miles apart, and rising behind one of them a third and higher hill, whose peak was still buried in the fog. All three seemed sharp and conical in figure.

So much I saw, almost in a dream, for I had not yet recovered from my horrid fear of a minute or two before. And then I heard the voice of Captain Smollett issuing orders. The *Hispaniola* was laid a couple of points nearer the wind, and now sailed a course that would just clear the island on the east.

"And now, men," said the captain, when all was sheeted home, "has any one of you ever seen that land ahead?"

"I have, sir," said Silver. "I've watered there with a trader I was cook in."

"The anchorage is on the south, behind an islet, I fancy?" asked the captain.

"Yes, sir; Skeleton Island they calls it. It were a main place for pirates once, and a hand we had on board knowed all their names for it. That hill to the nor'ard they calls the Fore-mast Hill; there are three hills in a row running south'ard—fore, main, and mizzen, sir. But the main—that's the big 'un with the cloud on it—they usually calls the Spy-glass, by reason of a look-out they kept when they was in the anchorage cleaning; for it's there they cleaned their ships, sir, asking your pardon."

"I have a chart here," says Captain Smollett. "See if that's the place."

Long John's eyes burned in his head as he took the chart; but, by the fresh look of the paper, I knew he was doomed to disappointment. This was not the map we found in Billy Bones's chest, but an accurate copy, complete in all things—names and heights and soundings—with the single exception of the red crosses and the written notes. Sharp as must have been his annoyance, Silver had the strength of mind to hide it.

"Yes, sir," said he, "this is the spot to be sure; and very prettily drawed out. Who might have done that, I wonder? The pirates were too ignorant, I reckon. Ay, here it is: 'Capt. Kidd's Anchorage'—just the name my shipmate called it. There's a strong current runs along the south, and then away nor'ard up the west coast. Right you was, sir," says he, "to haul your wind and keep the weather of the island. Leastways, if such was your intention as to enter and careen, and there ain't no better place for that in these waters."

"Thank you, my man," says Captain Smollett. "I'll ask you, later on, to give us a help. You may go."

I was surprised at the coolness with which John avowed his knowledge of the island; and I own I was half-frightened when I saw him drawing nearer to myself. He did not know, to be sure, that I had overheard his council from the apple barrel, and yet I had, by this time, taken such a horror of his cruelty, duplicity, and power, that I could scarce conceal a shudder when he laid his hand upon my arm.

"Ah," says he, "this here is a sweet spot, this island-a sweet spot for a lad to get ashore on. You'll bathe, and you'll climb trees, and you'll hunt goats, you will; and you'll get aloft on them hills like a goat yourself. Why, it makes me young again. I was going to forget my timber leg, I was. It's a pleasant thing to be young, and have ten toes, and you may lay to that. When you want to go a bit of exploring, you just ask old John, and he'll put up a snack for you to take along."

And clapping me in the friendliest way upon the shoulder, he hobbled off forward, and went below.

Captain Smollett, the squire, and Dr Livesey were talking together on the quarter-deck, and, anxious as I was to tell them my story, I durst not interrupt them openly. While I was still casting about in my thoughts to find some probable excuse, Dr Livesey called me to his side. He had left his pipe below, and, being a slave to tobacco, had meant that I should fetch it; but as soon as I was near enough to speak and not to be overheard, I broke out immediately: "Doctor, let me speak. Get the captain and squire down to the cabin, and then make some pretence to send for me. I have terrible news."

The doctor changed countenance a little, but next moment he was master of himself.

"Thank you, Jim," said he, quite loudly, "that was all I wanted to know," as if he had asked me a question.

And with that be turned on his heel and rejoined the other two. They spoke together for a little, and though none of them started, or raised his voice, or so much as whistled, it was plain enough that Dr Livesey had communicated my request; for the next thing that I heard was the captain giving an order to Job Anderson, and all hands were piped on deck.

"My lads," said Captain Smollett, "I've a word to say to you. This land that we have sighted is the place we have been sailing to. Mr Trelawney, being a very open-handed gentleman, as we all know, has just asked me a word or two, and as I was able to tell him that every man on board had done his duty, alow and aloft, as I never ask to see it done better, why, he and I and the doctor are going below to the cabin to drink *your* health and luck, and you'll have grog served out for you to drink *our* health and luck. I'll tell you what I think of this: I think it handsome. And if you think as I do, you'll give a good sea cheer for the gentleman that does it."

The cheer followed—that was a matter of course; but it rang out so full and hearty, that I confess I could hardly believe these same men were plotting for our blood.

"One more cheer for Cap'n Smollett," cried Long John, when the first had subsided.

And this also was given with a will.

On the top of that the three gentlemen went below, and not long after, word was sent forward that Jim Hawkins was wanted in the cabin.

I found them all three seated round the table, a bottle of Spanish wine and some raisins before them, and the doctor smoking away, with his wig on his lap, and that, I knew, was a sign that he was agitated. The stern window was open, for it was a warm night, and you could see the moon shining behind on the ship's wake.

"Now, Hawkins," said the squire, "you have something to say. Speak up."

I did as I was bid, and, as short as I could make it, told the whole details of Silver's conversation. Nobody interrupted me till I was done, nor did any one of the three of them make so much as a movement, but they kept their eyes upon my face from first to last.

"Jim," said Dr Livesey, "take a seat."

And they made me sit down at table beside them, poured me out a glass of wine, filled my hands with raisins, and all three, one after the other, and each with a bow, drank my good health, and their service to me, for my luck and courage.

"Now, captain," said the squire, "you were right, and I was wrong. I own myself an ass, and I await your orders."

"No more an ass than I, sir," returned the captain. "I never heard of a crew that meant to mutiny but what showed signs before, for any man that had an eye in his head to see the mischief and take steps according. But this crew," he added, "beats me."

"Captain," said the doctor, "with your permission, that's Silver. A very remarkable man."

"He'd look remarkably well from a yard-arm, sir," returned the captain. "But this is talk; this don't lead to anything. I see three or four points, and, with Mr Trelawney's permission, I'll name them."

"You, sir, are the captain. It is for you to speak," says Mr Trelawney, grandly.

"First point," began Mr Smollett. "We must go on, because we can't turn back. If I gave the word to go about, they would rise at once. Second point, we have time before us—at least, until this treasure's found. Third point, there are faithful hands. Now, sir, it's got to come to blows sooner or later; and what I propose is, to take time by the forelock, as the saying is, and come to blows some fine day when they least expect it. We can count, I take it, on your own home servants, Mr Trelawney?"

"As upon myself," declared the squire.

"Three," reckoned the captain, "ourselves make seven, counting Hawkins, here. Now, about the honest hands?"

"Most likely Trelawney's own men," said the doctor; "those he had picked up for himself, before he lit on Silver."

"Nay," replied the squire, "Hands was one of mine."

"I did think I could have trusted Hands," added the captain.

"And to think that they're all Englishmen!" broke out the squire. "Sir, I could find it in my heart to blow the ship up."

"Well, gentlemen," said the captain, "the best that I can say is not much. We must lay to, if you please, and keep a bright look-out. It's trying on a man, I know. It would be pleasanter to come to blows. But there's no help for it till we know our men. Lay to, and whistle for a wind, that's my view."

"Jim here," said the doctor, "can help us more than anyone. The men are not shy with him, and Jim is a noticing lad."

"Hawkins, I put prodigious faith in you," added the squire.

I began to feel pretty desperate at this, for I felt altogether helpless; and yet, by an odd train of circumstances, it was indeed through me that safety came. In the meantime, talk as we pleased, there were only seven out of the twenty-six on whom we knew we could rely; and out of these seven one was a boy, so that the grown men on our side were six to their nineteen.

PART III

MY SHORE ADVENTURE

CHAPTER XIII

HOW I BEGAN MY SHORE ADVENTURE

The appearance of the island when I came on deck next morning was altogether changed. Although the breeze had now utterly failed, we had made a great deal of way during the night, and were now lying becalmed about half a mile to the south-east of the low eastern coast. Grey-coloured woods covered a large part of the surface. This even tint was indeed broken up by streaks of yellow sandbreak in the lower lands, and by many tall trees of the pine family, outtopping the others—some singly, some in clumps; but the general colouring was uniform and sad. The hills ran up clear above the vegetation in spires of naked rock. All were strangely shaped, and the Spy-glass, which was by three or four hundred feet the tallest on the island, was likewise the strangest in configuration, running up sheer from almost every side, and then suddenly cut off at the top like a pedestal to put a statue on.

The *Hispaniola* was rolling scuppers under in the ocean swell. The booms were tearing at the blocks, the rudder was banging to and fro, and the whole ship creaking, groaning, and jumping like a manufactory. I had to cling tight to the backstay, and the world turned giddily before my eyes; for though I was a good enough sailor when there was way on, this standing still and being rolled about like a bottle was a thing I never learned to stand without a qualm or so, above all in the morning, on an empty stomach.

Perhaps it was this—perhaps it was the look of the island, with its grey, melancholy woods, and wild stone spires, and the surf that we could both see and hear foaming and thundering on the steep beach—at least, although the sun shone bright and hot, and the shore birds were fishing and crying all around us, and you would have thought anyone would have been glad to get to land after being so long at sea, my heart sank, as the saying is, into my boots; and from that first look onward, I hated the very thought of Treasure Island.

We had a dreary morning's work before us, for there was no sign of any wind, and the boats had to be got out and manned, and the ship warped three or four miles round the corner of the island, and up the narrow passage to the haven behind Skeleton Island. I volunteered for one of the boats, where I had, of course, no business. The heat was sweltering, and the men grumbled fiercely over their work. Anderson was in command of my boat, and instead of keeping the crew in order, he grumbled as loud as the worst.

"Well," he said, with an oath, "it's not for ever."

I thought this was a very bad sign; for, up to that day, the men had gone briskly and willingly about their business; but the very sight of the island had relaxed the cords of discipline.

All the way in, Long John stood by the steersman and conned the ship. He knew the passage like the palm of his hand; and though the man in the chains got everywhere more water than was down in the chart, John never hesitated once.

"There's a strong scour with the ebb," he said, "and this here passage has been dug out, in a manner of speaking, with a spade."

We brought up just where the anchor was in the chart, about a third of a mile from either shore, the mainland on one side, and Skeleton Island on the other. The bottom was clean sand. The plunge of our anchor sent up clouds of birds wheeling and crying over the woods; but in less than a minute they were down again, and all was once more silent.

The place was entirely land-locked, buried in woods, the trees coming right down to high-water mark, the shores mostly flat, and the hill-tops standing round at a distance in a sort of amphitheatre, one here, one there. Two little rivers, or, rather, two swamps, emptied out into this pond, as you might call it; and the foliage round that part of the shore had a kind of poisonous brightness. From the ship, we could see nothing of the house or stockade, for they were quite buried among trees; and if it had not been for the chart on the companion, we might have been the first that had ever anchored there since the island arose out of the seas.

There was not a breath of air moving, nor a sound but that of the surf booming half a mile away along the beaches and against the rocks outside. A peculiar stagnant smell hung over the anchorage—a smell of sodden leaves and rotting tree trunks. I observed the doctor sniffing and sniffing, like someone tasting a bad egg.

"I don't know about treasure," he said, "but I'll stake my wig there's fever here."

If the conduct of the men had been alarming in the boat, it became truly threatening when they had come aboard. They lay about the deck growling together in talk. The slightest order was received with a black look, and grudgingly and carelessly obeyed. Even the honest hands must have caught the infection, for there was not one man aboard to mend another. Mutiny, it was plain, hung over us like a thunder-cloud.

And it was not only we of the cabin party who perceived the danger. Long John was hard at work going from group to group, spending himself in good advice, and as for example no man could have shown a better. He fairly outstripped himself in willingness and civility; he was all smiles to everyone. If an order were given, John would be on his crutch in an instant, with the cheeriest "Ay, ay, sir!" in the world; and when there was nothing else to do, he kept up one song after another, as if to conceal the discontent of the rest.

Of all the gloomy features of that gloomy afternoon, this obvious anxiety on the part of Long John appeared the worst.

We held a council in the cabin. "Sir," said the captain, "if I risk another order, the whole ship'll come about our ears by the run. You see, sir, here it is. I get a rough answer, do I not? Well, if I speak back, pikes will be going in two shakes; if I don't, Silver will see there's something under that, and the game's up. Now, we've only one man to rely on."

"And who is that?" asked the squire.

"Silver, sir," returned the captain; "he's as anxious as you and I to smother things up. This is a tiff; he'd soon talk 'em out of it if he had the chance, and what I propose to do is to give him the chance. Let's allow the men an afternoon ashore. If they all go, why, we'll fight the ship. If they none of them go, well, then, we hold the cabin, and God defend the right. If some go, you mark my words, sir, Silver'll bring 'em aboard again as mild as lambs."

It was so decided; loaded pistols were served out to all the sure men; Hunter, Joyce, and Redruth were taken into our confidence, and received the news with less surprise and a better spirit than we had looked for, and then the captain went on deck and addressed the crew.

"My lads," said he, "we've had a hot day, and are all tired and out of sorts. A turn ashore'll hurt nobody—the boats are still in the water; you can take the gigs, and as many as please can go ashore for the afternoon. I'll fire a gun half an hour before sundown."

I believe the silly fellows must have thought they would break their shins over treasure as soon as they were landed; for they all came out of their sulks in a moment, and gave a cheer that started the echo in a far-away hill, and sent the birds once more flying and squalling round the anchorage.

The captain was too bright to be in the way. He whipped out of sight in a moment, leaving Silver to arrange the party; and I fancy it was as well he did so. Had he been on deck, he could no longer so much as have pretended not to understand the situation. It was as plain as day. Silver was the captain, and a mighty rebellious crew he had of it. The honest hands—and I was soon to see it proved that there were such on board—must have been very stupid fellows. Or, rather, I suppose the truth was this, that all hands were disaffected by the example of the ringleaders—only some more, some less; and a few, being good fellows in the main, could neither be led nor driven any further. It is one thing to be idle and skulk, and quite another to take a ship and murder a number of innocent men.

At last, however, the party was made up. Six fellows were to stay on board, and the remaining thirteen, including Silver, began to embark.

Then it was that there came into my head the first of the mad notions that contributed so much to save our lives. If six men were left by Silver, it was plain our party could not take and fight the ship; and since only six were left, it was equally plain that the cabin party had no present need of my assistance. It occurred to me at once to go ashore. In a jiffy I had slipped over the side, and curled up in the fore-sheets of the nearest boat, and almost at the same moment she shoved off.

No one took notice of me, only the bow oar saying, "Is that you, Jim? Keep your head down." But Silver, from the other boat, looked sharply over and called out to know if that were me; and from that moment I began to regret what I had done.

The crews raced for the beach; but the boat I was in, having some start, and being at once the lighter and the better manned, shot far ahead of her consort, and the bow had struck among the shore-side trees, and I had caught a branch and swung myself out, and plunged into the nearest thicket, while Silver and the rest were still a hundred yards behind.

"Jim, Jim!" I heard him shouting.

But you may suppose I paid no heed; jumping, ducking, and breaking through, I ran straight before my nose, till I could run no longer.

CHAPTER XIV

THE FIRST BLOW

I was so pleased at having given the slip to Long John, that I began to enjoy myself and look around me with some interest on the strange land that I was in.

I had crossed a marshy tract full of willows, bulrushes, and odd, outlandish, swampy trees; and I had now come out upon the skirts of an open piece of undulating, sandy country, about a mile long, dotted with a few pines, and a great number of contorted trees, not unlike the oak in growth, but pale in the foliage, like willows. On the far side of the open stood one of the hills, with two quaint, craggy peaks, shining vividly in the sun.

I now felt for the first time the joy of exploration. The isle was uninhabited; my shipmates I had left behind, and nothing lived in front of me but dumb brutes and fowls. I turned hither and thither among the trees. Here and there were flowering plants, unknown to me; here and there I saw snakes, and one raised his head from a ledge of rock and hissed at me with a noise not unlike the spinning of a top. Little did I suppose that he was a deadly enemy, and that the noise was the famous rattle.

Then I came to a long thicket of these oak-like trees—live, or evergreen, oaks, I heard afterwards they should be called—which grew low along the sand like brambles, the boughs curiously twisted, the foliage compact, like thatch. The thicket stretched down from the top of one of the sandy knolls, spreading and growing taller as it went, until it reached the margin of the broad, reedy fen, through which the nearest of the little rivers soaked its way into the anchorage. The marsh was steaming in the strong sun, and the outline of the Spy-glass trembled through the haze.

All at once there began to go a sort of bustle among the bulrushes; a wild duck flew up with a quack, another followed, and soon over the whole surface of the marsh a great cloud of birds hung screaming and circling in the air. I judged at once that some of my shipmates must be drawing near along the borders of the fen. Nor was I deceived; for soon I heard the very distant and low tones of a human voice, which, as I continued to give ear, grew steadily louder and nearer.

This put me in a great fear, and I crawled under cover of the nearest live-oak, and squatted there, hearkening, as silent as a mouse.

Another voice answered; and then the first voice, which I now recognised to be Silver's, once more took up the story, and ran on for a long while in a stream, only now and again interrupted by the other. By the sound they must have been talking earnestly, and almost fiercely; but no distinct word came to my hearing.

At last the speakers seemed to have paused, and perhaps to have sat down; for not only did they cease to draw any nearer, but the birds themselves began to grow more quiet, and to settle again to their places in the swamp.

And now I began to feel that I was neglecting my business; that since I had been so foolhardy as to come ashore with these desperadoes, the least I could do was to overhear them at their councils; and that my plain and obvious duty was to draw as close as I could manage, under the favourable ambush of the crouching trees.

I could tell the direction of the speakers pretty exactly, not only by the sound of their voices, but by the behaviour of the few birds that still hung in alarm above the heads of the intruders.

Crawling on all-fours, I made steadily but slowly towards them; till at last, raising my head to an aperture among the leaves, I could see clear down into a little green dell beside the marsh, and closely set about with trees, where Long John Silver and another of the crew stood face to face in conversation.

The sun beat full upon them. Silver had thrown his hat beside him on the ground, and his great smooth, blond face, all shining with heat, was lifted to the other man's in a kind of appeal.

"Mate," he was saying, "it's because I thinks gold dust of you—gold dust, and you may lay to that! If I hadn't took to you like pitch, do you think I'd have been here a-warning of you? All's up—you can't make nor mend; it's to save your neck that I'm a-speaking, and if one of the wild 'uns knew it, where 'ud I be, Tom now, tell me, where 'ud I be?"

"Silver," said the other man—and I observed he was not only red in the face, but spoke as hoarse as a crow, and his voice shook, too, like a taut rope—"Silver," says he, "you're old, and you're honest, or has the name for it; and you've money, too, which lots of poor sailors hasn't; and you're brave, or I'm mistook. And will you tell me you'll let yourself be led away with that kind of a mess of swabs? not you! As sure as God sees me, I'd sooner lose my hand. If I turn agin my dooty—"

And then all of a sudden he was interrupted by a noise. I had found one of the honest hands—well, here, at that same moment, came news of another. Far away out in the marsh there arose, all of a sudden, a sound like the cry of anger, then another on the back of it; and then, one horrid, long-drawn scream. The rocks of the Spy-glass re-echoed it a score of times; the whole troop of marsh-birds rose again, darkening heaven, with a simultaneous whirr; and long after that death-yell was still ringing in my brain, silence had re-established its empire, and only the rustle of the redescending birds and the boom of the distant surges disturbed the languor of the afternoon.

Tom had leaped at the sound, like a horse at the spur; but Silver had not winked an eye. He stood where he was, resting lightly on his crutch, watching his companion like a snake about to spring.

"John!" said the sailor, stretching out his hand.

"Hands off!" cried Silver, leaping back a yard, as it seemed to me, with the speed and security of a trained gymnast. "Hands off, if you like, John Silver," said the other. "It's a black conscience that can make you feared of me. But, in Heaven's name, tell me what was that?"

"That?" returned Silver, smiling away, but warier than ever, his eye a mere pin-point in his big face, but gleaming like a crumb of glass. "That? Oh, I reckon that'll be Alan."

And at this poor Tom flashed out like a hero.

"Alan!" he cried. "Then rest his soul for a true seaman! And as for you, John Silver, long you've been a mate of mine, but you're mate of mine no more. If I die like a dog, I'll die in my dooty. You've killed Alan, have you? Kill me, too, if you can. But I defies you!"

And with that, this brave fellow turned his back directly on the cook, and set off walking for the beach. But he was not destined to go far.

With a cry, John seized the branch of a tree, whipped the crutch out of his armpit, and sent that uncouth missile hurtling through the air It struck poor Tom, point foremost, and with stunning violence, right between the shoulders in the middle of his back. His hands flew up, he gave a sort of gasp, and fell.

Whether he were injured much or little, none could ever tell. Like enough, to judge from the sound, his back was broken on the spot. But he had no time given him to recover. Silver, agile as a monkey, even without leg or crutch, was on the top of him next moment, and had twice buried his knife up to the hilt in that defenceless body. From my place of ambush, I could hear him pant aloud as he struck the blows.

I do not know what it rightly is to faint, but I do know that for the next little while the whole world swam away from before me in a whirling mist; Silver and the birds, and the tall Spy-glass hill-top, going round and round and topsy-turvy before my eyes, and all manner of bells ringing and distant voices shouting in my ear.

When I came again to myself, the monster had pulled himself together, his crutch under his arm, his hat upon his head. Just before him Tom lay motionless upon the sward; but the murderer minded him not a whit, cleansing his blood-stained knife the while upon a wisp of grass. Everything else was unchanged, the sun still shining mercilessly upon the steaming marsh and the tall pinnacle of the mountain, and I could scarce persuade myself that murder had been actually done, and a human life cruelly cut short a moment since, before my eyes.

But now John put his hand into his pocket, brought out a whistle, and blew upon it several modulated blasts, that rang far across the heated air. I could not tell, of course, the meaning of the signal; but it instantly awoke my fears. More men would be coming. I might be discovered. They had already slain two of the honest people; after Tom and Alan, might not I come next?

Instantly I began to extricate myself and crawl back again, with what speed and silence I could manage, to the more open portion of the wood. As I did so, I could hear hails coming and going between the old buccaneer and his comrades, and this sound of danger lent me wings. As soon as I was clear of the thicket, I ran as I never ran before, scarce minding the direction of my flight, so long as it led me from the murderers; and as I ran, fear grew and grew upon me, until it turned into a kind of frenzy.

JUST BEFORE HIM TOM LAY MOTIONLESS UPON THE
SWARD

Indeed, could anyone be more entirely lost than I? When the gun fired, how should I dare to go down to the boats among those fiends, still smoking from their crime? Would not the first of them who saw me wring my neck like a snipe's? Would not my absence itself be an evidence to them of my alarm, and therefore of my fatal knowledge? It was all over, I thought. Good-bye to the *Hispaniola*; good-bye to the squire, the doctor, and the captain! There was nothing left for me but death by starvation, or death by the hands of the mutineers.

All this while, as I say, I was still running, and, without taking any notice, I had drawn near to the foot of the little hill with the two peaks, and had got into a part of the island where the live-oaks grew more widely apart, and seemed more like forest trees in their bearing and dimensions. Mingled with these were a few scattered pines, some fifty, some nearer seventy, feet high. The air, too, smelt more freshly than down beside the marsh.

And here a fresh alarm brought me to a standstill with a thumping heart.

Chapter XV

THE MAN OF THE ISLAND

From the side of the hill, which was here steep and stony, a spout of gravel was dislodged, and fell rattling and bounding through the trees. My eyes turned instinctively in that direction, and I saw a figure leap with great rapidity behind the trunk of a pine. What it was, whether bear or man or monkey, I could in nowise tell. It seemed dark and shaggy; more I knew not. But the terror of this new apparition brought me to a stand.

I was now, it seemed, cut off upon both sides; behind me the murderers, before me this lurking nondescript. And immediately I began to prefer the dangers that I knew to those I knew not. Silver himself appeared less terrible in contrast with this creature of the woods, and I turned on my heel, and, looking sharply behind me over my shoulder, began to retrace my steps in the direction of the boats.

Instantly the figure reappeared, and, making a wide circuit, began to head me off. I was tired, at any rate; but had I been as fresh as when I rose, I could see it was in vain for me to contend in speed with such an adversary. From trunk to trunk the creature flitted like a deer, running manlike on two legs, but unlike any man that I had ever seen, stooping almost double as it ran. Yet a man it was, I could no longer be in doubt about that.

I began to recall what I had heard of cannibals. I was within an ace of calling for help. But the mere fact that he was a man, however wild, had somewhat reassured me, and my fear of Silver began to revive in proportion. I stood still, therefore, and cast about for some method

"I'M POOR BEN GUNN, I AM. MAROONED THREE YEARS
AGONE, AND LIVED ON GOATS SINCE THEN"

of escape; and as I was so thinking, the recollection of my pistol flashed into my mind. As soon as I remembered I was not defenceless, courage glowed again in my heart; and I set my face resolutely for this man of the island, and walked briskly towards him.

He was concealed by this time, behind another tree trunk; but he must have been watching me closely, for as soon as I began to move in his direction he reappeared and took a step to meet me. Then he hesitated, drew back, came forward again, and at last, to my wonder and confusion, threw himself on his knees and held out his clasped hands in supplication.

At that I once more stopped.

"Who are you?" I asked.

"Ben Gunn," he answered, and his voice sounded hoarse and awkward, like a rusty lock. "I'm poor Ben Gunn, I am; and I haven't spoke with a Christian these three years."

I could now see that he was a white man like myself, and that his features were even pleasing. His skin, wherever it was exposed, was burnt by the sun; even his lips were black; and his fair eyes looked quite startling in so dark a face. Of all the beggar-men that I had seen or fancied, he was the chief for raggedness. He was clothed with tatters of old ship's canvas and old sea cloth; and this extraordinary patchwork was all held together by a system of the most various and incongruous fastenings, brass buttons, bits of stick, and loops of tarry gaskin. About his waist he wore an old brass-buckled leather belt, which was the one thing solid in his whole accoutrement.

"Three years!" I cried. "Were you shipwrecked?"

"Nay, mate," said he—"marooned."

I had heard the word, and I knew it stood for a horrible kind of punishment common enough among the buccaneers, in which the offender is put ashore with a little powder and shot, and left behind on some desolate and distant island.

"Marooned three years agone," he continued, "and lived on goats since then, and berries, and oysters. Wherever a man is, says I, a man can do for himself. But, mate, my heart is sore for Christian diet. You mightn't happen to have a piece of cheese about you, now? No? Well, many's the long night I've dreamed of cheese—toasted, mostly—and woke up again, and here I were."

"If ever I can get aboard again," said I, "you shall have cheese by the stone."

All this time he had been feeling the stuff of my jacket, smoothing my hands, looking at my boots, and generally, in the intervals of his speech, showing a childish pleasure in the presence of a fellow-creature. But at my last words he perked up into a kind of startled slyness.

"If ever you can get aboard again, says you?" he repeated. "Why, now, who's to hinder you?"

"Not you, I know," was my reply.

"And right you was," he cried. "Now you—what do you call your-self, mate?"

"Jim," I told him.

"Jim, Jim," says he, quite pleased apparently. "Well, now, Jim, I've lived that rough as you'd be ashamed to hear of. Now, for instance, you wouldn't think I had had a pious mother—to look at me?" he asked.

"Why, no, not in particular," I answered.

"Ah, well," said he, "but I had—remarkable pious. And I was a civil, pious boy, and could rattle off my catechism that fast, as you couldn't tell one word from another. And here's what it come to, Jim, and it begun with chuck-farthen on the blessed grave-stones! That's what it begun with, but it went further'n that; and so my mother told me, and predicked the whole, she did, the pious woman! But it were Providence that put me here. I've thought it all out in this here lonely island, and I'm back on piety. You don't catch me tasting rum so much; but just a thimbleful for luck, of course, the first chance I have. I'm bound I'll be good, and I see the way to. And, Jim"—looking all round him, and lowering his voice to a whisper—"I'm rich."

I now felt sure that the poor fellow had gone crazy in his solitude, and I suppose I must have shown the feeling in my face; for he re-peated the statement hotly:—

"Rich! rich! I says. And I'll tell you what: I'll make a man of you, Jim. Ah, Jim, you'll bless your stars, you will, you was the first that found me!"

And at this there came suddenly a lowering shadow over his face, and he tightened his grasp upon my hand, and raised a forefinger threateningly before my eyes.

"Now, Jim, you tell me true: that ain't Flint's ship?" he asked.

At this I had a happy inspiration. I began to believe that I had found an ally, and I answered him at once.

"It's not Flint's ship, and Flint is dead; but I'll tell you true, as you ask me—there are some of Flint's hands aboard; worse luck for the rest of us."

"Not a man—with one—leg?" he gasped.

"Silver?" I asked.

"Ah, Silver!" says he; "that were his name."

"He's the cook; and the ringleader, too."

He was still holding me by the wrist, and at that he gave it quite a wring.

"If you was sent by Long John," he said, "I'm as good as pork, and I know it. But where was you, do you suppose?"

I had made my mind up in a moment, and by way of answer told him the whole story of our voyage, and the predicament in which we found ourselves. He heard me with the keenest interest, and when I had done he patted me on the head.

"You're a good lad, Jim," he said; "and you're all in a clove-hitch, ain't you? Well, you just put your trust in Ben Gunn—Ben Gunn's the man to do it. Would you think it likely, now, that your squire would prove a liberal-minded one in case of help—him being in a clove-hitch, as you remark?"

I told him the squire was the most liberal of men.

"Ay, but you see," returned Ben Gunn, "I didn't mean giving me a gate to keep, and a shuit of livery clothes, and such; that's not my mark, Jim. What I mean is, would he be likely to come down to the toon of, say, one thousand pounds out of money that's as good as a man's own already?"

"I am sure he would," said I. "As it was, all hands were to share."

"*And* a passage home?" he added, with a look of great shrewdness.

"Why," I cried, "the squire's a gentleman. And, besides, if we get rid of the others, we should want you to help work the vessel home."

"Ah," said he, "so you would." And he seemed very much relieved.

"Now, I'll tell you what," he went on. "So much I'll tell you, and no more. I were in Flint's ship when he buried the treasure; he and six along—six strong seamen. They was ashore nigh on a week, and us standing off and on in the old *Walrus*. One fine day up went the signal, and here come Flint by himself in a little boat, and his head done up in a blue scarf. The sun was getting up, and mortal white he looked about the cutwater. But, there he was, you mind, and the six all dead—

dead and buried. How he done it, not a man aboard us could make out. It was battle, murder, and sudden death, leastways—him against six. Billy Bones was the mate; Long John, he was quarter-master; and they asked him where the treasure was. 'Ah,' says he, 'you can go ashore, if you like, and stay,' he says; 'but as for the ship, she'll beat up for more, by thunder!' That's what he said.

"Well, I was in another ship three years back, and we sighted this island. 'Boys,' said I, 'here's Flint's treasure; let's land and find it.' The cap'n was displeased at that; but my messmates were all of a mind, and landed. Twelve days they looked for it, and every day they had the worst word for me, until one fine morning all hands went aboard. 'As for you, Benjamin Gunn,' says they, 'here's a musket,' they says, 'and a spade, and pickaxe. You can stay here, and find Flint's money for yourself,' they says.

"Well, Jim, three years have I been here, and not a bite of Christian diet from that day to this. But now, you look here; look at me. Do I look like a man before the mast? No, says you. Nor I weren't, neither, I says."

And with that he winked and pinched me hard.

"Just you mention them words to your squire, Jim"—he went on: "Nor he weren't, neither—that's the words. Three years he were the man of this island, light and dark, fair and rain; and sometimes he would, maybe, think upon a prayer (says you), and sometimes he would, maybe, think of his old mother, so be as she's alive (you'll say); but the most part of Gunn's time (this is what you'll say)—the most part of his time was took up with another matter. And then you'll give him a nip, like I do."

And he pinched me again in the most confidential manner.

"Then," he continued—"then you'll up, and you'll say this:—Gunn is a good man (you'll say), and he puts a precious sight more confidence—a precious sight, mind that—in a gen'leman born than in these gen'lemen of fortune, having been one hisself."

"Well," I said, "I don't understand one word that you've been saying. But that's neither here nor there; for how am I to get on board?"

"Ah," said he, "that's the hitch, for sure. Well, there's my boat, that I made with my two hands. I keep her under the white rock. If the worst come to the worst, we might try that after dark. Hi!" he broke out, "what's that?"

For just then, although the sun had still an hour or two to run, all the echoes of the island awoke and bellowed to the thunder of a cannon.

"They have begun to fight!" I cried. "Follow me."

And I began to run towards the anchorage, my terrors all forgotten; while, close at my side, the marooned man in his goatskins trotted easily and lightly.

"Left, left," says he; "keep to your left hand, mate Jim! Under the trees with you! Theer's where I killed my first goat. They don't come down here now; they're all mast-headed on them mountings for the fear of Benjamin Gunn. Ah! and there's the cetemery"—cemetery, he must have meant. "You see the mounds? I come here and prayed, nows and thens, when I thought maybe a Sunday would be about doo. It weren't quite a chapel, but it seemed more solemn like; and then, says you, Ben Gunn was short-handed—no chapling, nor so much as a Bible and a flag, you says."

So he kept talking as I ran, neither expecting nor receiving any answer.

The cannon-shot was followed, after a considerable interval, by a volley of small arms.

Another pause, and then, not a quarter of a mile in front of me, I beheld the Union Jack flutter in the air above a wood.

PART IV

THE STOCKADE

CHAPTER XVI

NARRATIVE CONTINUED BY THE DOCTOR:

HOW THE SHIP WAS ABANDONED

It was about half-past one—three bells, in the sea phrase—that the two boats went ashore from the *Hispaniola*. The captain, the squire, and I were talking matters over in the cabin. Had there been a breath of wind we should have fallen on the six mutineers who were left aboard with us, slipped our cable, and away to sea. But the wind was wanting; and, to complete our helplessness, down came Hunter with the news that Jim Hawkins had slipped into a boat and was gone ashore with the rest.

It never occurred to us to doubt Jim Hawkins; but we were alarmed for his safety. With the men in the temper they were in, it seemed an even chance if we should see the lad again. We ran on deck. The pitch was bubbling in the seams; the nasty stench of the place turned me sick; if ever a man smelt fever and dysentery, it was in that abominable anchorage. The six scoundrels were sitting grumbling under a sail in the forecastle; ashore we could see the gigs made fast, and a man sitting in each, hard by where the river runs in. One of them was whistling "Lillibullero."

Waiting was a strain; and it was decided that Hunter and I should go ashore with the jolly-boat, in quest of information.

The gigs had leaned to their right; but Hunter and I pulled straight in, in the direction of the stockade upon the chart. The two who were left guarding their boats seemed in a bustle at our appearance; "Lillibullero" stopped off, and I could see the pair discussing what they ought to do. Had they gone and told Silver, all might have turned out differently; but they had their orders, I suppose, and decided to sit quietly where they were and hark back again to "Lillibullero."

There was a slight bend in the coast, and I steered so as to put it between us; even before we landed we had thus lost sight of the gigs. I jumped out, and came as near running as I durst, with a big silk handkerchief under my hat for coolness' sake, and a brace of pistols ready primed for safety.

I had not gone a hundred yards when I came on the stockade.

This was how it was: a spring of clear water rose almost at the top of a knoll. Well on the knoll, and enclosing the spring, they had clapped a stout log-house, fit to hold two score people on a pinch, and loopholed for musketry on every side. All round this they had cleared a wide space, and then the thing was completed by a paling six feet high, without door or opening, too strong to pull down without time and labour, and too open to shelter the besiegers. The people in the log-house had them in every way; they stood quiet in shelter and shot the others like partridges. All they wanted was a good watch and food; for, short of a complete surprise, they might have held the place against a regiment.

What particularly took my fancy was the spring. For, though we had a good enough place of it in the cabin of the *Hispaniola,* with plenty of arms and ammunition, and things to eat, and excellent wines, there had been one thing overlooked—we had no water. I was thinking this over, when there came ringing over the island the cry of a man at the point of death. I was not new to violent death—I have served his Royal Highness the Duke of Cumberland, and got a wound myself at Fontenoy—but I know my pulse went dot and carry one. "Jim Hawkins is gone!" was my first thought.

It is something to have been an old soldier, but more still to have been a doctor. There is no time to dilly-dally in our work. And so now I made up my mind instantly, and with no time lost returned to the shore, and jumped on board the jolly-boat.

By good fortune Hunter pulled a good oar. We made the water fly; and the boat was soon alongside, and I aboard the schooner.

I found them all shaken, as was natural. The squire was sitting down, as white as a sheet, thinking of the harm he had led us to, the good soul! and one of the six forecastle hands was little better.

"There's a man," says Captain Smollett, nodding towards him, "new to this work. He came nigh-hand fainting, doctor, when he heard the cry. Another touch of the rudder and that man would join us."

I told my plan to the captain, and between us we settled on the details of its accomplishment.

We put old Redruth in the gallery between the cabin and the forecastle, with three or four loaded muskets and a mattress for protection. Hunter brought the boat round under the stern-port, and Joyce and I set to work loading her with powder-tins, muskets, bags of biscuits, kegs of pork, a cask of cognac, and my invaluable medicine-chest.

In the meantime, the squire and the captain stayed on deck, and the latter hailed the coxswain, who was the principal man aboard.

"Mr Hands," he said, "here are two of us with a brace of pistols each. If any one of you six make a signal of any description, that man's dead."

They were a good deal taken aback; and, after a little consultation, one and all tumbled down the fore companion, thinking, no doubt, to take us on the rear. But when they saw Redruth waiting for them in the sparred gallery, they went about-ship at once, and a head popped out again on deck.

"Down, dog!" cries the captain.

And the head popped back again; and we heard no more, for the time, of these six very faint-hearted seamen.

By this time, tumbling things in as they came, we had the jolly-boat loaded as much as we dared. Joyce and I got out through the stern-port, and we made for shore again, as fast as oars could take us.

This second trip fairly aroused the watchers along shore. "Lillibullero" was dropped again; and just before we lost sight of them behind the little point, one of them whipped ashore and disappeared. I had half a mind to change plan and destroy their boats, but I feared that Silver and the others might be close at hand, and all might very well be lost by trying for too much.

We had soon touched land in the same place as before, and set to provision the block-house. All three made the first journey heavily laden, and tossed our stores over the palisade. Then, leaving Joyce to guard them—one man, to be sure, but with half a dozen muskets—Hunter and I returned to the jolly-boat, and loaded ourselves once more. So we proceeded without pausing to take breath, till the whole cargo was bestowed, when the two servants took up their position in the block-house, and I, with all my power, sculled back to the *Hispaniola.*

That we should have risked a second boat-load seems more daring than it really was. They had the advantage of numbers, of course, but we had the advantage of arms. Not one of the men ashore had a musket, and before they could get within range for pistol shooting, we flattered ourselves we should be able to give a good account of a half-dozen at least.

The squire was waiting for me at the stern window, all his faintness gone from him. He caught the painter and made it fast, and we fell to loading the boat for our very lives. Pork, powder, and biscuit was the cargo, with only a musket and a cutlass apiece for squire and me and Redruth and the captain. The rest of the arms and powder we dropped overboard in two fathoms and a half of water, so that we could see the bright steel shining far below us in the sun, on the clean, sandy bottom.

By this time the tide was beginning to ebb, and the ship was swinging round to her anchor. Voices were heard faintly halloaing in the direction of the two gigs; and though this reassured us for Joyce and Hunter, who were well to the eastward, it warned our party to be off.

Redruth retreated from his place in the gallery, and dropped into the boat, which we then brought round to the ship's counter, to be handier for Captain Smollett.

"Now, men," said he, "do you hear me?"

There was no answer from the forecastle.

"It's to you, Abraham Gray—it's to you I am speaking."

Still no reply.

"Gray," resumed Mr Smollett, a little louder, "I am leaving this ship, and I order you to follow your captain. I know you are a good man at bottom, and I dare say not one of the lot of you's as bad as he makes out. I have my watch here in my hand; I give you thirty seconds to join me in.

There was a pause.

"Come, my fine fellow," continued the captain, "don't hang so long in stays. I'm risking my life and the lives of these good gentlemen every second."

There was a sudden scuffle, a sound of blows, and out burst Abraham Gray with a knife-cut on the side of the cheek, and came running to the captain, like a dog to the whistle.

"I'm with you, sir," said he.

And the next moment he and the captain had dropped aboard of us, and we had shoved off and given way.

We were clear out of the ship, but not yet ashore in our stockade.

Chapter XVII

NARRATIVE CONTINUED BY THE DOCTOR: THE JOLLY-BOAT'S LAST TRIP

This fifth trip was quite different from any of the others. In the first place, the little gallipot of a boat that we were in was gravely overloaded. Five grown men, and three of them—Trelawney, Redruth, and the captain—over six feet high, was already more than she was meant to carry. Add to that the powder, pork, and bread-bags. The gunwale was lipping astern. Several times we shipped a little water, and my breeches and the tails of my coat were all soaking wet before we had gone a hundred yards.

The captain made us trim the boat, and we got her to lie a little more evenly. All the same, we were afraid to breathe.

In the second place, the ebb was now making—a strong rippling current running westward through the basin, and then south'ard and seaward down the straits by which we had entered in the morning. Even the ripples were a danger to our overloaded craft; but the worst of it was that we were swept out of our true course, and away from our proper landing-place behind the point. If we let the current have its way we should come ashore beside the gigs, where the pirates might appear at any moment.

"I cannot keep her head for the stockade, sir," said I to the captain. I was steering, while he and Redruth, two fresh men, were at the oars. "The tide keeps washing her down. Could you pull a little stronger?"

"Not without swamping the boat," said he. "You must bear up, sir, if you please—bear up until you see you're gaining."

I tried, and found by experiment that the tide kept sweeping us westward until I had laid her head due east, or just about right angles to the way we ought to go.

"We'll never get ashore at this rate," said I.

"If it's the only course that we can lie, sir, we must even lie it," returned the captain. "We must keep up-stream. You see, sir," he went on, "if once we dropped to leeward of the landing-place, it's hard to say where we should get ashore, besides the chance of being boarded by the gigs; whereas, the way we go the current must slacken, and then we can dodge back along the shore."

"The current's less a'ready, sir," said the man Gray, who was sitting in the fore-sheets; "you can ease her off a bit."

"Thank you, my man," said I, quite as if nothing had happened: for we had all quietly made up our minds to treat him like one of ourselves.

Suddenly the captain spoke up again, and I thought his voice was a little changed.

"The gun!" said he.

"I have thought of that," said I, for I made sure he was thinking of a bombardment of the fort. "They could never get the gun ashore, and if they did, they could never haul it through the woods."

"Look astern, doctor," replied the captain.

We had entirely forgotten the long nine; and there, to our horror, were the five rogues busy about her, getting off her jacket, as they called the stout tarpaulin cover under which she sailed. Not only that, but it flashed into my mind at the same moment that the round-shot and the powder for the gun had been left behind, and a stroke with an axe would put it all into the possession of the evil ones aboard.

"Israel was Flint's gunner," said Gray, hoarsely.

At any risk, we put the boat's head direct for the landing-place. By this time we had got so far out of the run of the current that we kept steerage way even at our necessarily gentle rate of rowing, and I could keep her steady for the goal. But the worst of it was, that with the course I now held, we turned our broadside instead of our stern to the *Hispaniola,* and offered a target like a barn door.

I could hear, as well as see, that brandy-faced rascal, Israel Hands, plumping down a round-shot on the deck.

"Who's the best shot?" asked the captain.

"Mr Trelawney, out and away," said I.

"Mr Trelawney, will you please pick me off one of these men, sir?—Hands, if possible," said the captain.

Trelawney was as cool as steel. He looked to the priming of his gun.

"Now," cried the captain, "easy with that gun, sir, or you'll swamp the boat. All hands stand by to trim her when he aims."

The squire raised his gun, the rowing ceased, and we leaned over to the other side to keep the balance, and all was so nicely contrived that we did not ship a drop.

They had the gun, by this time, slewed round upon the swivel, and Hands, who was at the muzzle with the rammer, was, in consequence, the most exposed. However, we had no luck; for just as Trelawney fired, down he stooped, the ball whistled over him, and it was one of the other four who fell.

The cry he gave was echoed, not only by his companions on board, but by a great number of voices from the shore, and looking in that direction I saw the other pirates trooping out from among the trees and tumbling into their places in the boats.

"Here come the gigs, sir," said I.

"Give way then," cried the captain. "We mustn't mind if we swamp her now. If we can't get ashore, all's up."

"Only one of the gigs is being manned, sir," I added, "the crew of the other most likely going round by shore to cut us off."

"They'll have a hot run, sir," returned the captain. "Jack ashore, you know. It's not them I mind; it's the round-shot. Carpet bowls! My lady's maid couldn't miss. Tell us, squire, when you see the match, and we'll hold water."

In the meanwhile we had been making headway at a good pace for a boat so overloaded, and we had shipped but little water in the process. We were now close in; thirty or forty strokes and we should beach her; for the ebb had already disclosed a narrow belt of sand below the clustering trees. The gig was no longer to be feared; the little point had already concealed it from our eyes. The ebb-tide, which had so cruelly delayed us, was now making reparation, and delaying our assailants. The one source of danger was the gun.

"If I durst," said the captain, "I'd stop and pick off another man."

But it was plain that they meant nothing should delay their shot. They had never so much as looked at their fallen comrade, though he was not dead, and I could see him trying to crawl away.

"Ready!" cried the squire.

"Hold!" cried the captain, quick as an echo.

And he and Redruth backed with a great heave that sent her stern bodily under water. The report fell in at the same instant of time. This was the first that Jim heard, the sound of the squire's shot not having reached him. Where the ball passed, not one of us precisely knew; but I fancy it must have been over our heads, and that the wind of it may have contributed to our disaster.

At any rate, the boat sank by the stern, quite gently, in three feet of water, leaving the captain and myself, facing each other, on our feet. The other three took complete headers, and came up again, drenched and bubbling.

So far there was no great harm. No lives were lost, and we could wade ashore in safety. But there were all our stores at the bottom, and, to make things worse, only two guns out of five remained in a state for service. Mine I had snatched from my knees and held over my head, by a sort of instinct. As for the captain, he had carried his over his shoulder by a bandoleer, and, like a wise man, lock uppermost. The other three had gone down with the boat.

To add to our concern, we heard voices already drawing near us in the woods along shore; and we had not only the danger of being cut off from the stockade in our half-crippled state, but the fear before us whether, if Hunter and Joyce were attacked by half a dozen, they would have the sense and conduct to stand firm. Hunter was steady, that we knew; Joyce was a doubtful case—a pleasant, polite man for a valet, and to brush one's clothes, but not entirely fitted for a man of war.

With all this in our minds, we waded ashore as fast as we could, leaving behind us the poor jolly-boat, and a good half of all our powder and provisions.

Chapter XVIII

NARRATIVE CONTINUED BY THE DOCTOR:

END OF THE FIRST DAY'S FIGHTING

We made our best speed across the strip of wood that now divided us from the stockade; and at every step we took the voices of the buccaneers rang nearer. Soon we could hear their footfalls as they ran, and the cracking of the branches as they breasted across a bit of thicket.

I began to see we should have a brush for it in earnest, and looked to my priming.

"Captain," said I, "Trelawney is the dead shot. Give him your gun; his own is useless."

They exchanged guns, and Trelawney, silent and cool as he had been since the beginning of the bustle, hung a moment on his heel to see that all was fit for service. At the same time, observing Gray to be unarmed, I handed him my cutlass. It did all our hearts good to see him spit in his hand, knit his brows, and make the blade sing through the air. It was plain from every line of his body that our new hand was worth his salt.

Forty paces farther we came to the edge of the wood and saw the stockade in front of us. We struck the enclosure about the middle of the south side, and, almost at the same time, seven mutineers—Job Anderson, the boatswain, at their head—appeared in full cry at the south-western corner.

They paused, as if taken aback; and before they recovered, not only the squire and I, but Hunter and Joyce from the block-house, had time to fire. The four shots came in rather a scattering volley; but they did the business: one of the enemy actually fell, and the rest, without hesitation, turned and plunged into the trees.

After reloading, we walked down the outside of the palisade to see to the fallen enemy. He was stone dead—shot through the heart.

We began to rejoice over our good success, when just at that moment a pistol cracked in the bush, a ball whistled close past my ear, and poor Tom Redruth stumbled and fell his length on the ground. Both the squire and I returned the shot; but as we had nothing to aim at, it is probable we only wasted powder. Then we reloaded, and turned our attention to poor Tom.

The captain and Gray were already examining him; and I saw with half an eye that all was over.

I believe the readiness of our return volley had scattered the mutineers once more, for we were suffered without further molestation to get the poor old gamekeeper hoisted over the stockade, and carried, groaning and bleeding, into the log-house.

Poor old fellow, he had not uttered one word of surprise, complaint, fear, or even acquiescence, from the very beginning of our troubles till now, when we had laid him down in the log-house to die. He had lain like a Trojan behind his mattress in the gallery; he had followed every order silently, doggedly, and well; he was the oldest of our party by a score of years; and now, sullen, old, serviceable servant, it was he that was to die.

The squire dropped down beside him on his knees and kissed his hand, crying like a child.

"Be I going, doctor?" he asked.

"Tom, my man," said I, "you're going home."

"I wish I had had a lick at them with the gun first," he replied.

"Tom," said the squire, "say you forgive me, won't you?"

"Would that be respectful-like, from me to you, squire?" was the answer. "Howsoever, so be it, amen!"

After a little while of silence, he said he thought somebody might read a prayer. "It's the custom, sir," he added, apologetically. And not long after, without another word, he passed away.

In the meantime the captain, whom I had observed to be wonderfully swollen about the chest and pockets, had turned out a great many various stores—the British colours, a Bible, a coil of stoutish rope, pen, ink, the log-book, and pounds of tobacco. He had found a longish fir-tree lying felled and cleared in the enclosure, and, with the help of Hunter, he had set it up at the corner of the log-house where the trunks crossed and made an angle. Then, climbing on the roof, he had with his own hand bent and run up the colours.

This seemed mightily to relieve him. He re-entered the log-house, and set about counting up the stores, as if nothing else existed. But he had an eye on Tom's passage for all that; and as soon as all was over, came forward with another flag, and reverently spread it on the body.

"Don't you take on, sir," he said, shaking the squire's hand. "All's well with him; no fear for a hand that's been shot down in his duty to captain and owner. It mayn't be good divinity, but it's a fact."

Then he pulled me aside.

"Dr Livesey," he said, "in how many weeks do you and squire expect the consort?"

I told him it was a question, not of weeks, but of months; that if we were not back by the end of August, Blandly was to send to find us; but neither sooner nor later. "You can calculate for yourself," I said.

"Why, yes," returned the captain, scratching his head, "and making a large allowance, sir, for all the gifts of Providence, I should say we were pretty close-hauled."

"How do you mean?" I asked.

"It's a pity, sir, we lost that second load. That's what I mean," replied the captain. "As for powder and shot, we'll do. But the rations are short, very short—so short, Doctor Livesey, that we're, perhaps, as well without that extra mouth."

And he pointed to the dead body under the flag.

Just then, with a roar and a whistle, a round-shot passed high above the roof of the log-house and plumped far beyond us in the wood.

"Oho!" said the captain. "Blaze away! You've little enough powder already, my lads."

At the second trial, the aim was better, and the ball descended inside the stockade, scattering a cloud of sand but doing no further damage.

"Captain," said the squire, "the house is quite invisible from the ship. It must be the flag they are aiming at. Would it not be wiser to take it in?"

"Strike my colours!" cried the captain. "No, sir, not I;" and, as soon as he had said the words, I think we all agreed with him. For it was not

107

I RAN TO THE DOOR IN TIME TO SEE JIM HAWKINS, SAFE AND SOUND, COME CLIMBING OVER THE STOCKADE only a piece of stout, seamanly, good feeling; it was good policy besides, and showed our enemies that we despised their cannonade.

All through the evening they kept thundering away. Ball after ball flew over or fell short, or kicked up the sand in the enclosure; but they had to fire so high that the shot fell dead and buried itself in the soft sand. We had no ricochet to fear; and though one popped in through the roof of the log-house and out again through the floor, we soon got used to that sort of horse-play, and minded it no more than cricket.

"There is one thing good about all this," observed the captain: "the wood in front of us is likely clear. The ebb has made a good while; our stores should be uncovered. Volunteers to go and bring in pork."

Gray and Hunter were the first to come forward. Well armed, they stole out of the stockade; but it proved a useless mission. The mutineers were bolder than we fancied, or they put more trust in Israel's gunnery. For four or five of them were busy carrying off our stores, and wading out with them to one of the gigs that lay close by, pulling an oar or so to hold her steady against the current. Silver was in the stern-sheets in command; and every man of them was now provided with a musket from some secret magazine of their own.

The captain sat down to his log, and here is the beginning of the entry:—

"Alexander Smollett, master; David Livesey, ship's doctor; Abraham Gray, carpenter's mate; John Trelawney, owner; John Hunter and Richard Joyce, owner's servants, landsmen—being all that is left faithful of the ship's company—with stores for ten days at short rations, came ashore this day, and flew British colours on the log-house in Treasure Island. Thomas Redruth, owner's servant, landsman, shot by the mutineers; James Hawkins, cabin-boy—"

And at the same time I was wondering over poor Jim Hawkins's fate.

A hail on the land side.

"Somebody hailing us," said Hunter, who was on guard.

"Doctor! squire! captain! Hullo, Hunter, is that you?" came the cries.

And I ran to the door in time to see Jim Hawkins, safe and sound, come climbing over the stockade.

CHAPTER XIX

NARRATIVE RESUMED BY JIM HAWKINS:
THE GARRISON IN THE STOCKADE

A s soon as Ben Gunn saw the colours he came to a halt, stopped me by the arm, and sat down.

"Now," said he, "there's your friends, sure enough."

"Far more likely it's the mutineers," I answered.

"That!" he cried. "Why, in a place like this, where nobody puts in but gen'lemen of fortune, Silver would fly the Jolly Roger, you don't make no doubt of that. No; that's your friends. There's been blows, too, and I reckon your friends has had the best of it; and here they are ashore in the old stockade, as was made years and years ago by Flint. Ah, he was the man to have a headpiece, was Flint! Barring rum, his match were never seen. He were afraid of none, not he; on'y Silver—Silver was that genteel."

"Well," said I, "that may be so, and so be it; all the more reason that I should hurry on and join my friends."

"Nay, mate," returned Ben, "not you. You're a good boy, or I'm mistook; but you're on'y a boy, all told. Now, Ben Gunn is fly. Rum wouldn't bring me there, where you're going—not rum wouldn't, till I see your born gen'leman, and gets it on his word of honour. And you won't forget my words: 'A precious sight (that's what you'll say), a precious sight more confidence'—and then nips him."

And he pinched me the third time with the same air of cleverness.

"And when Ben Gunn is wanted, you know where to find him, Jim. Just wheer you found him to-day. And him that comes is to have a white thing in his hand: and he's to come alone. Oh! and you'll say this: 'Ben Gunn,' says you, 'has reasons of his own.'"

"Well," said I, "I believe I understand. You have something to propose, and you wish to see the squire or the doctor; and you're to be found where I found you. Is that all?"

"And when? says you," he added. "Why, from about noon observation to about six bells."

"Good," said I, "and now may I go?"

"You won't forget?" he inquired, anxiously. "Precious sight, and reasons of his own, says you. Reasons of his own; that's the mainstay; as between man and man. Well, then"—still holding me—"I reckon you can go, Jim. And, Jim, if you was to see Silver, you wouldn't go for to sell Ben Gunn? wild horses wouldn't draw it from you? No, says you. And if them pirates camp ashore, Jim, what would you say but there'd be widders in the morning?"

Here he was interrupted by a loud report, and a cannon ball came tearing through the trees and pitched in the sand, not a hundred yards from where we two were talking. The next moment each of us had taken to his heels in a different direction.

For a good hour to come frequent reports shook the island, and balls kept crashing through the woods. I moved from hiding-place to hiding-place, always pursued, or so it seemed to me, by these terrifying missiles. But towards the end of the bombardment, though still I durst not venture in the direction of the stockade, where the balls fell oftenest, I had begun, in a manner, to pluck up my heart again; and after a long detour to the east, crept down among the shore-side trees.

The sun had just set, the sea breeze was rustling and tumbling in the woods, and ruffling the grey surface of the anchorage; the tide, too, was far out, and great tracts of sand lay uncovered; the air, after the heat of the day, chilled me through my jacket.

The *Hispaniola* still lay where she had anchored; but, sure enough, there was the Jolly Roger—the black flag of piracy—flying from her peak. Even as I looked, there came another red flash and another report, that sent the echoes clattering, and one more round-shot whistled through the air. It was the last of the cannonade.

I lay for some time, watching the bustle which succeeded the attack. Men were demolishing something with axes on the beach near the stockade; the poor jolly-boat, I afterwards discovered. Away, near the mouth of the river, a great fire was glowing among the trees, and between that point and the ship one of the gigs kept coming and going, the men, whom I had seen so gloomy, shouting at the oars like children. But there was a sound in their voices which suggested rum.

At length I thought I might return towards the stockade. I was pretty far down on the low, sandy spit that encloses the anchorage to the east, and is joined at half-water to Skeleton Island; and now, as I rose to my feet, I saw, some distance farther down the spit, and rising from among low bushes, an isolated rock, pretty high, and peculiarly white in colour. It occurred to me that this might be the white rock of which Ben Gunn had spoken, and that some day or other a boat might be wanted, and I should know where to look for one.

Then I skirted among the woods until I had regained the rear, or shoreward side, of the stockade, and was soon warmly welcomed by the faithful party.

I had soon told my story, and began to look about me. The log-house was made of unsquared trunks of pine-roof, walls, and floor. The latter stood in several places as much as a foot or a foot and a half above the surface of the sand. There was a porch at the door, and under this porch the little spring welled up into an artificial basin of a rather odd kind—no other than a great ship's kettle of iron, with the bottom knocked out, and sunk "to her bearings," as the captain said, among the sand.

Little had been left besides the framework of the house; but in one corner there was a stone slab laid down by way of hearth, and an old rusty iron basket to contain the fire.

The slopes of the knoll and all the inside of the stockade had been cleared of timber to build the house, and we could see by the stumps what a fine and lofty grove had been destroyed. Most of the soil had been washed away or buried in drift after the removal of the trees; only where the streamlet ran down from the kettle a thick bed of moss and some ferns and little creeping bushes were still green among the sand. Very close around the stockade—too close for defence, they said—the wood still flourished high and dense, all of fir on the land side, but towards the sea with a large admixture of live-oaks.

The cold evening breeze, of which I have spoken, whistled through every chink of the rude building, and sprinkled the floor with a continual rain of fine sand. There was sand in our eyes, sand in our teeth, sand in our suppers, sand dancing in the spring at the bottom of the kettle, for all the world like porridge beginning to boil. Our chimney was a square hole in the roof; it was but a little part of the smoke that found its way out, and the rest eddied about the house, and kept us coughing and piping the eye.

Add to this that Gray, the new man, had his face tied up in a bandage for a cut he had got in breaking away from the mutineers; and that poor old Tom Redruth, still unburied, lay along the wall, stiff and stark, under the Union Jack.

If we had been allowed to sit idle, we should all have fallen in the blues, but Captain Smollett was never the man for that. All hands were called up before him, and he divided us into watches. The doctor, and Gray, and I for one; the squire, Hunter, and Joyce upon the other. Tired as we all were, two were sent out for firewood; two more were set to dig a grave for Redruth; the doctor was named cook; I was put sentry at the door; and the captain himself went from one to another, keeping up our spirits and lending a hand wherever it was wanted.

From time to time the doctor came to the door for a little air and to rest his eyes, which were almost smoked out of his head; and whenever he did so, he had a word for me.

"That man Smollett," he said once, "is a better man than I am. And when I say that it means a deal, Jim."

Another time he came and was silent for a while. Then he put his head on one side, and looked at me.

"Is this Ben Gunn a man?" he asked.

"I do not know, sir," said I. "I am not very sure whether he's sane."

"If there's any doubt about the matter, he is," returned the doctor. "A man who has been three years biting his nails on a desert island, Jim, can't expect to appear as sane as you or me. It doesn't lie in human nature. Was it cheese you said he had a fancy for?"

"Yes, sir, cheese," I answered.

"Well, Jim," says he, "just see the good that comes of being dainty in your food. You've seen my snuff-box, haven't you? And you never saw me take snuff; the reason being that in my snuff-box I carry a piece of Parmesan cheese—a cheese made in Italy, very nutritious. Well, that's for Ben Gunn!"

Before supper was eaten we buried old Tom in the sand and stood round him for a while bare-headed in the breeze. A good deal of firewood had been got in, but not enough for the captain's fancy; and he shook his head over it, and told us we "must get back to this to-morrow rather livelier." Then, when we had eaten our pork, and each had a good stiff glass of brandy grog, the three chiefs got together in a corner to discuss our prospects.

It appears they were at their wits' end what to do, the stores being so low that we must have been starved into surrender long before help came. But our best hope, it was decided, was to kill off the buccaneers until they either hauled down their flag or ran away with the *Hispaniola.* From nineteen they were already reduced to fifteen, two others were wounded, and one, at least—the man shot beside the gun—severely wounded, if he were not dead. Every time we had a crack at them, we were to take it, saving our own lives, with the extremest care. And, besides that, we had two able allies—rum and the climate.

As for the first, though we were about half a mile away, we could hear them roaring and singing late into the night; and as for the second, the doctor staked his wig that, camped where they were in the marsh and unprovided with remedies, the half of them would be on their backs before a week.

"So," he added, "if we are not all shot down first they'll be glad to be packing in the schooner. It's always a ship, and they can get to buccaneering again, I suppose."

"First ship that ever I lost," said Captain Smollett.

I was dead tired, as you may fancy; and when I got to sleep, which was not till after a great deal of tossing, I slept like a log of wood.

The rest had long been up, and had already breakfasted and increased the pile of firewood by about half as much again, when I was awakened by a bustle and the sound of voices.

"Flag of truce!" I heard someone say; and then, immediately after, with a cry of surprise, "Silver himself!"

And, at that, up I jumped, and, rubbing my eyes, ran to a loophole in the wall.

CHAPTER XX

SILVER'S EMBASSY

Sure enough, there were two men just outside the stockade, one of them waving a white cloth; the other, no less a person than Silver himself, standing placidly by.

It was still quite early, and the coldest morning that I think I ever was abroad in; a chill that pierced into the marrow. The sky was bright and cloudless overhead, and the tops of the trees shone rosily in the sun. But where Silver stood with his lieutenant all was still in shadow, and they waded knee deep in a low, white vapour, that had crawled during the night out of the morass. The chill and the vapour taken together told a poor tale of the island. It was plainly a damp, feverish, unhealthy spot.

"Keep indoors, men," said the captain. "Ten to one this is a trick."

Then he hailed the buccaneer.

"Who goes? Stand, or we fire."

"Flag of truce," cried Silver.

The captain was in the porch, keeping himself carefully out of the way of a treacherous shot should any be intended. He turned and spoke to us:—

"Doctor's watch on the look out. Dr Livesey, take the north side, if you please; Jim, the east; Gray, west. The watch below, all hands to load muskets. Lively, men, and careful."

And then he turned again to the mutineers.

"And what do you want with your flag of truce?" he cried.

This time it was the other man who replied.

"Cap'n Silver, sir, to come on board and make terms," he shouted.

"Cap'n Silver! Don't know him. Who's he?" cried the captain. And we could hear him adding to himself: "Cap'n, is it? My heart, and here's promotion!"

Long John answered for himself.

"Me, sir. These poor lads have chosen me cap'n, after your desertion, sir"—laying a particular emphasis upon the word "desertion." "We're willing to submit, if we can come to terms, and no bones about it. All I ask is your word, Cap'n Smollett, to let me safe and sound out of this here stockade, and one minute to get out o' shot before a gun is fired."

"My man," said Captain Smollett, "I have not the slightest desire to talk to you. If you wish to talk to me, you can come, that's all. If there's any treachery, it'll be on your side, and the Lord help you."

"That's enough, cap'n," shouted Long John, cheerily. "A word from you's enough. I know a gentleman, and you may lay to that."

We could see the man who carried the flag of truce attempting to hold Silver back. Nor was that wonderful, seeing how cavalier had been the captain's answer. But Silver laughed at him aloud, and slapped him on the back, as if the idea of alarm had been absurd. Then he advanced to the stockade, threw over his crutch, got a leg up, and with great vigour and skill succeeded in surmounting the fence and dropping safely to the other side.

I will confess that I was far too much taken up with what was going on to be of the slightest use as sentry; indeed, I had already deserted my eastern loophole, and crept up behind the captain, who had now seated himself on the threshold, with his elbows on his knees, his head in his hands, and his eyes fixed on the water, as it bubbled out of the old iron kettle in the sand. He was whistling to himself, "Come, Lasses and Lads."

Silver had terrible hard work getting up the knoll. What with the steepness of the incline, the thick tree stumps, and the soft sand, he and his crutch were as helpless as a ship in stays. But he stuck to it like a man, in silence, and at last arrived before the captain, whom he saluted in the handsomest style. He was tricked out in his best; an immense blue coat, thick with brass buttons, hung as low as to his knees, and a fine laced hat was set on the back of his head.

"Here you are, my man," said the captain, raising his head. "You had better sit down."

"You ain't a-going to let me inside, cap'n?" complained Long John. "It's a main cold morning, to be sure, sir, to sit outside upon the sand."

"Why, Silver," said the captain, "if you had pleased to be an honest man, you might have been sitting in your galley. It's your own doing. You're either my ship's cook—and then you were treated handsome —or Cap'n Silver, a common mutineer and pirate, and then you can go hang!"

"Well, well, cap'n," returned the sea cook, sitting down as he was bidden on the sand, "you'll have to give me a hand up again, that's all. A sweet pretty place you have of it here. Ah, there's Jim! The top of the morning to you, Jim. Doctor, here's my service. Why, there you are together like a happy family, in a manner of speaking."

"If you have anything to say, my man, better say it," said the captain.

"Right you were, Cap'n Smollett," replied Silver. "Dooty is dooty, to be sure. Well, now, you look here, that was a good lay of yours last night. I don't deny it was a good lay. Some of you pretty handy with a handspike-end. And I'll not deny neither but what some of my people was shook—maybe all was shook; maybe I was shook myself; maybe that's why I'm here for terms. But you mark me, cap'n, it won't do twice, by thunder! We'll have to do sentry-go, and ease off a point or so on the rum. Maybe you think we were all a sheet in the wind's eye. But I'll tell you I was sober; I was only dog tired; and if I'd awoke a second sooner I'd a' caught you at the act, I would. He wasn't dead when I got round to him, not he."

"Well?" says Captain Smollett, as cool as can be.

All that Silver said was a riddle to him, but you would never have guessed it from his tone. As for me, I began to have an inkling. Ben Gunn's last words came back to my mind. I began to suppose that he had paid the buccaneers a visit while they all lay drunk together round their fire, and I reckoned up with glee that we had only fourteen enemies to deal with.

"Well, here it is," said Silver. "We want that treasure and we'll have it—that's our point! You would just as soon save your lives, I reckon; and that's yours. You have a chart, haven't you?"

"That's as may be," replied the captain.

"Oh, well, you have, I know that," returned Long John. "You needn't be so husky with a man; there ain't a particle of service in that, and you may lay to it. What I mean is, we want your chart. Now, I never meant you no harm, myself."

"That won't do with me, my man," interrupted the captain. "We know exactly what you meant to do, and we don't care; for now, you see, you can't do it."

And the captain looked at him calmly, and proceeded to fill a pipe.

"If Abe Gray—" Silver broke out.

"Avast there!" cried Mr Smollett. "Gray told me nothing, and I asked him nothing; and what's more, I would see you and him and this whole island blown clean out of the water into blazes first. So there's my mind for you, my man, on that."

This little whiff of temper seemed to cool Silver down. He had been growing nettled before, but now he pulled himself together.

"Like enough," said he. "I would set no limits to what gentlemen might consider ship-shape, or might not, as the case were. And seein' as how you are about to take a pipe, cap'n, I'll make so free as do likewise."

And he filled a pipe and lighted it; and the two men sat silently smoking for quite a while, now looking each other in the face, now stopping their tobacco, now leaning forward to spit. It was as good as the play to see them.

"Now," resumed Silver, "here it is. You give us the chart to get the treasure by, and drop shooting poor seamen, and stoving of their heads in while asleep. You do that, and we'll offer you a choice. Either you come aboard along of us, once the treasure shipped, and then I'll give you my affy-davy, upon my word of honour, to clap you somewhere safe ashore. Or, if that ain't to your fancy, some of my hands being rough, and having old scores, on account of hazing, then you can stay here, you can. We'll divide stores with you, man for man; and I'll give my affy-davy, as before, to speak the first ship I sight, and send 'em here to pick you up. Now you'll own that's talking. Handsomer you couldn't look to get, not you. And I hope"—raising his voice—"that all hands in this here block-house will overhaul my words, for what is spoke to one is spoke to all."

Captain Smollett rose from his seat, and knocked out the ashes of his pipe in the palm of his left hand.

"Is that all?" he asked.

"Every last word, by thunder! answered John. "Refuse that, and you've seen the last of me but musket balls."

"Very good," said the captain. "Now you'll hear me. If you'll come up one by one, unarmed, I'll engage to clap you all in irons, and take you home to a fair trial in England. If you won't, my name is Alexander Smollett, I've flown my sovereign's colours, and I'll see you all to Davy Jones. You can't find the treasure. You can't sail the ship—there's not a man among you fit to sail the ship. You can't fight us—Gray, there, got away from five of you. Your ship's in irons, Master Silver; you're on a lee shore, and so you'll find. I stand here and tell you so; and they're the last good words you'll get from me; for, in the name of Heaven, I'll put a bullet in your back when next I meet you. Tramp, my lad. Bundle out of this, please, hand over hand, and double quick."

Silver's face was a picture; his eyes started in his head with wrath. He shook the fire out of his pipe.

"Give me a hand up!" he cried. "Not I," returned the captain.

"Who'll give me a hand up?" he roared.

Not a man among us moved. Growling the foulest imprecations, he crawled along the sand till he got hold of the porch and could hoist himself again upon his crutch. Then he spat into the spring.

"There!" he cried, "that's what I think of ye. Before an hour's out, I'll stove in your old block-house like a rum puncheon. Laugh, by thunder, laugh! Before an hour's out, ye'll laugh upon the other side. Them that die'll be the lucky ones."

And with a dreadful oath he stumbled off, ploughed down the sand, was helped across the stockade, after four or five failures, by the man with the flag of truce, and disappeared in an instant afterwards among the trees.

CHAPTER XXI

THE ATTACK

As soon as Silver disappeared, the captain, who had been closely watching him, turned towards the interior of the house, and found not a man of us at his post but Gray. It was the first time we had ever seen him angry.

"Quarters!" he roared. And then, as we all slunk back to our places, "Gray," he said, "I'll put your name in the log; you've stood by your duty like a seaman. Mr Trelawney, I'm surprised at you, sir. Doctor, I thought you had worn the king's coat! If that was how you served at Fontenoy, sir, you'd have been better in your berth."

The doctor's watch were all back at their loopholes, the rest were busy loading the spare muskets, and every one with a red face, you may be certain, and a flea in his ear, as the saying is.

The captain looked on for a while in silence. Then he spoke.

"My lads," said he, "I've given Silver a broadside. I pitched it in red-hot on purpose; and before the hour's out, as he said, we shall be boarded. We're outnumbered, I needn't tell you that, but we fight in shelter; and, a minute ago, I should have said we fought with discipline. I've no manner of doubt that we can drub them, if you choose."

Then he went the rounds, and saw, as he said, that all was clear.

On the two short sides of the house, east and west, there were only two loopholes; on the south side where the porch was, two again; and on the north side, five. There was a round score of muskets for the seven of us; the firewood had been built into four piles—

tables, you might say—one about the middle of each side, and on each of these tables some ammunition and four loaded muskets were laid ready to the hand of the defenders. In the middle, the cutlasses lay ranged.

"Toss out the fire," said the captain; "the chill is past, and we mustn't have smoke in our eyes."

The iron fire basket was carried boldly out by Mr Trelawney, and the embers smothered among sand.

"Hawkins hasn't had his breakfast. Hawkins, help yourself, and back to your post to eat it," continued Captain Smollett. "Lively, now, my lad; you'll want it before you've done. Hunter, serve out a round of brandy to all hands."

And while this was going on, the captain completed, in his own mind, the plan of the defence.

"Doctor, you will take the door," he resumed. "See and don't expose yourself; keep within, and fire through the porch. Hunter, take the east side, there. Joyce, you stand by the west, my man. Mr Trelawney, you are the best shot—you and Gray will take this long north side, with the five loopholes; it's there the danger is. If they can get up to it, and fire in upon us through our own ports, things would begin to look dirty. Hawkins, neither you nor I are much account at the shooting; we'll stand by to load and bear a hand."

As the captain had said, the chill was past. As soon as the sun had climbed above our girdle of trees, it fell with all its force upon the clearing, and drank up the vapours at a draught. Soon the sand was baking, and the resin melting in the logs of the block-house. Jackets and coats were flung aside; shirts thrown open at the neck, and rolled up to the shoulders; and we stood there, each at his post, in a fever of heat and anxiety.

An hour passed away.

"Hang them!" said the captain. "This is as dull as the doldrums. Gray, whistle for a wind."

And just at that moment came the first news of the attack.

"If you please, sir," said Joyce, "if I see anyone am I to fire?"

"I told you so!" cried the captain.

"Thank you, sir," returned Joyce, with the same quiet civility.

Nothing followed for a time; but the remark had set us all on the alert, straining ears and eyes—the musketeers with their pieces balanced in their hands, the captain out in the middle of the block-house, with his mouth very tight and a frown on his face.

So some seconds passed, till suddenly Joyce whipped up his musket and fired. The report had scarcely died away ere it was repeated and repeated from without in a scattering volley, shot behind shot, like a string of geese, from every side of the enclosure. Several bullets struck the log-house, but not one entered; and, as the smoke cleared away and vanished, the stockade and the woods around it looked as quiet and empty as before. Not a bough waved, not the gleam of a musket-barrel betrayed the presence of our foes.

"Did you hit your man?" asked the captain.

"No, sir," replied Joyce. "I believe not, sir."

"Next best thing to tell the truth," muttered Captain Smollett. "Load his gun, Hawkins. How many should you say there were on your side, doctor?"

"I know precisely," said Doctor Livesey. "Three shots were fired on this side. I saw the three flashes—two close together—one farther to the west."

"Three!" repeated the captain. "And how many on yours, Mr Trelawney?"

But this was not so easily answered. There had come many from the north—seven, by the squire's computation; eight or nine, according to Gray. From the east and west only a single shot had been fired. It was plain, therefore, that the attack would be developed from the north, and that on the other three sides we were only to be annoyed by a show of hostilities. But Captain Smollett made no change in his arrangements. If the mutineers succeeded in crossing the stockade, he argued, they would take possession of any unprotected loophole, and shoot us down like rats in our own stronghold.

Nor had we much time left to us for thought. Suddenly, with a loud huzza, a little cloud of pirates leapt from the woods on the north side, and ran straight on the stockade. At the same moment the fire was once more opened from the woods, and a rifle-ball sang through the doorway, and knocked the doctor's musket into bits.

The boarders swarmed over the fence like monkeys. Squire and Gray fired again and yet again; three men fell, one forwards into the enclosure, two back on the outside. But of these, one was evidently more frightened than hurt, for he was on his feet again in a crack, and instantly disappeared among the trees.

Two had bit the dust, one had fled, four had made good their footing inside our defences; while from the shelter of the woods seven or eight men, each evidently supplied with several muskets, kept up a hot though useless fire on the log-house.

The four who had boarded made straight before them for the building, shouting as they ran, and the men among the trees shouted back to encourage them. Several shots were fired; but, such was the hurry of the marksmen, that not one appears to have taken effect. In a moment, the four pirates had swarmed up the mound and were upon us.

The head of Job Anderson, the boatswain, appeared at the middle loophole.

"At 'em, all hands—all hands!" he roared, in a voice of thunder.

At the same moment, another pirate grasped Hunter's musket by the muzzle, wrenched it from his hands, plucked it through the loophole, and, with one stunning blow, laid the poor fellow senseless on the floor. Meanwhile a third, running unharmed all round the house, appeared suddenly in the doorway, and fell with his cutlass on the doctor.

Our position was utterly reversed. A moment since we were firing, under cover, at an exposed enemy; now it was we who lay uncovered, and could not return a blow.

The log-house was full of smoke, to which we owed our comparative safety. Cries and confusion, the flashes and reports of pistol shots, and one loud groan, rang in my ears.

"Out, lads, out, and fight 'em in the open! Cutlasses!" cried the captain.

I snatched a cutlass from the pile, and someone, at the same time snatching another, gave me a cut across the knuckles which I hardly felt. I dashed out of the door into the clear sunlight. Someone was close behind, I knew not whom. Right in front, the doctor was pursuing his assailant down the hill, and, just as my eyes fell upon him, beat down his guard, and sent him sprawling on his back with a great slash across the face.

"Round the house, lads! round the house!" cried the captain; and even in the hurly-burly I perceived a change in his voice.

THE ATTACK

Mechanically I obeyed, turned eastwards, and, with my cutlass raised, ran round the corner of the house. Next moment I was face to face with Anderson. He roared aloud, and his hanger went up above his head, flashing in the sunlight. I had not time to be afraid, but, as the blow still hung impending, leaped in a trice upon one side, and missing my foot in the soft sand, rolled headlong down the slope.

When I had first sallied from the door, the other mutineers had been already swarming up the palisade to make an end of us. One man, in a red night-cap, with his cutlass in his mouth, had even got upon the top and thrown a leg across. Well, so short had been the interval, that when I found my feet again all was in the same posture, the fellow with the red night-cap still half way over, another still just showing his head above the top of the stockade. And yet, in this breath of time, the fight was over, and the victory was ours.

Gray, following close behind me, had cut down the big boatswain ere he had time to recover from his lost blow. Another had been shot at a loophole in the very act of firing into the house, and now lay in agony, the pistol still smoking in his hand. A third, as I had seen, the doctor had disposed of at a blow. Of the four who had scaled the palisade, one only remained unaccounted for, and he, having left his cutlass on the field, was now clambering out again with the fear of death upon him.

"Fire—fire from the house!" cried the doctor. "And you, lads, back into cover."

But his words were unheeded, no shot was fired, and the last boarder made good his escape, and disappeared with the rest into the wood. In three seconds nothing remained of the attacking party but the five who had fallen, four on the inside, and one on the outside, of the palisade.

The doctor and Gray and I ran full speed for shelter. The survivors would soon be back where they had left their muskets, and at any moment the fire might recommence.

The house was by this time somewhat cleared of smoke, and we saw at a glance the price we had paid for victory. Hunter lay beside his loophole stunned; Joyce by his, shot through the head, never to move again; while right in the centre, the squire was supporting the captain, one as pale as the other.

"The captain's wounded," said Mr Trelawney.

"Have they run?" asked Mr Smollett.

"All that could, you may be bound," returned the doctor; "but there's five of them will never run again."

"Five!" cried the captain. "Come, that's better. Five against three leaves us four to nine. That's better odds than we had at starting. We were seven to nineteen then, or thought we were, and that's as bad to bear."*

*The mutineers were soon only eight in number, for the man shot by Mr Trelawney on board the schooner died that same evening of his wound. But this was, of course, not known till after by the faithful party.

PART V

MY SEA ADVENTURE

Chapter XXII

HOW I BEGAN MY SEA ADVENTURE

There was no return of the mutineers—not so much as another shot out of the woods. They had "got their rations for that day," as the captain put it, and we had the place to ourselves and a quiet time to overhaul the wounded and get dinner. Squire and I cooked outside in spite of the danger, and even outside we could hardly tell what we were at, for horror of the loud groans that reached as from the doctor's patients.

Out of the eight men who had fallen in the action, only three still breathed—that one of the pirates who had been shot at the loophole, Hunter, and Captain Smollett; and of these the first two were as good as dead; the mutineer, indeed, died under the doctor's knife, and Hunter, do what we could, never recovered consciousness in this world. He lingered all day, breathing loudly like the old buccaneer at home in his apoplectic fit; but the bones of his chest had been crushed by the blow and his skull fractured in falling, and some time in the following night, without sign or sound, he went to his Maker.

As for the captain, his wounds were grievous indeed, bus not dangerous. No organ was fatally injured. Anderson's ball—for it was Job that shot him first—had broken his shoulder-blade and touched the lung, not badly; the second had only torn and displaced some muscles in the calf. He was sure to recover, the doctor said, but, in the meantime and for weeks to come, he must not walk nor move his arm, nor so much as speak when he could help it.

My own accidental cut across the knuckles was a flea-bite. Doctor Livesey patched it up with plaster, and pulled my ears for me into the bargain.

After dinner the squire and the doctor sat by the captain's side a while in consultation; and when they had talked to their hearts' content, it being then a little past noon, the doctor took up his hat and pistols, girt on a cutlass, put the chart in his pocket, and, with a musket over his shoulder, crossed the palisade on the north side, and set off briskly through the trees.

Gray and I were sitting together at the far end of the block-house, to be out of earshot of our officers consulting; and Gray took his pipe out of his mouth and fairly forgot to put it back again, so thunderstruck he was at this occurrence.

"Why, in the name of Davy Jones," said he, "is Dr Livesey mad?"

"Why, no," says I. "He's about the last of this crew for that, I take it"

"Well, shipmate," said Gray, "mad he may not be; but if *he's* not, you mark my words, *I* am."

"I take it," replied I, "the doctor has his idea; and if I am right, he's going now to see Ben Gunn."

I was right, as appeared later; but, in the meantime, the house being stifling hot, and the little patch of sand inside the palisade ablaze with midday sun, I began to get another thought into my head, which was not by any means so right. What I began to do was to envy the doctor, walking in the cool shadow of the woods, with the birds about him, and the pleasant smell of the pines, while I sat grilling, with my clothes stuck to the hot resin, and so much blood about me, and so many poor dead bodies lying all around, that I took a disgust of the place that was almost as strong as fear.

All the time I was washing out the block-house, and then washing up the things from dinner, this disgust and envy kept growing stronger and stronger, till at last, being near a bread-bag, and no one then observing me, I took the first step towards my escapade, and filled both pockets of my coat with biscuit.

I was a fool, if you like, and certainly I was going to do a foolish, over-bold act; but I was determined to do it with all the precautions in my power. These biscuits, should anything befall me, would keep me, at least, from starving till far on in the next day.

The next thing I laid hold of was a brace of pistols, and as I already had a powder-horn and bullets, I felt myself well supplied with arms.

As for the scheme I had in my head, it was not a bad one in itself. I was to go down the sandy spit that divides the anchorage on the east from the open sea, find the white rock I had observed last evening, and ascertain whether it was there or not that Ben Gunn had hidden his boat; a thing quite worth doing, as I still believe. But as I was certain I should not be allowed to leave the enclosure, my only plan was to take French leave, and slip out when nobody was watching; and that was so bad a way of doing it as made the thing itself wrong. But I was only a boy, and I had made my mind up.

Well, as things at last fell out, I found an admirable opportunity. The squire and Gray were busy helping the captain with his bandages; the coast was clear; I made a bolt for it over the stockade and into the thickest of the trees, and before my absence was observed I was out of cry of my companions.

This was my second folly, far worse than the first, as I left but two sound men to guard the house; but, like the first, it was a help towards saving all of us.

I took my way straight for the east coast of the island, for I was determined to go down the sea side of the spit to avoid all chance of observation from the anchorage. It was already late in the afternoon, although still warm and sunny. As I continued to thread the tall woods I could hear from far before me not only the continuous thunder of the surf, but a certain tossing of foliage and grinding of boughs which showed me the sea breeze had set in higher than usual. Soon cool draughts of air began to reach me; and a few steps farther I came forth into the open borders of the grove, and saw the sea lying blue and sunny to the horizon, and the surf tumbling and tossing its foam along the beach.

I have never seen the sea quiet round Treasure Island. The sun might blaze overhead, the air be without a breath, the surface smooth and blue, but still these great rollers would be running along all the external coast, thundering and thundering by day and night; and I scarce believe there is one spot in the island where a man would be out of earshot of their noise.

I walked along beside the surf with great enjoyment, till, thinking I was now got far enough to the south, I took the cover of some thick bushes, and crept warily up to the ridge of the spit.

Behind me was the sea, in front the anchorage. The sea breeze, as though it had the sooner blown itself out by its unusual violence, was already at an end; it had been succeeded by light, variable airs from the south and south-east, carrying great banks of fog; and the anchorage, under lee of Skeleton Island, lay still and leaden as when first we entered it. The *Hispaniola,* in that unbroken mirror, was exactly portrayed from the truck to the water-line, the Jolly Roger hanging from her peak.

Alongside lay one of the gigs, Silver in the stern-sheets—him I could always recognise—while a couple of men were leaning over the stern bulwarks, one of them with a red cap—the very rogue that I had seen some hours before stride-legs upon the palisade. Apparently they were talking and laughing, though at that distance—upwards of a mile—I could, of course, hear no word of what was said. All at once, there began the most horrid, unearthly screaming, which at first startled me badly, though I had soon remembered the voice of Captain Flint, and even thought I could make out the bird by her bright plumage as she sat perched upon her master's wrist.

Soon after the jolly-boat shoved off and pulled for shore, and the man with the red cap and his comrade went below by the cabin companion.

Just about the same time the sun had gone down behind the Spyglass, and, as the fog was collecting rapidly, it began to grow dark in earnest. I saw I must lose no time if I were to find the boat that evening.

The white rock, visible enough above the brush, was still some eighth of a mile farther down the spit, and it took me a goodish while to get up with it, crawling, often on all-fours, among the scrub. Night had almost come when I laid my hand on its rough sides. Right below it there was an exceedingly small hollow of green turf, hidden by banks and a thick underwood about knee-deep, that grew there very plentifully; and in the centre of the dell, sure enough, a little tent of goatskins, like what the gipsies carry about with them in England.

I dropped into the hollow, lifted the side of the tent, and there was Ben Gunn's boat—home-made if ever anything was home-made: a rude, lop-sided framework of tough wood, and stretched upon that a covering of goat-skin, with the hair inside. The thing was extremely small, even for me, and I can hardly imagine that it could have floated with a full-sized man. There was one thwart, set as low as possible, a kind of stretcher in the bows, and a double paddle for propulsion.

I had not then seen a coracle, such as the ancient Britons made, but I have seen one since, and I can give you no fairer idea of Ben Gunn's boat than by saying it was like the first and the worst coracle ever made by man. But the great advantage of the coracle it certainly possessed, for it was exceedingly light and portable.

Well, now that I had found the boat, you would have thought I had had enough of truantry for once; but, in the meantime, I had taken another notion, and become so obstinately fond of it, that I would have carried it out, I believe, in the teeth of Captain Smollett himself. This was to slip out under cover of the night, cut the *Hispaniola* adrift, and let her go ashore where she fancied. I had quite made up my mind that the mutineers, after their repulse of the morning, had nothing nearer their hearts than to up anchor and away to sea; this, I thought, it would be a fine thing to prevent; and now that I had seen how they left their watchmen unprovided with a boat, I thought it might be done with little risk.

Down I sat to wait for darkness, and made a hearty meal of biscuit. It was a night out of ten thousand for my purpose. The fog had now buried all heaven. As the last rays of daylight dwindled and disappeared, absolute blackness settled down on Treasure Island. And when, at last, I shouldered the coracle, and groped my way stumblingly out of the hollow where I had supped, there were but two points visible on the whole anchorage.

One was the great fire on shore, by which the defeated pirates lay carousing in the swamp. The other, a mere blur of light upon the darkness, indicated the position of the anchored ship. She had swung round to the ebb—her bow was now towards me—the only lights on board were in the cabin; and what I saw was merely a reflection on the fog of the strong rays that flowed from the stern window.

The ebb had already run some time, and I had to wade through a long belt of swampy sand, where I sank several times above the ankle, before I came to the edge of the retreating water, and wading a little in, with some strength and dexterity, set my coracle, keel downwards, on the surface.

I FELT WILLING RATHER TO STARVE AT SEA THAN
TO CONFRONT SUCH PERILS

Chapter XXIII

THE EBB-TIDE RUNS

The coracle—as I had ample reason to know before I was done with her—was a very safe boat for a person of my height and weight, both buoyant and clever in a seaway; but she was the most cross-grained, lop-sided craft to manage. Do as you pleased, she always made more leeway than anything else, and turning round and round was the manœuvre she was best at. Even Ben Gunn himself has admitted that she was "queer to handle till you knew her way."

Certainly I did not know her way. She turned in every direction but the one I was bound to go; the most part of the time we were broadside on, and I am very sure I never should have made the ship at all but for the tide. By good fortune, paddle as I pleased, the tide was still sweeping me down; and there lay the *Hispaniola* right in the fairway, hardly to be missed.

First she loomed before me like a blot of something yet blacker than darkness, then her spars and hull began to take shape, and the next moment, as it seemed (for, the farther I went, the brisker grew the current of the ebb), I was alongside of her hawser, and had laid hold.

The hawser was as taut as a bowstring—so strong, she pulled upon her anchor. All round the hull, in the blackness, the rippling current bubbled and chattered like a little mountain stream. One cut with my sea-gully, and the *Hispaniola* would go humming down the tide.

So far so good; but it next occurred to my recollection that a taut hawser, suddenly cut, is a thing as dangerous a kicking horse. Ten to one, if I were so foolhardy as to cut the *Hispaniola* from her anchor, I and the coracle would be knocked clean out of the water.

This brought me to a full stop, and if fortune had not again particularly favoured me, I should have had to abandon my design. But the light airs which had begun blowing from the south-east and south had hauled round after nightfall into the south-west. Just while I was meditating, a puff came, caught the *Hispaniola,* and forced her up into the current; and to my great joy, I felt the hawser slacken in my grasp, and the hand by which I held it dip for a second under water.

With that I made my mind up, took out my gully, opened it with my teeth, and cut one strand after another, till the vessel only swung by two. Then I lay quiet, waiting to sever these last when the strain should be more lightened by a breath of wind.

All this time I had heard the sound of loud voices from the cabin; but, to say truth, my mind had been so entirely taken up with other thoughts that I had scarcely given ear. Now, however, when I had nothing else to do, I began to pay more heed.

One I recognised for the coxswain's, Israel Hands, that had been Flint's gunner in former days. The other was, of course, my friend of the red night-cap. Both men were plainly the worse of drink, and they were still drinking; for, even while I was listening, one of them, with a drunken cry, opened the stern window and threw out something, which I divined to be an empty bottle. But they were not only tipsy; it was plain that they were furiously angry. Oaths flew like hailstones, and every now and then there came forth such an explosion as I thought was sure to end in blows. But each time the quarrel passed off, and the voices grumbled lower for a while, until the next crisis came, and, in its turn, passed away without result.

On shore, I could see the glow of the great camp fire burning warmly through the shore-side trees. Someone was singing, a dull, old, droning sailor's song, with a droop and a quaver at the end of every verse, and seemingly no end to it at all but the patience of the singer. I had heard it on the voyage more than once, and remembered these words:—

> *"But one man of her crew alive,*
> *What put to sea with seventy-five."*

And I thought it was a ditty rather too dolefully appropriate for a company that had met such cruel losses in the morning. But, indeed, from what I saw, all these buccaneers were as callous as the sea they sailed on.

At last the breeze came; the schooner sidled and drew nearer in the dark; I felt the hawser slacken once more, and with a good, tough effort, cut the last fibres through.

The breeze had but little action on the coracle, and I was almost instantly swept against the bows of the *Hispaniola*. At the same time the schooner began to turn upon her heel, spinning slowly, end to end, across the current.

I wrought like a fiend, for I expected every moment to be swamped; and since I found I could not push the coracle directly off, I now shoved straight astern. At length I was clear of my dangerous neighbour; and just as I gave the last impulsion, my hands came across a light cord that was trailing overboard across the stern bulwarks. Instantly I grasped it.

Why I should have done so I can hardly say. It was at first mere instinct; but once I had it in my hands and found it fast, curiosity began to get the upper hand, and I determined I should have one look through the cabin window.

I pulled in hand over hand on the cord, and, when I judged myself near enough, rose at infinite risk to about half my height, and thus commanded the roof and a slice of the interior of the cabin.

By this time the schooner and her little consort were gliding pretty swiftly through the water; indeed, we had already fetched up level with the camp fire. The ship was talking, as sailors say, loudly, treading the innumerable ripples with an incessant weltering splash: and until I got my eye above the window-sill I could not comprehend why the watchmen had taken no alarm. One glance, however, was sufficient; and it was only one glance that I durst take from that unsteady skiff. It showed me Hands and his companion locked together in deadly wrestle, each with hand upon the other's throat.

I dropped upon the thwart again, none too soon, for I was near overboard. I could see nothing for the moment but these two furious, encrimsoned faces, swaying together under the smoky lamp; and I shut my eyes to let them grow once more familiar with the darkness.

The endless ballad had come to an end at last, and the whole diminished company about the camp fire had broken into the chorus I had heard so often:—

"Fifteen men on the dead man's chest—
Yo-ho-ho and a bottle of rum!
Drink and the devil had done for the rest—
Yo-ho-ho, and a bottle of rum!"

I was just thinking how busy drink and the devil were at that very moment in the cabin of the *Hispaniola,* when I was surprised by a sudden lurch of the coracle. At the same moment she yawed sharply and seemed to change her course. The speed in the meantime had strangely increased.

I opened my eyes at once. All round me were little ripples, combing over with a sharp, bristling sound and slightly phosphorescent. The *Hispaniola* herself, a few yards in whose wake I was still being whirled along, seemed to stagger in her course, and I saw her spars toss a little against the blackness of the night; nay, as I looked longer, I made sure she also was wheeling to the southward.

I glanced over my shoulder, and my heart jumped against my ribs. There, right behind me, was the glow of the camp fire. The current had turned at right angles, sweeping round along with it the tall schooner and the little dancing coracle; ever quickening, ever bubbling higher, ever muttering louder, it went spinning through the narrows for the open sea.

Suddenly the schooner in front of me gave a violent yaw, turning, perhaps, through twenty degrees; and almost at the same moment one shout followed another from on board; I could hear feet pounding on the companion ladder; and I knew that the two drunkards had at last been interrupted in their quarrel and awakened to a sense of their disaster.

I lay down flat in the bottom of that wretched skiff, and devoutly recommended my spirit to its Maker. At the end of the straits, I made sure we must fall into some bar of raging breakers, where all my troubles would be ended speedily; and though I could, perhaps, bear to die, I could not bear to look upon my fate as it approached.

So I must have lain for hours, continually beaten to and fro upon the billows, now and again wetted with flying sprays, and never ceasing to expect death at the next plunge. Gradually weariness grew upon me; a numbness, an occasional stupor, fell upon my mind even in the midst of my terrors; until sleep at last supervened, and in my sea-tossed coracle I lay and dreamed of home and the old "Admiral Benbow."

Chapter XXIV

THE CRUISE OF THE CORACLE

It was broad day when I awoke, and found myself tossing at the southwest end of Treasure Island. The sun was up, but was still hid from me behind the great bulk of the Spy-glass, which on this side descended almost to the sea in formidable cliffs.

Haulbowline Head and Mizzen-mast Hill were at my elbow; the hill bare and dark, the head bound with cliffs forty or fifty feet high, and fringed with great masses of fallen rock. I was scarce a quarter of a mile to seaward, and it was my first thought to paddle in and land.

That notion was soon given over. Among the fallen rocks the breakers spouted and bellowed; loud reverberations, heavy sprays flying and falling, succeeded one another from second to second; and I saw myself, if I ventured nearer, dashed to death upon the rough shore, or spending my strength in vain to scale the beetling crags.

Nor was that all; for crawling together on flat tables of rock, or letting themselves drop into the sea with loud reports, I beheld huge slimy monsters—soft snails, as it were, of incredible bigness—two or three score of them together, making the rocks to echo with their barkings.

I have understood since that they were sea-lions, and entirely harmless. But the look of them, added to the difficulty of the shore and the high running of the surf, was more than enough to disgust me of that landing-place. I felt willing rather to starve at sea than to confront such perils.

In the meantime I had a better chance, as I supposed, before me. North of Haulbowline Head, the land runs in a long way, leaving, at low tide, a long stretch of yellow sand. To the north of that, again, there comes another cape—Cape of the Woods, as it was marked upon the chart—buried in tall green pines, which descended to the margin of the sea.

I remembered what Silver had said about the current that sets northward along the whole west coast of Treasure Island; and seeing from my position that I was already under its influence, I preferred to leave Haulbowline Head behind me, and reserve my strength for an attempt to land upon the kindlier-looking Cape of the Woods.

There was a great, smooth swell upon the sea. The wind blowing steady and gentle from the south, there was no contrariety between that and the current, and the billows rose and fell unbroken.

Had it been otherwise, I must long ago have perished; but as it was, it is surprising how easily and securely my little and light boat could ride. Often, as I still lay at the bottom, and kept no more than an eye above the gunwale, I would see a big blue summit heaving close above me; yet the coracle would but bounce a little, dance as if on springs, and subside on the other side into the trough as lightly as a bird.

I began after a little to grow very bold, and sat up to try my skill at paddling. But even a small change in the disposition of the weight will produce violent changes in the behaviour of a coracle. And I had hardly moved before the boat, giving up at once her gentle dancing movement, ran straight down a slope of water so steep that it made me giddy, and struck her nose, with a spout of spray, deep into the side of the next wave.

I was drenched and terrified, and instantly fell back into my old position, whereupon the coracle seemed to find her head again, and led me as softly as before among the billows. It was plain she was not to be interfered with, and at that rate, since I could in no way influence her course, what hope had I left of reaching land?

I began to be horribly frightened, but I kept my head for all that. First, moving with all care, I gradually baled out the coracle with my sea-cap; then getting my eye once more above the gunwale, I set myself to study how it was she managed to slip so quietly through the rollers.

I found each wave, instead of the big, smooth, glossy mountain it looks from shore, or from a vessel's deck, was for all the world like any range of hills on the dry land, full of peaks and smooth places and valleys. The coracle, left to herself, turning from side to side, threaded, so to speak, her way through these lower parts, and avoided the steep slopes and higher, toppling summits of the wave.

"Well now," thought I to myself, "it is plain I must lie where I am, and not disturb the balance; but it is plain, also, that I can put the paddle over the side, and from time to time, in smooth places, give her a shove or two towards land." No sooner thought upon than done. There I lay on my elbows, in the most trying attitude, and every now and again gave a weak stroke or two to turn her head to shore.

It was very tiring, and slow work, yet I did visibly gain ground; and, as we drew near the Cape of the Woods, though I saw I must infallibly miss that point, I had still made some hundred yards of easting. I was, indeed, close in. I could see the cool, green tree-tops swaying together in the breeze, and I felt sure I should make the next promontory without fail.

It was high time, for I now began to be tortured with thirst. The glow of the sun from above, its thousandfold reflection from the waves, the sea-water that fell and dried upon me, caking my very lips with salt, combined to make my throat burn and my brain ache. The sight of the trees so near at hand had almost made me sick with longing; but the current had soon carried me past the point; and, as the next reach of sea opened out, I beheld a sight that changed the nature of my thoughts.

Right in front of me, not half a mile away, I beheld the *Hispaniola* under sail. I made sure, of course, that I should he taken; but I was so distressed for want of water, that I scarce knew whether to be glad or sorry at the thought; and long before I had come to a conclusion, surprise had taken entire possession of my mind, and I could do nothing but stare and wonder.

The *Hispaniola* was under her main-sail and two jibs, and the beautiful white canvas shone in the sun like snow or silver. When I first sighted her, all her sails were drawing; she was lying a course about north-west; and I presumed the men on board were going round the island on their way back to the anchorage. Presently she began to fetch more and more to the westward, so that I thought they had sighted me and were going about in chase. At last, however, she fell right into the wind's eye, was taken dead aback, and stood there a while helpless, with her sails shivering.

"Clumsy fellows," said I; "they must still be drunk as owls." And I thought how Captain Smollett would have set them skipping.

Meanwhile, the schooner gradually fell off, and filled again upon another tack, sailed swiftly for a minute or so, and brought up once more dead in the wind's eye. Again and again was this repeated. To and fro, up and down, north, south, east, and west, the *Hispaniola* sailed by swoops and dashes, and at each repetition ended as she had begun, with idly-flapping canvas. It became plain to me that nobody was steering. And, if so, where were the men? Either they were dead drunk, or had deserted her, I thought, and perhaps if I could get on board, I might return the vessel to her captain.

The current was bearing coracle and schooner southward at an equal rate. As for the latter's sailing, it was so wild and intermittent, and she hung each time so long in irons, that she certainly gained nothing, if she did not even lose. If only I dared to sit up and paddle, I made sure that I could overhaul her. The scheme had an air of adventure that inspired me, and the thought of the water-breaker beside the fore companion doubled my growing courage.

Up I got, was welcomed almost instantly by another cloud of spray, but this time stuck to my purpose; and set myself, with all my strength and caution, to paddle after the unsteered *Hispaniola*. Once I shipped a sea so heavy that I had to stop and bale, with my heart fluttering like a bird; but gradually I got into the way of the thing, and guided my coracle among the waves, with only now and then a blow upon her bows and a dash of foam in my face.

I was now gaining rapidly on the schooner; I could see the brass glisten on the tiller as it banged about; and still no soul appeared upon her decks. I could not choose but suppose she was deserted. If not, the men were lying drunk below, where I might batten them down, perhaps, and do what I chose with the ship.

For some time she had been doing the worst thing possible for me— standing still. She headed nearly due south, yawing, of course, all the time. Each time she fell off her sails partly filled, and these brought her, in a moment, right to the wind again. I have said this was the worst thing possible for me; for, helpless as she looked in this situation with the canvas cracking like cannon, and the blocks trundling and banging on the deck, she still continued to run away from me, not only with the speed of the current, but by the whole amount of her leeway, which was naturally great.

But now, at last, I had my chance. The breeze fell, for some seconds, very low, and the current gradually turning her, the *Hispaniola* revolved slowly round her centre, and at last presented me her stern, with the cabin window still gaping open, and the lamp over the table still burning on into the day. The main-sail hung drooped like a banner. She was stock-still but for the current.

For the last little while I had even lost; but now, redoubling my efforts, I began once more to overhaul the chase.

I was not a hundred yards from her when the wind came again in a clap; she filled on the port tack, and was off again, stooping and skimming like a swallow.

My first impulse was one of despair, but my second was towards joy. Round she came, till she was broadside on to me—round still till she had covered a half, and then two-thirds, and then three-quarters of the distance that separated us. I could see the waves boiling white under her forefoot. Immensely tall she looked to me from my low station in the coracle.

And then, of a sudden, I began to comprehend. I had scarce time to think—scarce time to act and save myself. I was on the summit of one swell when the schooner came stooping over the next. The bowsprit was over my head. I sprang to my feet, and leaped, stamping the coracle under water. With one hand I caught the jib-boom, while my foot was lodged between the stay and the brace; and as I still clung there panting, a dull blow told me that the schooner had charged down upon and struck the coracle, and that I was left without retreat on the *Hispaniola*.

Chapter XXV

I STRIKE THE JOLLY ROGER

I had scarce gained a position on the bowsprit, when the flying jib flapped and filled upon the other tack, with a report like a gun. The schooner trembled to her keel under the reverse; but next moment, the other sails still drawing, the jib flapped back again, and hung idle.

This had nearly tossed me off into the sea; and now I lost no time, crawled back along the bowsprit, and tumbled head-foremost on the deck.

I was on the lee side of the forecastle, and the main-sail, which was still drawing, concealed from me a certain portion of the after-deck. Not a soul was to be seen. The planks, which had not been swabbed since the mutiny, bore the print of many feet; and an empty bottle, broken by the neck, tumbled to and fro like a live thing in the scuppers.

Suddenly the *Hispaniola* came right into the wind. The jibs behind me cracked aloud; the rudder slammed to; the whole ship gave a sickening heave and shudder, and at the same moment the main-boom swung inboard, the sheet groaning in the blocks, and showed me the lee afterdeck.

There were the two watchmen, sure enough: Red-cap on his back, as stiff as a handspike, with his arms stretched out like those of a crucifix, and his teeth showing through his open lips; Israel Hands propped against the bulwarks, his chin on his chest, his hands lying open before him on the deck, his face as white, under its tan, as a tallow candle.

145

For a while the ship kept bucking and sidling like a vicious horse, the sails filling, now on one tack, now on another, and the boom swinging to and fro till the mast groaned aloud under the strain. Now and again, too, there would come a cloud of light sprays over the bulwark, and heavy blow of the ship's bows against the swell: so much heavier weather was made of it by this great rigged ship than by my home-made, lop-sided coracle, now gone to the bottom of the sea.

At every jump of the schooner, Red-cap slipped to and fro; but—what was ghastly to behold—neither his attitude nor his fixed teeth-disclosing grin was anyway disturbed by this rough usage. At every jump, too, Hands appeared still more to sink into himself and settle down upon the deck, his feet sliding ever the farther out, and the whole body canting towards the stern, so that his face became, little by little, hid from me; and at last I could see nothing beyond his ear and the frayed ringlet of one whisker.

At the same time, I observed, around both of them, splashes of dark blood upon the planks, and began to feel sure that they had killed each other in their drunken wrath.

While I was thus looking and wondering, in a calm moment, when the ship was still, Israel Hands turned partly round, and, with a low moan, writhed himself back to the position in which I had seen him first. The moan, which told of pain and deadly weakness, and the way in which his jaw hung open, went right to my heart. But when I remembered the talk I had overheard from the apple barrel, all pity left me.

I walked aft until I reached the main-mast.

"Come aboard, Mr Hands," I said ironically.

He rolled his eyes round heavily; but he was too far gone to express surprise. All he could do was to utter one word, "Brandy."

It occurred to me there was no time to lose; and, dodging the boom as it once more lurched across the deck, I slipped aft, and down the companion-stairs into the cabin.

It was such a scene of confusion as you can hardly fancy. All the lockfast places had been broken open in quest of the chart. The floor was thick with mud, where ruffians had sat down to drink or consult after wading in the marshes round their camp. The bulkheads, all painted in clear white, and beaded round with gilt, bore a pattern of dirty hands. Dozens of empty bottles clinked together in the corners to the rolling of the ship. One of the doctor's medical books lay open on the table, half of the leaves gutted out, I suppose, for pipe-lights. In the midst of all this the lamp still cast a smoky glow, obscure and brown as umber.

I went into the cellar; all the barrels were gone, and of the bottles a most surprising number had been drunk out and thrown away. Certainly, since the mutiny began, not a man of them could ever have been sober.

Foraging about, I found a bottle with some brandy left, for Hands; and for myself I routed out some biscuit, some pickled fruits, a great bunch of raisins, and a piece of cheese. With these I came on deck, put down my own stock behind the rudder-head, and well out of the coxswain's reach, went forward to the water-breaker, and had a good, deep drink of water, and then, and not till then, gave Hands the brandy.

He must have drunk a gill before he took the bottle from his mouth.

"Aye," said he, "by thunder, but I wanted some o' that!"

I had sat down already in my own corner and begun to eat.

"Much hurt?" I asked him.

He grunted, or rather, I may say, he barked.

"If that doctor was aboard," he said, "I'd be right enough in a couple of turns; but I don't have no manner of luck, you see, and that's what's the matter with me. As for that swab, he's good and dead, he is," he added, indicating the man with the red cap. "He warn't no seaman, anyhow. And where mought you have come from?"

"Well," said I, "I've come aboard to take possession of this ship, Mr Hands; and you'll please regard me as your captain until further notice."

He looked at me sourly enough, but said nothing. Some of the colour had come back into his cheeks, though he still looked very sick, and still continued to slip out and settle down as the ship banged about.

"By the bye," I continued, "I can't have these colours, Mr Hands; and, by your leave, I'll strike 'em. Better none then these."

And, again dodging the boom, I ran to the colour lines, handed down their cursed black flag, and chucked it overboard.

"God save the king!" said I, waving my cap; "and there's an end to Captain Silver!"

He watched me keenly and slyly, his chin all the while on his breast

"I reckon," he said at last—"I reckon, Cap'n Hawkins, you'll kind of want to get ashore, now. S'pose we talks."

"Why, yes," says I, "with all my heart, Mr Hands. Say on." And I went back to my meal with a good appetite.

"This man," he began, nodding feebly at the corpse—"O'Brien were his name—a rank Irelander—this man and me got the canvas on her, meaning for to sail her back. Well, *he's* dead now, he is—as dead as bilge; and who's to sail this ship, I don't see. Without I gives you a hint, you ain't that man, as far's I can tell. Now, look here, you gives me food and drink, and an old scarf or ankecher to tie my wound up, you do; and I'll tell you how to sail her; and that's about square all round, I take it."

"I'll tell you one thing," says I: "I'm not going back to Captain Kidd's anchorage. I mean to get into North Inlet, and beach her quietly there."

"To be sure you did," he cried. "Why, I ain't sich an infernal lubber, after all. I can see, can't I? I've tried my fling, I have, and I've lost, and it's you has the wind of me. North Inlet? Why, I haven't no ch'ice, not I! I'd help you sail her up to Execution Dock, by thunder! so I would."

Well, as it seemed to me, there was some sense in this. We struck our bargain on the spot. In three minutes I had the *Hispaniola* sailing easily before the wind along the coast of Treasure Island, with good hopes of turning the northern point ere noon, and beating down again as far as North Inlet before high water, when we might beach her safely, and wait till the subsiding tide permitted us to land. Then I lashed the tiller and went below to my own chest, where I got a soft silk handkerchief of my mother's. With this, and with my aid, Hands bound up the great bleeding stab he had received in the thigh, and after he had eaten a little and had a swallow or two more of the brandy, he began to pick up visibly, sat straighter up, spoke louder and clearer, and looked in every way another man.

The breeze served us admirably. We skimmed before it like a bird, the coast of the island flashing by, and the view changing every minute. Soon we were past the high lands and bowling beside low, sandy country, sparsely dotted with dwarf pines, and soon we were beyond that again, and had turned the corner of the rocky hill that ends the island on the north.

I was greatly elated with my new command, and pleased with the bright, sunshiny weather and these different prospects of the coast. I had now plenty of water and good things to eat, and my conscience, which had smitten me hard for my desertion, was quieted by the great conquest I had made. I should, I think, have had nothing left me to desire but for the eyes of the coxswain as they followed me derisively about the deck, and the odd smile that appeared continually on his face. It was a smile that had in it something both of pain and weakness—a haggard, old man's smile; but there was, besides that, a grain of derision, a shadow of treachery, in his expression as he craftily watched, and watched, and watched me at my work.

CHAPTER XXVI

ISRAEL HANDS

The wind, serving us to a desire, now hauled into the west. We could run so much the easier from the north-east corner of the island to the mouth of the North Inlet. Only, as we had no power to anchor, and dared not beach her till the tide had flowed a good deal farther, time hung on our hands. The coxswain told me how to lay the ship to; after a good many trials I succeeded, and we both sat in silence, over another meal.

"Cap'n," said he, at length, with that same uncomfortable smile, "here's my old shipmate, O'Brien; s'pose you was to heave him overboard. I ain't partic'lar as a rule, and I don't take no blame for settling his hash; but I don't reckon him ornamental, now, do you?"

"I'm not strong enough, and I don't like the job; and there he lies, for me," said I.

"This here's an unlucky ship—this *Hispaniola,* Jim," he went on, blinking. "There's a power of men been killed in this *Hispaniola*—a sight o' poor seamen dead and gone since you and me took ship to Bristol. I never seen sich dirty luck, not I. There was this here O'Brien, now—he's dead, ain't he? Well, now, I'm no scholar, and you're a lad as can read and figure; and to put it straight, do you take it as a dead man is dead for good, or do he come alive again?"

"You can kill the body, Mr Hands, but not the spirit; you must know that already," I replied. "O'Brien there is in another world, and maybe watching us."

"Ah!" says he. "Well, that's unfort'nate—appears as if killing parties was a waste of time. Howsomever, sperrits don't reckon for much, by what I've seen. I'll chance it with the sperrits, Jim. And now, you've spoke up free, and I'll take it kind if you'd step down into that there cabin and get me a—well, a—shiver my timbers! I can't hit the name on't; well, you get me a bottle of wine, Jim—this here brandy's too strong for my head."

Now, the coxswain's hesitation seemed to be unnatural; and as for the notion of his preferring wine to brandy, I entirely disbelieved it. The whole story was a pretext. He wanted me to leave the deck—so much was plain; but with what purpose I could in no way imagine. His eyes never met mine; they kept wandering to and fro, up and down, now with a look to the sky, now with a flitting glance upon the dead O'Brien. All the time he kept smiling, and putting his tongue out in the most guilty, embarrassed manner, so that a child could have told that he was bent on some deception. I was prompt with my answer, however, for I saw where my advantage lay; and that with a fellow so densely stupid I could easily conceal my suspicions to the end.

"Some wine?" I said. "Far better. Will you have white or red?"

"Well, I reckon it's about the blessed same to me, shipmate," he replied; "so it's strong, and plenty of it, what's the odds?"

"All right," I answered. "I'll bring you port, Mr Hands. But I'll have to dig for it."

With that I scuttled down the companion with all the noise I could, slipped off my shoes, ran quietly along the sparred gallery, mounted the forecastle ladder, and popped my head out of the fore companion. I knew he would not expect to see me there; yet I took every precaution possible; and certainly the worst of my suspicions proved too true.

He had risen from his position to his hands and knees; and, though his leg obviously hurt him pretty sharply when he moved—for I could hear him stifle a groan—yet it was at a good, rattling rate that he trailed himself across the deck. In half a minute he had reached the port scuppers, and picked, out of a coil of rope, a long knife, or rather a short dirk, discoloured to the hilt with blood. He looked upon it for a moment, thrusting forth his underjaw, tried the point upon his hand, and then, hastily concealing it in the bosom of his jacket, trundled back again into his old place against the bulwark.

This was all that I required to know. Israel could move about; he was now armed; and if he had been at so much trouble to get rid of me, it was plain that I was meant to be the victim. What he would do afterwards—whether he would try to crawl right across the island from North Inlet to the camp among the swamps, or whether he would fire Long Tom, trusting that his own comrades might come first to help him, was, of course, more than I could say.

Yet I felt sure that I could trust him in one point, since in that our interests jumped together, and that was in the disposition of the schooner. We both desired to have her stranded safe enough in a sheltered place, and so that, when the time came, she could be got off again with as little labour and danger as might be; and until that was done I considered that my life would certainly be spared.

While I was thus turning the business over in my mind, I had not been idle with my body. I had stolen back to the cabin, slipped once more into my shoes, and laid my hand at random on a bottle of wine, and now, with this for an excuse, I made my reappearance on the deck.

Hands lay as I had left him, all fallen together in a bundle, and with his eyelids lowered, as though he were too weak to bear the light. He looked up, however, at my coming, knocked the neck off the bottle, like a man who had done the same thing often, and took a good swig, with his favourite toast of "Here's luck!" Then he lay quiet for a little, and then, pulling out a stick of tobacco, begged me to cut him a quid.

"Cut me a junk o' that," says be, "for I haven't no knife, and hardly strength enough, so be as I had. Ah, Jim, Jim, I reckon I've missed stays! Cut me a quid, as'll likely be the last, lad; for I'm for my long home, and no mistake."

"Well," said I, "I'll cut you some tobacco; but if I were you and thought myself so badly, I would go to my prayers, like a Christian man."

"Why?" said he. "Now, you tell me why."

"Why?" I cried. "You were asking me just now about the dead. You've broken your trust; you've lived in sin and lies and blood; there's a man you killed lying at your feet this moment; and you ask me why! For God's mercy, Mr Hands, that's why."

I spoke with a little heat, thinking of the bloody dirk he had hidden in his pocket, and designed, in his ill thoughts, to end me with. He, for his part, took a great draught of the wine and spoke with the most unusual solemnity.

"For thirty years," he said, "I've sailed the seas, and seen good and bad, better and worse, fair weather and foul, provisions running out, knives going, and what not. Well, now I tell you, I never seen good come o' goodness yet. Him as strikes first is my fancy; dead men don't bite; them's my views—amen, so be it. And now, you look here," he added, suddenly changing his tone, "we've had about enough of this foolery. The tide's made good enough by now. You just take my orders, Cap'n Hawkins, and we'll sail slap in and be done with it."

All told, we had scarce two miles to run; but the navigation was delicate, the entrance to this northern anchorage was not only narrow and shoal, but lay east and west, so that the schooner must be nicely handled to be got in. I think I was a good, prompt subaltern, and I am very sure that Hands was an excellent pilot; for we went about and about, and dodged in, shaving the banks, with a certainty and a neatness that were a pleasure to behold.

Scarcely had we passed the heads before the land closed around us. The shores of North Inlet were as thickly wooded as those of the southern anchorage; but the space was longer and narrower, and more like, what in truth it was, the estuary of a river. Right before us, at the southern end we saw the wreck of a ship in the last stages of dilapidation. It had been a great vessel of three masts, but had lain so long exposed to the injuries of the weather that it was hung about with great webs of dripping seaweed, and on the deck of it shore bushes had taken root, and now flourished thick with flowers. It was a sad sight, but it showed us that the anchorage was calm.

"Now," said Hands, "look here; there's a pet bit for to beach a ship in. Fine flat sand, never a catspaw, trees all round of it, and flowers a-blowing like a garding on that old ship."

"And once beached," I enquired, "how shall we get her off again?"

"Why, so," he replied: "you take a line ashore there on the other side at low water: take a turn about one o' them big pines; bring it back, take a turn round the capstan, and lie-to for the tide. Come high water, all hands take a pull upon the line, and off she comes as sweet as natur'. And now, boy, you stand by. We're near the bit now, and she's too much way on her. Starboard a little—so—steady—starboard—larboard a little—steady—steady!"

So he issued his commands, which I breathlessly obeyed; till, all of a sudden, he cried, "Now, my hearty, luff!" And I put the helm hard up, and the *Hispaniola* swung round rapidly, and ran stem on for the low wooded shore.

The excitement of these last manœuvres had somewhat interfered with the watch I had kept hitherto, sharply enough, upon the coxswain. Even then I was still so much interested waiting for the ship to touch, that I had quite forgot the peril that hung over my head, and stood craning over the starboard bulwarks and watching the ripples spreading wide before the bows. I might have fallen without a struggle for my life, had not a sudden disquietude seized upon me, and made me turn my head. Perhaps I had heard a creak, or seen his shadow moving with the tail of my eye; perhaps it was an instinct like a cat's; but, sure enough, when I looked round, there was Hands already half-way towards me, with the dirk in his right hand.

We must both have cried out aloud when our eyes met; but while mine was the shrill cry of terror, his was a roar of fury like a charging bull's. At the same instant he threw himself forward, and I leapt sideways towards the bows. As I did so, I left hold of the tiller, which sprang sharp to leeward; and I think this saved my life, for it struck Hands across the chest, and stopped him, for the moment, dead.

Before he could recover, I was safe out of the corner where he had me trapped, with all the deck to dodge about. Just forward of the mainmast I stopped, drew a pistol from my pocket, took a cool aim, though he had already turned and was once more coming directly after me, and drew the trigger. The hammer fell, but there followed neither flash nor sound; the priming was useless with sea water. I cursed myself for my neglect. Why had not I, long before, reprimed and reloaded my only weapons? Then I should not have been, as now, a mere fleeing sheep before this butcher.

Wounded as he was, it was wonderful how fast he could move, his grizzled hair tumbling over his face, and his face itself as red as a red ensign with his haste and fury. I had no time to try my other pistol, nor, indeed, much inclination, for I was sure it would be useless. One thing I saw plainly: I must not simply retreat before him, or he would speedily hold me boxed into the bows, as a moment since he had so nearly boxed me in the stern. Once so caught, and nine or ten inches of the blood-stained dirk would be my last experience on this side of eternity. I placed my palms against the main-mast, which was of a goodish bigness, and waited, every nerve upon the stretch.

Seeing that I meant to dodge, he also paused; and a moment or two passed in feints on his part, and corresponding movements upon mine. It was such a game as I had often played at home about the rocks of

THE COXSWAIN LOOSED HIS GRASP UPON THE SHROUDS
AND PLUNGED HEAD FIRST INTO THE WATER

Black Hill Cove; but never before, you may be sure, with such a wildly beating heart as now. Still, as I say, it was a boy's game, and I thought I could hold my own at it, against an elderly seaman with a wounded thigh. Indeed, my courage had begun to rise so high, that I allowed myself a few darting thoughts on what would be the end of the affair; and while I saw certainly that I could spin it out for long, I saw no hope of any ultimate escape.

Well, while things stood thus, suddenly the *Hispaniola* struck, staggered, ground for an instant in the sand, and then, swift as a blow, canted over to the port side, till the deck stood at an angle of forty-five degrees, and about a puncheon of water splashed into the scupper holes, and lay, in a pool, between the deck and bulwark.

We were both of us capsized in a second, and both of us rolled, almost together, into the scuppers; the dead Red-cap, with his arms still spread out, tumbling stiffly after us. So near were we, indeed, that my head came against the coxswain's foot with a crack that made my teeth rattle. Blow and all, I was the first afoot again; for Hands had got involved with the dead body. The sudden canting of the ship had made the deck no place for running on; I had to find some new way of escape, and that upon the instant, for my foe was almost touching me. Quick as thought I sprang into the mizzen shrouds, rattled up hand over hand, and did not draw a breath till I was seated on the cross-trees.

I had been saved by being prompt; the dirk had struck not half a foot below me, as I pursued my upward flight; and there stood Israel Hands with his mouth open and his face upturned to mine, a perfect statue of surprise and disappointment.

Now that I had a moment to myself, I lost no time in changing the priming of my pistol, and then, having one ready for service, and to make assurance doubly sure, I proceeded to draw the load of the other, and recharge it afresh from the beginning.

My new employment struck Hands all of a heap; he began to see the dice going against him; and after an obvious hesitation, he also hauled himself heavily into the shrouds, and, with the dirk in his teeth, began slowly and painfully to mount. It cost him no end of time and groans to haul his wounded leg behind him; and I had quietly finished my arrangements before he was much more than a third of the way up. Then, with a pistol in either hand, I addressed him.

"One more step, Mr Hands," said I, "and I'll blow your brains out! Dead men don't bite, you know," I added, with a chuckle.

157

He stopped instantly. I could see by the working of his face that he was trying to think, and the process was so slow and laborious that, in my new-found security, I laughed aloud. At last, with a swallow or two, he spoke, his face still wearing the same expression of extreme perplexity. In order to speak he had to take the dagger from his mouth; but, in all else, he remained unmoved.

"Jim," says he, "I reckon we're fouled, you and me, and we'll have to sign articles. I'd have had you but for that there lurch; but I don't have no luck, not I; and I reckon I'll have to strike, which comes hard, you see, for a master mariner to a ship's younker like you, Jim."

I was drinking in his words and smiling away, as conceited as a cock upon a wall, when, all in a breath, back went his right hand over his shoulder. Something sang like an arrow through the air: I felt a blow and then a sharp pang, and there I was pinned by the shoulder to the mast. In the horrid pain and surprise of the moment—I scarce can say it was by my own volition, and I am sure it was without conscious aim—both my pistols went off, and both escaped out of my hands. They did not fall alone; with a choked cry, the coxswain loosed his grip upon the shrouds, and plunged head-first into the water.

Chapter XXVII

"PIECES OF EIGHT"

Owing to the cant of the vessel, the masts hung far out over the water, and from my perch on the cross-trees I had nothing below me but the surface of the bay. Hands, who was not so far up, was, in consequence, nearer to the ship, and fell between me and the bulwarks. He rose once to the surface in a lather of foam and blood, and then sank again for good. As the water settled, I could see him lying huddled together on the clean, bright sand in the shadow of the vessel's sides. A fish or two whipped past his body. Sometimes, by the quivering of the water, he appeared to move a little, as if he were trying to rise. But he was dead enough, for all that, being both shot and drowned, and was food for fish in the very place where he had designed my slaughter.

I was no sooner certain of this than I began to feel sick, faint, and terrified. The hot blood was running over my back and chest. The dirk, where it had pinned my shoulder to the mast, seemed to burn like a hot iron; yet it was not so much these real sufferings that distressed me, for these, it seemed to me, I could bear without a murmur; it was the horror I had upon my mind of falling from the cross-trees into that still green water, beside the body of the coxswain.

I clung with both hands till my nails ached, and I shut my eyes as if to cover up the peril. Gradually my mind came back again, my pulses quieted down to a more natural time, and I was once more in possession of myself.

It was my first thought to pluck forth the dirk; but either it stuck too hard or my nerve failed me; and I desisted with a violent shudder.

159

Oddly enough, that very shudder did the business. The knife, in fact, had come the nearest in the world to missing me altogether; it held me by a mere pinch of skin, and this the shudder tore away. The blood ran down the faster to be sure; but I was my own master again, and only tacked to the mast by my coat and shirt.

These last I broke through with a sudden jerk, and then regained the deck by the starboard shrouds. For nothing in the world would I have again ventured, shaken as I was, upon the overhanging port shrouds, from which Israel had so lately fallen.

I went below, and did what I could for my wound; it pained me a good deal, and still bled freely; but it was neither deep nor danger-ous, nor did it greatly gall me when I used my arm. Then I looked around me, and as the ship was now, in a sense, my own, I began to think of clearing it from its last passenger—the dead man, O'Brien.

He had pitched, as I have said, against the bulwarks, where he lay like some horrible, ungainly sort of puppet; life-size, indeed, but how different from life's colour or life's comeliness! In that position, I could easily have my way with him; and as the habit of tragical adventures had worn off almost all my terror for the dead, I took him by the waist as if he had been a sack of bran, and, with one good heave, tumbled him overboard. He went in with a sounding plunge; the red cap came off, and remained floating on the surface; and as soon as the splash subsided, I could see him and Israel lying side by side, both wavering with the tremulous movement of the water. O'Brien, though still quite a young man, was very bald. There he lay, with that bald head across the knees of the man who had killed him, and the quick fishes steering to and fro over both.

I was now alone upon the ship; the tide had just turned. The sun was within so few degrees of setting that already the shadow of the pines upon the western shore began to reach right across the anchor-age, and fall in patterns on the deck. The evening breeze had sprung up, and though it was well warded off by the hill with the two peaks upon the east, the cordage had begun to sing a little softly to itself and the idle sails to rattle to and fro.

I began to see a danger to the ship. The jibs I speedily doused and brought tumbling to the deck; but the mainsail was a harder matter. Of course, when the schooner canted over, the boom had swung out-board, and the cap of it and a foot or two of sail hung even under water. I thought this made it still more dangerous; yet the strain was so heavy that I half feared to meddle. At last, I got my knife and cut the halyards. The peak dropped instantly, a great belly of loose canvas floated broad upon the water; and since, pull as I liked, I could not budge the downhaul, that was the extent of what I could accomplish. For the rest, the *Hispaniola* must trust to luck, like myself.

By this time the whole anchorage had fallen into shadow—the last rays, I remember, falling through a glade of the wood, and shining bright as jewels, on the flowery mantle of the wreck. It began to be chill; the tide was rapidly fleeting seaward, the schooner settling more and more on her beam-ends

I scrambled forward and looked over. It seemed shallow enough, and holding the cut hawser in both hands for a last security, I let myself drop softly overboard. The water scarcely reached my waist; the sand was firm and covered with ripple marks, and I waded ashore in great spirits, leaving the *Hispaniola* on her side, with her main-sail trailing wide upon the surface of the bay. About the same time the sun went fairly down, and the breeze whistled low in the dusk among the tossing pines.

At least, and at last, I was off the sea, nor had I returned thence empty-handed. There lay the schooner, clear at last from buccaneers and ready for our own men to board and get to sea again. I had nothing nearer my fancy than to get home to the stockade and boast of my achievements. Possibly I might be blamed a bit for my truantry, but the recapture of the *Hispaniola* was a clenching answer, and I hoped that even Captain Smollett would confess I had not lost my time.

So thinking, and in famous spirits, I began to set my face homeward for the block-house and my companions. I remembered that the most easterly of the rivers which drain into Captain Kidd's anchorage ran from the two-peaked hill upon my left; and I bent my course in that direction that I might pass the stream while it was small. The wood was pretty open, and keeping along the lower spurs, I had soon turned the corner of that hill, and not long after waded to the mid-calf across the water-course.

This brought me near to where I had encountered Ben Gunn, the maroon; and I walked more circumspectly, keeping an eye on every side. The dusk had come nigh hand completely, and, as I opened out the cleft between the two peaks, I became aware of a wavering glow against the sky, where, as I judged, the man of the island was cooking his supper before a roaring fire. And yet I wondered, in my heart, that he should show himself so careless. For if I could see this radiance, might it not reach the eyes of Silver himself where he camped upon the shore among the marshes?

Gradually the night fell blacker; it was all I could do to guide myself even roughly towards my destination; the double hill behind me and the Spy-glass on my right hand loomed faint and fainter; the stars were few and pale; and in the low ground where I wandered I kept tripping among bushes and rolling into sandy pits.

Suddenly a kind of brightness fell about me. I looked up; a pale glimmer of moonbeams had alighted on the summit of the Spy-glass, and soon after I saw something broad and silvery moving low down behind the trees, and knew the moon had risen.

With this to help me, I passed rapidly over what remained to me of my journey; and, sometimes walking, sometimes running, impatiently drew near to the stockade. Yet, as I began to thread the grove that lies before it, I was not so thoughtless but that I slacked my pace and went a trifle warily. It would have been a poor end of my adventures to get shot down by my own party in mistake.

The moon was climbing higher and higher; its light began to fall here and there in masses through the more open districts of the wood; and right in front of me a glow of a different colour appeared among the trees. It was red and hot, and now and again it was a little darkened—as it were the embers of a bonfire smouldering.

For the life of me, I could not think what it might be.

At last I came right down upon the borders of the clearing. The western end was already steeped in moonshine; the rest, and the blockhouse itself, still lay in a black shadow, chequered with long, silvery streaks of light. On the other side of the house an immense fire had burned itself into clear embers and shed a steady, red reverberation, contrasted strongly with the mellow paleness of the moon. There was not a soul stirring, nor a sound beside the noises of the breeze.

I stopped, with much wonder in my heart, and perhaps a little terror also. It had not been our way to build great fires; we were, indeed, by the captain's orders, somewhat niggardly of firewood; and I began to fear that something had gone wrong while I was absent.

I stole round by the eastern end, keeping close in shadow, and at a convenient place, where the darkness was thickest, crossed the palisade.

To make assurance surer, I got upon my hands and knees, and crawled, without a sound, towards the corner of the house. As I drew nearer, my heart was suddenly and greatly lightened. It is not a pleasant noise in itself, and I have often complained of it at other times; but just then it was like music to hear my friends snoring together so loud and peaceful in their sleep. The sea-cry of the watch, that beautiful "All's well," never fell more reassuringly on my ear.

In the meantime, there was no doubt of one thing; they kept an infamous bad watch. If it had been Silver and his lads that were now creeping in on them, not a soul would have seen daybreak. That was what it was, thought I, to have the captain wounded; and again I blamed myself sharply for leaving them in that danger with so few to mount guard.

By this time I had got to the door and stood up. All as dark within, so that I could distinguish nothing by the eye. As for sounds, there was the steady drone of the snorers, and a small occasional noise, a flickering or pecking that I could in no way account for.

With my arms before me I walked steadily in. I should lie down in my own place (I thought, with a silent chuckle) and enjoy their faces when they found me in the morning.

My foot struck something yielding—it was a sleeper's leg; and he turned and groaned, but without awaking.

And then, all of a sudden, a shrill voice broke forth out of the darkness:

"Pieces of eight! pieces of eight! pieces of eight! pieces of eight! pieces of eight!" and so forth, without pause or change, like the clacking of a tiny mill.

Silver's green parrot, Captain Flint! It was she whom I had heard pecking at a piece of bark; it was she, keeping better watch than any human being, who thus announced my arrival with her wearisome refrain.

I had no time left me to recover. At the sharp, clipping tone of the parrot, the sleepers awoke and sprang up; and with a mighty oath, the voice of Silver cried:

"Who goes?"

I turned to run, struck violently against one person, recoiled, and ran full into the arms of a second, who, for his part, closed upon and held me tight.

"Bring a torch, Dick," said Silver, when my capture was thus assured.

And one of the men left the log-house, and presently returned with a lighted brand.

PART VI

CAPTAIN SILVER

Chapter XVIII

IN THE ENEMY'S CAMP

The red glare of the torch, lighting up the interior of the block-house, showed me the worst of my apprehensions realised. The pirates were in possession of the house and stores: there was the cask of cognac, there were the pork and bread, as before; and, what tenfold increased my horror, not a sign of any prisoner. I could only judge that all had perished, and my heart smote me sorely that I had not been there to perish with them.

There were six of the buccaneers, all told; not another man was left alive. Five of them were on their feet, flushed and swollen, suddenly called out of the first sleep of drunkenness. The sixth had only risen upon his elbow: he was deadly pale, and the blood-stained bandage round his head told that he had recently been wounded, and still more recently dressed. I remembered the man who had been shot and had run back among the woods in the great attack, and doubted not that this was he.

The parrot sat, preening her plumage, on Long John's shoulder. He himself, I thought, looked somewhat paler and more stern than I was used to. He still wore the fine broadcloth suit in which he had fulfilled his mission, but it was bitterly the worse for wear, daubed with clay and torn with the sharp briers of the wood.

"So," said he, "here's Jim Hawkins, shiver my timbers! dropped in, like, eh? Well, come, I take that friendly."

And thereupon he sat down across the brandy cask, and began to fill a pipe.

"Give me a loan of the link, Dick," said he; and then, when he had a good light, "That'll do, lad," he added; "stick the glim in the wood heap; and you, gentlemen, bring yourselves to!—you needn't stand up for Mr Hawkins; *he'll* excuse you, you may lay to that. And so, Jim"—stopping the tobacco—"here you were, and quite a pleasant surprise for poor old John. I see you were smart when first I set my eyes on you; but this here gets away from me clean, it do."

To all this, as may be well supposed, I made no answer. They had set me with my back against the wall; and I stood there, looking Silver in the face, pluckily enough, I hope, to all outward appearance, but with black despair in my heart.

Silver took a whiff or two of his pipe with great composure, and then ran on again.

"Now you see, Jim, so be as you *are* here," says he, "I'll give you a piece of my mind. I've always liked you, I have, for a lad of spirit, and the picter of my own self when I was young and handsome. I always wanted you to jine and take your share, and die a gentleman, and now, my cock, you've got to. Cap'n Smollett's a fine seaman, as I'll own up to any day, but stiff on discipline. 'Dooty is dooty,' says he, and right he is. Just you keep clear of the cap'n. The doctor himself is gone dead again you—'ungrateful scamp' was what he said; and the short and the long of the whole story is about here: you can't go back to your own lot, for they won't have you; and, without you start a third ship's company all by yourself, which might be lonely, you'll have to jine with Cap'n Silver."

So far so good. My friends, then, were still alive, and though I partly believed the truth of Silver's statement, that the cabin party were incensed at me for my desertion, I was more relieved than distressed by what I heard.

"I don't say nothing as to your being in our hands," continued Silver, "though there you are, and you may lay to it. I'm all for argyment; I never seen good come out o' threatening. If you like the service, well, you'll jine; and if you don't, Jim, why, you're free to answer no—free and welcome, shipmate; and if fairer can be said by mortal seaman, shiver my sides!"

"Am I to answer then?" I asked, with a very tremulous voice. Through all this sneering talk, I was made to feel the threat of death that overhung me, and my cheeks burned and my heart beat painfully in my breast.

"Lad," said Silver, "no one's a-pressing of you. Take your bearings. None of us won't hurry you, mate; time goes so pleasant in your company, you see."

"Well," says I, growing a bit bolder, "if I'm to choose, I declare I have a right to know what's what, and why you're here, and where my friends are."

"Wot's wot?" repeated one of the buccaneers, in a deep growl. "Ah, he'd be a lucky one as knowed that!"

"You'll, perhaps, batten down your hatches till you're spoken to, my friend," cried Silver truculently to the speaker. And then, in his first gracious tones, he replied to me: "Yesterday morning, Mr Hawkins," said he, "in the dogwatch, down came Dr Livesey with a flag of truce. Says he, 'Cap'n Silver, you're sold out. Ship's gone.' Well, maybe we'd been taking a glass, and a song to help it round. I won't say no. Leastways one of us had looked out. We looked out, and, by thunder: the old ship was gone. I never seen a pack o' fools look fishier; and you may lay to that, if I tells you that looked the fishiest. 'Well,' says the doctor, 'let's bargain.' We bargained, him and I, and here we are: stores, brandy, block-house, the firewood you was thoughtful enough to cut, and, in a manner of speaking, the whole blessed boat, from cross-trees to kelson. As for them, they've tramped; I don't know where's they are."

He drew again quietly at his pipe.

"And lest you should take it into that head of yours," he went on, "that you was included in the treaty, here's the last word that was said: 'How many are you,' says I, 'to leave?' 'Four,' says he—'four, and one of us wounded. As for that boy, I don't know where he is, confound him,' says he, 'nor I don't much care. We're about sick of him.' These was his words."

"Is that all?" I asked.

"Well, it's all that you've to hear, my son," returned Silver.

"And now I am to choose?"

"And now you are to choose, and you may lay to that," said Silver.

"Well," said I, "I am not such a fool but I know pretty well what I have to look for. Let the worst come to the worst, it's little I care. I've seen too many die since I fell in with you. But there's a thing or two I have to tell you," I said, and by this time I was quite excited; "and the first is this: here you are, in a bad way: ship lost, treasure lost, men lost; your whole business gone to wreck; and if you want to know who did it—it was I! I was in the apple barrel the night we sighted land, and

I heard you, John, and you, Dick Johnson, and Hands, who is now at the bottom of the sea, and told every word you said before the hour was out. And as for the schooner, it was I who cut her cable, and it was I that killed the men you had aboard of her, and it was I who brought her where you'll never see her more, not one of you. The laugh's on my side; I've had the top of this business from the first; I no more fear you than I fear a fly. Kill me, if you please, or spare me. But one thing I'll say, and no more; if you spare me, bygones are bygones, and when you fellows are in court for piracy, I'll save you all I can. It is for you to choose. Kill another, and do yourselves no good, or spare me and keep a witness to save you from the gallows."

I stopped, for, I tell you, I was out of breath, and, to my wonder, not a man of them moved, but all sat staring at me like as many sheep. And while they were still staring, I broke out again.

"And now, Mr Silver," I said, "I believe you're the best man here, and if things go the worst, I'll take it kind of you to let the doctor know the way I took it."

"I'll bear it in mind," said Silver, with an accent so curious that I could not, for the life of me, decide whether he were laughing at my request, or had been favourably affected by my courage.

"I'll put one to that," cried the old mahogany-faced seaman—Morgan by name—whom I had seen in Long John's public-house upon the quays of Bristol. "It was him that knowed Black Dog."

"Well, and see here," added the sea cook. "I'll put another again to that, by thunder! for it was this same boy that faked the chart from Billy Bones. First and last, we've split upon Jim Hawkins!"

"Then here goes!" said Morgan, with an oath.

And he sprang up, drawing his knife as if he had been twenty.

"Avast there!" cried Silver. "Who are you, Tom Morgan? Maybe you thought you was cap'n here, perhaps. By the powers, but I'll teach you better! Cross me, and you'll go where many a good man's gone before you, first and last, these thirty year back—some to the yard-arm, shiver my sides! and some by the board, and all to feed the fishes. There's never a man looked me between the eyes and seen a good day a'terwards, Tom Morgan, you may lay to that."

Morgan paused; but a hoarse murmur rose from the others.

"Tom's right," said one.

"I stood hazing long enough from one," added another. "I'll be hanged if I'll be hazed by you, John Silver."

"Did any of you gentlemen want to have it out with *me*?" roared Silver, bending far forward from his position on the keg, with his pipe still glowing in his right hand. "Put a name on what you're at; you ain't dumb, I reckon. Him that wants shall get it. Have I lived this many years, and a son of a rum-puncheon cock his hat athwart my hawse at the latter end of it? You know the way; you're all gentlemen o' fortune, by your account. Well, I'm ready. Take a cutlass, him that dares, and I'll see the colour of his inside, crutch and all, before that pipe's empty."

Not a man stirred; not a man answered.

"That's your sort, is it?" he added, returning his pipe to his mouth. "Well, you're a gay lot to look at, anyway. Not much worth to fight, you ain't. P'r'aps you can understand King George's English. I'm cap'n here by 'lection. I'm cap'n here because I'm the best man by a long sea-mile. You won't fight, as gentlemen o' fortune should; then, by thunder, you'll obey, and you may lay to it! I like that boy, now; I never seen a better boy than that. He's more a man than any pair of rats of you in this here house, and what I say is this: let me see him that'll lay a hand on him—that's what I say, and you may lay to it."

There was a long pause after this. I stood straight up against the wall, my heart still going like a sledge-hammer, but with a ray of hope now shining in my bosom. Silver leant back against the wall, his arms crossed, his pipe in the corner of his mouth, as calm as though he had been in church; yet his eye kept wandering furtively, and he kept the tail of it on his unruly followers. They, on their part, drew gradually together towards the far end of the block-house, and the low hiss of their whispering sounded in my ear continuously like a stream. One after another they would look up, and the red light of the torch would fall for a second on their nervous faces; but it was not towards me, it was towards Silver that they turned their eyes.

"You seem to have a lot to say," remarked Silver, spitting far into the air. "Pipe up and let me hear it, or lay to."

"Ax your pardon, sir," returned one of the men; "you're pretty free with some of the rules; maybe you'll kindly keep an eye upon the rest. This crew's dissatisfied; this crew don't vally bullying a marlin-spike; this crew has its rights like other crews, I'll make so free as that; and by your own rules, I take it we can talk together. I ax your pardon, sir, acknowledging you to be capting at this present; but I claim my right, and steps outside for a council."

And with an elaborate sea-salute, this fellow, a long, ill-looking, yellow-eyed man of five-and-thirty, stepped coolly towards the door and disappeared out of the house. One after another, the rest followed his example; each making a salute as he passed; each adding some apology. "According to rules," said one. "Fo'c's'le council," said Morgan. And so, with one remark or another, all marched out, and left Silver and me alone with the torch.

The sea cook instantly removed his pipe.

"Now, look you here, Jim Hawkins," he said, in a steady whisper, that was no more than audible, "you're within half a plank of death, and, what's a long sight worse, of torture. They're going to throw me off. But, you mark, I stand by you through thick and thin. I didn't mean to, no, not till you spoke up. I was about desperate to lose that much blunt, and be hanged into the bargain. But I see you was the right sort. I says to myself: You stand by Hawkins, John, and Hawkins'll stand by you. You're his last card, and, by the living thunder, John, he's yours! Back to back, says I. You save your witness, and he'll save your neck!"

I began dimly to understand.

"You mean all's lost?" I asked.

"Ay, by gum, I do!" he answered. "Ship gone, neck gone—that's the size of it. Once I looked into that bay, Jim Hawkins, and seen no schooner—well, I'm tough, but I gave out. As for that lot and their council, mark me, they're outright fools and cowards. I'll save your life—if so be as I can—from them. But, see here, Jim—tit for tat— you save Long John from swinging."

I was bewildered; it seemed a thing so hopeless he was asking—he, the old buccaneer, the ringleader throughout.

"What I can do, that I'll do," I said.

" It's a bargain!" cried Long John. "You speak up plucky, and, by thunder! I've a chance."

He hobbled to the torch, where it stood propped among the fire-wood, and took a fresh light to his pipe.

"Understand me, Jim," he said, returning. "I've a head on my shoulders, I have. I'm on squire's side now. I know you've got that ship safe somewheres. How you done it, I don't know, but safe it is. I guess Hands and O'Brien turned soft. I never much believed in neither of *them*. Now you mark me. I ask no questions, nor I won't let others. I know when a game's up, I do; and I know a lad that's staunch. Ah, you that's young—you and me might have done a power of good together!"

He drew some cognac from the cask into a tin cannikin.

"Will you taste, messmate?" he asked; and when I had refused: "Well, I'll take a drain myself, Jim," said he. "I need a caulker, for there's trouble on hand. And, talking o' trouble, why did that doctor give me the chart, Jim?"

My face expressed a wonder so unaffected that he saw the needlessness of further questions.

"Ah, well, he did, though," said he. "And there's something under that, no doubt—something, surely, under that, Jim—bad or good."

And he took another swallow of the brandy, shaking his great fair head like a man who looks forward to the worst.

Chapter XXIX

THE BLACK SPOT AGAIN

The council of the buccaneers had lasted some time, when one of them re-entered the house, and with a repetition of the same salute, which had in my eyes an ironical air, begged for a moment's loan of the torch. Silver briefly agreed; and this emissary retired again, leaving us together in the dark.

"There's a breeze coming, Jim," said Silver, who had, by this time, adopted quite a friendly and familiar tone.

I turned to the loophole nearest me and looked out. The embers of the great fire had so far burned themselves out, and now glowed so low and duskily, that I understood why these conspirators desired a torch. About half-way down the slope to the stockade, they were collected in a group; one held the light; another was on his knees in their midst, and I saw the blade of an open knife shine in his hand with varying colours, in the moon and torchlight. The rest were all somewhat stooping, as though watching the manœuvres of this last. I could just make out that he had a book as well as a knife in his hand; and was still wondering how anything so incongruous had come in their possession, when the kneeling figure rose once more to his feet, and the whole party began to move together towards the house.

"Here they come," said I; and I returned to my former position, for it seemed beneath my dignity that they should find me watching them.

"Well, let 'em come, lad—let 'em come," said Silver cheerily. "I've still a shot in my locker."

The door opened, and the five men, standing huddled together just inside, pushed one of their number forward. In any other circumstances it would have been comical to see his slow advance, hesitating as he set down each foot but holding his closed right hand in front of him.

"Step up, lad," cried Silver. "I won't eat you. Hand it over, lubber. I know the rules, I do; I won't hurt a depytation."

Thus encouraged, the buccaneer stepped forth more briskly, and having passed something to Silver, from hand to hand, slipped yet more smartly back again to his companions.

The sea cook looked at what had been given him.

"The black spot! I thought so," he observed. "Where might you have got the paper? Why, hillo! look here, now: this ain't lucky! You've gone and cut this out of a Bible. What fool's cut a Bible?"

"Ah, there!" said Morgan—"there! Wot did I say? No good'll come o' that, I said."

"Well, you've about fixed it now, among you," continued Silver. "You'll all swing now, I reckon. What soft-headed lubber had a Bible?"

"It was Dick," said one.

"Dick, was it? Then Dick can get to prayers," said Silver. "He's seen his slice of luck, has Dick, and you may lay to that."

But here the long man with the yellow eyes struck in.

"Belay that talk, John Silver," he said. "This crew has tipped you the black spot in full council, as in dooty bound; just you turn it over, as in dooty bound, and see what's wrote there. Then you can talk."

"Thanky, George," replied the sea cook. "You always was brisk for business, and has the rules by heart, George, as I'm pleased to see. Well, what is it, anyway? Ah! 'Deposed'—that's it, is it? Very pretty wrote, to be sure; like print, I swear. Your hand o' write, George? Why, you was gettin' quite a leadin' man in this here crew. You'll be cap'n next, I shouldn't wonder. Just oblige me with that torch again, will you? this pipe don't draw."

"Come, now," said George, "you don't fool this crew no more. You're a funny man, by your account; but you're over now, and you'll maybe step down off that barrel, and help vote."

"I thought you said you knowed the rules," returned Silver contemptuously. "Leastways, if you don't, I do; and I wait here—and I'm still your cap'n, mind—till you outs with your grievances; and I reply, in the meantime, your black spot ain't worth a biscuit. After that, we'll see."

"Oh," replied George, "you don't be under no kind of apprehension; *we're* all square, we are. First, you've made a hash of this cruise—you'll be a bold man to say no to that. Second, you let the enemy out o' this here trap for nothing. Why did they want out? I dunno; but it's pretty plain they wanted it. Third, you wouldn't let us go at them upon the march. Oh, we see through you, John Silver; you want to play booty, that's what's wrong with you. And then, fourth, there's this here boy."

"Is that all?" asked Silver quietly.

"Enough, too," retorted George. "We'll all swing and sun-dry for your bungling."

"Well, now, look here, I'll answer these four p'ints; one after another I'll answer 'em. I made a hash o' this cruise, did I? Well, now, you all know what I wanted: and you all know, if that had been done, that we'd 'a' been aboard the *Hispaniola* this night as ever was, every man of us alive, and fit, and full of good plum-duff, and the treasure in the hold of her, by thunder! Well, who crossed me? Who forced my hand, as was the lawful cap'n? Who tipped me the black spot the day we landed, and began this dance? Ah, it's a fine dance—I'm with you there—and looks mighty like a hornpipe in a rope's end at Execution Dock by London town, it does. But who done it? Why, it was Anderson, and Hands, and you, George Merry! And you're the last above board of that same meddling crew; and you have the Davy Jones's insolence to up and stand for cap'n over me—you, that sank the lot of us! By the powers! but this tops the stiffest yarn to nothing."

Silver paused, and I could see by the faces of George and his late comrades that these words had not been said in vain.

"That's for number one," cried the accused, wiping the sweat from his brow, for he had been talking with a vehemence that shook the house. "Why, I give you my word, I'm sick to speak to you. You've neither sense nor memory, and I leave it to fancy where your mothers was that let you come to sea. Sea! Gentlemen o' fortune! I reckon tailors is your trade."

"Go on, John," said Morgan. "Speak up to the others."

"Ah, the others!" returned John. "They're a nice lot, ain't they? You say this cruise is bungled. Ah! by gum, if you could understand how bad it's bungled, you would see! We're that near the gibbet that my neck's stiff with thinking of it. You've seen 'em, maybe, hanged in chains, birds about 'em, seamen p'inting 'em out as they go down with the tide. 'Who's that?' says one. 'That! Why, that's John Silver. I knowed him well,' says another. And you can hear the chains a-jangle as you go about and reach for the other buoy. Now, that's about where we are, every mother's son of us, thanks to him, and Hands, and Anderson, and other ruination fools of you. And if you want to know about number four, and that boy, why, shiver my timbers! isn't he a hostage? Are we a-going to waste a hostage? No, not us; he might be our last chance, and I shouldn't wonder. Kill that boy? not me, mates! And number three? Ah, well, there's a deal to say to number three. Maybe you don't count it nothing to have a real college doctor come to see you every day—you, John, with your head broke—or you, George Merry, that had the ague shakes upon you not six hours agone, and has your eyes the colour of lemon-peel to this same moment on the clock? And maybe, perhaps, you didn't know there was a consort coming, either? But there is; and not so long till then; and we'll see who'll be glad to have a hostage when it comes to that. And as for number two, and why I made a bargain—well, you came crawling on your knees to me to make it—on your knees you came, you was that downhearted—and you'd have starved too, if I hadn't—but that's a trifle! you look there—that's why!"

And he cast down upon the floor a paper that I instantly recognised—none other than the chart on yellow paper, with the three red crosses, that I had found in the oilcloth at the bottom of the captain's chest. Why the doctor had given it to him was more than I could fancy.

But if it were inexplicable to me, the appearance of the chart was incredible to the surviving mutineers. They leaped upon it like cats upon a mouse. It went from hand to hand, one tearing it from another; and by the oaths and the cries and the childish laughter with which they accompanied their examination, you would have thought, not only they were fingering the very gold, but were at sea with it, besides, in safety.

"Yes," said one, "that's Flint sure enough. J. F., and a score below, with a clove-hitch to it; so he done ever."

"Mighty pretty," said George. "But how are we to get away with it! and us no ship?"

Silver suddenly sprang up, and supporting himself with a hand against the wall: "Now I give you warning, George," he cried. "One more word of your sauce, and I'll call you down and fight you. How? Why, how do I know? You had ought to tell me that—you and the rest, that lost me my schooner, with your interference, burn you! But not you, you can't; you hain't got the invention of a cockroach. But civil you can speak, and shall, George Merry, you may lay to that."

"That's fair enow," said the old man Morgan.

"Fair! I reckon so," said the sea cook. "You lost the ship; I found the treasure. Who's the better man at that? And now I resign, by thunder! Elect whom you please to be your cap'n now; I'm done with it."

"Silver!" they cried. "Barbecue for ever! Barbecue for cap'n!"

"So that's the toon, is it?" cried the cook. "George, I reckon you'll have to wait another turn, friend; and lucky for you as I'm not a revengeful man. But that was never my way. And now, shipmates, this black spot? 'Taint much good now, is it? Dick crossed his luck and spoiled his Bible, and that's about all."

"It'll do to kiss the book on still, won't it?" growled Dick, who was evidently uneasy at the curse he had brought upon himself.

"A Bible with a bit cut out!" returned Silver derisively. "Not it. It don't bind no more'n a ballad-book."

"Don't it, though?" cried Dick, with a sort of joy. "Well, I reckon that's worth having, too."

"Here, Jim—here's a cur'osity for you," said Silver; and he tossed me the paper.

It was a round about the size of a crown piece. One side was blank, for it had been the last leaf; the other contained a verse or two of Revelation—these words among the rest, which struck sharply home upon my mind: "Without are dogs and murderers." The printed side had been blackened with wood ash, which already began to come off and soil my fingers; on the blank side had been written with the same material the one word "Depposed." I have that curiosity beside me at this moment; but not a trace of writing now remains beyond a single scratch, such as a man might make with his thumb-nail.

That was the end of the night's business. Soon after, with a drink all round, we lay down to sleep, and the outside of Silver's vengeance was to put George Merry up for sentinel, and threaten him with death if he should prove unfaithful.

It was long ere I could close an eye, and Heaven knows I had matter enough for thought in the man whom I had slain that afternoon, in my own most perilous position, and, above all, in the remarkable game that I saw Silver now engaged upon—keeping the mutineers together with one hand, and grasping, with the other, after every means, possible and impossible, to make his peace and save his miserable life. He himself slept peacefully, and snored aloud; yet my heart was sore for him, wicked as he was, to think on the dark perils that environed, and the shameful gibbet that awaited him.

Chapter XXX

ON PAROLE

I was wakened—indeed, we were all wakened, for I could see even the sentinel shake himself together from where he had fallen against the door-post—by a clear, hearty voice hailing us from the margin of the wood:—

"Block-house, ahoy!" it cried. "Here's the doctor."

And the doctor it was. Although I was glad to hear the sound, yet my gladness was not without admixture. I remembered with confusion my insubordinate and stealthy conduct; and when I saw where it had brought me—among what companions and surrounded by what dangers—I felt ashamed to look him in the face.

He must have risen in the dark, for the day had hardly come; and when I ran to a loophole and looked out, I saw him standing, like Silver once before, up to the mid-leg in creeping vapour.

"You, doctor! Top o' the morning to you, sir!" cried Silver, broad awake and beaming with good nature in a moment. "Bright and early, to be sure; and it's the early bird, as the saying goes, that gets the rations. George, shake up your timbers, son, and help Dr Livesey over the ship's side. All a-doin' well, your patients was—all well and merry."

So he pattered on, standing on the hill-top, with his crutch under his elbow, and one hand upon the side of the log-house—quite the old John in voice, manner, and expression.

"We've quite a surprise for you too, sir," he continued. "We've a little stranger here—he! he! A noo boarder and lodger, sir, and look-

179

ing fit and taut as a fiddle; slep' like a super-cargo, he did, right alongside of John—stem to stem we was, all night."

Dr Livesey was by this time across the stockade and pretty near the cook; and I could hear the alteration in his voice as he said—

"Not Jim?"

"The very same Jim as ever was," says Silver.

The doctor stopped outright, although he did not speak, and it was some seconds before he seemed able to move on.

"Well, well," he said at last, "duty first and pleasure afterwards, as you might have said yourself, Silver. Let us overhaul these patients of yours."

A moment afterwards he had entered the block-house, and, with one grim nod to me, proceeded with his work among the sick. He seemed under no apprehension, though he must have known that his life among these treacherous demons depended on a hair; and he rattled on to his patients as if he were paying an ordinary professional visit in a quiet English family. His manner, I suppose, reacted on the men; for they behaved to him as if nothing had occurred—as if he were still ship's doctor, and they still faithful hands before the mast.

"You're doing well, my friend," he said to the fellow with the bandaged head, "and if ever any person had a close shave, it was you; your head must be as hard as iron. Well, George, how goes it? You're a pretty colour, certainly; why, your liver, man, is upside down. Did you take that medicine? Did he take that medicine, men?"

"Ay, ay, sir, he took it, sure enough," returned Morgan.

"Because, you see, since I am mutineers' doctor, or prison doctor, as I prefer to call it," says Dr Livesey, in his pleasantest way, "I make it a point of honour not to lose a man for King George (God bless him!) and the gallows."

The rogues looked at each other, but swallowed the home-thrust in silence.

"Dick don't feel well, sir," said one.

"Don't he?" replied the doctor. "Well, step up here, Dick, and let me see your tongue. No, I should be surprised if he did! the man's tongue is fit to frighten the French. Another fever."

"Ah, there," said Morgan, "that comed of sp'iling Bibles."

"That comed—as you call it—of being arrant asses," retorted the doctor, "and not having sense enough to know honest air from poison, and the dry land from a vile, pestiferous slough. I think it most probable—though, of course, it's only an opinion—that you'll all have the deuce to pay before you get that malaria out of your systems. Camp in a bog, would you? Silver, I'm surprised at you. You're less of a fool than many, take you all round; but you don't appear to me to have the rudiments of a notion of the rules of health."

"Well," he added, after he had dosed them round, and they had taken his prescriptions, with really laughable humility, more like charity school-children than blood-guilty mutineers and pirates—"well, that's done for to-day. And now I should wish to have a talk with that boy, please."

And he nodded his head in my direction carelessly.

George Merry was at the door, spitting and spluttering over some bad-tasted medicine; but at the first word of the doctor's proposal he swung round with a deep flush, and cried "No!" and swore.

Silver struck the barrel with his open hand.

"Si-lence!" he roared, and looked about him positively like a lion. "Doctor," he went on, in his usual tones, "I was a-thinking of that, knowing as how you had a fancy for the boy. We're all humbly grateful for your kindness, and, as you see, puts faith in you, and takes the drugs down like that much grog. And I take it, I've found a way as'll suit all. Hawkins, will you give me your word of honour as a young gentleman—for a young gentleman you are, although poor born— your word of honour not to slip your cable?"

I readily gave the pledge required.

"Then, doctor," said Silver, "you just step outside o' that stockade, and once you're there, I'll bring the boy down on the inside, and I reckon you can yarn through the spars. Good-day to you, sir, and all our dooties to the squire and Cap'n Smollett."

The explosion of disapproval, which nothing but Silver's black looks had restrained, broke out immediately the doctor had left the house. Silver was roundly accused of playing double—of trying to make a separate peace for himself—of sacrificing the interests of his accomplices and victims; and, in one word, of the identical, exact thing that he was doing. It seemed to me so obvious, in this case, that I could not imagine how he was to turn their anger. But he was twice the man the rest were; and his last night's victory had given him a huge preponderance on their minds. He called them all the fools and dolts you can imagine, said it was necessary I should talk to the doctor, fluttered the chart in their faces, asked them if they could afford to break the treaty the very day they were bound a-treasure-hunting.

"No, by thunder!" he cried, "it's us must break the treaty when the time comes; and till then I'll gammon that doctor, if I have to ile his boots with brandy."

And then he bade them get the fire lit, and stalked out upon his crutch, with his hand on my shoulder, leaving them in a disarray, and silenced by his volubility rather than convinced.

"Slow, lad, slow," he said. "They might round upon us in a twinkle of an eye, if we was seen to hurry."

Very deliberately, then, did we advance across the sand to where the doctor awaited us on the other side of the stockade, and as soon as we were within easy speaking distance, Silver stopped.

"You'll make a note of this here also, doctor," says he, "and the boy'll tell you how I saved his life, and were deposed for it, too, and you may lay to that. Doctor, when a man's steering as near the wind as me—playing chuck-farthing with the last breath of his body, like— you wouldn't think it too much, mayhap, to give him one good word? You'll please bear in mind it's not my life only now—it's that boy's into the bargain; and you'll speak me fair, doctor, and give me a bit o' hope to go on, for the sake of mercy."

Silver was a changed man, once he was out there and had his back to his friends and the block-house; his cheeks seemed to have fallen in, his voice trembled; never was a soul more dead in earnest.

"Why, John, you're not afraid?" asked Doctor Livesey.

"Doctor, I'm no coward; no, not I—not *so* much!" and he snapped his fingers. "If I was I wouldn't say it. But I'll own up fairly, I've the shakes upon me for the gallows. You're a good man and a true; I never seen a better man! And you'll not forget what I done good, not any more than you'll forget the bad, I know. And I step aside—see here— and leave you and Jim alone. And you'll put that down for me, too, for it's a long stretch, is that!"

So saying, he stepped back a little way, till he was out of earshot, and there sat down upon a tree-stump and began to whistle; spinning round now and again upon his seat so as to command a sight, some- times of me and the doctor, and sometimes of his unruly ruffians as they went to and fro in the sand, between the fire—which they were busy rekindling—and the house, from which they brought forth pork and bread to make the breakfast.

"So, Jim," said the doctor sadly, "here you are. As you have brewed, so shall you drink, my boy. Heaven knows, I cannot find it in my heart to blame you; but this much I will say, be it kind or unkind: when Captain Smollett was well, you dared not have gone off; and when he was ill, and couldn't help it, by George, it was downright cowardly!"

I will own that I here began to weep. "Doctor," I said, "you might spare me. I have blamed myself enough; my life's forfeit anyway, and I should have been dead by now, if Silver hadn't stood for me; and, doctor, believe this, I can die—and I dare say I deserve it—but what I fear is torture. If they come to torture me—"

"Jim," the doctor interrupted, and his voice was quite changed, "Jim, I can't have this. Whip over and we'll run for it."

"Doctor," said I, "I passed my word."

"I know, I know," he cried. "We can't help that, Jim, now. I'll take it on my shoulders, holus bolus, blame and shame, my boy; but stay here, I cannot let you. Jump! One jump, and you're out, and we'll run for it like antelopes."

"No," I replied, "you know right well you wouldn't do the thing yourself; neither you, nor squire, nor captain; and no more will I. Silver trusted me; I passed my word, and back I go. But, doctor, you did not let me finish. If they come to torture me, I might let slip a word of where the ship is; for I got the ship, part by luck and part by risking, and she lies in North Inlet, on the southern beach, and just above high water. At half tide she must be high and dry."

"The ship!" exclaimed the doctor.

Rapidly I described to him my adventures, and he heard me out in silence.

"There is a kind of fate in this," he observed, when I had done. "Every step, it's you that saves our lives; and do you suppose by any chance that we are going to let you lose yours? That would be a poor return, my boy. You found out the plot; you found Ben Gunn—the best deed that ever you did, or will do, though you live to ninety. Oh, by Jupiter, and talking of Ben Gunn! why, this is the mischief in person. Silver!" he cried, "Silver!—I'll give you a piece of advice," he continued, as the cook drew near again; "don't you be in any great hurry after that treasure."

"Why, sir, I do my possible, which that ain't," said Silver. "I can only, asking your pardon, save my life and the boy's by seeking for that treasure; and you may lay to that."

183

"Well, Silver," replied the doctor, "if that is so, I'll go one step further: look out for squalls when you find it."

"Sir," said Silver, "as between man and man, that's too much and too little. What you're after, why you left the block-house, why you given me that there chart, I don't know, now, do I? and yet I done your bidding with my eyes shut and never a word of hope! But no, this here's too much. If you won't tell me what you mean plain out, just say so, and I'll leave the helm."

"No," said the doctor, musingly, "I've no right to say more; it's not my secret, you see, Silver, or, I give you my word, I'd tell it you. But I'll go as far with you as I dare go, and a step beyond; for I'll have my wig sorted by the captain, or I'm mistaken! And, first, I'll give you a bit of hope: Silver, if we both get alive out of this wolf-trap, I'll do my best to save you, short of perjury."

Silver's face was radiant. "You couldn't say more, I'm sure, sir, not if you was my mother," he cried.

"Well, that's my first concession," added the doctor. "My second is a piece of advice: Keep the boy close beside you, and when you need help, halloo. I'm off to seek it for you, and that itself will show you if I speak at random. Good-bye, Jim."

And Dr Livesey shook hands with me through the stockade, nodded to Silver, and set off at a brisk pace into the wood.

Chapter XXXI

THE TREASURE HUNT—FLINT'S POINTER

"Jim," said Silver, when we were alone, "if I saved your life, you saved mine; and I'll not forget it. I seen the doctor waving you to run for it—with the tail of my eye, I did; and I seen you say no, as plain as hearing. Jim, that's one to you. This is the first glint of hope I had since the attack failed, and I owe it to you. And now, Jim, we're to go in for this here treasure-hunting, with sealed orders, too, and I don't like it; and you and me must stick close, back to back like, and we'll save our necks in spite o' fate and fortune."

Just then a man hailed us from the fire that breakfast was ready, and we were soon seated here and there about the sand over biscuit and fried junk. They had lit a fire fit to roast an ox; and it was now grown so hot that they could only approach it from the windward, and even there not without precaution. In the same wasteful spirit, they had cooked, I suppose, three times more than we could eat; and one of them, with an empty laugh, threw what was left into the fire, which blazed and roared again over this unusual fuel. I never in my life saw men so careless of the morrow; hand to mouth is the only word that can describe their way of doing; and what with wasted food and sleeping sentries, though they were bold enough for a brush and be done with it, I could see their entire unfitness for anything like a prolonged campaign.

Even Silver, eating away, with Captain Flint upon his shoulder, had not a word of blame for their recklessness. And this the more surprised me, for I thought he had never shown himself so cunning as he did then.

185

"Ay, mates," said he, "it's lucky you have Barbecue to think for you with this here head. I got what I wanted, I did. Sure enough, they have the ship. Where they have it, I don't know yet; but once we hit the treasure, we'll have to jump about and find out. And then, mates, us that has the boats, I reckon, has the upper hand."

Thus he kept running on, with his mouth full of the hot bacon: thus he restored their hope and confidence, and, I more than suspect, repaired his own at the same time.

"As for hostage," he continued, "that's his last talk, I guess, with them he loves so dear. I've got my piece o' news, and thanky to him for that; but it's over and done. I'll take him in a line when we go treasure-hunting, for we'll keep him like so much gold, in case of accidents, you mark, and in the meantime. Once we got the ship and treasure both, and off to sea like jolly companions, why, then, we'll talk Mr Hawkins over, we will, and we'll give him his share, to be sure, for all his kindness."

It was no wonder the men were in a good humour now. For my part, I was horribly cast down. Should the scheme he had now sketched prove feasible, Silver, already doubly a traitor, would not hesitate to adopt it. He had still a foot in either camp, and there was no doubt he would prefer wealth and freedom with the pirates to a bare escape from hanging, which was the best he had to hope on our side.

Nay, and even if things so fell out that he was forced to keep his faith with Dr Livesey, even then what danger lay before us! What a moment that would be when the suspicions of his followers turned to certainty, and he and I should have to fight for dear life—he, a cripple, and I, a boy—against five strong and active seamen!

Add to this double apprehension, the mystery that still hung over the behaviour of my friends; their unexplained desertion of the stockade; their inexplicable cession of the chart; or, harder still to understand, the doctor's last warning to Silver, "Look out for squalls when you find it;" and you will readily believe how little taste I found in my breakfast, and with how uneasy a heart I set forth behind my captors on the quest for treasure.

We made a curious figure, had anyone been there to see us; all in soiled sailor clothes, and all but me armed to the teeth. Silver had two guns slung about him—one before and one behind—besides the great cutlass at his waist, and a pistol in each pocket of his square-tailed coat. To complete his strange appearance, Captain Flint sat perched

"DARBY M'GRAW!" IT WAILED, "DARBY M'GRAW!"

upon his shoulder and gabbling odds and ends of purposeless sea-talk. I had a line about my waist, and followed obediently after the sea cook, who held the loose end of the rope, now in his free hand, now between his powerful teeth. For all the world, I was led like a dancing bear.

The other men were variously burthened; some carrying picks and shovels—for that had been the very first necessary they brought ashore from the *Hispaniola*—others laden with pork, bread, and brandy for the midday meal. All the stores, I observed, came from our stock; and I could see the truth of Silver's words the night before. Had he not struck a bargain with the doctor, he and his mutineers, deserted by the ship, must have been driven to subsist on clear water and the proceeds of their hunting. Water would have been little to their taste; a sailor is not usually a good shot; and, besides all that, when they were so short of eatables, it was not likely they would be very flush of powder.

Well, thus equipped, we all set out—even the fellow with the broken head, who should certainly have kept in shadow—and straggled, one after another, to the beach, where the two gigs awaited us. Even these bore trace of the drunken folly of the pirates, one in a broken thwart, and both in their muddied and unbaled condition. Both were to be carried along with us, for the sake of safety; and so, with our numbers divided between them, we set forth upon the bosom of the anchorage.

As we pulled over, there was some discussion on the chart. The red cross was, of course, far too large to be a guide; and the terms of the note on the back, as you will hear, admitted of some ambiguity. They ran, the reader may remember, thus:—

"Tall tree, Spy-glass Shoulder, bearing a point to the N. of N.N.E.
"Skeleton Island E.S.E. and by E.
"Ten feet."

A tall tree was thus the principal mark. Now, right before us, the anchorage was bounded by a plateau from two to three hundred feet high, adjoining on the north the sloping southern shoulder of the Spyglass, and rising again towards the south into the rough, cliffy eminence called the Mizzen-mast Hill. The top of the plateau was dotted thickly with pine-trees of varying height. Every here and there, one of a different species rose forty or fifty feet clear above its neighbours, and which of these was the particular "tall tree" of Captain Flint could only be decided on the spot, and by the readings of the compass.

Yet, although that was the case, every man on board the boats had picked a favourite of his own ere we were half-way over, Long John alone shrugging his shoulders and bidding them wait till they were there.

We pulled easily, by Silver's directions, not to weary the hands prematurely; and, after quite a long passage, landed at the mouth of the second river—that which runs down a woody cleft of the Spy-glass. Thence, bending to our left, we began to ascend the slope towards the plateau.

At the first outset, heavy, miry ground and a matted, marish vegetation greatly delayed our progress; but by little and little the hill began to steepen and become stony under foot, and the wood to change its character and to grow in a more open order. It was, indeed, a most pleasant portion of the island that we were now approaching. A heavy-scented broom and many flowering shrubs had almost taken the place of grass. Thickets of green nutmeg-trees were dotted here and there with the red columns and the broad shadow of the pines; and the first mingled their spice with the aroma of the others. The air, besides, was fresh and stirring, and this, under the sheer sunbeams, was a wonderful refreshment to our senses.

The party spread itself abroad, in a fan shape, shouting and leaping to and fro. About the centre, and a good way behind the rest, Silver and I followed—I tethered by my rope, he ploughing, with deep pants, among the sliding gravel. From time to time, indeed, I had to lend him a hand, or he must have missed his footing and fallen backward down the hill.

We had thus proceeded for about half a mile, and were approaching the brow of the plateau, when the man upon the farthest left began to cry aloud, as if in terror. Shout after shout came from him, and the others began to run in his direction.

"He can't 'a' found the treasure," said old Morgan, hurrying past us from the right, "for that's clean atop."

Indeed, as we found when we also reached the spot, it was something very different. At the foot of a pretty big pine, and involved in a green creeper, which had even partly lifted some of the smaller bones, a human skeleton lay, with a few shreds of clothing, on the ground. I believe a chill struck for a moment to every heart.

"He was a seaman," said George Merry, who, bolder than the rest, had gone up close, and was examining the rags of clothing. "Leastways, this is good sea-cloth."

"Ay, ay," said Silver, "like enough; you wouldn't look to find a bishop here, I reckon. But what sort of a way is that for bones to lie? 'Tain't in natur'."

Indeed, on a second glance, it seemed impossible to fancy that the body was in a natural position. But for some disarray (the work, perhaps, of the birds that had fed upon him, or of the slow-growing creeper that had gradually enveloped his remains) the man lay perfectly straight—his feet pointing in one direction, his hands, raised above his head like a diver's, pointing directly in the opposite.

"I've taken a notion into my old numskull," observed Silver. "Here's the compass; there's the tip-top p'int o' Skeleton Island, stickin' out like a tooth. Just take a bearing, will you, along the line of them bones."

It was done. The body pointed straight in the direction of the island, and the compass read duly E.S.E. and by E.

"I thought so," cried the cook; "this here is a p'inter. Right up there is our line for the Pole Star and the jolly dollars. But, by thunder! if it don't make me cold inside to think of Flint. This is one of *his* jokes, and no mistake. Him and these six was alone here; he killed 'em, every man; and this one he hauled here and laid down by compass, shiver my timbers! They're long bones, and the hair's been yellow. Ay, that would be Allardyce. You mind Allardyce, Tom Morgan?"

"Ay, ay," returned Morgan, "I mind him; he owed me money, he did, and took my knife ashore with him."

"Speaking of knives," said another, "why don't we find his'n lying round? Flint warn't the man to pick a seaman's pocket; and the birds, I guess, would leave it be."

"By the powers, and that's true!" cried Silver.

"There ain't a thing left here," said Merry, still feeling round among the bones, "not a copper doit nor a baccy-box. It don't look nat'ral to me."

"No, by gum, it don't," agreed Silver; "not nat'ral, nor not nice, says you. Great guns! messmates, but if Flint was living, this would be a hot spot for you and me. Six they were, and six are we; and bones is what they are now."

"I saw him dead with these here deadlights," said Morgan. "Billy took me in. There he laid, with penny-pieces on his eyes."

"Dead—ay, sure enough he's dead and gone below," said the fellow with the bandage; "but if ever sperrit walked, it would be Flint's. Dear heart, but he died bad, did Flint!"

"Ay, that he did," observed another; "now he raged, and now he hollered for the rum, and now he sang. 'Fifteen men' were his only song, mates; and I tell you true, I never rightly liked to hear it since. It was main hot, and the windy was open, and I hear that old song comin' out as clear as clear—and the death-haul on the man already."

"Come, come," said Silver, "stow this talk. He's dead, and he don't walk, that I know; leastways, he won't walk by day, and you may lay to that. Care killed a cat. Fetch ahead for the doubloons."

We started, certainly; but in spite of the hot sun and the staring daylight, the pirates no longer ran separate and shouting through the wood, but kept side by side and spoke with bated breath. The terror of the dead buccaneer had fallen on their spirits.

FOR ALL THE WORLD, I WAS LED LIKE A DANCING BEAR

CHAPTER XXXII

THE TREASURE HUNT—THE VOICE

AMONG THE TREES

Partly from the damping influence of this alarm, partly to rest Silver and the sick folk, the whole party sat down as soon as they had gained the brow of the ascent.

The plateau being somewhat tilted towards the west, this spot on which we had paused commanded a wide prospect on either hand. Before us, over the tree-tops, we beheld the Cape of the Woods fringed with surf; behind, we not only looked down upon the anchorage and Skeleton Island, but saw—clear across the spit and the eastern lowlands—a great field of open sea upon the east. Sheer above us rose the Spy-glass, here dotted with single pines, there black with precipices. There was no sound but that of the distant breakers, mounting from all round, and the chirp of countless insects in the brush. Not a man, not a sail upon the sea; the very largeness of the view increased the sense of solitude.

Silver, as he sat, took certain bearings with his compass.

"There are three 'tall trees,'" said he, "about in the right line from Skeleton Island. 'Spy-glass Shoulder,' I take it, means that lower p'int there. It's child's play to find the stuff now. I've half a mind to dine first."

"I don't feel sharp," growled Morgan. "Thinkin' o' Flint—I think it were—as 'as done me."

"Ah, well, my son, you praise your stars he's dead," said Silver.

"He were an ugly devil," cried a third pirate with a shudder; "that blue in the face, too!"

193

"That was how the rum took him," added Merry. "Blue! well, I reckon he was blue. That's a true word."

Ever since they had found the skeleton and got upon this train of thought, they had spoken lower and lower, and they had almost got to whispering by now, so that the sound of their talk hardly interrupted the silence of the wood. All of a sudden, out of the middle of the trees in front of us, a thin, high, trembling voice struck up the well-known air and words:—

> "*Fifteen men on the Dead Man's Chest—*
> *Yo-ho-ho, and a bottle of rum!*"

I never have seen men more dreadfully affected than the pirates. The colour went from their six faces like enchantment; some leaped to their feet, some clawed hold of others; Morgan grovelled on the ground.

"It's Flint, by—!" cried Merry.

The song had stopped as suddenly as it began—broken off, you would have said, in the middle of a note, as though someone had laid his hand upon the singer's mouth. Coming so far through the clear, sunny atmosphere among the green tree-tops, I thought it had sounded airily and sweetly; and the effect on my companions was the stranger.

"Come," said Silver, struggling with his ashen lips to get the word out, "this won't do. Stand by to go about. This is a rum start, and I can't name the voice: but it's someone skylarking—someone that's flesh and blood, and you may lay to that."

His courage had come back as he spoke, and some of the colour to his face along with it. Already the others had begun to lend an ear to this encouragement, and were coming a little to themselves, when the same voice broke out again—not this time singing, but in a faint distant hail, that echoed yet fainter among the clefts of the Spy-glass.

"Darby M'Graw," it wailed—for that is the word that best describes the sound—"Darby M'Graw! Darby M'Graw!" again and again and again; and then rising a little higher, and with an oath that I leave out, "Fetch aft the rum, Darby!"

The buccaneers remained rooted to the ground, their eyes starting from their heads. Long after the voice had died away, they still stared in silence, dreadfully, before them.

"That fixes it!" gasped one. "Let's go."

"They was his last words," moaned Morgan, "his last words above board."

Dick had his Bible out, and was praying volubly. He had been well brought up, had Dick, before he came to sea and fell among bad companions.

Still, Silver was unconquered. I could hear his teeth rattle in his head; but he had not yet surrendered.

"Nobody in this here island ever heard of Darby," he muttered: "not one but us that's here." And then, making a great effort, "Shipmates," he cried, "I'm here to get that stuff, and I'll not be beat by man nor devil. I never was feared of Flint in his life, and, by the powers, I'll face him dead. There's seven hundred thousand pound not a quarter of a mile from here. When did ever a gentleman o' fortune show his stern to that much dollars, for a boosy old seaman with a blue mug—and him dead, too?"

But there was no sign of re-awakening courage in his followers; rather, indeed, of growing terror at the irreverence of his words.

"Belay there, John!" said Merry. "Don't you cross a sperrit."

And the rest were all too terrified to reply. They would have run away severally had they dared; but fear kept them together, and kept them close by John, as if his daring helped them. He, on his part, had pretty well fought his weakness down.

"Sperrit? Well, maybe," he said. "But there's one thing not clear to me. There was an echo. Now, no man ever seen a sperrit with a shadow; well, then, what's he doing with an echo to him, I should like to know? That ain't in natur', surely?"

This argument seemed weak enough to me. But you can never tell what will affect the superstitious, and, to my wonder, George Merry was greatly relieved.

"Well, that's so," he said. "You've a head upon your shoulders, John, and no mistake. 'Bout ship, mates! This here crew is on a wrong tack, I do believe. And come to think on it, it was like Flint's voice, I grant you, but not just so clear-away like it, after all. It was liker somebody else's voice now—it was liker—"

"By the powers, Ben Gunn!" roared Silver.

"Ay, and so it were," cried Morgan, springing on his knees. "Ben Gunn it were!"

"It don't make much odds, do it, now?" asked Dick. "Ben Gunn's not here in the body, any more'n Flint."

But the older hands greeted this remark with scorn.

"Why, nobody minds Ben Gunn," cried Merry; "dead or alive, nobody minds him."

It was extraordinary how their spirits had returned, and bow the natural colour had revived in their faces. Soon they were chatting together, with intervals of listening; and not long after, hearing no further sound, they shouldered the tools and set forth again, Merry walking first with Silver's compass to keep them on the right line with Skeleton Island. He had said the truth; dead or alive, nobody minded Ben Gunn.

Dick alone still held his Bible, and looked around him as he went, with fearful glances; but he found no sympathy, and Silver even joked him on his precautions.

"I told you," said he—"I told you, you had sp'iled your Bible. If it ain't no good to swear by, what do you suppose a sperrit would give for it? Not that!" and he snapped his big fingers, halting a moment on his crutch.

But Dick was not to be comforted; indeed, it was soon plain to me that the lad was falling sick; hastened by heat, exhaustion, and the shock of his alarm, the fever, predicted by Doctor Livesey, was evidently growing swiftly higher.

It was fine open walking here, upon the summit; our way lay a little down-hill, for, as I have said, the plateau tilted towards the west. The pines, great and small, grew wide apart: and even between the clumps of nutmeg and azalea, wide open spaces baked in the hot sunshine. Striking, as we did, pretty near north-west across the island, we drew, on the one hand, ever nearer under the shoulders of the Spy-glass, and on the other, looked ever wider over that western bay where I had once tossed and trembled in the coracle.

The first of the tall trees was reached, and, by the bearing, proved the wrong one. So with the second. The third rose nearly two hundred feet into the air above a clump of underwood; a giant of a vegetable, with a red column as big as a cottage, and a wide shadow around in which company could have manœuvred. It was conspicuous far to sea both on the east and west, and might have been entered as a sailing mark upon the chart.

But it was not its size that now impressed my companions; it was the knowledge that seven hundred thousand pounds in gold lay somewhere buried below its spreading shadow. The thought of the money, as they drew nearer, swallowed up their previous terrors. Their eyes burned in their heads; their feet grew speedier and lighter; their whole soul was bound up in that fortune, that whole lifetime of extravagance and pleasure, that lay waiting there for each of them.

Silver hobbled, grunting, on his crutch; his nostrils stood out and quivered; he cursed like a madman when the flies settled on his hot and shiny countenance; he plucked furiously at the line that held me to him, and, from time to time, turned his eyes upon me with a deadly look. Certainly he took no pains to hide his thoughts; and certainly I read them like print. In the immediate nearness of the gold, all else had been forgotten; his promise and the doctor's warning were both things of the past; and I could not doubt that he hoped to seize upon the treasure, find and board the *Hispaniola* under cover of night, cut every honest throat about that island, and sail away as he had at first intended, laden with crimes and riches.

Shaken as I was with these alarms, it was hard for me to keep up with the rapid pace of the treasure-hunters. Now and again I stumbled; and it was then that Silver plucked so roughly at the rope and launched at me his murderous glances. Dick, who had dropped behind us, and now brought up the rear, was babbling to himself both prayers and curses, as his fever kept rising. This also added to my wretchedness; and, to crown all, I was haunted by the thought of the tragedy that had once been acted on that plateau, when that ungodly buccaneer with the blue face—he who died at Savannah, singing and shouting for drink—had there, with his own hand, cut down his six accomplices. This grove, that was now so peaceful, must then have rung with cries, I thought; and even with the thought I could believe I heard it ringing still.

We were now at the margin of the thicket.

"Huzza, mates, all together!" shouted Merry; and the foremost broke into a run.

And suddenly, not ten yards farther, we beheld them stop. A low cry arose. Silver doubled his pace, digging away with the foot of his crutch like one possessed; and next moment he and I had come also to a dead halt.

Before us was a great excavation, not very recent, for the sides had fallen in and grass had sprouted on the bottom. In this were the shaft of a pick broken in two and the boards of several packing-cases strewn around. On one of these I saw, branded with a hot iron, the name *Walrus*—the name of Flint's ship.

All was clear to probation. The *cache* had been found and rifled: the seven hundred thousand pounds were gone!

CHAPTER XXXIII

THE FALL OF A CHIEFTAIN

There never was such an overturn in this world. Each of these six men was as though he had been struck. But with Silver the blow passed almost instantly. Every thought of his soul had been set full-stretch, like a racer, on that money; well, he was brought up in a single second, dead; and he kept his head, found his temper, and changed his plan before the others had had time to realise the disappointment.

"Jim," he whispered, "take that, and stand by for trouble."

And he passed me a double-barrelled pistol.

At the same time he began quietly moving northward, and in a few steps had put the hollow between us two and the other five. Then he looked at me and nodded, as much as to say, "Here is a narrow corner," as, indeed, I thought it was. His looks were now quite friendly; and I was so revolted at these constant changes, that I could not forbear whispering, "So you've changed sides again."

There was no time left for him to answer in. The buccaneers, with oaths and cries, began to leap. one after another, into the pit, and to dig with their fingers, throwing the boards aside as they did so. Morgan found a piece of gold. He held it up with a perfect spout of oaths. It was a two-guinea piece, and it went from hand to hand among them for a quarter of a minute.

"Two guineas!" roared Merry, shaking it at Silver. "That's your seven hundred thousand pounds, is it? You're the man for bargains, ain't you? You're him that never bungled nothing, you wooden-headed lubber!"

"Dig away, boys," said Silver, with the coolest insolence; you'll find some pig-nuts and I shouldn't wonder."

"Pig-nuts!" repeated Merry, in a scream. "Mates, do you hear that? I tell you, now, that man there knew it all along. Look in the face of him, and you'll see it wrote there."

"Ah, Merry," remarked Silver, "standing for cap'n again? You're a pushing lad, to be sure."

But this time everyone was entirely in Merry's favour. They began to scramble out of the excavation, darting furious glances behind them. One thing I observed, which looked well for us: they all got out upon the opposite side from Silver.

Well, there we stood, two on one side, five on the other, the pit between us, and nobody screwed up high enough to offer the first blow. Silver never moved; he watched them, very upright on his crutch, and looked as cool as ever I saw him. He was brave, and no mistake.

At last, Merry seemed to think a speech might help matters.

"Mates," says he, "there's two of them alone there; one's the old cripple that brought us all here and blundered us down to this; the other's that cub that I mean to have the heart of. Now, mates—"

He was raising his arm and his voice, and plainly meant to lead a charge. But just then—crack! crack! crack!—three musket-shots flashed out of the thicket. Merry tumbled head foremost into the excavation; the man with the bandage spun round like a teetotum, and fell all his length upon his side, where he lay dead, but still twitching; and the other three turned and ran for it with all their might.

Before you could wink, Long John had fired two barrels of a pistol into the struggling Merry; and as the man rolled up his eyes at him in the last agony, "George," said he, "I reckon I settled you."

At the same moment the doctor, Gray, and Ben Gunn joined us, with smoking muskets, from among the nutmeg-trees.

"Forward!" cried the doctor. "Double quick, my lads. We must head 'em off the boats."

And we set off at a great pace, sometimes plunging through the bushes to the chest.

I tell you, but Silver was anxious to keep up with us. The work that man went through, leaping on his crutch till the muscles of his chest were fit to burst, was work no sound man ever equalled; and so thinks the doctor. As it was, he was already thirty yards behind us, and on the verge of strangling, when we reached the brow of the slope.

"Doctor," he hailed, "see there! no hurry!"

Sure enough there was no hurry. In a more open part of the plateau, we could see the three survivors still running in the same direction as they had started, right for Mizzen-mast Hill. We were already between them and the boats; and so we four sat down to breathe, while Long John, mopping his face, came slowly up with us.

"Thank ye kindly, doctor," says he. "You came in in about the nick, I guess, for me and Hawkins. And so it's you, Ben Gunn!" he added. "Well, you're a nice one, to be sure."

"I'm Ben Gunn, I am," replied the maroon, wriggling like an eel in his embarrassment. "And," he added, after a long pause, "how do, Mr Silver? Pretty well, I thank ye, says you."

"Ben, Ben," murmured Silver, "to think as you've done me!"

The doctor sent back Gray for one of the pickaxes, deserted, in their flight, by the mutineers; and then as we proceeded leisurely downhill to where the boats were lying, related, in a few words, what had taken place. It was a story that profoundly interested Silver; and Ben Gunn, the half-idiot maroon, was the hero from beginning to end.

Ben, in his long, lonely wanderings about the island, had found the skeleton—it was he that had rifled it; he had found the treasure; he had dug it up (it was the haft of his pickaxe that lay broken in the excavation); he had carried it on his back, in many weary journeys, from the foot of a tall pine to a cave he had on the two-pointed hill at the north-east angle of the island, and there it had lain stored in safety two months before the arrival of the *Hispaniola*.

When the doctor had wormed this secret from him, on the afternoon of the attack, and when, next morning, he saw the anchorage deserted, he had gone to Silver, given him the chart, which was now useless—given him the stores, for Ben Gunn's cave was well supplied with goats' meat salted by himself—given anything and everything to get a chance of moving in safety from the stockade to the two-pointed hill, there to be clear of malaria and keep a guard upon the money.

"As for you, Jim," he said, "it went against my heart, but I did what I thought best for those who had stood by their duty; and if you were not one of these, whose fault was it?"

That morning, finding that I was to be involved in the horrid disappointment he had prepared for the mutineers, he had run all the way to the cave, and, leaving squire to guard the captain, had taken

Gray and the maroon, and started, making the diagonal across the island, to be at hand beside the pine. Soon, however, he saw that our party had the start of him; and Ben Gunn, being fleet of foot, had been despatched in front to do his best alone. Then it had occurred to him to work upon the superstitions of his former shipmates; and he was so far successful that Gray and the doctor had come up and were already ambushed before the arrival of the treasure-hunters.

"Ah," said Silver, "it were fortunate for me that I had Hawkins here. You would have let old John be cut to bits, and never given it a thought, doctor."

"Not a thought," replied Doctor Livesey cheerily.

And by this time we had reached the gigs. The doctor, with the pickaxe, demolished one of them, and then we all got aboard the other and set out to go round by sea for North Inlet.

This was a run of eight or nine miles. Silver, though he was almost killed already with fatigue, was set to an oar, like the rest of us, and we were soon skimming swiftly over a smooth sea. Soon we passed out of the straits and doubled the south-east corner of the island, round which, four days ago, we had towed the *Hispaniola*.

As we passed the two-pointed hill, we could see the black mouth of Ben Gunn's cave, and a figure standing by it, leaning on a musket. It was the squire; and we waved a handkerchief and gave him three cheers, in which the voice of Silver joined as heartily as any.

Three miles farther, just inside the mouth of North Inlet, what should we meet but the *Hispaniola,* cruising by herself? The last flood had lifted her; and had there been much wind, or a strong tide current, as in the southern anchorage, we should never have found her more, or found her stranded beyond help. As it was, there was little amiss, beyond the wreck of the main-sail. Another anchor was got ready, and dropped in a fathom and a half of water. We all pulled round again to Rum Cove, the nearest point for Ben Gunn's treasure-house; and then Gray, single-handed, returned with the gig to the *Hispaniola,* where he was to pass the night on guard.

A gentle slope ran up from the beach to the entrance of the cave. At the top, the squire met us. To me he was cordial and kind, saying nothing of my escapade, either in the way of blame or praise. At Silver's polite salute he somewhat flushed.

"John Silver," he said, "you're a prodigious villain and impostor— a monstrous impostor, sir. I am told I am not to prosecute you. Well, then, I will not. But the dead men, sir, hang about your neck like mill-stones."

"Thank you kindly, sir," replied Long John, again saluting.

"I dare you to thank me!" cried the squire. "It is a gross dereliction of my duty. Stand back."

And thereupon we all entered the cave. It was a large, airy place, with a little spring and a pool of clear water, overhung with ferns. The floor was sand. Before a big fire lay Captain Smollett; and in a far corner, only duskily flickered over by the blaze, I beheld great heaps of coin and quadrilaterals built of bars of gold. That was Flint's treasure that we had come so far to seek, and that had cost already the lives of seventeen men from the *Hispaniola*. How many it had cost in the amassing, what blood and sorrow, what good ships scuttled on the deep, what brave men walking the plank blindfold, what shot of cannon, what shame and lies and cruelty—perhaps no man alive could tell. Yet there were still three upon that island—Silver, and old Morgan, and Ben Gunn—who had each taken his share in these crimes, as each had hoped in vain to share in the reward.

"Come in, Jim," said the captain. "You're a good boy in your line, Jim; but I don't think you and me'll go to sea again. You're too much of the born favourite for me. Is that you, John Silver? What brings you here, man?"

"Come back to my dooty, sir," returned Silver.

"Ah!" said the captain; and that was all he said.

What a supper I had of it that night, with all my friends around me; and what a meal it was, with Ben Gunn's salted goat, and some delicacies and a bottle of old wine from the *Hispaniola*. Never, I am sure, were people gayer or happier. And there was Silver, sitting back almost out of the firelight, but eating heartily, prompt to spring forward when anything was wanted, even joining quietly in our laughter—the same bland, polite, obsequious seaman of the voyage out.

Chapter XXXIV

AND LAST

The next morning we fell early to work for the transportation of this great mass of gold near a mile by land to the beach, and thence three miles by boat to the *Hispaniola*, was a considerable task for so small a number of workmen. The three fellows still abroad upon the island did not greatly trouble us; a single sentry on the shoulder of the hill was sufficient to ensure us against any sudden onslaught, and we thought, besides, they had had more than enough of fighting.

Therefore the work was pushed on briskly. Gray and Ben Gunn came and went with the boat, while the rest, during their absences, piled treasure on the beach. Two of the bars, slung in a rope's end, made a good load for a grown man—one that he was glad to walk slowly with. For my part, as I was not much use at carrying, I was kept busy all day in the cave, packing the minted money into bread-bags.

It was a strange collection, like Billy Bones's hoard for the diversity of coinage, but so much larger and so much more varied that I think I never had more pleasure than in sorting them. English, French, Spanish, Portuguese, Georges, and Louises, doubloons and double guineas and moidores and sequins, the pictures of all the kings of Europe for the last hundred years, strange Oriental pieces stamped with what looked like wisps of string or bits of spider's web, round pieces and square pieces, and pieces bored through the middle, as if to wear them round your neck—nearly every variety of money in the world must, I think, have found a place in that collection; and for

205

number, I am sure they were like autumn leaves, so that my back ached with stooping and my fingers with sorting them out.

Day after day this work went on; by every evening a fortune had been stowed aboard, but there was another fortune waiting for the morrow; and all this time we heard nothing of the three surviving mutineers.

At last—I think it was on the third night—the doctor and I were strolling on the shoulder of the hill where it overlooks the lowlands of the isle, when, from out the thick darkness below, the wind brought us a noise between shrieking and singing. It was only a snatch that reached our ears, followed by the former silence.

"Heaven forgive them," said the doctor; "'tis the mutineers!"

"All drunk, sir," struck in the voice of Silver from behind us.

Silver, I should say, was allowed his entire liberty, and, in spite of daily rebuffs, seemed to regard himself once more as quite a privileged and friendly dependant. Indeed, it was remarkable how well he bore these slights, and with what unwearying politeness he kept on trying to ingratiate himself with all. Yet, I think, none treated him better than a dog, unless it was Ben Gunn, who was still terribly afraid of his old quartermaster, or myself, who had really something to thank him for; although for that matter, I suppose, I had reason to think even worse of him than anybody else, for I had seen him meditating a fresh treachery upon the plateau. Accordingly, it was pretty gruffly that the doctor answered him.

"Drunk or raving," said he.

"Right you were, sir," replied Silver; "and precious little odds which, to you and me."

"I suppose you would hardly ask me to call you a humane man," returned the doctor with a sneer, "and so my feelings may surprise you, Master Silver. But if I were sure they were raving—as I am morally certain one, at least, of them is down with fever—I should leave this camp, and, at whatever risk to my own carcass, take them the assistance of my skill."

"Ask your pardon, sir, you would be very wrong," quoth Silver. "You would lose your precious life, and you may lay to that. I'm on your side now, hand and glove; and I shouldn't wish for to see the party weakened, let alone yourself, seeing as I know what I owes you. But these men down there, they couldn't keep their word—no, not supposing they wished to; and what's more, they couldn't believe as you could."

"No," said the doctor. "You're the man to keep your word—we know that."

Well, that was about the last news we had of the three pirates. Only once we heard a gun-shot a great way off, and supposed them to be hunting. A council was held, and it was decided that we must desert them on the island—to the huge glee, I must say, of Ben Gunn, and with the strong approval of Gray. We left a good stock of powder and shot, the bulk of the salt goat, a few medicines, and some other necessaries, tools, clothing, a spare sail, a fathom or two of rope, and, by the particular desire of the doctor, a handsome present of tobacco.

That was about our last doing on the island. Before that, we had got the treasure stowed, and had shipped enough water and the remainder of the goat meat, in case of any distress; and at last, one fine morning, we weighed anchor, which was about all that we could manage, and stood out of North Inlet, the same colours flying that the captain had flown and fought under at the palisade.

The three fellows must have been watching us closer than we thought for, as we soon had proved. For, coming through the narrows, we had to lie very near the southern point, and there we saw all three of them kneeling together on a spit of sand, with their arms raised in supplication. It went to all our hearts, I think, to leave them in that wretched state; but we could not risk another mutiny; and to take them home for the gibbet would have been a cruel sort of kindness. The doctor hailed them and told them of the stores we had left, and where they were to find them. But they continued to call us by name, and appeal to us, for God's sake, to be merciful, and not leave them to die in such a place.

At last, seeing the ship still bore on her course, and was now swiftly drawing out of earshot, one of them—I know not which it was—leapt to his feet with a hoarse cry, whipped his musket to his shoulder, and sent a shot whistling over Silver's head and through the main-sail.

After that, we kept under cover of the bulwarks, and when next I looked out they had disappeared from the spit, and the spit itself had almost melted out of sight in the growing distance. That was, at least, the end of that; and before noon, to my inexpressible joy, the highest rock of Treasure Island had sunk into the blue round of sea.

We were so short of men that everyone on board had to bear a hand—only the captain lying on a mattress in the stern and giving his orders; for, though greatly recovered, he was still in want of quiet.

We laid her head for the nearest port in Spanish America, for we could not risk the voyage home without fresh hands; and as it was, what with baffling winds and a couple of fresh gales, we were all worn out before we reached it.

It was just at sundown when we cast anchor in a most beautiful land-locked gulf, and were immediately surrounded by shore boats full of negroes, and Mexican Indians, and half-bloods, selling fruits and vegetables, and offering to dive for bits of money. The sight of so many good-humoured faces (especially the blacks), the taste of the tropical fruits, and, above all, the lights that began to shine in the town, made a most charming contrast to our dark and bloody sojourn on the island; and the doctor and the squire, taking me along with them, went ashore to pass the early part of the night. Here they met the captain of an English man-of-war, fell in talk with him, went on board his ship, and, in short, had so agreeable a time, that day was breaking when we came alongside the *Hispaniola*.

Ben Gunn was on deck alone, and, as soon as we came on board, he began, with wonderful contortions, to make us a confession. Silver was gone. The maroon had connived at his escape in a shore boat some hours ago, and he now assured us he had only done so to preserve our lives, which would certainly have been forfeit if "that man with the one leg had stayed aboard." But this was not all. The sea cook had not gone empty-handed. He had cut through a bulkhead unobserved, and had removed one of the sacks of coin, worth, perhaps, three or four hundred guineas, to help him on his further wanderings.

I think we were all pleased to be so cheaply quit of him.

Well, to make a long story short, we got a few hands on board, made a good cruise home, and the *Hispaniola* reached Bristol just as Mr Blandly was beginning to think of fitting out her consort. Five men only of those who had sailed returned with her. "Drink and the devil had done for the rest," with a vengeance; although, to be sure, we were not quite in so bad a case as that other ship they sang about:

> *"With one man of her crew alive,*
> *What put to sea with seventy-five."*

All of us had an ample share of the treasure, and used it wisely or foolishly, according to our natures. Captain Smollett is now retired from the sea. Gray not only saved his money, but, being suddenly smit with the desire to rise, also studied his profession; and he is now mate and part owner of a fine full-rigged ship; married besides, and the father of a family. As for Ben Gunn, he got a thousand pounds, which he spent or lost in three weeks, or, to be more exact, in nineteen days, for he was back begging on the twentieth. Then he was given a lodge to keep, exactly as he had feared upon the island; and he still lives, a great favourite, though something of a butt, with the country boys, and a notable singer in church on Sundays and Saints' Days.

Of Silver we have heard no more. That formidable seafaring man with one leg has at last gone clean out of my life; but I dare say he met his old negress, and perhaps still lives in comfort with her and Captain Flint. It is to be hoped so, I suppose, for his chances of comfort in another world are very small.

The bar silver and the arms still lie, for all that I know, where Flint buried them; and certainly they shall lie there for me. Oxen and wain-ropes would not bring me back again to that accursed island; and the worst dreams that ever I have are when I hear the surf booming about its coasts, or start upright in bed, with the sharp voice of Captain Flint still ringing in my ears: "Pieces of eight! pieces of eight!"

THE END

The Lives of Muhammad

The Lives of Muhammad

Kecia Ali

HARVARD UNIVERSITY PRESS
Cambridge, Massachusetts
London, England
2014

Copyright © 2014 by the President and Fellows of Harvard College
All rights reserved
Printed in the United States of America
First printing

Library of Congress Cataloging-in-Publication Data
Ali, Kecia.
    The lives of Muhammad / Kecia Ali.
        p. cm.
    Includes bibliographical references and index.
    ISBN 978-0-674-05060-0 (alk. paper)
        1. Muhammad, Prophet, –632—Biography—History and criticism.
    I. Title.

        BP75.3.A454 2014
        297.6'3092—dc23   2014009174

This book is dedicated to my children Saadia and Tariq, and to the memory of their sister Shaira (1996–2012). The standard biographies of Muhammad recount that seven of his eight children died during his lifetime. None of the miracles traditional sources ascribe to him impresses me more than his having survived such loss.

Contents

Chronology

*Conventional dating (approximate) of key events in
Muhammad's biography:*

570	Muhammad's birth
580s	Journey to Syria with his uncle Abu Talib
595	Marriage to Khadija
610	Qur'anic revelation begins
615	Some followers seek refuge in Abyssinia
619	Deaths of Khadija and Abu Talib
621	Night Journey and Ascension
622	Migration to Medina
624	Battle of Badr
625	Battle of Uhud
627	Siege of Medina and retaliation against the Banu Qurayza
630	Conquest of Mecca
632	Muhammad's death

Introduction

For a man who lived fourteen hundred years ago, Muhammad has been in the news a lot lately. From the 2005–2006 Danish cartoon debacle to the 2012 uproar over the *Innocence of Muslims* viral video, media coverage has often explained Muslim outrage by referencing long-standing prohibitions on the depiction of the Prophet and sensitivity to any insult directed at him. By the time this book appears there may have been another flash-in-the-pan incident, with these same tired explanations proffered alongside a portrait of irrational and fanatical Muslim rage, contrasted with a rational, pluralist, democratic West.

Rather than plunge into these recent controversies, which reinforce an unpersuasive clash of civilizations rhetoric, this book approaches Muhammad as he has been portrayed over the centuries. It is a book not about the life of Muhammad but about the ways in which his life has been told.

Biographies of the foundational figures of world religions are inherently controversial. The faithful prefer one biography, those outside the fold offer competing accounts, and experts often insist on other versions based on prevailing scholarly views. Muhammad,

alternately revered and reviled, has been the subject of hundreds if not thousands of biographies since his death in the seventh century.

Far from being uniform or unchanging, both non-Muslim and Muslim views of Muhammad have been diverse, multifaceted, and subject to dramatic changes over the centuries. This is widely known. Less well known is that since the nineteenth century they have become increasingly interdependent. In the twenty-first century, it makes no sense to speak of Muslim views of Muhammad in opposition to Western or Christian views. Instead, the images of Muhammad that contemporary Muslims hold fervently and defend passionately arose in tandem and in tension with western European and North American intellectuals' accounts of his life. At the same time, Muslim sensibilities and beliefs have affected the way many non-Muslim authors write his life. This book focuses on these interconnections, the circuitous routes that ideas about Muhammad have taken as they have circulated, and how these ideas have been shaped by shifting attitudes about human achievement, the nature and place of religion, and marriage and sexuality.

Interaction itself is nothing new. Muslims have always adopted and adapted material from their environments. Civilizational boundaries have always been porous, and were certainly so during the first two centuries of Islam's existence when the first accounts of Muhammad were written. The rapid evolution of his biography during the seventh and eighth centuries—shifting from biblical to Arabian motifs, merging the human and the heroic, engaging in contentious negotiations over identity and legacy—has its counterpart in the last two hundred years. Syriac Christian polemics against Islam motivated early refinements in Muhammad's biography.[1] Colonial-era missionizing by western European Christians

had a similar effect. There is a striking parallel between the major and disruptive transformations wrought by the advent of Islam in late antiquity and the coming of European colonialism to Muslim-majority societies in Asia and Africa. Specialized scholars are working hard to discover what sort of biography of Muhammad and knowledge of Islam one can retrieve from its first two centuries. *The Lives of Muhammad* describes an equally massive set of shifts in the last two centuries.

Just as boundaries between traditions have always been fluid, so traditions have always been internally heterogeneous. The nature of prophecy, the status of miracles, and—in a more mundane vein—the roles of those close to Muhammad are perennial issues in Muslim thought. These are not just matters of disagreement between insiders and outsiders, but litmus tests that raise the question of who is to be considered an insider and what is to count as tradition. In the modern era, European and American accounts and ideas are pressed into service for intra-Muslim debates. Understanding the multiple, sometimes contradictory, accounts of Muhammad's life requires close attention to the ways in which writers read and draw on their predecessors and antagonists: differing from them, depending on them, appropriating and repurposing their materials—at times narrowly imitative, in other moments strikingly innovative, in what Virginia Burrus, a historian of early Christianity, has called "writerly acts of textual recycling."[2]

A book like this requires authorial choices if it is not to run, as medieval Muslim histories typically did, to dozens of volumes. Some decisions are large, such as what to omit. I have chosen, among other things, Persian poetry, the Danish cartoons—in fact, any and all visual depictions—and whole swathes of the globe, including sub-Saharan Africa and Southeast Asia.[3] Others are

smaller, such as how to render foreign words and names, including that of the prophet. Earlier English-language authors generally preferred the French-inflected *Mahomet* but also wrote *Machomed, Mohamed, Mohammad, Muhammed,* and other variants, with little regard for consistency. *Muhammad* is now the usual English spelling, and I use it throughout except in quotations. Where I translate from modern French texts, in which *Mahomet* is standard, I use *Muhammad* to avoid accidentally imparting an archaic flavor. (One Indian biographer replaced *Mahomet* with *Muhammad* when quoting an earlier British work, "since the word Mahomet is derogatory.")[4] Texts also spell the names of people close to Muhammad in myriad ways. In quoting sources, I keep original spellings unless doing so seems likely to confuse readers. Otherwise, I use simplified versions of recurring names (for example, Khadija, Ali, Aisha, Abu Bakr). I usually skip the honorifics and blessings Muslim authors invoke at every mention of Muhammad and other prophets, and Muhammad's wives, close relatives, and associates. One becomes inured to these formulae when reading Arabic or devotional texts, but they distract those unaccustomed. Yet since their presence, especially in texts in European languages, tells about the intended audience for a work, I include them when it seems relevant.

I mostly dispense with diacritics in the body of the book, though quotes, notes, and bibliography retain full transliteration.

I draw primarily from English, Arabic, and French sources, occasionally dipping into works in other languages. I rely on published translations when appropriate; other translations are mine. (Where the nuances of the original language seem particularly relevant, I excerpt the key portion in the endnotes.) I do not read Persian, Turkish, or Urdu (or Dutch, Danish, or Latin) and am thus, like

many before me, at the mercy of translators when I consult texts composed in those languages. Translations themselves have been of major importance in the production and dissemination of knowledge and ideas about Muhammad, reshaping works in revealing ways. I discuss such changes, too, as one more way in which Muhammad's *Lives* proliferate, entering new spaces, reaching new audiences, and contributing to the voluminous literature about a man variously known as the Messenger of God, the Arabian impostor, an arch-heretic, an antichrist, a false prophet, the founder of Islam, Mahound, God's beloved, a hero, a Great Man, and—in the modern era—simply Muhammad.

The Historical Muhammad

The conventional narrative of Muhammad's life goes something like this:

> Muhammad was born in Mecca in 570 CE to a father, Abdullah, from a poor but noble background. He belonged to the Quraysh tribe. Abdullah died while Muhammad was still in the womb of his mother, Amina. She in turn died when Muhammad was about six. He was taken in by his grandfather Abd al-Muttalib and, after the old man's death, by his paternal uncle, Abu Talib, who raised him with his own sons. These cousins included Ali, to whom Muhammad grew close. Once grown to young manhood, Muhammad accepted employment on a trade caravan to Syria for a wealthy older widow, Khadija. The caravan prospered; on his return to Mecca, she proposed to him. He was twenty-five and she was forty. They married and were, by all accounts, happy. Muhammad took no other wife. They had two or three sons, who died in infancy, and four daughters. He also freed and adopted a male slave named Zayd, whom Khadija had given him.

After some years of married life, Muhammad took to meditating in a cave near Mecca. When he was forty, in 610, he had an experience during one such retreat: Muslim accounts say that an angel visited him and ordered him to recite what became the first verses of the Qur'an. He sought solace and reassurance from Khadija. Once convinced that he was receiving revelations and not going mad, in part through confirmation from a local Christian, he began to spread the message slowly. Its key points were the oneness of God—a rejection of Mecca's rampant polytheism—and the coming of a day of reckoning when all people would be held accountable for their deeds. His preaching, with its egalitarian undercurrents, attracted converts among the disadvantaged and hostility from local elites, in part because his nascent religion threatened the economy, which depended on pilgrims visiting the Kaaba, a bastion of idolatry.

Hostility turned to persecution after the deaths in 619 of both Khadija and Abu Talib, who had protected him. He remarried—Sawda, a widow, and Aisha, the young daughter of his close friend and follower Abu Bakr. The latter marriage was not consummated until after his flight, in 622, to Medina, accompanied by his family and followers. In Medina, Muhammad led the community politically as well as religiously. His years in Medina were turbulent, with periodic flare-ups of trouble from insincere converts to Islam, alternating cooperation and bloody conflict with local Jewish tribes, and periodic raids and pitched battles with Meccan opponents. He married several more times, including his (adoptive) son Zayd's ex-wife Zaynab. He captured Mecca in 630, encountering little resistance. He died in Medina two years later, Islam already dominating much of the Arabian Peninsula.

Today, most biographies—whether in Arabic or English, whether by Muslims or non-Muslims—cleave to this outline, providing more or less detail as the genre demands.[1] Wikipedia follows this general order. So do newspaper reporters and textbook writers and documentary filmmakers and authors of popular biographies. Hostile biographers weave a tapestry of improper actions around this weft, while pious accounts supplement it with evidence for Muhammad's prophethood and the authenticity of the revelation entrusted to him by God. But important differences in tone notwithstanding, polemicists and apologists and journalists and many scholars follow its contours.

This ubiquitous narrative is relatively recent, though. Most of its particulars can be found in Muslim accounts dating back to the eighth century, but the arrangement of these snippets into a birth-through-death narrative, which pauses at marriages, battles, and revelation, only became standard a century or two ago. Before that, Muslim and Christian accounts differed dramatically, not only on the question of whether Muhammad was a true prophet but in terms of what information was relevant, how it should be interpreted, and what weight—if any—should be given to alternate accounts. Medieval European polemics commingled "information from Muslim sources and defamatory legend."[2] Fact and fabrication coexisted happily, in proportions that varied from place to place, time to time, and author to author. Some "pseudo-historical" accounts aimed at accuracy as part of a broader project of refuting Muslim doctrine. "Literary" presentations of Muslims and Muhammad served different purposes.[3] None was concerned with presenting a full narrative of his life.

Muslim accounts likewise varied, some telling an encyclopedic but roughly chronological tale, others selective, thematic, and devo-

tional. All mixed miraculous events with daily interactions with family, followers, and foes.⁴ These tales elevated Muhammad's stature. They also exalted particular factions, promoted distinctive theological positions, and even served as a bulwark against Christian and Jewish apologetics. The range of concerns manifested in most works was broad, but they did not revolve around historical accuracy or source reliability, nor did most explicitly engage with anti-Muslim propaganda.

This tailoring of accounts for various audiences should not be surprising. Stories always serve purposes. Narrative, writes Christian Smith, "arranges human actions and events into organized wholes in a way that bestows meaning on the actions and events by specifying their interactive or cause-and-effect reactions to the whole." What Smith says about narrative in general applies to biography in particular. By placing the events of Muhammad's life "in a single, interrelated account," biographers "always have a point, are always about the explanation and meaning of events and actions in human life."⁵ The stories told about Muhammad's life have served a variety of purposes. At some point, however, the story itself— and its component parts—came to be called into question.

The Early Sources

Well into the twentieth century, scholars proceeded as if, in Ernest Renan's infamous phrase, Muhammad was "born in the full light of history."⁶ Orientalists confidently claimed to distinguish a factual biographical core from the overlay of legend or the underpinning of political-sectarian bias.⁷ Alford Welch pronounced the Qur'an "utterly reliable as a historical source, if it is properly interpreted," and drew from it a portrait of Muhammad's self-understanding.⁸ But in

recent decades, scholars have renewed their scrutiny of early Muslim history and turned a more skeptical lens on the textual record. The historian F. E. Peters has concluded that unlike scholarship on the historical Jesus, the "quest of the historical Muhammad" is unlikely to yield many certainties, because so little can be known for certain about the Arabian Peninsula of that era. Whereas the big wins of Jesus scholarship have to do with context, this is precisely what is missing from the sources for Muhammad's life.[9] Contemporaneous Arab sources are scanty, non-Arab sources are polemical, and Muslim sources are late and possibly untrustworthy. All attempts to radically rewrite the history of Islam face an uphill battle.

This, of course, has not stopped scholars from trying. Although the sanguine version of Muhammad's life story—an orphan of noble lineage challenging his tribe and the powers that be to proclaim God's oneness in an idolatrous wilderness—is widely accepted, there are reasons to question its accuracy. To begin with, Muhammad, "the praised one," sounds more like a title than a personal name.[10] And in an Arabia typically thought to have been suffused by paganism, it is odd that Muhammad's parents bore monotheist names: Abdullah means "servant of God" and Amina means "faithful one." One hypothesis, which requires only minor adjustments to the standard account, is that biographers whitewashed Muhammad's life to remove any pagan stain. And, indeed, the Muslim tradition preserves occasional traces of a Muhammad, who, before donning the mantle of prophet, worshipped in the manner of his people.[11] An isolated anecdote suggests that he once ate meat sacrificed to Mecca's idols.[12] Of course, most versions of the story tell precisely the opposite tale: even before his experience of revelation, he abstained from idolatry-tainted sacrifices.

Whether or not Muhammad ate the meat makes a great deal of difference to claims about his religious purity, but both variants reinforce the conventional view of Mecca as a hotbed of idolatry.

Other scholars, though, question this too, upending the standard narrative entirely. In 1977, Patricia Crone and Michael Cook published *Hagarism*, which, refusing to rely at all on Islamic sources, questioned the basic outlines of early Muslim history. Many of *Hagarism*'s suppositions have been convincingly refuted, and others more convincingly argued, but the basic questions it posed remain open: What can we really know about Muhammad, and how can we know it?[13] Did Muhammad exist? As to the latter question, though it is asked in the title of a new book by polemicist Robert Spencer, the answer, according to self-described "infidel" skeptic Cook, is an emphatic yes.[14] Even setting Muslim sources aside, early Greek and Syriac sources give sufficient evidence to remove "any doubts as to whether Muhammad was a real person."[15] Yet these same sources—themselves polemical—raise many other questions about Islam's early history. Scholars' theories are frequently incompatible. For instance, Gerald Hawting has argued that the Qur'an's references to idol worship and associating partners with God should be understood as intra-monotheistic polemic and not a description of an actual pagan environment.[16] Speculation of this sort understandably raises hackles.

Without seeking to discard the entire chronology and geography of early Islam, the historian Fred Donner argues that Muhammad's preaching was both apocalyptic and ecumenical, a movement of "believers" rather than "brand-name" Muslims.[17] Donner's view dovetails with other scholarship that sets Islam in a monotheistic context straddling the Red Sea.[18] He argues that Muhammad's community only later became a separate Arabo-centric

religion—capital *I* Islam, rather than *islam,* the ongoing human phenomenon of submission to God. At stake in these debates are not just particular biographical details but the validity of Islam as a religion and the viability of early Islamic history as an academic specialization.

Even among specialists who accept that the early Muslim sources have their own complex agendas, debate rages about how or, indeed, if one can use them for a reliable account of Muhammad's life.[19] There is a stalemate in the field.[20] Some hold that traditionally transmitted texts are tissue of fabrications, mere "salvation history."[21] Repetition, no matter how frequent, does not amount to corroboration. Others—though not accepting faith claims about the literal truth of these accounts, or even necessarily agreeing with the conventional story—remain optimistic about the prospect of retrieving an essential historical nucleus to Muhammad's biography from extant or reconstructed sources.[22] One specialist asserts that "we should be able to reconstruct without fanfare an outline of Muḥammad's life that can withstand all but the most extreme scholarly criticism."[23] Writing for a general audience, another remarks, "If we were to restrict ourselves entirely to the undisputed facts of Muhammad's biography, we would run out of information after only a few pages."[24] This seems overly strict to him, and he proceeds to write an entire book; others, however, doubt one could fill even those few pages with indisputable information.

Two recent studies centering on Muhammad's life illustrate the major challenges faced by revisionist projects. One centers on Muhammad's death date; the other, his sonlessness. In *The Death of a Prophet: The End of Muhammad's Life and the Beginnings of Islam,* Stephen Shoemaker, a historian of early Christianity, revisits early Arabic and non-Arabic sources to argue that Muhammad

may have lived through the conquest of Jerusalem in 634. When that conquest failed to bring about the large-scale conversion of its Christian and Jewish populace, the narrative of his life was rewritten to make Muhammad an Arabian prophet and to place his death before the conquest.[25] Like Donner, Shoemaker suggests that "during the century that elapsed between the end of Muhammad's life and the first recoverable narrative of Islamic origins," there was a "shift from an immanent eschatological belief focused on Jerusalem to . . . a sacred geography centered on the Hijāz."[26] (The Hijaz is the region of western Arabia encompassing Mecca and Medina.) In a different vein, scholar of early Islam David Powers argues that the doctrine of the finality of Muhammad's prophethood developed over a period of approximately fifty years following the Prophet's death.[27] After marrying, Muhammad had reportedly adopted a grown man named Zayd, making him the Prophet's sole male heir, his biological sons having reportedly died in infancy. Powers argues that Zayd's new status posed a challenge on two fronts: first, the issue of political succession, and second, the emerging doctrine of the finality of prophecy. Zayd would have arguably had a stronger claim to the caliphate than either Abu Bakr or Ali; more importantly, he would have been a prophet—compromising the doctrine that Muhammad was the last prophet. Powers argues that believers formulated two stories that, taken together, remove both challenges. One was the story of Muhammad's infatuation with, and eventual marriage to, Zayd's (ex-)wife Zaynab. Before marrying his (former) daughter-in-law, the Prophet repudiated Zayd, in accordance with a new Qur'anic passage declaring that "Muhammad is not the father of any of your men." The other story, that Muhammad appointed Zayd commander of a military expedition

and sent him to certain death—and martyrdom—on a battlefield in southern Jordan, served to establish that Zayd predeceased the Prophet. Scholarly reaction to the books by Donner, Shoemaker, and Powers, like those of other scholars of early Islam, has been mixed, alternately appreciative and deeply critical.

For all their erudition, these scholarly squabbles have had little effect on how Muhammad's story is told and retold. This is so even though modern accounts of Muhammad's life by Muslims and non-Muslims alike claim to rely on historical sources, and debates over the reliability of early sources permeate even nonspecialist engagement with writings about Islam. To wit: an online reader review of a general-audience book, *The Future of Islam*, criticized the author, Middle East studies scholar John Esposito, for omitting discussion of the earliest extant Muslim biographical account (by Ibn Ishaq), which, alongside his "quite laudable" qualities, "reveals Muhammad as a man that slaughtered captives, robbed caravans, sold women and children into slavery," and performed a litany of other abuses. Another reviewer replies that Ibn Ishaq's biography may say these things but the accusations are "unwarranted and baseless" because a "matured and discerning" reader would not accept its claims at "face value." Not only was it written at least a century and a half after Muhammad lived, but in that era, it was typical for facts to be presented "in [a] highly emotional, embellished, fanatacised [*sic*] and exaggerated manner, primarily to appeal to the emotions of the listeners rather than to leaving hard historical records for posterity."[28] The reviewers' opposing stances on one source's reliability result in their divergent assessment of Muhammad's character, but both agree that one derives knowledge of Muhammad from early texts, properly read.

The reviews share, too, the unspoken assumption that the present and future of Islam cannot be understood apart from its origins, which are inextricable from Muhammad's life. Thus, debates about Muslim origins form an inescapable backdrop for the modern Muhammad, whose biographers, Muslim and non-Muslim alike, portray a figure of human rather than cosmic import. How did we arrive at the common version of his life we have now? When and how did the Muslim and non-Muslim accounts become impossible to disentangle—indeed, in some cases impossible to distinguish?[29] To begin to answer such questions, we must address the sources themselves.

In his history of Western life writing, Nigel Hamilton informs readers that Islam is "a religion that eschewed individual life depiction as insulting to the majesty of Allah."[30] By employing the Arabic name for God and avoiding the simple possessive—"the majesty of Allah" rather than "God's majesty"—Hamilton conjures alien-ness and archaism. *We*, like our classical Mediterranean forebears, value individual lives; *they* single out only the deity to set apart from the mass of interchangeable humanity.

As it happens, Hamilton is flat-out wrong. Muslims have a voluminous biographical literature. Indeed, in one scholar's estimate, "No premodern civilization has ever produced so many biographies or biographical sketches of its men and women."[31] Biographical dictionaries, which the historian Hamilton Gibb calls "a wholly indigenous creation of the creation of the Islamic Community," assemble notices for groups of people.[32] The earliest surviving collection is the *Tabaqat* (Generations) of Ibn Sa'd (d. 845).[33] In addition to its biography of the Prophet, it has entries for Muhammad's wives, relatives, and Companions—those Muslims who had contact with him during his life.[34] Its entries, "arranged

more or less by religious importance,"[35] give genealogies and tell how people met the Prophet and when they became Muslim, in addition to other noteworthy facts. Later collections, of which there are many, focus on other groups: scholars of a particular city or intellectual subfield, notables of various types, or members of Sufi orders; each of these works contains hundreds or thousands of entries. Apart from these compendia, hagiographical works laud individuals, including founders of legal schools and local saints, or "friends of God." Rulers merited their own fawning biographies. Thousands upon thousands of pages depict lives singly and in aggregate. There are even medieval autobiographies.[36]

The Prophet stands at the center of these forms of life writing, often explicitly, otherwise implicitly. He is the paradigm of sanctity, the exemplar of manhood, the paragon of leadership, the model of devotion. His example is further fleshed out in the *sira* literature. The first such mostly continuous narrative is the "arabesque biography"[37] by Ibn Ishaq (d. 767), who lived a century before Ibn Saʻd. It was not a life story in the conventional sense. Its first book began with creation and the long lineage of biblical prophets, stretching back to God's first deputy on earth, Adam. Ibn Ishaq presented Muhammad as the culmination of that legacy, "plac[ing] Muhammad in the context of the history of the salvation of the world."[38] As Gordon Newby, a historian of religion, summarizes, "The form was universal history; the content was a mixture of Jewish Haggadah, Arab legend, and Christian martyrology; and the effect was hagiography and prophetology."[39] Ibn Ishaq's work survives primarily in a ninth-century epitome by Ibn Hisham (d. ca. 833). He viewed the entire first book as largely irrelevant and, more importantly, compromised by its extensive reliance on Jewish and Christian sources; thus, he cut it.[40] Ibn Hisham, like many

later biographers, did not discard these models or stories altogether but emphasized authentically Arabian contexts, and specifically Islamic theological and political rationales.[41] This work in turn was very successful; one scholar observes, "In the edition of Ibn Hisham, Ibn Isḥāq's biography of Muhammad has acquired almost the status of a sacred book all over the world of Islam."[42] Yet it was not without its detractors, and the veracity of some of its stories was debated well before an Amazon.com reviewer took it on: "Muslim regard for his biography has never risen to the level of canonicity."[43]

The question of how to refer to the text has given scholars pause. Scottish Orientalist and Bengal Civil Service official William Muir referred to the work as *Hishâmi;* Michael Edwardes, working from the handwritten translation of a Hungarian-born, India-based scholar, completed in 1898 and given to the Royal Asiatic Society, refers to it simply as "Ibn Ishaq's *Life.*" He cut the text substantially, removing the poetry that abounded in the original and providing occasional connective paragraphs; a handsomely bound version appeared in 1964 from London's Folio Society.[44] Alfred Guillaume, in his 1955 English translation, attempted to segregate the two men's words, exiling Ibn Hisham's additions to the end of the work and restoring some of what he had excised by ferreting out portions preserved by other authors.[45] For better or worse, the text as it has circulated for over a millennium is an amalgam; I occasionally have recourse to the cumbersome designation Ibn Ishaq/Ibn Hisham but, where possible, follow the attribution in the Arabic text as to what content belongs to which man.

Roughly contemporaneous with this reconstituted biography are the "expeditionary" writings or "war memoirs" of the historian Muhammad ibn Umar al-Waqidi (d. ca. 822), for whom Ibn Sa'd

served as scribe.[46] These recount Muhammad's military ventures, including minor skirmishes and major battles with Meccan opponents, and a protracted siege ending in brutal reprisal against a Jewish tribe.[47] Not exactly a biography, Waqidi's *Book of Campaigns* is full of stories about Muhammad, his Companions, and their neighbors and antagonists. Bernard Lewis describes writings of this type as "subjective and episodic, presenting a series of heroic figures and incidents without concern for chronology, sequence, or consistency—in a word, saga rather than history."[48] Its recent English translator describes it as "a work designed to show the role of Muhammad as the chosen messenger of God whose work led to the fulfillment of the will of God in establishing his community of Islam. It portrays . . . his image as a prophet and his status as a statesman."[49] If Ibn Ishaq had taken biblical motifs and themes as his model, Waqidi "works within typical models of story-telling devoted to continuing and enhancing cultural notions of heroes and legends."[50] Arab intellectual historian Tarif Khalidi's comment about other biographical works applies to Waqidi: the agglomerating impulse records "thousands of . . . men and women whose life stories were intertwined with Muhammad's own. . . . It is as if some early Christian Gospel writer had decided to fill out the Sermon on the Mount and the feeding of the five thousand with the names and life stories of every single one of those who were present, together with some account, long or short, of their life and subsequent fate."[51]

Muhammad through the Centuries

Although these early sources, along with one or two slightly later histories, provide a canon around which contemporary controver-

sies center—even among competing online reviewers—and which contemporary writers draw from, Muslim writing about the Prophet flowered bountifully through the centuries. Ibn Hisham and the rest were certainly known to scholars, but they did not determine or constrain the many and varied accounts of Muhammad's life and person, nor did they directly influence most lay Muslims. Muhammad's role as intercessor for Muslims on the day of judgment and his status as "the original light in creation," God's beloved, and the "perfect mirror of Divine Beauty," among similar attributes, "were far better known to the medieval Muslims than the historical facts of the Prophet's life."[52]

Though the facts of Muhammad's life may not have been the most important things to be known about him, some scholars pursued biography or *sira* seriously. In his *Images of Muhammad*, Khalidi divides Muslim biographies of the Prophet into three stages. First, in the late eighth through the early tenth centuries, there was the "*Sira* of primitive devotion," comprehensive in its impulse to preserve everything, including even "stories or anecdotes that may offend the sensibilities of Muslims." Khalidi argues that its "founding fathers"—the men mentioned earlier in this chapter plus historians Ahmad ibn Yahya al-Baladhuri (d. 892) and Muhammad ibn Jarir al-Tabari (d. 923)—"fixed the order of the *Sira* and determined much of its content for all later biographers."[53] Khalidi may overstate his case; Muslim authors through the centuries drew extensively on these thinkers but not uncritically. Indeed, in a second stage, "the Muhammadan *Sira* was subjected to critical assessment in order to prune it of superstition and heresy," resulting in a biographical tradition that was "canonical, moral, exclusivist, and rationalizing."[54] Though Khalidi refers to rationality and superstition, these biographies often presumed

"Muhammad's superhuman qualities—his pre-eternity, miraculous powers, and sinlessness"—as well as his suitability as "an object of love and devotion."[55] Khalidi's final stage, which he dates from the late nineteenth century, is "the polemical *Sira*, written largely to defend Muhammad's reputation against the attacks of the European Orientalists." It is this last period, and this genre, with which this book is primarily concerned. Not all present-day Muslim writings about Muhammad form part of "the polemical *Sira*." Other Muslim writings about Muhammad exist, including popular devotional works, compilations of *hadith* recounting his deeds, and works of guidance and reflection composed by lay believers and authorities of various sorts. Internal Muslim debates about who constitutes an authority, what role precedent plays, where it is reliably found, and who is qualified to interpret it are vibrant, vigorous, and sometimes vitriolic; these debates occur in sermons, online, and in a wide array of books, including biographies. To understand this modern Muslim approach to Muhammad's biography, we must know more about the millennium of writings about Muhammad's life that preceded it.

Like Christian writings about Muhammad, Muslim accounts of the Prophet's life were neither uniform nor static. Muslim thinkers engaged in subtle arguments and vigorous debate over such matters as the status of miracles and the relative prominence of various factions in Muhammad's community. Muslims told tales of the Prophet they required. Early texts depict Muhammad not as a psychologically unique individual but as a type, an exemplum, a manifestation, of a universal model. He represents an ideal: the "perfected human being" whose conduct people should try to emulate. Incidents and precedents drawn from his exemplary practice—snippets of life as reported, through authenticated

chains of reporters, in accounts called *hadith*—overlap with biographical retellings.

Birth and death inescapably bookend every human life, but not all life writing starts with the subject's birth or ends with her death. Muhammad's early Muslim biographies tend to start with his genealogy; his immediate lineage includes noble Arabs but stretches back through biblical prophets to the first human being, Adam. Some accounts tell of a light his father bore, shining, until Muhammad had been conceived; in some versions, this light was carried from father to son through the generations until it passed to Muhammad. His pregnant mother was granted a dream-vision, announcing the birth of a son; a light shone from her—or from the infant, after his birth—all the way to the castles of Bostra in Syria. These stories echo and amplify Qur'anic stories and, in the case of the annunciatory dream, have obvious parallels in biblical accounts.[56] Just as European polemicists mixed fact and fancy in their catalogs of Muhammad's failings, so, too, Muslim authors alternated between what we might think of as empirical (if unverifiable) fact—names, dates, kinship ties—and the aura of the miraculous, particularly surrounding Muhammad's birth. These events would form the centerpiece of devotional works associated with the *mawlid*, or celebration of his birthday.

Medieval Christian accounts say little of his birth but get mileage from his (usually humiliating and shameful) death. During the twelfth and thirteen centuries, Christians viewed Muhammad as "disgusting in life and, most of all, in the manner of his death."[57] Authors wrote Muhammad an undignified death—perhaps drunk or even murdered, in one account, by a cuckolded husband—and lingered on the dismemberment or desecration of his "smelly corpse"[58] by (unclean) animals, often

pigs or dogs.[59] This "ignominious death . . . followed by the desecration of his corpse" aimed to engender disgust."[60] These themes persisted into the early modern era, repeated in fifteenth-and sixteenth-century English works, one of which had him "gnaven by swine" after collapsing drunk.[61] Authors sought to provoke repugnance and also to highlight "the permanence of the 'pseudo'-prophet's death in contrast to Jesus' escape from decay through resurrection."[62]

Other hostile accounts drew on Muslim sources to link Muhammad's death to the ingestion of poisoned mutton. The poisoning by a Jewish woman allows critics to view Muhammad as bereft of God's protection and therefore clearly not what he claimed to be: "notwithstanding the Intimacy he pretended with the Angel *Gabriel,* and the continual *Revelations* which he brag'd that he received from him, he could not be preserved from thus perishing by the Snares of a silly Girl."[63] Those Muslims who favored the account used it to prove his martyrdom at the hands of one of Islam's enemies: an additional blessing by God.[64] In this and many other details, Muslim accounts aimed to depict an exemplary death. How Muhammad died had implications for the community he left behind. Sunni and Shi'i versions differed as to whether he had died in Aisha's arms—the version followed in nearly all Western biographies—or Ali's, and whether he had called for someone to record his words on succession. Accounts also differed as to who washed his corpse, how it was shrouded, and who lowered it into the grave.[65] These details indicated intimacy with the Prophet; they also bore on questions of proper procedure for later Muslims to follow and were thus found in legal works as well as biographical ones.

In comparing Islam with Christianity, historian Chase Robinson suggests that religious foci determined the emphases of early

narratives about Muhammad and Christ. It was Christ's death and resurrection, not "his birth or miracles," that held most significance for early followers; by contrast, "it seems that the earliest Muslims were principally interested in Muḥammad's charismatic career as God's prophet," not in "his childhood or career as a merchant."[66] (His gestation, birth, and infancy, including his fostering by a Bedouin woman, were central in *mawlid* texts, but less important in other sorts of works.) These elements "were central to their identity as Christians and Muslims" and therefore garnered the most attention within their respective communities. But "doubters and skeptics" questioned and probed, seeking stronger, more complete answers. Robinson writes that "having entered a market of competing ideas and polemics, early Christians and early Muslims eventually came to tell the *whole* story. What they could not remember they duly provided in the form of legends, myths, conjectures and reasonable guesses, all about things they had no real memory of, since they had not really mattered before."[67] Even though "by the standards of most historians, this is making things up," such details emerged in the eighth and ninth centuries to flesh out narratives.[68]

It was not necessarily Christian "doubters and skeptics" that Muslim biographers sought to convince, although interreligious debates and conversations were indeed taking place, and materials on miracles may have been oriented toward possible Christian audiences.[69] The primary audience for Muslim thinkers over the centuries has been other Muslims. Not as much effort was centered on the emerging sectarian divide between Sunni and Shi'a as one might expect; Shi'i authors focused on Ali and his descendants, the Imams, whom they believed were the rightful, though dispossessed, leaders of the community.[70] Sunni authors likewise praised

the members of Muhammad's household, including Ali, Fatima, and their offspring, whom later Shi'a would venerate.

Rather than produce a sectarian Muhammad, the biographical tradition gradually shifted from a prophet in the biblical tradition to an Arab hero, suitable for the imperial context developing as Muslim rule spread throughout the near east, across the Mediterranean, and into Asia. The "progression from signs to miracles, from eschatology to history, from figurative description to the literal," happened as part of this broader hero-building project.[71]

Over the next centuries, images of Muhammad oscillated between emphasizing Muhammad's saintly qualities and focusing on his humanity.[72] But it was not only biographers who remembered and celebrated Muhammad. In each field of Muslim intellectual endeavor, the Prophet was a central figure to be reckoned with.

Scriptural commentators fleshed out their interpretations of Qur'anic passages with copious references to Muhammad's life. Where was he when this verse was revealed? What circumstance of his life prompted this passage? How did he understand and apply a particular edict? Tabari, whose *History* is a prime source for prophetic biography, composed a massive Qur'anic commentary that provides much material on Muhammad, as it elaborates the backstory for events the Qur'an describes only elliptically and allusively.

Jurists, too, drew on numerous specifics about Muhammad's life as they delineated norms to govern ritual, personal, and communal conduct. From the way he washed before prayer to how he treated his wives to what he liked to eat to how he commanded troops in battle, no detail was insignificant. Some material had direct legal effect. For instance, how many nights Muhammad allocated to his brides helped determine standard doctrines on the question of a new husband's duties. Because Muhammad's

reported practice was central to ongoing debates among jurists, Joseph Schacht, a legal historian, suggested that "a considerable part of the standard biography of the Prophet in Medina" arose in response to these debates and is "without independent historical value."[73] Yet other biographical details yielded guidance rather than rules. His favorite foods and manner of eating provided material for pious emulation rather than legal rulings. The deep concern of Muslims with emulating Muhammad's behavior in every area of life meant that jurisprudence—an enterprise intertwining legal and ethical realms—was deeply informed by the prophetic model.

Pietistic movements developed alongside other forms of Muslim scholarly and popular activity. Storytellers and preachers recounted the lives of Muhammad and other prophets, combining entertainment and edification. Such stories could inspire a "mild asceticism" firmly grounded in law and ritual practice or, for others, lead to a preference for spiritual athleticism.

Sufi or mystical thinkers saw Muhammad not merely as someone whose balanced asceticism was to be imitated for the development of a virtuous character but as someone whose very existence suffused the cosmos with light, someone who served as a channel for grace and intercession.[74] The traditional response to quotation of the Qur'anic verse pronouncing Muhammad "a man like you" was to both accept and qualify this statement: "Yes, but like a ruby among stones."[75] Some mystical thinkers developed elaborate prophetologies, with Muhammad at their apex. Although allegorical and symbolic works of this sort were intended for the reflection of a small elite, this disposition toward the numinous was widely shared among premodern Muslims, including the idea that Muhammad was more than an ordinary man and that the universe contained more than was visible to the eye.

One type of vision widely believed to convey true knowledge was dreams. Sufis saw significance in dreams, but so did—and do—others.[76] As in many parts of the ancient and medieval Mediterranean, it was widely presumed that dreams were an accurate and important means for conveying information. They were available to pious laypeople, suggesting a breakdown of boundaries "between the exceptional few and the supposedly ignorant masses," though interpretation often relied (like legal queries) on expert guidance.[77] Some Muslims today continue to seek analysis from a spiritual authority; others post dreams to religious websites, offering them for collective comment and reflection. Dreams of the Prophet, perceived as a sign of the dreamer's piety, have always been particularly desirable, with various techniques employed to induce them. Such dreams were widely retold in hagiographical works about saintly figures, rulers, and scholars as a means of legitimation.[78] A widely quoted prophetic statement holds that anyone who sees Muhammad in a dream really sees him; Satan cannot take his form. Vision was a matter not only of the actual eyes but also of the "awakened heart."[79]

Dreams and pious emulation continue to shape Muslim belief and practice in many places and periods.[80] Yet a large swathe of Muslim thinking has been profoundly desacralized. This desacralization, contested in some quarters, is reflected in many biographies.[81] Although Muslims still put stock in dreams of the Prophet, unlike "true" dreaming's central role in Ibn Ishaq's biography, in which "dream accounts serve as narrative units . . . clearly integral to the themes of concern to the early transmission of traditions surrounding major events of the emerging Muslim community," contemporary biographers tend to pay it no mind.[82]

The demotion of dreams from a place of prominence is only one of many changes Muslim biographies have undergone. The ground for many of these transformations was laid by the Protestant Reformation, with its influential critique of authority structures, its assumptions about the accessibility of texts and the appropriate procedures for reading them, and the rise of vernacular scriptures. The composition of new sorts of *Lives* of Muhammad was precipitated, too, by European scholarship, beginning in the early modern era but developing under the aegis of Western European colonial power. German Jews and British Protestants engaged in the retrieval of early Muslim sources and, in doing so, shaped specialist, polemicist, and popular interest in Muhammad's life in the nineteenth century. From this point forward, Muslim *Lives*—engaged directly and indirectly with Western scholarship—are increasingly preoccupied with issues of achievement and historical significance. In order to understand these developments better, it will be helpful to know something about non-Muslim accounts of Muhammad up until that time.

Non-Muslim Accounts, from Late Antiquity to the Enlightenment

Nineteenth-century scholars were intent on discovering accurate, early information about Muhammad; their medieval counterparts were, for the most part, not.

During the first centuries of Islam's existence, many Europeans knew little and cared less about accuracy in their portrayal of Muhammad, whom they associated, as in the French epic *Song of Roland,* with paganism and idolatry. (As one might expect given their geographical proximity to early Muslims, Syriac Christian

polemics against Muhammad were more informed than European ones, if no less hostile.) As paganism became less of a concern than dissent and heresy, Muhammad was refashioned a heresiarch, an antichrist, a false prophet, and, eventually, a fraud. John Tolan, preeminent historian of European views of Muslims, points out the "carefully construct[ed]" nature of such medieval accounts: "Rather than presenting an inept hodge-podge, these authors forge clever and coherent—although inaccurate—polemics."[83] Writers, often clergy, tailored their accusations to current local theological and social worries, using Islam as a foil to address their preoccupations. For instance, Embrico of Mainz wrote his Latin life of Muhammad at a time when clergy worried about heretical "wandering preachers." Muhammad appears as "a trickster and a scoundrel, not an Antichrist but rather an anti-saint." He "feigns holiness and performs bogus miracles through magic and sleight-of-hand, hoodwinking the gullible Arab masses into deeming him holy."[84] Equating the reviled prophet of Islam with "itinerant visionaries closer to home," Embrico tars both with the same brush. For a feat like this, Embrico needed few concrete details. Fewer still were required by Alexandre du Pont for his twelfth-century Old French *Romance of Muhammad*. Adapting a Latin clerical rejoinder, the poet deliberately tweaked Muhammad's story to provide details and themes that would meet a lay audience's expectations.[85]

Around the same time, a translation project sponsored by Peter the Venerable, the abbot of Cluny, sought to improve knowledge about Muslim doctrines to combat heresy more effectively.[86] Robert of Ketton translated the Qur'an into Latin. Though Ketton's 1143 translation was free from deliberate distortion, its title, *The Law of the False Prophet Muhammad*, makes clear its framing.[87]

(Muhammad's role as lawgiver was stressed on and off for centuries, to varying effects. At one end of the spectrum, a late-fifteenth-century English text emphasizes "the falsity and fakery of Mahomet's 'lawe,'" while at the other, Muhammad appears with other lawgivers on the U.S. Supreme Court frieze.[88]) Other texts provided further information about Muslim doctrines and history. Even as they increasingly drew on Muslim sources for tidbits about Muhammad, Christian authors told dramatically different stories from their Muslim counterparts.[89] Neither lay nor scholarly Christian narratives tried to understand Muhammad or retell his life in full. His life was interesting only insofar as it illuminated the beastly nature of Islam as a religion and Muslims as a group. Selected incidents of Muhammad's life appeared "in a way meant to ridicule and discredit his followers."[90] Such works followed, in a way, the classical Western biographical tradition of treating "the individual persons portrayed [as] moral exempla, which should be followed or avoided, as the case might be."[91] But unlike the accounts of illustrious men composed by Suetonius and Plutarch, there was a metonymic dimension to biographies of Muhammad: he was both cause *and* example par excellence of the failings of Muslims as a whole.

In places where Muslims and Christians had ongoing contact—such as the Iberian Peninsula, which Arab armies had conquered in the early eighth century and where Christian control remained patchy through the fifteenth century—texts condemning Islam and Muhammad were sometimes meant to reassure Christians of their religion's superiority. Chronicles of Muhammad's life sought to demonstrate "the illegitimacy of Muslim dominion" by proving him "a heresiarch and a false prophet."[92] At other times, the usually fruitless aim was to convert Muslims, either directly or by giving

missionaries talking points "to demonstrate the superiority of Christianity."[93] A third function was to strengthen the "far from watertight" social barriers between Christians and Muslims by instilling "mutual repugnance."[94] Thus, Pedro Pascual's early fourteenth-century *On the Muhammadan Sect* "manipulates traditional anti-Muslim polemics, seeking to inspire in its readers hatred and disdain for Islam, in order to prevent them from crossing over to the rival faith." It also seeks to dissuade those Christians who "were ready to share their beds with the infidel." Although Muslims had been expelled from the Iberian Peninsula by the end of the fifteenth century, this gate-barring function was increasingly important as Muslim-ruled empires threatened Christian dominance in Africa, southern Europe, and western portions of Asia.

In Europe, from the fifteenth through the seventeenth centuries, one crucial way this happened was to portray Muslims— Muhammad chief among them—as monstrous. This might involve association with Jews, which "served a twofold polemical purpose, demonizing Judaism through its association with Islam, yet incorporating Islam into a grand Christian history through its connections with Judaism. Their shared monstrosity," Matthew Dimmock argues, "coalesces around two factors: the first, a continuing denial of the divinity of Christ . . . which transmuted in both cases into a responsibility for the murder of Christ, the second, the associated part both were to play in the events of apocalypse and revelation."[95]

The enemy within and the enemy without were two sides of the same coin. Especially after the start of the Protestant Reformation in the early sixteenth century, writers drew on Muhammad and Muslims for intra-Christian polemics. The accusations of debauched conduct launched against Muhammad had counterparts,

sometimes even more virulent, against purportedly heretical Christians. The Protestant/Catholic split, a "bitter dispute of unprecedented geographical range and chronological endurance," prompted a "level of vitriol [that] was, if not unprecedented, then not surpassed either."[96] Islam and Muhammad played a crucial role. Generally, theological enemies were likened to Muhammad or Muslims, but occasionally Islam or Muhammad were compared favorably to the opponent in question, to make the enemy seem worse. As Tolan suggests, "European discourse concerning Muḥammad is often best understood as a deforming mirror."[97]

If Muhammad had been the antichrist for some medieval critics, for Protestant polemicists, so was the Pope. The connection with Muhammad intensified anti-Catholic insults. A sixteenth-century Swedish church painting shows St. Christopher rescuing the Christ child "from the water in which the Pope and Muhammad perish. . . . The drowning, nameless pope is humiliated by being associated with Muhammad and Islam."[98] A Swiss tract from the same era against a Catholic monastic order bears the title *The Franciscans' Qur'an.*[99] Catholics, too, used Muhammad and Islam to denigrate Protestants, equating Martin Luther and other errant pastors to Muhammad and comparing "Calvinist and Muslim treachery."[100] Sixteenth-century French scholar Guillaume Postel put it particularly bluntly: "The spiritual sons of Luther are the little bastards of Mahom."[101] As Jonathan Lyons observes, "Each side in the European struggle over the Reformation sought to tar the other by rhetorical association with the violent and dangerous 'Turk.'"[102] Yet anti-Catholic and anti-Muslim sentiments were more consistently interwoven, perhaps because Luther himself had penned a condemnation of Islam and its prophet.[103] These associations between Muhammad and the Pope,

sometimes styled twin antichrists, persist well into the nineteenth century.[104]

Not only could Muhammad be marshaled to criticize Christian enemies, but he could also be linked rhetorically to Muslim political and military opponents. Renewed fears of Ottoman military advances led to villainous portraits of Turkish emperors. They were likened in their bad qualities to "the Arab pseudo-prophet Mohammed," to whom Philippus Meyerus's 1594 poetic Latin life assigns ruthlessness, cruelty, and a "diabolical combination of political astuteness and military strength." Other "dubious qualities in which the Ottoman sultans were perceived to emulate the founder of their religion were an extravagant lifestyle and sexual debauchery."[105]

The Ottoman threat revived the theological quandary Islam had posed centuries earlier for figures like Peter of Cluny. If Christianity was the true religion, why were Muslims enjoying worldly success? One answer was that God was punishing Christians for their failings; the catastrophe of Muslim military victory and widespread conversion to Islam was not because God had switched allegiance but because Muslims, just like Christians, were subject to God's broader plan.

This plan of God was under threat, too, from enemies closer to home. The early modern era, approximately from the Reformation to the French Revolution and the rise of Napoleon at the end of the eighteenth century, saw a series of intellectual and religious movements that challenged long-held ideas about God, humanity, and reason. The Enlightenment sought to replace irrationality and superstition with rationality. In addition to the Enlightenment's hostility toward religion generally, there was criticism of central Christian beliefs, including the Trinity, and widespread concern

with religious fraud. Given that, as Ziad Elmarsafy notes, "the Enlightenment holds a privileged position in the making of modernity writ large," the shifts it engendered were deeply influential in how Muhammad's biography came to be written.[106]

Imposture was the early modern era's characteristic preoccupation. William Bedwell's 1615 *Mohammedis imposturae; that is, A discovery of the manifold forgeries, falsehoods, and horrible impieties of the blasphemous seducer Mohammed* leveled the charge of fraud, which picked up steam as the seventeenth century wore on.[107] By the turn of the eighteenth century, three overlapping bodies of literature converged on the idea of the false prophet: Orientalist scholarship, Enlightenment thought, and Christian apologetic and polemic. As theology ceded some ground to secular humanism, some tried to set all religions and their founders on the same playing field, while others worked to exalt one religion by denigrating others. It was precisely this recognition, in some spheres unwelcome, that there were competing "religions" and not merely distortions or usurpations of the one true faith that marked the shift from medieval to modern ways of approaching Others. In the developing study of world religions, European scholarship on Islam was influential in forming the category of religion. Historian Guy Stroumsa argues that prejudices against Islam changed in the seventeenth century, allowing the "gradual emergence of a new, more open attitude that was most significant for the birth of the modern study of Islam."[108] The entry on Muhammad in Barthélemy d'Herbelot's *Bibliothèque orientale* begins, "This is the famous Impostor Mahomet, Author and Founder of a heresy which called itself Religion, and that we call Mahomedan."[109] Oxford Arabist Edward Pococke (1604–1691) applies Maimonides's notion of the false prophet to Muhammad, though he also holds that

"Muhammad should nonetheless be considered a remarkable man who brought moral reform to his people."[110]

Enlightenment thinkers extended the criticism of false prophets far beyond Muhammad, considering all religions equally false. The existence of and proofs for prophecy in general had been a significant topic of debate among philosophers and theologians for centuries, and Muslim figures had joined the fray between the ninth and eleventh centuries, with rationalist figures arguing that claims of revelation did not survive logical scrutiny. Defenders of Muhammad's role often found themselves laying the groundwork for their claims about him by arguing for the authenticity of previous prophets.[111]

The famous treatise on *The Three Impostors*, which the historian George Minois has called "an aggressive work, a frontal attack upon religion,"[112] takes the anti-revelation view to its logical end. This book was born of rumor and innuendo; a thirteenth-century pope accused the Holy Roman emperor of the time of having written a book condemning Moses, Jesus, and Muhammad. The emperor denied the accusation, but the shadow book persisted for four centuries: "nobody had seen it, nobody had read it, but almost everybody believed in its existence." Eventually, "it became such an obsession that it ended up by existing."[113]

Its basic premise was that Moses, Jesus, and Muhammad and their religions were equivalent, "full of hoaxes, trickery, and illusions that knock out critical thinking and cause senseless massacres." Their Gods were false, and the prophets, frauds. *The Three Impostors* was undoubtedly quite a different work than it would have been had it emerged from "virtual" to tangible existence two or three centuries earlier. Still, its references to central Christian,

Jewish, and Muslim figures continued the "triangularity of religious discourse" at evidence since the late seventh or eighth century.[114]

Whereas some antireligious tracts argued for the essential sameness of all religious teachings and religious founders, other thinkers clung to a bright division between true religion on the one hand and falsehood on the other. One Catholic cleric, for instance, sought to rehabilitate the reputations of Moses and Jesus but affirmed that Muhammad and Zoroaster had been impostors.

Accusations of fraud could also be levied against dissenters within a tradition. A concern with "simulation and dissimulation, pretending to be what one was not, concealing one's real identity and convictions," was everywhere. Writing about a seventeenth-century Catholic Italian laywoman, Cecilia Ferrazzi, Anne Schutte notes that the inquisitors who prosecuted her did not begin from the assumption that women (or anyone) claiming certain kinds of spiritual distinction were possessed or inspired or "deluded by the Devil," as would have been the case two centuries earlier. But "If the Devil could not have inspired them . . . they must be held responsible for fabricating, consciously and deliberately, evidence of a holiness they did not possess."[115]

Similar concerns guided the most famous early modern treatise on Muhammad: Humphrey Prideaux's *The True Nature of Imposture Fully Display'd in the Life of Mahomet*, published in 1697. Prideaux was an Anglican clergyman, serving as dean of the cathedral in Norwich, then England's third-largest town. Not himself an Oriental scholar, his treatise was "a pungent and polemical compilation of the oriental translations and researches of others."[116] Prideaux's book straddles two worldviews. It echoes medieval

accusations that Muhammad is an antichrist while debunking several popular legends and rejecting the enduring accusation that Muhammad was demonically possessed. Instead, Prideaux charges Muhammad with deliberate fraud.

Prideaux's treatise on Muhammad was mere preface to the real point: the accompanying refutation, long since fallen into obscurity, of Socinianism. Precursors of the Unitarians, Socinians levied radical criticisms of Trinitarian doctrine, prompting obvious comparisons to Islam and Muhammad. In the twenty-first century, Unitarianism has a reputation as wishy-washy liberalism. Prideaux, though, perceived Socinians as a major threat to his preferred kind of Christianity. The upstart Christians who were Prideaux's target were among those who viewed Islam and Muhammad positively—at least to a point. Muhammad's reformist monotheism was sufficiently distant that it could be used to critique Christians closer in for their irrationality and convoluted doctrines. Prideaux, too, used Muhammad to make his point because he was not admired by those Prideaux was attempting to persuade.

Within a century of Prideaux's polemic, shifting geopolitical realities sometimes enabled a more generous and nuanced appreciation of Muslims and Islam. Although "in regards to western views of Islam, the eighteenth and nineteenth centuries must be considered a prominent cultural and historical frontier,"[117] there was no clear transition from hostility to admiration. For one thing, earlier centuries' views of Muhammad were not entirely negative. Close study of earlier texts typically reveals more nuance than broad generalizations about Western portraits of the Prophet usually admit; even Théophane le Confesseur's early ninth century *Chronographie* treats Muhammad and Islam with relative "sobriety and

objectivity."[118] Early modern English texts contain more than "unchanging and relentless vitriol towards the Prophet."[119] Nor were generally positive eighteenth-century texts entirely praise filled.

Grand claims have been made for the originality of various texts' positive presentation of Islam and Muhammad. For instance, the Comte de Boulainvilliers 1731 *Life of Mahomet*, which praised Islam and its prophet "above all [as] a way of denigrating Christianity and favoring deism," has been called "the first frankly pro-Islamic text produced by European culture" and "the first genuinely sympathetic western biography of Muhammad."[120] Thomas Carlyle's "The Hero as Prophet," a century later, most commonly receives such accolades, with one scholar calling it "startlingly revisionist."[121]

Even if these declarations overstate the newness of the authors' approaches, failing to recognize traces of more inquisitive and less condemnatory work scattered through earlier European accounts of Muhammad, the seventeenth and eighteenth centuries did mark a change. Opposed approaches to the study of Muhammad and Islam came to coexist: recognizably positive, or at least deliberately non-hostile, alongside harsh condemnations. Scholarship on Arabic and Islam in western Europe played a key role in this process. To give just a few examples, André du Ryer published a French translation of the Qur'an, which was in turn rendered into a "less learned" but more widely read English version in 1649.[122] The next year, Pococke published *Specimen historiae Arabum*, a Latin edition of a medieval Muslim history, which included a brief sketch of Muhammad's life; it remained a vital resource for scholars into the nineteenth century.[123] This spate of publications continued into the first decades of the eighteenth century, with Boulainvilliers; Jean

Gagnier's 1723 translation of a medieval biography, followed by his multivolume *Life;* and George Sale's 1734 English translation of the Qur'an.[124]

Accompanying this growth of scholarly interest in Arabs and Islam was a shift in European perceptions of Muslims. In contrast to the beginnings of "the European relationship to the Orient . . . when . . . that relationship was one of anxiety and awe on the part of the Europeans,"[125] by the eighteenth century, "Fear of the Turks gave way to contempt, fascination, and a sort of cultural and historical tourism."[126] (French Marxist scholar Maxime Rodinson, whose 1961 biography of Muhammad was stricken from syllabi at the American University of Cairo, viewed the rise of "romantic exoticism" as the result of "a change within Western sensibilities" rather than as the outcome of changes in broader relationships between East and West.)[127]

Although serious scholarly work on Oriental languages and texts had begun centuries earlier, including that by monks intent on refutation of rival dogmas, it increased commensurately with European colonialism in Arab and Asian lands. Johann Fück divides European scholarship on Arabic and Islam into two periods. From its twelfth-century monastic origins through the late eighteenth century, with "rare exceptions" a "'Christian agenda'" governed such work, though for many scholars, a nominal profession of Christianity was sufficient to allow their work to have "fundamentally neutral content."[128] From then on, "modern scholarly studies of Arabic" came to dominate within a university system.[129] Most German researchers involved in the study of Arabic, Islam, and the Middle East worked in Oriental-language positions. Their research was "distinguished not only by an impressive number of outstanding scholars, but also by a heavy and persistent focus on

issues of language (in its classical form) and the early Islamic period."[130] In British universities as well, the study of Oriental languages, including Sanskrit and Arabic, ramped up dramatically.

Fascination with the East was by no means limited to universities. British and continental writers were drawn to partly known, mostly imagined exotic realms. The Romantic era, which spanned the last quarter of the eighteenth century and the first half of the nineteenth century, radiated out from Britain to affect much of Europe and "saw a crucial transition between an Enlightenment world view and the values of a modern, industrial society."[131] Romanticism was "a literary movement, and a profound shift in sensibility."[132] Early modern thinkers tried to unmask the impostor; Romantic thinkers instead aimed to reveal the genius. Concern with inner and outer, which had been focused on revealing the true hidden beneath the false, shifted to individuals' interior lives, not outward forms. Genius was the animating core of the Romantic vision, and its "prerequisites," in one early articulation, "were originality, passion, and enthusiasm."[133]

Ideas about genius and inner nature affected biography, a genre enjoying new popularity in Britain. Muhammad's biographers aimed to convey something of his "personality," as biographers did more generally. Beyond this concern for capturing a certain individual essence, biographers focused on Great Men and their Important Deeds. Military heroes (and antiheroes) figured large in the European imagination, and biography increasingly conveyed this information to a reading public. Philip Almond sums it up succinctly in his survey *Heretic and Hero: Muhammad and the Victorians:* "The Victorian penchant for great men coupled with the Western fascination for an exotic east engendered a sympathetic environment for the rehabilitation of Muhammad and Islam."[134]

As the next chapter will show, "rehabilitation" is too simplistic. Medieval obsession with disgust gave way to a modern scrutiny of deeds; concern with legend became preoccupation with fact. At the same time, churning away in the background were old ideas about Muhammad's calculating formulation of a false religion—and the even older notion, expressed in the view of an American clergyman who also served as Harvard's president, that "Muhammad had received his revelations straight from the devil."[135]

Chapter 2

A True Prophet

Orphaned of father then mother, bereaved of the grandfather who had taken him in, young Muhammad passed into the care of his paternal uncle Abu Talib. Not long thereafter, when he was nine or a little older, he accompanied his uncle on a caravan journey to Syria, during which he was miraculously shaded from the harsh desert sun. The caravan stopped at a monastery in Bostra, but Muhammad remained hidden until a monk asked Abu Talib to produce him. The monk, Bahira, questioned Muhammad closely and saw the seal of prophecy between his shoulder blades. Before sending him on his way, he predicted Muhammad's future greatness and warned Abu Talib to protect him from those who would harm him.

Muslim tradition views this encounter with Bahira as but one in a series of supernatural and non-Muslim affirmations of Muhammad's special status and future promise.[1] Extraordinary occurrences punctuated his life. Radiant light spilled from his father's forehead before his conception. His mother dreamed of illumination. Angels came and washed a speck from his breast when he was a boy in his foster mother's care. Classical sources elaborate at length on these portents, which surrounded Muhammad's birth and childhood with the luminous aura of the divine. Like the monk's recognition of the "seal of prophecy," which foreshadowed eventual confirmation of Muhammad's revelation by Khadija's Christian cousin Waraqa, these events indicated divine

favor and linked the nascent faith to the tradition of biblical prophecy.

The Bahira story has a distorted reflection in early Christian works, which often unspooled from this fateful encounter. In Syriac sources, a renegade monk usually called Sergius plots with Muhammad to deceive his compatriots. In European sources, the monk was often Nestur or occasionally Arius, attesting to the intertwining of ideas about Muhammad with Christian heresies.[2] Rather than serving as independent witness to Muhammad's legitimacy, as he does in Muslim accounts, the monk, sometimes alongside Waraqa or other Meccan Christians, is complicit in his scheme.

Early Muslims used biblical categories, proof texts, and miracle stories to affirm Muhammad's prophethood and the superiority of Islam, just as Christian opponents of the growing Muslim tradition used the same texts to affirm the opposite.[3] Early followers compared Muhammad to other prophetic figures in a bid to legitimate Muhammad in prevailing terms and, later, to prove his superiority. Once Muslim success was a fact, adherents of other traditions recast their foundational figures in Muhammad's image: Zoroastrians reimagined Zoroaster as a lone bearer of scripture.[4] The images of Muhammad held by Muslims altered and accreted, as did the images held by Christians—both Arabs who lived alongside Muslims and those in Europe who had never met one.

The question of the relation of Muhammad to other religious traditions, particularly Christianity, remained central even as medieval concern with heresy became early modern preoccupation with imposture. The Enlightenment critique of religion, the growth of academic Oriental studies, and the rise of colonialism led to increased connection between Muslim and non-Muslim accounts of Muhammad's life. A steady trickle of books on Mu-

hammad had appeared in western Europe during the seventeenth and eighteenth centuries, but the number of publications increased dramatically in the nineteenth century. In England and America—increasingly a locus of missionary fervor—popularizers supplemented scholarly publications based on newly available early Arabic sources with books and tracts targeting missionaries and general audiences. Although perennial themes persisted—miracles, sex, violence—non-Muslims posed new critiques of Muslim accounts and, even more fundamentally, focused attention on historical accuracy. The quest for correct information about Muhammad had precedent in the work of early clerical opponents of Islam, who aimed to know Muslim doctrines the better to refute them. In this era, however, a set of questions about historical fact came to dominate Western approaches to Muhammad's life. Their preoccupations intersected with those of Muslim religious thinkers, traditional scholars, and Western-educated reformers. In a series of exchanges, mostly occurring in English, among British scholars and missionaries, Indian Muslim elites, and Hindu reformers, new visions of Muhammad were hammered out.

The Original Sources

The battle over Muhammad's image was fought on the contested ground of history as preserved, more or less reliably, in "original sources." Despite significant disagreement over what kind of man Muhammad was and how he fit into narratives of biblical prophecy and world history, a set of largely implicit agreements came to govern claims about his life. Early texts gained new prominence; new methodological presuppositions fundamentally reshaped the way Muhammad's biography was written.

Historical chronicles and biographical dictionaries, like more straightforward biographies, use complex organizing principles and coded language to assert authoritative versions of events, even as they include information that is unlikely, contradictory, or unflattering. Today, those who study these texts tend to analyze the literary practices behind them, seeking to understand how their subjects, including Muhammad, were understood by those who wrote about them, fully aware that in many sources "the lines between outright history and devotion are blurred."[5] In the nineteenth century, however, scholars influenced by scholarship on the historical Jesus (and the historical Buddha) were primarily interested in ferreting out what was "true" or "untrue."

European biographies written in the previous century had relied on a small number of primary sources, including Jean Gagnier's 1723 Latin/Arabic edition of the biography of the Prophet by the Syrian Abu'l-Fida (1273–1331). That Abu'l-Fida's text became so central owed to the vagaries of manuscript circulation rather than any preeminence for medieval Muslims. Print made it available to Arabists who had no comparable manuscripts to consult; Latin made it accessible to scholars who did not read Arabic.[6] The Episcopal cleric William Murray published an English version for subscribers *(The Life of Mohammed Translated from the Arabic of Abulfeda)*, probably in the 1820s, accompanied by a scathing introduction and conclusion, together equaling the length of the translated source.[7] It found some use in the hands of Christian apologists but did not supplant Gagnier's Latin version.

Though Abu'l-Fida's text had not previously enjoyed great renown, it shared features with important medieval texts, such as the chronicle of Ibn al-Athir (d. 1233), on which it depended heavily, and through it, the standard early biographies.[8] Such chroni-

cles, in which Muhammad's life was only one element, were eclipsed in popularity among Muslims by highly stylized meditations on Muhammad's perfection, including devotional texts composed for celebrations of his birthday, which spanned the popular and the scholarly. One scholar notes that "among Muslims, the popularity of Muḥammad's biographies is based not on the historical evidence that they include but on their didactic, edifying, propagandistic, and entertaining features that address the needs of readers and listeners on various educational, psychological, and artistic levels."[9] This is certainly true for the premodern period, when "softer-edged Prophetic biography" was "in near constant demand by literate Muslims at large."[10] The *Shifa'* of Qadi 'Iyad, an Andalusian contemporary of these historians, was "an immensely popular compilation—indeed, arguably the single most popular Prophetic biography of the entire tradition."[11] To take a later example, in eighteenth-century Egypt, a collection of blessings and prayers for the Prophet by a fifteenth-century Moroccan Sufi "was the most commonly owned book after the Quran."[12] European scholars were largely uninterested in these sorts of texts; they wanted to know the facts of Muhammad's life, as closely as they could.

When Gustav Weil published his biography *Muhammad the Prophet, His Life and His Book* (1843) in German using Arabic manuscript sources, it ushered in "an entirely new era in Islamic studies in Europe."[13] It was the first major advance in about a century. (Weil, who was among a number of important Jewish Islamicists working in Germany, would go on to publish a two-volume German edition of Ibn Ishaq/Ibn Hisham, a history of the early caliphate, and a German translation of the *Arabian Nights*, which ended up being excerpted for American student use because it was, the editor said, "good modern German of an easy kind.")[14]

In the next two decades, the number of sources at the disposal of Europeans increased rapidly. Scholars working in India, where in some regions a Muslim minority constituted a ruling elite, were largely responsible for these developments. Europeans were instrumental in editing and publishing manuscripts of early texts, sometimes with accompanying translations.[15] Additionally, their own biographical writings drew on early sources, a fact advertised in their titles. Aloys Sprenger, an Austrian medical doctor who joined the British East India Company and became principal of Delhi College, wrote *The Life of Mohammad from Original Sources*, which the Presbyterian Mission Press published in Allahabad in 1851.[16] A longer German version, with extensive source material, appeared later but garnered substantially less attention from Muslim readers. Indeed, scholarly work in German—which had recently replaced Latin publications for university careers in Germany—was mostly read by other Europeans.[17] Despite their pioneering role in research on Muhammad's life, scholars like Weil were neglected by Indian and Egyptian authors, who were far more likely to read works in French or English. Sprenger was widely read in India in part because his *Life* appeared in English.

Anglo-Muhammadan *Lives*

Tarif Khalidi argues that two British *Lives* of the nineteenth century "haunt" modern Muslim biographers.[18] The first is Thomas Carlyle's 1840 lecture "The Hero as Prophet." Carlyle began by explaining, "We have chosen Mahomet not as the most eminent Prophet; but as the one we are freest to speak of."[19] He addressed an audience likely to be amenable to his claim that they were free to discuss Muhammad because "there is no danger of our becoming,

any of us, Mahometans."[20] His presumption that there was no danger of conversion was not entirely accurate—there were communities of Muslims in Britain, and a handful of Europeans did convert over the course of the nineteenth century—but unlike medieval Christians who had sought to reinforce boundaries, Carlyle considered a defensive stance unnecessary.[21] His view was not universally shared; less generous appraisals of Muhammad's life directed to Protestant missionaries in India or Sunday school children in America circulated widely. Carlyle, though, presumed a secure identity that would be neither offended nor threatened by any perceived slight to or glorification of Muhammad.

Carlyle delivered his lecture, in which he pronounced Muhammad "a true prophet"—if not the truest—in the heyday of British imperialism. The French invasion and occupation of Egypt in 1798 had marked a decisive shift in British and French colonial patterns. Western European provincial power struggles, such as the Napoleonic wars, played out on the world stage. French control spread in Africa and receded in India; the British expanded their control throughout India while maintaining African and Asian colonies. Eventually, the British came to dominate in Egypt as well, invading in 1882 and establishing a protectorate that, as the Ottoman Empire declined and eventually collapsed, took increasingly stringent measures to secure British commercial, diplomatic, and military interests. As later chapters will show, this interlude was decisive for the establishment of a colonialist party line on women and Islam, which is still broadly influential, and came to affect how people thought about Muhammad's marriages.

Biographical writing on Muhammad was also deeply shaped by the increasing popularity of the biographical genre in western Europe, particularly England, as well as by European scholarly

interest in the historical Jesus. The former, related to the country's national-heroic story line, concerned military figures of various sorts. The latter, part of a new biblical studies agenda, sought to integrate archaeology and critical textual methods with historical scholarship. Interwoven with these developments was a romantic sensibility.

Carlyle, deeply influenced by the German writer Goethe, linked ideas of genius with notions of greatness. Muhammad's unspoiled natural genius allows him to do things that will affect the world. Carlyle emphasized the primitive, the lack of artifice and artificiality, in his thinking about Muhammad's relation to environment as well as to his inner self. Muslims were not his target audience, though he became "the favorite author of all Islamic modernists in India."[22] Muslim authors appropriated his praise for apologetic purposes, a trend that only increased after the 1911 translation of his lecture into Arabic. An early twentieth-century Muslim author writes that "Carlyle unveiled, as it were, the beauty of the Holy Prophet to the Western eye."[23] Conventional wisdom deems his lecture, which includes its share of negative remarks, "a vehement and unusual rehabilitation of Muhammad."[24] It was not entirely unprecedented in its generally positive view of Muhammad; in addition to French works like that of Boulainvilliers, *An Apology for the Life and Character of the Celebrated Prophet of Arabia, Called Mohammed, or the Illustrious* by Godfrey Higgins predated it by more than a decade.[25] Yet is has become a touchstone for Muslims seeking Western support for their claims about Muhammad's greatness.

Carlyle was less interested in Muhammad himself than in what the Prophet allowed Carlyle to say about humanity as a whole. As he wrote to American essayist Ralph Waldo Emerson, describing

his lecture: "Beautiful people listened with boundless tolerance, eager attention" to his telling them that "man was still alive, Nature not dead or like to die; that all true men continued true to this hour." Muhammad—like Odin, "the Lama of Thibet," and others—was a "true" man. Truth was neither bound to Europe nor exclusive to Christianity. He was aware that in this latter claim, he was not merely stating an agreed-upon truth: "The Lecture on Mahomet . . . astonished my worthy friends beyond measure. It seems then that this Mahomet was not a quack? Not a bit of him! That he is a better Christian, with his "bastard Christianity," than the most of us shovel-hatted? I guess than almost any of you!"[26] Still, though Christianity might not have a monopoly on truth, it remained the byword for human morality: to say that Muhammad is "a better Christian" here means not that he accepted specific dogmas but that he embodied praiseworthy qualities.

If Carlyle synthesized the Romantic genius and the great man, William Muir represented the "Missionary-Orientalist complex."[27] It is widely recognized now that there was no one Orientalism.[28] Missionary, scholarly, and imperial aims were in tension and sometimes in conflict, both writ large and in individual lives. Muir's career intertwined evangelism, Orientalist scholarship, and service to the empire. He was a committed Christian, a serious Arabist, and a member of the Bengal Civil Service, serving nearly four decades in India (1837–1876) in former Mughal territory in the northwest, rising to the position of provincial lieutenant governor. He was good at his job, networking with other colonial officials— particularly those who shared his evangelical bent—and with "natives," including members of the Muslim scholarly class known as ulama. He skirted the formal policy requiring colonial officials' religious neutrality by supporting missionary activities in regions

where he was posted with both his money and, more importantly, his pen. An early article on "The Mahommedan Controversy," published in the *Calcutta Review* (1845) less than a decade into his stay in India, argued that the time was ripe for evangelism, since "at every point of contact with Islam, Christianity has the temporal ascendancy." His rousing challenge was aimed at conversion of Hindus and Muslims alike: "Britain must not faint until her millions in the East abandon both the false Prophet and the Idol shrines, and rally around that eternal truth which has been brought to light in the Gospel."[29]

The evangelizing intent behind Muir's *Life* was no secret. Muir tells how the Reverend Karl Pfander, stymied in his efforts to convert Muslims, implored him to write a biography suitable for evangelism. Muir reviewed extant missionary *Lives* and found them sorely wanting: error riddled and off-putting in tone.[30] Their outmoded or offensive ways of presenting Muhammad hampered conversion efforts. Pfander originally desired, and Muir set out to write, a synthetic, sensitive, Christianizing life in the vernacular. The project took on a life of its own, though, expanding and shifting in intent and audience as well as language.

The collision of Muir's evangelical aims and scholarly approach resulted in the magisterial four-volume *The Life of Mahomet from Original Sources*. Published between 1858 and 1861, and in abridged form in 1878, Muir's *Life* has been a major resource and reference for scholars and lay readers. Though ultimately unsuited for use as an evangelical tract, it was widely read by missionaries and by Indian Muslims with sufficient English competence. In 1905, nearly a half century after its publication, Muir's obituary called it "the standard presentment, in English, of the Prophet of Islam."[31] At the same time, it has come to symbolize what is bad

about Orientalist views of Muhammad.[32] Muir's biography was based on meticulous primary-source research as well as engagement with extant scholarship, but though he was faithful to his sources, he presented information gleaned from them in unflattering ways: "It is precisely because of its deadly accuracy," Khalidi writes, "that Muir's *Life* was found so distasteful by Muslim readership."[33]

Though Muslim writers have explicitly criticized Muir's approach and conclusions, the publication of his *Life* forever altered the enterprise of pious biography. It wove a handful of topics—authenticity of revelation, character, behavior with women—into a source-critical narrative history, fusing polemic and scholarship. What Muir ultimately accomplished was a grand restatement of Muhammad's life in his Arabian setting, grounding his study as firmly as possible in historical materials. Though far from aiming at any sort of apology, he rejected "the medieval polemic based on limited sources and an irrational bias against Islam and its prophet."[34] He sought to overcome both obstacles, though he was more successful at mining new sources than eliminating "irrational bias," at least in the views of his Muslim critics.

Muhammadan Controversies

The evangelical movement of which Muir formed part was far from the only religious contestation occurring in India. The nineteenth century was fertile ground for religious controversies and new identitarian movements both within and between religious communities. In keeping with broader currents of reform in the Arabian Peninsula and Arab world, Indian Muslims were engaged in debates over authority, tradition, and the proper approach to

matters of worship. Broader revivalist currents, including movements originating in the Arabian Peninsula, reverberated among Muslims in India.[35] The formation of the scholarly community at Deoband, as well as the Barelvi movement, resulted in internecine struggles and a flowering of scholarly and popular output. The proper way to celebrate Muhammad's life was one crucial node in those discussions.

The Ahmadiyya have their origin in the same period in the work and life of Mirza Ghulam Ahmad (1836–1908). Ahmad, from Qadian in India, came to prominence in the 1870s as a scholar and controversialist, who "attained wide fame in the subcontinent as one of Islam's foremost champions against the inroads of colonial missionaries and similar groups critical of Islam or committed to the conversion of Muslims."[36] He debated other Muslims, Hindu reformers, and Christians. Eventually, his claims to be the promised messiah alienated many of his supporters, but he continued to have active followers in colonial India. After his death, the movement split over whether he also fulfilled a prophetic role; both groups have proselytized actively, especially in the United States and Europe.

To discuss these as intra-Muslim shifts, as I have just done, already misrepresents the situation because it presumes that Muslim and Hindu were neatly distinguished at the outset and then fractured further. In fact, the development of these religious identities was less the precondition for than the outcome of nineteenth-century developments.[37] Some medieval Bengali tales of Muhammad's birth "placed the event within the all-embracing Indian religious scene by having Brahma, Vishnu, and others foretell the Prophet's coming."[38] In a Gujarati poem from the turn of the seventeenth century, a Brahmin gives the newly born Muhammad

his sacred thread.[39] Ronit Ricci finds similar congruences in seventeenth-century Tamil texts.[40] To call this "boundary blurring" implies that there were boundaries to be blurred rather than a complex topology of the sacred. Beginning in the eighteenth century, exclusivity and purity as religious values came to be increasingly celebrated by at least some elite thinkers, resulting in less crossover.[41]

New mechanisms for print interchange were intertwined with, and facilitated, these developments. A swifter process of polemical exchange in periodicals, pamphlets, and other print media characterized the middle decades of the nineteenth century. Hindus had vigorous interchanges concerning widow remarriage and other topics.[42] Intra-Muslim debates took place through the press, too. Print media facilitated the regular exchange between Indian Muslims and Europeans, as in the published fallout from and follow-up to the 1854 debates between missionaries and Muslim scholars.

In these writings, all parties presumed shared norms about evidence, facts, and proof, and appealed—intermittently—to ideals of objectivity, tolerance, and universalism. Though the transition was not without its rough moments, there came to be a shared notion that accuracy and insult were relevant categories for assessing portraits of Muhammad. One consistent key in modern Muslim treatments of Muhammad is the perceived need to combat negative portrayals—or, as one author puts it, "the misleading teaching and willful misrepresentations which are so common."[43]

The theme of rebutting (Western) misconceptions has become ubiquitous in studies of Islam, even those aimed primarily at Muslims.[44] This stated aim is such a predictable feature of writing about Islam in the twenty-first century, by both Muslims and sympathetic non-Muslims, that it is difficult to imagine that it once was

not so. Yet for centuries, people engaged in polemics felt free to point out the "errors" or "lies" of their opponents. Some Muslim writings still take this tone and refer to "refuting Orientalist calumnies"—often those by Muir. But the dominant approach, which has its origins in the nineteenth century, suggests that one's opponents are not so much in outright error as merely and sadly mistaken, and that if the facts can be clearly illustrated, they will abandon their "preconceptions" and recognize the legitimacy of Muslim assertions. As reformer Syed Ameer Ali puts it, the aim is "to disabuse the minds of many readers of false impressions and false prejudices."[45] Such claims may be partly rhetorical flourish, but they also indicate a (perceived) agreement on standards of proof to which one can appeal, and an ongoing dialogue—or the pretense of it—between Muslim and non-Muslim authors.[46]

Attempts by Muslims to correct Western "misunderstandings" also provided a means by which other objectives, including scoring points in internal Muslim debates and power struggles, could be pursued. Two of the authors whose engagement with Muir was most important were also deeply involved with projects for Muslim reform. The first, Syed Ahmad Khan (1817–1898), was a traditionally educated civil servant with whom Muir had a "close, complicated, fraught yet finally symbiotic relationship."[47] Ahmad Khan—who eventually became "Sir Sayyid"—was by birth a member of the Muslim scholarly class and by profession a member of the colonial service. Although he eventually became known as a modernist and an advocate of European-style education, founding the Mohammedan Anglo-Oriental College (now Aligarh Muslim University), Ahmad Khan had a fairly typical inculcation into the tradition, even penning a devotional text celebrating the Proph-

et's birthday. The second, Ameer Ali (1849–1928), was among the most prominent Indian Muslims who sought to talk back to their British colonizers—to rebut their claims about Islam in general and Muhammad in particular. Both men's English-language writings merged biography and polemic and, especially in Ameer Ali's case, became important resources for Muslims in India and elsewhere, including Egypt. British authors also read these works, though European authors did not engage with Muslim authors in nearly the proportions that the reverse happened. As Susan Buck-Morss has noted, "colonized people," including "Muslim intellectuals," have been "routinely required" "to argue for [their] beliefs on truly foreign, and in many ways unpalatable, discursive terrains" since Napoleon's invasion of Egypt in 1798.[48]

Tales of the Prophet

Three main things were at stake in nineteenth-century biographies. One was a matter of theology: Where (if anywhere) did Muhammad fit in a history of prophets sent by God to guide humanity? The second, without necessary confessional commitments, was where Muhammad fit in the history of human reformers or leaders. The third crucial issue, on which answers to the others depended, was epistemological: How do we know? What sources are available? Are they trustworthy? How should they be used, and by whom? As one might expect, European authors, most of whom were Christian, and Indian Muslim authors had varying views on the theological issues. Debates tended to hinge on the second and third points, with Muslim critics of scholars like Muir often arguing that their religious commitments biased them so strongly that

they could not use the sources properly, leading them to an unjust verdict on Muhammad's merits. Muslim authors also disagreed with one another about these questions.

The major problem for Muir and other British thinkers was how to understand Muhammad's claims to have received revelation from God. Ideas about demon possession were no longer in vogue, and claims of deliberate and total fraud were less easily accepted than they had been when Prideaux was writing a hundred and fifty years earlier. Few were, like Carlyle, willing to accept Muhammad's complete sincerity and attribute his revelations to a welling up within him from deep in nature. George Lathom Browne's question in his 1856 *The Æra of Mahomet*, is more typical: "Was this madness or imposture?"[49] Others refused these dichotomous positions and saw Muhammad as confused or conflicted. John Davenport, who collaborated with Ahmad Khan and whose 1869 *An Apology for Mohammed and the Koran* has been cited by Muslim authors, declares it "more than probable that he really and conscientiously believed himself to be the divinely inspired Apostle of God."[50]

Muir, on the other hand, believed that whatever legitimate stirrings of a prophetic impulse Muhammad may have once had, he made a fateful choice to present his proclamations as God's speech. Thus, a salutary reform effort became twisted by his ambition for worldly success. Muir connects Muhammad's "temptation" and slippage into believing himself a prophet of God with the temptation of Jesus by Satan: Jesus "rejected the suggestion, and throughout his life on earth refrained from bringing the divine power which he possessed to the relief of his personal wants." Muhammad, by contrast, "arrogated a spiritual power which the records of his life too plainly prove that he misused to subserve his personal

necessities and even his erring desires."[51] Here, though, Muir hesitates: Muhammad was "not, indeed, possessed of any supernatural energy," but perhaps his "early doubts . . . and his suspicion of being under the influence of genii or evil spirits, suggest the enquiry whether that suspicion rested on any real ground, or was the mere creation of a nervous and excited fancy."[52] The comparison with Jesus allows Muir to note that Muhammad claims to continue the legacy of the biblical prophets, among whom he numbers Jesus, but in fact clearly diverges.

Muhammad's mission is intimately connected with the Qur'an, about which nineteenth-century writers were not particularly complimentary. In this, they followed in the footsteps of their Enlightenment predecessors. As Swedish scholar Tor Andrae notes, "Voltaire called it 'an incomprehensible book which violates our common sense upon every page,' and since Voltaire most European readers have found that the Koran is the most boresome reading that can be imagined."[53] This notion that non-Muslims are likely to be left cold by the Qur'an has wide currency, perhaps owing to historian Edward Gibbon's influential formulation: "The harmony and copiousness of style will not reach, in a version, the European infidel; he will peruse, with impatience, the endless incoherent rhapsody of fable, and precept, and declamation, which seldom excites a sentiment or an idea, which sometimes crawls in the dust and is sometimes lost in the clouds."[54] Gibbon's words are self-fulfilling: others have called it "inexpressibly tedious" and "a mostly impossible book."[55]

Even Carlyle, convinced of the Qur'an's merits, denigrated its style, calling it "[a] wearisome confused jumble." This is fitting, though, since it is not really a book but "a bewildered rhapsody" whose "primary character" is "genuineness."[56] The unpolished

nature of the text corresponds to the unrefined messenger who brought it: "The rude message he delivered was a real one withal; an earnest confused voice from the enthusiastical unknown Deep."[57] In this view, Carlyle was influenced by Goethe, for whom "untamed, spontaneous authenticity was everything," and who declared, "The only true art is characteristic art. If its influence arises from deep, harmonious, independent feeling, from feeling peculiar to the self, oblivious, yes, ignorant of everything foreign, then it is whole and living, whether it be born from crude savagery or cultured sentiment."[58] Carlyle valued Muhammad's authentic barbarian originality.

Carlyle's view of the Qur'an as "a fiery mass of Life cast up from the great bosom of Nature herself" was not widely shared.[59] Most held more prosaic accounts of the Qur'an's origins. Muslim dogma, disdained only by some philosophers, held that the Qur'an was God's verbatim divine speech, delivered to Muhammad through the agency of the angel Gabriel.[60] Needless to say, non-Muslims rejected this characterization, though some accepted the Muslim belief that Muhammad was illiterate.[61] They were left with two options: either it came from inside Muhammad or outside. Medieval scholars who depicted Muhammad as a heresiarch favored a demonic origin. Muir entertains this option from time to time, but does not insist on it; some parts of the Qur'an may be explained by "the natural workings of the Prophet's mind,"[62] and others clearly derive in some part from biblical sources or monotheist communities.

Jewish scholars mostly assumed that Muhammad took a significant portion of the Qur'anic text as well as his religious ideas broadly from Jews, either those living on the Arabian Peninsula or those he encountered on his journeys. German Jewish Orientalist

Abraham Geiger even titled a study *What Did Muhammad Take from the Jews?* Susannah Heschel observes that like many of his colleagues, "Geiger was remarkably sympathetic to Islam: Muhammad was a genuine religious enthusiast, not a seducer or fraud or epileptic."[63] German Jewish scholars tended to view Islam positively—in part because, she argues, "imagin[ing] an Enlightened Islam" became a means "to insist on a 'purified,' rational Judaism."[64] For these scholars, Islam's Jewish origins were to be celebrated.

In strong contrast, Christian scholars typically thought Muhammad had help from errant Christians—like the Syrian monk and Khadija's cousin Waraqa—and believed his religion a perversion of Christianity, not a demonstration of its vitality and adaptability.[65]

Sometimes what was problematic about Muhammad's use of Christianity was not just his rejection of its main doctrine, the divinity of Christ, but also its confusion of Christianity with other sources: the admixture itself was impure and dangerous. Echoing medieval condemnations of Muslim monstrosity, which insisted on Islam's "unnatural hybridity," Browne refers to "the plausible creed which the fanatic concocted out of the idolatry of his native tribes, and the vagaries of the numerous Christian heretics with whom he met in his commercial journeys."[66] American Baptist John Walton thought Islam "was partly borrowed out of the Christian Bible, and partly hatched out of the enthusiastical Brain of Mahomet."[67] Tom Stecker, in his 1900 drama, puts his own view in the mouth of a merchant speaking to camel drivers. He describes "a curious mongrel creed / Concocted from the morsels he hath stolen / From Christian, Jew, and Gentile."[68] In *The False Prophet*, prepared for the Massachusetts Sabbath School Society, Harvey Newcomb listed perverted Christian dogma, Jewish scripture, and

Arabian superstition as Muhammad's sources.[69] Longtime missionary S. W. Koelle viewed Islam as "a compound of Jewish fanaticism and Roman despotism."[70]

Whatever its origins, few doubted that the Qur'an could be attributed to Muhammad himself. Stanley Lane-Poole, writing for a popular audience, was categorical: "The Korān is known beyond any doubt to be at this moment, in all practical respects, identical with the prophet's words as collected immediately after his death. . . . Its genuineness is above suspicion."[71] By "genuine," he means that it records Muhammad's own words, not that it is revelation. Lane-Poole saw the Qur'an as the product of "a simple enthusiast confronted with many and varied difficulties and trying to meet them as best he could by the inward light that guided him."[72] Browne, also writing for generalists, was in the dubious minority: "Of the Koran as given out by Mahomet, we have no means of judging. That Qur'an from which alone we have to decide, what is or is not the Islam faith, was the work of another generation, and no doubt grossly interpolated and corrupted."[73]

Muir's assessment falls in the middle. Though noting the careless way early Muslims collected and preserved written copies of its verses, he believes it was effectively safeguarded in the tenacious memory of early Muslims, whose culture cultivated memorization. He is confident of its essential reliability: "I have examined the Corân and admitted its authority as an authentic and contemporary record."[74] Though the Qur'an went through a complex and uneven process of compilation, it was reliable as a record not only of Muhammad's words but also of his life. Prophetic traditions were to be less easily trusted, but unlike Lane-Poole's judgment that Muslim methods were worthless ("a totally useless and preposterous criticism"),[75] Muir endorses them up to a point; tradi-

tion, properly scrutinized, can provide important facts about
Muhammad's life and career. Still, he subordinates them to the
Qur'an: "The sure light of the Corân will be the pole-star of the
historian; and by it he will judge tradition."[76]

That these accounts for scholars and the general public explicitly discussed source reliability is striking. Even if Lane-Poole
was ultimately casual in how he chose *hadith* ("those which strike
the attention and do not seem peculiarly improbable"), he nonetheless described the process for his readers.[77] Books about
Islam, Muslims, and Muhammad targeted to lay audiences ran
the gamut from novelistic renderings—such as that by Washington Irving (1783–1859), which also included occasional foot-
notes—to toned-down scholarly offerings. The abridged version
of Muir's opus (1878) ran to 613 pages, not counting the index;
more than a tenth was devoted to "Sources for the Biography of
Mahomet." This essay had come at the beginning of the original
edition, indicating its primacy; its inclusion in the abridgment,
even relegated to an appendix, shows that lay readers could be
expected to take an interest. When the third edition appeared
in 1894, Muir put it back at the beginning. In his preface, he
reasons that it should come first, "as the value of a history depends entirely on the credibility of the evidence on which it is
based."[78]

Historian of colonial South Asia Avril Powell suggests that the
removal of some of the technical source apparatus from "later editions reflects the *Life*'s transition from a serious scholarly challenge to Muslim readers into a popular reference book for readers
in Britain."[79] The book was indeed popular, but it is precisely its
"challenge to Muslim readers" wherein Muir made his most enduring impact, occasioning rejoinders.

The Muslim reaction of "amazed horror" to biographies by Muir and Sprenger spurred responses.[80] Ahmad Khan's came in the form of *A Series of Essays on the Life of Muhammad and Subjects Subsidiary Thereto*. Composed in Urdu while Ahmad Khan was in England in 1869, it was published in 1870 in English; an expanded Urdu version appeared later.[81] A lengthy essay on Arabian geography and topology kicks off the compendium, followed by an essay on Muhammad's ancestry. Later essays discuss Muslim "tradition": mostly *hadith* books and methods, Muslim "theological literature," the Prophet's birth, and the impact of Islam on humanity. Ahmad Khan's *Series of Essays* is not "a fully-fledged counter-biography."[82] Instead, the topics align with those Muir addressed. Ahmad Khan asks the same sorts of questions that European scholars were asking: Was Islam on balance beneficial to humanity? How does Islam compare to other religions? (This assumes, already, that there are discrete entities called "religions" that can be compared on their merits, whether doctrinal or historical.) And, most importantly, how does Muhammad compare to other prophets?

No incident better encapsulates the disagreement between Muir and his critics than the so-called Satanic verses controversy. During a period in Mecca when he was under pressure from elites, Muhammad reportedly pronounced a passage from the Qur'an that attributed intercessory powers to three Meccan goddesses who were known as "daughters of Allah"—Allah being, in pre-Islamic Arabia, the name of a major deity. According to Muslims who believe this incident happened, Satan cast these verses into the Prophet's mind; God, however, could not allow such corruption to stand, and revealed new verses that reject the very idea of God having daughters or other subordinate deities.

Such are the main features of the story as found in early and classical sources. Muslim tradition wavered as to whether to accept it as true. The problem of the Satanic verses is bound up with the question of the integrity of the Qur'anic text, the reliability of the *hadith* literature, and the deep theological issue raised by the Prophet's seeming fallibility.[83] Some, such as the fourteenth-century Syrian Ibn Taymiyya, saw in the ultimate resolution of this incident the proof of God's guarantee of safeguarding the Qur'an from corruption.[84] Modern Muslims, too, disagree about what really happened. Their debates take into consideration Western interlocutors and the fact that their writings might provide fodder for criticism of Muhammad and Islam.

For Muir, the story's inclusion in early books serves as guarantor of its truth—up to a point. Rather than seeing any Satanic intervention, he attributes these verses instead to Muhammad's attempt to placate the Meccans. However, when Muhammad eventually realizes that their content will compromise his core mission and message, he repudiates the verses and replaces them with the current set.[85] Referring to "the narratives of Wackidi and Tabari," Muir writes: "Pious Mussulmans of after days, scandalized at the lapse of their Prophet into so flagrant a concession, would reject the whole story. But the authorities are too strong to be impugned. It is hardly possible to conceive how the tale, if not in some shape or other founded in truth, could ever have been invented."[86] Unlike Sprenger, who believes that the biographical texts sometimes include wholesale fabrications about miracles and other unlikely goings-on, Muir sees a "kernel" of historical truth in all such stories, no matter how fantastical.[87] Ahmad Khan, on the other hand, rejects it wholesale, despite its presence in early biographies. He reasons that accounts of the supposed event contradict each other.

Their irreconcilability points to their untrustworthiness; they are not to be taken as authoritative.[88] In these debates, then, the question of source methodology is paramount.

At the opposite pole from the anxiety-provoking Satanic verses incident, the night journey and ascension are for Muslims a uniformly positive moment in Muhammad's life, perhaps the pinnacle of his prophetic experience.[89] Stories and images of the ascension were a central—perhaps *the* central—element of Muhammad's life story over the centuries. One night, not long before his migration to Medina, Muhammad lay down to sleep in his cousin Umm Hani's home; during the night he was transported to "the farthest mosque," traditionally situated in Jerusalem, and from there to the heavens, where he encountered past prophets, conversed with angels, and negotiated with God over the daily prayer obligations of Muslims—bargaining God down from fifty to five. Unlike the Satanic verses incident, which according to him has no *reliable* support in traditional texts, Ahmad Khan sees Qur'anic grounding for the ascension.[90] Was the ascension "a mere vision" or a "bodily" journey? Muslims have long debated this question.[91] Sprenger overstates the case when he declares, "All historical records are for the latter opinion; the former is upheld by some skeptics only."[92] Sprenger paints Muslims as credulous and the tradition as unreliable. But it is true that those who claim the journey was a vision were a minority.

Whether agreeing that it "really" happened or not, to focus on this point obscures earlier ways of treating the ascension. Muslims were attentive to the beauty and sublimity of the story itself and the spiritual truths it conveyed. Authors fleshed out the narrative in myriad ways. It figured prominently in preaching and proselytizing as well as sectarian conflict among Muslims.[93] It told

about the relation of Muhammad to other prophets, particularly Abraham and Moses. Its affirmation of Muslim ritual worked also to establish the superiority of Muhammad to other prophets, in part through narrating, though circumspectly, his vision of God. Mystics adopted the model of the ascension to describe spiritual progress. In a twist, the story of the ladder by which Muhammad ascended to heaven was known to medieval Europeans, including the author of the Divine Comedy.[94] "How ironic," renowned Islamic studies scholar Annemarie Schimmel observes, "that the hero of the true [ascension], the Prophet Muhammad, should have been placed by Dante among the schismatics in the lowest part of Hell!"[95]

The same dynamics at play in the story of the ascension also apply to the lesser-known story in which the boy Muhammad was playing near his foster mother's home when two angels approached him, held him down, opened his chest, and removed a miniscule black speck. This purified him and made him fit to receive the Qur'anic message. Non-Muslim scholars have sometimes seen this legend as an example of how Muslim tradition has sought to fill narrative gaps in the Qur'an, which alludes to having "opened [his] breast," by inventing stories to explain its obscure passages. Muslim tradition treats the Qur'anic statement as a reference to a real event, though Muslims again disagree over whether to understand it literally.[96] Muir, too, views the Qur'an and other early accounts as generally reflecting actual events of the Prophet's life: though his miracles are "puerile fabrications . . . we can generally trace in tradition some real incident on which they were engrafted, which prompted the idea, and gave to fancy a starting-point for its fairy creations and illusive colouring."[97]

The opening of the breast, which Ahmad Khan discusses in conjunction with the ascension, provides a useful counterpoint to the story of the seal of prophecy: in one account, something extraneous is removed from Muhammad's body; while in the other, something extra on his body is recognized not as superfluous or dangerous but as meaningful. The seal of prophecy—a bodily mark, mole, patch of hair, or "fleshy excrescence" the size of a pigeon egg—was between his shoulder blades. Ahmad Khan, like other modern Muslim scholars, downplays the role of this mark, but like the encounter with Bahira, it confirms objectively Muhammad's status as prophesied messenger.

As he interprets various facts about Muhammad's life, Ahmad Khan repeatedly attacks Muir's methods—from which sources he uses to how he interprets the materials he finds there. According to Ahmad Khan, Muir uses unreliable sources when it suits his purposes and repeats stories of miraculous occurrences or qualities credulously, when the right kind of Muslim would not accept them; he fails to grasp the more relaxed standards for biographical reports than for prophetic traditions with legal implications.[98] Just because accounts are *included* in the biographies does not mean that a good scholar will depend on them; the compilers' job was to collect, not to sort or discard them.[99] Sprenger, like Muir, depends on untrustworthy sources: "two Moslem authors (Wâkidi and his Kâtib [i.e., Ibn Sa'd]), regarded in the Mohammedan world as the least trustworthy and most careless biographers of Mohammed."[100] By contrast, he himself relies "on the writings of Ibn-Hishâm and Ibn-al-Athîr. The former, in spite of the animadversions of Muir, will always continue to occupy the position of the most careful and trustworthy biographer of the Prophet. The latter," Abu'l-Fida's main source, as noted earlier, "for his

critical acumen, the simple and chaste elegance of his style, and the extensive erudition displayed throughout his splendid history, might justly claim a place in the rank of the greatest historians of Europe."[101] How quickly Ahmad Khan moves from condemning Muir's misapprehension of the Muslim biographical tradition to holding up European scholars as the standard to which Muslim authors must be compared!

In Ahmad Khan's view, by accepting the wrong sorts of Muslim sources—out of ignorance, incompetence, or malice—Muir, Sprenger, and others come to erroneous and unwarranted conclusions about Islam.[102] Take a banal example, which Ahmad Khan approaches with absolute seriousness: Did the Prophet dye his hair? Muir sees contradictions within the tradition literature on this point. Ahmad Khan instead reconciles the various accounts, some of which suggest henna use and others that reject it. Muir's inability to reconcile the texts shows that he is unqualified to use them.[103]

Ahmad Khan may not consciously have been aware of the underlying problem. He was from a scholarly family, trained in traditional ways of reading texts. Although he makes unorthodox arguments in the course of his *Series of Essays* and other writings, his criticisms assume that Muir is hampered by not having a teacher to walk him through the texts, to point out what is to be trusted and what is not, to explain that mere inclusion does not guarantee reliability. As Timothy Mitchell puts it, discussing medieval historian Ibn Khaldun, "The entire practice of Arab scholarship revolved around the problem over overcoming the absence in writing of the author's unequivocal meaning."[104] The same is the case—indeed, is perhaps even more the case—for texts that are compilations, such as traditional biographies and *hadith* collections. Reading them involves more than an ability to decode the words.

Ahmad Khan does not articulate this point explicitly, instead appealing to methodological principles that he presumes Muir shares, including objectivity. Neatly reversing Muir's practice of taking unflattering or critical things from the Muslim tradition as unwilling witnesses, for Ahmad Khan, if antagonistic Christian scholars say something flattering about Muhammad, they are to be taken at face value.[105] Since they would not acknowledge it were it not indisputable, it can thus be taken as a given.[106] In incorporating European sources into his book, Ahmad Khan simultaneously bolsters his own authority by arrogating theirs and undermines (other) Indian and Muslim authors by favoring Western statements as authoritative. Use of non-Muslim sources by Muslim authors is, of course, an old tactic. Early Muslim authors used not only biblical models but also biblical passages as "sources of attestation."[107] Ahmad Khan follows in their footsteps, citing Western praise and also arguing for Muhammad's prophethood based on biblical scripture.[108]

His attempt to generate evidence for Muhammad's prophetic role on the basis of biblical texts was largely disregarded by Christian controversialists, who preferred to argue on other grounds, especially the Muslim biographical tradition. Where Ahmad Khan might claim that a particular fact about Muhammad's life, attested in the Qur'an or authentic traditions, illustrated his fulfillment of biblical prophecy, Muir read the same sources differently: either the event was not credible or it did not mean what Muslims wanted it to mean.[109] In particular, Muir dismissed arguments that presumed any supernatural influence on Muhammad (though he did not entirely rule out the possibility of demonic interference). Ahmad Khan insisted that Muir unfairly rejected stories about Muhammad similar to those that he accepted in the life stories of

Jesus and Moses. (This was the obverse of the argument found in *The Three Impostors:* "Whenever there is the same reason as in the case of Mahomet for charging any person with imposture . . . they should be placed in the same category. And, for example, in the case of Moses, there is the same reason.")[110]

Muir errs, in this view, by not approaching Moses and Jesus with the same skepticism that he brings to stories of Muhammad. Rather than undertaking "an unprejudiced and candid investigation [using] fair, just, and legitimate reasoning," Muir approaches the tradition literature prepared to find it affected by (in Muir's terms) "superstitious reverence" and "fond devotion," which distorted stories and inaccurately invested Muhammad "with supernatural attributes."[111] Ahmad Khan asks, with a great deal of vim, "May not all the miraculous deeds of Moses"—he lists quite a few—"be considered as only so many amusing tales, invented and fabricated by that prophet's ardent and zealous followers"? Or, for that matter, "What would become of Jesus and his devout and zealous followers were everyone to discard, as merely so many fabrications and idle inventions, the traditions which represent Christ as rising from the dead" and so forth?[112] Muhammad must be treated with the same impartiality. *The Three Impostors* argues for the men's equal fraudulence; Ahmad Khan argues for their equal validity.

Ameer Ali takes Ahmad Khan's work in a slightly different direction. Comfortable in English—he studied law in England, spent time there off and on for more than three decades, and then lived in England after his retirement from his position as a judge in India—Ali wrote several books, among them a popular *History of the Saracens* and works on Islamic law, including one about women. His two studies of Muhammad's life garnered him worldwide notice among Muslims. *A Critical Examination of the Life and*

Teachings of Mohammed first appeared in 1873.[113] A revised and edited version appeared in 1891 as *The Life and Teachings of Mohammed, or the Spirit of Islam;* it is by *The Spirit of Islam* that the book is commonly known.[114] Orientalist David Margoliouth thought it "probably the best achievement in the way of an apology for Mohammed that is ever likely to be composed in a European language."[115]

Ameer Ali situates Islam on the world stage and in an interreligious framework that is more cosmopolitan than that of Ahmad Khan. Where the latter argues that one must treat Muhammad in the same fashion that one treats Jesus or Moses—that is to say, within an Abrahamic, biblical paradigm—Ameer Ali's broader canvas includes Buddhists and Hindus in the religious history of the world. He focuses on human progress and universal norms. Some of Muhammad's seemingly questionable actions are perfectly understandable in context. Given the circumstances of time and place, he had to make certain compromises in order to accomplish what he did. His accomplishments are proof not only of his prophetic mission but of his superiority to other prophets in that he brought to fruition his vision. Muhammad was the last prophet, and there is no need for further prophecy, but there *is* a need for additional reform. Humanity's trajectory is toward enhanced freedom and vitality. Ameer Ali was among the first generations of people to be seduced by the idea of history as progress, laid out in the closing years of the eighteenth century by the Marquis de Condorcet. This view of history as forward movement merged with ideas about Muhammad as the "seal of the prophets," the last divinely sent messenger.

Muhammad's Muslim biographers would have experienced a tension between this model of Muhammad as a figure from the

past and that of Muhammad as someone to whom Muslims
should relate in an eternal present. What was the relationship between the Muhammad of history, increasingly at the center of
interreligious debates, and the Muhammad of devotion? Ahmad
Khan's own life illustrates a shift in emphasis if not a change of
heart: in his early twenties, he wrote a devotional text for the
Prophet's birthday celebration with the evocative (and, in the original language, rhyming) title "The Polishing of Hearts through
Remembrance of the Beloved One."[116] Although this text may
have had a reformist bent, the commemoration of Muhammad as
God's beloved is a strategy for individual spiritual progress; Ahmad
Khan's later work reflects a concern with Muhammad as someone
whose "benefit to humanity" can be determined once one sorts out
questions of evidence and bias.[117] Thinking of Islam as a religion
benefiting humanity in the sense of measurable human progress,
stacking civilizations up next to one another and comparing the reforms they wrought is a very different sort of strategy for human
betterment than is meditation on prophetic virtues as a tool for spiritual self-improvement.

Through the decades chronicled here, devotional texts, the sort
that Muir dismissed as "the veriest inanities which, by any possibility, could be imagined," continued to be written and to circulate.[118] At the same time, the language of humanity and progress
was widely adopted. Writing in India, probably in the 1930s,
Mohammad Ali Salmin writes that "the Great Holy Prophet . . .
worked for the benefit of humanity. . . . He identified himself entirely with his work for Humanity."[119] Such concepts did not entirely
displace effusive content; rather, "devotional" and "modernist" approaches came to coexist.[120] Salmin's biography, mostly apologetic
and engaged in contesting negative portrayals of Muhammad,

opens with a set of Arabic and English blessings on the Prophet, which evoke a believer's longing for closeness to him: "On account of the exceeding desire of seeing you, we have almost reached the point of death. . . . My poor heart . . . is now a martyr of love for the Prophet."[121]

"Competitive Hagiography"

Hybrid biography flourished with the ongoing proximity of Christians and Muslims in India and elsewhere.[122] The nineteenth and twentieth centuries may have their only parallel in the first two centuries of Islam, in terms of the speed and scope of transformation. The exchanges were not a one-sided imposition but a mutual if lopsided process.[123] And, indeed, it was not merely a two-player game: Hindu polemicists participated as well, as in the famous debates held, as public spectacles, in Shahjahanpur in northern India in 1875 and 1876. Sponsored by the British authorities, three men took the stage to argue for the truth of their religions—a Protestant scholar and school administrator; a Hindu reformer whose Arya Samaj movement played a crucial role in the transformation of Indian religion in the nineteenth century; and Qasim Nanautvi, a founder of the famous college at Deoband and "a towering figure in the intellectual history of Islam in South Asia."[124] (On other occasions, Arya Samaj representatives debated with Ahmadi controversialists; as noted previously, India's religious landscape was complicated with numerous lines of fracture within as well as between "religions.")[125]

Although the point of the Shahjahanpur convocation was to decide "the true God"—which, as SherAli Tareen points out, as-

sumes that the way one defines religion has to do with a set of dogmas and doctrines that can be logically argued, and moreover to which a public audience is crucial—participants debated the merits of their respective revered figures. When Muhammad's miracles came up for discussion, Nanautvi affirmed not only that Muhammad performed miracles well beyond bringing the Qur'an but that his miracles were superior to those performed by Jesus.

Nanautvi's emphatic praise for Muhammad's miracles was part of a long tradition. Comparisons between Jesus and Muhammad were not new, nor was the central place of miracles in those comparisons.[126] Byzantine Greek polemics against Muhammad had insisted that "Mahomet performed no miracles; his supposed miracles are the fruit of the imagination of his crude and barbaric adepts; the Qur'an, far from being one [that is, a miracle], is an incoherent and contradictory assemblage of doctrines borrowed from here and there; as to Mahomet's moral conduct, it is a tissue of debauchery, of carnal pleasures, of lies and of blood"; such accusations constitute "the ideological infrastructure under which concrete biographical elements are grafted."[127] Medieval European comparisons were likewise unflattering to Muhammad and agreed that he did not perform legitimate miracles.[128] One early Eastern polemic insisted that "of the three founders of religion, Moses, Jesus, and Muhammad, only this last did not perform miracles which have confirmed his status as God's envoy."[129] Both the growth of miracles in the Muslim biographical tradition and the denial of those miracles by Christians were spurred by the desire to enhance or detract from Muhammad's stature vis-à-vis other biblical figures and Christ himself.[130] (For Muslims, Christ

fit into the category of biblical prophet, not more special than others; for Christians, obviously, the case was different.)[131]

Ahmad Khan had objected to the unequal treatment of Muhammad and these other foundational figures in his *Series of Essays.* Yet he emphasized the natural nature of prophecy and Muhammad's humanity, seeing miracles as "unnecessary" and irrelevant to Muhammad's mission as God's messenger.[132] In this, he followed other Indian thinkers, such as the eighteenth-century figure Shah Wali Allah, who had begun to shy away from the miraculous elements of Muhammad's life. Muslim critique of the "extravaganzas" and "fables" found in traditional accounts of the Prophet's life gained steam in the late nineteenth and twentieth centuries.[133] Numerous Egyptian modernists would reject miracle stories as colorful additions to the biographical tradition. They had precedents among earlier Muslims, a minority of whom have always held that Muhammad's only miracle was the Qur'an, although various special signs and portents attached themselves to him.

By the mid-nineteenth century, many European authors looked on claims of miraculous deeds dismissively—not just by Muhammad but by anyone. They used Muhammad's reported insistence that he did not work miracles to critique their own traditions. Although Muhammad's (supposed) lack of miracles figured prominently in evangelical anti-Muslim tracts, other European thinkers treated Islam as a more rational religion precisely because it (supposedly) minimized miracles. Higgins did not deny that many Muslims attributed miracles to Muhammad, but he absolved the Prophet himself for any such claim: "some of his followers, long after his death, believing that he performed miracles, declared that he professed to have that power: a thing he certainly never pretended to."[134] In fact, he "totally denied from the beginning any

supernatural endowment of this kind . . . , and in the Koran the working of miracles is repeatedly disclaimed."[135]

The (minority) denial of miracles by Muslims was used by polemicists, who always exploit divergence within a tradition to their advantage, as evidence that Muhammad was not a legitimate prophet. Though popular Muslim belief clung to the notion of prophetic miracles, learned Muslims rejected them, and Muhammad himself had equivocated or temporized or denied them altogether.[136] Another strand of argument was that Muhammad's miracles were only trickery. Christian evangelists in nineteenth-century India continued to cite Muhammad's lack of miracles as proof that he was not a prophet.[137] (When the miraculous status of the Qur'an was raised, non-Muslims, not particularly complimentary about it, scoffed.)

Koelle compares Muhammad and Jesus in his 1889 *Mohammed and Mohammedanism Critically Considered*.[138] He declares that only from the viewpoint of the superior religion—that is, Christianity—can one truly judge Islam, since "only by the light of the higher religion can the lower be rightly estimated."[139] The missionary's task of conversion is made more difficult by "the transcendent halo of the mythical Mohammed."[140] Muslims must be brought to realize "that all the boasted equality or superiority of Mohammed to Christ rests on mere fiction, devoid of all foundation in fact."[141] Like recent historians who attend to the early Muslim biographical literature, Koelle focuses on the ways in which Muhammad is modeled after Jesus and, more broadly, on using Muslim sources "to illustrate how the glowing imagination and devout admiration of the Moslem believers have metamorphosed him, and enveloped the genuine natural original in the fictitious halo of a dazzling radiance and a supernatural glory."[142] Koelle laments not merely the

invention of miracle tales by credulous followers (encouraged, in his lifetime, by Muhammad himself) but their fantastical excesses in comparison to biblical miracles.[143] The bible's "wonders resemble beautiful flowers of Paradise, springing up from a purely ethical ground," while "Mohammedan marvels look like unreal phantoms of the air, produced for the purpose of ostentatious display, and result from an unethical trifling with the supernatural."[144] Thus, these exaggerated accounts of Muhammad's miracles prevent Muslims from recognizing the true glory of Jesus.[145]

Muhammad's miracles also had staunch defenders, and the arrival of the East India Company and missionaries at the turn of the nineteenth century prompted some to highlight them.[146] Nanautvi, the Deobandi representative at the Shahjahanpur festival, waxed eloquent about Muhammad's miracles. Not only did he perform miracles like Moses and Jesus, as Ahmad Khan had suggested, but his miracles were superior to theirs. What Koelle had seen as exaggeration in this case indicated the superiority not only of Muhammad but of Islam.

Evolution of Religion

The Shahjahanpur festival, juxtaposing Christian, Hindu, and Muslim arguments for the superiority of each faith, took place in a context in which new ideas about hierarchies of religious life framed debates. The Bombay Tract and Book Society's *Life of Mahomet*, a work Muir panned for its scholarly inadequacies, placed Islam on a spectrum of non-Christian religions arrayed by relative sophistication.[147] Instead of understanding Islam as being worse than paganism because its manner of being false allows it to be

mistaken for truth, here Islam is perceived as better because it is closer to Christianity (and Judaism, having drawn from both of them), while both Hinduism and Greek mythology are further from the truth. American Baptist missionary Frances Mason held a similar attitude: Islam was superior to idolatrous Hinduism.[148]

This view of Islam as better than pagan religions because it is a step on the path toward Christianity stands opposed to earlier centuries' view of Muhammad as an antichrist. The Antichrist is dangerous precisely because his seeming closeness to the true faith allows him to lead believers astray. An evolutionist logic, elaborated further over the course of the nineteenth century, helped portray Islam as an improvement, but a partial and incomplete one, over non-monotheistic faiths.[149] As Irvin Schick points out, "Europe's exploration of the world during the colonial age was always productive of power asymmetries" that functioned "within an evolutionist hierarchy."[150] Even if the Bombay Society missionaries would have rejected Darwin's hypothesis, they were shaped by many of its constituent ideas.[151]

In contrast to Christian views that positioned Islam as having begun to ascend the ladder of monotheism toward Christianity, some Muslim authors predictably situated Islam at monotheism's apex. Ameer Ali, for instance, concludes that Islam represents monotheism's fullest flowering. "Neither Christianity nor Judaism had succeeded in raising" the debased "moral and religious condition of the Arabs."[152] (He quotes Muir at some length to support this claim.) Both idolatry and human sacrifices were practiced by pre-Islamic Arabs.[153] Muhammad used the folklore and legends "floating among his people" and "adopted them as the lever for raising the Arabs as well as the surrounding nations from the depth of

social and moral degradation into which they had fallen."[154] Yet Ameer Ali does not proclaim that Islam supersedes Judaism and Christianity doctrinally. Such a tactic would ill suit his audience and betray the universal creed he rhetorically espouses. Instead, as Chapter 3 will explore further, Ameer Ali is among those using Muhammad's success in social transformation to elevate Islam over other religions.

Chapter 3

Eminent Muslims

Five years after the emigration, Muslims in Medina
faced ongoing hostilities with Meccan opponents. When
the Meccans threatened to attack, the Medinan community
was struggling with hypocrites—untrustworthy nominal
Muslims—and fickle Jewish allies, whose support could
not be ensured. The Muslims were grossly outnumbered
and outmatched in horses and weapons. How could they
hold off the Meccans? A Persian convert suggested a
strategy new to the region: dig a trench to supplement
Medina's natural fortifications. It was backbreaking
work, in which the Prophet assisted, but it paid off when
the ditch stymied the attacking cavalry. The Meccans
tried to persuade an allied Jewish tribe, the Banu
Qurayza, to attack on another front, but Muhammad
thwarted that plan. The Meccans eventually lifted their
siege, and the Banu Qurayza were punished for their
treachery: an arbiter they chose ordered the women and
children enslaved and the men executed.

In Medina, Muhammad was not only a prophet but also—and in
some contexts, primarily—a community leader and military
commander. These latter elements of his role were long taken for
granted by Muslims. His military expeditions were among the
earliest stories recorded; Waqidi's *Book of Campaigns* was devoted
to them. In thirteenth-century Egyptian Sufi Muhammad al-
Busiri's famous *Burda* ("Cloak Ode"), an edition of which was
printed in Leiden in 1761, the Prophet's "military achievements are

elaborated in gruesome detail." He leads "an ocean of an army on floating steeds / That threw up clashing waves of heroes / Each of them entrusted to God and expecting heavenly reward / Assailing, and completely devoted to the extirpation of idolatry."[1] Although al-Busiri spends far more time enumerating Muhammad's matchless excellence ("ascribe to his person whatever you want in terms of nobility / And ascribe to his power every greatness you want") than his battle prowess, it was Muhammad leading warriors that permeated anti-Muslim writing; the claim that Islam was spread by the sword recurred in Christian polemics throughout the centuries.[2]

In the nineteenth and twentieth centuries, however, a few essential things changed.

First, *Lives* of military heroes and other "great men" came to form a regular part of British biography. Second, and in tension with the first development, the use of violence came to be seen by large sections of the educated public and scholars as illegitimate unless justified by a compelling interest, such as self-defense (a notoriously elastic concept). The first meant that Muhammad's military exploits and, far more importantly, his and his followers' success in conquering and ruling large swathes of territory made him a figure of interest. The second meant that Muslim accounts of his military endeavors sought to justify his use of force in terms that would resonate with European Christian and other critics who charged that he was too wrapped up in worldly ambition and plans for military domination. In tension with this attempt to downplay Muhammad's military victories and to play up his defensive use of force, Muslims subject to foreign occupation treated Muhammad as a successful general partly as a way to envision alternative realities for subject peoples.

It was not just Muhammad. Early Islamic figures, including his successors, were relevant to problems of leadership that bedeviled modern Muslim societies chafing under colonial rule. Heroic figures—for Sunnis, Abu Bakr, Umar, Uthman, and Ali, the four so-called "rightly guided" successors to Muhammad who ruled from 632 to 661—were models for action. These men's success in the politico-military sphere made them tempting subjects, and their religious credentials mattered as well. Just as Europeans of earlier centuries had struggled to comprehend how Muslims, so clearly in the wrong religiously, could have managed to wrest away the Holy Land and, from the city formerly known as Constantinople, threaten the heart of Europe, Muslims in northern Africa and South Asia were confronted with the loss of sovereignty to powers they had, not long before, seen as barbaric and inferior. Some Muslim thinkers responded, just as medieval Christians had, by criticizing their own societies for moral and other failures that had led to foreign domination. In a new twist on old patterns of reformist thought, some Sunni thinkers turned to ideas of a pristine early tradition, before it was corrupted by improper innovations and the accretions of a scholarly tradition that, they thought, was collapsing under its own weight. Salafism, which prioritized the purported conduct of the first Muslim community, was a broad trend that developed into both Islamic modernism and puritanical Wahhabism. Both reform movements owe a profound debt to Protestantism, including its assumptions about authority and texts. These movements and tendencies predated and coexisted with colonialism, and developed alongside Orientalist scholarship and in engagement with it. Its assumptions affected those modern accounts of Muhammad and his Companions. Alternately sectarian and ecumenical tendencies among Muslims led to the glorification of early figures in ways that

consolidated and affirmed preferred versions of early Muslim history, including the roles of Muhammad's wives and kin, which resonated with the new emphasis on Muhammad the man as well as Muhammad the prophet.

Success and Succession

Perhaps paradoxically, given that Christian Europeans were now in power over vast tracts of Muslim-inhabited land, Islam's worldly success was a major preoccupation for Muhammad's biographers from the mid-nineteenth century to the mid-twentieth century. William Muir repeatedly warns his readers not to adopt the commonsensical view that Muhammad's success validates his religion. Although Muhammad's teachings had obvious and immediate impact on the world, whereas Jesus's career did not lead swiftly to perceptible external change, one should not take this for an indication of the relative importance of the two figures. Jesus "ministered . . . among the Jews, whose law he came not to destroy but to fulfill, and in whose *outer* life, therefore, there was no marked change to be affected." In other words, the lack of *visible* social change actually attests to Jesus's success. By contrast, Muhammad's success in winning adherents and dramatically reshaping the practices of "a nation of idolaters sunk in darkness and vice" is to be taken for granted, since "converts to exhibit any consistency whatever must go forth with a bold and distinctive separation."[3] Muir dismisses or highlights Muhammad's real-world legacies where it suits him, downplaying the end of idolatry but lambasting the interconnected evils of polygamy and slavery, which he attributes to Muhammad.

Aloys Sprenger approaches the spread of Islam differently, granting the premise that the faith's success has some bearing on the merit of those responsible for it. If Muhammad himself had led a revolution, he would have had an "irrefutable" case for his religion: "we should be obliged to acknowledge his doctrine as absolute truth because it was victorious." But the "false religion" had other historical causes for its success,[4] most notably in the role of a group of advisors, foremost among whom was Abu Bakr. As he describes it, "after his death they founded an empire which surpassed that of the Romans." Rather than being "hot headed fanatics," these men used "wisdom and perseverance" and "were guided by the most consunmate [sic] prudence and by cool reflection; and their objects were in most cases noble, and the means which they employed were rarely objectionable."[5] Broadly, where Muir is suspicious of worldly success—an odd position for one in the employ of the British Empire—Sprenger connects it to virtue.

Unlike Sprenger, Ameer Ali attributes Muslim successes to Muhammad himself rather than to his successors. Like Muir, success for Ameer Ali is manifested in Muhammad more than in Jesus, but this is a good thing rather than a sign of corruption. In an extended passage, Ameer Ali quotes Muir regarding the "spiritual torpor" of Arabia at the time of Muhammad. Previous monotheistic revelations had worked but "slight and transient influences . . . upon the Arab mind" and "people were sunk in superstition, cruelty, and vice." (The words are Muir's.) Muir notes the "arousing of spiritual life" reawakened for the first time "since the days when primitive Christianity startled the world from its sleep and waged a mortal conflict with Heathenism." Muhammad, according to Ameer Ali, completed his "Mission," and

in this fact—the fact of the whole work being achieved in his life-time—lies his distinctive superiority over the prophets, sages, and philosophers of other times and countries;—Jesus, Moses, Zoroaster, Sakya-Muni [i.e., Buddha], Plato, all had their notions of Realms of God, their Republics, their Ideas— through which degraded humanity was to be elevated into a new moral life. All had departed from this world with their as-pirations unfulfilled, their bright visions unrealized; or had be-queathed the task of elevating their fellow-men to sanguinary disciples or monarch-pupils. It was reserved for Mohammed to fulfil his mission and that of his predecessors. It was reserved for him alone to see accomplished the work of amelioration.[6]

In praising Muhammad's elevation of "degraded humanity . . . into a new moral life," he ignores Muir's arguments in favor of Jesus's goodness and Muhammad's rank ambition and instead uses Muir's dismal portrait of pre-Islamic Arabia to highlight the immensity of Muhammad's task and, therefore, the glory of his accomplishments. He goes further, however. Muhammad is more impressive than Jesus not only because he manages to fulfill his mission during his own lifetime but also because he finishes the job that earlier messengers, including Jesus, had left incomplete.[7] In emphasizing Muhammad's accomplishments, Ameer Ali also tries to refute criticism of his methods in accomplishing them, explaining Muhammad's use of force through the measures of man in wide circulation at the time: He acted in self-defense. Had he not, he could have held lofty principles but not made a dramatic change in the world, bringing his vision to fruition. Muhammad was justified in using force not because he had God on his side (though he did), but because his movement required

lifting a people out of ignorance. To do this in the face of Meccan opposition necessitated defensive military action. He undertook social reform and betterment, using force in legitimate ways, and was ultimately successful. He was, in other words, a great man of history by the categories of the British overlords. Indeed, accepting the use of force for social amelioration, and viewing its success as proof of the greatness of those who wield it, might seem to tacitly justify British rule over India. In his assessment of Muhammad's goals and means, Ameer Ali may have had in mind John Davenport's summary: "Mohammed, a simple Arab, united the distracted, scanty, naked, and hungry tribes of his country into one compact and obedient body, and presented them with new attributes and a new character among the people of the earth."[8] But Davenport sees Muhammad as a happy medium between the excessively spiritual (and therefore impractical) Christianity and the example of Moses, who not only had a more limited mission but also employed rough means to achieve it.[9]

Davenport's *Apology* fits within a spectrum of diverse publications on Islam appearing in Britain; in the United States, Christian tracts dominated. In the newly independent United States—in the early nineteenth century the country was but a few decades old—few Americans had met Muslims. American authors of evangelical works on Muhammad and Islam were not bound by the same imperative as British missionaries in India not to offend lest they lose out on converts. Most American books about Islam and Muhammad were addressed to other Christians, and Islam was often a foil for promoting the superiority of Protestantism—or one branch of it—over other traditions, particularly Catholicism within the United States and other forms of Christianity outside of it.

As the nineteenth century progressed, American missionizing in the Middle East increased dramatically. The official stance of the American Board of Commissioners for Foreign Missions was not unlike that of many other American Protestants concerned with proper doctrine: "the great pillars of the Papal and Mahometan impostures are now tottering to their fall."[10] When they did go on missions to convert those whom Palestine-bound Boston missionary Pliny Fisk called "the followers of that artful impostor, who arose in Arabia," they were often equally concerned with making converts from local forms of Orthodox Christianity.[11] Very few Muslims converted, and in one estimate, "probably only a few hundred eastern Christians became Protestants."[12]

Even once Americans became concerned with real-world Muslims, they lagged far behind Europe in the production of scholarship on Islam and Muhammad. Instead, publishers in New York and Boston churned out popular accounts, the best known of which was probably George Bush's *Life of Mohammed*. Bush, a Methodist preacher and a distant relation of the presidents Bush, followed Humphrey Prideaux closely in much of his content, but his framing was very different. Prideaux, whose work had appeared in several American editions, had been concerned with heretical Christians; Bush, like early modern English authors, saw in Muhammad and Islam the fulfillment of biblical prophecies about the end times.

Take his explanation of Islam's success, for example. Rather than attributing it to either the sincerity of its founder (Carlyle) or the virtues of his successors (Sprenger), or deeming it unimportant when compared to Christ's purity of motives (Muir), for Bush, how "an obscure individual, sprung from the roving tribes of Arabia, following no higher occupation than that of a caravan-trader,

possessing no peculiar advantages of mental culture, nor distinguished in the outset by any pre-eminence of power or authority" came to found a religion and empire that swayed millions and has persisted for more than a millennium "presents a phenomenon which increases our wonder the more steadily it is contemplated." It can only be explained, in Bush's estimate, by "the intended providential bearings of the entire fabric of Mohammedan delusion upon the church of Christ."[13] That Muhammad's success must be understood as part of a divine plan that will ultimately result in the triumph of Christianity is echoed by Murray in his translation of Abu'l-Fida.[14]

The Man Mahomet

Though Bush is strongly negative toward Islam—at least as much as anyone can be when convinced it is part of a divine plan—he, like Muir, allows Muhammad some virtues. Bush views him as "by nature a man of a superior cast of character," but according to a relative rather than an absolute measure: "the age and the country in which he arose and shone were rude and barbarous; and the standard which would determine him great among the roving tribes of Arabia might have left him little more than a common man in the cultivated climes of Europe. Men's characters are moulded as much by their circumstances and fortunes as by their native genius and bias."[15]

In addition to basic virtues of honesty, chastity, truthfulness, and resolve, there was the more complicated question of manliness. Stanley Lane-Poole saw Muhammad as effective in his exercise of power, displaying "manly bearing under obloquy and reproach," but also as effeminate and having a "nervous and

excitable" disposition.[16] This combination of "weakness and strength" was, for him, one of "the inevitable inconsistencies of a great man."[17] Sprenger believed Muhammad "unmanly" and even prone to hysterical oversensitivity.[18] According to Sprenger, he was very sensitive to bad smells, having a surprisingly "delicate constitution" for one of "semi-barbarous habits."[19] Muir objected to Sprenger's characterization of the prophet as "of weak and cunning mind," since that sort of man "could never have accomplished the mighty mission which Mahomet wrought."[20] Yet he alternated between terming him womanish and linking him with the masculine virtues of the Arab wilderness.[21] Such vacillation carried over from early modern European thinking about "Turks" (largely "synonymous with Muslim and Islamic"): indeed, one scholar suggests it was the "principle of inner-contradiction, of inconstancy," that defined views of the Turkish character.[22] This allowed "Turks"—and by extension, Muhammad—"to represent for European men both a self-denying virility that was appealing, and yet also everything they imagined themselves not to be."[23]

For these nineteenth-century thinkers, his status as "The Arabian Prophet"[24] helps to account for Muhammad's genius: his authentic, pure, uncosseted character developed in and was suited to the austere and wild Arabian desert. Yet barbarity (or "rudeness") only tells part of the story. Contradictory visions of Muhammad coexisted. Just as he could be weak and hysterical while also being strong and virile, simplicity could coexist with luxury.[25] With "Muhammad" as a metonym for Muslims in general and Muslim leaders in particular, Arabian harshness and defiant Bedouin independence morph into decadent palaces and harems and silks and tyrannical sultans. Muhammad and the Abbasid caliphs and the Ottoman sultans blended into one another, the decadence and

corruption and lust of one explaining, justifying, and exemplifying the same qualities in the other. In the East, sexuality was tied to power, and power to (potential) immorality. Passion improperly channeled was kin to, or perhaps even led to, power improperly wielded. Yet passion, simplicity, and even a measure of savagery informed what spiritual merit Muhammad possessed. These two models—austerity versus extravagance, wilderness versus urbanity—clashed, but the power of the model was not in its coherence but in the authority of the author to impose (his) authority over it, to define people and places authoritatively for his audience.[26]

Muir vacillates in his presentation of Muhammad, cataloging Muhammad's virtues but only to make the reader accept more readily his ultimate conclusions about his lapses. For Muir, Muhammad—perhaps led by a good impulse early on—comes to believe in his divine commission and thus is led to commit various acts out of "the grand conception that he was destined to be the Reformer of his people and of the whole world."[27] Praiseworthy descriptions occupy several sections: He displays "unwavering stedfastness [sic]" at both Mecca and Medina, where he offers a "denunciation of polytheism and idolatry." But despite the "earnestness and honesty of Mahomet at Mecca," "at Medina, worldly motives mingle with his spiritual objects," with "rapid moral declension: the natural consequences."[28] Following Edward Gibbon, Muir links the gradual decline of Muhammad's character and morality to the shift from Mecca to Medina. As Peirce Johnstone remarks, "as his power grew, his character suffered."[29] Muir ultimately renders the sweeping verdict, moving from Muhammad's (inconsistent) character and actions to Islam as a whole. By acknowledging Muhammad's "moral courage" and personal qualities, he

aims to lead the reader to trust his judgment, so the reader will accept his verdict that Muhammad's vices outweigh his virtues and that the "benefits of Mahometanism" are "outweighed by its evils."[30]

Like Napoleon, but Better

Although these biographers aimed at a comprehensive assessment of Muhammad's character, they were preoccupied by his achievements. British biographers had come to measure a life largely by impact: territory conquered or governed, making one's mark on the map. No longer did goodness or sanctity or proximity to the divine merit attention. *Lives* of military heroes such as Nelson or Wellington were largely concerned with their subjects' accomplishments, including the world-changing reverberations of their deeds; character was important but primarily in relation to actions.[31] Even antiheroes such as Napoleon were vital for people to understand. British authors may have deplored Old Boney, but he also inspired a certain awe.

By the twentieth century, time and distance had dimmed Napoleon's association with evil, leaving untarnished his reputation for military and political brilliance. This reputation spread beyond Europe. During his student years, the Pakistani scholar Fakir Syed Waheed-Ud-Din was assigned a brief biography of Napoleon, which led him to a long-standing fascination with and admiration for the general. Many years later, Waheed-Ud-Din read a biography of Muhammad, which led him to a similar fascination. Describing these encounters with books in the preface to *The Benefactor*—his Urdu biography of Muhammad and the first four caliphs—Waheed-Ud-Din affirms that he came to judge

the Prophet superior to Napoleon, since the former combined achievement with religious merit.[32] Works such as *The Benefactor* reflect a century's accumulated shifts in view of Muhammad's significance—and, indeed, the significance of any prominent figure. Though Muhammad's political and military deeds, as well as his acts in community, had been the subject of a great deal of reflection and retelling, especially by Muslims, they were not why he mattered for most of Muslim history.

In his study, translated into English in 1964 and published by the Nation of Islam, a Black Muslim religious movement, Waheed-Ud-Din emphasizes social rather than spiritual achievements. *The Benefactor* was among a number of Pakistani-produced Islamic books that were sold and circulated by members of the Nation of Islam in the 1960s.[33] Aiming at "the lay reader, both Muslim and non-Muslim," Waheed-Ud-Din avoids, according to the translator's foreword, "apocryphal and theological controversies," focusing "instead on those progressive and social values which motivated the early Muslim community and its outstanding leaders"—most centrally, Muhammad, but also his rightly-guided successors.[34]

Though obscure in comparison to some other twentieth-century biographies of Muhammad, Waheed-Ud-Din's book showcases some key features of hybrid *Lives*, including the increasingly global nature of intra-Muslim conversations, in which English-language publications, such as those by South Asians, played a growing role. *The Benefactor* targets a mixed audience, stakes a position on when a life is of merit, and illustrates the interplay of reading and writing in the formation and transmission of ideas. We may well begin with the book's explicit address to both Muslim and non-Muslims. Pious biographies of the Prophet were clearly written for Muslims. Medieval tracts against Muhammad were read primarily by

non-Muslims looking for useful arguments and strategies, even if those arguments were theoretically aimed at Muslims.[35] Like the Bombay Tract and Book Society's anonymously authored and generally unremarkable *Life*—by 1856 in its third edition—*The Benefactor*'s claim to a mixed audience is unlikely, certainly before it was translated into English but even after that; still, we should note its assumption that the same work *could* be meaningful to and appreciated by Muslims and non-Muslims.

Waheed-Ud-Din's address to both groups is plausible only because there has come to be common ground about what makes a life significant. He sets the religious dimensions of Muhammad's mission aside and focuses on social values. This goes beyond the idea that Muhammad was historically significant, which Carlyle and others had agreed about. Waheed-Ud-Din contends that Muhammad's program of social reform and betterment ought to elicit approval from non-Muslims. It is not (only) as prophet that he can be evaluated but also as statesman.[36] In a similar vein, Ghulam Malik titles the final chapter of his late twentieth-century biography "Greatness," meaning both prominence and social improvement. He writes, "Muhammad's mission was not confined to religion alone, but included other germane roles he played as a soldier, statesman, teacher, reformer, and prayer leader. He established social justice by introducing socio-economic reforms. He banned alcohol, gambling, prostitution, and usury; also he did away with the abominable female infanticide." Moreover, Muhammad anticipated abolition, human rights ("the Universal Declaration of Human Rights, proclaimed by the United Nations in 1948, echoes the Quran about the inalienable rights of human beings"), and women's rights: "The Prophet Muhammad pioneered and recognized women's rights in the Islamic society."[37]

Concern with improvements wrought in society has always been present in the *sira* literature to some degree, and these merits are inextricably bound up with Muhammad's personal acts. It finds anchor in the Qur'anic statement that Muslims have in God's messenger "a beautiful example."[38] In the last two centuries, this notion of ethical exemplarity has become bound up with the notion of historical importance. Muhammad *acted* in ways that one can use as a template for one's own behavior, as Muslims have always held, but he also *did* great things that are out of reach for ordinary people. Yet Waheed-Ud-Din is not just writing about Muhammad the great man; he is writing about Muhammad the *reformer*. He was a man with a plan, and that plan will reshape society in positive ways.

Omid Safi observes that modern biographers have focused on "Muhammad as a community leader and social engineer," whose role as "nation-builder" has overshadowed the "cosmic and mystical" role that he played in previous centuries. Rather than a "cosmic being whose intercession is to be hoped for, a channel of mercy and grace to this world," Muhammad is a "great man," a "genius," and a different sort of model.[39]

The most important modern biography of Muhammad reflects this transformation. Like *The Benefactor*, Muhammad Husayn Haykal's *Life of Muhammad* stands at the intersection of two bodies of literature and is deeply influenced by ideas about "greatness." Unlike *The Benefactor*, it has itself become a classic text. It draws on early Arabic sources, but the textual underpinnings of Haykal's *Life* are modern and Western, in details like the choice of topics and phrases and more fundamentally in assumptions about what makes men great. Haykal's *Life of Muhammad* marks a watershed moment, the point at which Western and Muslim writings have

become so intertwined that one can no longer speak of influence or reaction but interaction and fusion.

India, Egypt, and British Rule

There were key linkages between the Indian subcontinent, where Waheed-Ud-Din wrote, and Egypt, where Haykal did. British rule in India shaped the occupation and governance of Egypt, both because many officers had experience in India and because "the Indian experience provided the only real model for ruling people understood as having an ancient civilisation and deeply entrenched, stable forms of self government."[40] Although French became and remained the language of elite Egyptian social discourse until sometime in the twentieth century, English was increasingly important in intellectual life from the late nineteenth century on, providing a vehicle for Indian Muslim texts to have an impact beyond the circles of Urdu readers.

Building on the engagement with prophetic biography of figures like Ahmad Khan, Ameer Ali, Qasim Nanautvi, and Ahmadi leader Muhammad Ali, Indian Muslim writers expressed themselves in both languages from the late nineteenth century through the interwar period: "Between the two World Wars, in the subcontinent the market was flooded with biographies of Muhammad written in both Urdū and English. The Sīrat movement, which started in the Panjab in the 1920s, made a deep impression throughout all of India. The movement was designed to glorify the civilizing mission of Muḥammad."[41] Scholars marshalled traditional learning for new pedagogical purposes. Urdu was taking on a religious cast, used increasingly as a vernacular language for Muslims rather than only for Persian-speaking literati.[42] Among

the most influential works for later generations of Muslims in the Indian subcontinent was the multivolume biography by Shibli Nu-mani (d. 1914), completed and published posthumously by Sule-man Nadvi (d. 1953). It was eventually translated into both Arabic and English, but the immediate influence of Urdu publications on Egyptian intellectuals was negligible. South Asian Muslim scholars often read Arabic because of its centrality to religious scholarship, but the reverse seldom occurred. Haykal and his cohort continued to read Ameer Ali and other Indian works composed or published in English. They also read the European interlocutors—mostly French and English—with which their Indian Muslim counterparts engaged, particularly Carlyle, Muir, and Washington Irving.[43] Gustav Weil was occasionally cited but rarely read.

English and, to a lesser extent, French were used to communicate not only between Europeans and colonial subjects but also between and among colonized peoples who did not otherwise share a language. Arabic had long served this purpose for Muslim scholars, much as Latin had for medieval Christian scholars. The shift owed in part to the rise of a new class of Muslim intellectuals, some of whom had no formal religious scholarly training. Their approaches to prophetic biography challenged the monopoly of the traditional scholarly classes, and experimented with new forms. These authors, some of whom had studied in Europe, were extensively engaged with European writers in European languages.[44] Well into the twentieth century, female writers, even those whose primary spoken language was Arabic, sometimes bypassed literary Arabic in favor of French. Another factor was the rise of new reading publics: even if important Indian *sira* authors could read and write in Arabic, their non-clerical audiences could not.

A handful of books influenced Egyptian and South Asian writers disproportionately. When it came to books about Islam in general and Muhammad in particular, Muslim intellectuals "preferred and neglected books quite out of proportion to what was available."[45] In the first decade of the twentieth century, Haykal was part of a circle of intellectuals reading works by such British thinkers as John Stuart Mill (*On Liberty*), Herbert Spencer (*Justice*), and Thomas Carlyle (*Heroes and Hero Worship*), all of whom shared "the assumption of the unique role of the individual or great man in social development. This man was not only able to embrace the dictates of reason set against the ingrained conservatism of his society which was often founded on religious belief; he was destined to do so as part of a sociohistorical law of evolution. Conversely, the people should follow obediently."[46] Haykal was interested in French thinkers, too, and wrote a lengthy study of Jean Jacques Rousseau in the 1920s, valuing the philosopher not for his ideals about equality but because his ideas could help quell social unrest.[47] But it was exceptional individuals that preoccupied Haykal. In 1929, he published *Egyptian and Western Biographies*, a series of profiles of Egyptians and Europeans. His selections included Khedive Ismail (he, like seven others among the ten Egyptian figures, bears the title "Pasha"); Cleopatra, the first person and only woman profiled; and Qasim Amin, whose entry mentions the "liberation of women in Egypt."[48] Western figures were "giants of literature and the arts," including Beethoven, Shakespeare, and Percy Bysshe Shelley, to whom he devotes the book's longest entry.[49]

As this list of political and artistic figures demonstrates, Haykal's preoccupation with extraordinary individuals only later manifested in focus on early Islamic figures. *An Essay on Eight*

Words—an 1881 book by a scholar at Cairo's teacher training college—considered key terms "'current on the tongues of the younger generation today,' nation, homeland, government, justice, oppression, politics, liberty and education."[50] Conspicuously absent are *religion, faith, shariah,* and *Islam*. By the 1920s and 1930s, however, biographies of the early caliphs were part of a broader trend of "popular Islamic literature about early Islamic society and the exploits of Islamic founding fathers."[51] A few works came to focus on founding mothers—the Prophet's wives—as well.

What was the connection between Islam, Muhammad, and topics such as liberty and nation? Haykal's preface makes clear that success is the linchpin: "Muḥammad did not have to wait long for his religion to become known, or for his dominion to spread. God has seen fit to complete the religion of Islam even before his death."[52] Haykal merges Ameer Ali's argument that Muhammad brought his assignment to fruition during his lifetime with Carlyle's rousing conclusion about the spread of Islam in the century after Muhammad's death. He frames his argument about Muslims under domination: "no religion has ever conquered Islam despite the fact that its people have fallen under all kinds of tyrannies and unjust governments. Indeed, reduction of their worldly power has made the Muslims more strongly attached to their faith, to their Islamic way of life, and to their Islamic hope."[53] To escape from the current unjust tyranny of diminished power, Islam provides the path, and Muhammad, the example. Again, Muhammad emerges from and is surrounded by other heroic figures. Though he is certainly different from them, his role depends on them. The tension in Haykal's oeuvre, and that of his contemporaries, is between Muhammad's peerless genius and the greatness of his close companions.

The Hero and His Sidekicks

Before the last few decades, it was common for European books about Muhammad to contain chapters recounting the stories of his successors, at least through the first four caliphs. Thus, Irving wrote *Mahomet and His Successors*. Other authors joined the story of his life to the story of his religion (*Mohammed and Mohammedanism*). Centuries earlier, authors like Ibn Ishaq had situated Muhammad in a lineage of biblical prophets tracing back to Adam, and of Muslim leaders stretching to their present. Ibn Hisham emphasized the Abrahamic and Arabian genealogies. Ibn Saʿd placed Muhammad in the midst of followers and opponents, telling us a great deal about them.[54] Shiʿi authors included his biography in works devoted to the Imams.[55] Other influential biographies of Muhammad, like that of Tabari, were embedded in larger universal histories. Today, some have been extracted from those larger works to circulate in discrete editions, such as that by the fourteenth-century scholar Ibn Kathir.[56] In Haykal's work, the Prophet, though interacting with others, stood alone—as did, in his subsequent books, early Muslim heroes: Abu Bakr (*Abu Bakr the Righteous*), Umar (*Umar the Just*), and Uthman (*Uthman ibn ʿAffan: Between Caliphate and Kingship*).[57] Haykal died before getting to Ali.

Haykal was not the only Egyptian thinker of his era to write about these early figures. ʿAbbas Mahmud al-ʿAqqad, author of the 1942 book *The Genius of Muhammad*, also wrote *The Genius of the Righteous One* (referring to Abu Bakr), *The Genius of Umar*, and *The Genius of the Imam* (Ali), as well as volumes on Amr ibn al-ʿAs, the conqueror of Egypt; legendary swordsman and prophetic Companion Khalid ibn al-Walid; and Aisha (*The Righteous Woman*,

Daughter of the Righteous One).[58] (Despite the fact that he published biographies of Aisha and Muhammad's daughter Fatima, al-'Aqqad was widely perceived as a misogynist and known as the "enemy of woman."[59]) His series concluded with a 1954 biography of Uthman, perhaps left for last because he did not present as dynamic a figure of leadership.[60] Although Muhammad's successors were figures of interest, and had been so to Western authors since the nineteenth century, it was the Prophet's life above all that preoccupied Egyptian intellectuals and resonated with their audiences. No longer could one observe, as Muir had, that Muslims were not particularly concerned with the Prophet's biography.[61] Yet it was not primarily the traditional scholars who were rewriting that biography. Rather, in Egypt at least, a new intellectual class engaged with European writings was spurred to take up the topic. Al-'Aqqad reports that his interest in the idea of genius was sparked by a conversation he had about Carlyle's lecture—at a celebration of the Prophet's birthday.

The juxtaposition of a popular devotional gathering with a clearly politically inspired and oriented biography, derived from a British author's lecture to a British audience, suggests that in the era of printed books, the proper celebration of Muhammad was to be textual, not ritual. There is no necessary separation of the two; devotional texts associated with the *mawlid* had been written for centuries and printed as technology allowed. Devotional biographies continued to be written, telling miracle stories and lavishing prayerful praise on the Prophet. Still, there was a demonstrable shift in emphasis to biographies that focused on Muhammad's stellar qualities as a political leader, as a husband, and as a military figure.

The turn to Islamic subjects, then, was not primarily about belief or doctrine, and it intersected with the trend toward publishing

biographies of historical, political, and military figures. Some explorations of these figures took creative forms, including a drama not quite suitable for the stage, a historical novel, and eventually an allegorical novel. As Ruth Roded has noted, "From the 1930s, virtually every major literary figure in Egypt composed a modern biography of the Prophet."[62] In addition to Haykal and al-'Aqqad, Taha Husayn, Ahmad Amin, Tawfiq al-Hakim, and, somewhat later, Naguib Mahfouz are among those who wrote.

In a way, so did Aisha 'Abd al-Rahman (1913–1998), writing under the pen name Bint al-Shati' ("Daughter of the Shore"). A literary scholar within interests and training in the religious sciences—she memorized the Qur'an as a child—like most women who have written Muhammad's life, she did so obliquely, through portraits of the women surrounding him. In addition to her best-known work, *The Prophet's Wives* (1959), she published *The Prophet's Daughters* (1963) and *The Prophet's Mother* (1966).[63] Though accounts of the life of Muhammad and his inner circle went back more than a millennium, her books were not full biographies of the women in his life. Instead, she aimed to give another perspective on Muhammad through exploring his relationships with them. She was responding, too, to the work of her countrymen, staking a position on both Muhammad's nature and the appropriate way to engage with European literature about Muhammad.

Among male Egyptian intellectuals of the era, respect for and engagement with European—French, British, and occasionally German—ideas and thinkers competed, clashed, and became interwoven with concern for and interest in Islamic history and precedents. Also in the mix were ideas about Eastern spirituality in contrast to Western rationality. These tensions can be seen in the career of Ahmad Amin (1886–1954).[64] Amin, who exemplified "the

tornness of the Arab conservative,"[65] did not write extensively about Muhammad, but his writings include some "'self-consciously Islamic'" work and others with "the 'East-is-spiritual' theme."[66] Among the latter was his *The East and the West*, published a year after his death, in which "he expresses the opinion that Eastern civilization is based on religion and is more durable, whereas Western civilization is based on material pleasure and results in wars."[67] Seven years earlier, in 1948—the same year he, al-'Aqqad, and Haykal shared the King Fu'ad Prize[68]—he published a collection of profiles of modern Muslim reformers that "expresses the hope that the awakening East will become strong again without experiencing the defects that have marred the civilization of the West."[69]

This emphasis on Eastern spirituality, which Haykal shared, stood in tension with the social, political, and military accomplishments for which authors celebrated Muhammad. Al-'Aqqad's idea that Muhammad was simply the best at everything he did echoes in later works. Muhammad's battles were one arena for this. In a 1980 biography published in London, Afazlur Rahman writes, "A cursory study of the three battles of Badr, Uhud, and Azab shows superiority of Muhammad's war strategy, military tactics and defence plans over that of his enemies. He was always ahead of his enemies in military tactics and strategical moves. He always managed to know the plans of his enemies, forced them to attack at [the] most unsuitable position and time, commit mistakes and show their weaknesses and vulnerable points. Then he attacked them with determination and full force and rendered all their plans in vain."[70] The language here sounds much like that used in the Qur'an to describe God's foreknowledge and victories; it echoes the triumphalist tone of most accounts of Badr (624), where Muslims

won a decisive victory, but it is a bit surprising to have it applied to the Battle of Uhud (625), which was almost a rout. Salmin's *The Holy Prophet Mohammad*, whose subtitle emphasizes Muhammad's role as *The Commander of the Faithful*, likewise affirms Muhammad as "the best and the greatest General" but places less stress on Muhammad's superior military strategy and more on the nature of his fighting: "in self-defence, and self-protection."[71]

This insistence on the justifiable nature of his conduct is in large part a response to the sort of polemic that, for instance, George Lathom Browne offered. After the conquest of Mecca, "Mahomet was now virtually a king, at whose command an army of fanatical warriors . . . was ready to enforce at the point of a sword submission to the prophet, and adhesion to his creed."[72] Yet for all that they repeatedly insist on Islam's having been spread by the sword, hostile biographers devoted surprisingly little attention to the particulars of Muhammad's conduct in battle. When Browne does report the next battle, Muhammad is first overconfident, "march[ing] heedlessly" into an indefensible position, from which many of his troops "turned and fled with the utmost precipitancy." He then displays "commendable courage" and, following a tactical error on his enemy's part, is able to win "an easy victory."[73]

Twentieth-century Muslim authors contested these kinds of portraits. They largely bypassed supernatural explanations for Muslim victory, instead attributing Muslim victories to the justness of their cause and the brilliance of Muhammad's leadership. Salmin, for instance, presents his actions as "part of a religious programme," attested to not only in "religious books" but also in "the history of the world."[74] He insists, echoing Haykal's stress on scientific method, that "the events related here or those about

his life are not imaginary or mythical, but are historical acts faithfully recorded by authentic, and reliable people."[75]

Clash of Civilization

This insistence on authentic and scientific history suffuses Haykal's *Life,* standing somewhat at odds with its combative tone. Frequently pausing in its narrative to take Western authors to task, it epitomizes the essentially reactive and defensive tone of modern Muslim prophetic biography. Western works had set the agenda, and though Muslim authors might oppose the valuations set, the areas of focus—women, war, revelation—were largely predetermined. In an even more fundamental way, Haykal's *Life* owes its existence to European writings about Muhammad: it originated in a series of review essays of Émile Dermenghem's *Vie de Mahomet* (1929), which Maxime Rodinson called "a well-informed work, though without the trappings of scholarship."[76] He moved beyond mere review partway through the series of over a dozen articles (1932–1934). They appeared in book form in 1935 and shortly thereafter with expanded prefatory essays, which added a great deal of heft; depending on the edition, it contains between five and six hundred pages.[77] Haykal's use of Dermenghem was, he recalls in his *Memoirs,* suggested during a conversation "at a party when he asked for a European account of Muhammad's life which he could use in defending the Prophet against missionary attacks."[78]

Haykal includes Dermenghem as one of thirteen "foreign"—that is, non-Arabic—entries in his bibliography. Eight are English—including Ameer Ali, Irving, Muir, David Margoliouth, and Carlyle, but excluding Ahmad Khan—and five are French. A more extensive list of Arabic authors—including Ibn Hisham; Ibn Sa'd,

Waqidi's scribe; Waqidi; and Tabari—also appear, though he sometimes seems to have started with the Western sources and had reference to the Arabic originals as a second step; notably, a few of the Arabic texts were printed in Europe.[79]

It was not only in this respect that Haykal's biography was unusual. Today, conventional wisdom treats Haykal "as a convinced believer and as a modern man" and grants his *Life* a cherished place in the Muslim canon.[80] Yet the original title directly translates the standard Western *Life of Muhammad*. When Haykal's work appeared in Urdu several decades later, it bore the title *Sirat-i Rasul* (Biography of the Messenger).[81] The Urdu version harks back to centuries of tradition, drawing on the "connotative nimbus" of the term *sira*, linking Haykal's work to its "literary antecedents."[82] However, historian and biographer Charles Smith has argued that to read Haykal as offering an Islamic vision fundamentally misunderstands him.[83] For Smith, Haykal continued to promote thoroughly Western ideas about progress, science, individuality, and intellectuals. His criticisms of Western Orientalists aim to make his arguments palatable to a mass audience, while "attack[ing] the ulama and their authority" and appealing instead to "the true Islamic society established by Muhammad and experienced" during the reign of his first four successors.[84]

Haykal and his contemporaries were drawing on Muslim reform movements that looked to an early Islamic past and sought to bypass the clerical elite and its traditional forms of knowledge at the same time they were engaged in "a search for philosophical and legal norms from the Muslim past thought to be more appropriate to Egypt's needs as it confronted European military and economic expansion." Situating Haykal in context, Smith argues that "the notion that Western ideas might be isolated from Muslim

thought and considered valid in themselves appeared only in the last decade of the nineteenth century and the first decade of the twentieth, the transitional period in which Muhammad Husayn Haykal was reared."[85]

Haykal's unpublished diaries show that by 1910 he was already thinking of Muhammad as just a man and not divinely inspired. During his heady Paris years (1909–1912), he grappled with big ideas about religion and reform. "He concluded," writes Smith, "that religions were not inspired by a divine being. Rather they were social phenomena reflecting historical circumstances. Likewise, prophets such as Muhammad were products of their time, self-inspired men despite their sincere beliefs that they had been chosen by God."[86] Haykal saw "the prophet as representative of the superior individual in history." Haykal thought that a small number of "superior" people would be inspired.[87] Swedish scholar and Lutheran bishop Tor Andrae, writing at the same time in German, held a similar view of the process of prophetic inspiration.

Smith posits that Haykal smuggles in Western ideologies in the guise of anti-Orientalist scholarship, but Haykal's complicated relationship to the Western materials he uses finds its basis at least partially in his writing practices.[88] Haykal borrows structure, plot, and theme—and sometimes entire sentences—from his sources. Understanding Haykal's effect requires close exploration of what he keeps, what he jettisons, and what he modifies from the texts on which he relies.

The two *Lives* Khalidi mentions as crucial—those of Muir and Carlyle—were influential for Haykal and his peers. Muir's *Life* had "provoked a new Muslim orientation towards the study of the life of the Prophet,"[89] in large part through its choice of sources as well as subject matter. Meanwhile, Carlyle's "lasting effect on the

imaginary horizons of modern Muslim *Sira*" owes in part to a 1911 Arabic translation of *The Hero as Prophet*.[90] Serious translation is "the result of a series of creative decisions and imaginative acts of criticism."[91] Muhammad al-Siba'i's Arabic Carlyle is more nationalist and less romantic.[92] Fittingly, al-'Aqqad was less concerned with inner sincerity than with Muhammad's function as a model for conduct in personal, spiritual, military, and political spheres.[93]

Al-Hakim, another literary figure, had studied law in Paris for three years in the 1920s.[94] When he drew censure for his fictionalizations of Qur'anic stories, he responded by writing a play, *Muhammad* (1936). As one commentator notes, "that was the period when the leading Western-educated Egyptian writers, formerly accused of heresy and of polluting Islamic culture, were vying with one another and with the fundamentalists in turning to the Islamic legacy for their literary material, as though to prove to public opinion that they were no less Muslim than their fundamentalist critics."[95] This "avalanche of religious writings" was responding to its own Egyptian context while engaging with Western precursors— Voltaire and Goethe had, after all, written dramas of the same name.[96] As for the play itself, though "orthodox enough . . . it raised the problem of the permissibility of adapting sacred Islamic figures and themes to artistic treatment. . . . The question still remains unsolved in Arabic letters and the arts, but al-Hakim's *Muhammad* stirred no [significant] storm in the thirties . . . for the simple reason that al-Hakim never sought to have it performed. Artistically, too, it has no special merit."[97]

Haykal thus wrote among peers who were reading French and English authors and working out new ways of thinking and writing about early Islamic figures. Haykal's engagement with Western authorities carries on an intra-Muslim conversation by proxy:

What will a modern Muslim society look like? What sort of model does Muhammad provide for a proud people in a bad situation? Yaseen Noorani's account of the rise of Arab nationalist sentiments argues that "what took place in the rise of these values was not a clash of two irreconcilable cultures—the onslaught of secular Western modernity against an Islamic patriarchal premodernity—but the transformation of traditional cultural ideals from within, a process whose central dynamic lay in the transformation of virtue into nationality."[98] He sees a shift in "the traditional model of the self and its relation to collective order," increasingly "arising from innate human dispositions rather than from the sovereign authority of virtuous figures."[99] Noorani's insight helps clarify the role Muhammad's domestic arrangements played in modern Egyptian biographies. If the nuclear family and a companionate couple were central to the social order, so Muhammad—*innately* the best model for humanity—must also exemplify the best relationships. And yet his comportment would seem, on the surface, to be incompatible with precisely the sorts of arrangements seen as desirable.

Domestic matters were the subject of a great deal of scrutiny in early twentieth-century Egypt. Rifaʻa al-Tahtawi had broached some of these topics in the 1870s, and Muhammad ʻAbduh, a key reformist scholar of the era, made them a centerpiece of his writing. ʻAbduh railed against arranged marriage as "utterly and completely incompatible with modern subjectivity" and insisted on love as the necessary basis for marriage, which should be monogamous and centered on a nuclear family household.[100] Although he was primarily concerned with the pernicious effects of polygamy, he also assumed the need for females to be old enough and involved in the process of choosing spouses: if marriage is for the establishment of families, which are necessary to the nation, then

wives must be competent and loving partners, not subordinates. Not everyone held this view. Al-ʿAqqad devoted part of his substantial chapter in *The Genius of Muhammad* on Muhammad as a husband to explaining how Muhammad maintained a salutary discipline in his household. Although he objects to Western perceptions of Muslim backwardness, al-ʿAqqad by no means advocates egalitarian marriages.

Haykal's way of approaching questions about Muhammad's marriages as well as other issues often depended on what he read, and his decisions to focus on or ignore issues seems to emerge from his composition practices. To perhaps a greater extent than these other scholars, "Haykal read widely but not intensively."[101] He often marked up only the first two or three chapters of a book, and sometimes a lone paragraph. He does what all writers do to a greater or lesser degree: he presents his own versions of the books he reads, emphasizing and ignoring selectively, unable to ever account for all that they contain.[102] Throughout his book, even where he gives the impression of drawing on a broader source base, he relies "almost exclusively" on Ibn Ishaq/Ibn Hisham "as his classical source."[103] He "consults Ibn Hishām constantly . . . borrows much material from him, and cites him extensively, primarily in direct quotations, [and] also when he does not expressly acknowledge it."[104] Of course, the selections of particular texts from the Muslim tradition were a capitulation to the "scientific" sensibilities of the Orientalists: Haykal accepted the premise, articulated so clearly by Muir, that early texts mattered.

Indeed, Haykal at times takes his early Islamic texts through the mediation of Orientalist biographies, particularly that of Muir.[105] Of more recent Muslim texts, he draws on Ameer Ali's *The Spirit of Islam* and borrows its practice of including lengthy

apologetic sections alongside and interwoven with biographical material. (Dermenghem had also read Ameer Ali, as well as 'Abduh.)[106] Haykal starts with a contentious introduction and closes with two polemical essays. If Ameer Ali's text was in conversation with European scholarship, Haykal's was a more direct engagement. One commentator says that Haykal was "deeply read in anti-Islamic literature."[107] Given Haykal's scattershot reading practices, it is probably more accurate to say that he was deeply preoccupied by it.

Though Dermenghem takes pride of place in the *Life*'s origin story, Prideaux's famous polemic bleeds through the background, and Muir's *Life* serves as both foil and resource for Haykal.[108] He engages with Muir and Carlyle in ways beyond what he indicates directly in the text.[109] Haykal's use of Irving perhaps provides the clearest glimpse of what he was attempting. Irving features prominently in Haykal's closing essay on "Islamic Civilization and the Western Orientalists." Haykal calls him "one of the greatest writers" of nineteenth-century America and alternately praises and criticizes Irving's *Life*. Irving's theological understanding "fell short of grasping the spirit of Islam and its civilization. Hence his false interpretation of the problem of divine providence and predestination. Perhaps Irving had some excuse in that some of the Islamic books which he may have read do in fact point in the direction of his interpretation."[110] This criticism is only superficially about Irving's failure to understand Islamic teachings. The real problem is that some Muslim scholars hold erroneous views; Irving picks the wrong side in an intra-Muslim controversy. To acknowledge this, though, Haykal would have to admit that there is a legitimate debate, not just the correct view and a few Muslim authors who got it wrong. Here again, Western scholars become a means to attack

views held by Muslims: by associating the erring Muslims with Orientalists, the opprobrium can be shared.

Haykal used Muslim sources equally selectively, relying most heavily on Ameer Ali's *Spirit of Islam*.[111] His relationship to the classical sources is equivocal and he sometimes misrepresents them. For instance, regarding the Satanic verses incident, in which Muhammad was induced temporarily to allow the worship of three Meccan goddesses, Haykal writes, "These are the arguments on which stands the claim for veracity of the story of the goddesses. They are all false, incapable of standing any scrutiny or analysis. Let us begin with the argument of the Orientalist Muir."[112] The refutation that follows admits that the story appears in some early Muslim sources (Ibn Sa'd, Tabari) but places blame for repeating it on European scholars: it "arrested the attention of the western Orientalists who took it as true and repeated it ad nauseam."[113] Haykal rejects Muir's analysis on rational grounds and also asserts that the story is rejected by Ibn Ishaq, who, Haykal tells us, "did not hesitate at all to declare it a fabrication by the heretics."[114] Here, as with his criticism of Irving's view of free will, Haykal takes a Westerner to task for his reliance on the wrong Arab sources, a strategy that Ahmad Khan also employed to generally good effect. Haykal insists that his discernment among Muslim sources owes to a scientific approach to the tradition.

Ashis Nandy argues that "empire succeeded only when the colonized found—or were made to find—something to love in imperial culture."[115] In the case of biographers of Muhammad, it was often a critical, historical, or scientific method, for which European scholars stood as exemplars. The historian Abd al-Aziz Duri called for careful appraisal of early sources, such as Ibn Ishaq/Ibn

Hisham, to extract facts about "the Prophet's life" by means of "a sound evaluation of the sources" and "a critical historical approach to the accounts in which this material has been preserved."[116] Influenced by the work of Orientalists but also aiming to rebut some of their global criticisms, Duri attempts to salvage a core of historically accurate prophetic biography, as well as to rehabilitate the reputation of historians as a class. Much like Ahmad Khan praises a medieval Muslim historian by saying he ranks with the best European historians, "Haykal's exploitation of Islamic history in the 1930s, although including apologetic attacks on the West duly emphasized in Western studies of Egyptian modernism, was founded expressly on a glorification of the Western historical method and its concern for scientific accuracy."[117]

Character and Cohort

Premodern biographies had things to say about Muhammad the individual and his character. Haykal's title reflects and enacts a shift from the individual as model to the individual as personality. Muhammad becomes a man with temperament and traits that comprise a personality unique to him and capable of explaining in some vital way his "contribution" or "impact" or "genius." This is a dramatic departure from Ibn Ishaq's aim to model Muhammad after the biblical prophets who served as the touchstone for his notion of legitimacy, and led to the incorporation of such legends as that he spent time working as a shepherd in his youth.[118]

The interest in Muhammad's Companions, wives, and kin tended to reflect similar concerns with social and familial issues of the day. The Companions attest to his sterling qualities; their

virtues, including trustworthiness, guarantee his, and vice-versa. (Aisha's summation: "His character was the Qur'an.")[119] This only works to the extent that the Companions are revered. Yet although figures such as Aisha and Umar—the latter the subject of a massive biography by Numani as well as al-'Aqqad and Haykal—are particularly disparaged by the Shia, their emergence as vital figures in the middle of the twentieth century seems less intended to kindle sectarian fires and more to appeal to a seemingly simple, straightforward, early past that can provide lessons for a Muslim society in a turbulent time.

These lessons are about the proper shape of the family and the proper shape of society. Although Haykal and his countrymen insist on the religious resonance or authenticity of Muhammad and his close associates as models, they simultaneously present a less religious Muhammad. Or, as in Waheed-Ud-Din's *The Benefactor*, one whose religious successes are at least as noteworthy for their worldly effects as for their spiritual merit. To what extent Haykal's aim was to arrive at "a more secular culture through the undermining of Islam,"[120] despite his use of Islam as a language through which he could communicate to the masses, is unclear. Smith's contrarian interpretation posits Haykal as an elitist figure, caught between nostalgia for a hierarchical village power structure of patronage on the one hand, and an allegiance to European rationalism on the other, with suspicion of the Egyptian masses and their increasing power to disrupt the existing social order.[121] However, he concludes, "Paradoxically, Haykal's search for progress with order and his attempt to use Islam for that purpose encouraged retention of the values he hoped to undermine."[122]

Whether this is so can be debated. What seems clear, however, is that in India and Egypt, and broadly throughout the Arab world,

the terms in which success and truth are discussed are no longer primarily indigenous. As Shaden Tageldin puts it in discussing a different set of texts, "an Islam once taken for granted by its adherents as self-evident *sign* has become subject to external verification by European Orientalism: to the *proof* of the Orientalist's translated text."[123] Nowhere is this clearer than in the material on Muhammad's marriages, the subject of Chapters 4 and 5.

The Wife of Muhammad

By the time Muhammad had grown to manhood, he had gained a reputation as trustworthy and judicious. A wealthy widow named Khadija hired him to accompany her caravan to Syria. His performance so impressed her that she proposed marriage to him. He accepted. She was forty and he was twenty-five. They were happily married for twenty-five years. While she lived, he took no other wife. Her wealth and companionship gave him the support he needed to undertake his spiritual reflection and, eventually, his prophetic mission. After her death, he married other women, but she retained a special place in his memories.

A version of this story, often in nearly these exact words, appears in a striking proportion of books about Muhammad written in the last century, whether aimed at pious Muslim readers, American middle schoolers, college students, or the general reading public.[1] Phrases like "wealthy older widow" and "remained faithful" recur. Whatever the exact words, the same points surface repeatedly: their respective ages, that she was a widow, her wealth, the Syrian caravan expedition, her positive impression, and that the marriage took place at her instigation. We learn that her wealth gave him the leisure for retreat and reflection.[2] We are told that he took no other wives while she lived, and sometimes how unusual this was in the Arabian context. Authors sometimes mention that she bore him two or three or, occasionally, four sons who died in infancy

and four daughters.[3] After she died, her memory "cast a long shadow over" his later marriages.[4]

All of these bits of information about Khadija are gleaned from early Muslim biographies. Other things in those sources drop out, leaving a few overlapping facts.[5] The formulaic repetition of these facts paints Khadija as "the pattern of a Musalman matron," as one nineteenth-century scholar phrased it, and reinforces an image of Muhammad as a model husband.[6] A similarly coherent but substantively different portrait dominated early modern English accounts, which consistently portrayed Muhammad's "cynical wooing of, and marriage to, the widow Cadygan [Khadija], to gain earthly power."[7] Those accounts, though, did not dwell extensively on the marriage; it was one more bit of evidence for Muhammad's craftiness and ambition. For early Muslim biographers, the marriage was a narrative way station on Muhammad's journey to prophethood, recounted in terms that emphasized his prophetic role. For modern authors, the marriage to Khadija becomes a key to showing who Muhammad "really was." Her role in his character formation is increasingly important as people write about Muhammad the *man* rather than Muhammad the *prophet*.

The recognition that Muhammad was both man and messenger was not new, but a palpable shift in emphasis occurred in the nineteenth and especially the twentieth centuries. It can be seen clearly in the title of Muhammad Husayn Haykal's biography, discussed in Chapter 3. Narratives of Muhammad's life had customarily borne the title *Biography (sira) of the Prophet* or *Biography of the Messenger of God*.[8] Haykal's title directly translates to *The Life of Muhammad*, the usual title for European biographies and the one used by Dermenghem in the *Life* that Haykal was reviewing. That he retained it when he expanded his review articles

into an independent book suggests that he intended a different sort of biography than usual. The shift from "biography" to "life," and from a religious title ("the prophet" "God's messenger") to a personal name, indicates that we are no longer dealing with an account of a course of action (*sira* in its early meaning of "practice, procedure") but a life story.[9] Moreover, its subject is not a prophet or, rather, *the* Prophet but a man: Muhammad. The shift is from exemplar to individual, from type to personality.

Muhammad's modern biographers saw his character manifested in his relationships with women—first and foremost Khadija, but also, and as a clear counterpoise, his other wives as a group. Their centrality can be appreciated if we note that 'Abbas Mahmud al-'Aqqad's *Genius of Muhammad*, written at a time when questions about sovereignty, politics, and power were roiling the Egyptian public, devotes five pages to Muhammad as leader and forty-eight to Muhammad as husband.[10]

A Much-Married Man

Over the course of his life, Muhammad had about a dozen wives, depending on how one counts.[11] This is a large number of wives but an infinitesimally small portion of the hundreds of millions of Muslim women who have lived throughout history. Yet the two topics have become inseparable. Discussion of his wives is fraught with the weight of expectations about "the woman question" in Islam; many conversations about this latter topic, in turn, hinge on Muhammad's own married life as well as the example of the women of his household.

For contemporary Westerners, the association between Islam and women's oppression is strongly ingrained.[12] This has not al-

ways been the case. Muhammad's wives become more important as the idea of Muslim women becomes more important to discussions about Islam. The oppressed but alluring Muslim woman is a creature of the last few centuries. So is her counterpart: the pious, active female role model, of whom Khadija is the ideal example. And if she is a new kind of woman, Muhammad, as her husband, must be a new kind of man.

Muhammad's *Lives* have come to dwell at some length on his marriage to Khadija and to grant it prominence as the prime example of his married life. This might seem like an obvious thing to do; after all, by the usual reckoning, she was married to him for more than twice as long as any other woman. Yet premodern accounts tend to say little about their conjugal life beyond the proposal and marriage, the comfort and reassurance she provided to him at the outset of his mission, and his reaction to her death—scant details compared to the wealth of information about his later marriages and domestic arrangements, which transpired during the course of his public prophetic mission and communal leadership.

Khadija the Grand

Khadija may have been merited relatively few pages in early Muslim accounts of Muhammad's life, but they were important ones. She was associated with several turning points in his life: his first marriage; becoming a father; his prophetic commission; and, in the wake of her death, his departure from Mecca to Medina. Biographers recognized her exceptional nature and distinguished between her and his other wives. Ibn Sa'd set her apart in his compendium of early Muslim women, putting her first and leaving

the rest of Muhammad's wives until after chapters on his daughters and other female relatives.[13]

Traditionally, she bears epithets including "the Grand" and "the Pure." As the member of the Prophet's household least subject to partisan wrangling, she draws allegiance from Sunni and Shia alike. The same is true, in a limited way, for Fatima: daughter of Muhammad and Khadija, and the only one of his children to survive him, though only by a few months. Yet if Fatima is never precisely deprecated by Sunnis, her marriage to Ali and motherhood of Hasan and Husayn establish her as a potent symbol for the Shia, who hold that legitimate rulers come through Ali's line. Hence, Sunni tradition sometimes disregards or marginalizes her.[14] Khadija poses no sectarian threat and may be praised with impunity.

Her noble genealogy and stellar personal qualities reflect well on Muhammad. That a woman of her caliber, whom Ibn Ishaq calls the richest woman of the Quraysh of her time, would choose him proves that she recognized his impressive character.[15] This much, we get from the traditional texts. (It is no surprise that contemporary authors forgo her extensive genealogy; the prolonged recitation of anyone's ancestry is of little interest to modern readers.) They also say, though few modern authors repeat, that not everyone was impressed with the match; Khadija might have gotten her father drunk to gain his approval (a story frequently retold by pre-modern polemicists). In other versions, he was already deceased, and her uncle stood in for him.[16] Modern Muslim authors often skim over the father's or uncle's involvement in the marriage because it sits ill with the image of Khadija as a self-assured and independent woman. Moreover, the question of paternal involvement in any adult woman's marriage is jarring to some readers;

works for general readers published in America almost uniformly omit any discussion of her kin. Works aimed at Muslims may mention it, especially if they were published in South Asia.[17] It is an open question whether such authors note her father's or uncle's role because they are determined to rebut the slander that Khadija deceived her guardian, which some earlier hostile biographers highlight, or because custom still presumes a level of familial involvement in marriages that is alien to contemporary Westerners, including Muslims living in Europe or the Americas.

Contemporary biographers almost uniformly make Khadija forty and Muhammad twenty-five; some do the math for their readers and note the fifteen-year difference. Many use this "fact" to present interpretations about Muhammad's character: evidence that he was not consumed by lust and that he was comfortable with a powerful woman. Traditional accounts sometimes stick with the ages twenty-five and forty, as Tabari does, and sometimes register disagreement about Khadija's age at the time of her marriage; though the age forty is mentioned, another view is that she was twenty-eight. Ibn Ishaq gives Muhammad's age as twenty-five, but notes that he might have been twenty-one or thirty.[18] Ibn Sa'd reports that someone asked Khadija's nephew, "which of them was older, the Messenger of Allah or Khadija?" He said, "Khadija was fifteen years older than him. The prayer was unlawful for my aunt before the Messenger of Allah was born."[19] Ibn Sa'd explains the anachronistic response, "'The prayer was unlawful for her' means she menstruated, but he is speaking as the people of Islam speak." To understand this response, one must know that menstruants abstain from ritual worship; Khadija had reached menarche before Muhammad's birth.[20]

Why forty? As anyone familiar with the biblical tradition knows, forty is a potent number. In the Hebrew bible, the flood lasts forty

days, and the Israelites wander in the wilderness for forty years. Jesus fasts forty days and forty nights, according to the Gospel of Matthew, before the devil tempts him. And in Muslim tradition, Muhammad is usually said to have been forty when he received the first revelation from Gabriel in the cave on Mount Hira (though a few versions put him at forty-three).[21] One scholar suggests that the Prophet's age at revelation relies on the symbolic significance of the number forty: "In matters involving measurement of time, this usage of 'forty' is clearly devoid of specific chronological content."[22] For Khadija, this seems likely as well; that she supposedly bore Muhammad six or seven children suggests that it should not be taken literally.[23] We cannot assume, of course, that earlier scholars were ignorant of this point, since the facts of reproductive biology were no doubt more or less the same.[24] Instead, we ought to assume that they were aware of the symbolic resonance of forty and, further, that they expected their readers to be aware of it as well.

The suggestion that the symbolism matters more than factual accuracy suggests a rationale, too, for the devoted attention to Aisha's age that one finds in the early sources; Muhammad's marriage to Aisha, however, must await the next chapter.

Khadija the Comforter

If one were to construct a short list of candidates for the most important moment of Muhammad's life, the encounter with Gabriel in the cave would head the list. (Other contenders would include the migration to Medina and the ascension, though his marriage to Khadija appears in some accounts, particularly the more recent ones, as a pivotal point.)[25] Though Khadija was not on Mount Hira, she became a key part of the story shortly afterward.

In Ibn Ishaq's account, Muhammad turns to Khadija after his encounter with the angel leaves him shaken and wondering whether he was "poet or possessed."[26] Khadija does three things to restore Muhammad's equanimity and faith.[27] First, she comforts him physically ("I came to Khadīja and sat by her thigh and drew close to her") and reassures him of his excellent character and her confidence that God would not allow such a thing to happen to him. Then, she goes to her cousin Waraqa ibn Nawfal, "who had become a Christian and read the scriptures and learned from those who follow the Torah and the Gospel." Waraqa affirms that if Khadija's tale is true, then Muhammad is a prophet like Moses, "the prophet of his people."[28] Khadija conveys this message to Muhammad, who then meets Waraqa himself and is both reassured of the legitimacy of his visitor and warned that people will oppose him. Third, Khadija devises a test to see if Muhammad's "visitant" is angelic or demonic. She asks Muhammad to move progressively closer to her, and he continues to see the angel until she begins to disrobe and make sexual advances toward him; the visitor departs, confirming that "he is an angel and not a satan."[29]

Khadija's role as comforter extends beyond this moment. When Ibn Ishaq tells of Khadija's accepting of Islam ("she was the first of those who believed in God and His Messenger and the truth of what he brought from Him"), he refers to both the opposition and insults Muhammad encountered and the ways in which she supported and comforted him "when he returned to her." Alfred Guillaume, translating this phrase, gives a domestic twist: "when he went home."[30] Modern authors build on these ancient descriptions of Khadija as comforter to depict the act of comforting as a wifely duty, and marriage as an institution designed to nurture emotional closeness. For instance, Pakistani author G. N. Jalbani, in his

English-language *Life of the Holy Prophet* (1988), treats the aftermath of Muhammad's first revelation. He returned to Khadija,
who wrapped him up and comforted him by expressing her confidence in his merits. Jalbani comments: "She no doubt knew him
better, as no one can be better informed of the ways of a man than
his own wife, who is in a position to have free access to his heart."[31]
Similarly, British Muslim Ahmad Thompson: "No one—except
Allah of course—knows more about a man than his wife, both his
good and bad qualities, his strengths and his weaknesses."[32]

These descriptions of marital intimacy and wifely succor even
take on religious overtones. Haykal calls Khadija an "angel of
mercy," a coinage unusual enough that even though Arabic books
typically omit vowel markers, the text includes them on the word
angel to forestall confusion or misreading.[33] More frequent is the
stock Victorian phrase "angel of hope and consolation" used by
Stanley Lane-Poole in an introduction to selections from the
Qur'an.[34] It passed into English-language South Asian Muslim
works; Ameer Ali uses it.[35] More than a century later, Abdul
Hameed Siddiqui writes, "for a quarter of a century *Khadījah*
remained his angel of hope and consolation."[36] (Slightly later, Jalbani mangles the phrase: "He was much attached to Khadījah
who was his angel of hope and consolidation [*sic*].")[37] The imagery
of a wife as an "angel," however metaphorical, at least partially
displaces the actual angel whose appearance led Muhammad to
seek her comfort. As with Guillaume's translation, the emphasis
has changed from the irruption of the divine into Muhammad's
life to the importance of a domestic sanctuary, where an angel of
the hearth awaits him. This imagery links the spiritual and the
domestic—in John Davenport's *Apology*, "his soul and his hearth."
These ways of speaking about Khadija draw on early texts that

celebrate her pivotal role, yet they are decisively modern in their view of marriage as the center of one's emotional life, and the couple and nuclear household as the proper pattern for family living. Though he ultimately arrives at negative conclusions about Muhammad and Islam, a Christian author writing in 1895 had only praise for their union: "The home of Mahomet and Khadija was a bright and happy one, and their marriage fortunate and fruitful."[38] A recent self-published work on Muhammad and his family makes a similar point: "After his marriage with Khadijah, he had a happy family life."[39] Similarly, Driss Chraibi's 1995 French novella *Man of the Book* refers to Muhammad's "happy household" with Khadija, who provided both friendship and "a woman's love."[40] These authors envision households and families in familiar familial ways, which require forgetting the fostered cousin Ali, the presence of slave servants, and the adoptive adult son Zayd.

A rare objection to this view of conjugal life as the center of individual emotional life was raised by the Iraqi scholar and writer Amina bint Haydar al-Sadr, the sister of noted Shiʻi jurist Muhammad Baqir al-Sadr (both d. 1980). One of the relatively few Muslim women to write biographically about Muhammad, Bint al-Huda (Daughter of the Right Path), as she was widely known, wrote a lengthy essay, "Women and the Prophet." Though she generally avoided the topic of polygamy in her copious writings, she had to confront it in writing about Muhammad's life and wives. Like other authors, Sadr places Khadija in a central position: "It is only Muhammad's first, long-term, monogamous marriage with Khadija" that Sadr presents "in unambiguously positive terms. The polygamous marriages contracted after Khadija's death are represented as deficient in various [ways] and/or as examples of the Prophet's charity."[41] She, too, stresses "love and

companionship" between the spouses. However, emphasizing that Muhammad did not forget about other important women in his life when he married Khadija, Sadr "challenge[s] marriage as a private institution between two people, founded on a rupture with their previous lives and relationships."

Love Marriage

When Haykal wrote his biography in the mid-1930s, he was directly engaging French and Anglo-Muhammadan *Lives*. At the same time, he was responding to the circumstances of early twentieth-century Egypt. In addition to the shift of emphasis to religious topics, active debates about marriage served as a backdrop to his writing. The climate of ideas about companionate marriage, marriage age, and the "marriage crisis" could not but affect his portrayal of the Prophet. Haykal focuses on the inward and emotional dimensions of Muhammad's personhood, his character as manifested in his relationships with women. To do so, he borrows from the attribution of motives and feelings to Muhammad that had begun to emerge in nineteenth-century Western lives. In other words, he talks about love.

Moderns posit a primary role for sexual acts and identities in the constitution and definition of a self.[42] Marriage is often viewed as the single most central adult relationship. Classical authors placed less stress on marital conduct as a laboratory for evaluating the self or on the emotional bond between spouses as the prime locus for strong ties of love and obligation. That is not to say that conjugal love was unimportant before the modern era. The question of what Muhammad felt for which wife appeared from time to time in accounts of his life.[43] Yet friendships and kin ties

might be equally or more important. Where early biographies mention Muhammad's affection for this or that male figure—Zayd, Ali, or Abu Bakr, most often—there is an implicit contest about closeness and legitimacy in succession.[44] In modern biographies, Khadija has the greatest emotional and even spiritual resonance. In a passage that also shows Shi'i emphasis on Muhammad's descendants, Seyyed Hossein Nasr writes,

> The marriage with Khadījah was of very great significance in the life of the Prophet of Islam for it provided for him the companion on whom he could rely completely in the most difficult period of his life and who was endowed with the necessary moral and spiritual virtues to act as the perfect wife of God's most perfect creature and the mother of the prophetic family—the *Ahl al-bayt* [people of the household]—whose light was later to illuminate the world.[45]

Here, Khadija's virtues make her not only Muhammad's ideal partner but also a key player in the transmission of Muhammad's light.

Focusing on Khadija's politico-religious activities as well as her role as "partner" and "life companion," Pakistani lawyer Muhammad Anis-ur-Rahman goes so far as to make Khadija "the right hand of the Holy Prophet" in establishing Islam.[46] *The Historical Role of the Venerable Woman* describes her and Muhammad as "twin preachers."[47] Her courage and, not least, her wealth, "which financed the revolution," were vital for the spread of Islam.[48] The emphasis on Khadija's wealth is in keeping with focus on her business success—she was divinely chosen for marriage, he asserts, in order to show that Islam supports working women.[49] Nonetheless, her wifely virtues earn lavish praise: "The unique success of the

mission of the Holy prophet was achieved on account of the woman who provided peace and tranquility, inspiration and encouragement, solace and comfort to the messenger of Allah."[50]

Joining the domestic and the religious, American writer-poet Tamam Kahn imagines Khadija as "the rock upon which Muhammad built his family and his religion" as well as his "closest confidant."[51]

Similar qualities surface in other accounts. Siddiqui writes of Khadija: "She gave *Muhammad* ease of circumstances, freedom from the cares of daily life, strength, and comfort of deep mutual love, factors which contributed to the furtherance of the mission of the Prophet." And he adds, "In spite of conspicuous difference in age, *Muhammad's* love for *Khadijah* never wavered."[52] Also mentioning the age difference, Malik calls it "a perfect match" and claims that "they were deeply devoted to each other and much in love."[53] This attention to the difference in their ages as a factor that *should* have led to Muhammad's disinterest or wandering eye is alien to the classical Muslim tradition—perhaps because no one actually thought of Khadija as being forty. Western authors who discuss this marriage linger on the question of her "youthful charm" or lack thereof. Davenport, for instance, calls her "his beloved partner" and notes, "Notwithstanding that at so advanced an age she must have lost every youthful charm, yet Mohammed had remained faithful to the last, and refrained, as already said, from taking other wives."[54] Thomas Carlyle, and others following him, notes not that she was beautiful but that despite her age she was "still beautiful."[55] Washington Irving describes her as "past the bloom of years when women are desirable in the East."[56] Émile Dermenghem, too, comments on her presumably faded attractiveness, which makes Muhammad's faithfulness and devotion all the

more remarkable. Rodinson speculates that since her wealth put her "in a position to make demands," she might have insisted on a clause in their marriage contract preventing him from taking an additional wife.[57] Less cynically, Nasr attributes his abstention from taking other wives despite the fact that "she was fifteen years older than he and polygamy was a very common practice" to the marriage's perfection: "a marriage which was so complete and in a sense absolute that the Blessed Prophet did not marry another wife as long as Khadījah was alive."[58]

A Series of Unfortunate Events

Khadija's death provides biographers with another chance to emphasize her centrality in Muhammad's story. The narrative connection between her death and that of Muhammad's uncle, Abu Talib, who had raised him after his grandfather's death, provides an opportunity for authors to once again comment on the significance of their tie and the role Khadija played for him; to move the narrative of Muhammad's life forward with his move to Medina; and—not least important—to transition to the second stage of his life as a husband, beginning with his marriages to others.

The joining of Khadija and Abu Talib's deaths is at least as much literary artifact as historical fact: two events happen in temporal proximity and become, through their insistent juxtaposition in biographical writings, thematically conjoined as the Year of Sadness.[59] Elsa Marston's 2001 "book report biography" describes this as "a double blow—truly disastrous" under the subheading "Loss of Some Vital Support."[60] This link is ancient, going back at least to Ibn Ishaq/Ibn Hisham, which reads, in part: "Khadīja and Abū Ṭālib died in the same year, and with Khadīja's death

troubles followed fast on each other's heels, for she had been a faithful support to him in Islam, and he used to tell her of his troubles. With the death of Abū Ṭālib he lost a strength and a stay in his personal life and a defence and protection against his tribe."[61] Tabari, though he draws on Ibn Ishaq, is less effusive about Khadija's role, noting, "After this, Abū Ṭālib and Khadījah died in a single year. . . . Their death was a great affliction to the messenger of God. This is because after the death of Abū Ṭālib, Quraysh went to greater lengths in molesting him then they had ever done during his lifetime."[62] He makes no mention of any particular loss occasioned by Khadija's death. George Sale, in the preliminary discourse that introduces his 1734 translation of the Qur'an, signals these deaths as unfortunate but does not wax lyrical about either loss.[63]

Martin Lings, a British convert to Islam, weighs the relative impact of the two deaths differently in *Muhammad: His Life Based on the Earliest Sources* (1983). One scholar calls this book, popular among English-reading Muslims, "an uncritical English conflation of the traditional Muslim accounts" and a "curious undertaking," while another, more diplomatic scholar deems it "a traditional history based on Muslim sources."[64] Referring to the Year of Sadness, Lings writes that "the Prophet suffered a great loss in the death of his wife Khadījah. She was about sixty-five years old and he was nearing fifty. They had lived together in profound harmony for twenty-five years, and she had been not only his wife but also his intimate friend, his wise counselor, and mother to his whole household including 'Alī and Zayd." Lings emphasizes the length of their marriage as well as the tenor of their relationship: intimate, friendly, harmonious. He presumes a patriarchal family

unit—it is *his* household—and assigns her the maternal role. (Others play up Muhammad's role as paterfamilias: "Muhammad was a loving and affectionate husband, as well as a loving and deeply attached father.")[65] He then contrasts it with the next "loss [which] followed closely upon the death of Khadījah, a loss less great and penetrating in itself, but at the same time less consolable and more serious in its outward consequences. Abū Ṭālib fell ill, and it soon became clear that he was dying."[66] Similarly, Nasr acknowledges, with Tabari, the practical impact of the loss of Abu Talib, "his most powerful protector," but emphasizes the emotional impact of Khadija's death during "the bleakest period of his life": "The loss was almost unbearable at the beginning and practically nothing could console him."[67]

Though Muhammad's grief at Khadija's death has antecedents in the classical sources, the emotional tone for these twentieth-century Muslim writers was set by nineteenth-century British commentators. Davenport's *Apology*, for instance, says, "The death of this his beloved partner was indeed a heart-rending calamity for him. For twenty years she had been his counselor and supporter, and now his soul and his hearth had become desolate."[68]

Several life transitions happen in the wake of Khadija's and Abu Talib's deaths. Most significant for early biographers is the emigration from Mecca to Medina. Yet it is difficult to parse the relationship between narrative transitions and life transitions: the story has been told so often with these events connected that they seem causally linked, even though the emigration happened two or three years after these deaths. The other transition that concerns us here is Muhammad's remarriages, which happened more quickly.

The narrative link between Khadija's death and Muhammad's remarriages, specifically those to Aisha and Sawda, is also ancient. The story, based on a *hadith* account, appears in early works. This conjunction was used by hostile biographers—Humphrey Prideaux, for example, in a passage that many copied. Haykal's version owes at least as much to Prideaux's account, filtered through later authors, as it does to that of Ibn Hisham.

Prideaux frames the remarriages to make a moral point. He ignores the prophet's tender feelings and focuses instead on his calculations and plotting:

> And now *Cadigha*, his Wife, being dead, after she had lived Two and twenty Years with him; to strengthen himself the more, he took Two other Wives in her stead, *Ayesha*, the Daughter of *Abu Beker*; and *Sewda*, the Daughter of *Zama*; and a while after he added to them *Haphsa*, the Daughter of *Omar*; whereby making himself Son in law to Three of the Principal Men of his Party, he did by that Alliance the more firmly tie them to his Interest.[69]

In modern accounts, Muhammad's remarriages only reinforce Khadija's centrality. Traditional sources often mention the intervention of a matchmaker, who suggests Aisha if he wishes to marry a virgin and Sawda if he wishes a matron; Muhammad charges her to pursue both matches.[70] This focus on priority—most sources agree that the marriage to Aisha was first, though it was consummated only after a delay—and intervention tend to drop out of more recent accounts, which instead raise the question of motivations.[71] That polygamy itself needed justification never occurred to Muhammad's premodern Muslim biographers.

The Wives of Muhammad

Prideaux and earlier authors had seen improper motives for his marriage to Khadija. By the modern era, however, non-Muslim as well as Muslim authors had come to see that marriage as at least unobjectionable and, more often, admirable. As a result, those who would condemn Muhammad's marital conduct face a conundrum. Muhammad's conduct after Khadija's death gives a very different impression of Muhammad as a husband than does his conduct up to that point.[72] (As Carlyle put it, "He seems to have lived in a most affectionate, peaceable, wholesome way with his wedded benefactress; loving her truly, and her alone.")[73] How, then, to explain his behavior in taking many wives? Some Western authors have held, essentially, that power corrupts; Muhammad's changed marital conduct is of a piece with a larger change in his morals. He moves from ethical exemplar to bloodthirsty warrior. Among Muslim authors, the Iranian Ali Dashti, in his *Twenty-Three Years,* is an unusual example of this approach, though Dashti—who was part of a broader tradition of deliberately controversial writing—tempers his criticism by positing that Muhammad never really recovered from his grief at Khadija's death.[74] W. Montgomery Watt—whose *Muhammad at Mecca, Muhammad at Medina,* and abridged overview, *Muhammad: Prophet and Statesman,* are widely accepted as generally reliable accounts in the usual mode—hypothesizes that after the loss of "his faithful wife and helpmate Khadījah," Muhammad was compelled "to be more self-reliant, and that may have been necessary for the ultimate success of the religious movement." Watt speculates that even though he remarried, it was less for "spiritual companionship" than for political reasons; "there are signs that deepening religious experiences

were taking the place of human companionship."[75] For Watt, just as it was for Siddiqui, Jalbani, and many others, the marriage to Khadija was exceptional, emotionally and spiritually supportive, and companionate. Would Khadija's faithful and devoted husband have taken a dozen wives in a decade? (An American doctor writing shortly before World War I opined, in his work on "the lives of three great epileptics," that Muhammad's "veering from the monogamous ideal" resulted from "the setting in . . . of premature mental decay.")[76]

The centrality of Muhammad's multiple marriages to critical biographies led to a reactive focus on refuting criticisms. Prideaux had used Muhammad's marriages as an illustration of the role of (blameworthy) ambition and political interest in his actions and, thus, as part of a broader condemnation of his imposture, fraud, and general degeneracy.[77] Muir's tone is different; he focuses on polygamy, divorce, and slavery as core problems with Islamic morality, judged not just as personal failings of the Prophet, who had fathered Ibrahim by the slave woman Mariya, but as characteristic ills of Muslim civilization, blame for which may be laid in part at Muhammad's door. As Arthur Wollaston, also a British colonial official, echoes, after Khadija's death and Muhammad's remarriages, "henceforward polygamy became an institution in the Muslim world, hallowed as the custom thus was by the example of their Prophet who, it should be kept in mind, up to this period had limited himself to a single wife."[78]

Muslim authors took up the pen in response. Although some, like Ameer Ali, chose to address slavery, most allowed that charge to pass largely in silence. Often there was a tacit shift in the way Muhammad's slaves were referred to—Mariya becomes a wife—or an occasional pugnacious remark. But what stood out for Muslim

apologists was by and large polygamy, and they devoted themselves to explaining Muhammad's multiple marriages. (Only in the middle of the twentieth century did concern about polygamy begin to be overshadowed by concern about Aisha's age.)

It was not only the increased entanglement of pious biography with scholarly, popular, and polemical Western writing about Muhammad that led to an increased focus on polygamy. Questions about marriage were part of larger ongoing debates in societies such as India and Egypt, as well as in European nations. Religious thinkers, including Muhammad 'Abduh in Egypt, were formulating opposition to polygamy in religious terms at the same time legislatures were deciding about Muslim women's access to divorce and minimum marriage ages. Although legal reforms to limit polygamy were ultimately unsuccessful in most Muslim-majority societies during the first half of the twentieth century, there were vocal critics of the practice, both male and female. It is one thing, though, to suggest that a practice has no place in a modern Muslim society, that its costs outweigh its benefits; it is quite another to attach any opprobrium to deeds of the Prophet. Thus, whatever broader concerns about polygamy Muslim authors may have had, when they discussed it in the context of Muhammad's life, they defended his actions.

Often, the reactive framing is explicit. Hafiz Ghulam Sarwar's 1961 biography, published in Lahore, contains an appendix on Muhammad's marriages bearing the subtitle "A Refutation of the Lying Accusations of European Writers." Siddiqui's Indian biography from 1969 includes a section entitled "Fabrication of the Orientalists," concerned with Muhammad's marriage to Zaynab.[79] An early example, also from the Indian subcontinent, is Syed M. H. Zaidi's 1935 *Mothers of the Faithful,* subtitled: *Being a Discourse*

on Polygamy with a Biographical Sketch of the Wives of Muhammad refuting the allegations of the non-Muslims against them and the Prophet himself. Published in Calcutta the same year as Haykal's *Life*, it shares its preoccupation with perceived Western attacks. Zaidi's preface details two intended audiences, the second of which is Muslim women, whom he hopes to inspire with the life stories of the prophet's wives. His first aim, however, is "to explain to the non-Muslims, especially the European Christians, the circumstances connected with Muhammad's numerous spousals [*sic*] after the death of his first wife, the noble Khadija."[80] It is not just Muhammad's polygamy that is of interest, but specifically his polygamy *after* Khadija's death. His monogamous marriage to her serves as Exhibit A for the defense.

Although formulated as a response to outside criticism, the "allegations of the non-Muslims" have become troubling to Muslims as well. Zaidi's "European Christians" allow him to address justifications for Muhammad's marriages to Muslim readers without acknowledging that Muslims may wonder about the prophet's actions. By positing the non-Muslim addressee when making apologetic arguments, authors like Zaidi externalize their own anxieties. These anxieties, whatever their origin, testify to new Muslim sensibilities.

In Zaidi's book, polygamy takes center stage. More than anything else about Muhammad's marriages, their sheer number requires explanation or refutation: "circumstances" serve to "explain" (and perhaps excuse) his conduct. The information Zaidi gives has long since become predictable: Western criticisms are unjust and unfounded; Muhammad married repeatedly to protect vulnerable widows and strengthen alliances. As S. M. Abbasi puts it, "The accusation that he was a licentious man because he mar-

ried so many wives is absolutely false and mischievous. His marriages were all forced upon him, by circumstances. . . . In every
case of such marriage . . . it was a personal sacrifice on the part of
the Holy Prophet to have contracted the marriage, or the circumstances obliged him to do so."[81]

Zaidi's book straddles genres: it is a polemical engagement
with Western literature and a collective biography of the Prophet's
wives. It is this engagement with critics that compels extensive
attention to Zaynab, ex-wife of Muhammad's (ex-)son Zayd.[82]
This marriage has been the focus of a good deal of contention
over the centuries; Watt, writing in 1961, could still call this "the
most controversial of all Muḥammad's marriages."[83] Siddiqui
makes the claim, "So far as the fanciful stories and calumnies of
the Orientalists are concerned, we can only say that these are so
absurd that any one having even a grain of sense in him would
unhesitatingly reject them as mere fabrications." In particular, he
singles out "Muir and so many others like him," who repeat the
story of Muhammad beguiled by a glimpse of a disheveled Zaynab. There is, he writes, "absolutely no truth in these stories
which have been fabricated in this connection."[84] Siddiqui seems
to be unaware that these stories, rather than being invented by
Orientalists, appear in Arab sources, where they are treated with
varying degrees of acceptance and endorsement by compilers.[85]
He proposes a somewhat novel rationale for Muhammad's marriage to Zaynab: "to give a fatal blow to the distinctions of high
birth."[86] Zayd was a freed slave, and Zaynab, an aristocrat. On
their divorce, Siddiqui writes, "Muhammad (peace be upon him)
was generous enough to marry her himself and thus retrieved for
her family lost prestige and also removed the false conception that
the divorce of a woman at the hand of a freed slave ever degraded

her position."[87] Most importantly, in a rationale also described by other authors, "the real objective behind this marriage was to bury forever the un-Islamic custom of adoptive kinship which had taken a deep root in the minds of the people. As the Holy Prophet was the last link in the golden chain of prophethood, he was required to purge human society of all those customs and superstitions which ran counter to the canons of *Islam*."[88] Aisha 'Abd al-Rahman, however, sees Muhammad's attraction to Zaynab as reliably reported by Tabari and considers it "proof of his humanity" that "his heart went out to Zaynab."[89]

Apologetics and Mainstream Writing

The more frequent arguments, however, were not specific to this marriage, nor did they revolve around the undoing of deleterious custom. Muhammad's multiple marriages were usually explained as creating alliances or caring for vulnerable widows. Custom, too, could also be an exculpating argument—Sale saw it as a good enough reason for Muhammad's entanglements. So did George Bush.

Of course, not everyone was content to skip lightly over his many marriages. Departing from the incident of Muhammad's marriages to Aisha and Sawda, American Harvey Newcomb's *The False Prophet* (1844)—written as a dialogue between a mother and her children, and drawing heavily from Bush—leads into a discussion of Christianity's superior sexual ethic: "Christianity," the mother tells her daughter, "is the only religion in the world, which does not allow men to have more than one wife." The daughter declares: "Oh how unnatural . . . I think it must destroy the peace and happiness of families." Through a rhetorical sleight, something

defined as universal among non-Christians is nonetheless stigmatized as unnatural; it follows, then, that only Christianity accords with human nature. Polygamy's "effects upon society . . . have always been debasing. It has done more, perhaps than any other custom, to degrade the female character. . . . And whatever debases female character injures the whole face of society. Yet, this odious practice prevails throughout the whole heathen world."[90] After a pause, during which her daughter explains that she is weeping because "I was thinking what we owe to the Lord Jesus, and how ungrateful I have been to him for the benefits he has purchased for me with his own blood," the mother continues:

> Among the heathen, females are generally degraded almost to the condition of slaves. . . . In some places, their condition is so wretched that life is considered a burden; and parents often destroy their female children, to save them from the miseries of life. Among the Mohammedans, women are not allowed to appear in public. Some of their great men have many wives. They keep them shut up in a kind of prison, which they call *harems*. These women are subject to the will of their lordly master; and if he is displeased with them he has power to cut off their heads! In India, when a man died, they used to make a great pile of dry wood, and put his dead body upon it, and bind all his wives and lay them by his side, and then set the wood on fire and burn them all together.[91]

Newcomb's anti-Muslim tract wanders fairly far from the specific focus on Muhammad's biographical material; his polygamy is an entrée into the larger problem of polygamy, which segues into the degraded status of heathen women more generally. Bush, from

whom Newcomb draws much of his narrative and some of his language, is more sanguine about one element of Muhammad's conduct, and does not blame him for "the mere circumstance of multiplying his wives," since "a heathen people cannot be fairly judged by the rules of Christian morality."[92] A universalist model, in which all are judged according to the same standard, exists in tension here with a relativist standard, which, though it may save heathens from particular sorts of blame, nonetheless does so by viewing them as insufficiently advanced morally. Both Bush and Newcomb, however, draw the line in religious terms: heathen versus Christian. Yet Bush's absolution lays the groundwork for a heavier charge of failing to *observe those rules of morality which he himself laid down, and which he enforced upon others by such terrible sanctions.*[93] That is, "under the pretence of a special revelation, dispensing him from the laws imposed by his own religion, had the female sex abandoned without reserve to his desires."[94] He titillates but refuses to provide particulars of "how completely the prophet's imposture was made an engine for promoting the gratification of sensual passion," citing the requirements of "decorum."[95]

Monogamy and Polygamy

For most of the twentieth century, monogamy and polygamy were the poles that defined Muhammad's marital conduct and therefore character. His monogamous and happy companionate marriage to Khadija, now conventional wisdom, was to be understood as the norm for his conduct. His other marriages were attributed to pity, protection, or politics.

In traditional accounts, Muhammad's wives appear from time to time throughout the narrative. He gets married to one after a

battle, or an interpersonal crisis prompted by illness, jealousy, or some external event occurs and is documented in its chronological place. Anecdotes likewise appear in other types of works. Stories about intra-household conflict illuminate the revelation of particular verses of the Qur'an, some of which might otherwise remain opaque. *Hadith* accounts detail mundane incidents with legal implications. Though quite a few works have a chapter or section that lists Muhammad's wives and provides some biographical detail, they are typically instead woven into the narrative fabric.

As Muslim biography became increasingly responsive to Western critique, Muhammad's marriages become a worthy topic of discussion in and of themselves. Muir talks about his marriages along the way, but Dermenghem includes a separate chapter on "The Harem." Haykal follows, with a chapter on "The Prophet's Wives" and another on "Ibrāhīm and the Wives of Muhammad." Ameer Ali devotes an extensive section to addressing criticisms of Muhammad's marriages, and Ahmad Khan talks about polygamy and divorce at length when weighing the impact of Islam on human society.

Prior to the last two centuries, biographers did not concern themselves with *justifying* Muhammad's marriages—why defend something no one found objectionable?—but they did sometimes report motivations, implicitly or explicitly. Sometimes, for instance, Muhammad was struck by a woman's beauty. At other times, there was speculation about practical motives: perhaps his marriage to Sawda made sense in part since he was a widower with four daughters and she was an older woman with experience,[96] or his marriage to Umm Habiba might have been to strengthen an alliance with her father, his Meccan antagonist Abu Sufyan.

The explanation that many marriages took place for the forging or strengthening of alliances with staunch supporters and former

antagonists makes perfect sense. We can see the extent to which leadership was a family matter if we recall that among the first four men to lead the community after Muhammad's death—those the Sunnis retrospectively came to recognize as rightly guided caliphs—the first two, Abu Bakr and Umar, were Muhammad's fathers-in-law (he was married to their daughters, Aisha and Hafsa, respectively); the second two, Uthman and Ali, were his sons-in-law. Family ties matter even more for the Shi'a, who recognize Ali—also Muhammad's paternal cousin and, with Muhammad and Khadija's daughter Fatima, progenitor of Muhammad's only surviving descendants—as Muhammad's legitimate successor. When reading these accounts, it is vital to recall that the stories about Muhammad's wives reported by early biographers and *hadith* compilers were told by those who had a stake in enhancing or denigrating the reputations of the wives and their relatives—and the factions with which they were associated—in the aftermath of Muhammad's death and the ensuing contests over political leadership of the community. These reports were not transparent reflections of fact but narratives aimed at conveying particular notions about which women were trustworthy or favored. (As historian Chase Robinson observes, "Whereas late antique Christians quarreled about Christology, Muslims quarreled about the conduct of seventh-century Muslims as it was remembered and recorded in history.")[97]

These texts, however, have been plundered by modern biographers with different agendas. Ignoring the complex structures and motivations of those who wrote those early texts, modern writers treat them as straightforward storehouses of data that are either reliable or unreliable. Stories about the wives that may have been told for particular reasons now become understood in different ways.

Although lists of wives frequently appear as supplements to texts (as do lists of battles in which Muhammad participated, names of his horses, and the like), premodern authors did not concern themselves with how Muhammad treated women as a class, his wives as a group, or his female Companions. When they do play up one or another episode, or praise one wife over and against another, the point might be competition between factions (or a hermeneutical motive relating to explicating the Qur'anic text), not any kind of broader claim about gender or a desire to show anything particular about women's status. In fact, women as a collectivity, defined by their gender, seldom appears in the early biographies. Modern non-Muslim biographies often seek to derive something about Muhammad's character from how he related to women, as well as how his relations with his wives might have influenced his views on women more generally. Apologetic Muslim biographies illustrate the shift even more clearly, as they seek to define and defend his noble character by showing how he was enlightened in his relationships with his wives: he had impeccable motives for marrying them, he treated them with scrupulous fairness when allocating his time, he never hit them or spoke harshly, and he shared household chores. Again, apart from the concern with justifying his polygamy, the other elements are present in premodern biographies as well, but there they illustrate other things: his status as legal exemplar, his gentle manner, his humility, his concern for the vulnerable.

The defensive and reactive treatment of Muhammad's polygamy is typified in *The Holy Prophet Mohammad: The Commander of the Faithful* by Muhammad Ali-Al-Haj Salmin, written in the 1930s. In the section on "The Home Life of the Prophet," Salmin writes, "A charge, that he practiced polygamy and allowed his followers

the same, is levelled against him; but it can easily be explained." Salmin, using the passive voice and legalistic phrasing, attributes to unnamed accusers the "charge . . . levelled against him."[98] Salmin mounts his defense: "This is a fact that he contracted these marriages due to political circumstances and with a higher humanitarian consideration in view to save the honour of the women of those followers who laid their lives in sacrifice in the cause of Islam. That the motive of sensuality had nothing to do with these marriages, will be clear enough to any one who studies his private life dispassionately."[99] These sentences mix appeals to rationality ("fact," "clear," "studies," "dispassionately") with references to sentiments both praiseworthy and not ("humanitarian," "honour," "sacrifice," "sensuality"). He goes on to describe the Prophet's character as it relates to his treatment of his wives: "the Prophet was the model of a husband and householder, being courteous, kind and just to all of them, often helping them in their household duties." Note that in Salmin's presentation, the household work properly belongs to the wives.[100]

Ghulam Malik (1996) sounds the same broadly apologetic note, although with somewhat less attention to lust and a slightly less defensive tone. He, too, appeals to the need to correct improper views: "One of the most misunderstood aspects of the Prophet Muhammad's life has been the plurality of his marriages. Before passing any superficial judgment, it is necessary to delve into the socio-economic condition and political situation of Arabia in general, and particularly of the Muslim community, for a careful study of his marriages."[101] In a move adopted by both European apologists and essayists like Ahmad Khan and Ameer Ali, Malik notes that Islam does not link celibacy and piety and, further, that Old Testament prophets "practice[ed] polygyny without the

slightest detriment to their character or deviation from fulfilling their divinely ordained missions."[102] He then moves on to the defense of Muhammad's premarital chastity, as mentioned previously, and turns to his marriage to Khadija.

Though Khadija herself was wealthy, widows were typically destitute, making Muhammad's marriages charitable. (This desire to emphasize Muhammad's role in protecting the downtrodden leads some authors to a palpable contradiction, stressing Khadija's wealth and independence but in the next breath explaining how women were chattels before the coming of Islam.[103]) Vulnerable widows were simply an extreme instance of female need for protection. Malik writes: "Women had not rights or economic security" but depended on their husbands or fathers.[104] In the first Muslim community, "the widows and orphans of the small Muslim community posted serious problems." This made polygamy "a necessity in Muslim society at that time."

Protection was joined by political motives. Thus, Malik concludes, "Objectively speaking, the Prophet Muhammad's marriages were motivated mainly by economic and political factors to the benefit of his Call and the community."[105] He quotes Watt to support his claim: "Doubtless, Muhammad's own marriages and those of his close companions as well were contracted to improve relations with his opponents and consolidate his political power."[106] This explanation is typical of much twentieth-century biography: pragmatic political justifications for plural marriages are viewed as positive. British Muslim author Ziauddin Sardar's 2012 biography emphasizes the social function of Muhammad's marriages: "Marriage is the lubricant of a society based on kinship. . . . It should not surprise us, then, that most of Muhammad's marriages had a political context." This is the case both for marriages, such as those

to Aisha and Hafsa, that "constituted the glue that bound his companions to Muhammad" and for marriages that "cemented tribal alliances or served as a rationale for reconciliation."[107] Indeed, the translators of the volume of Tabari's history that deals with the first years after the migration to Medina devote a portion of the foreword to "The Marriage with 'Ā'ishah," in which they declare, "All Muḥammad's marriages and those he arranged for his daughters were made for political reasons."[108]

Author after author, Muslim and non-Muslim, insists that Muhammad's motives were political and therefore salutary rather than lustful and therefore deplorable. For earlier critics, though, political motives for marriage proved despicable scheming. Marrying women to promote alliances revealed a calculating disposition: Muhammad crafted a fraudulent persona to bolster his fraudulent religion. Ambition might not be worse than lustfulness, but neither was it a vast improvement. In their haste to defend Muhammad from charges of debauchery, writers argue that he was not attracted to these women—or, if he was, it was a happy bonus to be passed over as swiftly as possible. Few acknowledge his genuine attraction to several women. If they do, it is typically to downplay it and to stress the other factors, political or charitable, promoting his marriages.[109] For example, of Juwayriyya, Jewish captive from the Banu Mustaliq, Thompson writes, "Although Juwayriyya was young and beautiful and of noble lineage, the Prophet Muhammad was thinking of how to save her and all her tribe from an ignoble fate."[110] It is striking how frequently Muslim authors and sympathetic non-Muslim authors writing since the middle of the twentieth century overlap on these points. Dashti is virtually alone, in his *Twenty-Three Years*, when he suggests that Muhammad's multiple marriages signal "human weakness."[111]

Chastity and Caretaking

Muhammad's marriage to Khadija has always been worthy of note, though not always for the same reasons. Ibn Ishaq saw the marriage as confirming Muhammad's noble qualities and implicitly honoring the mother of his children and the resulting progeny, all of whom descend through Khadija. For more recent authors, she represents a companionate and monogamous marriage. Muhammad's monogamy with Khadija was already noteworthy for Ibn Hisham, who declares, "She was the first woman the Messenger of God married and he did not take another wife until she died."[112] But in this view, it proved her specialness, not Muhammad's continence. In contrast, after centuries of European criticisms of Muhammad's lustfulness, in modern apologetic works Muhammad's premarital chastity and longtime marital fidelity to Khadija serve as proof that he was not, as one author puts it, "sex-minded."[113]

In works from the Indian subcontinent from the late nineteenth century into the twenty-first century, authors tend to accept the model of the world in which climactic conditions lead to early puberty and strong desire. Thus, Muhammad's chastity—he "spent his 25 years like an angel"—is especially notable, given both the loose morals of pagan Meccan society and the fact that he lived in "tropical Arabia where puberty comes early."[114] Similarly, Muhammad Ali's *Muhammad the Prophet*—first published in 1924, revised half a century later, and by 1993 in its seventh edition—invokes the climate of Arabia to emphasize Muhammad's restraint and chastity: "If he had not been a complete master of his passions, he could not have led, up to the age of twenty-five, the exceptionally chaste and pure life . . . in a hot country like Arabia where

development must necessarily take place early and passions are generally stronger."[115] Ali—who led the Lahore branch of the Ahmadiyya—notes that "even according to Muir," Muslim sources agree that Muhammad displayed rare "'modesty of deportment and purity of manners.'"[116] Ali's views about Muhammad's marital and sexual life are echoed by those who disagreed with the Ahmadi viewpoint on other religious issues. For instance, Ghulam Malik similarly defends Muhammad's sexual honor: he "had no romance in his life" and "preserved his chastity at a time when the Arab society was enmeshed in immorality." In fact, he improbably asserts that "the first time Muhammad came into contact with a female outside his family was with Khadijah" when he was twenty-five: "And soon they got married."[117]

Ali is concerned generally with polygamy: he argues that Muhammad's heart was "free . . . of all base and sensual thoughts" and ascribes his multiple marriages after Khadija largely to a desire to protect widows.[118] This protection does not consist merely or even primarily in providing the women food and shelter but in ensuring their chastity through satisfaction of their sexual needs, since "the statesman who neglects sex requirements leads society to moral corruption, ending ultimately in the ruin of the whole nation."[119] Polygamy was necessary so that sexually deprived widows would not cause social chaos. (Siddiqui likewise attributes Muhammad's marriages to "the feeling of compassion for the widows of his faithful followers" but stresses not their sexual needs but that "they were bereft of the love and care of their husbands.")[120] Both the permission for polygamy in general and the Prophet's personal practice emerged from the need to keep widows chaste. Ali goes further to convince his readers that the Prophet's motives were pure: "Nearly all of his wives were widows. Where self-indulgence is the motive,

the choice does not fall on widows." Muhammad could have had virgins had he wanted them; there was "no dearth of virgins," and it "would have been an enviable privilege for any Muslim to be father-in-law of the Holy Prophet."[121] Ali assumes that fathers would make decisions about marrying off their daughters, placing the honor not on the wives but on their fathers. A 1994 Pakistani biography echoes this argument: "All his companions, male and female, had been so devoted to him that if he wanted to marry only virgin girls he could have done it and if he wished to keep any girl with him for a couple months for enjoyment, there was none to object him, but he never did so."[122]

So, Muhammad's "object was a far nobler one" than self-indulgence: "the protection of the widows of his friends" and "the moral safety of the Muslim society situated as it then was."[123] Additionally, in the cases of Juwayriyya and Safiyya, "widow of a Jewish chieftain," Ali cites "certain political reasons" for the marriages: "The Holy Prophet wanted to conciliate both tribes and that was the only motive in these marriages."[124] Zaynab's marriage was a special case, since she was Muhammad's cousin, originally "offered in marriage to the Holy Prophet by her brother" when she arrived at majority.[125] Muhammad "wedded her to Zaid, a slave whom he himself had freed"—note that nothing is said of their filial/parental tie, only that Zaid was "deeply attached to him." The marriage ultimately failed, but Muhammad did not want the stigma of divorce to taint her, especially since she was superior in social status to her ex-husband. Again, he felt it necessary to act personally:

> By this act, to which he was morally bound because the lady had been at first offered in marriage to him, he elevated the

whole class of divorced women who would otherwise suffer life-long humiliation in society. If he had any desire of self-gratification or if he had any passion for the lady, he would not have refused her when she was offered to him as a virgin. Refusal of her hand in the first instance, and taking her in marriage when being divorced she was lowered in general estimation, shows conclusively that his motive in this marriage was anything but self-gratification.[126]

These authors assume that men make decisions and "offer" their virgin female kin—daughters or sisters—in marriage, as Zaynab's brother had done and as fathers of virgins would have done out of a desire to make the Prophet their son-in-law. Ali also presumes that female inexperience is crucial to male desire and satisfaction: "Lust must needs have virginity for its gratification."[127] Widows and divorcees, who have had husbands before, must be protected and given an outlet for their own sexual desires in order to prevent rampant immorality. However, Ali assumes that they are not desirable in and of themselves. Zaynab's marriage, which gets special attention because of the "calumny" attached to it, is explained as aiming at removing the stigma surrounding divorce; nothing is said about Zayd's ambiguous kinship, the issue that preoccupied others.

Ali sums up his defense of Muhammad thus: "By disposition he was not inclined to polygamy, living a celibate life of unexampled purity up to twenty-five years and a married life of a monogamous husband up to fifty-four, but when duty called him to take more women under his shelter, he answered the call of duty."[128] Nasr offers a similar litany in *Muhammad: Man of God*, insisting that "the multiple marriages of the Blessed Prophet . . . were certainly not for sensual pleasure. He did not marry until he was

twenty-five and then during all the years when the sexual passions are strongest in the male, he lived with one wife who was fifteen years older than he."[129] Muhammad's "attitude toward sexuality," which he views as "the basis of the Islamic attitude in this domain," must be discussed because "so much criticism has been made of it by Western writers."[130] His marriages were for political and social reasons: "If the Blessed Prophet had contracted marriages just for sensual pleasure, as so many adverse Western biographers have written, surely he would have married many women when he himself was young and at the prime of manhood and also chosen all of his wives from among young women. But a study of his life reveals very different facts."[131] Khadija's age renders her less a proper object of "sensual pleasure": Nasr alludes twice to her age in this passage as evidence that Muhammad was not motivated by passion in his marriages.

These passages draw their structure and main points from Godfrey Higgins's 1829 *Apology*. Ameer Ali quoted him on a number of points, including the relative maturation rates of men and women in hot climes. Higgins seems to have originated the argument based on the fact that when Muhammad married Khadija, it was at "the very time of life when youthful passion may be supposed to be at its height; and though, by the laws of his country, he was entitled to have a plurality of wives, he neglected to avail himself of this permission, and continued faithful to her as long as she lived." He goes on to criticize those who see his behavior as resulting merely from "gratitude to his kindest friend, the maker of his fortune."[132]

Through quotation in Ameer Ali's influential work, arguments by a British non-Muslim survive to be used two centuries later by Muslim apologists in works read by Muslims, though ostensibly

directed toward refuting Western critics. Repeatedly, in works written by Muslims for Muslims, authors declare their aim to "answer allegations" of misconduct. Abbasi's prefatory words describing his objectives are typical: "The first and the foremost is to present the account of the lives of the Holy family objectively and secondly to rebut the false and malicious but sustained propaganda of the Western writers against Islam, its Holy Prophet (S.A.W.) and his family members."[133]

These rebuttals devote disproportionate attention to Khadija, not just in number of pages but in terms of psychic centrality.[134] Malik says it "would not be incorrect" to call their union "a love marriage between a wealthy widow and a poor young man." Nasr refers to this marriage as "perfect": it was "a marriage which was so complete and in a sense absolute that the Blessed Prophet did not marry another wife as long as Khadījah was alive. This fact is particularly important since she was fifteen years older than he and polygamy was a very common practice in Arabian, as in most other parts of the world, at that time."[135] For Karen Armstrong, "She had been Muhammad's closest companion, and nobody—not even Abu Bakr or the fervent 'Umar—would ever be able to provide Muhammad with the same intimate support."[136] Here and elsewhere, biographers enumerate Khadija's virtues but discount her attractiveness. Both her age and her nonvirgin status diminish her appeal for these mostly South Asian authors. Abbasi writes, for instance, of him marrying "a woman who is 15 years senior to him and has been widowed twice before."[137] Muhammad's faithfulness despite Khadija's diminished attractiveness proves that he was not motivated by lust.

Motives, of course, are notoriously tricky things. In fictionalization common to recent biographies, some authors imagine Khadija's

feelings too. American convert Yahiya Emerick attributes to her both love ("she was falling deeper and deeper in love with him") and self-doubt: Would Muhammad reject her overtures? New-age guru Deepak Chopra envisions her inner monologues, which reveal Khadija as insecure, including about her sexual appeal.[138] Yet her outstanding qualities cannot pass unremarked. Emerick shifts between emphasizing Khadija's nobility and wealth and por-traying Muhammad as having the upper hand: "Although Khadi-jah was neither young nor a virgin, which were essential traits in a wife in pre-Islamic Arabia, Muhammad treated her as his loving life-partner from the start."[139] Emerick makes the reader feel that Muhammad was quite forbearing in failing to exercise his privi-leges to marry again. In contrast, early biographies stress that Mu-hammad, despite his moral excellence, was lucky to make such an advantageous alliance: "Khadījah was then the most distinguished of the Quraysh women in lineage, the most highly honored, and the wealthiest," Tabari reports, "and all the men of her tribe would have been eager to accept this proposal had it been made to them."[140]

In something of a contrast to Khadija's exalted status, both Emerick and Nasr—like many other authors—portray women's existence in pre-Islamic Arabia as downtrodden.[141] In a similar vein, Ameer Ali paints a deplorable picture of the "condition" of women in ancient India; already bad "during that vague and mythic period which passes under the name of the Vedic age," it "arrived at the depth of degradation under Brahmanic domination."[142] Since the nineteenth century, Muslim apologists tout the improvement to women's status brought about by Islam: "All know that before his prophethood the condition of women was a very pitiable one. She was the most degraded of Allah's creations, but the Holy Prophet

raised her high, and set her up on a pedestal of her own high and sweet queendom."[143] But also striking is the way in which Muslim apologists adopt the condescending attitude of Western scholars toward Khadija, insisting on their happy companionate marriage, or her status as a trusting and comforting helpmate, while simultaneously downplaying her attractiveness—something that the early sources do not do. Premodern Muslim sources admittedly sometimes celebrate the attractions of young and especially virginal females; one could cite numerous examples, including references to Aisha. What is new is the application of this valuation to Khadija and the implicit view that because she was older and a widow—here, the acceptance of her age as given in the early biographies as literal rather than symbolic bolsters the idea that she was old and had lost her charms—it would have been charitable for Muhammad to marry her.[144]

A Different Perspective

Aloys Sprenger noted that "the amorous disposition of the messenger of God is considered as a virtue by most of his followers."[145] This was much more the case in 1850, when he was writing, than in 1950, when the discourse of politics, pity, and protection had taken hold. Yet there were exceptions to the reach of this delibidinizing discourse, which, in any case, was more prevalent in South Asia than in Egypt.

Pulitzer Prize winner Naguib Mahfouz's allegorical novelization *Children of the Alley* retells Abrahamic history, concluding with a figure named Qassem, who represents Muhammad.[146] Like his modernist countrymen, Mahfouz immersed himself in early Muslim sources and transmuted them into something

quite distinctive. As a novelist, Mahfouz was more interested in truth than in fact. But though his presentation of Qassem/ Muhammad is in keeping with the classical tradition's celebration of Muhammad's sexual prowess—in contrast to Haykal's ambivalence, wavering between defensiveness and denial—in other respects he is thoroughly modern. Some modern Egyptian authors including 'Abd al-Rahman had been matter-of-fact about the Prophet's (post-Khadija) penchant for women, but Mahfouz's reference to earlier "hot-blooded adventures in the desert with their blind, burning hunger and their sad, transient satisfaction" are explicitly denied by other authors, who emphasize Muhammad's premarital chastity. But if Mahfouz posits premarital "adventures," he also makes Khadija loom disproportionately large—first as presence, then as absence. This is manifestly not the case in *hadith* collections, works of exegesis, or premodern Muslim biographies, though it is typical for modern accounts of Muhammad's life.[147] Indeed, almost all modern accounts repeat an anecdote in which Aisha is jealous of Khadija's memory and Muhammad chastises her, enumerating Khadija's virtues.[148]

Mahfouz goes on to write erotically of the connection between Qassem and the Aisha figure, who becomes the first of his wives after Qamar, the Khadija figure. Most other Muslim authors downplay love and desire in Muhammad's later marriages, even as they emphasize his model behavior toward his wives. Highlighting his charitable and political motives for these marriages, authors depict Khadija as special. He was a good husband to his other wives, but those marriages were not the ideal "example of married life" that his monogamous marriage to Khadija was. Thus, Golam Choudhury's praise, written in the 1990s:

The Prophet was a model of good family life. As a husband, he had a unique relationship with his first wife, Khadijah, and his subsequent marriages after the death of his first wife were based on a number of considerations. As an ideal husband, Muhammad had set a good example of married life and showed how the relationship between a husband and wife should be based on the injunctions of the Qur'an: on the basis of tenderest devotion on both sides and on mutual love and attachment.[149]

Chapter 5

Mother of the Faithful

Muhammad grieved Khadija deeply, but he did not remain unmarried for long. A matchmaker approached him and offered to find him a new wife. Did he want a woman who had been previously married or one who never had? She had in mind Sawda, fairly recently widowed, or Aisha, daughter of his intimate friend and early convert Abu Bakr. He asked her to arrange matches with both of them. Sawda agreed, and that marriage took place immediately. Aisha's situation was more complicated. Securing her release from an earlier betrothal was easy; her intended's family had not become Muslim and was glad to back out. A contract was then made between Muhammad and Abu Bakr, but Aisha remained with her family. Two or three years later, after the migration to Medina, the marriage was consummated and Aisha moved into quarters attached to the mosque, next to Sawda's apartment. By most accounts, she was then nine years old.

If Khadija represents the positive role model and the linchpin of Muhammad's maturation as a man and a prophet in Mecca, Aisha is the wife whose presence most colors his Medinan years and whose story continues to unfold after Muhammad's death. She was a vital, if sometimes problematic, figure for the construction of Sunni orthodoxy, a major reporter of prophetic traditions, and a jurist of some note. Her chastity was impugned during her lifetime and her participation in an intra-Muslim civil war put

her at the center of debates over women's public roles. Humphrey Prideaux sees the political motivations behind their marriage as evidence of Muhammad's warped morality. For many nineteenth-century Christian authors, Aisha's status as a polygamous wife illustrated Muslim depravity. Since the middle of the twentieth century, it is Aisha's age that demands explanation, justification, or refutation. Tracking the attention to her age over the course of the last two centuries reveals a tension between models that treat Muslims as irreducibly different and irredeemably evil or as simply backwards and capable of reform—properly guided, of course.

The Muslim Textual Tradition

The two most trusted Sunni *hadith* compilations, those of Bukhari and Muslim, say that Aisha was six or seven at the time her marriage was contracted, and nine at consummation, as do Ibn Sa'd's sources. Ibn Hisham says nine or ten: "The Messenger of God, may God's blessings and peace be upon him, married Aisha daughter of Abu Bakr the Righteous in Mecca when she was a girl of seven years and he consummated the marriage with her in Medina when she was a girl of nine or ten years. The Messenger of God, may God's blessings and peace be upon him, did not marry a virgin other than her."[1]

Tabari provides some information on the ages of Muhammad's wives, including Aisha, as part of the biographical supplement to his massive history, in which ages are sometimes relevant but rarely important.[2] He expends a good deal more energy clarifying the women's genealogies and other facts about their lives, as well as the circumstances of their alliances with the Prophet. Still, it

can be helpful to see how unusual Aisha is in this context. Only
four entries mention age explicitly. Aisha was nine at consummation, which took place three years after the marriage and less than
a year after the emigration. Umm Habiba, the daughter of Muhammad's Meccan antagonist Abu Sufyan, was "thirty-odd years
old";[3] and Juwayriyya declares, "I was twenty years old when the
Prophet married me." Safiyya, the youngest of those whose age
Tabari gives, was "not even seventeen" or "just seventeen," according to her reported words "the night [she] entered the Prophet's room."[4] She was by that time once divorced and once widowed, the latter at Muslim hands. One can calculate rough ages
at marriage for five other women from their birth or death dates;
all were in their twenties or thirties. Aisha and possibly Khadija
are the only wives whose ages have been the focus of any real interest. In both cases, any attempt to corroborate or refute specific
figures is doomed to failure. Better to ask why the sources care.
Given the generalized indifference to birth dates—even for the
Prophet, let alone other key figures—the mention of ages must be
significant, aimed at something other than mere informing.[5]

Early Muslims intent on recording Muhammad's life story
paid attention to Aisha's age because she was a controversial figure. If biographers settled fairly rapidly on Khadija as a positive
force in Muhammad's life, Aisha's presence was substantially
more contentious. In a rivalry that may have given rise to later
infighting—or that may have been written into the sources in the
wake of that fighting—the dyad Aisha/Abu Bakr competed with
the dyad Fatima/Ali for prestige and authority. In her magisterial
study of the shifting treatment of Aisha over the centuries, the
historian Denise Spellberg suggests that competition over status
may have generated a need to affirm Aisha's youth and purity:

"All of these specific references to the bride's age reinforce 'A'isha's pre-menarcheal status and, implicitly, her virginity."[6] Insistence on her chastity is likely to have been prompted by other accounts that embroil her in scandal, such as the "affair of the necklace," during which she fell behind on an expedition in looking for a misplaced necklace, was brought back to the group by a young man, and was the subject of ugly rumors before a revelation exonerated her (in the Sunni version). Aisha's association with contests over succession to the caliphate made arguments over her excellence inevitable. Pointing to another passage in Tabari's *History* in which Aisha is said to have been born before the coming of Islam, Spellberg says she might have been twelve or thirteen at the time of marriage (and older at its consummation).[7] One explanation as to why a younger age would be preferable: It would mean that she was born into a Muslim household. Thus, insisting on her youth might prove her *religious* purity over and above concern with her sexual purity.

Aisha's age preoccupied early Sunni scholars but generated no significant reflection by later Muslims. Nor did medieval or early modern Christian polemicists care; they were bothered instead by Muhammad's general debauchery, as manifested in his polygamy, his followers' practice of sodomy, and—if they had to single out any—his marriage to Zaynab, which raised the specter of incest.

Prideaux viewed the marriage to Aisha as part of Muhammad's massive fraud: marrying Aisha as well as Sawda and Hafsa was part of a strategy to shore up alliances with their fathers.[8] Prideaux's account describes Muhammad's remarriages after Khadija's death. The link between Khadija's death and his remarriage to Sawda and Aisha (typically listed in that order in recent works) is

ubiquitous.[9] Hafsa, whose marriage came somewhat later, is not usually listed in this series. Prideaux includes it because it provides further evidence for his claim that Muhammad was marrying to cultivate powerful allies, the better to perpetrate his imposture. Aisha's youth causes him no qualms: "*Ayesha* was then but six Years old, and therefore he did not bed her till two Years after, when she was full eight Years old. For it is usual in those hot Countries, as it is all *India* over, which is in the same *Clime* with *Arabia*, for Women to be ripe for Marriage at that Age, and also bear Children the Year following."[10]

Two American authors writing a century and a half later draw from this passage extensively to quite different effect. George Bush's discussion of the marriages is separate from that of Aisha's age and disconnected from his discussion of Muhammad's marriage to Khadija.[11] He sums up the situation in language clearly adapted from Prideaux: "in order to strengthen his interest in Mecca, he married Ayesha, the daughter of Abubeker, and shortly after Sawda, the daughter of Zama. By thus becoming the son-in-law of two of the principal men of his party he secured their patronage to his person and his cause."[12] Bush highlights Muhammad's political aims; Aisha's age and personal qualities hold no interest for him. He also omits Hafsa. This passage neither connects Muhammad's remarriages to Khadija's death nor mentions Muhammad's emotions. Aisha's age merits a brief remark only in the final full chapter of the work, which treats Muhammad's wives and concubines. Bush accepts climate's effect on female maturation: "Ayesha was married—such is the surprising physical precocity peculiar to an eastern climate—at the early age of nine; and survived her husband forty-eight years."[13]

Washington Irving takes a similar view of Aisha's age, though he expresses a concern alien to Prideaux or Bush—that of Muhammad's emotional needs:

> The family with Mahomet in Medina consisted of his recently wedded wife Sawda, and Fatima and Um Colthum, daughters of his late wife Cadijah. He had a heart prone to affection, and subject to female influence, but he had never entertained much love for Sawda; and though he always treated her with kindness, he felt the want of some one to supply the place of his deceased wife Cadijah. . . . He now turned his eyes upon his betrothed spouse Ayesha, the beautiful daughter of Abu Beker. Two years had elapsed since they were betrothed, and she had now attained her ninth year; an infantine age it would seem, though the female form is wonderfully precocious in the quickening climates of the east.[14]

Irving adds exotic details of their simple "nuptials": a "wedding supper" of milk and "twelve okk of silver" for the bride's dowry. He acknowledges possible political motivations ("Perhaps he sought, by this alliance, to grapple Abu Beker still more strongly to his side") but notes Aisha's beauty (which Prideaux had said nothing about), calling her "a beautiful child" and noting that she was "chosen in the very blossom of her years."[15] John Davenport's *An Apology for Mohammed and the Koran* (1869) likewise highlights her appearance: "About two months after the death of Khadijah, Mohammed married Sawda, a widow, and nearly at the same time Ayesha, the young and beautiful daughter of his bosom friend Abu-Bekr, the principal object of this last union being to cement still more strongly their mutual attachment."[16] Although he structures his account of

the marriages like Prideaux, where Prideaux sees a power play ("he did by that Alliance the more firmly tie them to his Interest"), Davenport adapts Muir's language about Abu Bakr ("an alliance mainly designed to cement the attachment of his bosom friend") to highlight the reciprocal nature of their friendship.[17]

Other authors were both more critical of Muhammad's marital conduct and less interested in titillating accounts of the precocious development of young girls in the "*Torrid Zone*."[18] But these authors still did not object to Aisha's age. Muir, not one to miss an opportunity to criticize Muhammad for any perceived moral lapses, notes the standard ages of six or seven in discussing what he calls a betrothal.[19] He refers to her as a "precocious bride" or a "precocious maiden."[20] What bothers him about the consummation of the marriage when she was ten or eleven is not her age but the polygamous nature of the union; since Sawda had been for three or four years Muhammad's only wife, his consummation of the marriage with Aisha moves him decisively away from Christianity: "The unity of his family was now broken, and never again restored."[21]

Arthur Wollaston—like Muir, engaged in British imperial work in India—objects to polygamy and laments Muhammad's departure from monogamous precepts but nonetheless gives a romanticized description of the marriage, which began with a betrothal when "Ayisha [was] a child of about six or seven years of age."[22] After the immigration to Medina, Muhammad "celebrated his nuptials with Ayisha, to whom, as before stated, he had now been affianced upwards of three years." Aisha is a somewhat troubling figure—she "had from the first possessed an inscrutable hold over the affections of her husband"—but their devotion was mutual: "Faithful to her charge, the youthful wife—she was at this time but twenty years of age—watched and tended the bedside of

her aged lord and master; the affection of so young and beautiful a damsel for the aged and infirm Prophet was touching and pathetic. It was," he says, "the *romance* of Islam."[23] (In striking contrast, thirteenth-century Dominican friar Ramón Martí cites this "touching" scene of Muhammad dying with his head on Aisha's breast as further proof of his lack of holiness: "the death or end of Muḥammad was vile, unclean, and abominable. And such a death is in no way appropriate for a prophet or a messenger of God.")[24]

David Margoliouth, whose biography is strongly negative in tone about all aspects of Muhammad's life—in one commentator's words, "no other work in the world was such a compendium of lies and calumny"[25]—plays up the negative traits to which Wollaston alludes, describing Aisha pejoratively as a "blooming girl who claimed premiership in the harem" and a "pert minx."[26] Her scheming overshadows her youth: "from the time of her emergence from childhood till her death at the age of sixty-six, she exhibited a degree of ability and unscrupulousness which should earn her a place beside Agrippinas and Elizabeths of history."[27] Margoliouth's Aisha is no victimized child. When Margoliouth refers to the marriage as an "ill-assorted union" because it joined "a man of fifty-three to a child of nine," he dramatically declares that she was "dragged from her swing and her toys."[28] Still, it is likely that he was primarily objecting to the disparity itself. In his catechistic *The False Prophet,* Harvey Newcomb has his mouthpiece condemn the age difference between Muhammad and Khadija in similar terms: a marriage with such a significant age gap "is transgressing a law of propriety which is found in the nature of things."[29]

Other twentieth-century authors describe her childishness without becoming overwrought. Gladys Draycott's 1916 biography is unperturbed by Aisha's youth, referring elliptically to her age

on three occasions: "Abu Bekr's small daughter," "a merry child," and "his girl-bride."[30] She mentions her vitality, her beauty, and Muhammad's preference for her over his other wives (apart, of course, from Khadija, whom he mourns). Even as late as the 1970s and 1980s, biographers mentioned Aisha's childish habits without extensive condemnation. Martin Lings is matter-of-fact about the spouses' discrepant ages. He uses the age of nine without hesitation, and mentions her dolls and playmates.[31] John Glubb, whose main claim to expertise was having lived among the Bedouin for decades, wrote a popular biography (*The Life and Times of Muhammad*) in 1970, and he includes a reference to the marriage to Aisha in discussing the migration and the construction of the mosque and housing for Muhammad's family: "She was nine years old, while the Apostle was fifty-three. When she was married she brought her toys with her to her room in the Apostle's house, where she used to sit playing with them on the floor. Until the end of his life, Aisha was to be the dearest of his wives."[32] Glubb attributes the marriage to customary practice, noting that girls were often given for first marriages between eight and ten. He also suggests that Muhammad "enjoyed the company of mature, sensible women rather than that of young girls."[33] He does not say how this relates to Muhammad's favoritism of Aisha. Glubb's mention of "the Apostle's house" is notable for its unusual presentation of Muhammad as householder, given others' insistence that Muhammad had no rooms of his own but took turns among his wives.[34]

Muir and others took note of Aisha's youth in part because youthful female sexuality was on many people's minds. European and American attitudes were undoubtedly conditioned by broader portrayals of exotic sexualities and customs. In the late nineteenth and early twentieth centuries, some travelers and military officials

posted in Egypt, for instance, partook of sex with young females: "a British officer on the Nile in 1884 'bought a very lady like little girl for £16' for the duration of his voyage."[35] Among the slaves Englishman James Burton had bought a few decades earlier were girls of about ten and twelve, whom he used for sex.[36] Other Europeans, however, were appalled: another mid-nineteenth-century traveler, Bayle St. John, observing "two ten year old apprentice dancers" being ogled lustfully by Egyptian Arabs "'could not help feeling saddened by beholding childhood thus profaned.'"[37]

For authors of this era, Muslims represent only one instance of a category of backward or primitive Others who diverge from Western Christian norms. Both titillated and condemnatory accounts appeal to the idea of an erotic East. Irvin Schick points out that "Western attitudes" about Islam have "been shaped by a combination of moral outrage and irrepressible concupiscence focused on the trope of 'oriental sexuality.'"[38] The idea goes back at least to Hippocrates that climate has an effect on sexuality, with heat linked to excessive and potentially deviant sensuality. The "orient" is hot, which affects its inhabitants.[39] Irving refers to "the quickening climates of the east," Bush calls them "eastern climates," and Prideaux, referring to "those hot Countries," affirms that India is "in the same *Clime* with *Arabia*." Prideaux shows most clearly "a trademark of xenological writing, where the similarity of the fundamentally dissimilar is taken for granted so long as each is different from 'us.'"[40] Sexuality was an essential element of what made these Others different, whether it was idyllic and sensuous, or depraved and decadent. Females in this imagined Orient are "wonderfully precocious" and are "ripe for *Marriage*" and childbearing when their Western counterparts would not be. Not scandalous, not repellent, but intriguing.

Both Irving and Prideaux think that there are two kinds of people: us, and those who live in hot places and mature rapidly. As Sprenger put it: "The Arabs, like all southern nations, marry early."[41] No universal morality or set of uniform standards applies. Gender and power play out in concrete places and in *ideas* about places, which slip into ideas about people. "East" and "savage" and "hot" describe the Other. If two groups are both "hot" and "savage," then, in a colonial equivalent of Euclid's first Common Notion ("Things which equal the same thing also equal one another"), they are alike, perhaps interchangeable.

Polygamy, too, can be linked to climactic effects on female development. Higgins, in a passage recycled by Ameer Ali to interesting effect, quotes from a book by W. Ouseley:

> "The warm regions of Asia make a difference between the sexes not known to the climates of Europe, where the decay of each is mutual and gradual; whereas in Asia it is given to man alone to arrive at a green old age." If this be true, it goes far to excuse Mohamed in allowing a plurality of wives, and it sufficiently accounts for the fact that Jesus never expressly declared himself on this subject, but left it to the regulation of the governments of countries; as it is evident that what would be proper for Asia would be improper for Europe.[42]

Similarly, Ahmad Khan quotes a British apologist who cites Montesquieu to the effect that polygamy owes to women's aging more rapidly than men: "women, in hot countries, are marriageable at eight, nine, or ten years of age;—thus, in those countries, infancy and marriage almost always go together. They are old at twenty. . . . It is, therefore, extremely natural that in these places

a man, when no law opposes it, should leave one wife to take another, and that polygamy should be introduced."[43]

All of these thinkers assume that different places have different
behavioral rules. They also share a broader presumption about
men's sexual appetites: women age more rapidly, and so men take
younger wives to satisfy themselves when they are not prevented
from doing so by stringent rules of morality or religion.

Unlike some thinkers who view Muslim practice as a concession to the natural order of things, Newcomb foregrounds the
lack of appropriate religious restrictions in *The False Prophet*.
Muhammad's example provides a jumping-off point to blame
heathens not only for sexual immorality but also for want of maternal feeling: in discussing the allegiance oath taken by pagan
converts, in which they forswore idolatry, fornication, and infanticide, "as the Pagan Arabs used to do,"[44] the mother responds to
her daughter's horrified questioning by connecting all heathen
peoples. Just as her last discussion on the subject of morality joined
"Mohammedans" and Indians, here she links the pagan Arabs to
Polynesians and Chinese: "Yes, my dear; it is a common thing for
heathen women to kill their children. Before the missionaries
went to the South Sea Islands, there were scarcely any mothers,
who were not guilty of this horrible crime; and now, in China,
and many other parts of the world, multitudes of children are
destroyed as soon as they are born."[45] Rather than discuss the
improvement purportedly wrought by Muhammad in Arabia
with the Qur'anic prohibition of female infanticide, which she
had just mentioned, she sweepingly condemns heathen savagery.
Like Oriental sexuality, Eastern women's sufferings were fungi-
ble, one gliding into the other, so long as all of them were different
from "us."

These discussions reflect a never-resolved tension between a universal standard, against which all can be judged, and a particularist ethnic ideal, where some groups are simply insufficiently advanced to be held to the same standard. It has been argued that the development of a historical consciousness arose in the late eighteenth century in Europe and that "paradoxically, one of the consequences of this new historical consciousness in Europe was an *ahistorical* perspective on non-European societies."[46] I would suggest instead that over the course of the nineteenth and early twentieth centuries, the notion that non-European societies are backward reflects the view that they are capable of change. Rather than being incommensurable, they are laggards on a universal trajectory of progress.

Or, they are simply and irreparably different: condemnations of Muhammad's debauchery had long included the claim that he had tolerated homosexuality—specifically, sodomy.[47] In the early modern era, accusations of Turkish sodomitical practices were widespread. (Protestants also accused Catholics and American Indians of sodomy: all who were not them.)[48] In the late eighteenth century, fears of sodomy were displaced by obsession with female slavery and the harem. This shift from concern with the potential violation of male seamen to the plight of captured women and girls reflects changes in the region's power balance: "with Ottoman decline and British ascendancy, and the presumed safety of the latter's soldiers and sailors, came a new interest in the harem and stories highlighting not male but female vulnerability."[49]

Something else happened, as well, with the shift to women's plight: a connection between concern with "the woman question" in Islam and the rise of a humanitarian consciousness. In previous centuries, condemnation of Others' immoral practices did not

require any concern for reforming them. But alongside nineteenth-century fascination with the effects of "sultry climates" on female sexuality, there was a developing interest in protecting young womanhood. A series of campaigns arose against child marriage—first in India, where reformers tried to raise the age of consent from ten to twelve in 1891, and later in Egypt and elsewhere.[50]

These campaigns owed in part to sometimes ill-conceived and badly implemented European intervention. Alongside the much-noted hypocrisy of some Victorians, who publicly espoused prudish morals while embracing libertinism behind closed doors, there arose a notion of social improvement, the necessity for certain members of the elite to actively work for the amelioration of social conditions: "a widening of sympathies . . . the birth of a modern social conscience. Among other things, this involves an imaginative awareness of what it means to be at the bottom of the heap . . . and this in turn imposes new responsibilities toward such people."[51] Previously, one could condemn immorality without seeking to reform the society that tolerated it. This shift to fix the root problems decisively shaped European intervention into Muslim societies, both directly, in colonial policies and interventions, and indirectly, in the intellectual arena—including in discussions of Muhammad's life.

If the diminished power of the Ottoman Empire allowed Muslims to be "transformed from demons to curiosities"[52] during the early modern era, European domination was an inescapable backdrop for nineteenth-century portraits of Muhammad and—inevitably—of Muslim women.[53] Mohja Kahf has argued that contrary to modern emphasis on the pitiful plight of Muslim women, medieval and early modern writings often depicted them as termagants: warlike, powerful, a little scary, and sometimes

wanton, certainly not demure or ladylike. (Prideaux, for instance, called Aisha "a very wanton woman."[54]) Although Muhammad's pre-nineteenth-century critics denigrated his sensualism, his lustfulness, and his polygamy, they did not condemn the oppression of Muslim women in general or his wives in particular. Sexual immorality was a major concern for medieval and early modern thinkers, but women's sexual (or for that matter, social) oppression was not. "By the nineteenth century," however, "descriptions of the sufferings of women in the East had become a commonplace of xenological discourse."[55] Newcomb linked polygamy to female slavery, infanticide, and the immurement of women in harems.[56] Child marriage was primarily identified as a "Hindoo" practice and criticized as such in both Britain and the United States.

Coomar Roy's 1888 defense of the practice resonates with more recent Muslim apologetic literature on women's status.[57] He refers extensively to female seclusion, modesty, chastity, and so forth. His rhetoric departs from that of more recent writings when he asserts the goodness and propriety of wifely subordination; he assumes, probably correctly, that his audience shares his view, since he appeals to it as an obvious advantage of child marriage: being married early inculcates proper reverence for the husband in the child-wife. Mrs. Marcus B. Fuller's blistering polemic *The Wrongs of Indian Womanhood* (1900) presents the opposite view in its chapter "Child Marriage."[58] Belief in the superiority of the nuclear family unit over the joint family undergirds Fuller's argument; she defends personal, individual, companionate, love-based marriage.[59] Fuller argues against what she views as Hindu religious doctrine. Although Indian women were among the important activists for legal reform—including as advocates for the 1929

Child-Marriage Restraint Act—their writings on the subject did not make it into wide circulation in the West.[60]

At the close of the nineteenth century, India was generally perceived as the prime offender in child marriage, but it was frequently enough associated with Muslims that Fuller, in her screed about Indian women's oppression, denies that child marriage came from "the Mohammedan invasion." Muslims brought "the Zenana system," she says, but child marriage is woven into Hindu religion.[61] A slightly later document does make a specific reference to Islam: the 1909 U.S. Census Bureau's entry on Algeria affirms that "Mohammedan laws and customs respecting marriage are essentially different from any that obtain in Christian countries, and serve to emphasize the vast difference between Mohammedan and Christian civilization. . . . Polygamy is allowed, child marriage is common, and marriage has the character of a sale, in which the woman either sells herself to her husband or is sold to him by her father." It not only makes a broad statement about child marriage but connects it to prophetic precedent: "As a result of the efforts of the French Government to suppress the evil, child marriage is probably less frequent than it was formerly, but it has not been entirely stamped out; it has the sanction of Mohammedan law and the Koran, for the prophet Mohammed himself married his favorite wife when she was only 7 years of age."[62]

In the case of both India and "Mohammedan civilization," scholars make a concerted effort to insist that reform is generally impossible; here, the Census Bureau weighs in on the "sanction" of "the evil" of child marriage by scripture, law, and prophetic practice. This conceptual move to insist that religious texts be read literally, without interpretive gloss, and applied directly is not limited to Islamic texts. Some Indian reformers had insisted that

"'child marriage is not a religious ordinance, but an irreligious enactment, and an inhuman innovation upon ancient customs.'"[63] However, C. N. Barham insists that this is not the case. Rather, one must confront such "lying sophists" and "those who take their opinion from the transient colouring of the daily press" with the facts. One should appeal to texts ("the laws, prophets, and Scriptures of the East") to prove that child marriage *is* a Hindu practice.[64] Part of what is at stake here is the acceptability of Hindu scripture (as canonized by European scholars): if to be a Hindu *means* to follow the Laws of Manu, then one cannot be both Hindu and modern.[65] A well-meaning falsehood that treats child marriage as mere custom is unacceptable, even if this allows one to oppose it. The author insists on recognizing and rejecting the irremediable barbarism (the "diabolical evil") of child marriage, which taints Hindu religion and Indian culture.[66] (Of course, the notion that one can discard custom is itself an artifact of modern approaches to scripture, which give texts sanctioning power greater than the weight of practice. Indeed, to view custom and scripture as separate and separable in the first place is innovative.) Similar arguments are put forth today by critics of Islam and Muhammad who argue that since Muhammad is known to have behaved in particular ways, or since the Qur'an or early jurists say particular things, Muslims must obey them and are not allowed to rethink their tradition. Of course, in Barham's view, if Hinduism cannot be reformed, then to reform, Indians must cease being Hindu.

Child Marriage and Modern Society

Marriage of minors in both India and Egypt served as an entry point into larger questions of worldview. In Egypt, a 1914 proposal

to set a minimum age for marriage was, after much hue and cry about the intolerability of interfering with religious law and, notably, parental privilege, rejected. One opponent of the reform brought up Muhammad's marriage to Aisha.[67] A 1923 law set an age of sixteen for females and eighteen for males, below which no marriage could be registered or judicial relief obtained.[68] The Egyptian case illustrates a vision in which a national, modern Egypt is compatible with the notion of adult marriage and liberal subjects, with little attention to religion. A religious objection to establishing a minimum marriage age was enough to derail the 1914 legislative reform, but by 1923, it no longer was.

As the historian Hanan Kholoussy points out, this was less about protecting the interests of vulnerable girls than about "the role of the state in the production and promotion of modern nuclear families"—families that would be the "foundation stone of the emerging nation."[69] The three areas in which states attempted reform—polygamy, divorce, and marriage of minors—were of varying relevance.[70] Kholoussy points out: "That members of the state felt compelled to regulate the marriage of minors at this time is particularly significant because such unions appear to have been in decline by the early twentieth century.[71] "This suggests," she writes, "that some Egyptians wanted the government to establish a new means of monitoring the marital habits of the population to ensure that only adult Egyptians would marry and reproduce."[72] I would argue for an additional variable: the symbolic value of such reforms, regardless of their real or perceived practical impact. In India, marriage-age reform became a central project of the nation-state, which established a minimum age for marriage and required registration.[73] Marriage is a way of making proper citizens, proper national subjects, proper modern people—and, as a collectivity, a

proper nation. And in the case of Egypt, it required a proper religious precedent, or the incorporation into religious rhetoric of new ideas about family and marriage.

Chapter 4 illustrated that companionate marriage and Muhammad as Khadija's husband—and her as his beloved partner, mother to his children, and domestic comforter—became central to his life story. The same narrative was not readily available for Aisha, who had co-wives and no children and was not, because of her youth, a suitable "partner." How, then, could this marriage be discussed in terms compatible with the new ideals about marriage and family that were circulating? As decades passed, Muslim thinkers came increasingly to rely on engagement with, and definition against, the works of Western thinkers.

Vituperative criticisms similar to those directed at barbarous Hindu practices have more recently been aimed at Islam and Muslims. These have emerged against a backdrop of paranoia about Muslim fanaticism and legitimate concerns about Muslim extremism. In the late twentieth century, in a renewed climate of criticism of Islam, divergent tendencies emerge in Muslim and non-Muslim sources. Muslim scholars engage in apologetics to justify Aisha's marriage. The dominant strategy is to contextualize it as historically appropriate to its time and place and to play up, as with the multiple marriages, the political motivations behind it. A less common strategy recalculates Aisha's age at marriage based on other indicators in the sources.[74] Only a few authors, mostly traditionalist South Asian biographers, celebrate her youthful purity, sometimes also making practical arguments about what her youth made possible. Enhancing and upholding her reputation is undoubtedly part of the late South Asian scholar Syed Suleman Nadvi's objective when he connects Aisha's age with her virginal

status, mentioning "wedlock" at the "tender" age of six and consummation when Aisha was "only nine years of age."[75]

These few writers aside, most accounts of Aisha's marriage historicize assiduously. Purportedly objective American and European accounts may wax somewhat less rhapsodic about Muhammad's sterling virtues as a husband, but like apologetic biographers, they still emphasize both the connection with Abu Bakr forged by the marriage and the context of early Arabia, in which, as one Western survey puts it, the marriage was "not in the least improper."[76] Ziauddin Sardar frames the marriage with Aisha as being controversial now, but not at the time: "She was said to be 9 or 10 and he was 53. Conventions about the age of marriage are culturally determined and have changed radically over time."[77] His "was said to be" distances him from treating it as fact, while the mention of changing cultural standards suggests that even if it is true one should withhold judgment.

This fixation on changing standards of human conduct, on contextual explanation, has become commonsensical. We hear it so frequently we no longer really *hear* it. Certainly it is the case that people in the past recognized that different places/customs might call for different rules or conduct (when in Rome . . .). But the notion that social arrangements would change over time and, furthermore, that this change might be in the direction of progress rather than a decline from a pristine early stage is a recent development. It emerges in Muslim thinking in the nineteenth century and can be seen particularly in Ameer Ali's rebuttals to Muir and others' criticisms of Muhammad. This tendency is especially pertinent with regard to Muhammad's marital practices.

Modern texts, regardless of author, seldom bother with the anecdote according to which Gabriel came to the Prophet with a de-

piction of Aisha and told Muhammad that she was to be his wife. Ibn Sa'd includes the following report in his compendium: "The Messenger of Allah was so grieved about Khadija that people feared for him, until he married 'A'isha."[78] Another account concerns not his followers' worries but God's concern: "When Khadija died, the Prophet was terribly grieved over her, and Allah sent Jibril who brought him the picture of 'A'isha. He said, 'Messenger of Allah, this one will remove some of your sorrow. This one has some of the qualities of Khadija.'"[79] The comparison between the qualities of Aisha and Khadija is unusual, clearly meant to shore up Aisha's reputation; nonetheless, the link between Muhammad's fragile state ("people feared for him") and his remarriage to Aisha, who "remove[d] some of [his] sorrow," is significant. Recent authors tend to omit these plaudits and rationales, either because religious arguments are irrelevant to their audiences or because they are concerned with the practical dimension of the marriage.[80] Even in books ostensibly directed to Muslim audiences, arguments are framed in ways that respond at least implicitly to Western criticism; thinking about Muhammad's life is directly shaped by Western polemic and critique.

Western scholarship appears in apologetics around Aisha's age, in sometimes surprising ways. For instance, Syed M. H. Zaidi writes, in *Mothers of the Faithful:* "Ayesha was the young daughter of Muhammad's bosom friend Abu Bakr. . . . Her father was one of the most powerful, popular and well-to-do citizens. By this alliance, Muhammad's principal object was to cement Abu Bakr more strongly to his side." (He cites Davenport and Irving as authorities and follows the former almost verbatim in places.)[81] Note that Zaidi views Muhammad having his "principal object" be a political "alliance" as a *good* thing, precisely the opposite of Prideaux's

view. He continues: "In response to his politic dictate and in acceptance of the earnest solicitations of his noble disciple [i.e., Abu Bakr], the betrothal was announced when Ayesha was 7 years of age; and she was married over 2 years later when about 10 as such is the ripeness of the climate and such too is the custom of the country."[82] He cites, for this information, Edward Gibbon, whose work he mistitles *Downfall of the Roman Empire,* and recommends to his readers also Ameer Ali and Prideaux. Astonishingly, then, a work explicitly framed as a refutation of non-Muslim criticisms of Muhammad's marriages draws on Prideaux's polemic. Though he replaces Prideaux's ages of betrothal and consummation (six and eight) with his own (seven and ten), Zaidi agrees with Prideaux about climate's impact on "ripeness" for marriage and the connection between the marriage to Aisha and the alliance with Abu Bakr. "Custom" is a more recent addition.

Zaidi's use of Prideaux might seem preposterous, but it highlights the wide variety of ways Muslim scholars read, cite, and repurpose Western works. A more recent biography takes from a different sort of Western authority. A 1969 work published in India, reprinted as recently as 2002 and distributed in the United States, devotes a section to Aisha's youth at marriage. The "new bride," Abdul Hameed Siddiqui writes, "was just attaining her puberty and was still in the house of her father. She was a precocious girl" (here, he references Nadvi's biography of Aisha; the term precocious was a favorite of Muir's) "and was developing both in mind and body with rapidity peculiar to such rare personalities." Muhammad "decided to consummate the marriage" after it was suggested by Aisha's parents.[83] The marriage strengthened the ties of friendship between Muhammad and Abu Bakr and abolished the idea "that it was contrary to religious ethics to

marry the daughter of a man whom one declared to be one's brother."[84] Aisha's youth was particularly important: she entered "the *haram* of the Prophet at an impressionable age" and was thus guided appropriately in her development. Marriage at this "highly formative age" (Siddiqui avoids specific numbers) is good for the bride herself and the marital union. Siddiqui cites a Dutch doctor, to the effect that "the marriage of an elderly (senescent)—not, of course an old (senile)—man to a quite young girl, is often very successful and harmonious. The bride is immediately introduced and accustomed to moderate sexual intercourse."[85] Following this medical wisdom about sexuality, Siddiqui proceeds to lambaste "those Western critics of *Islam* who have criticized this marriage" for "los[ing] sight of the fact that this marriage did not involve sexual considerations alone." A crucial consideration was that Muhammad's other wives "were all of advanced age, and thus could neither share the feelings of the younger generation nor could they properly appreciate their point of view." They could not communicate with "the ladies of younger ages." Aisha's marriage "when she was at the threshold of puberty was a great necessity, as it was through her that instructions could successfully be imparted to the young ladies who had newly entered the fold of Islam."[86]

Siddiqui here combines tones, strategies, and sources of authority. Aisha's exceptional qualities led her to develop rapidly. Her youth enabled her to be of service to a broader Muslim population. Early consummation aided her moral development as well as her sexual initiation—a claim for which he cites a European figure. Like earlier authors, Siddiqui selectively incorporates Western authorities even as his justification shifts from climactic to medical. (Climate-based explanations persist in Muslim apologetics; S. M. Abbasi explains: "the climactic conditions in a tropical country like

Arabia, were conducive to the early development of human beings and the females in particular were precocious toward the growth of their body and faculties.")[87] Apparently without any sense of dissonance, Siddiqui moves swiftly from presenting the Dutch doctor's wisdom to railing against the ignorant pronouncements of "Western critics of Islam."[88]

Ghulam Malik's biography contains a chapter on "His Wives," which uses different but similarly overlapping strategies to discuss Aisha. He writes, "Aisha bint Abu Bakr was betrothed in Makkah when she was seven or eight years old. After nine months of the Hijrah, in 623, Muhammad married her, the only virgin among his wives, when she was only nine or ten." His use of "seven or eight" and "nine or ten" is slightly unusual. More typical is his claim that "at that time, such wide gaps in the ages of couples were not unusual or uncommon." His reference to a remote time period—"at that time"—suggests something archaic. Something else noteworthy becomes clear in Malik's biography: Muslim authors had adopted, even for works aimed at fellow believers, the terminology of betrothal or occasionally "engagement," which European authors from the nineteenth century forward used.[89]

By the standards of later Islamic jurisprudence—which had yet to develop during Muhammad's lifetime—the contract made between Muhammad and Abu Bakr was a binding marriage. Muslim biographers treated it as such for many centuries. Prideaux follows Muslim sources when he refers to it that way, as does Bush. But others, including Sprenger and particularly Irving, use the language of betrothal. Even if it was legally a marriage, it functioned like a betrothal: Western understandings become the crucial deciding factor rather than standard Muslim legal catego-

ries. Hence, the late-twentieth-century scholarly translators of a volume in Tabari's *History* in which Aisha's marriage is discussed explain that "what seems properly to be a betrothal was apparently called a marriage by the Arabs."[90]

Traduttore Tradittore

Similar issues of terminology crop up in Muhammad Husayn Haykal's discussion of Aisha's marriage, which reflects a complex engagement with Western writings. It avoids the sorts of apologetics used by twentieth-century authors, including those just discussed, but clearly reflects some level of unease about Aisha's youth; this is even more true for its English translation. Haykal mentions Aisha's age three times, once when he discusses Muhammad's marriages after Khadija's death, again when he discusses consummation of the marriage to Aisha, and a third time in his larger discussion of Muhammad's marriages, giving different ages each time.

Haykal depends on, and borrows heavily from, Prideaux, Irving, and Émile Dermenghem, but molds their material in keeping with his presumptions about sexuality, marriage, and the emotional life of the biographical subject. Prideaux sought to account for the influence of drives or motives (lust, ambition) on Muhammad's actions. Thomas Carlyle, nearly a century and a half later, had insisted, against Prideaux and his ilk, on Muhammad's sincerity but, like Prideaux, was not especially interested in Muhammad's feelings. In Irving's *Mahomet*, published not very long after Carlyle's lectures, the enduring preoccupation with the Prophet's sex life had become also concern with his feelings.

Irving brought his novelist's sensibility to his treatment of Muhammad's life.[91] Haykal, though primarily a journalist, had also written a novel, *Zaynab* (1913).[92] These writers' sensibilities—and perhaps the broader influence of novels on reader expectation—meant that in both works, life stories were premised on a coherent character revealed throughout and held a largely continuous rather than an episodic structure.

Haykal's *Life* retains some thematic sections—including one on Muhammad's wives, likely modeled on Dermenghem's chapter on "The Harem."[93] But two snippets on the marriages woven into the chronological narrative are especially revealing. He discusses Muhammad's marriages following Khadija's death in the context of Meccan tribes' rejection of Islam, which intensified his "pain and grief" at his loss:

> The mourning period for Khadija ended, and he thought of marrying, perhaps to find in his wife some of the solace he had when Khadija nursed his wounds. He thought he could strengthen the ties of kinship between himself and the early converts to Islam. He proposed to Abu Bakr for his daughter Aisha, but since she was still a child of seven years of age, he contracted marriage to her and did not consummate [the marriage] with her until two years later when she had turned nine. During these two [years] he married Sawda, widow of one of the Muslims who had emigrated to Abyssinia, returned to Mecca, and died there.[94]

Haykal revisits the marriage to Aisha three years later, again prefacing it with a summation of the religio-political situation and its effect on Muhammad's state. Whereas previously Muhammad was

persecuted, insulted, and grieving, here he is "satisfied" and his community "tranquil in its religion":

> At this time, Muhammad consummated [the marriage] with Aisha, daughter of Abu Bakr, who was then age ten or eleven. She was a slender girl, sweet of feature, an agreeable companion, crossing from childhood into maidenhood. She craved play and merriment and was growing beautifully.[95]

In both passages, marriages fulfill emotional needs. In the first, Muhammad seeks the kind of companionship that Khadija had provided, yet neither a contract with Aisha nor marriage to Sawda suffices. In the second, Aisha becomes "a source of relaxation" from the burdens of government. Haykal conjures a domestic sphere, where Muhammad can shed his communal responsibilities and indulge his young wife's childish inclinations. She is described here in terms that most authors reserve for Khadija, as a domestic comfort to him. Interestingly, Haykal also attends to how Muhammad meets Aisha's need for shelter and "play and merriment," serving as "a sympathetic and loving husband but also a compassionate father" to her.[96]

In both what they say and what they omit, these excerpts from Haykal draw extensively on the facts and tone of the Western *Lives* Haykal has read. The range of "ten or eleven" set out in the second passage does not appear in any of these sources, so far as I can tell, but the ages of seven and nine, which he gives in the earlier passage, are attested by early Muslim authorities and, not coincidentally, mirror Dermenghem.[97] (In his later chapter "The Prophet's Wives," Haykal places the "proposal" at age nine and the consummation two years later.)[98] He takes nearly verbatim

from Dermenghem Aisha's relationship to Abu Bakr, the two-year delay prior to consummation, and even the phrasing "thought of marrying," with which the text introduces his near-simultaneous arrangements with Sawda and Aisha.

Haykal plays up the emotional resonance of Muhammad's bond with Khadija, though he skims over Dermenghem's assertions that he lacked love and affection for most of his subsequent wives. Haykal omits Dermenghem's reference to Muhammad's "obstinate fidelity" to the aging Khadija, who had provided him comfort and tenderness.[99] Haykal generally treats Sawda in ways similar to Dermenghem, though he leaves out the name of Sawda's previous husband and the fact that, according to Dermenghem, Muhammad "seems to have had but little love for her."[100] He leaves out, too, the French scholar's titillating remark that "Aisha was the only one who went to his bed a virgin."[101] (Early Muslim sources remark on Aisha's virginity more circumspectly.)

Although Haykal downplays any criticism of Muhammad for withholding love from later wives, his emphasis on Muhammad's love for and bond with Khadija makes the contrast clear. Where love does emerge more explicitly, in the context of critiquing "Orientalists," he discounts its significance as a motivation: "If what is said about Aisha and his love for her is true, it was love that grew after marriage and not at the time of it. He proposed to her father for her when she was still nine years of age and waited two years before he consummated [the marriage] with her. It defies logic that he would have loved her when she was so young."[102] (Similarly, Muir had written: "The yet undeveloped charms of Ayesha could hardly have swayed the heart of Mahomet.")[103] Although Haykal here shifts the ages he provides, his main concern is not refuting Western critics who condemn Muhammad for Aisha's

youth but insisting that this marriage, like that to Hafsa, daughter of Umar, was motivated by neither love nor desire; instead, Muhammad aimed to strengthen his "ties" to the fathers, his "two viziers."[104]

Haykal uses different language to describe Muhammad's connection to Sawda than he does when describing his connection to Aisha. The first passage is subtitled "Proposal to Aisha and marriage to Sawda." In the text, he uses the term "marrying" for Sawda, whereas for Aisha he uses "proposing," "contracting," and (not) "consummating."[105] He titles the second section "The marriage of the Prophet to Aisha." Haykal thus creates four possible ways of discussing a union: proposal, contract, consummation, and simply marriage. The classical Islamic texts Haykal cites distinguish between two events, marriage and consummation, and do not typically render the linkage with Aisha in three parts. Ibn Kathir, for instance, acknowledges that scholars debate which marriage occurred first but agree unanimously that the marriage with Sawda was consummated first.

There are two complementary explanations for Haykal's choice to treat Muhammad's connection to Aisha as a marriage only upon its consummation. We may speculate that as arranged marriages became somewhat less frequent in Egypt, more marriages took place when the spouses were mature, with little or no separation between the contract and the commencement of married life. Becoming legally married meant becoming socially married. To apply the legal term *marriage* to an arrangement that was not its social equivalent may have seemed confusing. Thus, writing of the proposal and contract and avoiding the term *marriage* gets around the legal category retrospectively applied to Muhammad's union with Aisha by earlier generations of Muslims. The second explanation

is simpler: the word for "proposal" became associated with "betrothed" or "affianced" or "engaged" and was used in the English and French texts Haykal relied on (and, later, in their Arabic translations). It is likely that the accounts that used the term "betrothal," like Irving's and Muir's, affected his vocabulary.

If Haykal's departures from the classical Arabic tradition are relatively easily explained, Ismail Al Faruqi's English translation of Haykal's *Life*, which appeared four decades after its initial publication, takes substantially greater liberties, particularly with Aisha's age.[106] Al Faruqi places Aisha's age firmly in double digits; other changes make Aisha seem older and play down any sexual element of the relationship. Haykal had written, explaining the time elapsed between the contract and its consummation: "since she was still a child of seven years of age, he [Muhammad] contracted a marriage to her but did not consummate [the marriage] until two years later when she had turned nine."[107] Al Faruqi renders this as: "Since she was still too young to marry, the engagement was announced, but the marriage was postponed for three more years until 'Ā'ishah reached the age of eleven."[108] This "translation" omits the ages Haykal uses, giving no actual age for the "engagement" (a term not present in the original); adds in the number eleven; and says that "three more years" (rather than the original "two years") passed before "the marriage" (rather than *consummation*) took place. Al Faruqi's version sidelines sex entirely.

The less dramatic changes Al Faruqi makes to the second passage have similar effects. Both here and in the chapter "The Prophet's Wives," in which Haykal writes that Muhammad "consummated [the marriage] with Aisha," Al Faruqi states only that he "married" her. Although Al Faruqi refers to her youth when he calls her "a beautiful, delicate, and amiable young girl," Haykal's

Arabic, which I have rendered as "a slender girl, sweet of feature, an agreeable companion," alludes to physicality: the shape of her body, the lineaments of her face. The third element of the description, which might also be rendered "pleasant for companionship" or "desirable for intimacy," connotes specifically conjugal intimacy, a connection Al Faruqi's bland "amiable" forestalls. Haykal says she was "crossing from childhood into maidenhood," suggesting liminality.[109] Al Faruqi writes "emerging out of childhood and blossoming into full womanhood," going on to assert that she was "fully grown." His term "blossoming" suggests a process of transition, but "full womanhood" and "fully grown" evoke an adulthood at odds with other elements of the passage, which Al Faruqi renders more faithfully: Aisha's continued attachment to "play and amusement" and Muhammad's paternal affection.[110] His choice of modifiers is particularly surprising given that the phrase he translates as "full womanhood" denotes "youth, maidenhood." The phrase he renders as "fully grown" (in my version, "growing beautifully") contains no word for "full" or "complete" but hints at *incompleteness;* the word he translates "grown" can indicate growth or progress but is an active participle also used for "developing," as in the phrase "developing countries."

Of course, my renderings of these words are not the only possible ones, and with the exception of his alterations to the numbers given in the first passage, each of Al Faruqi's choices is individually defensible. One might even argue that given Haykal's self-contradiction as to Aisha's age at consummation, Al Faruqi is merely harmonizing the text to prevent reader confusion. Taken cumulatively, though, these choices result in a quite different overall effect. Presumably, Al Faruqi's aim was not to reproduce the text faithfully for scholarly readers but to translate an authoritative

religious text for a community of believers for whom a more literal rendering of Haykal's text would cause consternation. On a spectrum of translations, from conservative (or mediatory) to additive (or creative), Al Faruqi's falls closer to the creative end.[111] Notably, however, rather than adding to the text, Al Faruqi often modifies by subtraction. About Muhammad's Coptic slave Mariya, reportedly the only woman to bear him a child apart from Khadija, Haykal had been equivocal, stating that she became a wife but also indicating that he visited her as men visit their slaves. Al Faruqi simply omits this line, while maintaining the surrounding text.[112] For Haykal's Egyptian audience in the 1930s, the practice of concubinage among the elite was a recent memory; Al Faruqi adapts the text for a 1970s American audience, for whom Muhammad's having a sexual relationship with a female he owned would have been deeply troubling.

As a counterpoint to this consideration of Haykal in English, let us take a brief look at the Arabic version of Irving's *Life of Mahomet*. It came out in 1960, with a second edition in 1966—three decades after Haykal consulted the original and around the same time Al Faruqi began his translation endeavor.[113] The Arabic translation of Irving's account of Muhammad's marriages to Sawda and Aisha makes two sorts of changes. The first concerns the emotional dimensions of Muhammad's relationship to Sawda. It omits the reference to Muhammad's "heart prone to affection, and subject to female influence" and merely says that he did not have a "strong love" for Sawda.[114] The second concerns Aisha's age. The translator keeps Irving's original numbers. However, he adds a footnote about the matter of Aisha's age at "betrothal" and marriage.[115] Aisha's youth, unproblematic for Irving's American readers in the mid-nineteenth century, posed difficulties for Egyptian readers a century later.

Panic and Polemic

More broadly, in speaking of Muhammad's marriage to Aisha, books published in the United States around the time Haykal's *Life* appeared in English and Irving's *Life* appeared in Arabic tended to adopt either condescending or condemnatory tones; the latter increased in frequency and stridency as the twentieth century wore to a close. Betty Kelen, in a popular biography (1975), wrote of a "betrothal" at age seven, placing the "marriage" shortly after the move to Medina, when Aisha was nine: "We need not dwell on the abuse to the child of such a marriage," since it was customary; further, "Ayesha was dear to Muhammad, and she loved the Prophet. We can conclude that the relationship between the two was free from outrage."[116] W. Montgomery Watt makes a similarly unperturbed assessment in *Muhammad: Prophet and Statesman*, though he allows that "This relationship between a man of fifty-three and a girl of ten must have been a strange one. . . . We must remember, of course, that girls matured much earlier in seventh-century Arabia."[117] These authors were writing before hysteria about child sexual abuse had taken hold in the American imagination. By the last decade of the twentieth century and especially the first decade of the twenty-first, Aisha's age had become a favorite argument of anti-Islam polemicists, especially but not exclusively online.[118]

In the wake of this public wrangling over Aisha's age, in which accusations of pedophilia have become part of a broader public discourse about Muhammad, those who wish to rescue Islam and Muhammad from blanket condemnation attempt to contextualize the marriage. Muslim apologists online and in print often repeat some variant of the physical-precocity argument, sometimes

with a mention of climate; non-Muslim authors and those writing for mainstream general readers tend to stick with arguments from custom. Colin Turner's 2006 introduction *Islam: The Basics* mixes both. Fully aware of how such marriages are seen today, Turner mentions "paedophilia" and "child abuse" but hastens to reassure his readers that Muhammad's marriage to Aisha was common for the era and that "such marriages were almost certainly not consummated until both parties had entered adulthood, which seventh century Arabs tended to reach earlier than Westerners today."[119] (Turner says that Aisha was perhaps ten, though he also says, inaccurately, that the sources are not explicit about her age, then goes on to declare it "highly unlikely that Muhammad would have taken Aisha into his bed until she was at least in her early teens, which was wholly in keeping with the customs of the day, and in context not the least improper.")[120] This reference to Aisha as a teenager is, of course, highly anachronistic; Lesley Hazelton uses the term frequently in her recent biography *The First Muslim: The Story of Muhammad*. She suggests that in claiming that she was "six years old when she was betrothed and nine years old when the marriage was celebrated and consummated," Aisha may have played up her youth to appear extraordinary, since "to have been married at the customary age would make Aisha normal, and that was the one thing she was always determined not to be." Hazelton adds, without citing any specific sources, that "more restrained reports have her aged nine when she was betrothed and twelve when she was actually married."[121] Prolific religion writer Karen Armstrong's two biographies present similar accounts of Muhammad's remarriages. In the first, she denies a sexual motivation ("Aisha was only a little girl and at thirty Saw-

dah was past her first youth and was beginning to run to fat"—
pedophilia was not on anybody's radar, or she would have contested that claim) and plays up their "political dimension."[122] She
writes later that the wedding occurred when Aisha was nine but
"made little difference to Aisha's life. Tabari says that she was so
young that she stayed in her parents' home and the marriage was
consummated there later when she had reached puberty."[123]

Armstrong's later biography, like Al Faruqi's version of
Haykal, never mentions consummation, only a shift of residence.
Introducing Muhammad's marriages after Khadija's death, Armstrong writes that "Muhammad made some changes in his
household. He needed a wife." He married Sawda, and Abu
Bakr, "anxious to forge a closer link with the Prophet," took the
initiative "and proposed that he should marry his daughter 'A'isha
who was then six years old. 'A'isha was formally betrothed to
Muhammad in a ceremony at which the little girl was not present." She goes on to explain that "there was no impropriety in
Muhammad's betrothal to 'A'isha. Marriages conducted in ab-
sentia to seal an alliance were often conducted at this time between adults and minors who were even younger than 'A'isha."
Not only did they happen in Europe, too, "well into the early
modern period," but "there was no question of consummating
the marriage until 'A'isha reached puberty, when she would have
been married off like any other girl."[124] When it comes time for
the union to be sealed, however, Armstrong does not mention
consummation. Instead, among "changes in Muhammad's family life" that occurred in Medina was Aisha's (possible) reloca-
tion. Again, Armstrong invokes Tabari: she "may by this time
have moved into the apartment that had been prepared for her in

the mosque, though Tabari says that because of her youth she was allowed to remain for a while longer in her parents' house."[125] (Tabari includes several reports that that the marriage took place when she was six or seven.[126] He once notes that "when he married her she was young, unfit for intercourse."[127] However, he says nothing about puberty and consistently states that consummation occurred when she was nine.[128])

By the time of Armstrong's second biography, other writings had begun to accuse Muhammad of pedophilia and abuse, extending the characterization to cover Islamic civilization as a whole. In his *The Truth about Muhammad: Founder of the World's Most Intolerant Religion* (2006), Robert Spencer—front man for Jihad Watch and grand pooh-bah of the legion of American Islamophobes—qualifies the accusation of pedophilia as "a bit anachronistic" but makes an argument similar to that made by Barham a century earlier about the Laws of Manu. Under the provocative subtitle "Pedophile Prophet?" Spencer points out that although child marriage did not bother anyone at the time, its existence in Muslim communities today can be blamed on the insistence that Muhammad's model is to be literally followed.[129] Citing deplorable statistics about child marriage, Spencer writes: "This is the price that women have paid throughout Islamic history, and continue to pay, for Muhammad's status as 'an excellent example of conduct' (Qur'an 33:21)."

With this view of child marriage, which circulated in online polemics about Muhammad a decade before Spencer's book, we move from hierarchical rankings of societies, where some persist in primitive practices, to pedophilia. However, rather than viewing pedophilia as an individual perversion, all of Islam and every Muslim is tainted because Muhammad is the perpetrator. Pedophilia is

not (as polygamy once was) merely sensuality or lustfulness unrestrained, nor is it (as polygamy came to be) an indication of women's low status or the broader oppressiveness of Muhammad and Islam toward females. Here Muhammad's practice is viewed as justification for evil, meaning that in order to progress, one must reject his legacy.

Muhammad's marriage to Aisha has become, for contemporary polemicists, evidence of pedophilia not as a medical diagnosis but as an archaic and evil force. Sodomy had served, both in the early modern period and the Renaissance era, as a similar device.[130] As the historian Nabil Matar writes, "No other accusation needed less explanation or demonstration than sodomy. To mention it was to confirm it and to condemn the perpetrator; sodomy was a self-explanatory judgment, a cognitive keyword that proved that Muslims had no family structure, no 'natural' sexuality, and therefore no place in the civilized world."[131] Because the point being made in invoking this term is not, in fact, one about its diagnostic accuracy, a rebuttal like the one offered by Yahiya Emerick ("If *Muhammad* were a *pedophile,* he would not have waited for A'ishah to reach puberty before completing the marriage, nor would he have stopped at only one marriage to a young girl") is utterly ineffective.[132]

Deepak Chopra's attempt, in his fictionalized biography, to address concerns about Aisha's age in an afterword is neither quite so combative nor quite so hateful as Spencer's approach, but it draws equally false causal links between prophetic precedent and Muslim practice.[133] Chopra notes that on certain issues, Muslim perspectives differ from those of non-Muslims. He singles out, and thereby connects, two issues that have caused a great deal of consternation to contemporary observers: the reprisal against the

Banu Qurayza and the marriage to Aisha. The former is accepted by Muslim historians: "After his death, the ranks closed around absolute truth, which meant that it was a test of faith to turn any act by the Prophet, even the beheading of his enemies, into something right and good." He then continues:

> On this point, the critics of Muhammad cite his marriage to Aisha. She was the youngest daughter of Abu Bakr. . . . At the age of six Aisha was betrothed to a husband, until Muhammad had a revelation that she was meant for him. The prospective groom was persuaded to give her up. The marriage to Muhammad took place but wasn't consummated until Aisha was nine. Beyond Islam, this episode is more than distasteful. Within the faith, however, it is praised. None of Muhammad's other wives were virgins, and the rationale is that Aisha served as a kind of Virgin Mary, made all the more pure because she was so young. To the outside world, this is a prescription for blind fanaticism.[134]

Many things about Chopra's statement cry out for analysis, beginning with the link between a mass beheading and Aisha's age. The two are also intertwined in a biography by Adil Salahi, published by the UK-based Islamic Foundation. Originally published in 1995, the 2008 edition of *Muhammad: Man and Prophet* contains major changes in precisely these two sections. In the first, Salahi rejects Ibn Ishaq's version and thereby reports "a certain event . . . in a new light that totally negates what has been held as true by most people, including the present author." He also adds an appendix treating Aisha's age at marriage. In the case of the

Banu Qurayza, he acknowledges that his current view runs counter to his previous belief. With regard to Aisha's age, however, he explains, "I have always felt that the common notion concerning her age is wrong."[135]

Returning to Chopra and the comparison he draws between Aisha and Mary: If any one woman is parallel to Mary in Muslim tradition, it is Muhammad's daughter Fatima, who pious Shi'a call "the virgin," her offspring by Ali having been born, it is said, from her side or thigh; she was also exempt from menstruation. Alternately, some have drawn a parallel between Mary and Muhammad himself, each made into a pristine vessel to receive the Word of God.[136] Chopra is correct about the concern with purity (connected in South Asian texts with her youth), though it is probably asserted so forcefully because it was questioned so vigorously. Chopra writes, "The bald fact is that we cannot identify with customs that exist across such a yawning abyss."[137] To the contrary, it is precisely our acute preoccupation with the sexualization of young girls and the sexual abuse of children that leads to recent worry over Aisha's age.

Although Chopra makes a strange bedfellow for contemporary right-wing and evangelical figures who treat Islam as "an evil and wicked religion,"[138] he, like them, avoids notions of backwardness and progress and appeals instead to earlier notions of Truth and Error. Yet none of these figures merely re-creates medieval distinctions. In associating "pedophile" and "pervert" with demonic characterizations, they medicalize and pathologize religious valuations. In doing so, they draw on decidedly modern discourses about both illness and children. Contemporary polemics about Muhammad's marriages then draw from an

unwieldy jumble of incompatible discourses, which have in common mostly that they can provide a language with which to denigrate Others.[139]

Women Writing Women's *Lives*

Let me close with a brief foray into fiction, which provides an important window onto historical events. Modern Muslim women writing about marriage and celebrating Muhammad's precedent-setting example as a feminist have typically chosen to write about Khadija, seeing this marriage as the crucial model. For those writers interested in Muhammad's life and the issue of women's authority, however, Aisha figures much more prominently, including in several novels.

Chapter 4 noted how Mahfouz's allegorical novel *Children of the Alley* deals with the relationship between Muhammad/Qassem and Khadija/Qamar. The same novel contains an Aisha figure, a girl named Badriya, whom Mahfouz introduces in an erotic though chaste encounter when she brings Qassem coffee. He is thinking of Qamar then. "Between sips their smiling eyes meet." (Mahfouz coyly deflects the question of her age: "'How old are you, Badriya?' She bit her lip. 'I don't know,' she murmured.")[140] Qassem then reflects on his life, acknowledging a spectrum of emotions. No confusion appears between his paternal emotions and his sexual needs:

> His lasting happiness was Ihsan [his daughter by Qamar]
> when he played with her, rocked her, and sang to her, but this
> was not the case when she reminded him of his late wife; those

occasions immersed him in gloom and the hot sighs of yearning. She had been taken from him at the outset of the journey,
and left him prey to terrible depression whenever he was alone,
to regret, as when he had been on the mountainside, the day
he drank the coffee, the day of the shy smile, as soft as an
afternoon breeze.[141]

His "tormented depression and insomnia" lead him out to walk,
where he encounters one of his men; Qassem confesses, "Sometimes I can't stand being alone," and his companion notes,
"Most of your men are married or have families. . . . They're
never lonely."[142] He advises Qassem: "Someone like you cannot
do without a woman."[143] Qassem is divided: "'Marry, after Qamar?'
The objection in his voice was as strong as his feeling that the man
was right."

Sexual energy pulses through Mahfouz's prose. The thought
of remarrying leaves him "disturbed," as it would seem to be a betrayal "after her love and caring." At the same time, he is left with
"hot sighs of yearning" and roiling with "excitement." Whatever
conflict this collision of emotional residue and passionate impulses
produces for him, it does not make his followers anxious, even as he
marries several more wives. Qassem likes women, and his community finds his obvious virility a source of pride rather than a black
mark on his character.

This is a far cry from the insistent disclaimer of any sexual motive to his marriage to Aisha or other marriages prominent in more
recent apologetics. These attempts to explain Muhammad's conjugal relationships in terms that make him an indulgent husband and
an ideal companion, focusing on friendly feelings (or gratitude, in

Khadija's case), render him unlike either the classical Arabic tradition of prophetic biography, which celebrates his virility, or the Western model that Haykal, among others, outwardly deplores and nonetheless emulates.[144] Aisha 'Abd al-Rahman had criticized Haykal for his apologetic stance on Muhammad's polygyny; in her view, Muhammad's wives were lucky: better to have only a fraction of the attention of a great man than all the attention of a lesser one.[145]

More recent female authors have tended to spend less time on polygyny, even if they treat the wives as a collective. More dramatically, many focus their attention on one wife, typically Aisha, who has been the chief protagonist of sprawling novels. One is the historical romance by Sherry Jones, *The Jewel of Medina* (2008), which occasioned a kerfuffle when its first publisher dropped it at the last minute, reportedly afraid of possible reprisals. Jones, who calls the tale of Muhammad and his "favorite wife" "one of the most touching love stories ever recorded," surrounds her novel with a paratext which explicitly sets up Aisha as a compelling figure.[146] She claims that Aisha was engaged at age six and "according to numerous accounts" married at nine, though "they consummated the marriage later, when she had begun her menstrual cycle. Although the tender age may seem shocking to us now, scholars generally agree that the marriage was motivated by politics." The other is Kamran Pasha's *Mother of the Believers* (2009), generally better received, whether because the author is Muslim or male, or because it fell outside the generally scorned romance genre.[147]

Neither was as critically well-regarded as their precursor. Assia Djebar (b. 1936) published *Far from Medina*, which "retold the

early years from the voices of women, about women and for women," and in which Fatima and Aisha played key roles, the former "an outspoken, fighting feminist" and the latter recalling and narrating events. Djebar, in one view, "reclaim[ed] women's history of the advent of Islam . . . [seeking] out and privilege[ing] the female voices in the Islamic sources, and used her literary skill to imagine what the women of the time transmitted orally to future generations."[148] One critic, however, asserts that she gets it wrong, that she misreads the Arabic sources and, indeed, is not qualified to read them.[149] The charge is that Djebar adopts Western stereotyped images of Muslim women as silenced, and finds in the historical sources only what she intends. As much as any other perceived failing on Djebar's part, it is her critical stance toward the canonical Arabic historiographical tradition that provokes this attack.

Not quite a novel, but also a marked departure from the classical historical tradition, Nadia Yassine, a Moroccan Islamist with a complicated relationship to feminism, has written an online series of "vignettes of the life of the Prophet" in which she treads a course between minutely documented historical sources and "iconoclastic critic[ism]" of those texts, presenting a deliberately feminine perspective on the incidents she recounts.[150] She "did not challenge the authority of Muslim men—whether the classical scholars, modern authorities, or her contemporaries," although "perhaps there is a subtext" in her reimagining of Muhammad's life, "implying that Muslim men have been wanting in telling the story of the Prophet."[151] This view lies behind Tamam Kahn's *Untold*, in which she aims to join "the historical and the intuitive as respectfully as possible."[152]

These women's works rely on the same sources used by male biographers throughout the centuries, with very different results. If 'Abd al-Rahman, as one scholar notes, "has written no 'life' of Muḥammad"—and, indeed, strikingly few Muslim women have authored *Lives* in forms typically used for the purpose—then it is worth thinking about what forms of life story count as proper biography.[153] Samira al-Zaiyyid, a scholar in the exclusively female traditionalist Qubaysiyyat network in Syria, has published a ten-volume encyclopedia, as well as a two-volume abridgment (*The Collective Epitome of Prophetic Biography*), used for teaching.[154] Her use of this format is in keeping with the Qubaysi preference for traditionalist (male) forms and norms, with the salient difference being the all-female nature of their scholarly communities. The only stand-alone biography of Muhammad I have encountered written by a Muslim woman is *The Book of Muhammad:* a small volume in English, unencumbered by scholarly apparatus, by Austrian journalist Mehru Jaffer.

A handful of other women have published English-language lives of Muhammad, including Armstrong and journalist Hazelton, whose *The First Muslim: The Story of Muhammad* appeared in 2013.[155] Women are overrepresented among authors of children's books in European languages. These books by women include Demi's lushly illustrated and generally well-received *Muhammad,* Marston's biography for secondary students, and Sarah Conover's 2013 "young adult" biography, brought out by the Unitarian Universalist publishing house. *Muhammad: The Story of a Prophet and Reformer* imaginatively reconstructs his infancy, childhood, and teen years and chronicles his early prophetic career. It closes with the emigration, avoiding controversial topics. (The issue of wives,

for instance, is disposed of summarily in a way that emphasizes his monogamous bond: "He married a number of times after his wife of twenty-five years, Khadija, died."[156]) Apart from these introductory biographies, which aim at a different target audience, all recent biographies by women participate in the contemporary marketplace of ideas about spirituality, politics, and pluralism, which are the subject of Chapter 6.

Chapter 6

An Enlightened Man

*On his way to see his wife Amina, Abdullah, son of 'Abd
al-Muttalib, passed by the Kaaba. Though he did not
realize it, a light shone from his forehead. A woman he
encountered along the path tried to entice him to her bed.
He declined, and continued his journey, visiting Amina
and conceiving Muhammad. Returning home, he saw
the woman again. She made no overture this time. When
he asked why, she told him that the white light that had
blazed between his eyes the previous day was gone.*

This story has long been a staple of Muslim accounts of Muhammad's life. Ibn Ishaq gives two versions, which confirm that there was something special about Muhammad even before he was born. In one, the woman is the sister of Waraqa, Khadija's Christian cousin. He had told her to expect a prophet to arise from among their people; recognizing the sign, she proposes to Abdullah, even trying to sweeten the deal with one hundred camels. In the other version, the woman is another wife of Abdullah. He approaches her, but she turns him down because he needs a bath. He leaves her, bathes, and visits Amina instead. The woman's finicky attitude showed her unfit to bear God's prophet.[1] As Ibn Ishaq concludes: "So the apostle of God was the noblest of his people in birth and the greatest in honor both on his father's and his mother's side."[2]

Muhammad's conception was unusual, marked by the transmission of the light—in some later accounts, safeguarded since

creation and passed down through his ancestors—but in other respects ordinary. Unlike the conception of Jesus, which the Qur'an says took place by means of the Holy Spirit and with the intervention of an angel, both of Muhammad's parents were human, though exceptional.

What do moderns do with this story of the Muhammadan light? Some devout believers and writers still relish the tale, embellishing it and connecting it to other miraculous events surrounding Muhammad's birth and childhood, including the angel removing the black speck from his breast. These stories are told in celebrations of the Prophet's birthday. Although there has long been concern among some scholars about how precisely Muslims celebrate, in the last two centuries puritanical opposition to any commemoration has increased substantially. In a related development, tales that have long furnished material for pious devotion as well as theological elaboration about the preexistence of Muhammad and his importance to creation have become less central to Muslim accounts of Muhammad.[3]

Why this marginalization? Muir wrote, describing one such "fanciful fiction" recounting "how the Light of Mohammed, created a thousand years before the world, passed from father to son, down to the Prophet's birth," that it "forms a kind of celestial romance, the playful fantasy of an uncontrolled imagination."[4] Muir's rejection, which regards the Muhammadan light—like other supernatural elements in Muhammad's life—as an invention, garnered few direct rebuttals. Those who engaged directly with his work were more concerned with arguing for Muhammad's social and moral virtues than his cosmic status. Many Muslim authors strip miraculous occurrences and portents from Muhammad's story without any outright denial; this practice of simple omission of popular superstition, unworthy of

retelling, is in keeping with a broader "desanctification of the Prophet."[5]

Stories of holy figures across religious traditions use light motifs, of course. This book has noted comparison for purposes of denigration, and comparison for purposes of exaltation, but one also finds comparison for purposes of illustrating a broader truth. Religious studies scholars have attempted to remain attentive to the specificity of stories while analyzing shared elements. Marilyn Waldman's posthumously polished and published *Prophecy and Power: Muhammad and the Qur'an in the Light of Comparison* argues for a more thorough rethinking of categories; the act of comparison ought not to be to apply a preexisting notion of prophethood or prophecy to Muhammad (or biblical figures) but to do two things. The first is to use those figures and the ways in which they have been understood to rethink the categories used for comparison. Second, and more intriguingly, is to look at the ways figures, including Muhammad, used comparison as part of their rhetorical strategies.

In addition to scholarly comparison, which attempts to understand rather than to find religious truth, one finds appreciative outsiders with devotional sensibilities who may not believe in the literal truth of such tales as the Muhammadan light but who expect to gain spiritual wisdom from the encounter with it. In similar ways to the deracinated versions of Buddhism or yoga that flourish in America, some non-Muslims approach the Muslim tradition as a source of enlightenment, and Muhammad as a spiritual teacher from whom they can learn. In her first biography of Muhammad, Karen Armstrong wrote: "In all the great religions, seers and prophets have conceived strikingly similar visions of a transcendent and ultimate reality. . . . I believe that Muhammad

had such an experience and made a distinctive and valuable contribution to the spiritual experience of humanity."[6] More generally, "the Muslim interpretation of the monotheistic faith has its own special genius and has important things to teach us."[7] Fifteen years later, in her second biography, she made a similar case that Westerners need to know about Muhammad, but focused less on spirituality and more on social issues: "As a paradigmatic personality, Muhammad has important lessons, not only for Muslims but also for Western people." The example of his "tireless campaign against greed, injustice, and arrogance," his "effort to bring peace to war-torn Arabia," and his "creative effort to evolve an entirely new solution" when "the old way of thinking would no longer suffice" are vital today: "We entered another era of history on September 11, and must strive with equal intensity to develop a different outlook."[8]

Muhammad, Jesus, and the Buddha

A superficial but not unimportant difference between comparisons done in the eighteenth and nineteenth centuries and comparisons done in the twentieth and twenty-first centuries is the shift from the triad of Moses, Jesus, and Muhammad to Muhammad, Jesus, and the Buddha.[9] Whereas the early eighteenth century featured Moses, Jesus, and Muhammad as a trio of impostors—and whereas for much of the nineteenth century others were keen to join Muhammad to or separate him from biblical figures—by the late nineteenth century, the landscape had shifted: Buddhism had made its debut on the stage of world religions (as Indian author Ameer Ali acknowledged), and Moses was comparatively less important.

Today, authors often treat Muhammad, Jesus, and the Buddha in parallel. Peter Manseau's chronicle of holy relics advertises, on the inside flap, "postmortem accounts of Jesus, Buddha, Muhammad, and a crowd of other holy souls."[10] Jane Dammen McAuliffe prefaces her discussion of "prediction motifs" in "Al-Ṭabarī's Prelude to the Prophet," with nods to Buddhist biographies and Christian exegesis.[11] Jonathan Brockopp introduces his *Cambridge Companion to Muhammad* by observing that "the popular veneration of Muḥammad is quite similar to that offered to Jesus, the Buddha, and countless other religious figures around the world."[12] In *Memories of Muhammad,* Omid Safi draws a parallel between the spiritual centrality of Muhammad's ascension and "the crucifixion of Jesus and the enlightenment of the Buddha"; he also notes that "Muslims' perceptions of the Prophet have remained no more static over the centuries than have Christians' estimations of Christ or the Buddhists' engagement with Gautama Buddha."[13]

The Enlightenment-era linkage of Moses, Jesus, and Muhammad as three impostors fraudulently claiming inspiration stands in sharp contrast to the joining of Muhammad, Jesus, and the Buddha in Deepak Chopra's Enlightenment series, a volume on each man available in a boxed set. Chopra's approach attests to their joint truthfulness, or at least usefulness. In *Muhammad,* Chopra writes of his own "fascination with the way in which consciousness rises to the level of the divine. This phenomenon links Buddha, Jesus, and Muhammad."[14] However, he still treats Muhammad differently. *Buddha: A Story of Enlightenment* and *Jesus: A Story of Enlightenment* are joined by *Muhammad: A Story of the Last Prophet.*

Though this is not Chopra's aim in his fictionalized accounts, others have attempted to find the "true" historical figures behind the legends of these three men. The archaeological and textual

quest for the historical Jesus had a parallel in the Orientalist search for the man behind the statue—that is, the historical Buddha.[15] A tension between doctrine and biography meant that a distinction between the Jesus of history and the Christ of faith came to be accepted in many circles as a functional compromise. Buddhists have been less interested in the connection between the Buddha's life and his teaching, in part because that teaching downplayed the role of his own life.[16]

Muhammad is a slightly different case. Muslims have long sought guidance from records of Muhammad's human deeds, though in the modern era far more people attribute far greater weight to those acts in comparison with other elements of his role. What has changed is primarily the celebration of Muhammad's historicity, sometimes contrasted directly with the comparatively scarce evidence of other prophets' lives. In his 1925 Madras Lectures, Syed Suleman Nadvi signaled "historicity" as the first criterion by which to judge anyone's claim to be a model for humanity.[17] A related assumption is that the facts of Muhammad's life can be known independently of the authoritative and charismatic lineages of teachers and spiritual guides, and indeed apart from Muhammad's cosmic status as the jewel of creation. The historical Muhammad siphons attention from the luminous ethical exemplar: the lessons adhere in recorded facts. Very recently, moreover, some biographies written for non-Muslims have sought to connect the life and the lesson.

Where does the miraculous fit in to this picture? Scholars who quest for the historical Muhammad treat legends as "incrustations from fairyland" overlaying factual biographies.[18] Removing mythical debris, one uncovers the historical figure. Influenced by the "historical Jesus" scholarship, which sought to determine what

could be precisely known of Jesus's life, Michael Edwardes introduces the London Folio Society's translation of Ibn Ishaq's *Life*
with an attempt to extract a factual core from later embellish-
ments. He distinguishes between objective facts and the "aura of
the miraculous" that early biographers added, "a rich accretion of
myth and miracle, mysterious portents and heavenly signs," all of
which are present in the story of the "legendary Muhammad." Edwardes is confident that "behind the legendary Muhammad there
lies one of the great figures of history . . . [and that] it is possible to
build up the events of his real, as distinct from his symbolic life."[19]

In addition to attempting to discover the man in question, there
was an attempt to understand the faith that grew up around him.

Pointing out the centrality of "the historical person of the Buddha and the incipient period of [Buddhism's] history" to early
study of that tradition, historian of religion Tomoko Masuzawa
gives a list of *Lives* published over the nineteenth century. They
bear titles like *Buddha and His Religion; Buddha: His Life, His Doctrine, His Order;* and simply *Life of the Budd'a.* One could easily
substitute "Mahomet" for "Buddha" in any of the titles. She notes,
too, the "two typical, nearly requisite, means of identifying an
individual religious tradition as distinct, unique, and irreducible to
any other: the naming of an extraordinary yet historically genuine
person as the founder and initiator of the tradition, on the one
hand, and the recognition of certain ancient texts that could be
claimed to hold a canonical status, on the other."[20]

Unlike with Buddhism, Muslim tradition and Western scholarship had long recognized Muhammad as this "extraordinary yet
historically genuine person." Yet similar dynamics were at work.
The term *Mohammedanism*, already in limited circulation, displaced loaded phrases like "the Saracen heresy" and "Arabian im-

postor." Scholars—occasionally the same ones who worked on Buddhist texts—sought to delimit a universe of reliable texts from which to extract the basic facts of Muhammad's biography and the Mohammedan faith.[21] (The term *Islam* would only come into its own in the twentieth century as the name for the "religion" founded by Muhammad.) The well-studied textualization of Buddhism and Hinduism in the nineteenth century—owing a great deal to the energy and labor of Orientalist scholars, whose focus on ideals and doctrines expressed in purportedly authentic texts led to the study and description of particular religions ("isms") at the expense of lived practice—had a parallel in Islam. This was neither entirely successful—people's religious practice remains messy and difficult to classify—nor a one-way imposition. The newly canonical texts were taken up by some insider elites as "true" Buddhism or Hinduism or, in this case, "Islam." Stripped-down sets of religious norms became a criterion in intra-Muslim debates, as did these desanctified biographies of Muhammad. Not everyone was so quick to jettison the mythical and symbolic elements, however.

Instead of searching for facts underneath myths, another approach sought to uncover a different sort of truth *by means of* the myths. Stories about founders conveyed something of the "person in history." John Fenton, in the late nineteenth century, applied this method to the births and awakening experiences (revelation on the one hand, enlightenment on the other) of Muhammad and the Buddha. He sought to show that, despite key differences, the myths that arose about them had universal elements. Moreover, Fenton saw both as examples of the "great man." He argued that "great men are creatures of the times which they themselves help to modify," and that by looking at myths, "we may obtain some

knowledge of the man himself in history, as he appeared to his followers and contemporaries." This glimpse of the "person in history" does not correspond precisely to him as a "historic person" but as an idealized version, stripped of most of his "failings, weaknesses, peculiarities" and reenvisioned through the lens of core biographical motifs.[22] Although not factual, the mythological elements in the *Lives* of religious founders help us understand the impulses of followers, the lenses through which they seek to make sense of their towering figures. As historian of religion John Stratton Hawley notes, "Within each religion a powerful body of tradition emphasizes not codes but stories, not precepts but personalities, not lectures but lives."[23] These narratives serve a communal function, as did, in some views, the prophetic and religious impulses themselves.

Miracles, Founders, and Figureheads

Other scholars of religion were interested not in the venerating community but in how religious inspiration functioned within the psyche of extraordinary individuals. Acknowledging them as great men who did great things, these scholars sought to understand the "prophetic impulse" and its origins and effects on those who received or wielded it.

The broader transformations in ideas about religious figures that changed how Muhammad's purported miracles (or lack thereof) were viewed also made possible the attempt—rocky at first—to set such figures on a level field and judge them by the same criteria. The transition from religious polemic to "comparative religion" was halting and bumpy. Marcus Dods's 1877 book *Mohammed, Buddha, and Christ* sits at the cusp, torn between two aims. His

title establishes the three men's equivalence. The contents, however, betray this superficial equality: two chapters on Mohammedanism and one on Buddhism are followed by a chapter on "The Perfect Religion." (Sometime in the last century, a reader of the University of Michigan's copy crossed out "Perfect" and wrote in "Christian"; the scribble is now digitized for posterity.)

For all that he named individuals in his title, Dods primarily used the men as metonyms for their religions. The book originated as a series of lectures to students of London's English Presbyterian College. How Islam, Buddhism, and Christianity have been and ought to be studied is one of its key concerns:

> One cannot fail to notice in the literature of the day a tendency more or less pronounced to put all religions, including the Christian, more nearly on one level, and especially to deal with them as if they were all alike outgrowths from the same root, man's religious faculty. This tendency has been stimulated by the comparative study of religions, which has brought to light the large number of resemblances existing in the various religions of the world but which has as yet been backward in detecting, analyzing, and defining essential distinctions.[24]

Dods lamented this development. Despite common impulses in Islam, Christianity, and Buddhism, the distinctions matter more.

Later authors were less wary of comparison and less willing to explicitly advocate one religion over another—even as they continued to appeal to the newfangled trinity of Muhammad, Jesus, and the Buddha. For instance, Edwardes begins by setting Muhammad in parallel to other figures: "It is always extremely difficult to be objective about the life of the founder of a great religion—his

personality is inevitably blurred by an aura of the miraculous. Early biographers are preoccupied, not with historical fact, but with glorifying in every way the memory of one they believe to have been a Messenger of God or even God Himself." Edwardes lumps together a *presumed* "Messenger of God" and one *presumed* to be "God Himself" as instances of a larger category: "founder[s] of . . . great religion[s]."[25]

Edwardes implicitly sets Jesus in line with others, in sharp contrast to the Bombay Tract and Book Society's *Life of Mahomet* from the previous century, which used Jesus to illustrate Muhammad's myriad shortcomings. In nineteenth-century India, the question of Muhammad's performance of miracles was a central element of religious polemics, as was more direct comparison between Muhammad and Jesus. The missionary *Life* compares Jesus and Muhammad in its final pages. The section begins with a disclaimer about the endeavor of viewing Muhammad and Jesus side by side: "It is difficult to make a fair comparison of Mohammad with Jesus Christ. Even if religious reverence towards 'the Son of God' did not restrain us, how could we compare the licentious polygamist, the robber, the fiery warrior, the inexorable bigot, with the benevolent and majestic 'Son of Man?'"[26] Muhammad's polygamy, relatively little discussed in the book, became the first means of distinguishing the two men, perhaps because the entire passage echoes Alexander Ross's 1653 treatment of "Mahumetanisme," in which "Islam provides the foil for Ross's version of Christian Orthodoxy."[27] Despite reticence about comparing the "Son of God" with a human being, the author manages to compare on several notes: "Mohammad was a leader of Arabian plunderers: Jesus went about doing good. Mohammad became a warrior at the head of armies: Jesus was 'the Prince of peace.' Mohammad was a man of

unbounded sensuality: Jesus was 'holy, harmless, undefiled, separate from sinners.' Mohammad was ambitious: Jesus was 'meek and lowly in heart.' Mohammad rested his claims on secret revelations: Jesus did 'the works which none other man did,' healing the sick, and raising the dead."[28]

Like other nineteenth-century texts, the tract is preoccupied by themes of purity and corruption. It tells of secrecy, changeability, conflict, and contradiction in Muhammad's life, in contrast to the constancy of Jesus's life. Jesus "lived and died in Judea," while Muhammad "travelled and mingled with men of varying nations, and of conflicting religions." Sameness is safe; difference is dangerous. Positing intercultural contact as inherently problematic might seem an awkward position for a British Christian living in mostly Hindu India communicating to Indian Muslims to take. Yet lest there be any doubt that commingling and contamination can lead to devastating consequences, the final sentence of the work sums it up: "Mohammad was a destroyer: Jesus is THE SAVIOUR."[29]

We find a generally similar approach delivered in a more diplomatic tone from English evangelical Thomas Patrick Hughes, who had gradually became less vociferous in his criticism of Muhammad and Islam after returning from two decades of missionary work in India. Hughes connects Muslims' defective spirituality with their inferior exemplar. If Islam "has failed in raising the hearts of men to the high level of a spiritual Christianity, it must be because it does not possess in the character of Muhammad what Christianity possesses in the character of the Divine Jesus—a living example of purity and truth."[30]

Muslim comparisons of Muhammad and Jesus take a different tack, since Muslims revere Jesus as one of God's prophets. There are, of course, anti-Christian currents in Muslim thought, but no

blame accrues to Jesus himself. Jesus is a divine messenger to whom Christians have inappropriately ascribed divinity. They corrupted the Gospels he brought, but Jesus remains unsullied. Muslims tend to treat Jesus's reputation more respectfully than do many inhabitants of nominally Christian countries of the West today. However, some modern biographies venture a tentative line of argument in which Muhammad compares favorably to Jesus.[31] These involve no denigration of Jesus but they suggest that Muhammad is a better model for humanity. Since he was a man with wives, family, and worldly concerns, he can be an appropriate guide and model in a way that Jesus, who lived an *unusual* and, in particular, celibate life, cannot be.[32] As Aisha 'Abd al-Rahman observes, while Christians claim that Jesus has a divine nature, "the Islamic message has insisted upon admitting the human nature of the Prophet. . . . He is attracted to a wife, becomes involved in family life, and suffers from love and hate, desire and abstinence, fear and hope. What applies to any human applies also to him, such as daily toil, being orphaned, bereavement, disease and death." The only exception to his susceptibility to human "frailties" is in those matters directly concerning his role as prophet.[33] Here, the elements of Muhammad's life that served as fodder for criticism by earlier thinkers become the basis for his elevation. Jesus's set-apartness renders him less exemplary. In her view, Muhammad's humanity makes his role that much more meaningful: "What honour, that a Prophet carrying the Message of Heaven should be a part of mankind itself."[34]

The decades between Hughes and 'Abd al-Rahman saw extensive debates over the precise nature of Jesus's historicity and humanity. Ernest Renan's famous *Life of Jesus*, published in French in 1863—almost exactly a century prior to Edwardes's edition of Ibn

Ishaq and shortly after the Bombay Book and Tract Society's *Life*—laid a new foundation for thinking about Jesus, and therefore about comparison between him and Muhammad. Given Renan's writings on Islam, his famous declaration about Muhammad and the full light of history, and his engagement in debate with Ahmad Khan, his *Life* was not only a "critical text in the intellectual history of France" but also a milestone in Egypt and India.[35] Shortly after the book's publication, Renan spoke of Jesus publicly as "that incomparable man." A century and a half later, it is difficult to comprehend the scandal of that utterance. "Incomparable" sounds like praise. But for pious inhabitants of the nineteenth century, the key term was *man:* "incomparable" or not, to call Jesus "that . . . man" was itself offensive.

By the 1960s, things had changed dramatically in popular approaches to Jesus and in views about religious pluralism, including about the inclusion of Islam. Edwardes's introduction to the *Life* assumes this parity, even as it substitutes Buddhism for Judaism in its appeal to tradition.

Armstrong adopts a similar framing technique in *Muhammad: A Prophet for Our Time.* Her two poles, though, are not legend and fact, but "transcendent reality" and "current events in the mundane sphere." She believes in a "sacred past," neither opposed to nor circumscribed by a factual one; historicity is not the holy grail. Rather, she looks for an insider's perspective: "The faithful scrutinize the sacred past, looking for lessons that speak directly to the conditions of their lives." She continues:

> Most religions have a figurehead, an individual who expresses the ideals of the faith in human form. In contemplating the serenity of the Buddha, Buddhists see the supreme reality of

Nirvana to which each of them aspires; in Jesus, Christians glimpse the divine presence as a force for goodness and compassion in the world. These paradigmatic personalities shed light on the often dark conditions in which most of us seek salvation in our flawed world. They tell us what a human being can be.[36]

Armstrong views the Buddha and Christ as "figurehead[s]" "in human form"—"paradigmatic personalities," like Muhammad, who "tell us what a human being can be." The three figures are equivalent only insofar as one understands Jesus as a human manifestation of divine ideals. Renan's "incomparable man" begins to look utterly ordinary.

Unlike Dods, Edwardes and Armstrong presume that readers can and should evaluate Muhammad in nonconfessional terms, just as non-Christians evaluate Jesus in nonreligious terms. As W. Montgomery Watt, author of three biographies of Muhammad, puts it: "What Muslim and other non-Christians are asked to accept in this world where religions mix is this core of historical fact about the teaching and achievement of Jesus as a human being but without the theological interpretations."[37] They should extend the same courtesy to Muhammad.

Great Moral Teacher(s)?

Civic and academic discourse in purportedly secular societies of North America and Europe demands that one separate the praiseworthy historical achievements from the religious message delivered by a religious "founder" or "figurehead." Whether this is possible remains an open question. Still more fraught, however, is the

question of how religious believers ought to approach competing religious claims.

Given that the issue at stake is comparison, perhaps the question can best be addressed by a comparative example. C. S. Lewis, who died in 1963, was by training a scholar of medieval literature, though he is perhaps best known as the author of the Narnia series of children's books. He was also an amateur theologian and a popular Christian apologist. His commonsensical theology includes a famous argument, which he did not invent but popularized. In *Mere Christianity,* he targets those who proclaim their admiration for Jesus as a "great moral teacher" but reject his divinity and his status as savior. This, Lewis says, is untenable. Either Jesus was telling the truth about being the Son of God or he was lying. If he was lying, either he was insane, "on a level with the man who says he is a poached egg," or he was purposefully, maliciously misleading people: "the Devil from Hell." Since one cannot, Lewis insisted, admire a madman or an evil fraud, one must either reject Jesus entirely or accept him as the Son of God and savior of humankind. What one must not do, he said, is say "the really foolish thing that people often say about Him: 'I'm ready to accept Jesus as a great moral teacher, but I don't accept His claim to be God.'"[38] Lewis's trilemma has attracted plaudits and rebuttals that do not concern us here.[39] What matters is the problem itself.

Such willingness to accept Jesus as a human moral teacher tout court would have been unintelligible to medieval Christians or nineteenth-century missionaries. It is possible because of intertwined developments in European thought. Enlightenment rationality and Romantic ideas about genius had humans seeing profound truths without any necessary Divine hand. The Enlightenment leveling of the religious playing field and the rise of academic

religious studies led to the treatment of various traditions as instances of a larger phenomenon called religion. Related, the men (and they are nearly always men) associated with the origins of these religions came to be investigated on a par as "founders," whose lives or, for the skeptical, life stories bore crucial commonalities. And yet there were numerous ways of envisioning any given founder. Thomas Jefferson's Jesus (a "mild, humanitarian moralizer") is distinct from the gospel radical, the medieval savior, and related to, though not quite the same as, the great moral teacher to whom Lewis objects.[40]

Since at least the eighteenth century, some who reject Muhammad's claims to prophethood nonetheless see in him something admirable, worthy, and respectable. In a recent twist, some have come to see in him not only the founder of a great religion or a man who reformed his society, but also a spiritual leader and exemplar from whom even non-Muslims can learn. Not everyone subscribes to this view, of course; images of Muhammad as deluded or demonic continue to circulate. And just as Lewis argues for taking Jesus's words at face value, there are those who hold that Muhammad was precisely what he purported to be: a prophet from God entrusted with a revelation that will lead those members of humanity who accept it on the straight path to eternal felicity. My concern here is the muddy middle ground: those who reject Muhammad's prophethood but celebrate his qualities and accomplishments.

It is not just from the perspective of academic religious studies that the founders of great religions, in Edwardes's phrase, have been subjects of investigation. Believers from other traditions or no tradition have weighed in. Tom Stecker's oddball biography *The Man Mohammed: A Dramatic Character Sketch* (1900) takes the form of a play, which is mostly concerned with scandals and chal-

lenges in Muhammad's household. He articulates a larger purpose in his preface, pleading:

> Let scholars of all religious confessions include among their researchers the study of men who deserve the name of religious leaders; let them consider them not as either demigods or demons, but as men; let them endeavor to extract cogent truths and virtues from human follies and inconsistencies in doctrine and career of their subjects; let them remove the nimbus and halo of mystery from the brows of these humble tutors and present them as our peculiarly constituted brothers, who have imparted to us their diversely conceived convictions concerning truths of the metaphysical realm—and even the greatest curse of the ages, religious antagonism, which even in our day continues to culminate in massacre and war, will, in time, become an obsolete barbarism, while an approaching step toward uniformity of worship among the nations will be accomplished.

This is an extraordinary program of action, particularly coming from a man who penned the cheesy line for Muhammad, on seeing Zaynab: "O heavenly nymph! Thy beauty dazzles me!"[41] Overblown rhetoric aside, Stecker is committed to understanding a common religious impulse, stripped of miracle and mystery, which could unite humanity.

Pluralism and Exclusivity

Some Christian figures, including prominent theologian Hans Kung, have moved toward a more inclusive view of Islam that

may include recognition of Muhammad's prophethood *for Muslims*.[42] One sign of progress is "evangelical Baptist theologian Timothy George's measured Christian conservatism regarding Islam." Rejecting other evangelicals' pronouncements that the Qur'an resulted from demon possession, George "affirmed that Muhammad's establishment of monotheism was 'in keeping with biblical faith'."[43] At the same time, he insisted that there were certain irreconcilable "truth-claims" made by each religion, particularly having to do with the nature of Jesus.[44] This awareness that there are limits to how far such recognition can proceed is absent from some Muslim writings. Ahmad Gunny, in his history of French and English depictions of Muhammad, complains that although "in 1965, Vatican Council II stressed in positive terms those aspects of his preaching that are acceptable to Christians . . . it kept silence over Muḥammad's claim to divine inspiration, and there still seems to be some ambivalence towards Islam and Muḥammad in Roman Catholic thinking."[45] Does the pope, the leader of a faith whose truth claims rule out Muhammad's prophethood, really err by remaining mum as to whether Islam's message is divinely inspired? (Indeed, given Pope Benedict's inflammatory 2006 remarks about Muhammad, silence seems the better option.) In contemporary Western societies, citizens widely agree on equal accommodations for religious belief and observance (or nonbelief and nonobservance) as a matter of civic law. Is it reasonable to suggest that private citizens, much less religious leaders, must go beyond tolerance to accept rival truth claims, some of which diminish or outright contradict their own beliefs?[46] Or, put a different way, "How much of the Islamic view of Muhammad can outsiders share, without becoming Muslims and ceasing to be outsiders?"[47]

These are large questions, beyond the scope of this book to answer. We may consider, however, how these questions manifest in biographical writings. There have been a few explicitly Christian attempts to grapple with Muhammad's life from a pluralist rather than a polemical perspective. One approach has been to see Muhammad as representing a kind of incomplete or inferior— in Carlyle's term, "bastard"—Christianity. Such *Lives* recognize something human and perhaps legitimately prophetic, neither deluded nor demonic. The largely unspoken view in these portraits is that he may have been connecting in some way to a divine current flowing through the universe, but he was not directly commissioned by God in the way that the Hebrew prophets were. In such attempts to explain Muhammad's religious-spiritual impulses, God is surprisingly absent. Despite their Christian origins, they often smack of broader Romantic sensibilities. Watt, for instance, disclaiming any particular theological expertise, discusses in broad terms a "creative imagination" shared by artists, in which universal themes emerge. "Prophets and prophetic religious leaders," he suggests, "share in this creative imagination" and "proclaim ideas connected with what is deepest and most central in human experience, with special reference to the particular needs of their day and generation." Watt here combines the notion of a creative current running through the universe that poets and prophets alike tap into with a sense of the social utility of their works.

Tor Andrae, a Lutheran bishop, attempts to connect the larger question of how to think about religion and religious figures with the personal story of Islam's prophet.[48] *Mohammed: The Man and His Faith* was originally published in German in 1932, the same

year Haykal's first review article on Dermenghem appeared. Andrae writes:

> There was a time when it was considered in accordance with good scientific method to interpret all religious development as due to ... social and economic factors, which operated with the simple inevitability of natural law, or to ideas and conceptions which, by their necessary and reciprocal interaction, gave rise to religious dogmas and systems. . . . No place was really left for the great, leading, creative religious personalities. To go back to the particular personal experience, or the prophetic initiative, as the source of the new religious creation, was regarded as an act of scientific bankruptcy.[49]

He argues instead for the force and impact of "the creative spiritual life" of extraordinary people: "In all religious movements whose history we can really survey the awakening power proceeded from an individual personality."[50]

In recounting Muhammad's creative shaping of what the title ambiguously calls "his faith" (is it his inner certainty or the religion he founded?), Andrae neither takes Muslim claims about revelation at face value nor assumes that Islam can be reduced to a mash-up of earlier religions:

> The development of Islam ... presents us with yet another proof that the prophetic personality is the original source of new religious creation. . . . That the fundamental ideas of Islam were borrowed from the Biblical religions is a fact which requires no further discussion. . . . And yet it is cheap wisdom to think that this disposes of the question of Mohammed's

originality. . . . There is originality enough in Mohammed's achievement in catching up into a vital and adaptable personal synthesis the spiritual potentialities of his age.[51]

The traditional biographies allow glimpses of Muhammad's inner life, as does the Qur'an; reading it "enables us to trace a soul which wrestles with its fate, and with naïve candour reveals its aims and hopes, as well as its faults and accomplishments, its weakness and courage."[52]

In Andrae's view, "That Muhammad acted in good faith can hardly be disputed by anyone who knows the psychology of inspiration."[53] Yet this does not rule out his conscious shaping of what was "originally spontaneous inspiration."[54] For Muir, this had been the crux of the problem, the moment when Muhammad turned from spiritual seeker to grasping striver—or, as Peirce Johnstone put it, when his "sincere . . . desire to reform his countrymen" led him to take "the false, fatal step of proclaiming himself the Apostle of God," and then "to exalt his personal authority he used the Holy Name."[55] For Andrae, that "the Prophet gradually grew accustomed to think of ideas that emerged in his consciousness and decisions that matured in his soul as direct expressions of the Divine will" did not make him an impostor. Rather, Andrae concludes, "A genuine prophet is one who really has a message to deliver, one in whose soul some of the great questions of his age have stimulated a restlessness which compels him to speak and for whom the ecstasy and prophetic inspiration are but the natural and inevitable expression of a strong lasting conviction and a genuine passion."[56]

There are limitations, though, to this celebration of Muhammad's creative soul, which come in the connection between his inner resources and his outer actions, which mix, unpredictably,

forbearance and violence. Andrae concludes his reflections on a less flattering note: "We Christians are inclined to compare Mohammed with the unsurpassed and exalted figure whom we meet in the Gospels, and that we cannot avoid seeing his historical personality against the background of the perfect moral ideal to which the faith of his followers tried to exalt him. And when it is measured by such a standard, what personality is not found wanting?"[57]

Native Informants?

Similar questions about the relationship between Muhammad's actions and his character arise in more recent biographies. At least a dozen English-language biographies of Muhammad aimed at general audiences have been published in the United States and United Kingdom since the turn of the twenty-first century, undoubtedly spurred in part by interest in Islam after the September 11 terrorist attacks. Their authors include academics (Jonathan Brown, Tarif Khalidi, Daniel Peterson, Omid Safi), journalists (Lesley Hazelton, Barnaby Rogerson), public intellectuals (Karen Armstrong, Tariq Ramadan), and spiritual figures (Deepak Chopra), as well as a poet (Elliott Weinberger) and a professional polemicist (Robert Spencer). These categories are inadequate: Safi has a profile as a public intellectual; Ramadan, a doctorate and an Oxford professorship; Armstrong, a growing reputation as a purveyor of spiritual advice. What they share is that they are not divided strictly by religion. With the exception of Spencer, whose books provide reasonably accurate information framed and interpreted in relentlessly negative ways, these authors give at least somewhat positive accounts of Muhammad, which combine attention to historical fact with recognition of Muhammad's spiritual

agency, or initiative. They also tend to devote significant attention to the Banu Qurayza, and their diverse ways of approaching the bloodiest event of Muhammad's career are revealing.

These contemporary publications on Muhammad have mixed audiences, too. In some ways, this continues a pattern established a century and a half ago, when Muslims and non-Muslims began to regularly read one another's work. Muir aimed his biography at non-Muslims, and when Muslims read the work, it provoked anger rather than appreciation, along with extensive engagement. Yet when Zaidi aimed at correcting non-Muslim misunderstandings in his *Mothers of the Faithful* he was fooling himself; only scholars and polemicists paid heed to Muslim authors, and scholars were interested in premodern writings, the earlier the better. Since the late twentieth century, however, and in the last decade in particular, Muslim-authored works have been published to appeal to general non-Muslim audiences as well as Muslims. This shift has partly to do with the changing times and partly to do with the works themselves. Large numbers of Muslims live and write in Europe and North America, some holding academic positions and others working as journalists and public intellectuals. Works composed or published in French and, especially, English have a global reach. For some topics, books written by Muslims have additional cachet by virtue of "authenticity," but this is often true for books about women's experiences (particularly insofar as they conform to the "victim" or "escapee" model) rather than for those on topics on which one is expected to be "objective."[58]

One of the books with a legitimate claim to a crossover audience is Tariq Ramadan's *In the Footsteps of the Prophet*.[59] It is the anti-Haykal. The tone is confident, not combative; the narrative smooth, not choppy. Ramadan digresses at times to make points about

contemporary relevance but avoids direct engagement with critics. And the title itself harks back to the earlier tradition: it emphasizes Muhammad's role rather than his name and uses the imagery of a path, which is ubiquitous in Muslim writings on spiritual and legal conduct.[60] The appeal to non-Muslims is deliberate, with the idea that the subtitle's "Lessons from the Life of Muhammad"—a life that Ramadan recounts in roughly chronological fashion— are applicable to universal human struggles. (The original French subtitle puts it even more clearly: *Spiritual and Contemporary Teachings*.)[61]

Ramadan interweaves accounts of key events, such as the Battle of the Trench and the retaliation against the Banu Qurayza, with the lessons to be learned from them. The account of the siege of Medina is embedded in a chapter titled "Tricks and Treason"— both terms of which refer to Muhammad's enemies. When the chapter opens, Muhammad and his community are facing a "difficult" situation. Their defeat by the Quraysh at Uhud a few years earlier had led their opponents to believe them "vulnerable." Muhammad was able, sporadically, to ward off "planned attacks on Medina," but they were facing Meccans who "desire[d] to eradicate the Muslim community from the peninsula" and made alliances to that end.[62] All of these descriptors portray Muhammad's community as beleaguered and him as, alternately, a capable leader using his men to best advantage and someone forced reluctantly by circumstance into using military means of communal self-defense.[63]

Ramadan rejects the view of Muhammad as weak in Mecca, strong in Medina.[64] Rather than emphasizing Muhammad's strength, Ramadan illustrates Muslim vulnerability: "Many Muslims were taken prisoner during those years after falling into ambushes or simply being outnumbered by their enemies. They were

often tortured and dreadfully put to death, and tradition reports their courage, patience, and dignity in the face of death."[65] In this complex and treacherous milieu, the defection of allies such as the Banu Nadir tribe, "who lived inside Medina itself, made it impossible for the Muslims to set up a defense strategy."[66] Muhammad used "intuition," quick thinking, and decisive action to secure his community's safety by the "exceptional" expedient of cutting down tall palm trees. Once the tribe agreed to leave, he did not carry out "his threat to execute them" but instead let them leave with not only "their women and children" but also "a considerable amount of wealth."[67]

In similar fashion, Muhammad's next unanticipated military strategy was to ward off Meccan attackers by digging a trench to complement existing natural fortifications. In recounting Muhammad's adoption of the tactic from a Persian convert, Ramadan draws a lesson about creativity.[68] Ramadan has argued elsewhere that modern Muslims should borrow others' techniques and strategies.[69] Here, he roots such appropriations in Muhammad's precedent.

The expulsion of the Banu Nadir serves as a prelude to the bloodier story of the Banu Qurayza; the two form a thematic pair. Ramadan draws lessons from Muhammad's conduct in both. In the former, he lingers less on Muhammad's strategic vision or grasp of military tactics and more on care for the environment. About the palm trees, he writes: "Never again would the Prophet act in disrespect of creation, and he was to repeat again and again . . . that such respect must be complete, even in wartime."[70] (Yahiya Emerick likewise points out Muhammad's "green" bona fides; prior to this incident, "he had always ordered his men to refrain from harming the environment in their campaigns." In this instance, though, "in order to shorten the conflict, he took the drastic step, as men

in war sometimes must, of choosing expediency over principle."[71])
Ramadan is not preoccupied by strict follow-through on threats
or the question of Muhammad's decisiveness and resolve; rather,
as he writes in another context, beyond justice there is forbearance,
"the excellence of the heart, that offers forgiveness or gives people
more than their due."[72] Some of the lessons are about qualities like
generosity—the Banu Nadir story is about an individual's way of
being in the world—and others, like that of the Banu Qurayza,
emphasize communal action.

Deepak Chopra's novelized biography *Muhammad: A Story of
the Last Prophet,* told in nineteen chapters with different narra-
tors, makes an unexpected counterpart to Ramadan's book. Like
Ramadan, Chopra dispenses wisdom, and he too would probably
prefer the modifier "spiritual" to "religious." One similarity is superficial: both books' covers show desert scenes, Chopra's including
a distance view of a man walking through the sand. In fact, it
shows footsteps, presumably representing those of the Prophet.

Chopra focuses on Muhammad's humanity: not only the things
he shares with other important spiritual figures—Jesus and the
Buddha—but also the things he has in common with ordinary human beings. His Muhammad, like Ramadan's, is someone from
whom people can learn, not through formal dictates or the vision
of his conduct preserved by Muslim jurists but by understanding
his struggles in his confrontation with the Divine. However understanding Chopra is about Muhammad, he presents Islam and
Muslims as particularly linked to a backward past: though every
faith has its orthodoxy and fundamentalists (which he conflates),
he equates Muslims in toto with "fear of the modern world."[73] As
noted earlier, for him, Muhammad's conduct toward the Banu
Qurayza is, like his marriage to the young Aisha, incomprehen-

sible to non-Muslims but defended by Muslims as necessarily right and proper. (In fact, recent biographies by non-Muslims take a range of approaches to the conflict with the Banu Qurayza, from deflecting blame to signaling it as a regrettable but necessary demonstration of political will.[74] Salahi's revisionist discussion makes clear also that Muslims are not of one mind about the matter.)

British convert Muhammad Marmaduke Pickthall had already, in the concise biography which prefaced his 1930 English translation of the Qur'an, set the stage for deflecting blame for the slaughter of the "treacherous" Qurayza tribe, who were "conscious of their guilt" for having attempted to betray the Muslims. Muhammad, in a move that is described in straightforward military terms, "ordered war against" them. They "surrendered unconditionally" and "begged to be judged by a member of the Arab tribe to which they were affiliated. The Prophet granted their request and carried out the sentence of the judge: the execution of the men and the enslavement of the women and children."[75] In this account, Muhammad only acceded to the tribe's own wishes and followed through on established procedure.

In *Muhammad: A Biography of the Prophet*, Armstrong describes Muhammad's actions, contextualizing them but without exculpating him. Perhaps spurred by the desire to combat anti-Muslim sentiment in the wake of September 11, her later biography shifts blame onto the arbiter, emphasizing his responsibility for the decision to execute the men.[76] Hazelton is one of the few authors to suggest that Muhammad himself bore substantially more responsibility for the gruesome outcome. Although the arbiter made the decision, Muhammad selected him knowing he was a "militant hard-liner" who could not be expected to show clemency. In her view it was a political strategy that accomplished its purpose of instilling

respect and fear among other potential defectors precisely because it was a departure from customary modes of tribal dispute resolution.[77] Whether they themselves make explicit comparisons, these authors write in awareness that readers will undoubtedly compare Muhammad with other figures—Jesus, current national leaders, Muslim religious figures. Safi's *Memories of Muhammad* brings this comparative element to the fore.[78] It is also about communal boundaries and (mis)understanding. He makes the interreligious dimensions of his project explicit, and resists the monochromatic portrait of Islam and Muslims that Chopra paints. "Difficult" passages from scripture exist in all three "Abrahamic" traditions, but he lays out a constructive and positive path. "If," he writes, "we are willing to participate in a culture of generosity that affirms that *all* of our traditions contain verses, teachings, and practices that are at first glance—and sometimes at second and third glance— profoundly problematic, and that we must come to terms with them, and that all of our traditions also contain profound beauty and wisdom, then there is a journey we can take together." That journey involves recognition of the unpleasantness in Muhammad's life but also the triumph over difficulties; it also acknowledges that one's choice of lenses through which to view any tradition affect the resulting view.

Unlike the works of Anglo-Muhammadan authors of the late nineteenth century, or Egyptian writers of the first half of the twentieth century, Muhammad's world-altering accomplishments are not the centerpiece of these books. Yes, it matters that he accomplishes remarkable things. Chopra's back cover advertises "The Revelation That Changed the World." But the acts are connected also to interior changes: Muhammad "remade the world by going inward."[79] Nasr's *Muhammad: Man of God* refers to the impor-

tance of "the spiritual dimensions . . . of the life of the person who changed human history."[80] Safi writes of the "Muhammadi revolution," in which inward transformation must precede outward change: "before there can be a social movement, there has to be a spiritual awakening."[81] The crucial elements of Muhammad's story being offered to readers in these books are not recipes for starting a socialist revolution or standing up to colonial officials or being strong in the face of religious opposition. Instead, they have to do with being an ethical person, aware of God in times of adversity, and confronting complex social and moral dilemmas with an acute sense of both responsibility and wonder. Some decades earlier, Andrae and Watt were interested in the "creative spiritual life" of prophets, these extraordinary individuals. These contemporary biographies presume that readers themselves will have creative spiritual lives and that, whether Muslim or not, Muhammad's life can serve as a resource for their individual quests to develop and enhance those inner lives.

Defying Categorization

Recent biographies defy neat division into modern and traditional, Eastern and Western, or Muslim and non-Muslim; instead, they make a hash of those categories. None does so more completely than the lyrical, minimalist *Life* by Eliot Weinberger. *Muhammad* captures far better than most recent Salafi biographies the tone, at once reverent and matter-of-fact, of premodern Muslim accounts. He draws from Tabari's *History*, *hadith* collections, the Qur'an, and a seventeenth-century Persian Sufi treatise. He resuscitates the miraculous elements that Haykal and his ilk had dispensed with, resurrecting the Muhammad of devotion.[82] He recounts the

transmission of the primordial light, the splitting of the breast, the splitting of the moon, and his causing hair to grow on a bald man's head. Yet Weinberger's *Muhammad* is unmistakably modern in its organization and emphases. The first section narrates his life. The last, replete with miracles, recounts the night journey and ascension. The middle section describes his relationships with women. Though the material on wives and wonders is from traditional texts, its extraction from the quotidian details of expeditions, battles, and daily life results from an impulse toward thematic coherence indispensable to the modern biographical tradition. Weinberger sidesteps the contemporary impulse to contextualize or justify and instead merely relates; his characteristic authorial act is pruning. What is essential is the inclusion and placement of the material. Between the biography proper and the spiritual and legendary, Muhammad's relations with women are, quite literally, at the center of his story.

Conclusion

By the turn of the twentieth century, two largely separate streams of writing about Muhammad, one hagiographical and the other polemical, had converged in a single contentious body of literature. European and American portraits of the Prophet, shaped decisively by new notions of what made a man great and what counted as merit, set the agenda for Muslim depictions. Along the way, "authentic" historical sources from the first centuries of Islam became a touchstone for scholars and lay readers alike: all wanted to know the *facts* about Muhammad's life. Texts written symbolically came to be read literally. A shared rhetoric of evidence and objectivity pervaded biographies. So did a shared format—mostly narrative and chronological—and shared topics: pre-Islamic paganism, "revelation," violent encounters with hostile Meccans and Medinan Jews, and relationships with women—what Ziauddin Sardar calls "wives and warfare" and Omid Safi describes as "violence, sex, and heresy."[1] This does not mean, of course, that only one version of Muhammad appears in modern biographies. This is manifestly not the case. Both among Muslims and among non-Muslims, various approaches to the Prophet's life story coexist. Using raw materials

from a handful of early Muslim texts, biographers paint diverging portraits of their subject. No matter the author's background, the results "depar[t] dramatically from—without necessarily contradicting"—the sources on which they are based.[2]

The considerable overlap among modern biographies illustrates the futility of appealing to a timeless clash of civilizations between Islam and the West. In Muhammad's own era, identities were fluid and factionalized.[3] In the fourteen hundred years since then, neither Islamic nor Western civilization has been a unified entity politically, economically, or religiously. Intra-Muslim dissension exists over everything from whether one ought to stand when reciting blessings on the Prophet, to whether one can depict Muhammad's face, to which of his wives are trustworthy as sources of information, to whom, if anyone, he designated as his successor. Much less has Christianity or the West been a cohesive unit. The idea of "Europe" is of fairly recent origin. Christianity was perhaps more brutally riven by the Reformation than Islam was by the Sunni-Shi'a divide.[4] The repeated Protestant invocation of Muhammad and the Pope as twin antichrists foils any simple Christianity-versus-Islam story.

Not only is the notion of unified Muslim and Western civilizations baseless, but so is the presumption of timelessness in ideas about Muhammad. A comparison of Humphrey Prideaux's *The True Nature of Imposture*, published at the turn of the seventeenth century, and Robert Spencer's *Muhammad: Founder of the World's Most Intolerant Religion*, published at the turn of the twenty-first, shows that they differ vastly on questions of pluralism. Prideaux asserts, from an avowedly Christian perspective, that Muhammad is an impostor; he lambastes Muhammad's lustfulness, ambition, and fabrication of revelation. Spencer paints no more flattering a

portrait but proclaims Muhammad not an impostor but founder of a religion.[5] And, vitally, the main criticism of this religion is not that it is false but that it is intolerant. Prideaux would have scoffed at the idea of religious tolerance; he aimed to uphold singular religious truth.

Prideaux and Spencer differ on issues of pluralism but share an animating impulse: opposing *us* to *them*. In contrast, the Enlightenment tract *The Three Impostors* and Deepak Chopra's *Muhammad*, published around the same time, respectively, as Prideaux's and Spencer's books, assume an essential sameness of religions—the former, that all are similarly untruthful; the latter, that all contain truth.

In any survey, the choice to emphasize similarity or difference affects the end result profoundly. This study has toggled back and forth. Any body of work, looked at closely enough, reveals contradictory impulses and divergent tendencies. This is true for the views of Muhammad found in early modern English drama and Enlightenment-era French biography, late nineteenth century evangelical tracts and inter-war Egyptian *Lives*. Stepping back, one sees larger trends and patterns despite these internal variations.

A similarly irresolvable tension arises in considering continuity and change in Western approaches to Islam in general and Muhammad in particular. Two models compete. Jonathan Lyons believes that for the last millennium "the West's construction of Islam and Muslims has been essentialist, uniform, and not conducive to nuance and variation."[6] Change is minimal; positive ideas about Muhammad fail to catch on because of a pervasive "anti-Islam discourse." So powerful are recurring images of violence, backwardness, and misogyny that "the argument of any individual scholar is dissipated in the face of the overwhelming power of the broader

discourse at work."[7] My experiences attest to the impotence of facts alone to change people's beliefs; as another scholar notes, "Westerners and Western intellectuals often choose what they want to believe about Islam, rather than believing what the evidence suggests they believe."[8]

Lyons's pessimism seems warranted, too, by the persistence of old accusations. In American evangelical circles, references to Muhammad as false prophet, impostor, and demonically possessed continue, giving the lie to the suggestion that "connections between premodern and modern prejudices are tenuous."[9] If such terminology faded from polite discourse by the nineteenth and twentieth centuries, it continued in certain religious contexts and has made a comeback since the September 11 attacks, as with the reverend Jerry Vines's Southern Baptist Convention speech in 2002, in which he called Muhammad "a demon-possessed pedophile."[10]

Yet contrary to Lyons, there have been significant changes. In earlier periods, insults against Muhammad were typically used for rhetorical force in attacks on other Christians. Roger Williams referred to "that stupendous Cheater Mahomet" while criticizing Quaker leader George Fox in 1676.[11] An 1851 article denigrated Mormonism's prophet-founder Joseph Smith as "The Yankee Mahomet."[12] In contrast, Vines targets Muslims directly. And new accusations piled alongside the old attest to new worries: preacher Jerry Falwell's declaration that "Muhammad was a terrorist" would have made no sense in a premodern context (though it echoes accusations of violence),[13] nor would have Vines's accusation of pedophilia (though it draws on old themes of sexual perversion).

Vines combined one of the oldest accusations with one of the newest. How he defended his charges in the firestorm that followed illustrates the common ground he and his Muslim critics

stood on. When challenged, Vines cited authoritative *hadith* texts quoted in a book by putative "ex-Muslims." Rejoinders to Vines took two main forms. Some accepted the literal truth of his sources but stressed the need for historical contextualization ("things were different then"). Others insisted that these *particular* texts were not accurate, and alluded (vaguely) to different facts extractable from other texts. Thus, Vines and his Muslim critics might disagree about specific texts' reliability, but all share two presumptions. The first is that authentic early sources contain facts about what Muhammad did. The second is that by his deeds is how one judges him. In contrast to medieval emphases on personal habits or physical qualities, it is deliberate acts that matter. Medieval polemics associated objects of scorn with disgust-inducing filth; today, even the ugliest accusations hurled at Muhammad condemn his actions and not, for instance, his appearance or smell. Then, sloppy eating signaled degeneracy and animality, which were linked to violence and lust.[14] Today, it is marriage that matters, not table manners.

And yet, the accusation of pedophilia is meant to elicit not just condemnation but horror. Modern accounts are largely demythologized, written in terms of history, science, and fact as opposed to symbolism, myth, and legend.[15] In this case, though, Muhammad's sexual conduct becomes the locus for a renewed vision of Islam as an archaic and evil force. Medieval emphases on debauchery and lustfulness have become, since the colonial era, concern with oppression. Exactly which oppressive practices are singled out has also changed. William Muir, unbothered by Aisha's age, was troubled by polygamy and divorce, which, alongside slavery, debased women. Today, divorce carries little stigma in the United States and Europe, and even polygamy is quaint but unthreatening;

scripted television dramas like *Big Love* and reality shows like *Sister Wives* portray it as an exotic curiosity. On the other hand, child sexual abuse ranks with school shootings as a cause for condemnation. Sex with children is evil; thus, by implication, anyone who engages in it is evil. By the twentieth century, Muhammad had largely stopped being viewed as evil, even by people who did not much approve of him. The popularity of the pedophile epithet corresponds with a resurgence of the idea of evil, and the link between evil and Islam. Nor is it coincidental that the accusation surged after the clergy sex-abuse scandal: anti-Muslim and anti-Catholic sentiments remain connected.

Just as premodern polemics based on disgust were formulated about and by members of different communities, so, too, new conventions about sexuality and achievement are shared across communal and, increasingly, geographical boundaries. This sort of give-and-take has always been part of the Muslim biographical tradition. There was no pure "Islamic" tradition prior to the encounter with Western modernity. From the start, Muslim citizens of the late antique world borrowed from biblical and Near Eastern heroic motifs, praising Muhammad in the language of their times. Muhammad's biography included "ideational complexes whose mobility exceeded the limited reach of this or that ethnicity, linguistic group, or religious sect." This is not a question of corruption but merely a question of the circulation and interpenetration of ideas and style: certain "intellectual property was held in common" across sectarian lines.[16] This approach to Muhammad's life is not illegitimate but rather inevitable.

Yet although some authors always concerned themselves with responding to outsider claims and criticisms, and varied local traditions provided plentiful images with which to glorify Muhammad,

prior to the nineteenth century, one could speak about a tradition of Muslim biography that was, in meaningful ways, coherent and self-contained. There is something qualitatively different about the ways in which Muslim and non-Muslim portraits of Muhammad intermingle and intermarry from the nineteenth century forward. Some of this has to do with power: in responding to Muir, Ahmad Khan and Ameer Ali adopted the literary conventions, the styles of argument, and quite literally the language of their opponent.[17]

Such exchanges worked both ways. Muslim writings about Muhammad have also affected the way the majority of non-Muslim authors approach his life. Deference to the main contours of the newly homogenized story, as outlined in Chapter 1, prevails; the only ones who consistently buck it are scholars sometimes too quickly anathematized as revisionists. Often, what they are revising is not "the Muslim tradition" but the small slice of it consistently presented and represented as the story of his life.

Certain sorts of material were excluded from Muhammad's life story as it developed in the seventh through ninth centuries; things got left out, written off, forgotten.[18] Another round of narrowing took place in the last two centuries. A few things Muslim tradition had marginalized got pulled back to the center of the story when Western scholars resuscitated them, such as the Satanic verses; other things simply dropped out. Sunni-centrism infects mainstream Western biography: the Prophet invariably dies with his head on Aisha's shoulder;[19] the first four caliphs are always "rightly guided"; and if Ali converts first, he is usually the first "youth" to do so, making Abu Bakr the first "man."[20] And "first" means after Khadija, who is virtually always forty when she marries Muhammad. The range of anecdotes one finds in modern biographies is strikingly narrow.

So is the cast of characters. Muhammad's wives, particularly Khadija and Aisha, displace other figures, such as Muhammad's mother or foster mother. The emphasis on conjugal rather than kin relationships grows from shifting social norms but is reinforced by research practices. As Islamic studies scholar Marion Katz observes, though they are central to the *mawlid* narratives that celebrate Muhammad's birth and infancy, "Neither Āmina nor Ḥalīma is a major figure in the mainstream historical tradition dealing with the Prophet's life."[21] Since the early biographies and chronicles are the main sources used to write Muhammad's life, Amina and Halima recede.

That authors draw from a small pool of anecdotes owes partly to an understandable desire for narrative coherence. Modern readers want the story—they do not want seven versions of the tale of Aisha's necklace that repeat or, worse, contradict each other on major points or minor details. No one wants to wade through lengthy lists of authorities and weigh the information presented according to the trustworthiness of its reporters. There are, it is true, premodern examples of this sort of writing, and presumably oral storytellers preferred continuous narration. But the prevalence of smoothed-out written accounts, which proceed mostly forward in time from a determined starting point, is recent and has led to a homogenized story. If one is going to tell an incident once, it will be the majority version. The fact that there *were* alternate versions often drops out entirely.

Texts containing competing accounts of what happened, for instance, during the night journey and ascension present a problem. So do the "divergent and contradictory" accounts of Khadija's age at her marriage to Muhammad, the number of sons she bore him, and even her date of death.[22] If Ibn Hisham presents accounts that

report X *and* Y *and* Z about an event, what view does one impute to him? Modern practice treats *authors* as responsible for assessing material they report ("Ibn Hisham says"). By contrast, "traditional" readers saw compilers as responsible for collecting and presenting materials that readers, properly guided by their teachers, would assess.

Which raises the issues of reading, interpretation, and authority.

Modern Islam is a profoundly Protestant tradition.[23] Among Sunni Muslims in particular, core elements of post-Reformation Protestant textual practice enjoy widespread—though not universal—acceptance. Believers read scriptural texts in isolation from their commentarial traditions and often without expert guidance. Qur'an and *hadith* are widely translated into vernacular languages. Confronted by a difficulty or a question about religious doctrine or practice, a layperson is likely to turn to scripture—translations of the Qur'an often have a subject index, though keyword-searchable online texts are rendering other mechanisms obsolete.

These notions about texts, authority, and vernacular languages were influential in the encounters among scholars and texts which shaped interreligious and intra-Muslim debates. This does not mean that modern Islam was created by missionaries and Orientalists and imposed wholesale on hapless Muslims.[24] Reformers like Ameer Ali and Muhammad Husayn Haykal—as well as more "traditional" figures like Qasim Nanautvi—were not dupes of colonialism. Instead, they used Western texts, ideas, and strategies to present, or invent, a usable Muslim past—a past that differs in crucial respects from once-traditional visions of early Islam—and a viable Muslim future. With the *sira* movement in the Indian subcontinent and the explosion of works on Islamic topics in Egypt, prophetic biography became "a tool to combat the cultural

and intellectual onslaughts of the west."[25] And, even as "Modern Muslims' obsession with how Westerners represent the Prophet is inseparable from the issues of global power, hegemony, and colonialism,"[26] the form and content of Muslim prophetic biographies have been deeply conditioned by and implicated in those onslaughts. It "is not about an encounter between 'tradition' and 'modernity,' but about a peculiarly constituted modernity in which different traditions converge."[27]

The convergence of traditions which has been the subject of this book has occurred on a stage in which British and American writers and readers loom large, as does the English language itself. When Annemarie Schimmel published an expanded English version of *And Muhammad Is His Messenger* (1985)—her landmark study of poetic and mystical veneration of the Prophet—she omitted the images of him found in the German original. She explained that even though these were part of the medieval Muslim artistic tradition, contemporary Muslims might take offense. Unspoken is that although they were not likely to encounter them in the German edition, the English edition would have a global, and partly Muslim, readership.[28]

Muhammad's life continues to be central not only for ongoing exchanges—friendly and not-so-friendly—across confessional lines, but also for intra-Muslim polemical purposes. When the current head of one Ahmadi sect blames Muslim "misfortune" in the *Innocence of Muslims* debacle on the fact that "Muslims have no unity and no leadership," he is implicitly singling out his community as, unlike the majority of Muslims, unified around a single leader.[29] Debates of this sort existed long before Western political, military, and economic supremacy decisively altered the context for thinking about Muhammad. That said, the global preeminence of a hegemonic

Western order and its effect on Muslim thinking, including about Muhammad, are undeniable. Indonesian mogul Muhammad Syafii Antonio, using a team of authors from his Tazkia (piety) Institute, recently issued a glossy eight-volume encyclopedic biography of the Prophet.[30] It bears the title *Ensiklopedia Leadership & Manajemen Muhammad SAW, "The Super Leader Super Manager."* The first portion is technically in Bahasa, though loan words are so evident that one need not bother with a translation. The abbreviation "SAW" stands for the Arabic blessing that pious Muslims attach to every mention of Muhammad.[31] The last part is in English. The title is reminiscent of Labib Riyashi's 1934 Arabic biography *Muhammad: The World's First Superman* in that it attributes to Muhammad characteristics and qualities that bear little resemblance to the facts of his life as typically told.[32] Can Muhammad be seen as a model CEO? Perhaps. After all, early Muslims wrote about him as a shepherd, because all prophets were shepherds; and mid-twentieth-century Egyptians wrote about him as a socialist reformer, because that is what they needed. Why should a businessman not write about him as the epitome of executive skill? "Leadership" and "Manajemen" are not quite the same as annunciatory dreams and miracles, but they have a cosmic reverberation all their own.

Notes

Introduction

1. Jonathan A. C. Brown, *Muhammad: A Very Short Introduction* (New York: Oxford University Press, 2010), 89–93. For an overview of these sources, see Robert G. Hoyland, "The Earliest Christian Writings on Muḥammad: An Appraisal," in *The Biography of Muḥammad: The Issue of the Sources*, ed. Harald Motzki (Leiden: Brill, 2000): 276–297. Michael Penn's forthcoming book on Syriac Christian reactions to the rise of Islam addresses these issues in more detail. *Imaging Islam: Syriac Christianity and the Reimagining of Christian-Muslim Relations* (Philadelphia: University of Pennsylvania Press, forthcoming).

2. Virginia Burrus, *The Sex Lives of Saints: An Erotics of Ancient Hagiography* (Philadelphia: University of Pennsylvania Press, 2004), 12.

3. New research profitably explores visual depictions of Muhammad as well as the intersections between such depictions and verbal portraits. See, for example, Avinoam Shalem, ed. *Constructing the Image of Muhammad in Europe* (Berlin: De Gruyter, 2013).

4. Abdul Hameed Siddiqui, *The Life of Muhammad (P.B.U.H.)*, 2nd ed. (New Delhi: Islamic Book Service, 2002 [1975]), 340; 1st ed. 1969.

1. The Historical Muhammad

1. Tarif Khalidi's *Images of Muhammad: Narratives of the Prophet in Islam through the Centuries* (New York: Doubleday, 2009), 1–2, gives an even briefer summary of this "core story"; Matthew Dimmock's version, *Mythologies of the Prophet Muhammad in Early Modern English Culture* (Cambridge: Cambridge University Press, 2013), xiii, is shorter still.

2. John Tolan, *Sons of Ishmael: Muslims through European Eyes in the Middle Ages* (Jacksonville: University Press of Florida, 2008), 145.

3. Michelina Di Cesare, "Images of Muhammad in Western Medieval Book Culture," in *Constructing the Image of Muhammad in Europe*, ed. Avinoam Shalem (Berlin: De Gruyter, 2013), 11.

4. Nimrod Hurvitz, "Biographies and Mild Asceticism: A Study of Islamic Moral Imagination," *Studia Islamica* 85 (1997): 45; Chase Robinson,

Islamic Historiography (Cambridge: Cambridge University Press, 2002), 61–66.

5. Christian Smith, *Moral, Believing Animals: Human Personhood and Culture* (New York: Oxford University Press, 2003), 65.

6. A. Kevin Reinhart, "Juynbolliana, Gradualism, the Big Bang, and Ḥadīth Study in the Twenty-First Century," *Journal of the American Oriental Society* 130, no. 3 (July–September 2010): 413–444, at p. 416. Among Muslim biographers who incorporate this line—without citation—is Maulana Muhammad Ali; see Muhammad Ali, *Muhammad the Prophet* (Lahore: Ahmadiyya Anjuman Ishaat Lahore, 1993), 186.

7. Uri Rubin, *The Eye of the Beholder: The Life of Muhammad as Viewed by the Early Muslims; A Textual Analysis* (Princeton, NJ: Darwin, 1995), 1–3.

8. Alford T. Welch, "Muhammad's Understanding of Himself: The Koranic Data," in *Islam's Understanding of Itself,* ed. Richard G. Hovannisian and Speros Vyronis Jr. (Malibu: Undena, 1983), 15. Welch views the Qur'an as reflecting Muhammad's self-understanding, and the prophetic tradition (*ḥadīth*) and *sīra* literature as the product of the Muslim community's attempt to come to grips with Muhammad.

9. F. E. Peters, "The Quest of the Historical Muhammad," *International Journal of Middle East Studies* 23 (1991); see also his *Jesus and Muhammad: Parallel Tracks, Parallel Lives* (New York: Oxford University Press, 2011). Though pessimistic about prospects for Muhammad's biography, Peters is a great deal more optimistic about the textual history of the Qur'an. The scholarly literature on the Qur'an, even simply in relation to Muhammad's biography, is vast, and I have made no attempt to survey it here.

10. For the scholarly debate over whether Muhammad was in fact the Prophet's name, see Gabriel Said Reynolds, "Remembering Muhammad," *Numen: International Review for the History of Religions* 58, no. 2/3 (2011): 188–206. On the significance of the Prophet's name(s) for Muslims, see Annemarie Schimmel, *And Muhammad Is His Messenger: The Veneration of the Prophet in Islamic Piety* (Chapel Hill: University of North Carolina Press, 1985): 105–122.

11. Welch, "Muhammad's Understanding of Himself," 19; in Aloys Sprenger's view, "Up to his fortieth year Moḥammad devoutly worshipped the gods of his fathers." Sprenger, *The Life of Mohammad from Original Sources* (Allahabad: Presbyterian Mission Press, 1851), 94.

12. M. J. Kister, "'A Bag of Meat': A Study of an Early Ḥadīth," *Bulletin of the School of Oriental and African Studies* 33 (1970): 267–275.

13. See Fred Donner's retrospective review twenty years after *Hagarism*'s initial publication: *Middle East Studies Association Bulletin* 40, no. 2 (December 2006): 197–199.

14. Patricia Crone and Michael Cook refer to *Hagarism* as a book written "by infidels for infidels." *Hagarism: The Making of the Islamic World* (Cambridge: Cambridge University Press, 1977). Robert Spencer, *Did Muhammad Exist? An Inquiry into Islam's Obscure Origins* (Wilmington, DE: Intercollegiate Studies Institute, 2012).

15. Michael Cook, *Muhammad* (New York: Oxford University Press, 1996 [1983]), 74. Jonathan E. Brockopp notes that this book "is arguably less a biography of Muḥammad than it is a study of problems facing anyone who would write such a biography." Brockopp, ed., introduction to *The Cambridge Companion to Muḥammad* (Cambridge: Cambridge University Press, 2010), 13.

16. G. R. Hawting, *The Idea of Idolatry and the Emergence of Islam* (Cambridge: Cambridge University Press, 2002).

17. Fred Donner, *Muhammad and the Believers: At the Origins of Islam* (Cambridge, MA: Belknap, 2012); Donner, "Muhammad and the Debates on Islam's Origins in the Digital Age," in *Muhammad in the Digital Age*, ed. Ruqayya Y. Khan (Austin: University of Texas Press, forthcoming).

18. G. W. Bowersock, *Throne of Adulis: Red Sea Wars on the Eve of Islam* (New York: Oxford University Press, 2013).

19. At the level of mundane details, for instance, facts about Muhammad's father's death become suspiciously more specific as the tradition develops. See Cook, *Muhammad,* 63–64.

20. The term "stalemate" is Gregor Schoeler's. Schoeler, "Foundations for a New Biography of Muḥammad: The Production and Evaluation of the Corpus of Traditions from 'Urwah b. al-Zubayr," in *Method and Theory in the Study of Islamic Origins,* ed. Herbert Berg (Leiden: Brill: 2003), 21–28, at p. 21.

21. Schoeler, "Foundations for a New Biography of Muḥammad," 22. The phrase "salvation history" is John Wansborough's.

22. Herbert Berg, "Competing Paradigms in the Study of Islamic Origins: Qur'ān 15:89–91 and the Value of *Isnād*s," in *Method and Theory,* ed. Berg, 259–90.

23. Michael Lecker, "Glimpses of Muḥammad's Medinan Decade," in *Cambridge Companion,* ed. Brockopp, 75.

24. Daniel C. Peterson, *Muhammad: Prophet of God* (Grand Rapids, MI: Wm. B. Eerdmans, 2007).

25. Stephen J. Shoemaker, *The Death of a Prophet: The End of Muhammad's Life and the Beginnings of Islam* (Philadelphia: University of Pennsylvania Press, 2012); see also Robert G. Hoyland, *Seeing Islam as Others Saw It: A Survey and Evaluation of Christian, Jewish and Zoroastrian Writings on Early Islam* (Princeton, NJ: Darwin, 1998).

26. Shoemaker, *Death of a Prophet*, 87.

27. David S. Powers, *Muḥammad Is Not the Father of Any of Your Men: The Making of the Last Prophet* (Philadelphia: University of Pennsylvania Press, 2009).

28. John L. Esposito, *The Future of Islam* (New York: Oxford University Press, 2013). I quote from the reviews by Mohammed Shadman (August 20, 2010) and Andrew J. Stunich (April 1, 2010).

29. In a post-9/11 special issue of the *Message International* devoted to Muhammad, an article by "Abu Iqbal, Ph.D." refers to the centuries-long history of presenting Muhammad as an impostor. His list of recent contributions to that literature mentions Patricia Crone and Michael Cook, Tor Andrae, and Alfred Guillaume, whose *Life of Muhammad* is actually a translation of Ibn Isḥāq: *The Life of Muhammad: A Translation of Ibn Isḥāq's Sīrat Rasūl Allāh* (Karachi: Oxford University Press, 2003 [1955]). Abu Iqbal, "Muhammad in Rewrite," *Message International*, August–September 2002, 12–13, quotation from p. 12.

30. Nigel Hamilton, *Biography: A Brief History* (Cambridge, MA: Harvard University Press, 2008), 48.

31. Khalidi, *Images of Muhammad*, 16.

32. Hamilton Gibb, "Islamic Biographical Literature," in *Historians of the Middle East*, ed. Bernard Lewis and P. M. Holt (London: Oxford University Press, 1962), 54–58, at p. 54; see also Robinson, *Islamic Historiography*, xxiv–xxv.

33. On Ibn Saʿd's treatment of Muhammad's virtuous conduct in matters of manners and habits, see Hurvitz, "Biographies and Mild Asceticism." He notes that "the Traditionists projected onto the Prophet the behavioral patterns that they practiced or held in high esteem" (59). See also, with regard to food, Tor Andrae, *Mohammed: The Man and His Faith*, trans. Theopil Menzel, rev. ed. (New York: Harper and Row, 1960), 180.

34. There is an English translation of the entries for his wives, daughters, and female companions in Ibn Saʿd, *Women of Madina*, trans. Aisha Bewley (London: Ta-Ha Publishers, 1995).

35. Khalidi, *Images of Muhammad*, 16.

36. Dwight F. Reynolds, ed., *Interpreting the Self: Autobiography in the Arabic Literary Tradition* (Berkeley: University of California Press, 2001); see esp. pp. 38–51.

37. Leor Halevi, *Muhammad's Grave: Death Rites and the Making of Islamic Society* (New York: Columbia University Press, 2007), 50; in Halevi's view, it "reveals far too much about the concerns of Ibn Isḥāq, his informants, and his audience, even if it reveals nothing at all about the historical Muḥammad" (50–51).

38. Gordon D. Newby, *The Making of the Last Prophet: A Reconstruction of the Earliest Biography of Muhammad* (Charleston: University of South Carolina Press, 1989), 9.

39. Ibid., 2.

40. Newby, *Making of the Last Prophet*. Newby attempts to reconstruct the lost book from fragments in others' writings. On this reconstruction, see Ahmad Gunny, *The Prophet Muhammad in French and English Literature, 1650 to the Present* (Leicestershire: Islamic Foundation, 2010).

41. Uri Rubin, *The Eye of the Beholder: The Life of Muhammad as Viewed by the Early Muslims; A Textual Analysis* (Princeton, NJ: Darwin, 1995).

42. Bernard Lewis, "Gibbon on Muhammad," in "Edward Gibbon and the Decline and Fall of the Roman Empire," special issue, *Daedalus* 105, no. 3 (Summer 1976): 96.

43. Peter Matthews Wright, "Critical Approaches to the Farewell *Khutba* in Ibn Ishaq's Life of the Prophet," *Comparative Islamic Studies* 6, nos. 1–2 (2010): 217–249, at p. 220.

44. Ibn Ishaq, *The Life of Muhammad: Apostle of Allah*, ed. Michael Edwardes, trans. Edward Rehatsek (London: Folio Society, 1964); hereafter Ibn Ishaq, *Life of Muhammad*. A recent Dutch translation by Wim Raven, *Het leven van Mohammed: de vroegste Arabische verhalen* [The life of Muhammad: The earliest Arab stories] (Amsterdam: Bulaaq, 2000), likewise identifies the author simply as Ibn Ishaak.

45. Guillaume, *Life of Muhammad*.

46. The Arabic term is *maghāzī*. The first suggestion is Jaroslav Stetkevych, *Muhammad and the Golden Bough: Reconstructing Arabian Myth* (Bloomington: Indiana University Press, 1996), 30; the second, S. A. A. Rizvi, "Muḥammad in South Asian Biographies: Changes in Islamic Perceptions of the Individual in Society," in *Self and Biography: Essays on the Individual and Society in Asia*, ed. Wang Gungwu (Sydney: Sydney University Press), 103. Tarif Khalidi, *Arabic Historical Thought in the Classical Period* (Cambridge: Cambridge University Press, 1996), 44, sees Wāqidī and Ibn Saʿd as "a pair." See, more broadly, pp. 44–48.

47. H. R. Idris ("Réflexions sur Ibn Ishaq," *Studia Islamica* 17 [1962]) observes that al-Wāqidī "never cites Ibn Isḥāq" and attributes this to his competing work (26); Khalidi, *Arabic Historical Thought*, 48, n. 53, disagrees, citing not Wāqidī's *Maghāzī* but Ibn Saʿd's *Ṭabaqāt al-Kubrāʾ*.

48. Lewis, "Gibbon on Muhammad," 95.

49. Al-Wāqidī, *The Life of Muḥammad: Al-Wāqidī's Kitāb al-Maghāzī*, ed. Rizwi Faizer, trans. Rizwi Fazier, Amal Ismail, and AbdulKader Tayob (London: Routledge, 2011), xvi.

50. Ibid.

51. Khalidi, *Images of Muhammad*, 2; see also Khalidi, *Arabic Historical Thought*, 45.

52. Schimmel, *And Muhammad Is His Messenger*, 130–131.

53. Khalidi, *Images of Muhammad*, 58. On al-Ṭabarī, see also "Al-Ṭabarī: An Introduction," in *Al-Ṭabarī: A Medieval Muslim Historian and His Work*, ed. Hugh Kennedy (Princeton, NJ: Darwin), 1–9, though it is mostly focused on his Qurʾan commentary.

54. Khalidi, *Images of Muhammad*, 17, 18.

55. Ibid., 18.

56. On this dream in Ibn Hishām, see Sarah Mirza, "Dreaming the Truth in the *Sīra* of Ibn Hishām," in *Dreams and Visions in Islamic Societies*, ed. Özgen Felek and Alexander Knysh (New York: State University of New York Press, 2012), 21.

57. Alexandra Cuffel, *Gendering Disgust in Medieval Religious Polemic* (Notre Dame, IN: University of Notre Dame Press, 2007), 13.

58. Ibid., 77.

59. Tolan, *Sons of Ishmael*, 19–34.

60. Ibid., 20; Etan Kohlberg, "Western Accounts of the Death of Muḥammad," in *L'Orient dans l'histoire religieuse de l'Europe: L'invention des origines*, ed. Mohammad Ali Amir-Moezzi and John Scheid (Turnhout: Brepols, 2000), 165–195. Cuffel reports anecdotes where Muhammad's corpse would be "devoured by swine, dogs, or in one case vultures," "making him doubly filthy—unclean because these creatures ate unclean things, and impure because the animals themselves were contaminating." Cuffel, *Gendering Disgust*, 76, 226.

61. Dimmock, *Mythologies*, 37; see also 40, 59–60. Dimmock reproduces an image of "Machomeete" being consumed by swine (32).

62. Cuffel, *Gendering Disgust*, 77. A Jewish polemic makes use of this Christian anti-Islamic material; see Cuffel, *Gendering Disgust*, 134; Cuffel also (135–136) discusses Christian polemics that denigrate Muhammad and his death through association with Jews. In "Christian

antibiographies," Muhammad's "life and smelly death . . . stood as a kind of anti-incarnation against which they could contrast that of Jesus" (154).

63. Humphrey Prideaux, *The True Nature of Imposture Fully Display'd in the Life of Mahomet*, 8th ed., corrected (London: E. Curll, 1723 [1697]), 101.

64. For these stories, see Kohlberg, "Western Accounts," and, briefly, Shoemaker, *The Death of the Prophet*, 301–302, n. 75; al-Wāqidī, *The Life of Muḥammad*, 333–334. The use of poison and the martyr's death suggest important parallels to stories of the deaths of the Shi'i Imams. See Matthew Pierce, "Remembering the Infallible Imams: Narrative and Memory in Medieval Twelver Shi'ism" (Ph.D. diss., Boston University, 2013), esp. ch. 4, "Betrayal." Alfons Teipen shows that Jewish culpability in the poisoning shifted in early Muslim biographical sources from individual responsibility to a small group of culprits to a collective guilt, reflecting an increased anti-Jewish sentiment occasioned by polemical exchanges in the eighth and ninth centuries. "The 'Poisoning Jewess' Motif in Early Muslim Biographies of Muhammad," unpublished paper, presented at the American Academy of Religion Annual Meeting, November 2013.

65. Halevi, *Muhammad's Grave*; Shoemaker, *Death of a Prophet*, 90–99.

66. Robinson, *Islamic Historiography*, 11.

67. Ibid., 11.

68. Ibid., 12.

69. Brown, *Muhammad*, 90–91.

70. Khalidi, *Images of Muhammad*, 134; Pierce, "Remembering the Infallible Imams."

71. Uri Rubin, "Muḥammad's Message in Mecca: Warnings, Signs, and Miracles," in *Cambridge Companion*, ed. Brockopp, 39–56.

72. Khalidi, *Images of Muhammad*; Omid Safi, *Memories of Muhammad: Why the Prophet Matters* (New York: Harper One, 2009); Carl Ernst, "Muḥammad as the Pole of Existence," in *Cambridge Companion*, ed. Brockopp, 123–138.

73. He argues that biographical narratives about, for instance, Muhammad's marriage to Maimuna, who is largely absent from modern biographies, were formulated in support of (or against) particular legal views. Joseph Schacht, "A Revaluation of Islamic Traditions," *Journal of the Royal Asiatic Society of Great Britain and Ireland* 81, no. 3–4 (October 1949): 143–154.

74. On the hope for Muhammad's intercession, see Schimmel, *And Muhammad Is His Messenger*, 81–104.

75. Safi, *Memories of Muhammad*, 265; Schimmel, *And Muhammad Is His Messenger*, 135–137.

76. On contemporary Muslim dreams of Muhammad, see Leah Kinberg, "Dreams Online: Contemporary Appearances of the Prophet in Dreams," in *Dreams and Visions in Islamic Societies*, ed. Özgen Felek and Alexander D. Knysh (Albany: State University of New York Press, 2012), 139–157; Amira Mittermaier, *Dreams That Matter: Egyptian Landscapes of the Imagination* (Berkeley: University of California Press, 2011). Mittermaier discusses veneration of the Prophet more generally at pp. 113–114.

77. Mittermaier, *Dreams That Matter*, 168.

78. Leah Kinberg, "The Legitimization of the *Madhāhib* through Dreams," *Arabica* 32, no. 1 (March 1985): 47–79; Mimi Hanaoka, "Visions of Muhammad in Bukhara and Tabaristan: Dreams and Their Uses in Persian Local Histories," *Iranian Studies* 47, no. 2 (March 2014): 289–303. Shahzad Bashir, "Narrating Sight: Dreaming as Visual Training in Persianate Sufi Hagiography," in *Dreams and Visions in Islamic Societies*, ed. Felek and Knysh, 233–247. Bashir notes that "dream narratives need to be treated as literary artifacts placed strategically within larger textual arrangements" (233).

79. Jonathan G. Katz, "Dreams and Their Interpretation in Sufi Thought and Practice," in *Dreams and Visions in Islamic Societies*, ed. Felek and Knysh, 181–197, at p. 190; see also Meenakshi Khanna, "The Visionaries of a *Ṭarīqa:* The Uwaysī Sufis of Shāhjahānabād," in *Dreams and Visions in Islamic Societies*, ed. Felek and Knysh, 273–96, at p. 280. Dreams raised another question about Muhammad's status. Was he alive, dead, or not really either? A core distinguishing element between the Barelvis and the Deobandis in India today has to do with the status of the Prophet and the appropriate way to show reverence for him. For a brief summary, see Clinton Bennett, *In Search of Muhammad* (London: Cassell, 1998), 184; Ernst, "Muḥammad as the Pole of Existence," 138.

80. Kinberg, "Dreams Online." Kinberg emphasizes continuities between contemporary and classical ideas about the Prophet's appearance in dreams, while noting that the rise of the Internet makes individuals' narratives about such dreams accessible in an unprecedented way. Amira Mittermaier, drawing on others' work, suggests that there may be more emphasis on appearances of the Prophet in dreams from the eighteenth century forward.

81. Some reject the great man Muhammad of recent biographies, pointing out that such depictions fail to convey something crucial about

him. See, for example, the Egyptian shaykh discussed by Mittermaier (*Dreams That Matter,* 125) and the British Muslim Timothy Winter ("Jesus and Muḥammad: New Convergences," *Muslim World* 99, no. 1 [January 2009]: 31–33).

82. Mirza, "Dreaming the Truth," 26.

83. Tolan, *Sons of Ishmael,* xiv.

84. Ibid., xiii.

85. Reginald Hyatte, trans., *The Prophet of Islam in Old French: The Romance of Muhammad (1258) and The Book of Muhammad's Ladder (1264)* (Leiden: Brill, 1997).

86. See Tolan, *Sons of Ishmael,* 46–63; Ronit Ricci, *Islam Translated: Literature, Conversion, and the Arabic Cosmopolis of South and Southeast Asia* (Chicago: University of Chicago Press, 2012), 61–65.

87. *Lex Mahumet pseudoprophete;* it is also sometimes titled *Lex saracenorum* (Law of the Saracens). See Thomas E. Burman, *Reading the Qur'an in Latin Christendom, 1140–1560* (Philadelphia: University of Pennsylvania Press, 2007); Ziad Elmarsafy, *The Enlightenment Qur'ān* (Oxford: Oneworld, 2009), 2; Jonathan Lyons, *Islam through Western Eyes: From the Crusades to the War on Terrorism* (New York: Columbia University Press, 2012), 85.

88. Dimmock, *Mythologies,* 38.

89. One exception is the *Book of Muhammad's Ladder,* a retelling of the Muslim story of Muhammad's night journey and ascent into heaven, which was little more than a translation of Muslim material. See Hyatte, *The Prophet of Islam in Old French.*

90. Tolan, *Sons of Ishmael,* 145. Tolan is remarking specifically on Pedro Pascual, but the insight holds true more broadly.

91. Marc Laureys, "History and Poetry in Philippus Meyerus's Humanist Latin Portraits of the Prophet Mohammed and Ottoman Rulers (1594)," in *Latinity and Alterity in the Early Modern Empire,* ed. Yasmin Annabel Haskell and Juanita Feros Ruys (Tempe, AZ: Arizona Center for Medieval and Rennaisance Studies; Turnhout: Brepols, 2010), 286.

92. Tolan, *Sons of Ishmael,* 134.

93. Ibid.

94. Ibid.

95. Matthew Dimmock, "'A Human Head to the Neck of a Horse': Hybridity, Monstrosity and Early Christian Conceptions of Muhammad and Islam," in *The Religions of the Book: Christian Perceptions, 1400–1600,* ed. Matthew Dimmock and Andrew Hadfield (New York: Palgrave, 2008), 66–88, at p. 67.

96. Thomas Conley, *Toward a Rhetoric of Insult* (Chicago: University of Chicago Press, 2010), 69–70.

97. John Tolan, afterword to *Contextualizing the Muslim Other in Medieval Christian Discourse*, ed. Jerold C. Frakes (New York: Palgrave, 2011), 249.

98. Jonas Otterbeck, "The Depiction of Islam in Sweden: An Historical Overview," http://inhouse.lau.edu.lb/bima/papers/Jonas_Otterbeck.pdf.

99. In French, *L'Alcoran des Cordeliers*. Thomas Conley, *Toward a Rhetoric of Insult* (Chicago: University of Chicago Press, 2010), 71.

100. Laureys, "History and Poetry," 293 n. 59.

101. Quoted in Irwin, *Dangerous Knowledge: Orientalism and Its Discontents* (New York: Overlook, 2006), 70.

102. Lyons, *Islam through Western Eyes*, 135; Elmarsafy, *Enlightenment Qur'ān*, 3–7.

103. Thomas S. Kidd's *American Christians and Islam: Evangelical Culture and Muslims from the Colonial Period to the Age of Terrorism* (Princeton, NJ: Princeton University Press, 2009) shows how American Christian thinkers from what later became the evangelical tradition used Islam in intra-Protestant debates and in anti-Catholic works, continuing to use epithets like "impostor," "false prophet," and "Antichrist." See esp. pp. 8–14, 17–18. For a rarer instance of modern Catholic linking of Protestantism and Islam, see p. 81.

104. Prideaux, *True Nature of Imposture*, 13; George Bush, *The Life of Mohammed: Founder of the Religion of Islam, and of the Empire of the Saracens* (New York: Harper and Brothers, 1837).

105. Laureys, "History and Poetry," 278. Muslims also accused Christians of sexual improprieties of various sorts. See, for example, Cuffel, *Gendering Disgust*, 148.

106. Elmarsafy, *Enlightenment Qur'ān*, ix.

107. On Bedwell, see Matthew Birchwood, "Confounding Babel: The Language of Religion in the English Revolution," in *The Religions of the Book*, ed. Dimmock and Hadfield, 142–143; Guy G. Stroumsa, *A New Science: The Discovery of Religion in the Age of Reason* (Cambridge, MA: Harvard University Press, 2010), 129.

108. Stroumsa, *A New Science*, 125, and, broadly, ch. 6 ("From Mohammedis imposturae to the Three Impostors: The Study of Islam and the Enlightenment"), 124–144.

109. Quoted in ibid., 131.

110. Ibid., 130.

111. Khalidi, *Images of Muhammad*, 200–207.

112. George Minois, *The Atheist's Bible: The Most Dangerous Book That Never Existed* (Chicago: University of Chicago Press, 2012), x.

113. Ibid., xi.

114. Jacob Lassner, *Jews, Christians, and the Abode of Islam: Modern Scholarship, Medieval Realities* (Chicago: University of Chicago Press, 2012), 239.

115. Cecilia Ferrazzi, *Autobiography of an Aspiring Saint*, ed. and trans. Anne Jacobsen Schutte (Chicago: University of Chicago Press, 1996), 15.

116. Christopher J. Walker, *Islam and the West: A Dissonant Harmony of Civilizations* (London: Sutton, 2005), 184.

117. David R. Blanks and Michael Frasetto, introduction to *Western Views of Islam in Medieval and Early Modern Europe* (New York: St. Martin's, 1999), 3.

118. Astérious Argyriou, "Éléments biographiques concernant le prophète Muhammad dans la littérature grecque des trois premiers siècles de l'Hégire," in *La vie du prophète Mahomet*, ed. Toufic Fahd (Paris: Presses universitaires de France, 1983), 159–182, at p. 168.

119. Dimmock, *Mythologies*, 9.

120. Diego Venturino, quoted in Minois, *The Atheist's Bible*, 186; Tolan, *Sons of Ishmael*, 33. This biography was Voltaire's primary source for his 1742 play *Mahomet* (Ronald W. Tobin, "The Sources of Voltaire's 'Mahomet,'" *French Review* 34, no. 4 [February 1961]: 372–378). Voltaire's play condemns Muhammad to serve an anticlerical agenda. (Voltaire's later *Essay on the Moors* is substantially more approving of Muhammad.) The singling out of specific works as exceptional, unusual, and first is a frequent act of modern scholars, drawn to what is different and unusual. For instance, Kohlberg ("Western Accounts of the Death of Muḥammad," 180) remarks that Henry Stubbe's seventeenth-century biography (published only in the early twentieth century) is "exceptionally sympathetic for his time." See Henry Stubbe, *An Account of the Rise and Progress of Mahometanism with the Life of Mahomet and a Vindication of Him and His Religion from the Calumnies of the Christians*, ed. Hafiz Mahmoud Khan Shairani (London: Luzac, 1911). The fact that it was published "under the auspices of the Islamic Society" (v) attests to the perception that it was sympathetic, or, as the editor puts it in his introduction, "he was the first Englishman to cast from himself the trammels which, with the rest of his countrymen, he had inherited from the Middle Ages. There is no trace in him of that concession to preconceived ideas and malignant notions" (xvi). See the next chapter's discussion of the idea of

avoiding prejudice. For a new edition with a useful introduction, see Nabil Matar, ed. *Henry Stubbe and the Beginnings of Islam: The Originall & Progress of Mahometanism* (New York: Columbia University Press, 2014).

121. Shaden Tageldin, *Disarming Words: Empire and the Seductions of Translation in Egypt* (Berkeley: University of California Press, 2011), 173.

122. Gunny, *The Prophet Muhammad in French and English Literature*, 251.

123. On Pococke, see Birchwood, "Confounding Babel."

124. Voltaire used Gagnier's *Life* for his *Essay on the Moors*. He also borrowed Sale's translation of the Qur'an from the Bibliothèque Royale in 1747. Tobin, "Sources of Voltaire's 'Mahomet.'"

125. Daniel J. Vitkus, "Early Modern Orientalism: Representations of Islam in Sixteenth- and Seventeenth-Century Europe," in *Western Views of Islam*, ed. Blanks and Frasetto, 209–210.

126. Christopher Tyerman, *The Crusades: A Very Short Introduction* (Oxford University Press, 2005), 137; Ketton says "fear of the Turk was being replaced by impatience, contempt, and arrogance" (56). In Tolan, *Sons of Ishmael*, after 1683, "the Turk no longer seemed a threat to western European writers. . . . It was now possible to portray the Muslim as a sympathetic if benighted 'other,' rather than a threatening one. Gibbon . . . could portray Muhammad with an inimitable mix of praise and condescension" (34).

127. Maxime Rodinson, *Europe and the Mystique of Islam* (London: I. B. Tauris, 2002 [1987]), 52.

128. Ibid., 44.

129. Ursula Wokoeck, *German Orientalism: The Study of the Middle East and Islam from 1800 to 1945* (New York: Routledge, 2009), 4–5. Wokoeck mentions but is unconvinced by Rudi Paret's contrary claim that the study of Islam was more important than Arabic. On the early modern study of religion, see also Stroumsa, *A New Science*, 30.

130. Wokoeck, *German Orientalism*, 2. Wokoeck's study, focused on "professional scholars pursuing an academic career at the university" (18) in the "minor discipline" (27) of Oriental studies, takes seriously their practices, procedures, negotiations, and strategic considerations.

131. Stuart Curran, ed., *The Cambridge Companion to British Romanticism*, 2nd ed. (Cambridge: Cambridge University Press, 2010), xi. Curran gives a narrower date range, 1785–1825.

132. From the 1985 *Oxford Companion to English Literature,* quoted by Aidan Day, introduction to *Romanticism* (New York: Routledge, 1996), 1.

133. Timothy Blanning, *The Romantic Revolution: A History* (New York: Modern Library, 2012), 27.

134. Philip Almond, *Heretic and Hero: Muhammad and the Victorians* (Wiesbaden: Otto Harrassowitz, 1989), 95.

135. Kidd, *American Christians and Islam,* 28.

2. A True Prophet

1. On this story, see, for example, Maxime Rodinson, *Mahomet* (Paris: Éditions du Seuil, 1961), 70–71; Ruth Warren, *Muhammad: Prophet of Islam* (New York: Franklin Watts, 1965), 9–10. On the doctrine of Muhammad as "seal of the prophets" (Q. 33:40), see Powers, *Muhammad Is Not the Father,* 52–55. More generally, on the supernatural in Muhammad's life, see Rebecca R. Williams, *Muhammad and the Supernatural: Medieval Arab Views* (New York: Routledge, 2013), which appeared as this book was going to press.

2. On the Syriac sources, see Krisztina Szilágyi, "Muhammad and the Monk: The Making of the Christian Bahīrā Legend," *Jerusalem Studies in Arabic and Islam* 34 (2008): 169–214; for a brief discussion of some European versions of the story, see John Tolan, *Saracens: Islam in the Medieval European Imagination* (New York: Columbia University Press, 2002), 139, including one in which the monk is Nestur. See also Stubbe, *Account of the Rise,* 144; Dimmock, *Mythologies,* 29, 45.

3. Uri Rubin, *The Eye of the Beholder: The Life of Muhammad as Viewed by the Early Muslims; A Textual Analysis* (Princeton, NJ: Darwin, 1995).

4. Marilyn Waldman, *Prophecy and Power: Muhammad and the Qur'an in the Light of Comparison,* ed. Bruce B. Lawrence, with Lindsay Jones and Robert M. Baum (Sheffield, UK: Equinox, 2013), 131–135.

5. Safi, *Memories of Muhammad,* 243. See also Robinson, *Islamic Historiography.*

6. Today, when "English is the new Latin in much of Europe" and beyond, the availability of a text in English makes it more likely that its ideas will circulate. David Northrup, *How English Became the Global Language* (New York: Palgrave, 2013), 148.

7. William Murray, trans., *The Life of Mohammed Translated from the Arabic of Abulfeda* (Elgin, Scotland: A. C. Brander, n.d.). It was also printed in London, Edinburgh, and Aberdeen.

8. Lewis, "Gibbon on Muhammad," 94.

9. Lecker, "Glimpses of Muḥammad's Medinan Decade," 63.

10. Robinson, *Islamic Historiography*, 105.

11. Ibid., 65.

12. Brown, *Muhammad*, 87. The book is the *Dalā'il al-Khairāt* of Muḥammad ibn Sulaymān al-Jazūlī (d. 1465); on this, see also Schimmel, *And Muhammad Is His Messenger*, 86.

13. Gustav Weil, *Mohammed der Prophet, sein Leben und seine Lehre: Aus handschriftlichen Quellen und dem Koran geschöpft und dargestellt von Dr. Gustav Weil; mit Beilagen und einer Stammtafel* (Stuttgart: J. B. Metzler, 1843). Lewis, "Gibbon on Muhammad," 93.

14. On the Arabian nights, see Weil, *The Story of Ali Baba and the Forty Thieves: An Extract from Dr. Weil's German Translation of the Arabian Nights* (Boston: D.C. Heath and Co., 1889), 4.

15. In Calcutta, Alfred Kramer published in 1856 an edition of al-Wāqidī's *Book of Campaigns* as *The History of Mohammed's Campaigns by Aboo 'Abdollah Mohammad bin 'Omar al-Wakidy*. Al-Wāqidī, *Life of Muḥammad*, xiii. Julius Wellhausen published "an abbreviated translation" into German based on a different manuscript in 1882. An authoritative Arabic edition was printed in Europe some decades later.

16. Gail Minault, "Aloys Sprenger: German Orientalism's 'Gift' to Delhi College," *South Asia Research* 31 no. 1 (February 2011): 7–23.

17. The expanded German edition was published as *Das Leben und die Lehre des Moḥammad, nach bisher des grösstentheils unbenutzten Quellen bearbeitet*, 2 vols. (Berlin: Nicolaische Verlagsbuchhandlung, 1861). William Muir reviews the portion of the book that discusses his sources as "The Value of Early Mahometan Historical Sources" (1868), republished in Muir, *Mohammedan Controversy*, 103–151; on the shift to scholarly work in German, see Wokoeck, *German Orientalism*, 31; she also cites much of the extensive and growing literature on German Orientalism.

18. Khalidi, *Images of Muhammad*, 247.

19. Thomas Carlyle, *The Hero as Prophet: Mahomet; Islam (Lecture II: Heroes and Hero Worship)* (New York: Maynard, Merrill, and Co., 1882), 11.

20. Ibid.

21. On such conversions, see Umar F. Abd-Allah, *A Muslim in Victorian America: The Life of Alexander Russell Webb* (New York: Oxford University Press, 2006), 69–79.

22. Schimmel, *And Muhammad Is His Messenger*, 229.

23. Khwaja Kamal-ud-Din, *The Ideal Prophet: Aspects of the Life and Qualities of the Holy Prophet Muhammad* (Woking, UK: Ahmadiyya Anjuman Isha'at Islam Lahore, 1925), xii.

24. Ibid., 248.

25. Godfrey Higgins, *An Apology for the Life and Character of the Celebrated Prophet of Arabia, Called Mohammed, or the Illustrious* (London: Rowland Hunter, 1829).

26. Charles Eliot Norton, ed., *The Correspondence of Thomas Carlyle and Ralph Waldo Emerson, 1834–1872* (Boston: James R. Osgood, 1883), 1:293. See also Carlyle, *Hero as Prophet*, 25, where he declares Islam "a confused form of Christianity" and remarks that they share the same "soul," which is to adhere to "the great, deep Law of the World."

27. The phrase is from Khalidi's *Images of Muhammad*.

28. On Orientalism—the history of the term as well as the contests over its meaning—see Robert Irwin, *Dangerous Knowledge: Orientalism and Its Discontents* (New York: Overlook, 2006), esp. 2–8; later portions of the book are devoted to a critique of Edward Said, *Orientalism* (New York: Pantheon, 1978). See also Daniel M. Varisco, *Reading Orientalism: Said and the Unsaid* (Seattle: University of Washington Press, 2007).

29. Muir, "Biographies of Mohammed," in *Mohammedan Controversy*, 100. Avril Powell, *Scottish Orientalists and India: The Muir Brothers, Religion, Education and Empire* (Woodbridge, UK: Boydell, 2010), 94, argues that since he agreed to republish it in 1897, "it may be regarded as encapsulating views on Islam to which he had adhered from his mid-20s, throughout his Indian career and into his late 70s."

30. Muir, "The Mohammedan Controversy" and "Biographies of Mohammed," in *Mohammedan Controversy*.

31. C. J. Lyall, "Obituary Notice: Sir William Muir," *Journal of the Royal Asiatic Society of Great Britain and Ireland* 37 (1905): 875–879.

32. Jabal Muhammad Buaben, *Image of the Prophet Muḥammad in the West: A Study of Muir, Margoliouth, and Watt* (Leicester, UK: Islamic Foundation, 1996); Muhammad Mohar Ali, *Sirat al-Nabi and the Orientalists, with Special Reference to the Writings of William Muir, D. S. Margoliouth and W. Montgomery Watt*, vols. 1A and 1B (Medina: Kingdom of Saudi Arabia Ministry of Islamic Affairs, King Fahd Complex for the Printing of the Holy Qur'an, 1997).

33. Khalidi, *Images of Muhammad*, 249. Edward Said highlights this same element in Muslim readers' (or nonreaders') complaints about *The Satanic Verses*, linking them to Orientalist discourse: "Why must a Moslem . . . represent us so roughly, so expertly, and so disrespectfully to an audience already primed to excoriate our traditions, reality, history, religion, language, and origin? Why . . . must a member of our culture join

the legions of Orientalists in Orientalizing Islam so radically and unfairly?" Quoted in Wendy Steiner, *The Scandal of Pleasure: Art in an Age of
Fundamentalism* (Chicago: University of Chicago Press, 1995), 107; el-
lipses in Steiner.

34. Alan Guenther, "The Image of the Prophet Muhammad as Found
in Missionary Writings of the Late Nineteenth Century," *Muslim World*
90 (Spring 2000): 44.

35. Barbara Daly Metcalf, *Islamic Revival in British India: Deoband,
1860–1900* (New Delhi: Oxford University Press, 2002).

36. Abd-Allah, *A Muslim in Victorian America*, 61; more broadly, on
his correspondence with American convert Alexander Russell Webb,
see pp. 61–65. The major study on the Ahmadiyya is Yohanan Friedmann, *Prophecy Continuous: Aspects of Ahmadi Religious Thought and Its
Medieval Background* (Berkeley: University of California Press, 1989).

37. For an exploration of one such process, see Teena Purohit, *The Aga
Khan Case: Religion and Identity in Colonial India* (Cambridge, MA:
Harvard University Press, 2012).

38. Schimmel, *And Muhammad Is His Messenger*, 157.

39. Ibid.

40. Ricci, *Islam Translated*, 57–58, 231.

41. See Ricci, *Islam Translated*, 241. At the level of popular and especially shrine culture, these intersections and overlaps continue to be negotiated. Schimmel reports (*And Muhammad Is His Messenger*, 192) that a
Hyderabadi Hindu political figure from the first half of the twentieth century "expressed his love of the Prince of Medina [Muhammad] and his
longing for the Rauda [part of his tomb complex], in eloquent Urdu verse."

42. Ishvarchandra Vidyasagar, *Hindu Widow Marriage: An Epochal
Work on Social Reform from Colonial India*, trans. Brian A. Hatcher (New
York: Columbia University Press, 2011).

43. Foreword to Kamal-ud-Din, *Ideal Prophet*.

44. For instance, the introduction to the edited volume *Honor, Violence, Women and Islam* asks: "Why are honour killings and honour-
related violence (HRV) so important to understand? What do such
crimes represent? And how does HRV fit in with Western views and
perceptions of Islam?" Mohammad Mazher Idriss, "Honour, Violence,
Women and Islam: An Introduction," in *Honour, Violence, Women and
Islam*, ed. Mohammad Mazher Idriss and Tahir Abbas (Abingdon,
UK: Routledge 2011), 1–15, quote on p. 1.

45. Syed Ameer Ali, *A Critical Examination of the Life and Teachings of
Mohammed* (London: Williams and Norgate, 1873), viii.

46. Bulandshehri combines the two tacks: condemnation of Orientalist "propaganda" and correction of errors: "This book is also written," his final sentence declares, "keeping in view to correct our educated readers who fell pray [*sic*] to the propaganda spread by the infidels and pagans against Islam which they learn by reading the books of *seerah* written by the so-called European orientalists." Muhammad Ashiq Elahi Bulandshehri, *The Wives of the Prophet Muhammad (sallalahu alayhe wasallam): A Complete Book on the Biographies of the Wives of Holy Prophet Muhammad (sallallahu alayhe wasallam)*, trans. Mohammad Akram (Lahore: Idara-e-Islamiat, 1994), 174.

47. Powell, *Scottish Orientalists and India*, 102.

48. Susan Buck-Morss, *Thinking Past Terror: Islamism and Critical Theory on the Left* (London: Verso, 2006), viii.

49. G[eorge] Lathom Browne, *The Æra of Mahomet:* A.D. 527 to 629 (London: Society for Promoting Christian Knowledge, 1856), 174.

50. John Davenport, *An Apology for Mohammed and the Koran* (London: J. Davy and Sons, 1869), 16. Powell, *Scottish Orientalists and India*, 201, discusses their interactions, noting that in Britain, Davenport had a reputation as a plagiarist.

51. William Muir, *The Life of Mahomet from Original Sources*, 2nd ed. (London: Smith, Elder, and Co., 1878), 57.

52. Ibid.

53. Andrae, *Mohammed*, 115.

54. Quoted in Lewis, "Gibbon on Muhammad," 32. Carlyle writes, "Nothing but a sense of duty could carry any European through the Koran" (*Hero as Prophet*, 31).

55. P[eirce] De Lacy Johnstone, *Muhammad and His Power* (New York: Charles Scribner's Sons, 1908), 153; Matthew Woods, *In Spite of Epilepsy: Caesar, Mohammed, Lord Byron; The Founders Respectively of an Empire, a Religion, and a School of Poetry* (New York: Cosmopolitan Press, 1913), 184.

56. Carlyle, *Hero as Prophet*, 31, 32. See also Washington Irving, *Mahomet and His Successors*, 2 vols. (New York: G. P. Putnam and Son, 1868), 336–337.

57. Carlyle, *Hero as Prophet*, 13.

58. Timothy Blanning, *The Romantic Revolution: A History* (New York: Modern Library, 2012), 28.

59. Carlyle, *Hero as Prophet*, 13.

60. Some Muslim scholars held a more nuanced view of the process of revelation and saw some role, albeit subordinate, for Muhammad's

consciousness in the formulation of revelation. For one modern attempt to recuperate this view, see Fazlur Rahman, *Prophecy in Islam: Philosophy and Orthodoxy* (Chicago: University of Chicago Press, 2011). For the modern tendency to think of Muhammad as nothing more than a "UPS delivery man," see Omid Safi, *Memories of Muhammad: Why the Prophet Matters* (New York: Harper One, 2009), 265.

61. Prideaux had accepted that Muhammad "was in truth, what they say, an *Illiterate Barbarian*"—able neither to read nor to write, and like his countrymen doomed "to continue in the same Ignorance with which they came out of the Mothers Bellies unto their Lives end." Prideaux, *True Nature of Imposture*, 29.

62. Muir, *Life of Mahomet*, 2nd ed., 88.

63. Susannah Heschel, "German Jewish Scholarship on Islam as a Tool for De-Orientalizing Judaism," *New German Critique* 39, no. 3 (Fall 2012): 91–107, at p. 94.

64. Ibid., 91. The rational and purified Islam presented in this scholarship fed back into later Muslim attempts to present a streamlined, rational, purified Islam.

65. In addition to believing that Muhammad had teachers, including Waraqa, Sprenger thought Muhammad owned or at least had access to "a version of portions of the Scriptures, both of the genuine and some of the apocryphal works." Sprenger, *Life of Mohammad*, 100.

66. Dimmock, "Human Head," 83; Browne, *Æra of Mahomet*, iv. The biography of "Mahomet, the Fanatic" covers pp. 117–179, or about one-fourth of the book, which also includes sketches of "Justinian, the Legislator"; "Belisarius, the Conqueror"; "Gregory, the Pope"; "Augustine, the Missionary"; and "Benedict, the Monk."

67. Kidd, *American Christians and Islam*, 13.

68. Yet "he is withal, a moralist by nature"—prohibiting gambling, wine, and female infanticide. Tom Stecker, *The Man Mohammed: A Dramatic Character-Sketch* (n.p.: Co-operative Press, 1900), 15–16. He also refers to "the record of his hybrid creed, the Koran" (16).

69. Harvey Newcomb, *The False Prophet: or, An Account of the Rise and Progress of the Mohammedan Religion; Comprising the History of the Church, etc.*, 2nd ed. (Boston: Massachusetts Sabbath School Society, 1844), 105–106; Prideaux had listed Jews, Christians, and "heathen Arabs" as the sources of Muhammad's religion. Prideaux, *True Nature of Imposture*, 37–38.

70. S. W. Koelle, *Mohammed and Mohammedanism Critically Considered* (London: Rivingtons, 1889), xix.

71. Lane-Poole offers a biographical introduction to a volume of Qur'anic selections and selected hadith. *The Speeches and Table-Talk of the Prophet Mohammad* (London: Macmillan, 1882), liii–liv.

72. The overall assessment wavers: "The guidance was not perfect, we know, and there is much that is blameworthy in Mohammad; but whatever we believe of him, let it be granted that his errors were not the result of premeditated imposition, but were the mistakes of an ignorant, impressible, superstitious, but nevertheless noble and great man." Lane-Poole, *Speeches and Table-Talk*, lv.

73. Browne, *Æra of Mahomet*, 174.

74. Ibid., vol. 1, cv. See also Welch, "Muhammad's Understanding of Himself," 15: Welch declares himself "not yet prepared to render a final judgment" about the trustworthiness of hadith and *sīra* literature but expresses "confiden[ce] that the contents, although not the final arrangement, of the Koran date from the time of Muhammad, and that the Koran is utterly reliable as a historical source, if it is properly interpreted."

75. Lane-Poole, *Speeches and Table-Talk*, liv.

76. Muir, *Life of Mahomet*, 2nd ed., 603.

77. Lane-Poole, *Speeches and Table-Talk*, liv.

78. William Muir, *The Life of Mahomet from Original Sources*, 3rd ed. (London: Smith, Elder, and Company, 1894), v.

79. Powell, *Scottish Orientalists and India*, 128.

80. Schimmel, *And Muhammad Is His Messenger*, 228.

81. Syed Ahmad Khan, *A Series of Essays on the Life of Muhammad and Subjects Subsidiary Thereto* (Lahore: Premier Book House, 1968). The Urdu version was *Khutbat-i Ahmadiyya* [Essays pertaining to Ahmad]. The title is ambiguous; Ahmad can refer to Ahmad Khan but also to Muhammad. The translation was probably mostly done by his son.

82. Powell, *Scottish Orientalists and India*, 202.

83. Bruce Fudge makes a similar point. "Qur'an, Canon, and Literature," in *Sacred Tropes: Tanakh, New Testament, and Qur'an as Literature and Culture*, ed. Roberta Sterman Sabbath (Leiden: Brill, 2009), 41–52. Of the Satanic verses, he notes that they are "found in the Arabic historical tradition, present but not necessarily accepted (usually denied)" (47).

84. Shahab Ahmed, "Ibn Taymiyya and the Satanic Verses," *Studia Islamica* 87 (1998): 67–124.

85. Qur'an 53:20–23.

86. Muir, *Life of Mahomet*, 2nd ed., 88. Similarly, W. Montgomery Watt says that the story is "so strange that it must be true in essentials."

Muhammad: Prophet and Statesman (London: Oxford University Press, 1974 [1961]), 61.

87. Muir, *Mohammadan Controversy*, 123.

88. Ahmad Khan, *Series of Essays*, 221.

89. See Frederick S. Colby, *Narrating Muḥammad's Night Journey: Tracing the Development of the Ibn ʿAbbās Ascension Discourse* (Albany, NY: State University of New York Press, 2008).

90. Ahmad Khan, *Series of Essays*, esp. 347.

91. See, briefly, Schimmel, *And Muhammad Is His Messenger*, 161–162, on this question, and 159–175 on the ascension more generally.

92. Sprenger, *Life of Mohammad*, 136.

93. Colby, *Narrating Muḥammad's Night Journey*, 172–173.

94. See the thirteenth-century Old French *Book of Muhammad's Ladder*. Reginald Hyatte, trans., *The Prophet of Islam in Old French: The Romance of Muhammad (1258) and The Book of Muhammad's Ladder (1264)* (Leiden: Brill, 1997).

95. Schimmel, *And Muhammad Is His Messenger*, 174.

96. For Ahmad Khan, these events did not happen physically but were nonetheless real. On the perfect and divine nature of the Qur'an, which reports (he says) these events, see *Series of Essays*, 272.

97. Muir, "Of Moslem Tradition," in *Mohammedan Controversy*, 123.

98. Ahmad Khan, *Series of Essays*, 212.

99. Ibid., 182.

100. Ibid., vii.

101. Ibid., ix.

102. Ibid., 181.

103. Ibid., 234. Sprenger, *Life of Mohammad*, 118.

104. Timothy Mitchell, *Colonising Egypt* (Berkeley: University of California Press, 1991), 152.

105. In addition to Muir, see also Johnstone, *Muhammad and His Power*, 228–229.

106. Ahmad Khan, *Series of Essays*, 141.

107. Rubin, *Eye of the Beholder*, 66.

108. Ahmad Khan, *Series of Essays*.

109. The argument that Muhammad fulfilled biblical prophecies recurs in modern texts, including those aimed at conversion of non-Muslims to Islam. See, for example, the Ahmadi biography by Sufi Mutiur Rahman Bengalee, *The Life of Muhammad* (Chicago: Moslem Sunrise Press, 1941).

110. Alcofribas Nasier, *The Three Impostors*, trans. anon. (n.p.: privately printed, 1904), 132.

111. Ahmad Khan, *Series of Essays*, 205–206.

112. Ibid., 206.

113. Ali, *Critical Examination*.

114. Syed Ameer Ali, *The Life and Teachings of Mohammed, or the Spirit of Islam* (London: W. H. Allen, 1891).

115. David Samuel Margoliouth, *Mohammed and the Rise of Islam* (New York: G. P. Putnam's Sons, 1905), vii.

116. *Jalā al-qulūb bi dhikr al-mahbūb*. The text dates to 1839. See Powell, *Scottish Orientalists and India*, 31; Guenther, "Response of Sayyid Aḥmad Hān to Sir William Muir's Evaluation of *Ḥadīṯ* Literature," *Oriente Moderno* 82, no. 1 (2002): 221.

117. Schimmel describes this as a reformist text (*And Muhammad Is His Messenger*, 158). On Muhammad as God's beloved, see Schimmel, *And Muhammad Is His Messenger*, 87, 109.

118. Muir, *Mohammedan Controversy*, 76.

119. Mohammad Ali Salmin, *The Holy Prophet Mohammad: The Commander of the Faithful* (Bombay: M. A. Salmin, 1930s), 134.

120. These categories are Omid Safi's. Safi, *Memories of Muhammad*, 265.

121. Salmin, *Holy Prophet Mohammad*, 2. In a similar vein, the title of Indian scholar Ashraf Ali Thanvi's pamphlet on Muhammad's polygamy bears the title *Kasrat-e-Azwaaj-le-Sahib-e-Me'raj*. See Bulandshehri, *Wives of the Prophet Muhammad*, 174.

122. I borrow the phrase "Competitive Hagiography" from Steven Judd, who applies it to early legal figures, noting that one technique for ascribing merit and holiness to them is to liken them to Muhammad. Steven C. Judd, "Competitive Hagiography in Biographies of al-Awzā'ī and Sufyān al-Thawrī," *Journal of the American Oriental Society* 122, no. 1 (2002): 25–37.

123. Diane Robinson-Dunne, *The Harem, Slavery, and British Imperial Culture: Anglo-Muslim Relations in the Late Nineteenth Century* (Manchester, UK: Manchester University Press, 2006), x; Richard King, *Orientalism and Religion: Postcolonial Theory, India, and the Mystic East* (London: Routledge, 1999). See esp. his discussion of "intercultural mimesis."

124. SherAli Tareen, "The Polemic of Shahjahanpur: Religion, Miracles, and History," *Islamic Studies* 51, no. 1 (2012): 49–67, at p. 50. On the gathering, see also Metcalf, *Islamic Revival*, 221–234.

125. Muhammad Ali, "Dottrine e attività dei musulmani Aḥmadiyya di Lahore," *Oriente Moderno* 6, no. 2 (February 1926): 122.

126. For Muhammad's own use of comparative arguments, see Waldman, *Prophecy and Power*.

127. Astérious Argyriou, "Éléments biographiques concernant le prophète Muhammad dans la littérature grecque des trois premiers siècles de l'Hégire," in *La vie du prophète Mahomet*, ed. Toufic Fahd (Paris: Presses universitaires de France, 1983), 159–182, at pp. 162–163.

128. See, for example, Tolan, *Sons of Ishmael*; Cuffel, *Gendering Disgust*.

129. Argyriou, "Éléments biographiques," 166. Note that the author uses the anachronistic category "founders of religion," which is assuredly not in the dialogue attributed to Saint John of Damascus.

130. Argyriou, "Éléments biographiques," 162.

131. Theologically, Muslims believe something different about Muhammad's nature than Christians believe about Christ's nature, but as Clinton Bennett observes, the affective connection and modes of veneration can be similar. See Bennett, *In Search of Muhammad* (London: Cassell, 1998). On polemics about Muhammad, Jesus, and the idea of prophecy, see Mona Siddiqui, *Christians, Muslims, and Jesus* (New Haven, CT: Yale University Press, 2013), 43–50.

132. Rizvi, "Muḥammad in South Asian Biographies," 114.

133. Also, see Ali Dashti, *Twenty-Three Years: A Study of the Prophetic Career of Mohammad*, trans. F. R. C. Bagley (Santa Ana, CA: Mazda, 1994), 7.

134. Higgins, *Apology for the Life*, 21.

135. Ibid., 49–50. Quite a few Egyptian authors would, over the course of the following century, raise similar objections to miracle accounts.

136. For example, Prideaux, *True Nature of Imposture*, 25, 28. Browne, *Æra of Mahomet*, 173, similarly asserts, "Of miracles he makes no claim, beyond the transmission to him of the Koran."

137. Bombay Tract and Book Society, *Life of Mahomet*, 3rd ed. (Bombay, 1856); similarly, Murray, *Life of Mohammed*, 3.

138. Koelle, *Mohammed and Mohammedanism*.

139. Ibid., viii.

140. Ibid., vii.

141. Ibid., x.

142. Ibid., 242; on the modeling of Muhammad after Jesus, see, e.g., Jane Dammen McAuliffe, "Al-Ṭabarī's Prelude to the Prophet," in *Al-Ṭabarī: A Medieval Muslim Historian and His Work*, ed. Hugh Kennedy (Princeton, NJ: Darwin, 2008), 123–126, 129.

143. Sprenger absolves Muhammad of claiming an ability to perform most sorts of miracles; his enemies were responsible for circulating some of them: "When the conservatives of Makka had at length succumbed to the arms of Mohammad, he forced his religion on them, and they found it expedient to profess that they had been convinced by miracles, and not by the sword." He was not entirely blameless, though; Sprenger thought Muhammad himself "fostered" belief in the descent of the spirit to him in the form of Gabriel, and possibly about the night journey and ascension. *Life of Mohammad*, 138.

144. Koelle, *Mohammed and Mohammedanism*, 243–44.

145. Ibid., 245.

146. Rizvi, "Muḥammad in South Asian Biographies," 113.

147. Bombay Tract and Book Society, *Life of Mahomet*.

148. Kidd, *American Christians and Islam*, 47.

149. See, for example, ibid., 54: Cyrus Hamlin, once a leader of the American Board of Commissioners for Foreign Missions in Turkey, eventually left the organization, having come to believe that "direct evangelism was unnecessary and possibly counterproductive; civilization and educational and commercial progress would, over time, necessarily bring Christianization."

150. Irvin Schick, *The Erotic Margin: Spatiality and Sexuality in Alterist Discourse* (London: Verso, 1999), 25.

151. Tomoko Masuzawa, *The Invention of World Religions, or How European Universalism Was Preserved in the Language of Pluralism* (Chicago: University of Chicago Press, 2005).

152. Ameer Ali, *Critical Examination*, 19.

153. Ibid., 18.

154. Ibid., 25.

3. Eminent Muslims

1. Schimmel, *And Muhammad Is His Messenger*, 181–187, at p. 186. The quotations from the *Burda* are pp. 186–187, translated by Arthur Jeffery. A more recent translation has been done by American Muslim Hamza Yusuf, sold with CDs of performance of the ode (in Arabic) by the Fez Singers.

2. For example, in mid-eighteenth-century America, Jonathan Edwards wrote of "Mahomet's pretences to intercourse with heaven, and his success in rapine, murder, and violence" as the foundation of Islam. Edwards, quoted in Kidd, *American Christians and Islam*, 17. See also John Tolan, "European Accounts of Muḥammad's Life," in *Cambridge*

Companion, ed. Brockopp, 226–250; Tolan, *Saracens;* Frederick Quinn, *The Sum of All Heresies: The Image of Islam in Western Thought* (New York: Oxford University Press, 2008).

3. Muir, *Life of Mahomet,* 2nd ed., 172.

4. Sprenger, *Life of Mohammad,* 174.

5. Ibid., 184.

6. Ali, *Critical Examination,* 150.

7. This spirit is reflected in M. Sharif Ahmad Amini, *Muhammad: The Most Successful Prophet* (Calcutta: Asian Printers, 1978).

8. Davenport, *Apology for Mohammed,* 54.

9. Ibid., 81.

10. Quoted in Kidd, *American Christians and Islam,* 37.

11. Fisk, quoted in ibid., 37; Irwin, *Dangerous Knowledge,* 65.

12. Kidd, *American Christians and Islam,* 46.

13. Bush, *Life of Mohammed,* 18, 19.

14. Murray, *Life of Mohammed.*

15. Bush, *Life of Mohammed,* 160–161. This is at least the second use of the phrase "roving tribes of Arabia" (18).

16. Lane-Poole, *Speeches and Table-Talk,* xxxiii–xxxiv.

17. Ibid., xi. Rodinson, *Mahomet* (77), saw a passionate and nervous temperament behind a decorous and stately façade.

18. Sprenger, *Life of Mohammed,* vii, x, xi. Having declared his intent to "acquaint" his readers with Muhammad's character, Sprenger launches into a lengthy description of his physical appearance (84), habits, and "temperament," which he pronounces, like the physician he is, "melancholic, and in the highest degree nervous" (89). In some respects, Sprenger does recognize some positive behaviors in Muhammad, but assigns the praise to others. For instance, he credits Muhammad's "extraordinary firmness and perseverance" in the face of opposition to "the endurance of his wife Khadyjah" (91).

19. Ibid., 89.

20. William Muir, "Value of Early Mahometan Historical Sources," originally published in the *Calcutta Review* (1868), republished in *Mohammedan Controversy,* quote from pp. 103–104.

21. Ibid. See xii (Arab wildness) and xiv (wives).

22. Gerald MacLean, "Milton among the Muslims," in *The Religions of the Book: Christian Perceptions, 1400–1600,* ed. Dimmock and Hadfield (New York: Palgrave, 2008), 180–194, at p. 182.

23. Ibid., 183.

24. Andrae, *Mohammed,* 12. However, Andrae objects to a certain "calculating slyness" on Muhammad's part, saying that one incident "reveals a trait of his character which is particularly uncongenial to the ideals of manliness of the Nordic races" (142).

25. Carlyle, for instance, has Muhammad threatened and vulnerable, and then "the wild Son of the Desert resolved to defend himself, like a man and an Arab." Carlyle, *Hero as Prophet,* 29.

26. Said, *Orientalism;* Schick, *Erotic Margin.* Kidd, *American Christians and Islam,* 14, writes of "the multiple uses of Muhammad in early America: He could be portrayed as an example of a graceless legalist or a wild enthusiast, depending on the rhetorical need of the moment."

27. Woods, by contrast, asserts, "If he, Mohammed, assumed a false commission, it was in order to inculcate salutary doctrines." (*In Spite of Epilepsy,* 130)

28. Muir, *Life of Mahomet,* 2nd ed., 311–312, 315–316, 318–319.

29. Johnstone, *Muhammad and His Power,* 226; similarly, Irving, *Mahomet and His Successors,* 337.

30. Muir, *Life of Mahomet,* 2nd ed., 320, 321. For instance, in the final chapter of the final volume of Muir's *Life,* "The Person and Character of Mahomet," negative traits follow positive ones. After a few headings concerned with appearance, "gait," and habits, this alternation leaves the reader with a negative impression and the sense that the presentation has been thoughtful and balanced. For instance, "Urbanity and kindness of disposition," "Friendship," and "Moderation and magnanimity" are followed by "Cruelty towards his enemies" and "Craftiness and perfidy." The section "Domestic life; polygamy" begins: "In domestic life the conduct of Mahomet, with one grave exception, was exemplary."

31. Ghulam Malik, *Muhammad: An Islamic Perspective* (Lanham, MD: University Press of America, 1996), 153–154.

32. Fakir Syed Waheed-Ud-Din, *The Benefactor,* trans. Faiz Ahmed Faiz (World Community of Islam in the West, n.d. [1964]). This edition lists the publisher as World Community of Islam in the West, the name that Warith Deen Muhammad gave his community when he reshaped the Nation of Islam in the mid-1970s. It later became the American Muslim Mission and eventually the Muslim American Society. This book was published, with translation by Faiz Ahmed Faiz, in 1964, before that name was in use; presumably it is a later printing. One online source lists the publisher for the 1964 edition as the "Lost-Found Nation of Islam." Later editions (Chicago: Kazi Publications, 1987, 1995) give the

title as *The Benefactor and the Rightly Guided,* referring to the inclusion of accounts of the first four caliphs as well. For Napoleon's own view of Muhammad, see Tolan, "European Accounts," 244–245.

33. Edward E. Curtis IV, *Black Muslim Religion in the Nation of Islam, 1960–1975* (Chapel Hill: University of North Carolina Press, 2006), 79–85; Edward Curtis, personal communication, November 2013.

34. Waheed-Ud-Din, *Benefactor,* vi. The original Urdu publication mentioned the first four caliphs in the title, as did at least one later English edition.

35. Tolan, *Sons of Ishmael,* xi, discussing ninth- to fourteenth-century Christian European polemical texts: "Such texts were only rarely addressed to readers of the rival faith: more commonly, they were meant to persuade vacillating Christians of the superiority of their religion to Islam, in order to prevent them from converting to Islam or in order to convince them of the justice and necessity of wars against Muslims."

36. On Muhammad as statesman and prophet, see Cook, *Muhammad,* 2, 51. On another set of competing identities, between "ethnic warner" and "messenger sent to restore" the pure monotheistic faith of Abraham, see Cook, *Muhammad,* 39.

37. Malik, *Muhammad,* 153–154.

38. The Qur'anic phrase is *uswa ḥasana* (Q. 33:21), also meaning "a good pattern."

39. Safi, *Memories of Muhammad,* 290.

40. Robinson-Dunn, *Harem, Slavery and British Imperial Culture,* 8.

41. Rizvi, "Muḥammad in South Asian Biographies," 121. See also Muhammad Qasim Zaman, "A Venture in Critical Islamic Historiography and the Significance of Its Failure," *Numen* 41, no. 1 (January 1994): 26–50.

42. On the role of Urdu for Indian intellectuals, see Metcalf, *Islamic Revival.*

43. Schimmel, *And Muhammad Is His Messenger,* 229.

44. On these trends, see Northrup, *How English Became;* David Bellos, *Is That a Fish in Your Ear? Translation and the Meaning of Everything* (New York: Faber and Faber, 2011).

45. Ira D. Gruber, *Books and the British Army in the Age of the American Revolution* (Chapel Hill: University of North Carolina Press, 2010), 235; Gruber's context is different, but the observation applies.

46. Charles D. Smith, *Islam and the Search for Social Order in Modern Egypt: A Biography of Muhammad Husayn Haykal* (Albany: State University of New York Press, 1983), 38.

47. Ibid., 56–57.

48. Muḥammad Ḥusayn Haykal, *Tarājim Miṣrīyah wa-gharbīyah* [Egyptian and Western biographies] (Cairo: Maṭbaʿat al-Siyāsah, 1929), 144. The portrait of Cleopatra is an image of a Western sculpture, reclining and nude. See also Smith, *Islam and the Search*, 97; Smith observes Haykal's deliberate omission of "the Islamic period," instead jumping from pre-Islamic to "the Khedive who committed Egypt to the European path."

49. Quotation from back cover of book.

50. Mitchell, *Colonising Egypt*, 131. The partial quotation is from Ḥusayn al-Marsafī's 1881 *Risālat al-kalim al-thaman*.

51. Israel Gershoni, "Theory of Crises," in *Middle Eastern Historiographies: Narrating the Twentieth Century*, ed. Israel Gershoni, Amy Singer, and Y. Hakan Erdem (Seattle: University of Washington Press, 2006), 315.

52. Muḥammad Ḥusayn Haykal, *The Life of Muḥammad*, trans. Ismail Al Faruqi (Kuala Lampur: Islamic Book Trust, 2002 [1976]), xxviii.

53. Ibid.

54. Khalidi, *Images of Muhammad*.

55. Ibid.

56. On his near contemporary al-Dhahabī (d. 1348), see Robinson, *Islamic Historiography*, 64–65.

57. Muḥammad Ḥusayn Haykal, *Al-Ṣiddīq Abū Bakr* [Abū Bakr the Righteous], 6th ed. (Egypt: Dār al-Maʿārif, 1971); *Al-Fārūq ʿUmar* [ʿUmar the Just] (Cairo: Maktabat al-Nahḍah al-Miṣrīyah, 1963–1964); *ʿUthmān ibn ʿAffān: Bayna al-khilāfah wa-al-mulk* [ʿUthmān ibn ʿAffān: Between caliphate and kingship] (Beirut: Dār al-Kutub al-ʿIlmīyah, 2007). At 141 pages, the book on ʿUthmān is less than half the length of the earlier works.

58. On this book see Hoda Elsadda, "Discourses of Women's Biographies and Cultural Identity: Twentieth Century Representations of the Life of ʿAʾisha bint Abi Bakr," *Feminist Studies* 27, no. 1 (2001): 37–64, esp. pp. 47–50. On the controversy it generated over Aisha's age, see Jonathan A. C. Brown, *Misquoting Muhammad: The Challenges and Choices of Interpreting the Prophet's Legacy* (Oxford: Oneworld, forthcoming).

59. Mervat F. Hatem, "'Aʾisha Abdel Rahman: An Unlikely Heroine: A Post-Colonial Reading of Her Life and Some of Her Biographies of Women in the Prophetic Household," *Journal of Middle East Women's Studies* 7, no. 2 (Spring 2011): 1–26, at p. 12; Elsadda, "Discourses of Women's Biographies," 49.

60. Israel Gershoni and James P. Jankowsi, *Redefining the Egyptian Nation, 1930–1945* (Cambridge: Cambridge University Press, 2002), 59.

61. Muir, *Mohammedan Controversy*, 68.

62. Ruth Roded, "Gender in an Allegorical Life of Muḥammad: Mahfouz's *Children of Gebelawi*," *Muslim World* 93 (January 2003): 118; also Antonie Wessels, *A Modern Arabic Biography of Muḥammad: A Critical Study of Muḥammad Ḥusayn Haykal's* Ḥayāt Muḥammad (Leiden: Brill, 1972), 1–2. On these biographies, see also E. S. Sabanegh, *Muhammad b. Abdallah, "Le Prophete": Portraits contemporains, Egypte 1930–1950* (Paris: Librairie J. Vrin, n.d.).

63. 'Ā'isha 'Abd al-Raḥmān [Bint al-Shāṭi'], *The Wives of the Prophet*, trans. Matti Moosa and D. Nicholas Ranson (Lahore: Muhammad Ashraf, 1971); Wessels, *Modern Arabic Biography*, 31; Ruth Roded, "Bint Al-Shati's 'Wives of the Prophet': Feminist or Feminine?" *British Journal of Middle Eastern Studies* 33, no. 1 (May 2006): 51–66; and Roded, "Muslim Women Reclaim the Life-Story of the Prophet: 'Ā'isha 'Abd al-Raḥmān, Assia Djebar, and Nadia Yassine," *Muslim World* 103, no. 3 (July 2013): 334–346; see esp. 335, n. 6, which lists relevant recent publications.

64. On Amin, see William Shepard, *The Faith of a Modern Muslim Intellectual: The Religious Aspects and Implications of the Writings of Ahmad Amin* (New Delhi: Indian Institute of Islamic Studies/Vikas, 1982). See also his autobiography, Aḥmad Amīn, *Aḥmad Amīn: My Life*, trans. Issa J. Boullata (Leiden: Brill, 1978).

65. Gustave von Grunebaum, quoted in Issa J. Boullata, introduction to *Aḥmad Amīn*, ix.

66. Shepard, *Faith of a Modern Muslim Intellectual*, 194.

67. Boullata, introduction, xiii.

68. Amīn, *Aḥmad Amīn*, 220.

69. Boullata, introduction, xiii. Like others of his time, "by comparison of cultures, he arrived at a better understanding of his own and discovered for himself some salient areas of pride in it and others of necessary reform" (ix).

70. Afazlur Rahman, *Muhammad as a Military Leader* (London: Muslim Schools Trust, 1980), 190. A more measured assessment of Muhammad's military skills can be found in Rodgers, *The Generalship of Muhammad*.

71. Salmin, *Holy Prophet Mohammad*, 153.

72. Browne, *Æra of Mahomet*, 160.

73. Ibid., 161–162.

74. Salmin, *Holy Prophet Mohammad*, 152.

75. Ibid., 153. A studiously noncritical account of Muhammad as "military strategist and warrior" appears in Elsa Marston, *Muhammad of Mecca: Prophet of Islam* (New York: Franklin Watts, 2001), 71–73.

76. Maxime Rodinson, "A Critical Survey of Modern Studies on Muhammad," in *Studies on Islam*, ed. and trans. Merlin Swartz (New York: Oxford University Press, 1981), 23–85, at p. 27. On Dermenghem, see Gunny, *The Prophet Muhammad in French and English Literature*, 213–215.

77. Al Faruqi's 1976 English translation is just under six hundred pages of text, plus nearly one hundred pages of prefaces and additional endnotes.

78. Smith, *Islam and the Search*, 114.

79. Muḥammad Ḥusayn Haykal, *Ḥayāt Muḥammad* (Cairo: Maṭbaʻat Miṣr, 1935), 3–5.

80. Ch. Vial, "Muḥammad Ḥusayn Haykal," in *Encyclopaedia of Islam*, 2nd ed., ed. P. Bearman et al. (Leiden: Brill, 2011).

81. Muḥammad Ḥusayn Haykal, *Sirat-i Rasul*, trans. Muḥammad Vāris Kāmil. (Lahore: Maktabah-yi Kāravāṇ, 1964). A more recent edition bears the title *Hayat-i Muhammad*.

82. On Haykal's reception in contemporary Indonesia, see Anna M. Gade, "Religious Biography of the Prophet Muḥammad in Twenty-First-Century Indonesia," in *Cambridge Companion*, ed. Brockopp, 254–258, 272–273.

83. See also Gershoni, "Theory of Crises."

84. Charles D. Smith, "*Hayat Muhammad* and the Muslim Brothers: Two Interpretations of Egyptian Islam and Their Socioeconomic Implications," *Journal of the American Research Center in Egypt* 16 (1979): 175–181, at p. 175.

85. Smith, *Islam and the Search*, 9.

86. Ibid., 41.

87. Ibid., 41–42; he refers to "wahy."

88. These have been ably sketched in Wessels, *Modern Arabic Biography*.

89. Rizvi, "Muḥammad in South Asian Biographies," 113.

90. Khalidi, *Images of Muhammad*, 248; Smith, *Islam and the Search*, 17. On the translation, see Tageldin, "Secularizing Islam: Carlyle, al-Sibāʻī, and the Translations of 'Religion' in British Egypt," *PMLA* 126, no. 1 (January 2011), 124: "Nowhere is the power of the religious to attract the Egyptian Muslim intellect to secularity more evident than in al-Sibāʻī's seminal Arabic translation of Thomas Carlyle's *On Heroes, Hero-Worship, and the Heroic in History*, published in Cairo in 1911." Also see Tageldin, *Disarming Words*.

91. Edith Grossman, *Why Translation Matters* (New Haven, CT: Yale University Press, 2010), 8.

92. See Tageldin, "Secularizing Islam."

93. Louis Awad, *The Literature of Ideas in Egypt, Pt. 1* (Atlanta: Scholars Press, 1986), 169.

94. Ibid., 186.

95. Ibid., 187.

96. Ibid.

97. Ibid., 188.

98. Yaseen Noorani, *Culture and Hegemony in the Colonial Middle East* (New York: Palgrave, 2010), 1; Mittermaier, *Dreams That Matter,* likewise points out that we are not dealing with tradition versus modernity but a very specifically shaped modernity (168–174).

99. Noorani, *Culture and Hegemony,* 2.

100. Samira Haj, *Reconfiguring Islamic Tradition: Rationality, Reform, and Modernity* (Stanford, CA: Stanford University Press, 2009), 128–136, quotation at p. 128.

101. Smith, *Islam and the Search,* 204, n. 16.

102. Pierre Bayard, *How to Talk about Books You Haven't Read,* trans. Jeffrey Mehlman (New York: Bloomsbury, 2007).

103. Wessels, *Modern Arabic Biography,* 199.

104. Ibid., 196.

105. Wessels, *Modern Arabic Biography,* 228–229.

106. Gunny, *The Prophet Muhammad in French and English Literature,* 214.

107. Bernard E. Dold, *Carlyle, Goethe, and Muhammad* (Messina, Italy: Edizioni Dott. Anotonino Sfameni, 1984), 75.

108. For Haykal's reliance on Muir, see Wessels, *Modern Arabic Biography.* Broadly on Orientalist use of Arabic sources, and vice versa, with a specific reference to Theodor Nöldeke and Jalāl al-Dīn al-Suyūṭī, see Ahmad Atif Ahmad, *Islam, Modernity, Violence, and Everyday Life* (New York: Palgrave Macmillan, 2009), 29–34.

109. On a similar "intermingling of texts," see Lyons, *Islam through Western Eyes,* 170–171.

110. Haykal, *Life of Muḥammad,* 557.

111. Smith, *Islam and the Search,* 129.

112. Haykal, *Life of Muḥammad,* 108.

113. Ibid., 105. Similarly, he rejects the story of Muhammad's marriage to Zaynab. For ʿAbd al-Raḥmān's refutation of his analysis, see *Wives of*

the Prophet, 146–151. For other biographers on the marriage to Zaynab, see Chapter 4.

114. Haykal, *Life of Muhammad,* 107.

115. This succinct formulation is Tageldin's. Tageldin, *Disarming Words,* 173.

116. 'Abd al-'Aziz Duri, *The Rise of Historical Writing among the Arabs* (Princeton, NJ: Princeton University Press, 1983), 8–9.

117. Smith, *Islam and the Search,* 5.

118. See Ibn Ishaq, *Life of Muhammad,* 21. Ruth Warren takes the work of shepherding as a realistic possibility while treating the "miraculous happenings" recounted during Muhammad's youth with his foster mother as "legends similar to those which grow up in afteryears [*sic*] about great religious leaders." Warren, *Muhammad: Prophet of Islam,* 8.

119. Khalidi, *Images of Muhammad,* points to this phrase or a variant repeatedly (e.g., pp. 10, 158).

120. Smith, *Islam and the Search,* 5.

121. Ibid.

122. Ibid., 6.

123. Tageldin, *Disarming Words,* 164.

4. The Wife of Muhammad

1. A sampling, by no means comprehensive, would include the following: Peterson, *Muhammad,* 44–45; Warren, *Muhammad,* 11; Feisal Abdul Rauf, *Moving the Mountain: A New Vision of Islam in America* (New York: Free Press, 2012), 108; Marston, *Muhammad of Mecca,* 24; John Bagot Glubb, *The Life and Times of Muhammad* (New York: Cooper Square Press, 2001 [1970]), 72–75; G. N. Jalbani, *Life of the Holy Prophet* (Islamabad: National Hijra Council, 1988), 13 (mentioning, unusually, M. M. Pickthall, *The Life of the Prophet Muhammad: A Brief History* [Beltsville, MD: Amana Publications, 1998], 9 [originally published in 1930 as an introduction to his Qur'an translation]); Eliot Weinberger, *Muhammad* (New York: Verso, 2006), 29; Ziauddin Sardar, *Muhammad: All that Matters* (London: Hodder, 2012), 33–34; Rizvi, "Muhammad in South Asian Biographies," 100; Golam W. Choudhury, *The Prophet Muhammad: His Life and Eternal Message,* 2nd ed. (Kuala Lumpur: WHS Publications 1994 [1993]), 24–25; Watt, *Muhammad,* 12–13 (of her age, he writes, "perhaps this is only a round figure, and she may have been somewhat younger"); Karen Armstrong, *Muhammad: A Prophet for Our Time* (New York: Harper One, 2007), 25–26; Malik,

Muhammad, 10–11; Brown, *Muhammad*, 11. Similar material appears in a different format in Shahid Zafar Qasmi, *Questions and Answers on the Mothers of Believers (May Allah Be Pleased with Them)*, rev. Muhammad Tahir Salafi (Riyadh: Darussalam, 1997), 9–12; Siddiqui, *Life of Muhammad*, 52–53; and Mehru Jaffer, *The Book of Muhammad* (New Delhi: Penguin Global, 2010), 63, 65–66. Jaffer gives a slightly overwrought description of the interest Khadija ("a rich widow who was forty years old and managed a booming business in import and export") developed in Muhammad: "Khadija's curiosity was killing her. She wanted to see the man whose praises she heard sung by the whole town. She asked her minions to seek Muhammad out" (63). Armstrong, *Prophet for Our Time*, 24–25, is typical in every regard except that she puts Khadija's age "probably in her late thirties" without further comment. My entry on Khadija for the *Oxford Encyclopedia of Women in World History* ("Khadija bint Khuwaylid," 2007) follows much the same approach if in slightly more detail. Earlier English-language works present similar information but not usually in such a narrowly predetermined way. See, for example, Stubbe, *Account of the Rise*, 74–76, 139; George Sale, in the preliminary discourse introducing his English translation of the Qur'an, gives a slightly different account (Sale, *The Alcoran of Mohammed*, 1:50–51). Davenport, *Apology for Mohammed*, 13, gives Muhammad's age as twenty-eight and Khadija's as forty; Bush, *Life of Mohammed*, 43–44, gives the now-familiar account of Muhammad's marriage to "a rich trading widow of his native city, who had been twice married, and whose name was CADIJAH." Newcomb, *False Prophet*, 68, echoes Bush on their respective ages: she "forty" and he "twenty-eight."

2. Russ Rodgers emphasizes this element in his account of the marriage. *The Generalship of Muhammad* (Jacksonville: University Press of Florida, 2012), 35–36.

3. M. J. Kister, "The Sons of Khadīja," *Jerusalem Studies in Arabic and Islam* 16 (1993): 69–75, surveys premodern reports about Muhammad and Khadija's male children, which are, like reports about the spouses' respective ages, "divergent and contradictory" (83). He favors the early view that Khadija bore Muhammad only one male child (85).

4. Khalidi, *Images of Muhammad*, 76.

5. The use of an intermediary, derived from Ibn Sa'd and repeated by earlier authors, appears infrequently in recent texts. Emerick, who does mention it (*Muhammad*, 44) falls into anachronism when he describes Nafisa as Khadija's "best friend"; the most recent edition of Aḥmad, *Life of Muhammad*, 22, uses "a woman friend of hers." See also Deepak

Chopra, *Muhammad: A Story of the Last Prophet* (New York: Harper One, 2010), 98.

6. The quotation is from Sprenger, *Life of Mohammad*, 82.

7. Dimmock, *Mythologies*, 34. On the marriage to Khadija, see pp. 29, 40, 44, 46, 58–59, 62. The notion that Muhammad married Khadija seeking wealth may originate in the Iraqi Christian apology *Risālat al-Kindī*, probably from the tenth century. Tolan, "European Accounts," 233.

8. *Al-sīra al-nabawīya, Sīrat al-nabī*, or *Sīrat rasūl allāh*.

9. M. M. Bravmann, *The Spiritual Background of Early Islam: Studies in Ancient Arab Concepts* (Leiden: Brill, 2009 [1972]), 128–130; see, more generally, 123–139.

10. ʿAbbās Maḥmūd al-ʿAqqād, *Abqariyat Muḥammad* [The genius of Muhammad] (Cairo: Maṭbaʿat al-Istiqāma, 1942), 166–70 (*al-raʾīs*), 172–219 (*al-zawj*).

11. Variables include whether one counts unconsummated marriages and whether certain women were wives or enslaved concubines.

12. Lyons, *Islam through Western Eyes*, ch. 6 and literature cited there; for a rebuttal, see Ama F. Shabazz, "The Prophet on the Treatment of Women," *Message International*, August–September 2002, 37–39. Armstrong argues for Muhammad's concern: "the emancipation of women was a project dear to the Prophet's heart," though some male Muslims "resolutely opposed" it. *Muhammad: A Prophet for Our Time*, 135. See also Fatima Mernissi, *The Veil and the Male Elite: A Feminist Interpretation of Women's Rights in Islam*, trans. Mary Jo Lakeland (New York: Perseus, 1991). For a thorough exploration of these issues, see Lila Abu Lughod, *Do Muslim Women Need Saving?* (Cambridge, MA: Harvard University Press, 2013).

13. Ibn Saʿd, *Women of Madina*.

14. Matthew Pierce, "Remembering Fāṭimah: New Means of Legitimizing Female Authority in Contemporary Shīʿī Discourse," in *Women, Leadership, and Mosques: Changes in Contemporary Islamic Authority*, ed. Masooda Bano and Hilary Kalmbach (Leiden: Brill, 2012), 345–362.

15. Ibn Hishām, *Al-Sīra al-nabawīya* (Al-Mansura, Egypt: Dar al-Ghadd al-Jadeed, 2003), 157; also Guillaume, *Life of Muhammad*, 82.

16. The story is told in Ibn Saʿd and is reported by, among others, al-Ṭabarī, *The History of al-Ṭabarī*, vol. 6, *Muhammad at Mecca*, trans. W. Montgomery Watt and M. V. McDonald (Albany: State University Press of New York, 1989), 49, who reports it on the authority of al-Wāqidī, noting that he considers it an error. See also Andrae, *Mohammed*, 41; Sprenger, *Life of Mohammad*, 83. Betty Kelen, *Muhammad: The*

Messenger of God (New York: Pocket Books, 1997), 13–15, repeats it, confusing the uncle and the father.

17. Bulandshehri, *Wives of the Prophet Muhammad,* 16.

18. Al-Ṭabarī, *History of al-Ṭabarī,* vol. 6, 47. Ibn Hishām, *Al-Sīra al-nabawīya.* See also Kister, "Sons of Khadīja," 66–69. Khalidi, *Images of Muhammad,* 75, is among the rare modern scholars who include variant ages for Khadija. Tariq Ramadan likewise makes note of it, though he, too, ignores the symbolism. *In the Footsteps of the Prophet: Lessons from the Life of Muhammad* (New York: Oxford University Press, 2007), 23. See also Glubb, *Life and Times of Muhammad,* 75.

19. Ibn Saʿd, *Women of Madina,* 9.

20. Notably, Islamic jurists set fifteen as the presumptive age by which menarche will be assumed to have been reached; it is also the age at which a boy is presumed sufficiently mature to undertake jihad—though biological signs of maturity count as well.

21. Al-Ṭabarī, *History of al-Ṭabarī,* vol. 6, 60–61. One explanation of the discrepancy is a three-year gap between the commission of prophecy (at forty) and the commencement of Qurʾanic revelation (at forty-three).

22. Lawrence Conrad, "Abraha and Muḥammad: Some Observations Apropos of Chronology and Literary "Topoi" in the Early Arabic Historical Tradition," *Bulletin of the School of Oriental and African Studies, University of London* 50, no. 2 (1987): 225–240, at p. 230. For its symbolic associations, see esp. 231–232; on Khadija's age, 236. For a related point on Muhammad, Abu Bakr, and Umar's ages at death, see the "Chronology" in Rubin, *Eye of the Beholder,* 209–211. Similarly, the gospel statement "that Jesus was about thirty" was "just the conventional way of saying that he was fully adult." Garry Wills, *What Jesus Meant* (New York: Viking, 2006), 5. On the use of forty, see also Schimmel, *And Muhammad Is His Messenger,* 117; she points out that the number forty corresponds in Arabic numerology to the letter *m* for Muhammad.

23. Sprenger, *Life of Mohammad;* D. A. Spellberg, *Politics, Gender, and the Islamic Past* (New York: Columbia University Press, 1996), 216, n. 5. Betty Kelen, *Muhammad,* 15, gives the usual story and then suggests that "since she bore him seven children," she "might have been somewhat younger, perhaps in her thirties."

24. Of course, pious authors might note that divine intervention can override biological norms.

25. Safi, *Memories of Muhammad,* 100, for these three "movements." Lesley Hazelton views the Mount Hirāʾ encounter as "the pivotal point of his life." Hazelton, *The First Muslim: The Story of Muhammad* (New

York: Riverhead Books, 2013), 11. For the view that the *hijra* to Medina was the most significant act of Muhammad's career, see Ismail R. Al Faruqi, *The Hijrah: The Necessity of Its* Iqāmat *or Vergegenw'artigung* (Islamabad: National Hijra Council, 1985). Nasr, *Muhammad,* 37, refers to the ascension as "the spiritual crowning of the Blessed Prophet's life" but then emphasizes the migration as "a new phase in the life of the Blessed Prophet as leader of a human society and a person immersed in the life of action" (40).

26. Guillaume, *Life of Muhammad,* 107; the quoted phrase is Guillaume's interpolation from al-Ṭabarī.

27. Sale, *The Alcoran of Mohammed,* 1:56, gives the same general story but without any references to her comforting him; instead, she is gladdened.

28. For a polemical version of this story, see Tolan, "European Accounts," 228–229.

29. Guillaume, *Life of Muhammad,* 106–107; another version of the story is told near the section on Khadija's marriage (Ibn Hishām, *Al-Sīra al-nabawīya,* 159; Guillaume, *Life of Muhammad,* 83). For Khadija's role after the first revelation, see also al-Ṭabarī, *History of al-Ṭabarī,* vol. 6, 67–77.

30. Ibn Hishām, *Al-Sīra al-nabawīya,* 193, my translation; Guillaume, *Life of Muhammad,* 155.

31. Jalbani, *Life of the Holy Prophet,* 20.

32. Ahmad Thompson, *The Wives of the Prophet Muhammad: May the Blessings and Peace of Allah Be on Him and His Family and Companions* (London: Ta-Ha Publishers, 2004 [1993]), 1.

33. "Kānat malak raḥma." The Arabic text includes both *fatḥa*s (short vowel *a* markers) on the word *malak.* Haykal, *Ḥayāt Muḥammad,* 189; Haykal, *Life of Muḥammad,* 136.

34. Stanley Lane Poole, introduction to *Selections from the Ḳur-án,* by Edward William Lane, rev. ed. (London: Trübner, 1879), liii.

35. Syed Ameer Ali, *Spirit of Islam,* 115. The sentence "She was ever his angel of hope and consolation" appears in quotation marks but without attribution.

36. Siddiqui, *Life of Muhammad,* 53.

37. Jalbani, *Life of the Holy Prophet,* 15.

38. J. W. H. Stobart, *Islam and Its Founder* (London and New York: Society for Promoting Christian Knowledge, 1895), 57.

39. Shamim Aleem, *Prophet Muhammad (S) and His Family: A Sociological Perspective* (Bloomington, IN: AuthorHouse, 2007), 8.

40. Driss Chraibi, *L'homme du livre* (Paris: Éditions Denoël, 2011 [1995]), 16.

41. Sara Pursley, "Daughters of the Right Path: Family Law, Homosocial Publics, and the Ethics of Intimacy in the Works of Shi'i Revivalist Bint al-Huda," *Journal of Middle East Women's Studies* 8, no. 2 (Spring 2012): 51–77. Pursley points out that "the valorization of Khadija conforms to historical Shi'i evaluations of the Prophet's wives, though that may simply have made it a more effective vehicle for expressing the author's distaste for polygamy" (74, n. 7; 51–77).

42. Reynolds, *Interpreting the Self,* 79–80.

43. See, for example, al-Ṭabarī, *History of al-Ṭabarī,* vol. 39, *Biographies of the Prophet's Companions and Their Successors,* trans. Ella Landau-Tasseron, 176 (regarding Aisha and Umm Salama).

44. See David S. Powers, *Zayd* (Philadelphia: University of Pennsylvania Press, forthcoming); al-Ṭabari, *History of al-Ṭabarī,* vol. 39, 65, n. 299.

45. Nasr, *Muhammad,* 18.

46. Muhammad Anis-ur-Rahman, *The Historical Role of the Venerable Woman,* 3rd ed., enlarged (Karachi: Faran Publications, 2007), 44, 52.

47. Ibid., 32.

48. Ibid., 86. See also 44, 57, 63.

49. Anis-ur-Rahman writes, "*The first lady of Islam should be a working woman as to give lead to the women community of the world who were to come in the fold of Islam.* So a great woman was brought by the historical forces under the command of the providence to be married to the Holy Prophet." Ibid., 74. Italics in original.

50. Ibid., 57.

51. Tamam Kahn, *Untold: A History of the Wives of Prophet Muhammad* (Rhinebeck, NY: Monkfish, 2010), 16, 29.

52. Siddiqui, *Life of Muhammad,* 52–53. Italics in original.

53. Malik, *Muhammad,* 10.

54. Davenport, *Apology for Mohammed,* 23–24; quotation at p. 24.

55. Carlyle, *Hero as Prophet,* 22; Davenport, *Apology for Mohammed,* 13.

56. Irving, *Mahomet and His Successors,* 109.

57. Rodinson, *Mahomet,* 79; *Muhammad,* 55.

58. Nasr, *Muhammad,* 18–19.

59. There is some dispute over which death occurred first, or even when they happened. See Kister, "Sons of Khadīja." See also, briefly, Brown, *Muhammad,* 22.

60. Marston, *Muhammad of Mecca,* 41.

61. Guillaume, *Life of Muhammad,* 191. Numerous authors follow this, some quite closely. See, for example, Schimmel, *And Muhammad Is His Messenger,* 13.

62. Al-Ṭabari, *History of al-Ṭabarī*, vol. 6, 115; see also vol. 39, 3–4, 161. Or, in Ibn Isḥāq, "the Quraysh began to treat him in an offensive way which they would not have dared to follow in his uncle's lifetime" (Guillaume, *Life of Muhammad*, 191). See Stecker, *Man Mohammed*, 29–30, for the deaths, followed by persecution.

63. Sale, *The Alcoran of Mohammed*, 1:60

64. Peters, "Quest of the Historical Muhammad," 307; James E. Montgomery, "Editor's Introduction," in *The Oral and the Written in Early Islam*, ed. Gregor Schoeler, Uwe Vagelpohl, and James E. Montgomery (London: Taylor and Francis, 2006), 7. Nasr, *Muhammad*, 94, calls it "the most eloquent and moving biography of the Prophet" in English and recommends it "highly to those seeking to understand how the Prophet is seen in traditional Islamic sources."

65. Choudhury, *Prophet Muhammad*, 29. Stobart had called him "a faithful and affectionate husband." *Islam and Its Founder*, 64.

66. Martin Lings, *Muhammad: His Life Based on the Earliest Sources* (Rochester, VT: Inner Traditions International, 1983), 96.

67. Nasr, *Muhammad*, 26. See, similarly, Thompson, *Wives of the Prophet Muhammad*, 7.

68. Davenport, *Apology for Mohammed*, 23–24; quotation at p. 24.

69. Prideaux, *True Nature of Imposture*, 41.

70. Ibn Hishām, *Al-Sīra al-nabawīya;* al-Ṭabarī, *History of al-Ṭabarī.* Guillaume, *Life of Muhammad*, 792, n. 918, attributes this material to Ibn Hishām and not Ibn Isḥāq.

71. Ibn Kathīr, *The Life of the Prophet Muḥammad*, trans. Trevor Le Gassick (Reading, UK: Garnet, 1998), 2:92, insists that the contract with Aisha occurred before the marriage to Sawda, though he acknowledges at least one scholar who held a contrary opinion (2:97); the English translation reads, "his betrothal to 'Ā'isha preceded his marriage to Sawda." (On the particulars of this "translation," see Williams, *Muḥammad and the Supernatural*, ix.) See also al-Ṭabarī, *History of al-Ṭabarī*, vol. 9, 128, which notes dispute as to which marriage occurred first, but insists that "all those knowledgeable about the Messenger of God's life agree that the Messenger of God consummated his marriage with Sawda before [consummating his marriage with] 'Ā'ishah" (brackets in original). Some traditionalist accounts, however, retain the matchmaker's intervention. See, for example, Bulandshehri, *Wives of the Prophet Muhammad*, 31–33; Thompson, *Wives of the Prophet Muhammad*, 8–10.

72. For instance, Andrae, *Mohammed*, 188.

73. Carlyle, *Hero as Prophet*, 22.

74. Dashti, *Twenty-Three Years*.

75. Watt, *Muhammad*, 79.

76. Woods, *In Spite of Epilepsy*, 136. Hostile biographers suggested that Muhammad invented the story of revelations to explain his epileptic fits so that Khadija would still marry him. For a thirteenth-century Latin example, see Tolan, "European Accounts," 228–229. For early modern English examples, see Dimmock, *Mythologies*, 31.

77. Sometimes used interchangeably with motive, "interest" has a broader significance, not coterminous with ambition. In the eighteenth century, elite figures on both sides of the Atlantic used the term to mean personal "ties to men with social, political, and military power." Gruber, *Books and the British Army*, 8. In his biography of George Washington, who persistently worked to strengthen such ties, Paul Johnson explains that "interest was a connection through family ties, friendship, local ties, or clan, which put a man ahead of his immediate competitors in getting something he wanted—a place, a promotion, a contract, a favor." Paul Johnson, *George Washington: The Founding Father* (New York: Harper Collins, 2006), 12. Twenty-first-century Americans laud networking but frown on nepotism; their ancestors presumed it legitimate to draw on personal and family ties for economic and professional advancement. As a clergyman, Prideaux presumably saw "interest" less pragmatically than Washington and his British military counterparts. Yet it seems likely that Prideaux objected to Muhammad marrying to "strengthen himself" by "Alliance[s]," primarily because it was part of a larger imposture.

78. Arthur N. Wollaston, *Half-Hours with Muhammad, Being a popular Account of the Prophet of Arabia and of his more immediate Followers* (London: W.H. Allen, 1886), 48.

79. Siddiqui, *Life of Muhammad*. On this marriage, see also al-Ṭabarī, *History of al-Ṭabarī*, vol. 8, *The Victory of Islam*, trans. Michael Fishbein, 1–4.

80. Zaidi, *Mothers of the Faithful*, 1.

81. S. M. Madni Abbasi, *The Family of the Holy Prophet (S.A.W.)* (New Delhi: Adam, 2004), 67. Thompson, *Wives of the Prophet Muhammad*, 37, is unusual in mentioning—in addition to alliances, protection, or demonstration of marriage norms—that God's "decree" was the deciding factor.

82. For a treatment of this marriage in the earlier Muslim tradition, with some reference to modern Muslim thinking, see Ze'ev Maghen, "Zayd and Zaynab Revisited: Bowdlerizing the *Uswa Ḥasana*," chap. 3

in *Virtues of the Flesh: Passion and Purity in Early Islamic Jurisprudence* (Leiden: Brill, 2005), 75–110. Maghen suggests that "not only was Zayd's 'adoption by the Prophet' largely a symbolic gesture—such that we should not really think of Muḥammad as having married his adoptive *son's* wife—but marriage itself at the time could be an ephemeral affair, often failing to establish a close connection between newlywed couples—and thus we should not really think of Muḥammad as having married his adoptive son's *wife*, with all that the later title implies for us. In order to avail themselves of such a claim, however, modern Muslim apologists would have to admit that marriage among the *ṣaḥāba* did not adhere to today's ideal" (108–109, n. 80).

83. Watt, *Muhammad*, 156.

84. Siddiqui, *Life of Muhammad*, 226.

85. Wessels, *Modern Arabic Biography*, 133–141, on the marriage and some of the commentarial tradition.

86. Siddiqui, *Life of Muhammad*, 227.

87. Ibid., 225.

88. Ibid.; Thompson, *Wives of the Prophet Muhammad*, 49–52; Davenport, *Apology for Mohammed*, 35.

89. Quoted in Wessels, *Modern Arabic Biography*, 147.

90. Newcomb, *False Prophet*, 118–119.

91. Ibid., 119–120.

92. Bush, *Life of Mohammed*, 161.

93. Ibid., 162; italics in original.

94. Ibid.

95. Ibid., 163.

96. For instance, Jalbani, *Life of the Holy Prophet*, 44: "The Holy Prophet after [Khadija's] death married Saudah bint Zam'ah, one of the earliest Muslims and now a widow, so that, the minor children may be looked after with ease." See also Thompson, *Wives of the Prophet Muhammad*, 8–9; Dashti, *Twenty-Three Years*, 122–123; Qasmi, *Questions and Answers*, 24.

97. Robinson, *Islamic Historiography*, 104.

98. Salmin, *Holy Prophet Mohammad*, 122.

99. Ibid.

100. Ibid., 123.

101. Malik, *Muhammad*, 123.

102. Ibid. For Ahmad Khan, too, the links between Muhammad's polygamy and Jesus's celibacy and piety were central, but he wrote that "wives were not indicative of holiness and that Christ was holy because

he was a prophet, not because of his celibacy. Monogamy was not necessarily meritorious, and there occurred many situations in life which necessitated the practice of polygamy." Rizvi, "Muḥammad in South Asian Biographies," 115–116.

103. For a thoughtful attempt to reconcile these divergent assessments, see Kahn, *Untold*, 10–11.

104. Malik, *Muhammad*, 124.

105. Ibid.

106. Ibid., 125.

107. Sardar, *Muhammad*, 118, 120; see also Rauf, *Moving the Mountain*, 110, regarding Muhammad's marriages after he was widowed: "As was often the case in ancient times, he married for political reasons: to take care of a widow, say, or to strengthen his bond with certain key leaders. In purely religious terms, the Prophet's wives were major sources for many of the *hadiths*."

108. Al-Ṭabarī, *History of al-Ṭabarī*, vol. 7, xviii.

109. In contrast, Rodinson (*Mahomet*, 79) suggests that Muhammad remained faithful to Khadija at significant psychological cost, given the clash between his own "erotic temperament" and his conscience, which "prevented him from satisfying his desires." (My translation; the published translation [Rodinson, *Muhammad*, 55] uses the phrase "a highly sexed man.") Sardar, *Muhammad*, 122, is also frank: "There is no doubt that Muhammad himself enjoyed the company of women and a robust sex life."

110. Thompson, *Wives of the Prophet Muhammad*, 55. Compare to al-Ṭabarī, *History of al-Ṭabarī*, vol. 39, 183.

111. Dashti, *Twenty-Three Years*, 135; discussing Zaynab, 121.

112. Ibn Hishām, *Al-sīra al-nabawiya*.

113. Abbasi, *Family of the Holy Prophet*, 67. See also Bulandshehri, *Wives of the Prophet Muhammad*, 168: "These sexually perverted people of Europe can not comprehend the sublime and exalted designs of Islam. . . . If any person with clear and impartial vision tries to evaluate the life of the Prophet Muhammad *(sallallahu alayhe wasallam)*, he can not just think in the terms that he married so many wives just for sexual pleasures."

114. Abbasi, *Family of the Holy Prophet*, 67.

115. Ali, *Muhammad the Prophet*, 187.

116. Ibid.

117. Malik, *Muhammad*, 123–124.

118. Ali, *Muhammad the Prophet*, 192.

119. Ibid.

120. Siddiqui, *Life of Muhammad*, 251.

121. Ali, *Muhammad the Prophet*, 192.

122. Bulandshehri, *Wives of the Prophet Muhammad*, 170.

123. Ali, *Muhammad the Prophet*, 193.

124. Ibid.

125. Ibid.

126. An interesting case of reticence about her status as divorcee: Al-eem, *Prophet Muhammad (S)*, 105–106, includes an appendix on Muhammad's wives, including a column for marital status. Aisha is listed as a virgin; other women are listed as "W," for widow, with additional notations as to whether they have been twice or thrice married. Zaynab, in that column, has "N. A."

127. Ali, *Muhammad the Prophet*, 193.

128. Ibid., 196.

129. Nasr, *Muhammad*, 20; see also Bulandshehri, *Wives of the Prophet Muhammad*, 168–169, 170.

130. Nasr, *Muhammad*, 19.

131. Ibid., 20. See a similar argument in Higgins, *Apology for the Life*, 26; he suggests the desire for a son may have motivated his marriages.

132. Higgins, *Apology for the Life*, 26. Stubbe, *Account of the Rise*, 139, speculates that it was "perhaps out of gratitude to the raiser of his fortunes" that Muhammad did not marry again while Khadija lived.

133. Abbasi, *Family of the Holy Prophet*, 1.

134. Unusually, Qasmi, *Questions and Answers*, devotes more than twice as much space to Aisha (twenty pages) as to Khadija (nine); his work, however, is more catechism than biography.

135. Nasr, *Muhammad*, 18–19.

136. Armstrong, *Muhammad*, 75.

137. Abbasi, *Family of the Holy Prophet*, 67.

138. Chopra, *Muhammad*, 105. For Khadija's chapter, see 103–115. Other figures reflect on their marriage as well (e.g., 95–99). Emerick, *Muhammad*, 44. For an account of his conversion, see Yahiya Emerick, "Getting to Know a Friend: My Introduction to Muhammad," in *Message International*, August–September 2002, 21–25. For a different imagining of Khadija's developing love for Muhammad in a 2004 Indonesian biography, which perhaps draws on Haykal, see Gade, "Religious Biography," 261–263.

139. Emerick, *Muhammad*, 45.

140. Al-Ṭabarī, *History of al-Ṭabarī*, vol. 6, 48.

141. Emerick, *Muhammad*, 44: "An older woman . . . marrying a man fifteen years younger was unheard of in Arab society."

142. Ameer Ali, *Critical Examination*, 4–5. Note that his evidence, here, is the "Brahmanic legislator," as reported in a French history of comparative ancient criminal law; an excerpt from the Laws of Manu, published in *Tytler's Considerations on the State of India;* and a book, also French, on women in ancient India (5, n.).

143. Salmin, *Holy Prophet Mohammad*, 143; for a more recent example, see Shabazz, "Prophet on the Treatment of Women." Dashti, *Twenty-Three Years,* reports the degraded condition but does not present such a glowing portrait of Muhammad's reforms, saying only that he "blunted the edge of this savagery" (114).

144. Salmin nonsensically writes, "[He h]imself married a widow so that the remarriage of widows may not remain a taboo." But remarriage of widows in the Arabian Peninsula was not a taboo by conventional accounts which say Khadija was widowed twice—and hence remarried after being widowed—before Muhammad wed her. *Holy Prophet Mohammad*, 151. Bulandshehri makes a slightly different point in *The Wives of the Prophet*, 11: widow marriage was not sinful in the prophet's context but today "in certain nations, the re-marriage of a widow is considered as an evil. This is a colossal sin. A practice which the holy Prophet performed must not be considered wrong."

145. Sprenger, *Life of Mohammad*, 153–154.

146. *Awlād ḥāritnā* (Children of our quarter) appeared in serial form in 1959 and was first published in book form in 1967. See Roded, "Gender in an Allegorical Life," 117–134; Wessels, *Modern Arabic Biography,* 24–29.

147. For instance, Marston's *Muhammad of Mecca* discusses Khadija extensively on p. 24, throughout the next sections of the book, and then in the discussion of his family life, where Mariya, "his Egyptian concubine" (91), is mentioned; Aisha gets her own short section; and she discusses (without naming) Umm Habiba, the daughter of Abu Sufyan, because it enables her to illustrate how the marriage was for the purpose of "reconciliation" between Muhammad and her father, his "old enemy" (92–93). Wollaston mentions this marriage (*Half-Hours*, 62): "This fair matron was like all her predecessors in the apostle's harem a widow; her husband had long since died in Abyssinia, and it is conjectured that the Prophet was moved by motives of policy to add the lady to his long list of spouses, hoping that she might thereby be enabled to soften in some measure, the animosity of her father, a bitter, unrelenting, and withal power-

ful opponent to the faith of Islam." Armstrong, *Muhammad: A Prophet for Our Time*, calls this marriage "a shrewd political move" (181).

148. A sampling: Stecker, *Man Mohammed*, 37–38; Émile Dermenghem, *Life of Mahomet*, trans. Arabella Yorke (New York: Routledge, 1930), 286–287; Carlyle, *Hero as Prophet*, 26; Khalidi, *Images of Muhammad*, 75–76; Emerick, *Muhammad*, 45 (though he does not mention that it was Aisha); Andrae, *Mohammed*, 41; G. M. Draycott, *Mahomet: Founder of Islam* (New York: Dodd, Mead, and Company, 1916), 91–92; Thompson, *Wives of the Prophet Muhammad*, 6–7; Davenport, *Apology for Mohammed*, 24. Armstrong, *Muhammad: A Prophet for Our Time*, 26, writes that "after her death he used to infuriate some of his later wives by endlessly singing her praises."

149. Choudhury, *Prophet Muhammad*, 154.

5. Mother of the Faithful

1. Ibn Hishām, *Al-sīra al-nabawīya*, 668; Guillaume's version reads: "He married 'Ā'isha in Mecca when she was a child of seven and lived with her in Medina when she was nine or ten. She was the only virgin that he married" (*Life of Muhammad*, 792, n. 918). The phrase Guillaume translates as "lived with her" is *banā bihā;* the word he translates as child is *bint*.

2. Aisha's age is discussed in al-Ṭabarī, *History of al-Ṭabarī*, vol. 39, *Biographies of the Prophet's Companions and Their Successors*, trans. Ella Landau-Tasseron, 171–174, and vol. 9, *The Last Years of the Prophet*, trans. Ismail K. Poonawala, 129–131. In these accounts, she is usually six (sometimes seven) at the marriage and nine at consummation. The age at death (sixty-six) and death date (58/678) roughly corroborate this statement (39:173). In discussing whether, after Khadija's death, Muhammad married Sawda or Aisha first, al-Ṭabarī writes: "As for 'Ā'ishah, when he married her she was very young and not yet ready for consummation, whereas Sawdah was already married before" (9:128). Poonawala inserts a footnote directly after the word "consummation," in which he writes that she was six at the marriage during Shawwal, year 10, and nine when it was consummated in Shawwal. He cites Ibn Sa'd's *Ṭabaqāt* and Balādhurī's *Ansāb*. On Aisha's age, see also Brown, *Muhammad*, 24, 76–78, and al-Ṭabarī, *History of al-Ṭabarī*, vol. 39, 180.

3. Al-Ṭabarī, *History of al-Ṭabarī*, vol. 39, 180.

4. Ibid., 185.

5. Conrad, "Abraha and Muḥammad." He does not mention Aisha.

6. Spellberg, *Politics, Gender, and the Islamic Past*, 40.

7. Spellberg, *Politics, Gender, and the Islamic Past*, 197–198, n. 4.

8. One finds in Bulandshehri a rare echo of Prideaux in a discussion of Hafsa's marriage: "By this marriage, the Prophet strengthened the ties between two of his closest companions" (*Wives of the Prophet Muhammad*, 39).

9. "After the death of Khadija in 619, and while still in Mecca, he [Muhammad] married Sawda bint Zam'a, a recent widow, and Aisha, the daughter of his closest companion, Abu Bakr" (Sardar, *Muhammad*, 118). See also Nasr, *Muhammad*, 26. Siddiqui puts Sawda first, too: "After the sad demise of *Khadijah*, he again went in for a widow, this time a helpless one in great distress. She was one of the earliest converts to *Islam* who had suffered many hardships for the cause of truth." Only after that, "the Holy Prophet married *A'ishah*, the daughter of his devoted friend *Abu Bakr*. She was the only virgin wife of *Muhammad* (peace be upon him)." Siddiqui, *Life of Muhammad*, 250.

10. Prideaux, *True Nature of Imposture*, 41. Italics in original.

11. Bush, *Life of Mohammed*.

12. Ibid., 88. This passage is echoed nearly verbatim in Newcomb, *False Prophet*, 117–118. Here, Khadija's death does not serve as the lead-in. This section leads, predictably, to discussion of the degraded position of females in heathen areas.

13. Samuel Green plagiarizes this line, and much of its surrounding material, in *The Life of Mahomet: Founder of the Religion of Islamism and of the Empire of the Saracens* (London: William Tegg, 1877), 207. (Bush's *Life of Mohammed* is absent from his list of sources, vii.) Bush, in turn, borrows a great deal from Prideaux in this section.

14. Irving, *Mahomet and His Successors*, 151, 152.

15. Ibid., 109–110.

16. Davenport, *Apology for Mohammed*, 25.

17. Muir, *Life of Mahomet*, 2nd ed, 117.

18. Prideaux, *True Nature of Imposture*, 21, 85. Italics in original.

19. Muir, *Life of Mahomet*, 2nd ed, 117.

20. William Muir, *The Life of Mahomet, with Introductory Chapter on the Original Sources for the Biography of Mahomet, and on the Pre-Islamite History of Arabia* (London: Smith, Elder, 1861), 3:13, 22. Muir, *Life of Mahomet*, 2nd ed, 117, suggests that "there may have been something more than ordinarily interesting and precocious about the child." Also, Muir, *Life of Mahomet*, 2nd ed., 62: "Ayesha his daughter (born about this period, and destined while yet a girl to be the Prophet's bride)."

21. Ibid., 23.

22. Wollaston, *Half-Hours*, 42.

23. Ibid., 66–67. Italics in original. In discussing Ayesha's role at Muhammad's illness and death, Johnstone refers to her as "his best beloved, not yet twenty years old"; discusses how Muhammad "lay his weary head on Ayesha's loving breast"; and notes the "fond, faithful soothing of his young wife" (*Muhammad and His Power*, 144–146).

24. Quoted in Tolan, "European Accounts," 235–236.

25. Rizvi, "Muḥammad in South Asian Biographies," paraphrasing Shibli Numani, 117; see also Syed Suleman Nadvi [Saiyid Sulaiman Nadwi], *Muhammad: The Ideal Prophet. A Historic, Practical, Perfect Model for Humanity*, trans. Mohiuddin Ahmad (Kuala Lumpur: Islamic Book Trust, 1977 [n.d.]), 56.

26. Margoliouth, *Mohammed and the Rise of Islam*, 343.

27. Ibid., 450.

28. Ibid., 234–235.

29. Newcomb, *False Prophet*, 68.

30. Draycott, *Mahomet*, 95–96, 102, 182.

31. On the marriage to Aisha, see Lings, *Muhammad*, 105–106 (he does not use the term "betrothal"), and 132–133.

32. Glubb, *Life and Times of Muhammad*, 160.

33. Ibid., 239.

34. Sprenger also makes Muhammad a householder: "'A'yishah being only nine years of age when she married him, brought her toys into *his house;* and he occasionally played with her. She also used to race with him" (*Life of Mohammad*, 93; emphasis mine). But see, for example, Johnstone, *Muhammad and His Power*, 132.

35. Quoted in Ian Littlewood, *Sultry Climates: Travel and Sex* (Cambridge, MA: Da Capo, 2002), 52.

36. Neil Cooke, "James Burton and Slave Girls," in *Unfolding the Orient: Travellers in Egypt and the Near East*, ed. Paul and Janet Starkey (Reading, UK: Garnet, 2001), 209–217.

37. Schick, *Erotic Margin*, 137; the partial quotation is from St. John.

38. Ibid., 1.

39. On seventeenth-century British writers' views of the contribution of hot climates to "sodomitical" tendencies, see Nabil Matar, *Turks, Moors, and Englishmen in the Age of Discovery* (New York: Columbia University Press, 1999), 120. The effects of "sultry climates" are not limited to the Orient; see the discussions of tourism in Italy and Tahiti in Littlewood, *Sultry Climates;* on sexual precocity, see esp. 168, 194–196. Littlewood's occasional use or inclusion of "oriental" references—"sultanesque

fantasies," "seraglio," "bashaw" (pasha) (41, 52, 141, 156)—suggests the need for further investigation.

40. Schick, *Erotic Margin*, 108.

41. Sprenger, *Life of Mohammad*, 80.

42. Higgins, *Apology*, 34.

43. Quoted in Khan, *Essays*, 149; the ellipsis is Ahmad Khan's.

44. Newcomb, *False Prophet*, 124.

45. Ibid., 125.

46. Schick, *Erotic Margin*, 67.

47. Tolan, *Sons of Ishmael*, 144.

48. Mark Jordan, *The Ethics of Sex* (Malden, MA: Blackwell, 2002); Matar, *Turks, Moors, and Englishmen*, 112; Kidd, *American Christians and Islam*, 27.

49. Robinson-Dunn, *Harem*, 11, citing Miguel Cabrera.

50. Mrinali Sinha, *Specters of Mother India: The Global Restructuring of an Empire* (Durham, NC: Duke University Press, 2006); Schick, *Erotic Margin*, 138

51. Littlewood, *Sultry Climates*, 74.

52. Tyerman, *Crusades*, 137.

53. The relationship between overt imperial control and specific scholarship and writing is one subject to debate. See Wokoeck, *German Orientalism*.

54. Prideaux, *True Nature of Imposture*, 107.

55. Schick, *Erotic Margin*, 154.

56. Johnstone compares Islam's "enslaving women" to Christianity, which "has raised woman to her proper place as the equal of man." *Muhammad and His Power*, 159; see also: "the whole position of women was changed for the worse, and instead of the equal and help of her husband the wife was degraded to be his slave and his toy" (227).

57. Coomar Roy, with a prefatory note by Joel Benton, "Child Marriage in India," *North American Review* 147 (1888): 415–423. Though Coomar draws a number of parallels with Catholic marriage, he notably deemphasizes individual consent of spouses.

58. Mrs. Marcus B. [Jenny] Fuller, *The Wrongs of Indian Womanhood* (New York: Fleming H. Revell, 1900). "Child Marriage," 33, is followed by a chapter on widowhood. A number of authors, interestingly, connect Aisha's youth at marriage with the lengthy period she lived after Muhammad's death.

59. Fuller, *Wrongs of Indian Womanhood*, 47.

60. Sumit Sarkar and Tanika Sarkar, eds., *Women and Social Reform in Modern India: A Reader* (Bloomington: Indiana University Press, 2008), 464–465 and elsewhere; Sinha, *Specters of Mother India.*

61. Fuller, *Wrongs of Indian Womanhood,* 47.

62. Department of Commerce and Labor, Bureau of the Census, *Special Reports: Marriage and Divorce, 1867–1906,* Pt. 1: *Summary, Laws, Foreign Statistics* (Washington, DC: Government Printing Office, 1909). "Marriage and Divorce Laws: Algeria," 359. No one has yet undertaken a study of the history of the Western presentation of Aisha as Muhammad's "best-beloved wife" (Prideaux, *True Nature of Imposture,* 42, 103).

63. C. N. Barham, "Child Marriage in India," *Westminster Review* 135, no. 2 (January–June 1891): 113–124, at p. 118.

64. Ibid.

65. Such a move runs counter to the creative work that a scholar such as Isvarchandra Vidyasagar undertook, "redeploy[ing] premodern textual sources and interpretive strategies in the service of a modern reformist cause." Vidyasagar wrote on both the *Evils of Child Marriage* (1850) and *Hindu Widow Marriage* (1855). His work, as Brian Hatcher has shown, has been attacked from all directions (Hatcher, introduction to *Hindu Widow Marriage,* by Vidyasagar, 31).

66. Barham, "Child Marriage in India," 119.

67. Beth Baron, "The Making and Breaking of Marital Bonds in Modern Egypt," in *Women in Middle Eastern History: Shifting Boundaries in Sex and Gender,* ed. Nikki R. Keddie and Beth Baron (New Haven, CT: Yale University Press, 1992), 275–291; Jonathan Brown, *Misquoting Muhammad: The Challenges and Choices of Interpreting the Prophet's Legacy* (Oneworld, forthcoming), cites a few instances where Muhammad's precedent was mentioned.

68. Procedural reforms, to close loopholes and dissuade guardians and court officials from fudging girls' age, were passed in 1931 and 1933. See Hanan Kholoussy, "The Nationalization of Marriage in Monarchical Egypt," in *Re-Envisioning Egypt, 1919–1952,* ed. Arthur Goldschmidt, Amy J. Johnson, and Barak A. Salmoni (Cairo: American University in Cairo Press, 2005), 317–350, esp. 320–324.

69. Kholoussy, "Nationalization of Marriage," 317, 318.

70. Ibid., 319.

71. She cites Beth Baron, *The Women's Awakening in Egypt: Culture, Society, and the Press* (New Haven, CT: Yale University Press, 1997), 164, and says that 1907 and 1917 census numbers show that "most females

married between the ages of twenty and twenty-nine" and less than 10 percent of females married below that age. It is unclear whether this is the age at first marriage, or the age at which all marriages during that period took place.

72. Kholoussy, "Nationalization of Marriage," 320.

73. Sinha, *Specters of Mother India*.

74. Or to ignore it. Aḥmad, *Life of Muhammad*, mentions Aisha throughout but does not specifically discuss circumstances of the marriage to her or Sawda.

75. Syed Suleman Nadvi, *Women Companions of the Holy Prophet and Their Sacred Lives* (New Delhi: Islamic Book Service, 2001): 34–35.

76. Colin Turner, *Islam: The Basics* (New York: Routledge, 2006), 35.

77. Andrae, *Mohammed*, 162.

78. Ibn Sa'd, *Women of Madina*, 44.

79. Ibid., 54–55.

80. Thompson, *Wives of the Prophet Muhammad*, 14, is among the few who repeat the story of the portrait brought by the angel Gabriel. His collective biography of Muhammad's wives was published by the publisher of Ibn Sa'd's *The Women of Madina*.

81. Zaidi, *Mothers of the Faithful*, 37; Davenport, *Apology for Mohammed*, 25.

82. Zaidi, *Mothers of the Faithful*, 37.

83. Siddiqui, *Life of Muhammad*, 150.

84. Ibid., 151.

85. Ibid.

86. Ibid. See also Thompson, *Wives of the Prophet Muhammad*, 17. Bulandshehri, *Wives of the Prophet*, 167, provides a similar rationale for Muhammad's polygamy in a final chapter entitled "The Philosophy of Wedding So Many Wives." He writes, "There were so many intricate subjects which could only be explained to the general public, specially the women, through his wives alone. For [the] purpose of imparting information and rightly educating the public, it was very important for him to have too many wives."

87. Abbasi, *Family of the Holy Prophet*, 72–73.

88. For a discussion of how even critical works can function as sources of authority, see Tageldin, *Disarming Words*.

89. For betrothal: Abbasi, *Family of the Holy Prophet*, 72 (though he uses marriage on the same page); Nasr, *Muhammad*, 26 ("A short time later he married Sawdah and became betrothed also to the daughter of Abū Bakr, 'Ā'ishah, who was then only seven years old and whom the

Blessed Prophet was to marry when she came of age"); Thompson, *Wives of the Prophet Muhammad*, 10. For engagement, see Hafez Ghulam Sarwar, *Muhammad the Holy Prophet* (Lahore: Shaykh Muhammad Ashraf, 1980 [1961]).

90. M. V. McDonald, foreword to Al-Ṭabarī, *History of al-Ṭabarī*, vol. 7, *The Foundation of the Community*, trans. M. V. McDonald, xviii. For the marriage, see Al-Ṭabarī, *History of al-Ṭabarī*, vol. 7, 6–8, including the translators' note (6, n. 12), which says, "The original marriage . . . could be considered rather a betrothal."

91. Irving lists Weil among his sources (*Mahomet and His Successors*, vi) but makes little use of him, a point Muir notes (and for which he criticizes him). See "Biographies of Mohammed," in *Mohammedan Controversy*, 69.

92. Whether *Zaynab* counts as the "first" proper Arabic novel has been the subject of some debate; see, for example, Mohammad R. Salama, *Islam, Orientalism, and Intellectual History: Modernity and Politics of Exclusion since Ibn Khaldun* (London: I. B. Tauris, 2011), 175. Salama discusses a slightly earlier novel, Maḥmūd Ṭāhir Ḥaqqī's *The Virgin of Denshawai*, about which he states that it is "free from some of the restrictions of normal historical writing. He can be episodic and fragmentary, add or delete events altogether. This is not merely freedom from the constraints of the history of Denshawai [the town where the novel is set] but also freedom to choose and to foreground, and thus to offer an understanding that holds the immediacy of direct perception" (179). I would suggest that Salama's observation applies to both premodern and postmodern biography, as well as fiction.

93. Haykal, *Ḥayāt Muḥammad*, 311–320; Haykal, *Life of Muḥammad*, 285–298.

94. "Fa khaṭaba Abī Bakr ibnatahu 'Ā'isha, wa limmā kānat lā tazāla ṭifla fī al-sābi'a min 'umrihā 'aqada 'alayhā wa lam yabni bihā ilā ba'd sanatayn hīn balaghat al-tāsi'a, wa fī hadhihi al-ithnā' tazawwaja Sawda, armalat aḥad al-muslimīn aladhīna hājaru ilā al-ḥabasha wa 'ādū ilā Makka wa matū bihā." Haykal, *Ḥayāt Muḥammad*, 193. Compare Al Faruqi's version: "He therefore asked Abū Bakr for the hand of his daughter 'Ā'ishah. Since she was still too young to marry, the engagement was announced but the marriage was postponed for three more years until 'Ā'ishah reached the age of eleven. In the meantime, Muḥammad married Sawdah, the widow of one of the Muslim companions who emigrated to Abysinnia but died upon his return to Makkah." Haykal, *Life of Muḥammad*, 139. I discuss this translation below.

95. "Idh dhāk banā Muḥammad ṣalla Allāhu 'alayhi wa sallam bi 'Ā'isha bint Abī Bakr, wa kānat fī'l-'āshira aw al-ḥādiya 'ashira min 'umrihā, wa kānat fatā raqīqa, ḥalwat al-qasamāt, muḥabbabat al-'ishra, wa kānat takhṭū min al-ṭufūla ilā al-ṣiban wa kānat dhāt wala' bi'l-la'ib wa'l-maraḥ wa kānat nāmīya naman ḥasanan." Haykal, *Ḥayāt Muḥammad*, 231. Compare Al Faruqi's translation: "At this time Muḥammad married 'Ā'ishah, daughter of Abū Bakr, who was then ten or eleven years old. She was a beautiful, delicate, and amiable young girl, emerging out of childhood and blossoming into full womanhood. Although she was fully grown, she was still quite attracted by amusement and play." Haykal, *Life of Muḥammad*, 183. I discuss this translation below.

96. Al Faruqi's translation. See also Hazelton, *First Muslim*, 215: "It was as though [Muhammad] had granted her license for girlish mischief. Much as a fond father might indulge a spoiled daughter, he seemed diverted by her sassiness and charm."

97. Muir says she was ten, "though she had been three years affianced." Muir, *Life of Mahomet*, 2nd ed., 186. Elsewhere he says she was "six or seven" when betrothed and that "the marriage took place not more than three years afterwards" (117).

98. Haykal, *Ḥayāt Muḥammad*, 315; Haykal, *Life of Muḥammad*, 291.

99. Émile Dermenghem, *La vie de Mahomet* (Paris: Charlot, 1950), 145–146. "Elle avoit une soixantaine d'années et pourtant son mari n'avait pas songé à lui donner une co-épouse; il lui était resté obstinément fidèle."

100. He provides these details about Sawda's husband later. Haykal, *Ḥayāt Muḥammad*, 315; Haykal, *Life of Muḥammad*, 290.

101. Glubb, *Life and Times of Muhammad*, also refers a few times to Aisha's virginity (e.g., 237).

102. Haykal, *Ḥayāt Muḥammad*, 315. Al Faruqi's version reads: "If it is true that Muḥammad did in fact love 'Ā'ishah, it must have been a love which arose after marriage, surely neither before nor at the time of marriage. He had asked her hand from her father while she was only nine years old, and did not marry her until two years later. It is contrary to logic to claim that he could have fallen in love with her while she was at this tender age." Haykal, *Life of Muḥammad*, 291.

103. Muir, *Life of Mahomet*, 2nd ed, 117.

104. Haykal, *Ḥayāt Muḥammad*, 315; see Haykal, *Life of Muḥammad*, 290.

105. *Zawwaja* (marry or espouse); *khaṭaba* (propose); *'aqada* (contract); *banā* (consummate).

106. John Esposito, "Ismail al-Faruqi: Muslim Scholar-Activist," in *The Muslims of America*, ed. Yvonne Haddad (New York: Oxford University Press, 1991), 65–79; also Ali Zaidi, *Islam, Modernity, and the Human Sciences* (New York: Palgrave Macmillan 2011), 67–68; Imtiyaz Yusuf, ed., *Islam and Knowledge: Al Faruqi's Concept of Religion in Islamic Thought: Essays in Honor of Isma'il Al Faruqi* (London: I. B. Tauris, 2012).

107. *Lam yabni bihā ilā ba'd sanatayn hīn balaghat al-tāsi'a.*

108. Haykal, *Life of Muhammad*, 139.

109. *Min al-tufūla ilā al-siban.*

110. Haykal, *Life of Muhammad*, 183–184.

111. No translation is purely conservative or additive; rather, "the two models provide the notional poles of a scale of conformity." Sukanta Chaudhuri, *The Metaphysics of Text* (Cambridge: Cambridge University Press, 2010), 180–181.

112. Aysha Hidayatullah, "Māriyya the Copt: Gender, Sex and Heritage in the Legacy of Muhammad's *Umm Walad*," *Islam and Christian–Muslim Relations* 21, no. 3 (July 2010): 229. For a brief mention in the context of recounting Muhammad's children, see Ibn Hishām, *Al-Sīra al-nabawīya*, 158.

113. Washington Irving [Wāshinjtūn Irfinj], *Hayāt Muhammad*. Translated by 'Alī Husnī al-Kharbūtlī, 2nd ed. (Egypt: Dār al-Ma'ārif, 1966 [1960]), 196. For the particular issues where Haykal mentions Irving, see Wessels, *Modern Arabic Biography*, 235–237.

114. *Al-hubb al-shadīd.* Irving, *Hayāt Muhammad*, 132.

115. *Khitba* (betrothal), related to the word *khataba* (to propose); *zawāj* (marriage).

116. Kelen, *Muhammad*, 70.

117. Watt, *Muhammad*, 102.

118. Ruqayya Y. Khan, "Of Cyber Muslimahs: Wives of the Prophet and Muslim Women in the Digital Age" in *Muhammad in the Digital Age*, ed. Ruqayya Khan.

119. Colin Turner, *Islam: The Basics* (New York: Routledge, 2006), 34. Given the connection between maturation and nourishment, his argument about puberty seems unlikely.

120. Ibid., 34–35.

121. Hazelton, *First Muslim*, 214–215. References to Aisha as a teenager appear at 134, 216, 217, and 219.

122. Armstrong, *Muhammad: A Biography of the Prophet*, 145.

123. Ibid., 157.

124. Armstrong, *Muhammad: A Prophet for Our Time*, 92–93.

125. Ibid., 126–127.

126. Al-Ṭabarī, *History of al-Ṭabarī*, vol. 7, 7; vol. 9, 130, 131; vol. 39, 171 (implicitly).

127. "Fa-ammā ʿĀʾisha fa-kānat yawm tazawwajahā ṣaghīra lā tusliḥ li'l-jimāʿa." Abū Jaʿfar Muḥammad ibn Jarīr al-Ṭabarī, *Tārīkh al-Ṭabarī: tārīkh al-rusul wa-al-mulūk*, ed. Muḥmmad Abū al-Faḍl Ibrāhīm, 11 vols. (Egypt: Dār al-Maʿārif, 1960–[1977]), vol. 3, 161. The English translation, which Armstrong presumably relied upon, reads: "As for ʿĀʾishah, when he married her she was very young and not yet ready for consummation." The translator's note specifies that she was six at marriage and nine at consummation. Al-Ṭabarī, *History of al-Ṭabarī*, vol. 9, 128. See also Brown, *Muhammad*, 78.

128. Al-Ṭabarī, *History of al-Ṭabarī*, vol. 7, 7; vol. 9, 131; vol. 39, 171.

129. Robert Spencer, *The Truth about Muhammad: Founder of the World's Most Intolerant Religion* (Washington, DC: Regnery, 2007), 170–172. Abdulkader Tayob, "Epilogue: Muhammad in the Future," 305, points out that "the book promises to be saying something about the Prophet, but it intends to say something more specifically about Muslims."

130. Kecia Ali, *Sexual Ethics and Islam: Feminist Reflections on Qur'an, Hadith, and Jurisprudence* (Oxford: Oneworld, 2006), 135–150; Lyons, *Islam through Western Eyes*, 11–12.

131. Matar, *Turks, Moors, and Englishmen*, 126.

132. Yahiya Emerick, *Complete Idiot's Guide to Understanding Islam*, 3rd ed. (New York: Alpha, 2011), 311; see also Emerick, *Muhammad*.

133. Though he acknowledges that violence and abuses were found throughout the ancient world, "Islam has been branded with barbarity in a unique way, in part because, in its zeal to maintain the Prophet's world as well as his word, the customs of antiquity have been preserved into modern times" (1:xi). However, he concludes on a different note: "Muhammad can be judged by the worst of his followers or the best" (Chopra, *Muhammad*, 267).

134. Ibid., 264.

135. Adil Salahi, *Muhammad, Man and Prophet: A Complete Study of the Life of the Prophet of Islam.* (Leicestershire, UK: The Islamic Foundation, 2012), iv–v. The preface in this edition was originally included in the 2008 edition.

136. See, for example, Nasr, *Muhammad*, 24–25.

137. Chopra, *Muhammad*, 264.

138. Franklin Graham, son of evangelical preacher Billy Graham. Another example is Floridian Pastor Terry D. Jones, known for his

threat, eventually carried out, to burn copies of the Qur'an. Jones published a book titled *Islam Is of the Devil* (Lake Mary, FL: Creation House, 2010), which was "largely ignored." Peter Morey and Amina Yaqin, *Framing Muslims* (Cambridge, MA: Harvard University Press, 2010), 211.

139. Schick, *The Erotic Margin*, has pointed out very clearly the merger of decidedly incompatible notions in earlier accounts of "oriental sexuality." See also Tolan, "Afterword."

140. Naguib Mahfouz, *Children of the Alley: A Novel* (New York: Anchor, 1996), 333.

141. Ibid.

142. Ibid., 334.

143. Ibid., 335.

144. Wessels, *Modern Arabic Biography*, 146; Roded, "Alternate Images of the Prophet Muhammad's Virility," in *Islamic Masculinities*, ed. Lahoucine Ouzgange (London: Zed Books, 2006); Kecia Ali, "'A Beautiful Example': The Prophet Muḥammad as a Model for Muslim Husbands," *Journal of Islamic Studies* 43, no. 2 (Summer 2004): 273–291; Powers, *Muhammad Is Not the Father*, 49; Dashti, *Twenty-Three Years*, 66. On Muhammad as a model of masculinity and how this intersects with his marital and sexual life, see also Amanullah De Sondy, *The Crisis of Islamic Masculinities* (London: Bloomsbury, 2014), 110–115.

145. Ruth Roded, "Muslim Women Reclaim the Life-Story of the Prophet: 'A'isha 'Abd al-Raḥmān, Assia Djebar, and Nadia Yassine," *Muslim World* 103, no. 3 (July 2013): 334–346, at p. 343.

146. Sherry Jones, *The Jewel of Medina* (New York: Beaufort Books, 2008), vii. On this book, see Aysha Hidayatullah, "Behind Every Good (or Bad) Muslim Man: Representation of Muhammad's Wives after 9/11," in *Muhammad in the Digital Age*, ed. Ruqayya Khan.

147. Kamran Pasha, *Mother of the Believers: A Novel of the Birth of Islam* (New York: Washington Square, 2009). Pasha interweaves a good deal of material on sex and sexual jealousy, although he fades to black in his accounts of Aisha and Muhammad's intimate encounters. However, connecting sexual immorality with pagan unbelief, he recounts Hind's arrangement of a threesome among herself, her husband Abu Sufyan, and a fourteen-year-old dancer (89–91).

148. Roded, "Muslim Women Reclaim," 340.

149. Ibid., 342. Roded sees her acknowledgment of the help of a male poet with the Arabic texts as aimed "to cement her authority." Elsayed reads the same acknowledgment ("'Silence' and Historical Tradition,"

95) as evidence of Djebar's incapacity to properly read and interpret the texts.

150. Roded, "Muslim Women Reclaim," 334–335, 337.

151. Ibid., 340.

152. Kahn, *Untold*, 9.

153. Wessels, *Modern Arabic Biography*, 31.

154. Sara Omar, "Al-Qubaysiyyāt: Negotiating Female Religious Authority in Damascus," *Muslim World* 103, no. 3 (July 2013): 355, n. 21. I was unable to consult these works.

155. Demi, *Muhammad* (New York: Margaret K. McElderberry, 2003); Marston, *Muhammad of Mecca*; Sarah Conover, *Muhammad: The Story of a Prophet and Reformer* (Boston: Skinner House, 2013). Betty Kelen, whose 1975 biography, *Muhammad*, is discussed earlier, also published biographies of Buddha and Confucius.

156. Conover, *Muhammad*, 100.

6. An Enlightened Man

1. It may also convey another moral: do not turn down your husband when he wants sex, even if he is sweaty and dirty from work; he will visit another wife, and she will get the blessing.

2. Guillaume, *Life of Muhammad*, 69.

3. On the Muhammadan light, see Schimmel, *And Muhammad Is His Messenger*, 123–143; Marion Holmes Katz, *The Birth of the Prophet Muhammad* (New York: Routledge, 2007), 12–15; Ernst, "Muhammad as the Pole of Existence," 124–128. Uri Rubin, "Pre-Existence and Light: Aspects of the Concept of *Nūr Muhammad*," *Israel Oriental Studies* 5 (1975): 62–119, and republished in Rubin, *Muhammad the Prophet and Arabia* (Farnham, UK: Ashgate / Variorum, 2011) remains useful.

4. Muir, *Mohammedan Controversy*, viii.

5. Abdulkader Tayob, "Epilogue: Muhammad in the Future," in *Cambridge Companion*, ed. Brockopp, 307; see also Safi, *Memories of Muhammad*, 264–265.

6. Armstrong, *Muhammad: A Biography of the Prophet*, 14.

7. Ibid., 13.

8. Armstrong, *Muhammad: A Prophet for Our Time*, 7.

9. Giving a slightly different list, Ziauddin Sardar begins his biography of Muhammad by declaring: "Prophets are persons of renown. The greatest of them—Abraham, Moses, Buddha, Jesus, Muhammad—have indisputably changed the course of human history." *Muhammad*, 2.

10. Peter Manseau, *Rag and Bone: A Journey among the World's Holy Dead* (New York: Henry Holt, 2009).

11. McAuliffe, "Al-Ṭabarī's Prelude to the Prophet," 113.

12. Brockopp, introduction to *Cambridge Companion*, 1.

13. Safi, *Memories of Muhammad*, 115, 265. See also Waldman, *Prophecy and Power*, 77; on p. 83 she compares Moses, Jesus, Buddha, and Muhammad.

14. Chopra, *Muhammad*, xii. See also 255.

15. Whalen Lai, "The Search for the Historical Śakyamuni in Light of the Historical Jesus," *Buddhist-Christian Studies*, vol. 2 (1982), 79–91; Donald Lopez, *From Stone to Flesh: A Short History of the Buddha* (Chicago: University of Chicago Press, 2013). On the scholarly study of the Buddha, see Donald Lopez, *The Scientific Buddha: His Short and Happy Life* (New Haven, CT: Yale University Press, 2012).

16. Edward Shaner, "Biographies of the Buddha," *Philosophy East and West* 37, no. 3 (July 1987): 306–322, at p. 312. On the description of the "human Buddha" as depicted in early texts, see Lopez, *From Stone to Flesh*, 206.

17. Nadvi, *Muhammad*, 15; also chapter 3, "Historicity," 33–59.

18. John Fenton, "Biographical Myths; Illustrated from the Lives of Buddha and Muhammad," *Folk-Lore Record* 3, no. 1 (1880): 26–39, at p. 26.

19. Ibn Ishaq, *Life of Muhammad*, 5.

20. Masuzawa, *Invention of World Religions*, 132.

21. For instance, Edward Salisbury formulated an influential conception of the Buddha (Lopez, *Scientific Buddha*, 39–40) and wrote on technical aspects of Muslim *hadith* criticism.

22. Fenton, "Biographical Myths," 26.

23. John S. Hawley, "Introduction: Saints and Virtues," in *Saints and Virtues*, ed. Hawley (Berkeley: University of California Press, 1987), xi.

24. Marcus Dods, *Mohammed, Buddha, and Christ: Four Lectures on Natural and Revealed Religion* (London: Hodder and Stoughton, 1877), 189.

25. Ibn Ishaq, *Life of Muhammad*.

26. Bombay Tract and Book Society, *Life of Mahomet*, 173–174.

27. Birchwood, "Confounding Babel," 151.

28. Bombay Tract and Book Society, *Life of Mahomet*, 174.

29. Ibid. Emphasis in original.

30. Quoted in Guenther, "Image of the Prophet," 54.

31. For a discussion of Muḥammad 'Abduh on this point, see Tim Winter, "Jesus and Muḥammad: New Convergences," *Muslim World* 99 (January 2009): 21–38, at p. 24.

32. The Ahmadiyya hold that Jesus survived his crucifixion, traveled to Kashmir, married, and led a mortal life. This account is not widely accepted outside Ahmadi circles.

33. 'Abd al-Raḥmān, *Wives of the Prophet*, 4.

34. Ibid., 5.

35. Alan Pitt, "The Cultural Impact of Science in France: Ernest Renan and the Vie de Jésus," *Historical Journal* 43, no. 1 (March 2000): 79–101, at p. 79. On this life, see also Terence R. Wright, "The Letter and the Spirit: Deconstructing Renan's "Life of Jesus" and the Assumptions of Modernity," *Religion & Literature* 26, no. 2 (Summer 1994): 55–71.

36. Armstrong, *Muhammad: A Prophet for Our Time*, 1. Spencer, *Truth about Muhammad*, 6, calls this biography "hagiographical," not entirely without justification.

37. Quoted in Buaben, *Image of the Prophet Muḥammad*, 214.

38. C. S. Lewis, *Mere Christianity* (San Francisco: Harper San Francisco, 2001 [1952]), 52. For two different recent approaches to the range of ways Jesus's claims could be interpreted, see Wills, *What Jesus Meant*, and Daniel Boyarin, *The Jewish Gospels: The Story of the Jewish Christ* (New York: New Press, 2013).

39. For a discussion of an earlier, roughly parallel Muslim argument "that Mohammed must have been either a true prophet or a madman," see Muir, *Mohammedan Controversy*, 59.

40. Wills, *What Jesus Meant*, xxiv.

41. Stecker, *Man Mohammed*, 44.

42. "In truth, Muhammad was and is for persons in the Arabian world, and for many others, *the* religious reformer, lawgiver, and leader; the prophet *per se*. Basically Muhammad . . . is more to those who follow him than a prophet is to us." Quoted in Tolan, "European Accounts," 248. On this point, see also Bennett, *In Search of Muhammad*, who suggests that Muhammad is as much to his followers as Jesus is to his.

43. Kidd, *American Christians and Islam*, 152. On two nineteenth-century missionaries who wrestled with the issue of Muhammad's relationship to biblical prophecy, see Guenther, "Image of the Prophet."

44. Kidd, *American Christians and Islam*, 152.

45. Gunny, *The Prophet Muhammad in French and English Literature*, 252–253.

46. For two suggestive discussions, see Jerold C. Frakes, *Vernacular and Latin Literary Discourses of the Muslim Other in Medieval Germany* (New York: Palgrave, 2011), xi–xiv and Philip Jenkins, *God's Continent:*

Christianity, Islam, and Europe's Religious Crisis (Oxford: Oxford University Press, 2007), 267–269.

47. Bennett, *In Search of Muhammad*, 222.

48. Andrae, *Mohammed*. On Andrae, see Gunny, *The Prophet Muhammad in French and English Literature*, 215–218.

49. Andrae *Mohammed*, 10.

50. Ibid.

51. Ibid., 11.

52. Ibid., 114.

53. Ibid., 47.

54. Ibid., 52.

55. Johnstone, *Muhammad and His Power*, 150.

56. Andrae, *Mohammed*, 52.

57. Ibid., 191.

58. I owe the division of memoirs into "victim" and "escapee" to Mohja Kahf.

59. Ramadan, *In the Footsteps*.

60. For instance, *sharīʿa, ṭarīqa, madhhab, ṣirāṭ al-mustaqīm*.

61. Tariq Ramadan, *Muhammad: Vie du prophète: Les enseignements spirituels et contemporains* (Paris: Presses du Châtelet. 2006).

62. Ramadan, *In the Footsteps*, 129.

63. On Muhammad's "principles" and conduct concerning warfare, see also Aḥmad, *Life of Muhammad*, 182–186, which makes comparisons with Gandhi.

64. For instance, Nasr writes: "He was still molested and oppressed in every possible way in Makkah." Nasr, *Muhammad*, 37.

65. Ramadan, *In the Footsteps*, 130.

66. Ibid., 131.

67. Ibid., 132.

68. Sherry Jones takes creative license and attributes the tactic to Aisha. Jones, *Jewel of Medina*, 210.

69. Tariq Ramadan, *Radical Reform: Islamic Ethics and Liberation* (New York: Oxford University Press, 2008).

70. Ramadan, *In the Footsteps*, 132.

71. Emerick, *Muhammad*, 210.

72. Ramadan, *In the Footsteps*, 133.

73. I borrow the phrase from Mernissi, *Islam and Democracy*.

74. See, for example, Watt, *Muhammad*, 171–175. Brown writes that Muhammad "faced the question of the Banu Qurayza Jews," who "had betrayed their non-aggression pact with the Muslims." "Muhammad

offered them" the opportunity to convert, but nearly all declined and, eventually, "surrendered." At this point, "Muhammad allowed the chief of the Aws tribe, who had been closely allied with the Banu Qurayza before, to determine their punishment. He decided that the men should be executed and the women and children sold into slavery." *Muhammad*, 43.

75. Pickthall, *Life of the Prophet Muhammad*, 32.

76. Armstrong, *Muhammad: A Biography of the Prophet*, 206–209; Armstrong, *Muhammad: A Prophet for Our Time*, 148–152). I thank Galen Olson for calling the differences between these accounts to my attention.

77. Hazelton, *First Muslim*, 226–238.

78. It also takes Shi'i perspectives seriously, lingering on the martyrdom of Muhammad's grandson, acknowledging the contemporary Iranian fondness for iconic depictions of the Prophet, and suffusing the writing with mentions of Islam's "holy family"—Ali, Fatima, Hassan, and Husayn, the "people of the household," who have historically been a focus of Sunni devotion as well, but who get short shrift in most modern accounts, displaced in favor of Muhammad's wives (part of the turn from kin to spouses Amina bint Haydar al-Sadr, another Shi'i author, criticizes; see Chapter 4).

79. Chopra, *Muhammad*, xiii; see also Nasr, *Muhammad*, 40–41, on both individual and social change (e.g., on the imposition of Islamic law). Nasr here echoes, presumably unwittingly, the Lahori Ahmadi thinker Muhammad Ali, who wrote that "the political superiority of Islam should come after its spiritual supremacy." Ali, "Dottrine e attività," 108–123, at p. 119.

80. Nasr, *Muhammad*, 7.

81. Safi, *Memories of Muhammad*, 101.

82. Unlike Dashti, *Twenty-Three Years*, which ends with an appeal to consider Muhammad's achievements.

Conclusion

1. Sardar, *Muhammad*, 115; Safi, *Memories of Muhammad*, 6.

2. Pierce, "Remembering Fāṭimah," 355, writing about 'Ali Shariati's reworking of the classical narrative of Fatima's life.

3. Donner, *Muhammad and the Believers;* Waldman, *Prophecy and Power*.

4. For an early modern view of a "fundamental antagonism between Europe and Asia, provoked by the irreconcilable opposition between Christianity and Islam," see Laureys, "History and Poetry," 279–280.

5. The term "founder" in this sense was used by some of Prideaux's contemporaries. Stroumsa, *A New Science*, 131–134.

6. Lyons, *Islam through Western Eyes*, 9.

7. Ibid., 7–8.

8. Elmarsafy, *Enlightenment Qur'ān*, xii. Or, more simply, "bigotry rarely responds to empirical evidence." Frakes, *Vernacular and Latin Literary Discourses*, xiii.

9. David R. Blanks, "Western Views of Islam in the Premodern Period: A Brief History of Past Approaches," in *Western Views of Islam in Medieval and Early Modern Europe*, ed. David R. Blanks and Michael Frasetto (New York: St. Martin's, 1999), 11–53, at p. 16.

10. Kidd, *American Christians and Islam;* see, for example, the discussion of George Otis, 128–129. On Vines, see Ali, *Sexual Ethics and Islam*, ch. 8; Kidd, *American Christians and Islam*, 147–148.

11. Quoted in Kidd, *American Christians and Islam*, 11.

12. Kidd, *American Christians and Islam*, 26; a later writer, George Seibel, "saw Smith as even worse than Muhammad, with the former being a 'cunning impostor' and the latter 'a sincere fanatic.'"

13. Falwell made this assertion on *60 Minutes*. See Kidd, *American Christians and Islam*, 145.

14. One place where symbolic "language" remains crucial is cartoons/caricatures. On the sexual and animal nature in the cartoons added to the dossier with the Danish Jyllands-Posten cartoons, see Jytte Klausen, *The Cartoons That Shook the World* (New Haven, CT: Yale University Press, 2009), 91, 101; Lawrence Rosen, *Varieties of Muslim Experience: Encounters with Arab Political and Cultural Life* (Chicago: University of Chicago Press, 2008), 107–108.

15. For one counterexample, see Nasr, *Muhammad*, 30–31, 35–36.

16. Wright, "Critical Approaches," 245.

17. So do online authors today, engaged in a similar if more rapid direct exchange, with embedded links shuttling readers back and forth, and page titles and keywords structured to give their pages an advantage when search engines look for "Muhammad" or "Muhammad's marriages" or "Banu Qurayza." Vigorous and vicious online polemics truly have—at least in that brief moment before readers click away—a genuinely global, multireligious, mixed audience, the sort of thing that earlier texts proclaimed but seldom accomplished.

18. For instance, what of the Prophet's stepchildren? According to al-Ṭabarī's history, one of Khadīja's sons from a previous marriage "lived

to see [the advent of] Islam and was converted" (vol. 39, 80; bracketed text in original). See also Kister, "Sons of Khadīja," 61.

19. And many Muslim-authored biographies as well, for example, Haykal, *Life of Muhammad*, 502–503; Aḥmad, *Life of Muhammad*, 291–293. An exception, which notes disputes, is Hazelton, *First Muslim*, 292.

20. For an early view that Zayd was the first convert, see Powers, *Zayd*, 30. Aḥmad (*Life of Muhammad*, 383) lists all four: Khadija is the first woman, Abu Bakr the first free man, Ali "first among children" and Zayd "first among slaves." Similarly, Waheed-Ud-Din lists Khadija as his "first follower," after which she was joined by his "friend Abu Bakr, his cousin Ali, and his freed man, Zayd" (*Benefactor*, 10–11).

21. Marion Holmes Katz, "The Prophet Muḥammad in Ritual," in *Cambridge Companion*, ed. Brockopp, 143.

22. Kister, "Sons of Khadīja."

23. Safi, *Memories of Muhammad*, 264, makes a similar point using different evidence, remarking on modernist Muslims' "rationality" rather than their textual practices: they have "flattened the cosmos, both spiritually and metaphysically."

24. Haj, *Reconfiguring Islamic Tradition*; Noorani, *Culture and Hegemony*, 16–20, argues against a clear epistemic rupture between premodern and modern, or between East and West.

25. Taiyaba Nasrin, *The Prophet Muhammad as a Man: Islamic Modernism and Sirah Literature in Egypt* (Aligarh, India: Aligarh Muslim University Press, 2008 [1992]).

26. Safi, *Memories of Muhammad*, 41.

27. Mittermaier, *Dreams That Matter*, 174.

28. Schimmel, *And Muhammad Is His Messenger*, xi–xii. On Romanization and the use of English by non-Arabic-reading Muslims, see p. 98.

29. Mirza Masroor Ahmad, *True Love for the Holy Prophet* (Silver Spring, MD: Ahmadiyya Muslim Community, 2012), 25.

30. Muhammad Syafii Antonio, *Ensiklopedia Leadership & Manajemen Muhammad SAW, "The Super Leader Super Manager"* (Jakarta: Tazkia Publishing, 2010). For additional examples of hybrid titles, see Gade, "Religious Biography," 257, 263.

31. *Ṣalla Allāhu 'alayhi wa sallam:* "May God bless him and grant him peace," often rendered "peace be upon him" or abbreviated PBUH.

32. In the original Arabic title, the word "Superman" appears transliterated into Arabic (*subirman*). See Wessels, *Modern Arabic Biography*, 2. Riyāshī later published a two-volume study of *The Psychology* [or *Inner Life* or *Psyche*] *of the Arab Messenger*. Labīb Riyāshī, *Nafsīyat al-Rasūl al-'Arabī* (Beirut: Maṭba'at al-Kashshāf, 1937).

Bibliography

In my treatment of Muhammad's *Lives* I have drawn not only on scores of biographies but also on a substantial body of secondary literature about these biographies. Readers who want to explore further should begin with *The Cambridge Companion to Muhammad*, edited by Jonathan Brockopp. Tarif Khalidi's *Images of Muhammad* is a narrative history of the Muslim biographical treatment of the Prophet. Annemarie Schimmel's *And Muhammad Is His Messenger* explores devotion to the Prophet in Muslim tradition. Marion Katz's *The Birth of the Prophet Muhammad* addresses textual and ritual celebrations of the Prophet's birthday, past and present. John Tolan's writings, especially *Saracens* and the first chapters of *Sons of Ishmael*, are essential for medieval European views of Muhammad; Philip Almond's slim but richly documented *Heretic and Hero: Muhammad and the Victorians* is a treasure.

In alphabetizing entries, I ignore the prefix al- and the letter 'ayn.

Abbasi, S. M. Madani. *Family of the Holy Prophet (S.A.W.).* New Delhi: Adam, 2004.

Abd-Allah, Umar F. *A Muslim in Victorian America: The Life of Alexander Russell Webb.* New York: Oxford University Press, 2006.

'Abd al-Raḥmān, 'Ā'isha [Bint al-Shāṭi']. *The Wives of the Prophet.* Translated by Matti Moosa and D. Nicholas Ranson. Lahore: Muhammad Ashraf, 1971.

Abu Iqbal. "Muhammad in Rewrite." *Message International,* August–September 2002, 12–13.

Abu Lughod, Lila. *Do Muslim Women Need Saving?* Cambridge, MA: Harvard University Press, 2013.

Ahmad, Atif Ahmad. *Islam, Modernity, Violence, and Everyday Life.* New York: Palgrave Macmillan, 2009.

Aḥmad, Mirzā Bashīruddīn Maḥmūd. *Life of Muḥammad.* Tilford, UK: Islam International Publications, 2012.

Ahmad, Mirza Masroor. *True Love for the Holy Prophet.* Silver Spring, MD: Ahmadiyya Muslim Community, 2012.

Ahmad Khan, Syed. *A Series of Essays on the Life of Muhammad and Subjects Subsidiary Thereto.* Lahore: Premier Book House, 1968. First published 1870 by Trübner.

Ahmed, Shahab. "Ibn Taymiyya and the Satanic Verses." *Studia Islamica* 87 (1998): 67–124.

Aleem, Shamim. *Prophet Muhammad (S) and His Family: A Sociological Perspective.* Bloomington, IN: AuthorHouse, 2007.

Ali, Kecia. "'A Beautiful Example': The Prophet Muḥammad as a Model for Muslim Husbands." *Journal of Islamic Studies* 43, no. 2 (Summer 2004): 273–291.

———. "Khadija bint Khuwaylid." In *The Oxford Encyclopedia of Women in World History*, vol. 3, edited by Bonnie G. Smith. Oxford: Oxford University Press, 2007.

———. *Sexual Ethics and Islam: Feminist Reflections on Qur'an, Hadith, and Jurisprudence.* Oxford: Oneworld, 2006.

Ali, Muhammad. "Dottrine e attività dei musulmani Aḥmadiyya di Lahore." *Oriente Moderno* 6, no. 2 (February 1926): 108–23.

———. *Muhammad the Prophet.* Lahore: Ahmadiyya Anjuman Ishaat Islam, 1993.

Ali, Muhammad Mohar. *Sirat al-Nabi and the Orientalists, with Special Reference to the Writings of William Muir, D. S. Margoliouth and W. Montgomery Watt.* Vols. 1A and 1B. Medina: Kingdom of Saudi Arabia, King Fahd Complex for the Printing of the Holy Qur'an, 1997.

Ali, Syed Ameer. *A Critical Examination of the Life and Teachings of Mohammed.* London: Williams and Norgate, 1873.

———. *The Life and Teachings of Mohammed, or the Spirit of Islam.* London: W. H. Allen, 1891.

Almond, Philip. *Heretic and Hero: Muhammad and the Victorians.* Wiesbaden: Otto Harrassowitz, 1989.

Amīn, Aḥmad. *Ahmad Amin: My Life.* Translated by Issa J. Boullata. Leiden: Brill, 1978.

Amini, M. Sharif Ahmad. *Muhammad: The Most Successful Prophet.* Calcutta: Asian Printers, 1978.

Andrae, Tor. *Mohammed: The Man and His Faith.* Translated by Theophil Menzel. Rev. ed. New York: Harper and Row, 1960. (Original German publication 1932; first English ed. 1936, rev. ed. 1955.)

Andrea, Bernadette, and Linda McJannet, eds. *Early Modern England and Islamic Worlds.* New York: Palgrave, 2011.

Anis-ur-Rahman, Muhammad. *The Historical Role of the Venerable Woman.* 3rd ed., enlarged. Karachi: Faran Publications, 2007.

Antonio, Muhammad Syafii. *Ensiklopedia Leadership and Manajemen Muhammad SAW, "The Super Leader Super Manager."* Jakarta: Tazkia Publishing, 2010.

Al-'Aqqād, 'Abbās Maḥmūd. *'Abqariyyat Muḥammad* [The genius of Muhammad]. Cairo: Maṭbaʿat al-Istiqāma, 1942.

Argyriou, Astérious. "Éléments biographiques concernant le prophète Muhammad dans la littérature grecque des trois premiers siècles de l'Hégire." In *La vie du prophète Mahomet,* edited by Toufic Fahd, 159–182. Paris: Presses universitaires de France, 1983.

Armstrong, Karen. *Muhammad: A Biography of the Prophet.* New York: Harper, 1992.

———. *Muhammad: A Prophet for Our Time.* New York: Harper One, 2007.

Awad, George. "The Prophet Muhammad." In *The Crescent and the Couch: Cross-Currents between Islam and Psychoanalysis,* edited by Salman Akhtar. Lanham, MD: Jason Aronson, 2008.

Awad, Louis. *The Literature of Ideas in Egypt, Pt. 1.* Atlanta: Scholars Press, 1986.

Barham, C. N. "Child Marriage in India." *Westminster Review* 135, no. 2 (January–June 1891): 113–124.

Baron, Beth. "The Making and Breaking of Marital Bonds in Modern Egypt." In *Women in Middle Eastern History: Shifting Boundaries in Sex and Gender,* edited by Nikki R. Keddie and Beth Baron. New Haven, CT: Yale University Press, 1992.

———. *The Women's Awakening in Egypt: Culture, Society, and the Press.* New Haven, CT: Yale University Press, 1997.

Bashir, Shahzad. "Narrating Sight: Dreaming as Visual Training in Persianate Sufi Hagiography." In *Dreams and Visions in Islamic Societies,* edited by Özgen Felek and Alexander Knysh, 233–247. Albany: State University of New York Press, 2012.

Bayard, Pierre. *How to Talk about Books You Haven't Read.* Translated by Jeffrey Mehlman. New York: Bloomsbury, 2007.

Bellos, David. *Is That a Fish in Your Ear? Translation and the Meaning of Everything.* New York: Faber and Faber, 2011.

Bennett, Clinton. *In Search of Muhammad.* London: Cassell, 1998.

Berg, Herbert. "Competing Paradigms in the Study of Islamic Origins: Qur'ān 15:89–91 and the Value of Isnāds." In *Method and Theory*

in the Study of Islamic Origins, edited by Herbert Berg, 259–290. Leiden: Brill, 2003.

Birchwood, Matthew. "Confounding Babel: The Language of Religion in the English Revolution." In *The Religions of the Book: Christian Perceptions, 1400–1600,* edited by Matthew Dimmock and Andrew Hadfield, 140–158. New York: Palgrave, 2008.

Black, Jeremy. *Culture in Eighteenth-Century England: A Subject for Taste.* Hambledon, UK: Continuum, 2005.

Blanks, David R. "Western Views of Islam in the Premodern Period: A Brief History of Past Approaches." In *Western Views of Islam in Medieval and Early Modern Europe,* edited by David R. Blanks and Michael Frasetto, 11–53. New York: St. Martin's, 1999.

Blanks, David R., and Michael Frasetto. "Introduction." In *Western Views of Islam in Medieval and Early Modern Europe,* edited by Blanks and Frasetto.

Blanning, Timothy. *The Romantic Revolution: A History.* New York: Modern Library, 2012.

Bombay Tract and Book Society. *Life of Mahomet.* 3rd. ed. Bombay: Bombay Tract and Book Society, 1856.

Boullata, Issa J. Introduction to *Aḥmad Amīn: My Life,* by Aḥmad Amīn. Translated by Issa J. Boullata. Leiden: Brill, 1978.

Bowersock, G. W. *The Throne of Adulis: Red Sea Wars on the Eve of Islam.* New York: Oxford University Press, 2013.

Boyarin, Daniel. *The Jewish Gospels: The Story of the Jewish Christ.* New York: New Press, 2013.

Bravmann, M. M. *The Spiritual Background of Early Islam: Studies in Ancient Arab Concepts.* Leiden: Brill, 2009 [1972].

Brockopp, Jonathan E., ed. *The Cambridge Companion to Muḥammad.* Cambridge: Cambridge University Press, 2010.

Brown, Jonathan A. C. *Misquoting Muhammad: The Challenges and Choices of Interpreting the Prophet's Legacy.* Oxford: Oneworld, forthcoming.

———. *Muhammad: A Very Short Introduction.* New York: Oxford University Press, 2010.

Browne, G[eorge] Lathom. *The Æra of Mahomet: A.D. 527 to 629.* London: Society for Promoting Christian Knowledge, 1856.

Buaben, Jabal Muhammad. *Image of the Prophet Muḥammad in the West: A Study of Muir, Margoliouth, and Watt.* Leicester, UK: Islamic Foundation, 1996.

Buck-Morss, Susan. *Thinking Past Terror: Islamism and Critical Theory on the Left.* London: Verso, 2006.

Bulandshehri, Muhammad Ashiq Elahi. *The Wives of the Prophet Muhammad (sallalahu alayhe wasallam): A Complete Book on the Biographies of the Wives of Holy Prophet Muhammad (sallallahu alayhe wasallam).* Translated by Mohammad Akram. Lahore: Idara-e-Islamiat, 1994.

Burman, Thomas E. *Reading the Qur'an in Latin Christendom, 1140–1560.* Philadelphia: University of Pennsylvania Press, 2007.

Burrus, Virginia. *The Sex Lives of Saints: An Erotics of Ancient Hagiography.* Philadelphia: University of Pennsylvania Press, 2004.

Bush, George. *The Life of Mohammed: Founder of the Religion of Islam, and of the Empire of the Saracens.* New York: Harper and Brothers, 1837.

Carlyle, Thomas. *The Hero as Prophet: Mahomet; Islam (Lecture II: Heroes and Hero Worship).* New York: Maynard, Merrill, and Co., 1882.

Chaudhuri, Sukanta. *The Metaphysics of Text.* Cambridge: Cambridge University Press, 2010.

Chopra, Deepak. *Buddha: A Story of Enlightenment.* New York: Harper One, 2007.

———. *Jesus: A Story of Enlightenment.* New York: Harper One, 2008.

———. *Muhammad: A Story of the Last Prophet.* New York: Harper One, 2010.

Choudhury, Golam W. *The Prophet Muhammad: His Life and Eternal Message.* 2nd ed. Kuala Lumpur: WHS Publications, 1994 [1993].

Chraibi, Driss. *L'homme du livre.* Paris: Éditions Denoël, 2011 [1995].

Colby, Frederick S. *Narrating Muḥammad's Night Journey: Tracing the Development of the Ibn ʿAbbās Ascension Discourse.* Albany: State University of New York Press, 2008.

Coomar, Roy. With a prefatory note by Joel Benton. "Child Marriage in India." *North American Review* 147 (1888): 415–423.

Conley, Thomas. *Toward a Rhetoric of Insult.* Chicago: University of Chicago Press, 2010.

Conover, Sarah. *Muhammad: The Story of a Prophet and Reformer.* Boston: Skinner House, 2013.

Conrad, Lawrence. "Abraha and Muḥammad: Some Observations Apropos of Chronology and Literary 'Topoi' in the Early Arabic Historical Tradition." *Bulletin of the School of Oriental and African Studies* 50, no. 2 (1987): 225–240.

Cook, Michael. *Muhammad.* New York: Oxford University Press, 1996 [1983].

Cooke, Neil. "James Burton and Slave Girls." In *Unfolding the Orient: Travellers in Egypt and the Near East,* edited by Paul and Janet Starkey, 209–217. Reading, UK: Garnet, 2001.

Cooperson, Michael. "Images without Illustrations: The Visual Imagination in Classical Arabic Biography." In *Islamic Art and Literature*, edited by Oleg Grabar and Cynthia Robinson. Princeton, NJ: Markus Wiener, 2001.

Crone, Patricia, and Michael Cook. *Hagarism: The Making of the Islamic World.* Cambridge: Cambridge University Press, 1977.

Cuffel, Alexandra. *Gendering Disgust in Medieval Religious Polemic.* Notre Dame, IN: University of Notre Dame Press, 2007.

Curran, Stuart, ed. *Cambridge Companion to British Romanticism.* 2nd ed. Cambridge: Cambridge University Press, 2010.

Curtis, Edward E., IV. *Black Muslim Religion in the Nation of Islam, 1960–1975.* Chapel Hill: University of North Carolina Press, 2006.

Dashti, Ali. *Twenty-Three Years: A Study of the Prophetic Career of Mohammad.* Translated by F. R. C. Bagley. Santa Ana, CA: Mazda, 1994.

Davenport, John. *An Apology for Mohammed and the Koran.* London: J. Davy and Sons, 1869.

Day, Adrian. *Romanticism.* London: Routledge, 1996.

Demi. *Muhammad.* New York: Margaret K. McElderberry, 2003.

Department of Commerce and Labor, Bureau of the Census. *Special Reports: Marriage and Divorce, 1867–1906.* Pt. 1, *Summary, Laws, Foreign Statistics.* Washington, DC: Government Printing Office, 1909.

Dermenghem, Émile. *The Life of Mahomet.* Translated by Arabella Yorke. New York: Routledge, 1930.

———. *La vie de Mahomet.* Paris: Charlot, 1950.

De Sondy, Amanallah. *The Crisis of Islamic Masculinities.* London: Bloomsbury, 2014.

Di Cesare, Michelina. "Images of Muhammad in Western Medieval Book Culture." In *Constructing the Image of Muhammad in Europe*, edited by Avinoam Shalem, 9–32. Berlin: De Gruyter, 2013.

Dimmock, Matthew. "'A Human Head to the Neck of a Horse': Hybridity, Monstrosity and Early Christian Conceptions of Muhammad and Islam." In *The Religions of the Book: Christian Perceptions, 1400–1600*, edited by Matthew Dimmock and Andrew Hadfield, 66–88. New York: Palgrave, 2008.

———. *Mythologies of the Prophet Muhammad in Early Modern England.* Cambridge: Cambridge University Press, 2013.

Dods, Marcus. *Mohammed, Buddha, and Christ: Four Lectures on Natural and Revealed Religion.* London: Hodder and Stoughton, 1877.

Dold, Bernard E. *Carlyle, Goethe, and Muhammad.* Messina, Italy: Edizioni Dott. Antonino Sfameni, 1984.

Donner, Fred. *Muhammad and the Believers: At the Origins of Islam.* Cambridge, MA: Belknap, 2012.

———. "Muhammad and the Debates on Islam's Origins in the Digital Age." In *Muhammad in the Digital Age,* edited by Ruqayya Y. Khan. Austin: University of Texas Press, forthcoming.

———. *Review of Hagarism. In Middle East Studies Association Bulletin* 40, no. 2 (December 2006): 197–199.

Draycott, G. M. *Mahomet: Founder of Islam.* New York: Dodd, Mead and Company, 1916.

Duri, 'Abd al-'Aziz. *The Rise of Historical Writings among the Arabs.* Princeton, NJ: Princeton University Press, 1983.

Elmarsafy, Ziad. *The Enlightenment Qur'ān.* Oxford: Oneworld, 2009.

Elsadda, Hoda. "Discourses of Women's Biographies and Cultural Identity: Twentieth Century Representations of the Life of 'A'isha bin Abi Bakr." *Feminist Studies* 27, no. 1 (2001): 37–64.

Emerick, Yahiya. *Complete Idiot's Guide to Understanding Islam.* 3rd ed. New York: Alpha, 2011.

———. "Getting to Know a Friend: My Introduction to Muhammad." *Message International,* August–September 2002, 21–25.

———. *Muhammad.* Indianapolis: Alpha, 2002.

Ernst, Carl. "Muḥammad as the Pole of Existence." In *Cambridge Companion,* edited by Brockopp, 123–138.

Esposito, John L. "Ismail al-Faruqi: Muslim Scholar-Activist." In *The Muslims of America,* edited by Yvonne Haddad, 65–79. New York: Oxford University Press, 1991.

———. *The Future of Islam* (New York: Oxford University Press, 2013).

Al Faruqi, Ismail R. *The Hijrah: The Necessity of Its* Iqāmat *or Vergegenw'artigung.* Islamabad: National Hijra Council, 1985.

Fenton, John. "Biographical Myths; Illustrated from the Lives of Buddha and Muhammad." *The Folk-Lore Record* 3, no. 1 (1880): 26–39.

Ferrazzi, Cecilia. *Autobiography of an Aspiring Saint.* Edited and translated by Anne Jacobsen Schutte. Chicago: University of Chicago Press, 1996.

Frakes, Jerold C., ed. *Contextualizing the Muslim Other in Medieval Christian Discourse.* New York: Palgrave, 2011.

———. *Vernacular and Latin Literary Discourses of the Muslim Other in Medieval Germany.* New York: Palgrave, 2011.

Friedmann, Yohanan. *Prophecy Continuous: Aspects of Ahmadi Religious Thought and Its Medieval Background.* Berkeley: University of California Press, 1989.

Fuller, Mrs. Marcus B. [Jenny]. *The Wrongs of Indian Womanhood*. New York: Fleming H. Revell, 1900.

Gade, Anna M. "Religious Biography of the Prophet Muḥammad in Twenty-First-Century Indonesia." In *Cambridge Companion*, edited by Brockopp, 251–273.

Gershoni, Israel. "The Reader—'Another Production': The Reception of Haykal's Biography of Muhammad and the Shift of Egyptian Intellectuals to Islamic Subjects in the 1930s." *Poetics Today* 15, no. 2 (Summer 1994): 241–277.

———. "Theory of Crises." In *Middle Eastern Historiographies: Narrating the Twentieth Century*, edited by Israel Gershoni, Amy Singer, and Y. Hakan Erdem. Seattle: University of Washington Press, 2006.

Gershoni, Israel, and James P. Jankowsi. *Redefining the Egyptian Nation, 1930–1945*. Cambridge: Cambridge University Press, 2002.

Gibb, Hamilton. "Islamic Biographical Literature." In *Historians of the Middle East*, edited by Bernard Lewis and P. M. Holt, 54–58. London: Oxford University Press, 1962.

Glubb, John Bagot. *The Life and Times of Muhammad*. New York: Cooper Square Press, 2001 [1970].

Green, Samuel. *The Life of Mahomet: Founder of the Religion of Islamism and of the Empire of the Saracens*. London: William Tegg, 1877.

Grossman, Edith. *Why Translation Matters*. New Haven, CT: Yale University Press, 2010.

Gruber, Ira D. *Books and the British Army in the Age of the American Revolution*. Chapel Hill: University of North Carolina Press, 2010.

Guenther, Alan. "The Image of the Prophet Muhammad as Found in Missionary Writings of the Late Nineteenth Century." *Muslim World* 90 (Spring 2000): 43–70.

———. "Response of Sayyid Aḥmad Ḥān to Sir William Muir's Evaluation of *Ḥadīṯ* Literature." *Oriente Moderno* 82, no. 1 (2002).

Guillaume, Alfred, trans. *The Life of Muhammad: A Translation of Ibn Isḥāq's Sīrat Rasūl Allāh*. Karachi: Oxford University Press, 2003 [1955].

Gunny, Ahmad. *The Prophet Muhammad in French and English Literature, 1650 to the Present*. Leicestershire: Islamic Foundation, 2010.

Haj, Samira. *Reconfiguring Islamic Tradition: Rationality, Reform, and Modernity*. Stanford, CA: Stanford University Press, 2009.

Halevi, Leor. *Muhammad's Grave: Death Rites and the Making of Islamic Society.* New York: Columbia University Press, 2007.

Hamilton, Nigel. *Biography: A Brief History.* Cambridge, MA: Harvard University Press, 2008.

Hanaoka, Mimi. "Visions of Muhammad in Bukhara and Tabaristan: Dreams and Their Uses in Persian Local Histories," *Iranian Studies* 47, no. 2 (March 2014): 289–303.

Hatem, Mervat F. "'A'isha Abdel Rahman: An Unlikely Heroine: A Post-Colonial Reading of Her Life and Some of Her Biographies of Women in the Prophetic Household." *Journal of Middle East Women's Studies* 7, no. 2 (Spring 2011): 1–26.

Hawley, John S. "Introduction: Saints and Virtues." In *Saints and Virtues,* edited by John Stratton Hawley. Berkeley: University of California Press, 1987.

Hawting, G. R. *The Idea of Idolatry and the Emergence of Islam.* Cambridge: Cambridge University Press, 2002.

Haykal, Muḥammad Ḥusayn. *Al-Fārūq 'Umar* ['Umar the Just]. Cairo: Maktabat al-Nahḍah al-Miṣrīyah, 1963–1964.

———. *Ḥayāt Muḥammad.* Cairo: Maṭba'at Miṣr, 1935.

———. *Ḥayāt Muḥammad.* 8th ed. Cairo: Maktabat al-Nahḍah al-Miṣrīyah, 1963.

———. *The Life of Muḥammad.* Translated by Ismail Al Faruqi. Kuala Lumpur: Islamic Book Trust, 2002 [1976].

———. *Al-Ṣiddīq Abū Bakr* [Abu Bakr the Righteous]. 6th ed. Cairo: Dār al-Ma'ārif, 1971.

———. *Sirat-i Rasul.* Translated by Muḥammad Vāris Kāmil. Lahore: Maktabah-yi Kāravān, 1964.

———. *Tarājim Miṣrīyah wa-gharbīyah* [Egyptian and Western biographies]. Cairo: Maṭba'at al-Siyāsah, 1929.

———. *'Uthmān ibn 'Affān: Bayna al-khilāfah wa-al-mulk* ['Uthman ibn 'Affan: Between caliphate and kingship]. Beirut: Dār al-Kutub al-'Ilmīyah, 2007.

Hazelton, Lesley. *The First Muslim: The Story of Muhammad.* New York: Riverhead Books, 2013.

Heschel, Susannah. "German Jewish Scholarship on Islam as a Tool for De-Orientalizing Judaism." *New German Critique* 39, no. 3 (Fall 2012): 91–107.

Hidayatullah, Aysha. "Behind Every Good (or Bad) Muslim Man: Representation of Muhammad's Wives after 9/11." In *Muhammad in the Digital Age,* edited by Ruqayya Y. Khan.

———. "Māriyya the Copt: Gender, Sex and Heritage in the Legacy of Muhammad's *Umm Walad*," *Islam and Christian–Muslim Relations* 21, no. 3 (July 2010): 221–243.

Higgins, Godfrey. *An Apology for the Life and Character of the Celebrated Prophet of Arabia, Called Mohamed, or the Illustrious*. London: Rowland Hunter, 1829.

Hoyland, Robert G. "The Earliest Christian Writings on Muhammad: An Appraisal." In *The Biography of Muhammad: The Issue of the Sources*. Ed. Harald Motzki. 276–297. Leiden: Brill, 2000.

———. *Seeing Islam as Others Saw It: A Survey and Evaluation of Christian, Jewish and Zoroastrian Writings on Early Islam*. Princeton, NJ: Darwin, 1998.

Hurvitz, Nimrod. "Biographies and Mild Asceticism: A Study of Islamic Moral Imagination." *Studia Islamica* 85 (1997): 41–65.

Hyatte, Reginald, trans. *The Prophet of Islam in Old French: The Romance of Muhammad (1258) and The Book of Muhammad's Ladder (1264)*. Leiden: Brill, 1997.

Ibn Hishām, *Al-sīra al-nabawīya*. Al-Mansura, Egypt: Dar al-Ghadd al-Jadeed, 2003.

Ibn Ishaak. *Het leven van Mohammed: De vroegste Arabische verhalen*. Translated by Wim Raven. Amsterdam: Bulaaq, 2000.

Ibn Ishaq. *The Life of Muhammad: Apostle of Allah*. Edited by Michael Edwardes and translated by Edward Rehatsek. London: Folio Society, 1964.

Ibn Kathīr. *The Life of the Prophet Muhammad*. Translated by Trevor Le Gassick. Reading, UK: Garnet, 1998.

Ibn Sa'd. *Women of Madina*. Translated by Aisha Bewley. London: Ta-Ha Publishers, 1995.

Idris, H. R. "Réflexions sur Ibn Ishaq." *Studia Islamica* 17 (1962): 23–36.

Idriss, Mohammad Mazher. "Honour, Violence, Women and Islam: An Introduction." In *Honour, Violence, Women and Islam*, edited by Mohammad Mazher Idriss and Tahir Abbas, 1–15. Abingdon, UK: Routledge, 2011.

Irving, Washington [Wāshinjtūn Irfinj]. *Hayāt Muhammad*. Translated by 'Alī Husnī al-Kharbūtlī, 2nd ed. Egypt: Dār al-Ma'ārif, 1966 [1960].

———. *Mahomet and His Successors*. 2 vols. New York: G. P. Putnam and Son, 1868.

Irwin, Robert. *Dangerous Knowledge: Orientalism and Its Discontents*. New York: Overlook, 2006.

Jaffer, Mehru. *The Book of Muhammad*. New Delhi: Penguin Global, 2010.

Jalbani, G. N. *Life of the Holy Prophet*. Islamabad: National Hijra Council, 1988.

Jameelah, Maryam. *Islam and Orientalism*. Rev. ed. Lahore: Mohammad Yusuf Khan and Sons, 1981.

Jenkins, Philip. *God's Continent: Christianity, Islam, and Europe's Religious Crisis*. Oxford: Oxford University Press, 2007.

Johnson, Paul. *George Washington: The Founding Father*. New York: Harper Collins, 2006.

Johnstone, P[eirce] De Lacy. *Muhammad and His Power*. New York: Charles Scribner's Sons, 1908.

Jones, Sherry. *The Jewel of Medina*. New York: Beaufort Books, 2008.

Jones, Terry D. *Islam Is of the Devil*. Lake Mary, FL: Creation House, 2010.

Jordan, Mark. *The Ethics of Sex*. Malden, MA: Blackwell, 2002.

Judd, Steven C. "Competitive Hagiography in Biographies of al-Awzāʾī and Sufyān al-Thawrī." *Journal of the American Oriental Society* 122, no. 1 (2002): 25–37.

Kahf, Mohja. *Western Representations of the Muslim Woman: From Termagant to Odalisque*. Austin: University of Texas Press, 1999.

Kahn, Tamam. *Untold: A History of the Wives of Prophet Muhammad*. Rhinebeck, NY: Monkfish, 2010.

Kamal-ud-Din, Khwaja. *The Ideal Prophet: Aspects of the Life and Qualities of the Holy Prophet Muhammad*. Woking, UK: Ahmadiyya Anjuman Ishaʿat Islam Lahore, 1925.

———. *The Ideal Prophet, Incorporating a Portion of "Glimpses from the Life of the Prophet."* 4th ed. Woking, UK: Woking Muslim Mission and Literary Trust, 1956 [1925].

Katz, Jonathan G. "Dreams and Their Interpretation in Sufi Thought and Practice." In *Dreams and Visions in Islamic Societies*, edited by Felek and Knysh, 181–197.

Katz, Marion Holmes. *The Birth of the Prophet Muhammad*. New York: Routledge, 2007.

———. "The Prophet Muhammad in Ritual." In *Cambridge Companion*, edited by Brockopp, 139–157.

Kelen, Betty. *Muhammad: The Messenger of God*. New York: Pocket Books, 1997.

Khalek, Nancy. *Damascus after the Muslim Conquest: Text and Image in Early Islam*. New York: Oxford University Press, 2011.

Khalidi, Tarif. *Arabic Historical Thought in the Classical Period*. Cambridge: Cambridge University Press, 1996.

———. *Images of Muhammad: Narratives of the Prophet in Islam through the Centuries.* New York: Doubleday, 2009.

———. "Al-Ṭabarī: An Introduction." In *Al-Ṭabarī: A Medieval Muslim Historian and His Work,* edited by Hugh Kennedy, 1–9. Princeton, NJ: Darwin Press, 2008.

Khan, Ruqayya Y., ed. *Muhammad in the Digital Age.* Austin: University of Texas Press, forthcoming.

———. "Of Cyber Muslimahs: Wives of the Prophet and Muslim Women in the Digital Age." In *Muhammad in the Digital Age,* edited by Ruqayya Y. Khan.

Khanna, Meenakshi. "The Visionaries of a *Ṭarīqa:* The Uwaysī Sufis of Shāhjahānabād." In *Dreams and Visions in Islamic Societies,* edited by Felek and Knysh, 273–296.

Kholoussy, Hanan. *For Better, for Worse: The Marriage Crisis That Made Modern Egypt.* Stanford, CA: Stanford University Press, 2010.

———. "The Nationalization of Marriage in Monarchical Egypt." In *Re-Envisioning Egypt, 1919–1952,* edited by Arthur Goldschmidt, Amy J. Johnson, and Barak A. Salmoni, 317–350. Cairo: American University in Cairo Press, 2005.

Kidd, Thomas S. *American Christians and Islam: Evangelical Culture and Muslims from the Colonial Period to the Age of Terrorism.* Princeton, NJ: Princeton University Press, 2009.

———. "Is It Worse to Follow Mahomet Than the Devil? Early American Uses of Islam." *Church History* 72, no. 4 (December 2003): 766–790.

Kinberg, Leah. "Dreams Online: Contemporary Appearances of the Prophet in Dreams." In *Dreams and Visions in Islamic Societies,* edited by Felek and Knysh, 139–157.

———. "The Legitimization of the *Madhāhib* through Dreams." *Arabica* 32, no. 1 (March 1985): 47–79.

King, Richard. *Orientalism and Religion: Postcolonial Theory, India, and the Mystic East.* London: Routledge, 1999.

Kister, M. J. "'A Bag of Meat': A Study of an Early *Hadīth.*" *Bulletin of the School of Oriental and African Studies* 33 (1970): 267–275.

———. "The Sons of Khadīja." *Jerusalem Studies in Arabic and Islam* 16 (1993): 59–95.

Klausen, Jytte. *The Cartoons That Shook the World.* New Haven, CT: Yale University Press, 2009.

Koelle, S. W. *Mohammed and Mohammedanism Critically Considered.* London: Rivingtons, 1889.

Kohlberg, Etan. "Western Accounts of the Death of Muḥammad." In *L'Orient dans l'histoire religieuse de l'Europe: L'invention des origines*, edited by Mohammad Ali Amir-Moezzi and John Scheid, 165–195. Turnhout: Brepols, 2000.

Lai, Whalen. "The Search for the Historical Śakyamuni in Light of the Historical Jesus." *Buddhist-Christian Studies* 2 (1982): 79–91.

Lane, Edward William. *Selections from the Ḳur-án*. Rev. ed. London: Trübner, 1879.

Lane-Poole, Stanley. *The Speeches and Table-Talk of the Prophet Mohammad*. London: Macmillan, 1882.

———. Introduction to *Selections from the Ḳur-án*, by Edward William Lane, xi–cix. Rev. ed. London: Trübner, 1879.

Lassner, Jacob. *Jews, Christians, and the Abode of Islam: Modern Scholarship, Medieval Realities*. Chicago: University of Chicago Press, 2012.

Laureys, Marc. "History and Poetry in Philippus Meyerus's Humanist Latin Portraits of the Prophet Mohammed and Ottoman Rulers (1594)." In *Latinity and Alterity in the Early Modern Empire*, edited by Yasmin Annabel Haskell and Juanita Feros Ruys, 273–299. Tempe, AZ: Arizona Center for Medieval and Rennaisance Studies; Turnhout: Brepols, 2010.

Lecker, Michael. "Glimpses of Muḥammad's Medinan Decade." In *Cambridge Companion*, edited by Brockopp, 61–79.

Lee, Hermione. *Biography: A Very Short Introduction*. Oxford: Oxford University Press, 2009.

Lewis, Bernard. "Gibbon on Muhammad." In "Edward Gibbon and the Decline and Fall of the Roman Empire." Special issue, *Daedalus* 105, no. 3 (Summer 1976): 89–101.

Lewis, C. S. *Mere Christianity*. San Francisco: Harper, 2001 [1952].

Lings, Martin. *Muhammad: His Life Based on the Earliest Sources*. Rochester, VT: Inner Traditions International, 1983.

Littlewood, Ian. *Sultry Climates: Travel and Sex*. Cambridge, MA: Da Capo, 2002.

Lopez, Donald S., Jr. *From Stone to Flesh: A Short History of the Buddha*. Chicago: University of Chicago Press, 2013.

———. *The Scientific Buddha: His Short and Happy Life*. New Haven, CT: Yale University Press, 2012.

Lyall, C. J. "Obituary Notice: Sir William Muir." *Journal of the Royal Asiatic Society of Great Britain and Ireland* 37 (1905): 875–879.

Lyons, Jonathan. *Islam through Western Eyes: From the Crusades to the War on Terrorism*. New York: Columbia University Press, 2012.

MacLean, Gerald. "Milton among the Muslims." In *The Religions of the Book: Christian Perceptions, 1400–1600*, edited by Matthew Dimmock and Andrew Hadfield. New York: Palgrave, 2008: 180–94.

Maghen, Ze'ev. *Virtues of the Flesh: Passion and Purity in Early Islamic Jurisprudence*. Leiden: Brill, 2005.

Mahfouz, Naguib. *Children of the Alley: A Novel*. New York: Anchor, 1996.

Malik, Ghulam. *Muhammad: An Islamic Perspective*. Lanham, MD: University Press of America, 1996.

Manseau, Peter. *Rag and Bone: A Journey among the World's Holy Dead*. New York: Henry Holt, 2009.

Margoliouth, David Samuel. *Mohammed and the Rise of Islam*. New York: G. P. Putnam's Sons, 1905.

Marston, Elsa. *Muhammad of Mecca: Prophet of Islam*. New York: Franklin Watts, 2001.

Masuzawa, Tomoko. *The Invention of World Religions: Or, How European Universalism Was Preserved in the Language of Pluralism*. Chicago: University of Chicago Press, 2005.

Matar, Nabil. *Turks, Moors, and Englishmen in the Age of Discovery*. New York: Columbia University Press, 1999.

———, ed. *Henry Stubbe and the Beginnings of Islam: The Originall & Progress of Mahometanism*. New York: Columbia University Press, 2014.

McAuliffe, Jane Dammen. "Al-Ṭabarī's Prelude to the Prophet." In *Al-Ṭabarī: A Medieval Muslim Historian and His Work*, edited by Hugh Kennedy, 113–129. Princeton, NJ: Darwin, 2008.

Mernissi, Fatima. *Islam and Democracy: Fear of the Modern World*. Translated by Mary Jo Lakeland. New York: Perseus, 1992.

———. *The Veil and the Male Elite: A Feminist Interpretation of Women's Rights in Islam*. Translated by Mary Jo Lakeland. New York: Perseus, 1991.

Metcalf, Barbara Daly. *Islamic Revival In British India: Deoband, 1860–1900*. New Delhi: Oxford University Press, 2002.

Minault, Gail. "Aloys Sprenger: German Orientalism's 'Gift' to Delhi College." *South Asia Research* 31, no. 1 (February 2011): 7–23.

Minois, George. *The Atheist's Bible: The Most Dangerous Book That Never Existed*. Chicago: University of Chicago Press, 2012.

Mirza, Sarah. "Dreaming the Truth in the *Sīra* of Ibn Hishām." In *Dreams and Visions in Islamic Societies*, edited by Felek and Knysh, 15–30.

Mitchell, Timothy. *Colonising Egypt*. Berkeley: University of California Press, 1991.

Mittermaier, Amira. *Dreams That Matter: Egyptian Landscapes of the Imagination.* Berkeley: University of California Press, 2011.

Monroe, James T. "The Poetry of the *Sīrah* Literature." In *The Cambridge History of Arabic Literature: Arabic Literature to the End of the Umayyad Period,* edited by A. F. L. Beeston, T. M. Johnstone, R. B. Serjeant, and G. R. Smith, 368–373. Cambridge: Cambridge University Press, 1983.

Montgomery, James E. "Editor's Introduction." In *The Oral and the Written in Early Islam,* edited by Gregor Schoeler, Uwe Vagelpohl, and James E. Montgomery. London: Taylor and Francis, 2006.

Morey, Peter, and Amina Yaqin. *Framing Muslims.* Cambridge, MA: Harvard University Press, 2010.

Muir, William. *The Life of Mahomet from Original Sources.* 2nd ed. London: Smith, Elder, 1878.

―――. *The Life of Mahomet from Original Sources.* 3rd ed. London: Smith, Elder, 1894.

―――. *The Life of Mahomet, with Introductory Chapter on the Original Sources for the Biography of Mahomet, and on the Pre-Islamite History of Arabia.* London: Smith, Elder, 1858 (vols. 1–2) and 1861 (vols. 3–4).

―――. *The Mohammedan Controversy: Biographies of Mohammed; Sprenger on Tradition; the Indian Liturgy; and the Psalter.* Edinburgh: T. & T. Clark, 1897.

Murray, William, trans. *The Life of Mohammed Translated from the Arabic of Abulfeda.* Elgin, Scotland: A. C. Brander, n.d.

Nadvi, Syed Suleman [Saiyid Sulaiman Nadwi]. *Muhammad: The Ideal Prophet. A Historic, Practical, Perfect Model for Humanity.* Translated by Mohiuddin Ahmad. Kuala Lumpur: Islamic Book Trust, 1977 [n.d.].

―――. *Women Companions of the Holy Prophet and Their Sacred Lives.* New Delhi: Islamic Book Service, 2001.

Nasier, Alcofribas, trans. *The Three Impostors.* Privately printed, 1904.

Nasr, Seyyed Hossein. *Muhammad: Man of God.* Chicago: Kazi, 1995.

Nasrin, Taiyaba. *The Prophet Muhammad as a Man: Islamic Modernism and Sirah Literature in Egypt.* Aligarh, India: Aligarh Muslim University Press, 2008 [1992].

Nazik Saba Yared. *Arab Travellers and Western Civilization.* Translated by Sumayya Damluji Shahbandar. London: Saqi Books, 1996.

Newby, Gordon D. *The Making of the Last Prophet: A Reconstruction of the Earliest Biography of Muhammad.* Charleston: University of South Carolina Press, 1989.

Newcomb, Harvey. *The False Prophet; or, An Account of the Rise and Progress of the Mohammedan Religion; Comprising the History of the Church, etc.* 2nd ed. Boston: Massachusetts Sabbath School Society, 1844.

Noorani, Yaseen. *Culture and Hegemony in the Colonial Middle East.* New York: Palgrave, 2010.

Northrup, David. *How English Became the Global Language.* New York: Palgrave, 2013.

Norton, Charles Eliot, ed. *The Correspondence of Thomas Carlyle and Ralph Waldo Emerson, 1834–1872.* 2 vols. Boston: James R. Osgood, 1883.

Omar, Sara. "Al-Qubaysiyyāt: Negotiating Female Religious Authority in Damascus." *Muslim World* 103, no. 3 (July 2013): 347–362.

Otterbeck, Jonas. "The Depiction of Islam in Sweden: An Historical Overview." http://inhouse.lau.edu.lb/bima/papers/Jonas_Otterbeck .pdf.

Pasha, Kamran. *Mother of the Believers: A Novel of the Birth of Islam.* New York: Washington Square, 2009.

Pelikan, Jaroslav. *Jesus through the Centuries: His Place in the History of Culture.* New Haven: Yale University Press, 1999 [1985].

Penn, Michael. *Imaging Islam: Syriac Christianity and the Reimagining of Christian-Muslim Relations.* Philadelphia: University of Pennyslvania Press, forthcoming.

Peters, F. E. *Jesus and Muhammad: Parallel Tracks, Parallel Lives.* New York: Oxford University Press, 2011.

———. "The Quest of the Historical Muhammad." *International Journal of Middle East Studies* 23 (1991): 291–315.

Peterson, Daniel C. *Muhammad: Prophet of God.* Grand Rapids, MI: Wm. B. Eerdmans, 2007.

Pickthall, M. M. *The Life of Muhammad: A Brief History.* Beltsville, MD: Amana, 1998.

Pierce, Matthew. "Remembering Fāṭimah: New Means of Legitimizing Female Authority in Contemporary Shīʿī Discourse." In *Women, Leadership, and Mosques: Changes in Contemporary Islamic Authority,* edited by Masooda Bano and Hilary Kalmbach, 345–362. Leiden: Brill, 2012.

———. "Remembering the Infallible Imams: Narrative and Memory in Medieval Twelver Shiʿism." Ph.D. diss., Boston University, 2013.

Pitt, Alan. "The Cultural Impact of Science in France: Ernest Renan and the Vie de Jésus." *Historical Journal* 43, no. 1 (March 2000): 79–101.

Powell, Avril A. *Scottish Orientalists and India: The Muir Brothers, Religion, Education and Empire.* Woodbridge, UK: Boydell, 2010.

Powers, David S. *Muḥammad Is Not the Father of Any of Your Men: The Making of the Last Prophet.* Philadelphia: University of Pennsylvania Press, 2009.

———. *Zayd.* Philadelphia: University of Pennsylvania Press, forthcoming.

Prideaux, Humphrey. *The True Nature of Imposture Fully Display'd in the Life of Mahomet,* 8th ed. London: E. Curll, 1723 [1697].

Prothero, Stephen. *American Jesus: How the Son of God Became a National Icon.* New York: Farrar, Straus and Giroux, 2003.

Purohit, Teena. *The Aga Khan Case: Religion and Identity in Colonial India.* Cambridge, MA: Harvard University Press, 2012.

Pursley, Sara. "Daughters of the Right Path: Family Law, Homosocial Publics, and the Ethics of Intimacy in the Works of Shiʻi Revivalist Bint al-Huda." *Journal of Middle East Women's Studies* 8, no. 2 (Spring 2012): 51–77.

Qasmi, Shahid Zafar. *Questions and Answers on the Mothers of Believers (May Allah Be Pleased with Them).* Revised and checked by Muhammad Tahir Salafi. Riyadh: Darussalam, 1997.

Quinn, Frederick. *Sum of All Heresies: The Image of Islam in Western Thought.* New York: Oxford University Press, 2008.

Rahman, Afazlur. *Muhammad as a Military Leader.* London: Muslim Schools Trust, 1980.

Rahman, Fazlur. *Prophecy in Islam: Philosophy and Orthodoxy.* Chicago: University of Chicago Press, 2011.

Ramadan, Tariq. *In the Footsteps of the Prophet: Lessons from the Life of Muhammad.* New York: Oxford University Press, 2007.

———. *Muhammad: Vie du prophète; Les enseignements spirituels et contemporains.* Paris: Presses du Châtelet. 2006.

Rauf, Imam Feisal Abdul. *Moving the Mountain: A New Vision of Islam in America.* New York: Free Press, 2012.

Reinhart, A. Kevin. "Juynbolliana, Gradualism, the Big Bang, and Ḥadīth Study in the Twenty-First Century." *Journal of the American Oriental Society* 130, no. 3 (July–September 2010): 413–444.

Reynolds, Dwight F., ed. *Interpreting the Self: Autobiography in the Arabic Literary Tradition.* Berkeley: University of California Press, 2001.

Reynolds, Gabriel Said. "Remembering Muhammad." *Numen: International Review for the History of Religions* 58, no. 2/3 (2011): 188–206.

Ricci, Ronit. *Islam Translated: Literature, Conversion, and the Arabic Cosmopolis of South and Southeast Asia*. Chicago: University of Chicago Press, 2012.

Riyāshī, Labīb. *Nafsīyat al-Rasūl al-'Arabī*. Beirut: Maṭba'at al-Kashshāf, 1937.

Rizvi, S. A. A. "Muḥammad in South Asian Biographies: Changes in Islamic Perceptions of the Individual in Society." In *Self and Biography: Essays on the Individual and Society in Asia*, edited by Wang Gungwu, 99–122. Sydney: Sydney University Press, 1975.

Robinson, Chase. *Islamic Historiography*. Cambridge: Cambridge University Press, 2002.

Robinson-Dunn, Diane. *The Harem, Slavery and British Imperial Culture: Anglo-Muslim Relations in the Late Nineteenth Century*. Manchester, UK: Manchester University Press, 2006.

Roded, Ruth. "Alternate Images of the Prophet Muhammad's Virility." In *Islamic Masculinities*, edited by Lahoucine Ouzgane. London: Zed Books, 2006.

———. "Bint al-Shati's 'Wives of the Prophet': Feminist or Feminine?" *British Journal of Middle Eastern Studies* 33, no. 1 (May 2006): 51–66.

———. "Gender in an Allegorical Life of Muḥammad: Mahfouz's *Children of Gebelawi*." *Muslim World* 93 (January 2003): 117–134.

———. "Muslim Women Reclaim the Life-Story of the Prophet: 'A'isha 'Abd al-Raḥmān, Assia Djebar, and Nadia Yassine." *Muslim World* 103, no. 3 (July 2013): 334–346.

Rodgers, Russ. *The Generalship of Muhammad*. Jacksonville: University Press of Florida, 2012.

Rodinson, Maxime. "A Critical Survey of Modern Studies on Muhammad." In *Studies on Islam*, edited and translated by Merlin Swartz, 23–85. New York: Oxford University Press, 1981.

———. *Europe and the Mystique of Islam*. London: I. B. Tauris, 2002 [1987].

———. *Mahomet*. Paris: Éditions du Seuil, 1961. Translated by Anne Carter as *Muḥammad* (New York: Pantheon, 1980 [1971]).

Rosen, Lawrence. *Varieties of Muslim Experience: Encounters with Arab Political and Cultural Life*. Chicago: University of Chicago Press, 2008.

Roy, Coomar. With a prefatory note by Joel Benton. "Child Marriage in India," *North American Review* 147 (1888): 415–423.

Rubin, Uri. *The Eye of the Beholder: The Life of Muhammad as Viewed by the Early Muslims; A Textual Analysis*. Princeton, NJ: Darwin, 1995.

———, ed. *The Life of Muhammad*. Aldershot, UK: Ashgate / Variorum, 1998.

———. "Muhammad's Message in Mecca: Warnings, Signs, and Miracles." In *Cambridge Companion*, edited by Brockopp, 39–56.

———. *Muhammad the Prophet and Arabia*. Farnham, UK: Ashgate / Variorum, 2011.

———. "Pre-Existence and Light: Aspects of the Concept of *Nūr Muḥammad*." *Israel Oriental Studies* 5 (1975): 62–119.

Sabanegh, E. S. *Muhammad b. Abdallah, "Le prophete": Portraits contemporains, Egypte 1930–1950*. Paris: Librairie J. Vrin, n.d.

Sabbath, Roberta Sterman, ed. *Sacred Tropes: Tanakh, New Testament, and Qur'an as Literature and Culture*. Leiden: Brill, 2009.

Safi, Omid. *Memories of Muhammad: Why the Prophet Matters*. New York: Harper One, 2009.

Said, Edward. *Orientalism*. New York: Pantheon, 1978.

Salahi, Adil. *Muhammad, Man and Prophet: A Complete Study of the Life of the Prophet of Islam*. Leicestershire, UK: Islamic Foundation, 2012.

Salama, Mohammad R. *Islam, Orientalism, and Intellectual History: Modernity and the Politics of Exclusion since Ibn Khaldun*. London: I. B. Tauris, 2011.

Sale, George, trans. *The Koran: Commonly Called the Alcoran of Mohammed*. London: L. Hawes et al., 1734.

Salmin, Muhammad Ali-Al-Haj. *The Holy Prophet Mohammad: The Commander of the Faithful*. Bombay: M. A. Salmin, 1930s.

Sardar, Ziauddin. *Muhammad: All That Matters*. London: Hodder, 2012.

Sarkar, Sumit, and Tanika Sarkar, eds. *Women and Social Reform in Modern India: A Reader*. Bloomington: Indiana University Press, 2008.

Sarwar, Hafiz Ghulam. *Muhammad: The Holy Prophet*. Lahore: Shaykh Muhamamd Ashraf, 1980 [1961].

Schacht, Joseph. "A Revaluation of Islamic Traditions." *Journal of the Royal Asiatic Society of Great Britain and Ireland* 81, no. 3–4 (October 1949): 143–154.

Schick, Irvin. *The Erotic Margin: Spatiality and Sexuality in Alterist Discourse*. London: Verso, 1999.

Schimmel, Annemarie. *And Muhammad Is His Messenger: The Veneration of the Prophet in Islamic Piety*. Chapel Hill: University of North Carolina Press, 1985.

Schoeler, Gregor. "Foundations for a New Biography of Muhammad: The Production and Evaluation of the Corpus of Traditions from 'Urwah b. al-Zubayr." In *Method and Theory in the Study of Islamic Origins*, edited by Herbert Berg, 21–28. Leiden: Brill: 2003.

Shabazz, Ama F. "The Prophet on the Treatment of Women." *Message International*, August–September 2002, 37–39.

Shalem, Avinoam, ed. *Constructing the Image of Muhammad in Europe*. Berlin: De Gruyter, 2013.

Shaner, Edward. "Biographies of the Buddha." *Philosophy East and West* 37, no. 3 (July 1987): 306–322.

Shepard, William. *The Faith of a Modern Muslim Intellectual: The Religious Aspects and Implications of the Writings of Ahmad Amin*. New Delhi: Indian Institute of Islamic Studies / Vikas, 1982.

Shoemaker, Stephen J. *The Death of a Prophet: The End of Muhammad's Life and the Beginnings of Islam*. Philadelphia: University of Pennsylvania Press, 2012.

Siddiqui, Abdul Hameed. *The Life of Muhammad (P.B.U.H.)*. 2nd ed. New Delhi: Islamic Book Service, 2002 [1975]; 1st ed. 1969.

Siddiqui, Mona. *Christians, Muslims, and Jesus*. New Haven, CT: Yale University Press, 2013.

Sinha, Mrinali. *Specters of Mother India: The Global Restructuring of an Empire*. Durham, NC: Duke University Press, 2006.

Smith, Charles D. "*Hayat Muhammad* and the Muslim Brothers: Two Interpretations of Egyptian Islam and Their Socioeconomic Implications." *Journal of the American Research Center in Egypt* 16 (1979): 175–181.

————. *Islam and the Search for Social Order in Modern Egypt: A Biography of Muhammad Husayn Haykal*. Albany: State University of New York Press, 1983.

Smith, Christian. *Moral, Believing Animals: Human Personhood and Culture*. New York: Oxford University Press, 2003.

Spellberg, D. A. *Politics, Gender, and the Islamic Past*. New York: Columbia University Press, 1996.

Spencer, Robert. *Did Muhammad Exist? An Inquiry into Islam's Obscure Origins*. Wilmington, DE: Intercollegiate Studies Institute, 2012.

————. *The Truth about Muhammad: Founder of the World's Most Intolerant Religion*. Washington, DC: Regnery, 2006.

Sprenger, Aloys. *The Life of Mohammad from Original Sources*. Allahabad: Presbyterian Mission Press, 1851. Expanded German ed.: *Das Leben und die Lehre des Moḥammad, nach bisher des grösstentheils unbenutzten Quellen bearbeitet*. 2 vols. Berlin: Nicolaische Verlagsbuchhandlung, 1861.

Stecker, Tom. *The Man Mohammed: A Dramatic Character-Sketch*. Cambridge, MA: Co-operative Press, 1900.

Steiner, Wendy. *The Scandal of Pleasure: Art in an Age of Fundamentalism*. Chicago: University of Chicago Press, 1995.

Stetkevych, Jaroslav. *Muḥammad and the Golden Bough: Reconstructing Arabian Myth*. Bloomington: Indiana University Press, 1996.

Stobart, J[ames] W[illiam] H[ampson]. *Islam and Its Founder*. London: Society for Promoting Christian Knowledge, 1895.

Stroumsa, Guy G. *A New Science: The Discovery of Religion in the Age of Reason*. Cambridge, MA: Harvard University Press, 2010.

Stubbe, Henry. *An Account of the Rise and Progress of Mahometanism with the Life of Mahomet and a Vindication of Him and His Religion from the Calumnies of the Christians*. Edited by Hafiz Mahmoud Khan Shairani. London: Luzac, 1911.

Szilágyi, Krisztina. "Muḥammad and the Monk: The Making of the Christian Baḥīrā Legend." *Jerusalem Studies in Arabic and Islam* 34 (2008): 169–214.

Al-Ṭabarī, Abū Jaʿfar Muḥammad ibn Jarīr. *Tārīkh al-Ṭabarī: tārīkh al-rusul wa-al-mulūk*, edited by Muḥmmad Abū al-Faḍl Ibrāhīm. 11 vols. Egypt: Dār al-Maʿārif, 1960–[1977].

———. *The History of al-Ṭabarī*. Various translators. 39 vols. Albany: State University of New York, 1989–1998.

Tageldin, Shaden. *Disarming Words: Empire and the Seductions of Translation in Egypt*. Berkeley: University of California Press, 2011.

———. "Secularizing Islam: Carlyle, al-Sibāʿī, and the Translations of 'Religion' in British Egypt." *PMLA* 126, no. 1 (January 2011).

Tareen, SherAli. "The Polemic at Shahjahanpur: Religion, Miracles, and History." *Islamic Studies* 51, no. 1 (2012): 49–67.

Tayob, Abdulkader. "Epilogue: Muḥammad in the Future." In *Cambridge Companion*, edited by Brockopp, 293–308.

Teipen, Alfons. "The 'Poisoning Jewess' Motif in Early Muslim Biographies of Muhammad." Unpublished paper, presented at the American Academy of Religion Annual Meeting, November 2013.

Thompson, Ahmad. *The Wives of the Prophet Muhammad: May the Blessings and Peace of Allah Be on Him and His Family and Companions*. London: Ta-Ha Publishers, 2004 [1993].

Tobin, Ronald W. "The Sources of Voltaire's 'Mahomet.'" *French Review* 34, no. 4 (February 1961): 372–378.

Tolan, John. "Afterword." In *Contextualizing the Muslim Other in Medieval Christian Discourse*, edited by Jerold Frakes, 170–177. New York: Palgrave, 2011.

———. "European Accounts of Muḥammad's Life." In *Cambridge Companion*, edited by Brockopp, 226–250.

————. *Saracens: Islam in the Medieval European Imagination.* New York: Columbia University Press, 2002.

————. *Sons of Ishmael: Muslims through European Eyes in the Middle Ages.* Jacksonville: University Press of Florida, 2008.

Turner, Colin. *Islam: The Basics.* New York: Routledge, 2006.

Tyerman, Christopher. *The Crusades: A Very Short Introduction.* Oxford: Oxford University Press, 2005.

Varisco, Daniel M. *Reading Orientalism: Said and the Unsaid.* Seattle: University of Washington Press, 2007.

Vial, Ch. "Muḥammad Ḥusayn Haykal." In *Encyclopaedia of Islam,* 2nd ed., edited by P. J. Bearman, Th. Bianquis, C. E. Bosworth, E. van Donzel, and W. P. Heinrichs. Leiden: Brill, 2011.

Vidyasagar, Ishvarchandra. *Hindu Widow Marriage: An Epochal Work on Social Reform from Colonial India.* Translated by Brian A. Hatcher. New York: Columbia University Press, 2011.

Vitkus, Daniel J. "Early Modern Orientalism: Representations of Islam in Sixteenth- and Seventeenth-Century Europe." In *Western Views of Islam in Medieval and Early Modern Europe,* edited by David R. Blanks and Michael Frasetto, 207–230. New York: St. Martin's, 1999.

Waheed-Ud-Din, Fakir Syed. *The Benefactor.* Translated by Faiz Ahmed Faiz. World Community of Islam in the West, n.d. [1964].

Waldman, Marilyn. *Prophecy and Power: Muhammad and the Qur'an in the Light of Comparison.* Edited by Bruce B. Lawrence, with Lindsay Jones and Robert M. Baum. Sheffield, UK: Equinox, 2013.

Walker, Christopher J. *Islam and the West: A Dissonant Harmony of Civilizations.* London: Sutton, 2005.

Al-Wāqidī, Muḥammad b. 'Umar. *The Life of Muḥammad: Al-Wāqidī's Kitāb al-Maghāzī.* Edited by Rizwi Faizer and translated by Rizwi Fazier, Amal Ismail, and AbdulKader Tayob. London: Routledge, 2011.

Warren, Ruth. *Muhammad: Prophet of Islam.* New York: Franklin Watts, 1965.

Watt, W. Montgomery. *Muhammad: Prophet and Statesman.* London: Oxford University Press, 1974 [1961].

Weil, Gustav. *Mohammed der Prophet, sein Leben und seine Lehre: Aus handschriftlichen Quellen und dem Koran geschöpft und dargestellt von Dr. Gustav Weil; mit Beilagen und einer Stammtafel.* Stuttgart: J. B. Metzler, 1843.

————. *The Story of Ali Baba and the Forty Thieves: An Extract from Dr. Weil's German Translation of the Arabian Nights.* Boston: D. C. Heath, 1889.

Weinberger, Eliot. *Muhammad.* New York: Verso, 2006.

Welch, Alford T. "Muhammad's Understanding of Himself: The Koranic Data." In *Islam's Understanding of Itself,* edited by Richard G. Hovannisian and Speros Vyronis Jr., 15–52. Malibu, CA: Undena, 1983.

Wessels, Antonie. *A Modern Arabic Biography of Muḥammad: A Critical Study of Muḥammad Ḥusayn Haykal's* Ḥayāt Muḥammad. Leiden: Brill, 1972.

Williams, Rebecca R. *Muḥammad and the Supernatural: Medieval Arab Views.* New York: Routledge, 2013.

Wills, Garry. *What Jesus Meant.* New York: Viking, 2006.

Winter, Tim. "Jesus and Muḥammad: New Convergences." *Muslim World* 99 (January 2009): 21–38.

Wokoeck, Ursula. *German Orientalism: The Study of the Middle East and Islam from 1800 to 1945.* New York: Routledge, 2009.

Wollaston, Arthur N. *Half-Hours with Muhammad, Being a popular Account of the Prophet of Arabia and of his more immediate Followers.* London: W.H. Allen, 1886.

Woods, Matthew. *In Spite of Epilepsy: Caesar, Mohammed, Lord Byron; The Founders Respectively of an Empire, a Religion, and a School of Poetry.* New York: Cosmopolitan Press, 1913.

Wright, Peter Matthews. "Critical Approaches to the Farewell *Khutba* in Ibn Ishaq's Life of the Prophet." *Comparative Islamic Studies* 6, nos. 1–2 (2010): 217–249.

Wright, Terence R. "The Letter and the Spirit: Deconstructing Renan's "Life of Jesus" and the Assumptions of Modernity." *Religion & Literature* 26, no. 2 (Summer 1994): 55–71.

Yusuf, Imtiyaz, ed. *Islam and Knowledge: Al Faruqi's Concept of Religion in Islamic Thought; Essays in Honor of Isma'il Al Faruqi.* London: I. B. Tauris, 2012.

Zaidi, Ali. *Islam, Modernity, and the Human Sciences.* New York: Palgrave Macmillan, 2011.

Zaidi, Syed M. H. *Mothers of the Faithful: Being a Discourse on Polygamy with a Biographical Sketch of the Wives of Muhammad refuting the allegations of the non-Muslims against them and the Prophet himself.* Calcutta: N. Mukherjee at the Art Press, 1935.

Zaman, Muhammad Qasim. "A Venture in Critical Islamic Historiography and the Significance of Its Failure." *Numen* 41, no. 1 (January 1994): 26–50.

Acknowledgments

As the preceding pages attest, every book is in dialogue with its predecessors; every author with her contemporaries. Many people share credit for what is valuable in this study, though none of them bears blame for its inevitable shortcomings. Colleagues and friends near and far encouraged and challenged me, responded to queries, and suggested further points of investigation. They include Leila Ahmed, Ali Asani, Jonathan Brockopp, Edward Curtis, Farid Esack, Juliane Hammer, Susannah Heschel, Aysha Hidayatullah, Marion Katz, Ruth Roded, Omid Safi, Sa'diyya Shaikh, Laury Silvers, Harvey Stark, Abdulkader Tayob, and Alfons Teipen. Kevin Fogg, Gene Garthwaite, Nasir Rana, and Sameer Sabir called my attention to biographies they thought might interest me. Jonathan Brown, Mimi Hanaoka, Ruqayya Khan, Michael Penn, and David Powers generously shared forthcoming work.

Colleagues and students at Boston University were vital interlocutors. The Muslim Studies faculty listened to an early overview; Roberta Micallef organized a conference at which I presented an early version of Chapter 3; and the Department of Religion faculty heard a draft of Chapter 2. In each case, listeners asked probing questions and suggested productive areas to explore. David Frankfurter, Deeana Klepper, Steve Prothero, and Michael Zank made time for additional conversations; Teena Purohit read two chapters in draft form and provided incisive comments. Administrators Karen Nardella and Wendy Czik kept logistics running smoothly and coffee brewing. Students in my Fall 2010 seminar on Representations of Muhammad thought through some of these issues along with me: Gerry Dunn, Galen Olson, Alix Saba, and Monsura Sirajee. Najah Ahmad brought me a book from Cairo. Eric Dorman, Andi Ogier, Matthew Pierce, and Nik Zanetti helped at various times with research tasks small and large; Matt, whose own work

centrally addresses questions of biography, has also been a perceptive conversation partner throughout.

I spoke about this project as part of Arlington Community Education's Tuesday Night Conversations series and at Harvard University; the Islamic Center of Boston-Wayland; Macalester College, where I gave the 2014 Arnold Lowe Lecture; Mount Holyoke College; New York University; Transylvania University; the University of Johannesburg; the University of Cape Town; Wheaton College; and Wilson College, where I delivered the Orr Forum lectures in 2011. These audiences allowed me to field-test ideas, for which I am thankful.

Sharmila Sen at Harvard University Press went above and beyond the usual editor's duty as this book underwent twists and turns, while Heather Hughes kept the project on track. Two anonymous reviewers provided thoughtful and generous reports.

Most important, at the start and at the finish, was my family. More than ever, I am grateful beyond measure.

Index

In alphabetizing entries, I ignore the prefix al- and the letter 'ayn.